Lawrie Lough___

Sept. 1961.

& then to Tony Cross
from Penny & Ryan.
July '84

D1421172

THE LAST EXILE

By the same Author

Novels:

SIGNED WITH THEIR HONOUR
THE SEA EAGLE
OF MANY MEN
THE DIPLOMAT
THE HUNTER
HEROES OF THE EMPTY VIEW
I WISH HE WOULD NOT DIE

Short stories:

GOLD AND SAND

Non-fiction:

UNDERSEA HUNTING FOR INEXPERIENCED ENGLISHMEN

THE LAST EXILE

A NOVEL

BY

JAMES ALDRIDGE

HAMISH HAMILTON
LONDON

First published in Great Britain 1961
by Hamish Hamilton Ltd
90 *Great Russell Street London W.C.*1
Copyright © 1961 *by James Aldridge*

PRINTED IN GREAT BRITAIN BY
WESTERN PRINTING SERVICES LTD BRISTOL

Take up the White Man's burden—
  Send forth the best ye breed—
Go bind your sons to exile
  To serve your captives' need;
    *   *

Take up the White Man's burden—
  Ye dare not stoop to less—
Nor call too loud on Freedom
  To cloak your weariness;
By all ye cry or whisper,
  By all ye leave or do,
The silent, sullen peoples
  Shall weigh your Gods and you.

From *The White Man's Burden*
RUDYARD KIPLING (*The Five Nations*)

ACKNOWLEDGEMENTS

Acknowledgements are due to Mrs. George Bambridge and Messrs. Methuen for permission to reproduce an extract from Rudyard Kipling's 'The White Man's Burden'.

Part of the secondary action of this story concerns a plot to assassinate President Gamal Abd el Nasser of Egypt.

The Egyptian authorities have reported three such plots to kill Nasser. The first, soon after he came to power, was by a religious fanatic who fired at him with a revolver while he was giving a public speeech in Alexandria. Nasser was lightly wounded. The second was a scheme to machine-gun the entire Revolutionary Council, but the principals were caught before the attempt was made. These two attempts were planned before the Suez war. The third attempt was uncovered recently, and concerned Egyptians, Zionists, and several foreigners, who, it is said, were planning to poison Nasser.

Taken at their face value, these planned assassinations have been attributed by the Egyptians to three different factions : the first one by local enemies, the second by British agents, the third by Israeli agents.

The one I talk about in this book is entirely fictitious, and has nothing to do with any of these versions of real events.

CHAPTER ONE

SAM HASSOON watched his friend Captain Ali Zareef, an Egyptian and also a Mohammedan, landing a small Auster. Zareef's flying was rather like Zareef himself—rounded and friendly and professional.

'Tell Captain Ali I'm coming home with him,' Sam told Hefney the prop-swinger.

'Ho-kay!' Hefney replied.

Sam, who was Ali Zareef's wireless operator and mechanic on his Narcotics Co-operation flights, went into his office to lock it up.

'Ya Bey!' Hefney the prop-swinger had opened the door, and his black face was just inside it asking in Arabic: 'Are you flying tonight with Captain Ali?'

'God willing,' said Sam, 'and a passenger, Hefney.'

The passenger was illegal, and though Nasser had made Egypt stricter than it used to be, Sam had not yet been influenced by legalities. This passenger was a surprise he had for Scott, who rarely saw an Englishman these days and probably never saw old friends at all, excepting Sam himself.

The last plane, the Besterman, taxied past the window like a steady hooded bird with no more movement or sound or engine or rudder than was necessary. That was Captain Selim, Ali Zareef's rival. Captain Selim was *le chef* of Cairo Air Training. Zareef, everyone thought, ought to be *le chef*. Captain Selim was a secretive hooded-looking man and was probably anti-Semitic; but Sam could only dislike a man until he came face to face with him. Face to face with any man Sam brushed off antagonism the way he brushed the Cairo dust from his enormous black shoes, which his Aunt Nona (who was the same age as he was) had always called submarines.

'Sam!'

This was the engineer, and mechanic, Bambo, shouting through the window.

'If you go to Ghurdakha tomorrow, bring me back some fish.'

'Okay!' Sam shouted.

He shared this office with Bambo and with a Civil Aviation inspector, who came in once a month. Bambo never paid him for the fish. 'By now

B   I he must owe me twenty pounds for all that stinking fish,' Sam thought. But that would not be important until Sam needed money. Then he would think of Bambo's debts but would never mention them, although Sam himself was always in need of money.

'Ali!' Sam called through the window to Zareef. 'Wait for me.'

Zareef waved his short fingers. Captain Zareef liked to look (in his beret and blue air force coat) like J. P. Mermoz the famous French pilot who had flown the South Atlantic in 1933—wrapped up in his barrel shape against the cold; and happy.

Sam prepared Zareef's flight plan for the morning, wrote across it in English the letters NCER which meant Narcotics Co-operation Eastern Region, and then wrapped his earphones in his scarf and put them near the Very pistol box with the cartridges in it.

That was all, and he was ready to go. Somehow the dying red sun had soaked a soft haze out of the dry brown stubble of the airfield before it went down. Then it was done. That was how it always ended out here on the very edge of the fields and the desert. The day was simply done.

Sam was watching it sentimentally when two men he had never seen before came into the office and said to him in English, 'You are Sam Hassoon? Isn't that right?' They were young and neat; sure, and very polite. Sam guessed, in the fear and the sudden blow of it, that they were Egyptian Security police, and that they spoke English to him to show that they were insulting him.

'Yes?'

'Don't be alarmed. Are you going now?'

'Yes. Why? Who are you?'

'It doesn't matter,' one of them said in his good English. 'We are from the Ministry. You were going, you said?'

Sam was impulsive enough to lose his temper, but frightened enough not to. He wasn't surprised. He stooped over them a little from his very large physical advantage and said, 'I was leaving. Why? What's the matter?'

The pleased, cheerful, too-understanding policeman laughed and went on in insistent English. 'Don't worry. Go ahead. Off you go.' The other one was looking around the room at the few books, and at the charts on the walls.

'I've got to lock up,' Sam told them through his fear.

'We'll do that.'

Sam's instinct was pressing him to get out of the way as quickly as possible, but in the very fear that always came to him quickly in any sort of danger he actually found a delayed resistance to fear.

'No,' he said, resigning himself to English. 'I don't know what you want but I'll stay here until you've finished. What is it? What's the matter?'

2

The understanding fellow hit him on the shoulder lightly and laughed again. 'We need a few things,' he said. 'Do you mind? Which are yours?'

Sam indicated the few belongings in his corner of the room.

'Nothing else?' the policeman said, disappointed.

Then he raised his voice in a stronger version of himself and shouted for someone to come in. Four ordinary policemen came in and dragged a cane hamper behind them. Two or three words in Arabic and Sam was watching his corner being cleared out.

'What are you doing that for? Are you throwing me out? Is that it?'

The policeman loved to laugh, and Sam watched his tools and small library of code books and radio manuals go into the hamper. When they came to the headphones and thermos he said he would need those in the morning, but the policeman repeated that they would bring it all back; and then Sam knew he must go quickly before they changed their minds and took him as well.

At 3 a.m., when the Egyptian night was still hovering over the morning, Zareef started the starboard and then the port engines of the Gemini, and showed the Englishman beside him how to fasten his safety belt. He watched the oil-pressure rise in the already-warm engines, and then waved Hefney the old prop-swinger out of the way in the darkness.

'Lights!' Hefney shouted over the roar, but Zareef was too preoccupied to hear him.

He had Sam's important, illegal passenger, but not Sam. He taxied a few yards so that Hefney could get out of the gritty slipstream, and then he took off in the moonlight almost straight across the apron, making a climbing turn the moment the undercarriage was up, testing the magneto switches one at a time and watching the revolutions, and without looking at the compass setting the course over the neon dust of night-bound Cairo.

Then he tried to relax into it, to enjoy his early-morning flying; but he was worried about Sam, and after an hour he was still restless at the controls, still silent.

'Beautiful!' his passenger shouted to him suddenly. 'Look.'

Zareef had run into the dawn near Gimsa. He sailed right down it, down the muffled trough of early-morning Red Sea air (marking the chart and doing what Sam should be doing), and when he had lost height and skimmed up the granite valley of the hills called Ballaba, he landed in his own wheel tracks and dug his heels into the brakes a foot from Scott's two water-cans, which would act as wheel chocks.

When he had greeted Scott he excused himself and left the explanations, in all politeness, to his English passenger, Colonel Peacock. The Colonel could tell Scott that Sam had been arrested late last night.

3

CHAPTER TWO

'CAN you do anything about Sam?' Peacock asked his friend Scott. 'Anything at all, Scotty.'

Scott hid his eyes with his hat. 'I'll go back with you. It must be a mistake.'

'Do you think Nasser has started arresting all the Egyptian Jews? Poor old Sam.'

'It won't be that,' Scott told him. 'Probably it's Sam's gambling . . .'

'Then why would the Security police arrest him?'

'Who told you that?'

'Zareef.'

Scott strolled through the Red Sea sand and looked nostalgically at Peacock who had arrived like that with Zareef, stepping out of the Gemini on to the pale desert and saying *'Hello there. The same old chap!'* as if the days had gone and the weeks perhaps, but not thirteen years since the western desert war, when Peacock had last seen him being marched out of a court martial with loss of rank and six months' detention at Abu Suweir. Without Peacock's plea as his commanding officer for extenuating circumstance it might have been worse, if any punishment could have been worse for taking your own men out of a very fine trap a very bad General named Church had so carefully got them into.

'Is that Peacock the Tory M.P. worried about the Jews?' Scott asked. 'Or is it Tim Peacock the old Colonel worried about his friend Sam?'

'That's unfair. Sam's an old friend.'

Scott blushed. 'I'm sorry. Of course he is.'

He was pleased to see Peacock, but he could not help being suspicious. 'That's all right. I know how you must feel,' Peacock said forgivingly.

'No,' said Scott. 'It was stupid of me. I'm really sorry.'

'Never mind all that. I can't blame you for being suspicious,' Peacock said, trying to find out what there was of Scott under his large hat; but it was too difficult.

4

'Oh, I know what they've been doing to you lately,' Peacock told him. 'I suppose the combination of being court-martialled during the war and being a friend of Nasser's since the war is too much for them. Newspapers never bother to find out the real truth, you know that.'

'But it is the truth, anyway,' Scott said aggressively. 'I *was* court-martialled, and I do consider myself a friend of Nasser's.'

'Yes, but why do they drag it up all the time; and after all these years?' Peacock was also indignant. 'And anyway, the two things have nothing to do with each other.'

Scott lifted his hat and called out angrily in Arabic to his driver Ishaak not to handle a sack of rice from the plane with petrol-soaked hands. Zareef had brought it in the Gemini for them.

'How else can I lift it?' Ishaak complained back in Arabic.

'Don't handle it. Leave it. I'm tired of tasting petrol in everything I eat. Put it down!'

'But . . .'

'Put it down, Ishaak.'

'What was that about?' Peacock asked. 'Why did you bawl him out?'

'He's like a child,' Scott complained. 'You have to tell him twenty times not to do a thing. Then he goes right on and does it again anyway. He always washes his greasy hands with petrol. Afterwards, everything he handles smells of it and tastes of it . . .'

'Oh well . . .' Peacock had felt the isolated world at work, but he also recognized the familiar glow of temper in Scott—that sudden anger which had always flared up dangerously in him when he had to face something he considered stupid or wrong. Was the same underground volcano still dangerously there? Peacock laughed and pointed. 'Now you can bawl him out properly,' he said.

Ishaak had dropped the bag in a sulk, and it had burst open over the sand.

'Oh my God,' Scott groaned and lay back in the sand. 'I don't even want to see it.'

Peacock thought it very funny, and quite disproportionate. But it made him curious. Scott was obviously suppressing more than a second's impatience. He lay there under his hat as if he were trying to blot out all the small ways of the world which might threaten him.

'What do you do out here really?' Peacock asked him, peering with sudden distaste at the emptiness around them. But he felt already as if he were talking to himself, because Scott was under that hat again, and his powerful fingers were tied together tightly over his barrel of a chest.

'I'd hate to see that mass of bone and muscle in a towering rage,' Peacock decided. It was partly admiration, but it was partly a reminder.

But Scott had recovered. He sat up and smiled. He was, after all, a very

5

gentle man. 'When Zareef's finished with the plane I'll show you what I do,' he said.

'Fantastic! And to think of you spending all these years in the desert. I simply can't believe it. I didn't realize . . .'

Scott was pleased now to hear Peacock's gay voice, and he felt all wasteful suspicion of Peacock fading from his mind. 'I'm used to it out here,' he said. 'And anyway it's simply my job.'

Peacock shivered pictorially. 'It's so lonely when you look at the top of a hill, like that one over there, and know there's absolutely nothing on the other side except more hills, more sand, more wadis. Or maybe a few Bedouins rotting to death near the water-holes. What do you see in it?'

'Very sparse lines on an unfinished map,' Scott said. 'Are you ready, Ali?' he called down to Zareef who was doing what Sam usually did with the plane: some mystery of filters and oil pumps, which he insisted on doing himself without their help.

'This is where I miss Sam,' Zareef called up. 'Five minutes, Capten.'

'Are you really a Captain in the Egyptian Army?' Peacock asked him.

'No, no. The *Capten* is a nickname Sam brought with him. They call me Captain Scott, but I work for the Frontier Department now, under contract.'

'Doing what?'

'I'm finishing up one survey,' Scott's voice said, 'and laying the basis for another . . .'

'But I thought Egypt had been surveyed years ago,' Peacock said restlessly. 'By the British Army mostly.'

Scott could sit very still, but he watched Peacock wriggling and he knew that Peacock had not changed at all. He was still very much the same Peacock. 'There's never been a geodetic survey made of this part of Egypt.'

'What's the difference?'

'More exact.'

'How do you do it?' Peacock asked. 'I mean, what's so special about it?'

'Nothing much,' Scott said as if he were being very very cautious about it. 'Measurement with invar tapes, triangulation with theodolites, astronomic determinations of latitudes, longitudes and azimuths with precision instruments, determination of precise levels . . .'

'Okay, okay!' Peacock said quickly, feeling relieved because Scott was slyly teasing him. 'But seriously, Scotty, do you really feel you're doing something *useful* out here? What can you do in a desert, even with a survey?'

'That depends.' Scott shrugged. 'I'm only laying the basis, myself, for the proper geodetic survey to follow. That's what will be important. I did most of my real work in the Sinai.'

'I'd heard that you were there. But that was some years ago, surely.'

6

'I left it when it became too much like a front line,' Scott told him. 'I finished up all the field work quickly and shifted over here. But I'm still finishing the Sinai maps, even now; and while I work on them out here I go on checking and supplementing all the photogrammetry maps they've been making of these deserts and hills. That's why we need the plane.'

'But these patrols?'

'Oh . . . they're just the price we pay for borrowing the plane. We keep an eye on other things, for the Frontier Department.'

'On what? Israeli spies?'

Scott looked at him quickly but he laughed. 'I haven't seen one yet, Tim,' he said. 'But you'll see now. Ali is ready.'

Peacock finally managed to get a good look at him then, and he was surprised. This was not really the same Scott who had defied Church single-handed thirteen years ago; not that same determined man at all. This one looked very much like a man in careful hiding. The climate had baked him, and he was still built like the side of a mountain, but he seemed to be hidden by the tangle of troubled lines pressing down relentlessly from his forehead; and his manner was diffident but wary and very watchful.

'It must have been lonely all these years,' Peacock said involuntarily.

'Lonely? Why?'

'You couldn't have seen many English people out here, surely.'

'Not so many,' Scott agreed. 'But not many wanted to see me. In fact, no Englishman has ever wanted to see me at all, since the war.'

'Ho-kay,' Zareef called up. 'When you like, up there.'

They went down to the Gemini, and Scott told Ishaak to get out the plastic-chart board and use it as a scoop, and to get the rice back into the bag while they were away.

Zareef laughed up from his heart and said in English: 'He's going to sulk again.'

They got into the box-like plane and left Ishaak recklessly involved in the jeep, searching for the chart-board to act as a scoop to save that important sack of spilled rice which seemed to mean so much to Captain Scott.

Zareef took them over the hot pads of air rising from the red granite mountains to the place which Scott shouted into Peacock's ear was the Qattar slope. Zareef came down over one orb-like peak which Scott pointed out to him, and after shooting the long reaches of the wadi bed once, he landed gently and professionally between the salt-bushes and the bare wind-sore rocks, taxiing rapidly away from two Bedouin women who were minding a dozen arid camels.

'Isn't that good piloting?' Scott said to Peacock with a real pride.

7

'Marvellous,' Peacock groaned. 'I've never felt so frightened in my life.'

Scott smiled at his friend Zareef. 'Ali likes getting in and out of these death-traps. He scares me like that all the time.'

'*He* makes me do it,' Zareef said to Peacock, 'I'm afraid myself.'

Peacock watched one and then the other and knew that Scott was not exactly friendless.

'What do we do here?' he asked them.

'Sit down for a few minutes,' Scott told him. 'We'll wait and see how those women react. Or rather what happens up the side of the wadi.'

'Are those awful-looking women the smugglers you're looking for?'

'They're in the family,' Scott said. 'This is one of their camps on their short route to the sea.'

They sat down near the hot plane and watched the women who watched them, and Scott let his eyes wander carefully over the difficult slopes of the hills around them. A small yellow dog, filthy with mud and fleas, deserted the women and came sniffing towards them.

'Yalla! Yalla!' Ali shouted at it in a panic.

'No, Ali. Let's have a look at him,' Peacock said. 'I've never seen a dog in the desert, now that I think of it. I suppose he comes from a very long line of Levantine smuggling hounds. Looks just like a beagle.'

'Do you still keep dogs?' Scott asked him, eyes everywhere. 'Setters?'

Peacock sighed as if this had touched on an old argument. 'No. Eileen keeps a couple of corgis because they're small enough to keep in our London flat. But I refuse to keep dogs in the country. Eileen's mad on hunting, but I'm not. I went in for French bulldogs for a while but they're so disgustingly noisy and so full of energy that they wore me out. They were always nipping the children when we weren't looking, and when one of them got nasty with our eldest girl, Pam, we sent them all to Coventry. I mean literally. There was a breeder there who was anxious to have them, and he paid fifty pounds for each dog.'

'I didn't even know you were married,' Scott said.

'Didn't you?' Peacock pulled his crumpled summer coat over his head and said '*Service before elegance. Ah if only my tailor could see me now.* I married Eileen Bentinck, General Warren's daughter. You remember young Benty who was killed on that silly business with the Hurricane. Didn't you know I married her? That was ages ago—in forty-five.'

'I didn't know,' Scott said, surprised, 'but I always admired her very much. Lucy Pickering took me to her wedding reception.' Scott blushed. 'I mean, when she married young Bentinck.'

Peacock laughed.

Scott was still feeling embarrassed when a little cracking sound in the vastness from the hills, and a whining and snaking sound overhead, made Peacock duck involuntarily.

8

'That's somebody taking a shot at us,' he said indignantly. 'Surely?'

'Yes. We shouldn't be watching their women,' Scott said.

'Well, let's stop watching their women. What are we doing it for?'

'Because the men don't like it. They usually give themselves away like that.'

Peacock had been stroking the dog's ears nervously and he pushed it away. 'Well?'

'We can go down and talk to the women now. They're sure to be hiding something if their men ran off like that. And you'd better wash your hands at the well after handling the dog. Ali is religious, and you'll make his plane unclean if you go into it with that smell on your hands . . .'

'Oh, I'm awfully sorry, Ali.'

'The Capten is teasing; he's joking,' Zareef said as they went down to the women. 'Don't take any notice of him.'

But Peacock looked up at the hills expectantly. He didn't want another little reminder to come from up there.

'Are they really smugglers, those dirty black witches with the camels?'

'They're experts,' Scott told him. 'They're a mother and daughter. The husband and son-in-law are the ones sitting up in the sand hills watching us. But I suspect now that they're on their way to get the stuff rather than coming in with it.'

'Well I'll be damned. What a life you lead.'

Scott greeted the women formally, and then told them to strip their tattered bundles from one of the camels. When they refused he pointed to the plane and said something in Arabic, and the women took off their belongings and undid them. When Scott bent over them to look closer the younger woman with camel-dunged hair which looked like tarred rope raised her stick and threatened Scott.

'Mother! Mother!' Scott said delicately to her. 'Be ashamed.'

She spat, and she insulted them until Zareef (who said he insisted on respect from any woman) walked away covering his ears and shaking his head. 'God!' he said, and he meant it as useful information, 'that woman's an awful bitch, and not trustworthy either.'

Peacock was laughing at what he saw and he whispered to Scott: 'Is this what you do, Scotty? Poke around in women's pots looking for hashish?'

'I should poke something up the camel's backside, but that young woman will hit me with her club if I do.' Scott's eyes were on the sand hills. 'And I don't suppose you'd defend me.'

'I would not. I'd let you fight it out. I wouldn't have a chance if I had to fight a woman like that one.'

'Then let's go,' Scott said. 'I don't want to embarrass a British Member of Parliament by forcing him to fight a Qelali woman in that Savile Row suit. You're spoiling it, you know.'

'When I think of the care my poor old tailor took with this summer suit.' Peacock began to scratch himself as if he had been bitten. 'It's covered in fleas. . . .'

Another tinkling crack and a wisp of sound passed over.

'What about those chaps?' Peacock asked. 'Are you going to leave them like that?'

'I don't want to see them,' Scott told him. 'They'll keep me here talking all day if I call them down, and they'll insist that we eat with them and take coffee and God knows what.'

'You mean it's all a friendly game?'

'Not exactly,' Scott said. 'It's just the way it's done.'

'Why don't you carry a gun?'

'Never again,' Scott said. 'There's a Sten in the jeep, but I never touch it.'

'Really? What happens if one of those fellows begins to take exception?'

'That's what Sam was always worried about. When they play jokes like this on us Sam usually stands here and shouts up at them to come out in the open and fight like a man, flexing his arms and getting ready for them. Sam thinks he's got everybody in the desert frightened, but every man in the desert knows that Sam wouldn't hurt a flea. He would weep if he even bent someone's arm out of joint. Even here, in the desert, they call him the big sweetheart . . .'

'Damn! I hope he's not in any real trouble,' Peacock said sadly. 'He's such an innocent chap.'

'Sam'll be all right,' Scott said, under his hat once again.

When Zareef flew back over the wadi camp they could see another little aeroplane parked near the tarpaulin which Ishaak had erected that morning. Scott was surprised to see it and asked Zareef who it could be.

'It's an Auster from Gedida anyway,' Zareef told him. 'Perhaps it's Sam . . .'

It was not Sam.

Ishaak was waiting for them with the news that Captain Selim from Gedida airfield had arrived in the new plane with another Englishman who had been asking for Colonel Peacock and Captain Scott; they had gone off in the jeep.

'Didn't he say what he wanted or who he was?' Scott asked Ishaak.

'No. They didn't tell me.'

'Where are they now?'

'Captain Selim borrowed the jeep and they went off towards the old mines.'

'Are you sure they were looking for me?' Peacock asked.

'Yes, y'effendim.'

'Why did you give them the jeep?' Scott asked irritably.

'But it was Captain Selim, and we know Captain Selim.'

'I don't care who it was,' Scott answered. 'Don't ever do a thing like that, Ishaak. You know the rules in the desert . . .'

But Ishaak thought it unfair and defended his innocence, saying that he had only tried to help them because they were the Capten's friends, not his.

'All right, all right,' Scott said appeasingly. 'But you should have asked them at least where they were going . . .'

'Somebody who knows both of us?' Peacock said. 'I don't know who it can be.'

'If they don't come back soon I shan't be able to go to Cairo with you,' Scott told him. 'I have other things to do before I can leave here tonight.'

'But you must come back,' Peacock said firmly in the certainty of this friendship they had re-established, this old confidence which he had carefully won from Scott, 'otherwise Sam might rot in gaol for weeks.'

After a lunch of strong stewed mutton, Peacock felt that he could venture a little further into Scott's life.

'You know, I didn't come out here just to see you about Sam,' Peacock said to him. 'I had another reason as well.'

They were lying down in the heat of the day, the very hot afternoon of the day, under the tarpaulin's heavy shadow, digesting the mutton which Ishaak had cooked in rice, which had certainly tasted of petrol.

Scott was relaxed under this normal, grey, tarpaulin sky. 'Did you have to come out here for a reason?' he said. 'It's so pleasant just talking to you. Even to hear real English is a luxury out here.'

'Oh, damn it all, Scotty, it's such a colossal waste to see you hiding out here,' Peacock said impatiently. 'That's what I have always felt. Everybody who ever had anything to do with Tracks and Surveys, even the latecomers, never got over your court-martial. Nobody agreed with it.'

'Never mind that now,' Scott said. 'It's gone and forgotten.'

'*You* haven't forgotten it,' Peacock argued, 'otherwise you wouldn't have buried yourself out here.'

But Scott waved it away lazily, perhaps too lazily. 'Too late to worry about that now. Why drag back over that old ground?'

'But that's exactly what I came out to see you about.'

'About what?'

'About an appeal on your court-martial. I mean on the judgment—to revise it.'

Scott did not rise enthusiastically to it at all. 'After thirteen years'? he said.

'Does it matter how long ago it happened, so long as you can wipe it off the record? Your record should be absolutely clean,' Peacock said convincingly.

'But I went through all the appeals. Have you forgotten?'

'How could I ever forget. But now there is something new happening. They're going to change the Army law, or the regulation or something, about courts-martial; and when the change does go through you will be able to appeal against a court-martial judgment in a special appeal court, or in the House of Lords. The moment I heard of that I thought of you. We've already had some discussion about it in the House of Commons, only a few weeks ago, and I even mentioned your case—not by name of course, although everybody knew who I was talking about. So everybody would be on your side, if it did come up for review.'

'You mean they would review a court-martial decision which was handed down during the war?'

'But that's the very point,' Peacock said excitedly. 'Some of us are trying to put a rider or an amendment on it, so that certain war-time cases can be reviewed . . .'

'They'll never do it,' Scott said. 'Everybody would start appealing.'

'No they won't. We've thought up something that would make it difficult to do that, but which might satisfy the legal beans, particularly in your case. We want to add this bit about a war-time case being considered for appeal if the commanding officer at the time of the original trial—the C-in-C at the time—strongly recommends it. That narrows it considerably, but since the C-in-C at the time of your trial is now my father-in-law, and under very direct persuasion from Eileen who always liked you enormously, there's a good chance it will come off.'

'Just an appeal? Nothing more? No hearing?'

Peacock raised his hands reluctantly. 'You'd have to go through some sort of legal process, that's obvious. But I'd arrange for that.'

'Bring it all up in detail again?' Scott asked, almost deeply interested, but not quite.

'Inevitably, old chap. But surely it would be worth it.'

Scott felt hot. He sat up and began to take his boots off. Suddenly his blood seemed to have begun pumping itself violently into his face, his hands, and his feet in their thick boots.

'I don't know that I'd ever want to bring it up again,' he told Peacock, taking his socks off. 'Once was enough, Tim. I'm all right now. I've forgotten the worst of it . . .'

'But this time it would be quite different. This time they would clear the actual record. Everybody knows you were right that day at Agheila. But everybody also knows that you got the worse of it when they found you guilty. Everybody knows that you've never really had a fair chance since.'

12

'No thanks,' Scott said more determinedly now. 'If they start dragging it up again they might also make it worse.' He shook his head. 'People have forgotten it—almost anyway—and that's the best way for me. I don't think about it any more.'

'You're wrong.'

'Please leave it,' Scott appealed, undoing his shirt now. 'I've lived all right with it this far, so I don't really care any more, one way or the other. I used to care—I had to, because I couldn't get a decent job as an engineer or as a surveyor or even as cartographer after the war, even with the Americans. They wouldn't touch me. Nobody would except the Egyptians.'

'Then why not take this chance to clear it up once and for all?'

Scott was obviously avoiding any serious consideration of the idea. He was suddenly standing up and looking over the western horizon at the red hills, pressing his field-glasses into his eyes. 'They're very foolish to be out there now,' he said irritably. 'If someone takes a shot at them in fun, they'll probably panic—and they'll tip the jeep over. It's difficult country, even for a jeep. I hope they're hiding somewhere in the shade, and aren't upside-down in a heap.'

'Don't worry about them, whoever they are,' Peacock said. 'They'll be all right.'

Scott went on looking for a while, and then he sat down again and said thoughtfully: 'Did it ever occur to you, Tim, that I might have been wrong that day at Agheila, when I refused to carry out Church's order, and took everybody out?'

'How can you say that?' Peacock said, amazed. 'I didn't think I'd ever hear you say a thing like that.'

'Nevertheless, I did disregard an order in the field. I did, in the military sense, hazard an operation.'

'No you didn't. You actually saved it.'

'Did I? But Church didn't think so, and he was the General in charge of it.'

'But Church was wrong.'

Scott had buried his head a little between his knees and he kept it there while he talked. 'I know that he was wrong. But *I* should have done the wrong thing also. The plan was the plan, wasn't it? I should have done the wrong thing and had Rommel cut us up into little pieces if necessary and just shrugged it off. What difference does it make in a war, anyway?'

'I won't even listen to you,' Peacock protested. 'There are a couple of hundred men walking around today who would have been slaughtered quite uselessly if you hadn't pulled them out. In fact, it goes further than that. What if Church had really gone ahead? Can you imagine the colossal muck-up?'

13

'Then leave it like that, Tim,' Scott said resignedly. 'It's done.'

'I can't leave it like that. Don't you see . . .'

Scott wiped his large hands over his hot face and said, 'Wait a minute. Wait. You must know what the newspapers in England have already written about me out here,' he said.

'I know. I've seen them.'

'Then you know that they've started discovering the secret life of me—this doubly disgraced and ignoble character . . .'

'Oh, that's nothing.'

'. . . not only court-martialled in the field at the height of our difficult situation in the western desert in 1942 but involved in Egyptian politics to the point where an Egyptian tried to shoot me . . .'

'But that's nothing to do with it.'

'. . . and worst of all, now a well-known friend of Gamal Abd el Nasser.'

'I know all that. It's all nonsense. Why do you take any notice of it?'

'Don't you see? They've only got to dig a little deeper and they'll start writing all that sort of stuff again. The real details don't matter. They'll simply make it worse.'

'So what? You'll be cleared. Isn't that what counts?'

'I doubt it,' Scott said and got up again to look for the jeep, but his eyes were pushed firmly into the sockets of his field-glasses and as he spoke Peacock knew that he was under great strain now, and was trying to hide his worried face.

'Let me at least try,' Peacock said.

Scott shook his head. 'Thanks anyway, but I simply want them to leave me alone now. It's best left alone.'

'I can never agree. I know what it really means to you. I can *see* what you've been through.'

'Then leave me alone, Tim. You did your best at the time. Let's leave it like that. These things are only fatal to me. So what's the use?'

'But everybody is still indignant and angry about what happened to you.'

'Anger is a luxury other people can afford. But when I become indignant or angry, look what happens to me. It's fatal. So I don't let myself get angry any more . . .'

'But that was what made you so marvellous.'

'Not any more.' Scott smiled ruefully on the view of his pacifism. 'I can live safely here without indignation or anger. There's nothing much to get upset or angry about in the desert, is there?'

'That's all right for idiots,' Peacock said indignantly. 'But,' he sighed, 'stay out here and be safe if you want to.'

'It's a joke, Tim,' Scott told him. 'Don't take it too seriously.'

14

But Peacock knew he could take it in no other way but seriously.

'Anyway,' Scott was saying now, 'it's Sam we have to bother about now. I suppose he must be in real trouble this time—if it's the Security police who have arrested him.'

Peacock was still showing his disappointment.

Scott looked away. 'Then, there are these other fellows in the jeep,' he went on. 'If they don't get back soon I think we'll have to take off and look for them. Ali Zareef is still down there in the sun working his head off.'

Peacock shrugged. 'Just as you say. But I can't really believe you're all that uninterested in yourself.'

How could he believe that Scott was genuinely so reluctant about everything, particularly about clearing up the mess Church had made of him? Peacock refused to believe it. He was not defeated yet, and he was determined to go on trying to persuade Scott, because Peacock had always felt that as long as a man was not actually hurt by arguments he still remained open to persuasion.

To Peacock's surprise he found an unexpected ally for his persuasions in the man who had come to see them in the other plane.

The jeep returned in the late afternoon with Captain Selim and an Englishman who was another member of the group of British M.P.'s visiting Egypt.

'It's Monroe Mathieson,' Peacock said to Scott as the jeep stopped near the second plane. 'Can you beat that?'

'Who is he?'

'One of the M.P.s who are on our crazy tour of the Middle East.'

'What would he want out here?' Scott asked, suspicious again.

'I can't imagine. Don't worry about him.'

Monroe Mathieson, who was a short unsmiling man with horned-rimmed spectacles and very black hair, leapt off the jeep and greeted Peacock by his first name and then turned and said, without apparently meaning it as a joke:

'Captain Scott, I presume?'

'Yes.'

Mathieson shook hands with a purpose and he did not apologize for his surprise arrival, or his absence in the jeep, but explained to Peacock that, having heard him leave the hotel this early morning, and having discovered from the porter that he had gone to the little airfield at Gedida, and having guessed that something interesting was afoot, he had hurried out to Gedida himself, and after asking the right questions he had hired the plane which had brought him here.

'But I did it legally,' Mathieson said with his solemn eyes on Peacock.

15

'I rang up Nasser and he gave me permission, which is more than you did. You should have asked, you know.'

'But what did you come out here for?' Scott asked him.

'I guessed that Tim had come to see you, and I knew you wouldn't mind if I joined him.'

Where had they been in the jeep?

'To get petrol for the plane. We apparently used up too much looking for you. So Captain Selim went over to some dump near by and brought back a spare drum. We had a blow-out in the jeep on the way, so . . .' Mathieson took a deep hot breath and held up his greasy hands, 'here we are. I wanted very much to see you, Scott.'

Perhaps it was a fortunate thing after all, because Mathieson went on to tell Scott that he had always been interested in his exploits.

'At least, I have been lately,' he said. 'And though I've never spoken to Peacock about you, I did know that you were old friends. I knew that this would be the one chance, finally, to meet a man who has fascinated me in many ways.'

Fascinated him?

While Ishaak took Mathieson to the little muddy pool of the nearby well to wash his greasy hands and face, Peacock began to make full use of this unexpected support, to persuade Scott to make use also of this new and surprising ally.

'I don't really know the fellow very well, in fact, hardly at all,' he told Scott. 'I don't think anybody does. They say he's a decent fellow; and he's certainly a powerful man in the House sometimes, and on television. I do admit he's not exactly my type, though. He's all politician. It's funny how there's a whole group in the House, both sides, who take themselves so bloody seriously that it frightens me off . . .'

'Don't you take yourself seriously?' Scott joked.

'Not myself, only my job,' Peacock said. 'But some of us do it ambidextrously. You know—with both hands. But I think this chap is one of the ones who go at it all the time, nothing else. I mean he's a serious, singular, parliamentary type, and he takes it all as a sort of law unto himself. He and another chap from the House, whom I don't like at all, are always arguing on television, every week, and though I can't stomach it myself, he really is a good man to know. He's a sort of know-all expert . . .'

'He's ruined our chances of leaving before dark,' Scott said. 'I've got to wait now until they fix that other plane. Zareef has to help them, since we haven't got Sam.'

'Never mind that. Talk to him nicely, anyway.'

Scott shrugged, which he did often, but in the Egyptian fashion of *malesh*—it didn't matter. 'We have a couple of hours to kill.'

'Good.' Peacock was persuasive again, and they all sat down under the tarpaulin to wait for Selim and Zareef and Ishaak to finish refuelling the small plane and clean out the carburettor, and the air filter, while Peacock showed great interest in Monroe Mathieson's interest in Scott. How did he know about Scott? Had Mathieson been in the Eighth Army at the time?

'No,' Mathieson said, 'but I'm probably one of the few people who take a genuine interest in these things. We need to remind ourselves of the bad blunders we made during the war, so that we don't make them again.'

'Of course,' Peacock said. 'I'd forgotten your line on that; although I thought it was mainly political—how we lost the Balkans to the Russians and that sort of thing.'

'In this case,' Mathieson said solemnly, 'it's also military. Now,' he said to Scott in a legal manner, 'I've got a pretty fair picture of your court-martial, Scott, I even managed to get a look at the record before I left; but what I don't really understand is the actual sequence of the events themselves, at that time. How did you ever get to be at loggerheads with General Church in the first place?'

Scott did not want to hear this, and yet Peacock had affected him considerably. Perhaps he was also under the influence of this sudden upheaval in his normal life out here, or under the influence of their English voices under his greasy tarpaulin sitting on this little red Qellala hill eating uncooked peanuts which Ishaak had offered them from a biscuit tin he kept in his own pack. Perhaps he might be able to explain carefully enough to this man what had happened; and for a moment it looked, he even felt, as if he would try. But faced with those English, horn-rimmed eyes it simply would not emerge, and he looked at Peacock and shook his head slightly to show that it was hopeless to expect him to be drawn out by this man. He had made up his mind. But Peacock had also made up his mind, and he took it up quickly and told Mathieson how General Church had caused the original Tracks and Survey unit (under Pickering then) to be almost completely wiped out when he had sent them onto a British minefield accidentally, and had then ordered British guns to hack them to pieces in a blunder of military idiocy, thinking they were an enemy force.

'But that's the sort of mistake which was quite common in the desert war, surely,' Mathieson said. 'Even with good generals.'

'Good generals did *not* make that mistake,' Peacock said indignantly and then added sadly, 'but it was common enough though, because we had so many bad generals.'

'Is that when you took over the Tracks and Survey unit,' Mathieson said to Peacock, 'when the famous Pickering was killed?'

'Yes, but they offered it to Scotty first, and he turned it down, even then.'

17

'Why?'

'Because he wouldn't trust Church.'

'Did *you* trust him?' Mathieson asked Peacock.

'Who? Church? No, I didn't trust him either. Nobody did. But I'm not Scott,' Peacock said. 'I was a fool myself in those days.'

'Perhaps I was the real fool,' Scott put in to rescue a friend, 'for making such an issue of it.'

'Everybody seems to have been a fool,' Mathieson said solemnly without diverting at all from the serious to the ridiculous. Although both Scott and Peacock laughed, Mathieson looked at them as if they were being very frivolous.

'Didn't some Egyptian officer shoot you, at about that time also?' Mathieson asked Scott. 'Something to do with local politics?'

'Yes, but that was nothing to do with the court-martial. Absolutely nothing at all . . .'

'But you *were* involved in Egyptian politics in those days?'

'Not at all. I had by chance picked up an Egyptian officer outside my home. He had been wounded while attempting to assassinate an Egyptian politician . . .'

'Was that Gamal . . .'

'Shhh!' Peacock said, indicating the two Egyptian pilots and Ishaak who were working on the plane below; but voices carried.

'Yes. It was a young officer named Gamal.'

'But *he* didn't shoot you.'

'No, it was a lieutenant named Hakim Abdul Sadat who shot me.'

'They say he's the man you work for now.'

'He's in charge of the Frontier Department, and I work for the Frontier Department, that's all.'

'Why did he try to shoot you—if you weren't involved in their politics?'

'He thought, when I helped Gamal, that I was really betraying him to the British.'

'But you hadn't?'

'Of course not.'

'Shouldn't you have told the British authorities about him, if this Gamal was really an assassin, anyway? After all, you were a British officer.'

Scott shrugged. 'I don't think I had any right to betray him. Perhaps I might have if I had disagreed with him. But I didn't disagree with him at all. Not that much. I knew what he was really trying to do.'

'Then it *is* true,' Mathieson insisted.

'What is?'

'What they say in the press about you helping the Egyptian officers' revolution.'

18

'I didn't help it at all. I kept up their friendship, and they actually helped me get work in Egypt when no one else would touch me.'

'I understand that,' Mathieson said, sympathetically, as if he were taking on a great burden of understanding in this, trying hard to see what Scott meant in behalf of those million English eyes. He had changed his spectacles for sun-glasses because the reflection of the sloping desert sun off the sea of silica glints in the limestone gravel was now very glaring and harsh.

'But, as I recall it, didn't those shots which Hakim Sadat fired at you put you in hospital rather badly wounded?' Mathieson said, determined to get to the bottom of this.

'They thought I was badly wounded at the time, but I was out in two months,' Scott said, feeling that he was becoming too deeply entangled in this now, despite himself. Yet he could not leave it there. Some things had to be explained. 'That was the luck of the situation,' he said. 'Church had been forced by Rommel to postpone his original plans for Agheila, so I got out of the hospital just in time to join Tim and go through with the scheme anyway. If it hadn't been for Hakim putting those holes through me I would probably have gone to another unit, and all that followed would never have happened. I had already asked for a transfer. . . .'

Scott stopped abruptly. He decided, sharply, that he had gone as far as he could go. He simply left it there, and the more Mathieson pressed him now, asking about Church, the more his resentment and reluctance began to show, until Peacock rescued him again.

'Let me explain,' Peacock said then, before it was too late and Scott ruined his case, 'because I know Scott won't ever tell you the real details, Mathieson. But I will. You see, Church had this crazy plan for sending us hundreds of miles into Rommel's back yard, right up onto the road at Agheila, where we were supposed to make a mock attack the day before the real offensive was timed to start on the sea coast, farther back. Rommel, God help him, was supposed to think we were a fairly large force coming up on his flank from the south, so we had to use one of the tricks Wavell had tried before so successfully—mock-up guns and tanks and stuff like that, because we couldn't get a real force of any size so far in. That was Scott's job—to deliver the mock-up group to Agheila and make the attack.'

'Where were you?' Mathieson asked Peacock.

'I was sitting, dammit, in an A.C.V. miles away, in case the General changed his mind at the last moment.'

'But he didn't?'

'No! So Scotty changed it for him.'

'Why?'

'That was the point,' Peacock said a little irritably. 'When Scott got to the rendezvous at Agheila, undetected, where we already had a couple of road-watchers, he saw immediately that any attack there would fail to fool anyone, and would in fact give the rest of the show away, the real attack which was starting next day. It was practically telling Rommel that something was up.'

'Is that why you pulled out of it?' Mathieson asked Scott.

'Partly,' Scott said, but he was becoming rather morose now, and he watched Ishaak trying to lift the drum of petrol from the jeep to the top of the little Auster where Zareef and Captain Selim were quarrelling about how it should be done. He thought it a pity that these two men, Zareef and Selim, were always at loggerheads, because they were both such good pilots, although Selim could never be quite as good as Ali Zareef. But why did they quarrel, even with their eyes and their flying?

'It wasn't because you disliked Church, and wanted him to fail?' Mathieson was saying to him, and he barely heard it or believed it.

'Oh, Scott had had rows with Church,' Peacock put in quickly, 'but this Agheila mess was obvious, even to me and I was miles away. The trouble was that Scott had orders not to change the plan, no matter what happened. That was Church's real crime.'

'And you did change it?' Mathieson said to Scott.

'Yes, I did,' Scott said, interested now but wishing that it would stop. He was trying not to hear it, not to make it important—even out here after all these years. Why did they have to pick it up suddenly, and in detail like this?

'Why *did* you pull out?' Mathieson asked, as if promising that his confidence would not be mishandled. 'I mean the real reason.'

Scott chewed a few coffee-grounds from his cup, and wondered how he could ever tell this Englishman, whom Peacock called useful, that he had changed everything that day not calmly because it was going to be a bloody mess and another blunder, or because it would ruin the more important event of the next day; he had really done it simply because one man, one unimportant man among all of them, one man who should never have been there at all, had been caught unluckily across the other side of the road and was washed out by a surprising burst from some Afrika Corps soldier's carbine. Every death had hurt him, but it was the terrible vision of Atiya in his outsize greatcoat which had given him the anger to disobey Church, to recognize quite clearly his own responsibility, to withdraw; to take the rest of them out carefully that night without Rommel ever discovering that they had even been there. Could he ever explain that strange, freakish soldier, Atiya, to this man and make him coherent?

'I've forgotten the whole thing,' Scott said brusquely to Mathieson again.

It seemed to be very rude.

20

'I told you why he did it,' Peacock said. 'It was useless going ahead with Church's plan. Rommel could easily have knocked us out, and guessed the real intention behind it.'

'But is that really why?' Mathieson asked Scott. 'It was nothing to do with your feelings about Church, or because he had caused Colonel Pickering's death?'

'It might have been that,' Scott admitted carelessly knowing that he was now exposing himself in some way, yet reluctant even to show anger. 'I could not forget what Church had already done to my friends,' he said, and hated himself instantly for saying it, feeling crudely insincere, as if he had betrayed too much of himself and his friends to this man.

'I don't suppose you could rightly forget Church's mistake,' Mathieson said seriously. 'But that seems to have been your mistake also—being so directly personal about it. After all, the war was on.'

'But we all felt the same way as Scott did,' Peacock put in. 'Only none of us had the courage to do anything about it. Nobody else ever did.'

'That doesn't make it right, does it?' Mathieson suggested.

'Would you like to help me get this tarpaulin down,' Scott said. He was afraid of it now. He did not like this politician. What was he doing out here, asking these questions of him, as if he were specially ordained by some special English eye to do so? What an extraordinary manner he had —this curious, impersonal security in himself and in his own conscience. Could Peacock actually trust such a man, even though he did come from the House of Commons?

But Peacock saw that it was no longer worth pursuing, not for the moment, anyway, so he got up quickly and said, 'Okay, old chap.'

'With a bit of luck we'll be in Cairo soon after dark,' Scott told them.

Mathieson looked at Scott with his large eyes, and then held a corner of the tarpaulin while Scott dismantled the guy-ropes with a quick twist on the straining bobbins.

21

CHAPTER THREE

SAM HASSOON was not confined in a prison, but in a house on the out-skirts of Cairo where he listened to the Heliopolis metros go by, knowing that everybody was on the way to work in their clean clothes at eight in the morning. The Cairo girls in their dressmakers' clothes were going to their offices, and he was here, miserable, locked up in this empty, lifeless room, waiting.

But in the years before the gaol, before Cairo was burned and before Madame Zuzu Nahas could rig the Alexandria cotton exchange and rule the country as a pleasant sideline (it was said) for her lover; before the famous black Friday, a working Jewish family like the Hassoons was considered normally well-off if they had one or two native servants. They had lived like this for eighty years in Egypt, with many advantages you couldn't get in Europe unless you had plenty of money.

But now, being foreign and Jewish (Sam's mother had been Egyptian, but his father was an Aleppo Jew by origin) they were stateless in a Moslem country which did not want foreigners ruling them any more after eighty years of such subjection.

Sam, moaning softly at night against fate in this special gaol of the new republic, could not have escaped his fate anyway, because the fate of the Hassoons seemed to be the fate of British rule in Egypt. The Hassoons themselves had served British rule on the survival principle. To be an Egyptian had always meant being menial and in service to any and every foreigner. It was therefore much better to remain a foreigner (even a state-less one) than to become an Egyptian subject, because even the stateless foreigner had the right to despise and demand service of the Egyptian.

But Sam, in gaol with three Egyptian communists and the ex-King's bath-attendant and fourth barber, could not trace it back nor forward that far; and though he ground his big, square, yellow teeth against his folly and kept back his tears and crashed fistfuls of hard-worked knuckles together in dry arpeggios, he could not escape the realization of his own naïve treason.

22

'I couldn't help it,' Sam would tell himself over and over again.

If there was ever any question in his mind about this, it was always the same one:

'What else could I do?'

He had been led to treason. But by what? By history?

He had looked once, casually, at the black friendly face of his Sudanese gaoler bringing him lentil soup and he had experienced that hard, bright removal to space which is possible just once in anyone's lifetime. That was when he felt this long pressure of history against him. He didn't understand it, but he knew how hopeless his predicament was.

'I know they'll hang me if they ever find out what I've done,' he said, and the metros went by in the dewy dry mornings with the clerks and the typists and the daily life which went on without him. That was the worst part of it.

Clackety-clack the metros went, taking all those familiar Cairo people to work in a life which now seemed to have forgotten him, perhaps for ever.

CHAPTER FOUR

In order to get Sam out of trouble Scott knew he would need the helpful friendship of his old friend Hakim Abdul Sadat, although it was a helpful friendship he knew he might never really have. Hakim was in charge of the Frontier Department, and Hakim guarded his frontiers jealously against all enemies; even against Sam, even against himself.

'But my dear,' Hakim said, 'I had just telephoned this minute to Amin Fakhry in Ghurdakha to speak with you, and here you are.'

Hakim had pulled Scott to his desk with a thin handshake, holding it and drawing an intimacy over the division they knew would always be there.

'Did your friend Colonel Peacock find you?' Hakim asked.

'I came back in the Gemini with him,' Scott said, realizing that Hakim knew all about Peacock.

'I only heard accidentally this morning that he'd been to see you. We did not know.'

'I don't suppose he should have done it that way,' Scott apologized, 'but he's an old friend, and I know he did not mean to brush aside the legalities.'

'But if he'd asked me I would have arranged it for him,' Hakim protested. 'We don't mind. But we like to know.'

'I'm sorry,' Scott said.

'But why apologize?'

'I don't know why,' Scott said, sitting down. 'I seem to be apologizing quite a bit these days, for one reason or another. I wanted to see you about Sam Hassoon. You must know that he's been arrested.'

Hakim had subsided from the politeness, and he relaxed into the canvas chair which helped take the immovable look away from the big mahogany desk, and fitted in better with the barrack-square *hups* that filtered through the open windows. Hakim slouched a little too deliberately for a general, and he still looked too young for it and yet too sure of it. He smoked a cigarette between second and third fingers, and almost too lazily he

24

allowed the curling smoke to soften the air. It looked very conspiratorial even to Scott.

'Yes, I knew about Hassoon,' he said.

'What has he done now?'

Hakim was very gentle with it. 'It's very serious for your friend Hassoon.'

'I suppose it is, but what has he done, Hakim?'

'That I can't tell you exactly. At the moment he is outside my responsibility.'

'Oh! Why?'

'He's a civilian.'

'So am I,' Scott said, 'but I'm responsible to you. So is Sam.'

'Ah no, *ya effendim*!' Hakim said. 'You are under contract to the Frontier Department. But Hassoon has never been part of us. He is employed by the private company which owns the Gemini and hires it out to us. Like Captain Zareef the pilot, who is part of the flying school, Hassoon has never been part of us.'

'All right,' Scott accepted. 'But what difference does that make?'

'A great deal,' Hakim said and pushed a button and told a soldier to bring in files. 'I know you have come to ask me to help him. But I don't think I can. It is too serious to . . .'

That was all Scott heard of it. The collapsing roar of a Russian jet shot down low over the barracks and buried all sound lower than the eucalyptus trees. Hakim leaned back to look out of the window.

'Have you seen them? Our own pilots. In God's name look how they go. They're so much faster than those old English Vampires, or even the Americans. Look at them, habibi.'

'I've seen them over the town before.'

'At ground level they're too fast to see,' Hakim went on. 'One second and they've gone. Not at all like your war against the Germans.'

Scott agreed again. 'I suppose even wars are faster,' he said. 'Although it's war just the same.'

'Of course nobody wants war,' Hakim said. 'But . . .'

Another Mig went over and Hakim watched Scott with quick, unembarrassed, amused looks—one glance to the English face, another to the whole situation of Scott sitting there before him, and a third to his own neatly detached view of it.

'I don't think I can help Hassoon,' he said again. 'But *you* may be able to help him.'

Scott knew that he ought to break up Hakim's detached sort of humour, which always bothered him. He needed to keep his head when Hakim was like this, so he went to the window and watched a flock of noisy minahs eating flat bread thrown out of the windows by soldiers across the gardens which the British had left them at Abassia.

25

'If I can help, I'll do anything you suggest,' he said to Hakim.

Hakim laughed. It was such a thin face on a small body, and his smile was now a boy's smile. He waved his hand to ease the tension, which was all imaginary. Why be so serious about this?

'You're a faithful friend,' he said. 'You're very worried about your friend Sam. I know. But we too are worried. That's why we have him. We know, for instance, that there is some unpleasant trouble being organized against us.'

'By Sam?' Scott was incredulous, although it was impossible to be really surprised by anything Hakim ever said.

'By many people.'

'What sort of trouble, Hakim? Anyway, Sam isn't capable of doing anything that's troublesome. Not the way you mean it.'

Hakim drooped. A soldier entered from the painted white dirt of the barracks and saluted and placed with barrack-room respect two tattered files on Hakim's desk and went out again.

'Perhaps,' Hakim said. 'Nevertheless, something like terrible trouble is behind it. I assure you . . .'

'But what sort of trouble?' Scott insisted. 'Sam's never had anything to do with politics.'

'Perhaps it's even worse than politics,' Hakim said. 'Perhaps, for instance, it is an attempt to injure Gamal. What, for instance, would you say to that?'

'But by whom?'

Hakim shrugged gently. 'Old enemies, habibi. Foreign influences. Miserable people.'

'The British?'

'Oh, the British usually like more secretive affairs than this. Perhaps . . . anybody. Wouldn't the Jews also like to see Gamal removed? Or perhaps the British, as you suggest. But we've heard about it.'

'About Sam too? You think Sam is in it?'

'I will tell you honestly that Hassoon was actually denounced to us.'

'And you listen to people who denounce others? Ah—Hakim, it hasn't come to that, surely?'

'There is much more to it.' Hakim turned over the tattered files and said, 'There are also many old friends of yours. You remember though, it was you who got Hassoon the position with the Gemini company. Not so?'

'Sam was the only man who could be found to do it,' Scott reminded him. 'You couldn't find a wireless operator and a mechanic and a man with his sort of desert experience. They didn't exist. You wanted him, and you were lucky to get him.'

'Ah, yes. Your desert hero Pickering was a good teacher.'

26

'So he was, and Sam was a good pupil.'

'Perhaps too good.' Hakim closed the file. 'You know that your friend General Church is in Egypt now, in the desert? What would he be doing in the eastern zones?'

'Church?'

Hakim opened the other file. 'And a few days ago Mrs. Lucy Pickering asked for a visa for Egypt from Greece. She has gone there from Israel. She thinks she is being very clever. Now why does she want to come to Egypt? She loves the Israelis, it's well known.'

'And you put Sam into that sort of suspicion. Have a heart, Hakim.'

'But they are all old friends, including your friend Sam. Not so? Be honest . . .'

'You might as well put me into it. Of course we are all old friends!'

Hakim came around and tapped Scott's shoulder with gentle amusement and went to the door and gave the files through it to the clerk outside, saying:

'We could never put you into that. You, my dear, are *our* good friend. The very last Englishman in service to Egypt and a dear friend too.'

'What's it got to do with Sam Hassoon then?' Scott said impatiently. 'Don't go on around the point. I'd prefer that you came out with it.'

'We have been warned, I tell you honestly.'

Scott threw up his hands. 'Then it's exaggerated. I don't care what you say.'

Hakim was delightfully patient. 'It's really very logical. That's why we thought you might help. Mrs. Pickering will be here in a few days. We have allowed her to come. General Church is a regular visitor to Egypt. He is something of an archaeologist, although we didn't take much notice of him until a week ago. Colonel Peacock is already here, but he is a British M.P. and your good friend. Nevertheless, we know from very good sources that there is a reason for it all.'

'What reason?'

'That's what we thought you might hear about, if you chose to.'

Scott laughed. 'You want me to start spying on my old friends?'

Hakim waved a stained finger. 'Not on your old friends. General Church is not an old friend. I won't be personal about Mrs. Colonel Pickering. I'm not being rude, habibi, so please forgive me. Please! But the English hate Gamal, and they will do all they can to get rid of him. You know that, not so? Be honest.'

'Do you really believe that?'

Hakim threw down the pencil he had been playing with and paced up and down impatiently. 'Do you imagine that the English don't plot against us? Do you think they will give up the canal and the oil and their influence without some resistance? And the Israelis?'

'No, I don't think so. But that's nothing to do with me,' Scott said. 'You know I know nothing about politics. I keep out of politics.'

'Then don't weep if we shoot your friend Sam.'

Scott broke gently into Arabic. 'That would be inhuman, Hakim.'

Hakim shrugged. 'Just as you wish. But remember—I warned you. It's not funny. And I put you on your honour not to betray what I have said here.'

'That's understood, at least.'

'Why don't you go to your old friends and let *them* convince you that they are not here to scheme against us?'

'I don't even want to see my old friends.'

'We have been told all about them by someone who would know. Believe me. And about Hassoon too . . .'

Scott got up to leave because he knew he could do no good now.

But Hakim held him back and steered him through the french windows and walked with his arm through Scott's, down the avenue of conscript salutes and listless gum trees, down to the main gate which looked like a petrol station where the M.P.'s brusqued themselves into efficiency when they saw him coming.

'The sad thing is,' Hakim told him, 'we are all in a dilemma, not so?'

'The only man I'm worried about is Sam Hassoon.'

'But that's exactly it. He ought to expect help from his friends.'

'If I were Sam I don't think I'd expect help from anyone.'

'Except from his good old friend Scott,' Hakim said, 'with whom I would trust my own life, unworthy as it is. And Gamal's life also. Remember that! Gamal's life may be in your hands.'

'I don't know about that,' Scott said, stubbornly refusing that responsibility.

28

CHAPTER FIVE

HELEN MAMOON, Sam's aunt, was not a great deal older than Sam himself but everybody knew that she had been the support of her family since she was seventeen when both her parents had died and left her four sisters and two brothers, and cousins like Sam who were incapable of looking after themselves. She had grown from a firm, flower-like Egyptian girl into a self-possessed woman. She had to be self-possessed.

It was said that she had *shaitan* eyes. 'Slay me if you wish,' the young man says desperately in Arabic to the pale and delicate face quivering expectantly behind the shutters, 'but do it, for God's sake, with your *shaitan* eyes.' Her pale, Egyptian-looking face was overwhelmingly Egyptian only around the eyes, but once you had looked at them nothing else of her face seemed to be important. When Sam looked at her he was afraid of her; and in return she was bad-tempered with Sam most of the time, although behind his back she was anxious and protective and sorry for him.

'It's Sam who has always given me the worst moments,' she said to her older sister, Hanna. 'He's always been such a baby.'

Sam's own sister, Alicia, and his grandmother had just left Helen, weeping and begging her to do something to bring him back.

'I know I'm going to have a headache before this is over,' she said bitterly after them.

She suffered from migraines, and the thought of that old circuit of friends in the Government departments and ministries brought a shooting pain across her eyes. At first, even trying to find out what had happened to him had been difficult; but she had been spared a great deal of trouble by Captain Scott who had telephoned her, and now Colonel Peacock had also offered to do what little he could.

She did not like Scott, but she liked Peacock because he was well mannered and untroubled, honest and undoubting, charming and happy and important. That was how an Englishman ought to be and what she had once hoped to find in the one Englishman (the biggest mistake of her life) who had deserted her.

29

Also, Peacock remembered her very well.

'I remember when you worked for old Barker-Danderson during the war. You know? When he was in the Royal Engineers and smoked that stinking pipe all day at G.H.Q. with his feet out of the window because he couldn't stand the smell of them, while you were up at Immobilia keeping his powerhouse maintenance or whatever it was in apple-pie order and probably making him scads of money.'

She laughed. He was a very gay man to be with. 'How did you know all that?'

'Everybody knew, my dear. That lovely dark-eyed girl in Barky's office, they used to say. I remember you so well. You were a bit younger then, twenty-three or four or so, I suppose, and quite stunning, but a little bit unseeing. You always looked as if you were trying to find a worthy equal in some man, but I suspect you never did. I'll bet you didn't, not with those eyes.'

She knew she couldn't have found her equal in Peacock then, because she did not remember him. 'What a pity I didn't know you then,' she said.

He liked her for saying that, and they ate dinner on the damp tablecloth of Hati's. She could see that kufta and kebab and tamia in garlic and coarse native bread were probably not good for Peacock's delicately prejudiced English stomach, and she would remember not to bring him here again. She considered it a good thing to remember the requirement of men she enjoyed being with, and she preferred it that way to any kind of suffrage for its own sake, because she was not afraid of being a woman. Oh no! She could flatter a man and still feel superior to him.

'Did you know Scott then?' he asked her.

'No, but I knew of him, of course. Before the war in Cairo everybody knew everybody else. But why is he such a shy and mysterious and lonely man?'

'Mysterious? Good heavens, Scotty's as simple as an open book. And he's not nearly as shy or remote as he used to be,' he told her. 'Sam probably told you what happened to him in the war.'

'Sam never talks to me like that.'

'Not even about Scotty?'

'No.' She was smiling, yet it did not seem to him to be an easy smile. 'Sam always runs away from me as quickly as he possibly can,' she said, 'in case I have to be angry with him. But I know he gets terribly upset sometimes when he talks about the bluddy British and Scott.'

'If it wasn't for Scott the most unlikely and incompetent general of the war might have got the Eighth Army at a most critical time. But it cost Scotty his career, and a lot more besides. Scotty wasn't exactly cut out for disgrace . . .'

'Who is cut out for it?' she asked.

Peacock sucked some of the cheese off his fingers and washed his hands in a small bowl of water near him and said, 'Well, nobody. But he is particularly not cut out for it, if you see what I mean.'

'Captain Scott remains a mystery to me anyway,' she insisted. 'He came to ask me yesterday if I knew what Sam had done. He almost accused me of having been the cause of it. When I said I didn't know what Sam had been up to, he obviously didn't believe me. Why should he be so angry with me?'

'Oh, he's quite upset,' Peacock said lightly. 'He's one of those unlucky men who have a conscience that always pushes them into all sorts of silly situations. The trouble is he doesn't know it, so he always gets stung. Nobody thinks of their conscience these days, at least I don't. Do you?'

'Being a woman . . .' she began delicately.

'Oh, I don't mean that. We all have to have a conscience, but if we had any sense we would let the cursed thing operate without thinking too much about it. You know what I mean?'

'I think I do.' She sighed, as if admitting that she was being bothered by her own.

'But anyway,' Peacock said, 'let's not worry about old Scotty. What about you?' He was rubbing his hands over the kebab which was curled up into an attractive necklace where the waiter had unskewered it on the dish. He suddenly sat back from it. 'Pepper!' he said. 'My wife warned me not to eat anything with too much pepper. Has this got oodles of cayenne in it?' He sniffed it tastily.

'It's seasoned with pepper,' she told him. 'At least I think it is.'

He picked up his knife and fork and began eating. 'Once won't hurt,' he said. 'It's the green salads that are really dangerous.'

She watched him eating as she would watch a schoolboy enjoying himself, out on a treat with his favourite aunt. He caught her at it, and he smiled as if he could show the same frank pleasure in looking at her face as he had found in the sight of this kebab. All things were equal if you liked them.

'Are you really Egyptian?' he asked her.

'Of course.'

'Ah. Of course,' he repeated, chewing lustily. 'You know, only the French or the Orientals say *of course* like that. Do you mind me telling you? In English you should say, "As a matter of fact I am." Or, "I suppose I am."'

'But I *am* Egyptian. Why can't I say *of course*?'

'In English you should never emphasize what you are,' he said, teasing her deliberately, knowing he could disarm that aunt-like look with a little retaliation. 'You should emphasize what you are not.'

'What am I *not*?' she asked.

31

'Let me see. I could ask you: "Are you a bit of a blue-stocking?"'

'What should I answer?'

He looked at her appreciatively. 'Definitely not!' he said.

'All right,' she said. 'I am definitely not a blue-stocking. What does it mean?'

He laughed. 'Oh, you're lovely,' he said happily and then devoted himself to his kebab, enjoying it to its last little piece before saying to her again: 'But how are you Egyptian. I mean, Sam is Jewish, but you're not. How is that?'

'My sister married Sam's father, who was Jewish, that's all.'

'But your names are almost the same.'

'Our name is Mamoon which is a Circassian name, Sam's father's name was an unpronounceable Hebrew name, so he changed it to Hassoon when he married my sister, to make it sound similar and more acceptable in Egypt.'

'But what are you? You're not Moslem, you can't be. You must be Copt or Christian. Are you a Copt?'

'Part Copt, part Christian, if you can separate them.'

'Then you must be part European.'

'As European as Farouk was Turkish, I suppose. I'm not quite sure whether I'm emphasizing what I am, or what I'm not; but my great-grandfather came from the Caucasus. He was a Circassian—although he came here long after the original Circassians who once ruled Egypt. He went to Arabia first over a hundred years ago, and then came here, and after that we were Egyptian. My grandmother was an Egyptian Copt and my father was therefore a Christian Circassian and Copt mixed. My own mother was Sudanese . . . .'

'I always thought the Circassians in Egypt were Moslems.'

'Only the rich ones. The poorer ones were Christians, because they were the mountain people who were never defeated by the Moslems. So a Moslem is something I am not. Should I emphasize that?'

'My God,' he said. 'How dull it is to be English. What a mixture! But all Circassians were such marvellous horsemen, I know that much.'

'Aren't the English also famous horsemen?'

'Yes, but they don't wear those marvellous costumes.' He drew his hands down his well-tailored breast where cartridge folds might be seen among the wild men of the Caucasus, or perhaps buried on some English hussar on the Crimean peninsula. 'What's this?'

The waiter had brought them dessert.

'I remember seeing it before. That's that honey stuff with cream on top, isn't it? But I've forgotten the name of it.'

'Eck-meck,' she told him.

'Eck-meck? Oh, my God, yes. Let's get a few feet away from it. I

32

remember it. It sticks like glue. It's sure to add another couple of inches to the old girth. But here goes, Helen. Here goes.'

It went down very well; and when he had finished his coffee and paid the bill and tried once to forget his wife and discover the real fascination of those enticing eyes, he took her home in a taxi and sighed regretfully as they walked up the entrance of her apartment building, saying:

'You didn't really have to ask me to help Sam, you know. I was going to do what I could.'

'I know,' she said. 'But I wanted you to see that we were grateful for your help.'

'It's really Scotty who . . .' he began.

She was obviously not very patient with any talk of Scotty's special value. 'Oh, he'll disappear again, back to the desert,' she told him. 'They say he always does.'

'Don't be too hard on him.'

'All right,' she said. 'I'll be patient.' She gave him her hand and Peacock knew better than to do anything but shake it. 'Tell me,' she said in a gayer mood, 'if I came to England, would you know somebody who could give me a job?'

'Hundreds of people,' he said. 'Oh heavens . . . don't worry. Why? Are you thinking of leaving Egypt?'

'I haven't made up my mind yet.'

'You don't like Nasser either, I suppose,' he said in a whisper because the boabs were talking quietly at the dark entrance.

'The Moslems started to make it difficult for us long before Nasser,' she told him. 'He only makes it worse.'

'Then please come to England,' he told her. 'Just to see you walking down a London street. I'd follow you around just to see the general effect of that walk of yours.' He was half-way down the steps and into the taxi, while she stood at the lift door, laughing to herself.

CHAPTER SIX

SCOTT was careful about money. He saved the fare to Port Said by get-ting a ride in a Ford station-wagon from the Frontier Department's pool which left Cairo with a khamsin, the desert dust-storm which blew curtains of fine yellow shot across the green fields and into every pore of the skin, into pore against pore so that sweat became a painful abrasive.

He had felt the khamsin coming last night. It was an alienation which he never liked, and he had gone for comfort into the clean new bookshops along Emad el din where they sold English and French and American pocket books. He had bought four American novels which did not have this sort of vista or alienation about them—the little metropolis of Wines-burg and the tragedies of Cowperwood in Philadelphia and Chicago which he already knew well.

'Do you want to stop at Ismailia, Capten?' the Sudanese driver asked him.

Scott did not want to stop anywhere in this grit-world, but he would have to. The driver would want a drink of coca-cola from one of the street sellers.

'Five minutes,' he said.

He sat absolutely still in the sealed car trying to read in the bronze day-light while the Sudanese drank the iced drink. Scott paid for it and they went on through the hazy French town which had lost all its old prospect now that the British army had almost moved out of the Canal zone.

Just outside it they passed a white and sick-looking British Red Cap crouched into the lashing dust-storm on the road where the sign said *Brigade of Guards*. In two months he would not be there. Gamal Abd el Nasser had achieved that much by treaty. The last British soldier would definitely leave Egypt in two months' time never to return.

A car passed them with lights on, and two police officers stopped them on the canal road and asked them for a ride into Port Said.

'Get in the back,' Scott said.

They realized he was English but what was he doing in a Frontier

34

Department car? Scott was an old hand at giving no answers to this sort of question.

'Where are you going?' he asked them in Arabic.

'Our duty is in Port Said,' the younger of them in a green beret said.

He became charming then in his attempts to provoke Scott into defending the English for their murder of the police at Ismailia in 1952, the incident which had been the real spark for the officers' revolution. They realized, of course, that not all English were responsible.

'Why not?' Scott said, willing to accept it. 'Blame one and you might as well blame us all, don't you think?'

'That's true, that's true,' the older one sighed. He coughed through the dust, opened a back window and spat into the storm.

'What will you do in Port Said?' the young one asked him.

'My wife lives there,' Scott said.

It was one of those odd lies that trip out of a man's life without real reason. Françoise was not his wife, she was someone else's wife. But there was comfort in the lie at least.

Françoise would first of all open the door an inch on its chain, and if the children were there she would greet him formally, almost accusingly, like an old friend: 'You see, it's Monsieur Scott. Are you going to shake hands with him André or are you going to be impolite?' If the children were not there she would simply open the door wide, a little surprised to see him, and say calmly and teasingly in English, 'Come in.' He never thought it much of a greeting, but he knew he might have inspired something better himself if he could have attempted something more emotional. But that would come later and cause trouble.

'You should always telephone me first,' she said to him now in French and went on in French as he followed her inside.

'I was in too much of a hurry to get here,' he told her.

'But you are so reckless. What if somebody is here?'

'Then I am just Monsieur Scott calling to see how you are,' he told her. 'That's all I am anyway.'

'Cynique,' she said as if she were hiding a joke. 'Cher anglais,' she said, forgiving him. 'You are so nice sometimes.'

It was satisfying that someone thought him a little reckless. He did not feel reckless at all, coming here, although that was what he needed here, and what Françoise needed more than he did—more recklessness.

'This khamsin,' she complained in French. 'This terrible country.'

Françoise had known no other country, but it was a slip-shod phrase from her upbringing. Any European born in Egypt would say it, the words meant nothing and he knew it, but he took it up as if they had irritated him.

35

'London has fogs and I don't know what Paris has,' he told her. 'I've never been there, and neither have you, Françoise. So you'll have to put up with the khamsin.'

'That's not nice,' she said in French. 'Why do you say that?'

'Why do you always call this a terrible country?'

'But *un pays terrible* doesn't mean the same thing in French as it does in English—a terrible country. It's a different word. It's your bad French, cheri, and you mustn't get upset and you mustn't *attack* me.'

'I'm not upset,' he said; but he was, without being able to prevent it or understand why.

She shrugged and let it pass. 'I have some small veal cutlets,' she told him, 'which I had for the children when they come home from Ismailia tomorrow, but I can get some more. And some potatoes?'

'I'd like to take a shower first,' he said.

'Naturally. You are always so clean, aren't you?'

She was going to make it up to him by getting him a towel and by keeping herself amused with her friendly affection, which did not annoy him any more but made him feel thought-of and appreciated. But she drew back quickly when he tried to make it a little more than that.

'Not now,' she said and gave him soap to wash the khamsin off with.

'I'm sorry,' he said and went to the shower feeling guilty.

'Ah, my nice clean Monsieur Scott,' she said through the door when he was stepping out of the deliciously clean water. 'Your veal cutlet and potatoes are ready.'

He dried and dressed and sat down to eat, feeling better; and he let her tease him. He complained about it, but it did not really annoy him and she watched him eat and shook her head and looked at his face.

'That's when I know how you are a man. Look how you eat. You love it.'

'There are other ways, also, of showing you that I am a man,' he said.

But when she laughed, he blushed at his own unintentional innuendo.

'Comme je vous aime. Comme je vous adore,' she said, but she held up her hand like a policeman when he started to reply. 'Don't say anything. Let *me* say it,' she insisted. 'Grosse bête. I can be so much nicer than you.'

He would have felt better if she had said 'Comme je t'aime, comme je t'adore', but she could not *tu* him. She would only *tutoyer* her family and her children and Roberto, the husband who had deserted her.

'Why do you always like being so elusive?' he said. 'It doesn't help.'

'But that's the French in me,' she replied. 'And because you are sometimes too *brut*.'

'There's not a drop of French blood in you—only your husband and your passport,' he insisted. 'The rest is all Jewish, which I like better anyway.'

36

'No. That is why you *don't* like me.'

'Because you never allow me to. You make it so impossible.'

'Only because I am a married woman and you would be doing wrong.'

It remained a sort of safe protective joke as long as she did not mention the children. If she brought the children into their relationship she would mean it bitterly and seriously. But that would come later also. Now they were becoming intimate by quarrelling, although it always seemed to be a useless dead-end to Scott, because she would not plunge deeply into any sort of emotion, nor let him plunge.

'Anyway, you're a good cook,' he told her. 'Is that Jewish?'

'No. It is French. Roberto Rolland taught me.'

Roberto had been a very successful man for a local girl to marry. He was a pure Frenchman, not a local Frenchman, and he had worked in the Canal company's office at the mouth of the canal itself, to which he had come from the *sous-officierie* of the French Army. She had almost cut herself off from her Jewish family to marry him as a Roman Catholic, and her own aunt had screamed when she heard that Françoise had married a Christian as a Christian. If she had not been such a dutiful daughter her parents would have lost her by outside religious pressure on them, simply for the disgrace. Now they were dead, and Françoise survived in that half-way world of no religion, although she could never be anything but Jewish. She had nailed to the front door of her apartment a little mezuza with one word—Adonai—on it. God. That was a mere formality of Judaism, but it was enough.

'God is enough,' she would insist. 'I don't recognize anything else, except for the children. Their only hope, *les pauvres*, is to be French, I know that. And to be French,' she would say with a shrug, 'you must be Catholic, and so they will be Catholic which is simply one other way of tolerating God, isn't it? Wouldn't you say that?'

'Opportunism,' he would say lightly, not taking it seriously.

'*You* talk!' she would slash at him with her calm and unshakable reluctance. 'You are just a pure Englishman standing so upright. No problems of who you are and what you are. *You* talk. But it's not like that when you are born Jewish in Egypt under French protection, yet never one thing nor the other of anything.'

'I know,' he would say seriously then to stop this sort of discussion. 'I know all that, and I'm sorry, Françoise.'

'Are you sick?' she said to him now over the yaourt she had served him with a fruit salad.

'I was thinking of Roberto,' he replied. 'Have you heard at all where he is?'

She swivelled round on the kitchen stool to whip the coffee off the

37

stove before it boiled over, and then she got up to turn on the light because the khamsin had smothered the day right out of the sky, or rather had pulled down deep yellow curtains of dust over Port Said.

'Monsieur Beauvoir, who is always *stupide*, told me the other day that he had a letter from Roberto. He's gone back to the army, in North Africa. That man is stupid, Beauvoir, because he always liked Roberto, and he was really telling me I should write to him because he is doing his duty in Algeria for France. They are so patriotic, the Monsieur Beauvoirs, when they are so far away from France. But the patriotic thing for Monsieur Beauvoir to do is not to tell me to write to Roberto but to elevate me to Grade Four, which would give me more time and money for the children.'

She was a Grade Three employee of the Canal company and she wrote out all day in long-hand in purple ink, in a large green ledger the size of her desk, the shifting appointments and gradings of every employee of the Canal company in Egypt. It was a sinecure for her lost husband and her French children, but Monsieur Beauvoir (who had helped her get the job) would not upgrade her.

'He will never up-raise a Jew,' she said. 'Even Roberto's wife.'

'Then let me raise you up,' he said in the idiom.

'*Tttt! Tttt!*' The annoying and casual negative of Egypt. 'Let's not start that, chéri, it is too complicated.'

'Do you want me *not* to come and see you?' he said unhappily.

She shrugged. 'If you don't want to.'

'Don't be like that.'

'But I must be like that. If I let myself go, simply for a *plaisanterie*, what will be left of the little I have?'

'It ought to be more than a *plaisanterie*. I don't want a *plaisanterie* either.'

'If you'll only wait a little while longer,' she pleaded gently and seriously. 'I can't divorce Roberto unless I go to France, and you know if I go to France the Egyptians may not let me back in. And how will I live in France? How? I can get a divorce in the Moslem law, but it would not be real, and since the Tribunaux Mixtes are finished in Egypt I can't do anything here. I may not ever be able to do anything, so I am really of no use to you,' she told him. 'Am I?'

'I can be patient,' he said resignedly. 'If I know I am waiting . . .'

'But you shouldn't wait,' she went on sadly. 'I don't really wonder that Roberto went away like that. Sometimes I even understand it. It was only what he did afterwards that I could kill him for.'

Roberto had simply given up being her husband. But first he had made it public among the *clubistes* of the company that his wife was not simply elusive but hopelessly frigid. It had been a terrible effort to get his children born (he had complained). That was what came of marrying a Jewess. He

38

had abandoned her in a wild spree among the young wives and daughters and widows of the company clubs of Port Said. Everybody knew.

Françoise had long ago told Scott, tearfully, the worst of it. He had tried not to be told, but she had been ruthless with it because she needed to trust someone with herself, and she had never found anyone else, not even a woman, who could be trusted the way she could trust *l'anglais*.

'You will never hurt me like that,' she told him.

'Why should I hurt you?' he said gently. 'Moreover, you don't give me a chance to.'

They could laugh it off.

But he felt a sympathy for Roberto, although he knew that some day he might have what Roberto had never had of her, because he understood her better. He had lived in this country long enough to know what the mixtures meant. He could easily trace the gloss of one people imposed upon the race of another, even though they were so thoroughly intermingled at times that only the broadest outlines of each could be recognized. He knew what was semitic in Françoise and liked it; and he also knew what was French in her and liked it also, though in a different way and perhaps not so much. It was when she could not make up her own mind that she froze upon herself, so that she was neither delicately and cleverly French, nor generously and maternally Jewish, but trapped and nullified between both as she was now.

'But I know you will never insult me for being Jewish,' she was saying. 'Even when you are angry with me. Promise me that.'

'Why should I do a thing like that?' he said. 'You know . . .'

But he gave up explaining himself, and she gave him more coffee and sniffed gently into her handkerchief.

'You always expect the worst,' he accused. 'You mustn't do that.'

'Only a Jew understands that we *must* expect the worst,' she said. 'How can you blame us for being the way we are. You are at heart, all of you, anti-Jew. How can you avoid it when you are taught it from the cradle that the Jews murdered your Christ. If I was a Christian I would hate the Jews.'

'And André and Mireille, your own children who are Jewish?'

'I tell them every day of their lives that they are also Jews, that they must not forget it, whatever religion they grow up in.'

'I don't understand it,' he admitted, 'but I think you make too much of it.'

'With Nasser trying to murder us all in our beds?'

'That's silly.'

'Of course it is. But is it so impossible? Look at poor Sam Hassoon. What did he do wrong that did not begin by being born Jewish? You will never be able to save him, I know it.'

39

'You don't know anything.'

'I do! You all hate. Even you hate,' she said. 'And yet you don't know why you hate. Even Roberto who might have hated me for a real reason shouted out at the top of his voice that I was Jewish. Why did he do that? Perhaps you even say it yourself when you leave here, angry because I can't turn this into a pleasanterie between us, because I know if I did you would desert me quickly and think soon: *that Jewess!*'

'Now you are being stupid. Stop it. You'd spoil any man's feeling by saying things like that. Stop it. Please, Françoise. . . .'

'But it's true.'

'It's not true. I'll get up and leave if you go on like this, because it is not true at all.'

She shrugged offhandedly. 'All right,' she said obligingly. 'But you are too English and simple. I think I ought to find somebody to explain these things to you.'

He gave up against the superior French intellect. 'Do you think somebody else can explain my own feelings to me?'

'No. But feelings are wrong anyway. You need someone who understands these things about Nasser.' She touched him on the neck then—a cool embrace which only modified the desire instead of warming it up. 'But I wish there were someone else you would love.'

'There are plenty of others,' he said pacifically, always the pacifist, ultimately, in these situations between them, always willing to give in, to wait until she recovered.

'Then off you go,' she said.

But she was too confident of him to fear that she was releasing him once too often. He might take her up some day and leave her, but she doubted it. *L'anglais* was a very loyal man.

40

WHEN another set of young men questioned Sam, taking him out of his box-room in the old sandstone villa which smelled of dried-up sugar-cane and dead cockroaches, they were polite and encouraging, asking him who his friends in this were and why did he want to kill Gamal Abd el Nasser?

'If you could only explain, we would understand.'

When Sam heard this question he was less frightened of what they suspected than of the truth. The truth was not so stupid, although it was probably worse.

'But I'm innocent!' Sam cried in Arabic.

'Of course you are, Sam.'

'But in the name of God I am. I don't understand this at all.'

'Neither do we, Sam, but we will.'

It seemed very cunning to Sam that they should admit ignorance, and he did not like their honesty at all.

'If I knew anything to help you,' Sam offered, 'I swear by God I'd tell you.'

'You will tell us sooner or later,' they said.

They had not touched the truth, and yet he could not blame them for their purring cynicism because they were, after all, policemen, and they had not yet beaten him. If they ever did beat him he was not in good enough shape to take much punishment. He had grown fat lately because he had given up wrestling and gymnastics at the Maccabee Club and was following the basketball teams instead.

'What will your aunt, Miss Helen Mamoon, think of this, Mister Sam?' Mustafa the questioner said to him.

'She'll be very, very worried,' Sam admitted in English.

They laughed until the phone rang and there was suddenly a power outside of them at work. It brought the deference up from their stomachs.

'Iowa ya sidi, ya sa'atel bey, ya. . . .'

Sam waited for the exalted word *pasha*, now forbidden under Nasser, but it did not quite come which meant that Mustafa was probably talking

C*   41

to a new official of the regime. The other one, Mahmood, was half-listening and they were in the guard room, which looked as if it had once been a drawing-room but was now like any dried-up office in any Ministry—dusty, naked, and worn.

'I always greet your aunt,' Mahmood said, 'when I meet her in the street. I say *Goodmorning* to her, and she nods her head a little. I have always admired her. Look at how she walks. Is there anyone in the Ministries your aunt doesn't know, Mister Hassoon, *ya bey*, *ya basha*?'

'She knows everybody,' Sam agreed.

'And what's the use of that?' the policeman said with a shrug.

He was a good-looking man and Sam hated to mistrust him or think of him as an enemy, but he knew he must do so.

'She even speaks better Arabic than I do,' Mahmood said to Sam, 'but what good is that now? How good is your Arabic, Sam, who has lived here all his life and hates the Egyptians? How good is your Arabic, Sam?'

'Better than yours,' Sam said resentfully, tiring of the jibes. 'I wouldn't even say to you what I *could* say to you; because it would insult your mother, and it would be *shameful* for me to say it anyway. Believe me.'

His Arabic was the blacksmith's, the soldier's, the mechanic's, the fireman's and the sailor's; and the policeman laughed. They loved to laugh. The other one still talking on the phone told him to shut up.

'Hoss, hoss!' he said and looked worried.

When he hung up he looked threateningly at Sam, and for the first time since they had taken him Sam knew that something specific had happened which might or might not be in his favour. But he did not know what it was.

Another, more serious policeman at the airport was also questioning Captain Selim and Captain Serafi and the flying students about Sam. He knew he was being silly. Bambo the engineer looked puzzled and shrugged when he was asked about Sam. What could he know? The students laughed at the policeman and told him to talk to Captain Zareef.

Zareef had already seen the policeman among the students and knew what he wanted. But he was instructing, and he would not get out of the plane.

One after the other the students went into the plane and told Zareef what the policeman wanted, and they laughed at the stupidity of taking Sam or his predicament all that seriously. What fools the police were. They were all trying to reassure Zareef. They knew he was worried about Sam. That was normal. They were Arabs, brought up that way in Egypt where a brotherhood could still remain intact.

Also, Zareef was the man they liked.

Captain Selim, in charge of it all, was a good pilot and a man without a

42

temper, but he was not a good instructor. Zareef was still fascinated by flying. Teaching it (after twenty years at it) was still a vocation, and he always insisted on their notes. 'Write down your airspeed and revs, my dears, and draw the petrol system. Write it down not once-and-for-all but every month.'

Why did they admire him so much?

Only one of them had the secret of Zareef. He was Fahid Rahman, the son of a well-known eccentric, anarchistic old lawyer named Osman Rahman; but Fahid was a sharp and dry-tempered boy and the others ostracized him for his harsh peculiarities. It was simply impossible to tolerate him sometimes. 'He's *magnoon*,' Captain Selim would confide to the Director and suggest from time to time that Fahid be sent back to his father as a hopeless case.

Finally, after trying and failing to instruct Fahid in the rudiments of flying, Captain Selim had handed him over to Zareef, who discovered that the boy did not even know what the tail-trimmer was. He didn't work, he didn't want the belief of working. He was too suspicious of it, or perhaps he simply pictured himself making two flights a month as an airline pilot with good pay, like Waters the American airline pilot who kept a small private Cessna in the second hangar.

He was obviously a sharp-witted boy, but he hated the continuous adolescent joking of the other pupils and he was a bad student, almost as if to prove how stupid the good ones were; anything rather than conform to their tomfoolery. He saw it all. Everything. He noticed, for instance, that Captain Selim liked to put a plane down on the very border of the airfield, not even one-third of the way across; and that Captain el Kadir, the young relief instructor, liked to test the Ghoumariya himself, because it was the only time he could be alone in a plane. Captain Selim with his hooded eyes was afraid to allow a pupil to take the stick, whereas Captain Ali Zareef let the pupils do it always, all the time. The Austers were stiff left-handed planes; the Besterman, which the Egyptians built and called the Ghoumariya, was light to fly but noisy. He suspected, deeply, that Zareef wanted the feeling of being an airline captain himself, of being a man and flying the far distances. Zareef would walk up the corridor of the plane to the pilot's seat through the passengers—the captain of it, but above all the pilot of it. That was what Zareef cared about and was proud of. Instead, he was the world's best and most patient instructor, admired by his pupils, even by the stupid ones. And even when he was on the ground they would gather round Zareef like silly girls.

'Ya Capten,' the policeman said to Zareef when at last he stopped for the day.

Zareef, too sharpened and too tired after bumping all day in the Auster, lost his temper. 'What is it? Why do you wait for me like this all day?'

43

'Please understand . . .' the policeman began apologetically.

'I do understand. I know you've been waiting for me. I have seen you talking to them all.' But Zareef's dignity got the better of him. 'Why do you bother me, *ya effendim*?' he asked stiffly.

'Because they all say to ask you, ya Capten. You must know this Hassoon.'

'Yes, we all know him.'

'Ay then? Well, Captain?'

'He is a very good man. If you are asking me, that's what I am saying. Hassoon effendi is a very good man. I don't care what you say.'

44

'DID Helen Mamoon ever work for you?' Peacock was asking Peter Dukes, who now had a dry body that looked like pale old Japanese bamboo. Peter was not that old, but he looked thin from a lifetime of excess or restraint, and pale because he had hidden himself in terror from the sun, and he was freckled already with the large brown stains of early old age. 'And I don't mean in the cotton business,' Peacock added.

Peter shook his head. 'Helen hasn't exactly worked for me, but she's certainly helped me from time to time, particularly when she worked for old Barker-Danderson.'

'Do the Egyptians know she helped you?'

'Who knows what the Egyptians know these days?'

'But surely they must know who you are,' Peacock reminded him.

'Of course they do. After all, we once worked in close liaison with Egyptian security. We ran it . . .'

'Then I suppose they must suspect her of being a British agent, if she had anything to do with you.'

Peter Dukes smiled knowingly, and Peacock thought that smile a very annoying trade-mark of Peter's work.

'I doubt if they suspect her,' Peter said, and when he talked he pushed off his disguise of old age, as if he were still a little too coarse-grained for the transparency of a gentle old man. 'Anyone but Helen Mamoon. She knows everybody, including me, and that's all it amounts to. Or rather, I should say she used to know everybody; but probably none of her old friends counts in this regime. But she's had a remarkable career for a woman in this country. She might not have been the first woman official in the Egyptian government, but she was one of the first.'

'What about her nephew? Did Sam Hassoon ever work for you?' Peacock asked, admiring his own cunning in thus asking the really important question.

Peter, in his dim musty room, rubbed his bamboo nose and looked so

45

quickly and with such amusement at Peacock that he gave himself away, which was professionally unusual.

'I'm not a fool, Tim. That boy's an idiot.'

'He's in gaol.'

'I know that.'

'What *don't* you know, Peter?'

'Not much I do know these days,' he said regretfully. 'If you want the up-to-date Egyptian experts, full of inside stuff, you'll have to go to the marvellous young men Tony Mason is sending out. They're the experts London is counting on these days. Not the old hands.'

'You mean that ginger-headed fellow, Bateman?'

'Bateman and that young South African woman they've brought in from Beirut.' Peter snarled over it. 'She actually drives a Jaguar.'

'They can't help being young,' Peacock sighed.

Peter recovered himself, and he was a stickish old man again sitting calmly·and neatly at his cotton-broker's desk which seemed never used, never crossed by business or money or trouble.

'You really begin to look like one of those spiderish old millionaires,' Peacock said to him, 'sitting in the middle of it in your linen suit and manipulating everything by remote control. This place looks as if the noise of one typewriter would shatter it. Couldn't we have the shutter open just a little? All very well for you living out here all the time, keeping the sun out, but take pity on the poor sun-starved Englishman, Peter.'

Peter got up obligingly and opened the shutter an inch.

'Oh, go on,' Peacock said. 'Let's be reckless and open it right up.'

'Too much glare,' Peter said and left it barely open. 'No soft and azure skies here, no green and shaded lanes,' he mocked.

'How long is it since you were home, Peter?'

'Thirty years, and I'm not going to be sentimental about it, so don't expect it of me.'

Peacock stood by the window, looking for the daylight.

'What the devil is that supposed to mean? Don't you want to go home?'

'If England is turning out a generation like Bateman I don't think I want to see it in process. Poor old England.' Peter chuckled at his own despair.

'What's the matter with Bateman? He can't help being that way.'

'*I* don't know what's the matter with him,' Peter said in a matter-of-fact sort of contempt. 'Lack of bone marrow, lack of something. They're so milk-fed. They speak the language, and they're as busy as bees, but . . .' He twisted his head like a helpless praying mantis, looking at Peacock and warning him. 'If any of you ever do listen to Bateman we end up losing the little influence we have left here—you know that, don't you? Canal and all.'

46

'Get away with it. You're prejudiced.'

'Scum, that's exactly what they are,' Peter said calmly. 'Half-educated as they are, I'm not going to put up with them, believe me. I'm determined to get them out of here by any means. They're too bloody dangerous.'

'You take them too seriously,' Peacock said, amazed at the cold ferocity which appeared like a brittle crust on Peter's thin, coarse voice. 'After all, the bright young men have to grow up somehow, like Topsy.'

'This isn't the time for bright young Topsies,' Peter said contemptuously. 'Not with Nasser, at any rate. Nasser's different. And Nasser is not a Topsy. He's a very businesslike, determined, extremely calm, thoughtful and dedicated young bastard. Bateman and these young Joint School boobies haven't a hope of standing up to his methods. It's laughable. They've got no sense of the past, and they are even more ignorant of the present. They don't even realize that these Arabs are going through a dangerous process which young Bateman or the backsided patriotism of some of our politicians can't really interrupt for a second. No offence to you, Tim, but politicians *are* to blame '

'Of course we are. I know that.'

'But when these flimsy young know-alls think of facing up to Nasser and having a crack at him—oh, how I begin to quake. How I quake. And I think of the Arabs, not of Nasser.

'I'm a bit that way myself about Nasser,' Peacock said.

'Well, don't be that way,' Peter snapped. 'And if you're also thinking about having a crack at Nasser, go to Bateman, don't come to me.'

'I've already been to him,' Peacock admitted.

Peter's sense of humour came back. 'Nothing will change you, Timothy. Not even a soft-bench in parliament. But be careful. I'm not going to let these young fools make a mess here—politicians or no politicians.'

'Let's have dinner tomorrow and you can tell me more,' Peacock said. 'I have to rush off now to see Scott. You remember Scotty?'

'Having watched him being hounded into oblivion, how could I forget him?'

'It seems odd the way they've discovered him again.'

'Nothing odd about it,' Peter answered. 'It's all part of the same silly game of baiting Nasser. They're using him.'

'But has Scott really been mixed up with Nasser and the officers, Peter? Tell me honestly, because I must know that above all else.'

'Of course he's been mixed up with them. Didn't you yourself, during the war, arrange for me to get Scott into the Ministry to see Gamal when they arrested him? He knows them. I suppose he respects them and trusts them. Why shouldn't he, after what we did to him in the war and even after the war? Every time Scott tried to get a job with the English oil companies or even get a passport renewed they practically threw him out

47

of the place as if he had a contagious disease. That was probably his own fault. Nobody likes a stupid man, and Scott is sometimes very stupid. But that's no reason to hound him . . .'

'Perhaps they've hounded him because he's for Nasser, and plays politics here when he ought not to, seeing that we're up against it.' Peacock felt very hypocritical, but he had to know for sure. Was it true? Had Scott ever been deeply involved in Egyptian politics?

Peter drained a plastic cup of brandy he had been drinking, and he put it away unceremoniously and put his hand out for the cup he had given Peacock, so that Peacock also drank it down and pulled a face and wiped his mouth.

'Plastic and brandy just don't mix,' Peacock said. 'Tastes like horses' hooves.'

'Horses' hooves are good for you,' Peter said and went on. 'You needn't worry, Timothy. Scott doesn't know anything about politics here. It's all sentiment for him. Some other blind outlook perhaps, but not politics. But be careful of him just the same. He's not all that safe a man to be with in this country. Too complicated.'

'I know how complicated he is,' Peacock said, as he left.

When Peacock did try to find out about Sam Hassoon from Bateman, he began to see what Peter Dukes had meant about this young man with his ginger hair and his rather flamboyant self-confidence. It was the camel-hair waistcoat that worried Peacock.

'That idiotic schoolboy,' Peter Dukes had said.

'That silly old bastard,' Bateman moaned now. 'Merde on them all!'

Peacock did not understand it, remembering the good times of his own youth, his own generation, which had whooped it up gaily in the delight of being lost and abandoned by the previous and older generation. There wasn't much left now for the Batemans, only the welfare state; they groaned, they mocked, but they never really laughed.

'You've been talking to old Dukes,' Bateman said to him, as if it were already a good joke; everything for young Bateman seemed to be a good harsh joke to begin with. So far it seemed to be a little cruel, to Peacock. 'So he told you to ask me about Sam Hassoon?'

'That's true,' Peacock admitted. 'Peter is an old friend of mine, so don't be too hard on him.'

'I know he is. That's why it's all right for you to listen to him. But don't expect *me* to take any notice of that silly old bastard.'

'Really . . .'

'Did you know that the surveyor's report on his building (you know he owns that whole office building) says that the floor above him is about to

48

collapse on his head with borer or death-watch beetle or something?'
Bateman laughed erratically at the prospect and Peacock felt he was
actually picturing the real event, that horrifying crash. They drank orange
juice in a Greek café where Bateman was known and never paid a bill.
That was what contacts did for you.

'Aren't you being a bit hard on Peter?' Peacock suggested.

'That's impossible.'

'After all, he does know this part of the world, don't you think?'

'Before I came out here,' Bateman told him, 'I saw two hundred and
eighty reports Peter Dukes had made in thirty years. Reports doing what?
Why—giving it all away. Just simply giving it away, inch by inch, even
when there was never any reason to give up a damn thing. Now look what
it's come to.'

'What has it come to?'

'Nothing yet. But sooner or later it will reach a very low-level showdown
with Nasser.' Bateman wrinkled his unbothered forehead. 'The sort of
situation where you have to push it to the limit or chuck it all in and sink
into oblivion. It's going to be one or the other so why muck about with
the middle bits, old boy.'

Old boy!

Peacock was very amused. If he had not enjoyed it, and been flattered
by this low-level equality, he might have been as annoyed by it as Peter
Dukes was. But Peacock saw through it. From a twenty-five-year-old boy
to a forty-year-old politician, this was simply a generation being determined to get what was owed them. Who could blame them?

'I really think you ought to be a little more restrained about Peter,'
Peacock said, goaded into loyalty none the less. 'He was doing this, you
know, before you were born.'

'I've heard that one before.' Bateman's gold cigarette-holder jerked up
and down between his good teeth. 'Peter Dukes was also walking backwards before I was born. All very well for you to play the game here as it
used to be played. But what you don't realize is that it is not like it used
to be. The clowns have moved in . . .'

'The who?'

'The clowns. The goons.' Bateman's small laugh came from his small
mouth, and it did not sound like an intellectual joke.

'You mean Nasser?'

'Of course I mean Nasser!'

Having been forced into this age equality, Peacock supposed he must
also get used to a cruder political equality.

'Perhaps you're right,' he said. 'But Peter thinks most people here are
for Nasser.'

'Oh, shit on that,' Bateman said good-naturedly. 'If you like, I'll take you to all sorts of Egyptians here who will tell you otherwise, if you're interested.'

'I'm very interested,' Peacock said.

'Good. I'll fix it.'

'And about Sam?' Peacock asked.

'No. You ask Peter Dukes about him. He knows all about your Sam.'

'But that's exactly what Peter says about you.'

Bateman, with the gold cigarette-holder in his lips, wriggling it up and down gaily as he spoke, his good teeth gleaming and his green eyes burning away at the game he played, said:

'Did he? Well *he* played the dirty trick on your friend, not me. So now I'm batting you back to Peter.' He took a coin out of the fob-pocket of his camel-hair waistcoat and tossed it onto the marble-top table for the Greek waiter. 'It's all a bit of a football game anyway, don't you think? Isn't that what old Dukesy says?'

Peacock thought Bateman looked like a young tiger, and young tigers did not play football.

'You may think so, and Peter may think so,' he said to Bateman, 'but I, for one, don't feel like being the bloody ball. Nor does poor Sam Hassoon.'

Bateman enjoyed that. He laughed and elbowed Peacock's arm to show his appreciation, so that Peacock felt puzzled about his position for a moment. Then he realized that it was probably in the line of all things at his age—to be caught between an older Peter Dukes at one end, and a young Bateman at the other.

Was that the modern outlook for a forty-year-old—when you came right down to it?

'I think I'm going to hate this business of growing old,' Peacock told himself sadly as they left together.

CHAPTER NINE

WHEN Aunt Clothilde (everybody had called her that) had died in 1945, Scott had learned how to feed her pet tortoise, Felu.

'Felu, Felu, Felu,' he called gently, tapping the clam shell under the dripping garden tap, just as that blind old lady had done.

He held the breadcrumbs in his hand and fed Felu while he waited, after days of fruitless efforts, for a telephone call—a message from Gamal Abd el Nasser which would mean that he could ask Gamal directly about Sam.

Achmed the kitchen boy put the morning newspaper near his knee on the garden path, and he leaned over it and read on the front page that Gamal had already gone to Aswan with the Productivity Council. That was bad luck. But no doubt Gamal had gone to Aswan to prove to himself that the first stage of the High Dam could be completed in five years, instead of twelve. Fourteen engineers and surveyors and economists had gone with him to give him the arguments, because Mr. Wilson Close of the World Bank would be in Cairo on the fourteenth of the next month to decide whether or not to lend Egypt the first part of twelve million pounds sterling to get on with it.

Scott put the last crumbs on the paper and let Felu feed herself.

Aunt Clothilde was long dead, and the *pension* was not quite the same these days; but it was the only home he had known in twenty years, and he supposed that by now it was simply habit. For the last six years the *pension* had been owned by Madame Salz who denounced Sam Hassoon as the biggest vagabond in Cairo because he gambled all his money away and would not marry. But with one marriageable and dowryless daughter, little Becky, left unattached, she was willing to marry her off to Sam, and she had once gone to a marriage broker to arrange it. It was really a sin for Sam to go on the way he did.

But Sam thought otherwise.

'They only want my money,' Sam said, and though he never had any money he never came near the *pension* any more, not even to see Scott.

The other pensionnaires were not the same sort of friends they had all been once, either. They came and went too quickly for Scott to keep up a friendship with any of them. At the moment one was a divorced Palestinian who lived desperately by dressmaking, and her sewing-machine thundered on the top floor all day; another was a bank clerk whose family lived in Alexandria; and there were two brothers who had come from Halfaya to try to set up a carpet-weaving business in Cairo, and who talked only of the difficulties under Nasser of importing anything saleable, particularly if you weren't a Moslem. None was a Moslem, but the Zionism-versus-internationalist brotherhood of the Maccabee of Aunt Clothilde's table had died when Aunt Clothilde's friend had died, soon after her. That true Maccabaean (also half-blind) had believed in the revolutionary brother-hood of Jews against great wrong, and she had refused to be panicked into the narrow concept of Israel for the Jews. She had died in frail opposition to it.

'Captain Scott!'

He turned around, surprised. 'Yes?'

A woman and a stoutish man were on the garden path, the man with a black bakelite box slung off his shoulder like a camera.

'I'm sorry to startle you,' he said in an American voice, 'but your friend Colonel Peacock thought it would be a good idea to come and see you. I hate to interrupt that reverie down there . . .'

Scott was still squatting, Arab fashion, near Felu and the morning paper.

'I was feeding the tortoise,' Scott said, standing up in embarrassment.

'You were much farther away than that,' the man suggested, but the American voice seemed to suggest that anything in life was permissible. He was Jack de Brazio, he said, and this was his wife Ella. And the little black bakelite box was a German wire recorder which they would, with his permission, switch on at the battery, if the voyage out in the local taxi hadn't ruined the thing.

'I wonder if I can get a tape of a tortoise eating,' de Brazio said and put the small hand-microphone near Felu chewing the bread on Gamal's formal portrait. Felu ate a few mouthfuls and then pulled her head in.

Scott stood back to let it all pass him by, to escape if he could.

'It's still a new toy with him,' Ella de Brazio said to Scott. 'When the Germans built this one, they made it so sensitive that you can easily pick up anything remotely resembling a munch or a statement.'

'What's its name?' de Brazio asked Scott familiarly. 'The tortoise?'

'Felu.'

'Well, we got Felu anyway,' de Brazio said, but all this elaboration was not quite as elaborate as it seemed, and Scott asked him then what they wanted.

De Brazio made a pretence of apology and produced an English news-paper from his pocket, folded open at a war-time picture of Scott himself, and around it on almost the entire page a story with sensational headlines over it, written by Monroe Mathieson, M.P. and famous T.V. personality.

'Had you seen it?' Jack de Brazio asked him.

Scott held the paper before him but he saw only Monroe Mathieson's rich black hair and responsible eyes—those eyes which swore to be the conscience of a million other eyes.

'No . . .'

He took out his steel-rimmed spectacles and looked at the article, read-ing a few paragraphs with a detached fascination, not for himself but for the author of it. The story was simple. By some extraordinary power (the introduction said) which could not be revealed, Mathieson had managed to unearth and reach that mysterious Englishman Captain Scott who was now employed by Colonel Nasser to do secret work on the eastern fron-tiers of Egypt.

A description of the aeroplanes, the camp, the mysterious journeys in the mountains, the search for Scott, the whole adventurous episode, and finally the mysterious outline of the reluctant, secretive Captain Scott him-self, embittered by the old memories of his court-martial during the war, and strangely reluctant to respond to any suggestions that his case should be reopened. What was the real mystery of this strange Englishman?

Tomorrow, it promised, Monroe Mathieson (who was now on a tour of the Middle East and who had just flown on to Israel from Cairo and Cyprus) would tell exclusively the background of Captain Scott's disgrace and court-martial during the war, in Scott's own words.

'Hot stuff,' de Brazio was saying.

Scott looked at the American and his wife and remembered with an effort who they were and what they were here for.

'I think you'd better go,' he told them. 'In fact, you can go to the devil.'

'Don't be like that,' Ella de Brazio said. 'We really came out here be-cause Peacock was so angry with Mathieson. He rang us up all the way from Aswan and begged us to come out here first thing and get your answer to it.'

Scott put his glasses away carefully. 'My answer to what? To that?' he said, handing the paper back. 'Who can argue with that sort of thing?' he said angrily.

'You can,' Jack de Brazio told him with his microphone in his hand.

Scott looked at that little black tube and stepped hastily away from it.

'But please listen,' Ella de Brazio argued. 'We're not the British televi-sion. This is for an American programme, and you can say what you like

53

on it. We're not going to crucify you. On the contrary—Tim Peacock wanted to give you a chance to give your own version of what's been going on . . .'

'Nothing's been going on.'

'But you've read that article. Mathieson says you're more or less the pet Englishman Nasser keeps around.' De Brazio had it out of his pocket again with the microphone cradled in his hand.

'I tell you I'm not talking any more to you people.'

'We're not *you people*,' de Brazio replied indignantly. 'We're simply giving you a chance to reply to everything said in this article. Half America and heaven knows who else will probably hear it.'

'I don't want anyone to hear it. Go away,' Scott said.

'Don't go. Please!' the wife insisted, holding his arm. Her dark Italian face made it all for his own good. 'Look. These English papers have practically called you a deserter and a traitor. Many people know that you were neither. And simply because you still work in this country seems hardly excuse enough to drag up old histories of the war at this time. Why do you think they've done it?'

'I don't know and I don't care.'

'But you do care, Captain Scott,' Mrs. de Brazio said. 'Do you feel like a traitor and a deserter?'

'Do you expect me to answer questions like that? Look what that fellow did with the simple-minded questions he asked. How do I know what you will do?'

'Because it's all in here,' de Brazio said and tapped the black box.

'Just leave me out of it. I don't know why this sudden interest in anything I've done. If I'm a traitor, that's perfectly all right,' he said angrily. 'If I'm a deserter, that's good too. Now that's the end of it . . .'

'What about your friend Sam Hassoon?'

'Who told you about Sam?'

'Peacock told us. But don't worry, we're not going to broadcast that. We have to stay in this country. But at least you might tell us what's behind it all. What's suddenly happening in this country, Captain Scott?'

'I don't know anything. Nothing!'

'You're not helping yourself, you know,' Mrs. de Brazio said regretfully.

He had won his way to the brick staircase leading to his room and he could see Madame Salz smiling out of the front room window at Captain Scott and his friends.

De Brazio, who was obviously a man who liked to eat and drink well, lost his patience. 'Why not tell this Mathieson guy what you think of him? This is your chance.'

'Do you think it's as simple as that?'

54

'Absolutely!' de Brazio said. 'Just let him have it.'

Scott said nothing, but he avoided the eyes of Mrs. de Brazio which were accusing him for being a fool.

'Sooner or later the other guys will get to you, and you'll have lost your chance to say what you want,' de Brazio insisted.

'They'll never get to me,' he told them.

'That's what you think,' de Brazio said and put the microphone in his top pocket and turned it off in disgust.

'I'm sorry,' Scott told them. 'Nothing I say will do me any good, so leave it all alone.'

De Brazio shook his head. 'Can't,' he said. 'Whether you like it or not, you're worth the interest.'

They were talking from the top to the bottom of the brick stairs and back again. But the staircase was dangerous for such a big man and Scott warned them not to step on it any higher up.

'Some of the steps will break,' he said. 'Get off it.'

'If you won't talk to us,' his wife tried, 'would you just walk outside the garden gate onto the street so that we can get a picture of you from across the road.'

'No. Never.'

'What she means is,' de Brazio said with his cynical intimacy: 'will you walk out so that we can get a film of you where your boss, General Hakim Abdul Sadat, shot at you in 1942. You see, Captain, you can't hide the old . . .'

Scott had closed the door of his room.

De Brazio shrugged. 'If he wasn't such a hefty-looking guy I'd have hammered on his door, but why should I break my neck?'

Scott could not go out because he could not face the cameraman across the street waiting to take a film of him at the gatepost where Hakim had tried to kill him during the war. But Peacock, arriving at Almaza airport from his sightseeing tour of the Aswan Dam site, came straight to the *pension* and knocked on his door and found him working on maps and notes and reference books.

'I came straight from the airport,' Peacock told him breathlessly.

'Is that fellow with the camera still outside the gate?' Scott asked.

'Yes, but I sent them.'

'I know you did, and I don't think much of the idea.'

Peacock sat down wearily. 'But I was so mad when I picked up that paper last night at the airport. I tried to ring you then, but I didn't have time. I knew you wouldn't see anyone, even if I asked you, so I rang de Brazio this morning and told him to come straight out here.'

'What for?'

'I'll never get over that dirty trick Mathieson played. But that's the most incredible hypocrisy,' Peacock said helplessly, as if all those years in Parliament had sheltered him delicately from ever experiencing such perfidy. 'If I'd known he was writing for the press I would have stopped him; but really, Scotty, I didn't know. I didn't think he'd do a thing like that. It's such *barefaced* hypocrisy. That television conscience! You ought to sue him for libel. I trusted him, and I can't apologize enough. I'm terribly upset.'

Peacock was visibly upset. He looked as if he had raced down the garden path and up the stairs with his eyes burning with indignation and resentment, his own honour betrayed and in need of rescue. Scott tried to calm him, saying he could not feel angry about Mathieson because he had not trusted him anyway, whatever Peacock had thought.

'But why did he do it? I'll never speak to that fellow again. I'll never allow a word he says in the House to go unchallenged. I'll remind everyone every day of his dirty trick, his barefaced hypocrisy . . .'

Scott laughed. 'Don't bother, Tim. Don't. He can't hurt me.'

'But he hurts me,' Peacock said indignantly. 'I encouraged you to talk.' Peacock went on with his helpless discovery. How could a man be so vile? Scott tried again to reassure him and to make light of it, begging him to forget it. But Peacock was adamant.

'Never,' Peacock swore, and he would have gone on with it, but Scott refused to listen any further.

Peacock had relaxed by now. He had already charmed Madame Salz, in their brief encounter at the front door, and now in the winter afternoon she offered them tea with a knock at Scott's door.

Scott said, 'Yes, please: but put it in the garden, Madame Salz.'

'But it's cold in the garden,' she said in French.

'My friend wants the sun,' Scott said.

'That old lady's got a bit fatter since I saw her years ago,' Peacock said of her as they heard her going carefully down the brick stairs.

'That's Madame Salz. Aunt Clothilde died years ago.'

'Was this the twin, the friend, the one in the black dress and the thick glasses?'

'She died a few years ago, too. It's all been changed.'

'Except for you,' Peacock told him. 'You're a conservative type, you know.'

'I have to keep my belongings somewhere,' Scott said. 'It doesn't cost me much and they are all old friends. What you could do, Tim, is to tell that fellow on the other side of the street with a camera to go home, because I'm not going to be photographed.'

'But I tell you it's for your own good. Honest. I've known that American

56

de Brazio since he was in London after the war, and he'll give you a fair chance to defend yourself.'

'All I want is for them to forget it, to leave it alone.'

'But they won't. Don't you realize that? De Brazio says the others will get to you sooner or later.'

'By tomorrow night I'll be back at the Red Sea, and let them find me there if they can . . .'

'You're going back straight away?'

'Yes.'

'But what about Sam?'

'I can't do anything about Sam.'

Scott was leading the way down into the garden and Peacock looked on the hard head below him and he thought then: *He's going to be knocked about again if he's not careful. Or if I'm not careful. He's going to get the worst of this too.*

'But surely,' he said to Scott, 'you can say a word in the right place. You must have *some* influence here.'

'I told you I have no influence,' Scott said, sitting on the old banyan stump and sending Achmed away and pouring tea with hands so hard and so thick that they could hardly straighten on the handle of the teapot.

'Then what hope has old Sam got?'

'The same sort of hope he'd have anywhere,' Scott said.

'But I still think that one word in the right place . . .'

'Why do you think that? Don't you think there are laws here as there are in England? Sam's all right.'

'But let's be realistic. You know as well as I do that influence counts more than any law in this part of the world.'

'Not any more,' Scott argued. 'All very well, Tim, to come out here from the law-and-order of Britain and think that everything everywhere else is corrupt. It may have been once, but it isn't now. Could you put a word in the right place in England to get someone out of gaol?'

Peacock took the cup of tea and one of the doughnutty biscuits, which added to this plot to put weight on him. The change in climate seemed to have given him an appetite.

'But, Scotty! You're not going to abandon Sam to the mercies of the Egyptian law, such as it is; or to the Egyptian mentality, such as it is.'

'He's safe enough.'

'I wish I could believe it.'

'You'll have to believe it,' Scott said unhappily. 'Anyway, what do you think he's in trouble for?'

'I'm hanged if I know.'

'Let me tell you, then. Do you know what they asked me about here?'

'You mean the Egyptians?'

57

'Yes. They wanted to know what you are all doing in Egypt anyway,' Scott said. 'What is Church doing here, and why should Lucy Pickering be coming here from Israel?'

'I don't know about Lucy. Is she in Egypt? But what's that got to do with Sam?'

'Too many old friends, Tim. All of you once in the same line of business,' Scott said, not accusing him but warning him. 'If I knew what it was all about I suppose I'd get angry. But since I don't know what it's all about I'm going back tomorrow. You can try and get Sam out of gaol if you can, but I know now it's not possible at the moment—with all these suspicions about.'

'But you know I can't help. I'm probably more hindrance than help.'

Scott was too much in agreement with that comment to reply. But he gave Peacock another cup of tea, and Peacock also felt it was wiser not to press it any further, seeing how it was affecting Scott.

'Oh damn!' he complained. 'Why does this sort of thing have to happen?'

'Politics,' Scott said bitterly, and they said no more about it.

58

CHAPTER TEN

THERE was no need to leave at dawn. Zareef could fly him down later and then stay the night in the desert and then fly him, in the morning, over the last valleys near the Qena road where he would begin to work now, if Hakim agreed. Let anyone find him there if they could.

'Do you mind this boy?' Zareef said to him at eight in the morning. The ciné cameraman had gone, but a tall sharp-cheeked youth was standing near Zareef's Czech car. 'He is one of my pupils, Fahid Rahman.' Then he said in a whisper to Scott, 'He's the son of old Osman Rahman the lawyer and he's a little mad, but he's all right.'

So was his father a little mad, Scott remembered. Old Osman Rahman was a well-known religious anarchist who had been against every Government in power in Egypt for thirty years, and most violently against all women's suffrage movements. He hated them and blamed them for Nasser's existence.

In the car Scott felt Fahid looking at him from the back seat as if he wanted to find a flaw in his neck. He turned around, and the Egyptian boy smiled with his sharp bony face as if it were a joke, almost a cruel joke.

'Can you fly a plane, Capten Scott?' he said in English.

'I hold the stick of the Gemini for Captain Zareef sometimes when he drinks his coffee.'

'That's not flying,' Fahid said, 'that's camel driving.'

'Is it? Then I leave flying to our expert.' He nodded at Zareef.

'Captain Zareef is our best expert,' Fahid said with a fragile surface of mocking affection. 'Captain Haboob Selim is our worst expert.' That was definitely savage.

Scott nodded and watched the road and left the boy's remark alone, for Zareef's sake. He would not foster comments on this rivalry between Zareef and Selim. He had wanted to ask Zareef more about Sam Hassoon, but that would also have to wait now.

'Never mind, Capten,' Fahid said inexplicably, but in a comforting way as if he knew what Scott was thinking. 'I understand you.'

59

Fahid's gazelle eyes watched him, restlessly. He knew quite well (his eyes said so) that this Englishman did not realize how well known he was in Egypt for being Gamal's English friend. His quiet, stiff, English ways were watched with fascination by the flying pupils at Gedida because he looked so sure of what he was doing, and because Zareef would tell them how he admired Scott. A man must be a man; and Scott was very much a man in Zareef's point of view. 'He would have made such a great pilot,' Zareef had said, and wasn't that the highest possibility of flattery? The other and unknown side of Scott was also an attraction because it was a tempting mystery. What did he do out there? They say he had found every route a camel or a man could take across the Sinai, from the Red Sea and from the Gulf of Akaba all the way down to the Sudan border. They would watch him talking and walking with Zareef and know what he was, without really knowing, because he hid so much of it. When the Gemini took off to take him back to the Red Sea, the stupid ones would usually say, *'There he goes, back to the goats.'* Fahid would then tell them what idiots they were. 'If the Englishman ever barked at any of you,' he would say, 'you would all run like goats.'

'I don't suppose you would let me take it off?' Fahid asked Zareef now.

The Gemini was wheeled out in the Gedida morning and all was ready for them.

'I would not,' Zareef said.

Fahid shrugged, and Scott asked him how many flying hours he had.

'Twenty-five,' Fahid told him. 'But I had taken eighteen hours to solo. Even now Captain Zareef checks me every few days. I am the very worst here. They don't trust me. I am a bad pupil, very bad.' He laughed cruelly at himself.

'Perhaps you're not patient enough,' Scott told him. 'That's not so good.'

'Naturally I'm not patient,' Fahid agreed. 'I hate patience.'

'You'll have to be patient on this flight,' Scott said as Zareef checked the controls and fixed the seats. 'It's going to be cramped and boring . . .'

'I suppose it is. But it's my luck that Sam Hassoon was taken away like that. Poor Sam Hassoon. Poor very stupid Hassoon. Nothing much anyone can do for him, is there?'

Scott turned away from that.

Fahid obviously knew that Scott had been in Cairo to see about Hassoon. He had probably guessed that much. But he did not quite ask Scott what he had achieved. He thought about asking now, but then he shrugged. Very stupid Sam. Fahid knew what Sam had done. It was so foolish of him that no doubt Gamal Abd el Nasser would hang him as a traitor when he found out. His father thought so, and his father also knew what Sam had wanted and what Sam had got. But it was no use worrying

Zareef or Scott by talking about it. He wanted two days' flying with Zareef, not two days of Zareef worrying about Hassoon.

'I think, Captain Scott, that you're very happy on these co-operation flights,' Fahid said as they got into the small four-seater cockpit. 'Not so?'

'That's right.'

'I think too that Captain Zareef likes them.'

Zareef buckled his safety-belt. 'I think you should be less talkative.'

'Do the Bedu ever try to kill you for capturing them?' Fahid asked.

'They're all our friends,' Scott said. 'Why should they kill us?'

'Ah, but smugglers . . .'

'So are the smugglers our friends,' Scott said.

'Then why do you try to capture them and put them in gaol?'

'We try not to,' Scott said, giving the boy a chance.

'But you catch them.'

'Sometimes. But we don't like to.'

Zareef pushed the starter buttons.

'Then they must love you very much,' Fahid shouted above it and sat well back into the irony of the situation. 'You are all very brave men,' he said, and laughed heartily as the Gemini rattled into life.

Far way, beyond the coast and over the low bronzed hills, Scott pointed to a shadow below and shouted at Zareef that it was somewhere around here.

'Go down by the Roman ruins in the Mitgal. I want to see what's there.'

Mitgal was the Arab name for the coarse, sandy bottom that ran through some crushed-looking Eocene hills. In the middle of it stood the square outline of an ancient Roman outpost called the *mons claudianus castellum*. Mitgal simply meant mother-of-columns, and several half-finished Roman-quarried columns were still lying in the wadi.

'Do you want me to go right down?' Zareef asked.

Scott nodded, saving his voice from the Gemini's battling engines. When he had telephoned Hakim that he was going back to the desert, Hakim had been very anxious that he come this way. 'Anywhere on that line between Qena and the coast,' Hakim had said with a curious sense of humour about it. 'And if you see any trucks, go down and take a look at them, particularly if there's a bus with them.'

It was one of Hakim's unfathomable jokes, but they usually meant something.

'Are there trucks there?' he shouted to Zareef.

Fahid was leaning forward chewing gum and breathing down Scott's neck as Zareef banked down over the crumbling empty village in its sand-trap.

'Two trucks,' Fahid shouted and pointed them out.

They were hidden under the shade of an old quarry shelf he knew well. 'You had better land,' he told Zareef.

This was not far from the direct road between the Red Sea and the nearest Nile town of Qena. But it was really the back way—the same way the Romans themselves had used when they had carted the granite blocks over to Qena to ship them down the Nile to Alexandria and on to Rome to build the Pantheon and Trajan's forum. Smugglers had used trucks before this, even buses, and a Saudi Arabian gold smuggler had often used a small aeroplane from Jidda until a khamsin had caught him and blown him down into the desert where Scott had found him, eaten to the bone by desert rats.

Zareef shot up the wadi once, and then half-turned and landed bumpily over the camel scrub that was hidden by the softer sand.

'What do you think of them?' he asked Zareef as they stood near the plane looking at the trucks under the big shelf in the shade.

'They're English trucks,' Fahid told them.

They were small half-ton Bedfords, but one looked more like a bus than a truck, with windows and seats.

'At this distance they could be anything,' Zareef said. 'Let's look a little closer.'

Scott had his eyes on the sides of the wadi, but nothing could be hidden on either side, and when he looked at the trucks closer he said they looked harmless.

'They might be geologists from the Desert Institute. There are two or three wells around here the hydrologists are interested in.'

They walked cautiously into the quarry shade to see them.

Zareef chuckled into his blue coat. 'Department of Antiquities,' he said.

There was one small bus and a half-ton truck, but they were not from the Department of Antiquities as Zareef thought. On the bus was written the route in English: *Elephantine, Hermonthis, Thebes, Coptos, Leucos, Limen, and Memphis.*

Scott knew it now, or rather he knew the route. It would take them (whoever they were) from the Sudan border, northwards down the Nile to Qena, then across the mountains to the Red Sea at Safaga, back to the Nile, and on to Memphis and Cairo. He had heard of this bus. It took British and German and French and other foreign archaeologists from one site to the other—not as tourists but as experts looking at the work of other experts. They were usually well-known visiting professors who made the tour to see new work on the excavations.

'Who are they?' Fahid asked, ridiculing them sight unseen. 'Americans?'

'They're probably Germans mostly,' Scott told him. 'I've seen them in Ghurdakha at the Rest House sometimes.'

He had usually seen them from a distance, but he had never heard of them turning into *mons claudianus castellum* before. It seemed logical though, since it wasn't far from the main Qena road although it wasn't Pharaonic by any means.

'There they are.'

Scott tilted his big hat against the sun and saw the small group, drivers and professors presumably, emerging from the ruins a hundred and fifty yards away. They were walking half backwards, and two small old men were taking photographs. Scott admired their enthusiasm. None of the eight or nine of the group was young, and there were two women among them.

'So they are your hashish experts,' Fahid began, 'your gold smugglers.'

Zareef told him to be quiet.

A small authoritative Englishman was giving them history as they took photographs. Scott listened, but he was more interested in a large fat German-looking man who seemed ill and should not have been out in the heat of the day. He was fanning himself with his hat and breathing heavily. Scott felt like telling him to get into the shade quickly.

The Englishman's voice was explaining the system of quarrying.

'All this rock is foliated granodiorite,' he said. 'There's the loading ramp, and these were the square blocks and column bases that were never delivered.'

'But where are the columns?' one of the women asked.

'Farther up the wadi,' the Englishman said. 'One is lying at a loading ramp with an inscription on it that reads the second century A.D., cut in the time of Valvenius Priscus, centurion of the twenty-second Legion, by the architect Heracleides.'

He stopped and wiped his forehead with a silk bandanna. He was a neat, small Englishman with a very red face, wearing a well-pressed alpaca suit and hiding under a good panama hat. He was obviously in charge.

'Heracleides?' the woman asked again. 'Were there a lot of Greeks working here with the Romans?'

Scott squatted down, unwilling to interrupt this although they must have seen the plane landing higher up the wadi; but they were all fascinated with this small man's talk.

'Most of the quarry overseers were probably Greek,' he was saying. 'They usually cut their names into the quarries they were in charge of. But the real inscriptions are Roman. There is one very fine lintel, or there was one, marked in dedication to the God Seraphis in honour of Hadrian. There *is* one Greek inscription,' he said in his sharp rather military voice. 'Down there.'

They turned round as he pointed.

'A graveyard,' he said. 'One of the gravestones is marked in Greek. *Welcome*, it says, *anyone who wants to join me.*'

They laughed.

Then Scott felt himself recognizing a familiar voice, a familiar figure. The small red Englishman in charge of these curious people turned in time to make it sure. Scott felt a desire to hide, because it was General Church. No wonder Hakim had suggested that he come this way looking for trucks.

'Look!' one of the women said. 'Here are the people from the aeroplane.'

'Good morning,' Zareef said with his politest smile.

'Oh. You speak English,' this thin woman said carrying it on professionally for the others. 'Did you think we were trying to steal some of the pillars?'

It could not be avoided now and when Scott lifted his large hat to the ladies, General Church recognized him and coughed in amazement.

'Well, good heavens, Scott. It *is* you, isn't it? What an extraordinary thing. How are you, lad?'

'Very well, thank you,' Scott said.

They shook hands, and Scott knew then that something dangerous had happened to his life.

CHAPTER ELEVEN

NONA MAMOON (who was now Nona Quartermain) was Helen's young-est sister, and she looked like a brisker, sharper copy of Helen. She ex-pected admiration more than Helen did, but like Helen she was a little contemptuous of it when she got it. She was sure, anyway, that she was envied and admired and liked, which was mostly true. She had come back to Cairo to see her sisters, with two sons but without her husband, which worried Helen and the eldest sister, Hanna. When Helen asked a tactful question about it, Nona shrugged it off impatiently.

'He has to work. He's in Cyprus. He might come later.'

Helen suspected otherwise, but she would not ask about it or put her fears into another question. She would not believe there was trouble. Nona's unexpected war-time marriage to Quartermain, who had always been a little exaggerated, had been happy. Quartermain was by no means the man they had anticipated for her, but that made it more likely to succeed. Allowing for the normal flow and fall of marriage it had been happy for twelve years. The sort of children she had proved it.

'I shan't give them the evil eye by talking about it,' Helen said to Hanna. 'I won't even think about it.'

But Hanna, being the eldest, had to say something about it.

'Why don't you send him a telegram and tell him to come?' she said to Nona.

She was pleading for Quartermain—for Nona to forgive the unknown sin. Husband was next to God, even before the father and before the son. Hanna believed in a rootless Christian, Coptic, Catholic, Egyptian, uni-versal, all-hovering and on the whole semitic God, taking that part of each which protected the family and provided for the children.

'You mustn't imagine things, my darling,' Nona said very firmly.

'But he should be with you.'

'He's all right,' Nona said to end it; and when she talked to Hanna like this she could keep her affection and her sharp-tongued independence in one unit of speech without hurting Hanna. 'Don't fuss about it.'

That was all. Three Mamoon sisters would never quarrel anyway. They had burning consciences to protect each other. Their affection was of mutual indebtedness, and was always heartfelt. It had to be, living in a Moslem world which pushed them to the wall. In Cairo there was expectancy in every man's glance, and women were not safe without some sort of defence, of which the family was one, and ever-ready resistance another.

'And please, darling, you mustn't start by spoiling the children,' Nona warned the two of them. 'Their father spoils them enough.'

'That's nonsense,' Helen said. 'A little spoiling won't hurt them. You're too strict.'

Helen and Hanna both knew that they had the absolute right to win the boys over as quickly as they could by any means. What if it did involve a little indiscipline and spoiling? They had to make up for the disappointments of their own lives, for their long discipline and pride against men. The boys were six and three years of age, and boys were particularly valuable. It seemed therefore even more of a pity that their darling and successful and near-perfect Nona had developed a flaw in her marriage. Quartermain *ought* to be with her.

Nona had brought them both presents, which they were unpacking in the flat they had rented for her, near them in Gezira and overlooking the public gardens. English woollen skirts, which Helen started tucking and pinning, and which Hanna showed gratitude for by going to the kitchen to make sure that the servant, Ali, didn't spoil the roast. They ate a large lunch which Hanna had cooked herself and they gossiped in English, French, Italian and Arabic—depending on the nuances they wanted. When they began to talk about an Englishman they found it came more naturally in French.

'Have you never known,' Helen asked Nona over the rest of the unpacking later, 'this Englishman who calls himself Scott?'

'Of course I know him,' Nona replied, answering all questions as if they were borderline, almost silly.

'Oh, I knew that you'd heard of him. But himself!'

'How could I avoid knowing him?' Nona said. 'He and Quarts were such good friends, and in the same desert group in the Army. Doesn't everyone know Scott?'

'Yes, darling, but what is he? I mean as a man?'

'The English put him in prison during the war for disobeying orders,' Nona recalled. 'But you ought to hear Quarts on that subject. As far as he's concerned it was Scott who saved *the-bloody-British Army*, I mean from that General with the red face. But Quarts exaggerates, as you know.'

'I know all that. But is he nice or not nice?'

66

Nona's teasing suddenly danced into the realization of what was being asked her. 'Why?' she said. 'What is it?'

'Nothing,' Helen answered, 'except that for Sam he's the one we have to depend on. Now with Nasser. He knows Nasser.'

'You met Scott?'

'Of course I did. What are you asking? He came here.'

Nona's black eyes were all over the place and then they came back mischievously to Helen's poor defence. Her wish for Helen was always the same—not necessarily that Helen should have a husband, not necessarily so, because only a married woman knew that there were worse things in life than being husbandless; but all her life she had wished that Helen could at least find some relief from her bad luck, from constant duty, and from her defensive contempt for men which frightened them off whenever they became serious. She wanted Helen at least to find her equal.

'So you like Scott,' Nona said happily.

'No. Don't be silly. He is too difficult and too stiff. In fact I don't think I like him at all. Just to see him.' Helen made the shape with her hands and lowered her eyebrows to mimic the soft disguise of Scott's deeply hidden eyes and the enormity of his body and hands. 'Sometimes the English look as if they could easily carry the whole world on their necks,' she said. 'But I've found that too often it can be a deception. They are just as weak as every other man.'

'Perhaps this one is different,' Nona said and walked out to the balcony to shake out a skirt.

'That's not the point,' Helen insisted, following her. 'It's Sam I'm thinking about.'

'If Sam's in gaol it's his own fault,' Nona said, laying it down as a family law. 'Don't you start killing yourself for Sam.'

'You can't say that.'

'Yes I can. I know what will happen. You will wear yourself out and ruin yourself trying to get Sam out. What did he do anyway?'

'Oh, something stupid.'

'What?'

Helen shook her head. 'Don't ever ask me. Please!'

'I'm sorry, darling, but if it's that bad . . .'

'It's stupid. But don't ask me yet.'

'All right.' At least Nona would not press her, but she knew that Nona would go on worrying about her rather than about Sam. 'But it's so typical . . .'

Outside, from this balcony, they could see Hanna in the nearby public gardens, playing ball with little Hilal who had been given an Arabic name eaning new moon, a change of luck, because that was what they had

67

needed when he was born. He was holding Hanna's skirt. The other boy, the elder, who was called little Ben—although he too had been given an Arabic name, *Da-ud*—had apparently been born for the fun of it. He was dancing up the garden dust with his feet and trying to catch it, laughing at the sport, or at the sight of genuine Egyptian dust. Then he leapt affectionately at Hanna's legs for no apparent reason, and they both knew that Hanna's eyes were filling with delighted tears for that loving impulse.

'That devil little Ben is going to break Hanna's heart,' Nona said, 'and he'll also come home filthy.'

'At least it will give her something worth breaking her heart for,' Helen told her in English harshly. 'The Ministry still won't give her nationality. I think this time, with Nasser, everything is changing for the last time. They say she's nothing, simply because she was born in the Sudan. They worry me about her all the time now. In fact, they say she's British, because she was born in Khartoum. The fact that mother and father were Egyptian doesn't even count any more, because father was absent enough or Christian enough for these Moslems to be officious about it. They *always* find something to make it difficult for a non-Moslem. That's how they are now.'

'They've always been like that. Egyptian means Moslem, darling, so let's face it.'

'Yes, but this time it's worse. All the Jews, too, are leaving if they can leave. They get half their business taken away from them under this new law, which says they must have Egyptian partners. I can't blame the Egyptians. But what can the Jews do? Or the Copts, simply because they are Christians? What can we do?' Helen cried desperately. 'The Moslems are going to make it a Moslem country, pure and simple, and even the Copts are going to be pushed out. As for the half-and-half Copt-Christian mixtures like us, it's hopeless.'

'They really can't push out a million and a half Copts, who are more Egyptian than the Moslems anyway. How can they do it?'

'No, but a lot of the Italians and Armenians have gone. It's not the same for anyone, even us. You won't like it any more.'

'It's time all the foreigners went, Helen. You know that.'

'But why should *we* suffer for it? At least we're Egyptian . . .'

'Because we stuck to the English, that's why.'

'*You* can say that. You're English now. All right, you are! And you ought to be glad. I wonder what would have happened if I'd brought you up like a Moslem girl? It's no use damning the English like that. You and I wouldn't be as lucky as we are, without the English.'

'I didn't mean us,' Nona said, sitting down and looking at the dusty top of a mango tree. 'We're Egyptians, and you oughtn't to let them convince you that we're not. Even so, the Europeans have been here long enough.

68

You know what they all think of the Arabs—*les sales Arabes*. Look at our own relatives. Is there one among father's side of them who ever forgave grandfather for marrying grandmother because she came from the villages, even though he was Egyptian himself? They cling to their European quarter or eighth or twenty-eighth to prove that they're not dirty Egyptians. The Europeans corrupted us against our own people, so it's time they left us alone.'

'But where can they go, most of them?'

'I don't know. That's their problem.'

'But look at Hanna. Is she any less Egyptian than Gamal Abd el Nasser, except that she's not Moslem?'

'Don't get angry! Of course she isn't less Egyptian.'

'How can I help getting angry? Now they've started on Sam because his father's a Jew.'

It wasn't the anger or the argument or Sam that worried Nona, but the tears behind them. She felt she had heard the first faint beat of defeat in Helen's voice for the first time in her life.

'I didn't want to tell you so soon,' Helen said to her, ignoring her own tears, 'but I want to leave Egypt. I've made up my mind to go.'

'Leave for good?'

'It's hopeless here,' Helen said, leaning on the balcony to look at Nona and admire her. 'I do this miserable job now with the English oil company, but when they close up, as they will, I'll never be able to find anything else. I know it. This regime won't let anybody but Moslems into real work.'

'But surely, darling, you can find something.'

'Find what? You don't know what it's like here now, with the Moslems in full power. They are so determined to remove everybody but themselves from any kind of real work of responsibility. If I want to stay I'll have to become a shorthand-typist. At my age you can imagine me even trying to live on that salary, let alone surviving the work itself.'

'But if you left Egypt you wouldn't be much better off.'

'There wouldn't be Nasser and the Moslems asking you all the time to prove that you're Egyptian, and making trouble for innocents like Hanna and Sam. What am I to do if I can't get her papers? They'll make trouble for her.'

'My God,' Nona said. 'One forgets, being married to an Englishman, that half the world lives in terror of being without a piece of paper which says you are this or that race or religion, or giving you permission to go on living in this or that hole in the ground.'

'It's not even that,' Helen said. 'They won't take my passport away from me, because I'm as Egyptian as they are, and I'll never give in. But I've got to live, I've got to work. I'm getting on.'

'Don't say that, darling.'
'But look at me. Where does it end, Nona? You tell me.'

Where did Helen's bad luck end?

Where did her empire of troubles end? Or for that matter, what happened to any eastern woman, whatever her religion, in this Moslem world which treated women contemptuously if they did not fall into the only available rut of degrading, married life? One looked at the Egyptian middle-class women walking or riding around the streets of Cairo in their driven automobiles, and one despised them for their spinelessness, for their lack of resistance to such a stupid life. Why? Helen herself could have become one of them at any time in her life, plenty of these now-prosperous Moslems who had been her friends would have married her, Christian or not, and turned her into a plump, cream-skinned wife with fat spoiled children and half a dozen servants, and what else? *Oh, what else?* one wanted to shout aloud into their disinterested faces.

Nona knew, when she thought like this, that she had missed most of the secret struggles of Helen's character, somewhere in the past. She had been too young to know what had taken Helen, at nineteen or even younger, into a role which women did not easily manage in this Moslem country. Yet at nineteen, by some means known only to herself, probably by some deeply laid feminine upheaval of will-power, she had forced her way into an Egyptian Ministry, although admittedly it was still under British jurisdiction. There, by the time she was twenty-two, and certainly with the help of one intelligent English official, she had become the first woman Labour inspectress in Egypt.

Perhaps it was the British who had deliberately taken one lone sample of Egyptian womanhood to make an admirable example of. Nona could remember the man she had worked for, Colonel Braithwaite, who was now one of the British delegates to the ILO in Geneva. He had once taken Helen to Geneva as his secretary and assistant, probably because she spoke English, Arabic, French, Italian and Spanish so fluently, and possibly because she had been so lovely. It was Sir Colin Braithwaite himself who had obviously been attracted to her, perhaps in the noblest sense, perhaps in other ways as well, but the relationship as far as Nona remembered it had always been strict, whatever secret motivations might have been at work behind its façade. Helen in full bloom, in full youth, in full confidence was someone to admire, and one need not therefore be suspicious of motivations. In fact, it was impossible to be suspicious of either of them, looking back on it.

But the strange inter-effect of her uniqueness in an Egyptian Ministry had soon revealed itself. Nona's memory, even as a schoolgirl, could trace the change from an interested woman who was simply fascinated with her

70

work, into a woman with a vocation which suited her perfectly, almost God equipped and God given.

'They never really accepted me,' Helen had since told her, when she recalled the factories and tailors' shops and clothing ateliers she had visited to make sure that women's and children's labour conditions were adequate. Adequate? They could never be a thousandth part adequate. The most she had achieved were separate toilets for women in the tobacco factories, which had amounted to a revolution. And in the ten thousand back-rooms of Cairo, where women worked over machines, it was sometimes possible to shorten their day by an hour or to give them a safe exit from a fire-trap or to check once a month the appearance of the sick women who should never be working fourteen hours a day at all, not only the Egyptians and the native women, but poor Greeks, poor Italians, poor Jews, and above all—poor Armenians who made shoes and suitcases and God knows what in miserable top rooms jammed one against the other in the near-native quarters of the city, cold in winter and suffocating in summer.

They, the proprietors of these old-fashioned workshops, might not have accepted Helen, but they had gradually learned to fear her. What else could they do to make money but work the women hard? What was a woman's value if it wasn't her marvellous resilience and toughness and cheapness, when men themselves were available at a fraction of a piastre an hour, a shilling a day? What other chance did women have in a world where men themselves were so degraded and beastlike?

'I can't blame them,' Helen had said sadly, looking back on it. 'It was never their fault. The owners were often little better off than the women.'

She had never, in fact, learned or bothered with the political factors at all, and that was the disagreement Nona saw and felt between Helen and her own husband, Quartermain.

'If she'd ever seen it with even half a political eye,' Quartermain had once said, 'it would have given her something much more important than a vocation. When the Moslems pushed her out of the Labour Office they simply pushed her out of a job. She never did realize that she couldn't do much as one woman, fighting a woman's battle like that, alone, on behalf of several millions. What hope did she have?'

Helen had fought the battle as one woman and she had lost it as one woman, because the very moment the British had handed over the Labour Office to the Egyptians in Farouk's day, the Moslems had immediately ridded themselves of a woman in the Ministry.

The best work she could find thereafter was the sort of work she had done in Barker-Danderson's office, or the sort of work she did now, saving an English oil exploration company from the despairing job of getting their ten thousand requests for this or that through the various Egyptian

71

Government departments. She had protected their concession. She had used her friends in the Government departments, knowing how they could be used (in all honesty and by subtlety, without bribing or without any kind of corruption, but by appealing to the most subtle intelligence they had) and always winning the point in her oil company's favour. They wanted to import new electronic gear without import duties? She could argue the logic of it in governmental and departmental terms to an official who could not quite see what advantage untaxed equipment could mean to Egypt. She had probably saved them a million pounds, simply in time saved, and in petty official trouble avoided, and in taxes. They might or might not realize how valuable she was, but it didn't matter now. The day of the British oil concessions was also drawing to a close.

'I don't know where it ends,' Nona told her now. 'But I don't think you ought to leave Egypt. You'd never survive in England.'

'I'll learn how to survive. At least there I could earn my living.'

Nona doubted it, but she would not argue it now, so soon after her return, and when there was trouble with Sam and her husband to think about.

Hanna Mamoon, the eldest, whose body seemed too full and too power-ful for her gentle outlook, had, on the other hand, been in service most of her life to the memory of her dead parents. When they had died within the same year she had clung to their memory as long as she could by codifying their characters and behaviour into a tender perfection.

'Father used to say . . .'

She liked to begin like that, but the others would not always let her finish.

'That's all very well,' Helen would tell Nona in their evening walk along the Nile for Helen's health, 'but father gave mother too many children, and sometimes he had a violent temper. I remember him striking Emil once as if he would kill him.'

'I've never heard you talk like that about father,' Nona said. 'It's usually me who says things like that.'

'I know, but I think it's time we all looked at the truth of our family,' Helen told her. 'There's nothing left of it anyway, except the three of us. The boys were never very close to us, not after they married. And now they're disappeared all over the place. None of them is left in Egypt. So why should we always be thinking back on what it was? Who cares what the family was?'

'You can't blame Hanna,' Nona said, feeling Helen's defeat again. 'Hanna lost more than we did when they died like that. More than I did, anyway. I hardly remember them.'

'I'm not blaming her,' Helen said rather sharply. 'I'm simply reminding

72

myself that nothing is perfect or permanent. Why have we gone around all our lives looking for perfection? Why do you think Hanna never married? Simply because she could never find the equal respect and perfection to the man she thinks father was. Well, he was a marvellous man, but he wasn't all that perfect . . .'

'What man is, my dear? Let Hanna live with it.'

'Oh, I shan't argue with her about father now. But thank God,' Helen said, 'for the children. They will bring her up to the present a little.'

The children were with Hanna every day in the gardens, where she kept them off the freshly-watered and muddy grass, but a rascal of a native gardener was shouting at them angrily for stepping on the flower-beds.

'Don't shout at the children,' Hanna told him. 'There's no need to.'

'All-*ah*!' the old gardener said. 'If I don't shout how can they hear?'

'They're children. It's bad to shout at them. Don't do it.'

'They pick the flowers! It's forbidden, do you hear!'

The old man had lost his temper and was screaming violently through his muddy moustache, his bare feet stamping up and down on the wet path.

Hanna understood servants and she called the children and took them to the other end of the garden and sat down to watch them and ignore this new voice which now had the right to answer back.

'Come,' she said to the elder—to little Ben, who was looking at the fat hose of the gardener to see what he could do with it if he could get his hands on it, 'and I'll show you the sort of boats your grandfather built.'

'Why did he build them?' Ben asked. 'For himself?'

'No,' Hanna said. 'For the English.'

'What for?'

She did not want to tell him that her father had built gun-boat scows to slaughter the natives with. That was not quite right, taken as crudely as that. She might explain how her father, this handsome young Egyptian-Circassian, had left his family in Cairo and had helped build the railroad for General Kitchener to Wadi Halfa. She could tell them that he was a very good engineer who had been educated in France. But she could not say that when he had finished the railroad to Halfa, he had built the gun-boats which Kitchener had used to sail up-river to Omdurman to blow the Khalifa off the red cliffs and then take Khartoum for the British.

'The English were finding Africa,' she said to little Ben. 'It was not easy to go up the river then because there were no trains, so your grandfather built the English a big boat to sail in.'

'How big?'

She took a twig from the ground and drew a scow, so well-remembered at the dockside moorings at Khartoum where her father had kept it as a memento when the British had abandoned it as a weapon.

'It was like that,' she said. 'You see. Flat along the bottom, so that it

D*   73

could get up the river to Khartoum. That is where your grandfather met your grandmother. . . .'

'Where is she now? Why didn't she bring us something?'

No death and no violence. What could she say of her own mother, whose parents had been slaughtered twelve years before Kitchener reached Khartoum: murdered by the Mahdi? The Mahdi had killed every adult male in Khartoum when he defeated General Gordon, and among them was the family of a Christian Egyptian soap-maker from the Saïd, her mother's family. Not a male was left alive; only her mother, then a child, and her grandmother. At least the Mahdi had spared the women.

'Your grandmother is not here now.'

Little Ben walked over the lines of the boat and then got down on the path and began to make a decent-sized river for the scow to sail in.

'No, sweetheart,' Hanna said. 'Don't spoil the path.'

'*You* spoil it then,' little Ben suggested. 'You make it.'

She laughed and the younger one—this little new moon, this change of luck—got down from her lap and dug into the path. She shrugged and let them be. Let the gardener come, let the voice be raised. Some resistance was needed for one's own sake. The past could not be abandoned that easily, and the brown little river at her feet with Nona's children in the mud was a poor substitute for the large mud villa by the Nile at Khartoum where they had slept on the cool mud roof and had monkeys and snakes in the dirt gardens. Life had been settled there; eight children were born there; and they had slaughtered whole sheep for feast days and birthdays. Four servants had served there, and the bread had been baked in mud ovens in the sand garden where her mother's blind sister had chased the children with more devilry and more fun than anyone understood now.

'Don't get too dirty, my darlings,' she said, watching them make the river of red water run down the path, with their knees well into it.

'Take off my sandals,' little Ben ordered urgently. He was so like his mother in his firm intention, his clear requirement of life.

Hilal, who could not speak, also held up one foot. He fell on his backside into the mud, and she picked him up and sat him on the seat while little Ben abandoned the river.

'Thank God,' she said as she took off Hilal's well-made English sandals, 'that Nona's children are English. They will always know what they are.'

They would not suffer the insecurity she was going through now, simply because her father's papers had said *French-protected* instead of Egyptian or British. The Mamoons had come to Egypt long before Napoleon, but the French had simply taken over and *protégé* anyone not Moslem, because they had needed them to rule the Egyptians with. The English had also used the foreigners. Kitchener, the Englishman, had loved her father

74

and her father had given all his faith to the English. But even so, despite Kitchener's letters and decorations, her own father could not be British. Not that he had tried. In those days it had not mattered, so long as you were a European. No passport, no identity cards, no nationality. If you were the works engineer of the Sudan Government Dockyard, that was enough to live your life on, and when you'd finished there, you could live what was left of your life in the security of a Government pension.

'Tearing down trees, by God!'

The old gardener had come back, and he was dancing in the mud again and waving at little Ben who had climbed a fir tree. He fell and stripped off a small piece of bark as he tried to hold on.

'Ça, c'est vilain,' she admonished Ben.

'All you need in life is a hat, by God, and you can do as you please!' the gardener shouted.

Hanna picked up her bag and her sunglasses and moved away again.

'A hat, by God!' he shouted frantically waving his old arms.

He was ragged and covered in red mud. His own battered hat was the sort you found in the dust and pierced and put on a horse. His cry about the hat was an attack on the spoiled European, who always wore a hat— never the tarboush or the taiya.

'Come on, sweetheart,' Hanna said. 'We're going home.'

Little moon sucked his fingers for protection and carefully watched the gardener who followed them.

'So you're going, by God. Well. It's lucky for you . . .'

And in his gesticulating the old man accidentally knocked Hanna's sunglasses out of her hand.

'Ai-eee!' she cried in surprise, 'What are you doing?'

She watched him fearfully, knowing that when it reached the insulting stage it could also reach the hitting stage. She expected to be struck. If he struck her or the children she would kill him.

But the old man looked at her glasses and laughed.

'She's frightened of me,' he said, picking up his fat canvas hose and pulling it behind him like a sick boa-constrictor, limp and dying. 'She's frightened of an old man who earns half a piastre a day. Heh, heh! What a silly woman. Did she think I was going to water her? Ah, God, but think what I could have said to her if I'd been another sort of man . . . I could have told her something.'

Hanna left the sunglasses on the path. Dignity was worth more than the price of a pair of sunglasses. She snared Benjamin away from the trees, promising him a bag of peanuts at the gate where a native boy sold them hot, fresh and very salty. They were probably too indigestible for the children, and Nona had warned her not to give them anything to eat.

But one little bag couldn't possibly do them any harm.

75

CHAPTER TWELVE

SAM had learned to enjoy the lentil soup and fasoulya which the Sudanese gaoler served him now in a chipped and battered enamel bowl.

'God be with you, Said,' Sam said.

'May your morning be blessed, *ya hawaga*.'

'Do we have any new officers this morning?'

Said would warn him of what was coming. 'No, *ya effendi*. It's Captain Mahmood and Captain Hassan today.'

'Will they call me out today?'

'Yes. After your beans. Every day now. But why don't you think of your family, *ya effendim*? Why don't you tell them what they want? Then you will go home.'

'You think so? But there's nothing I can tell them, Said.'

Said shrugged. 'They only keep the communists now. What are communists but poor schoolteachers? All the King's men have been let out. All except the barber who is still sobbing every day. But now they'll let him stay out in the garden to cut everyone's hair for half a piastre a day.'

Said left the beans and Sam sipped at the hot fasoulya. It was obliging of Said to keep it so hot. An unpolished brass spoon had given his meals a green taste at first, but he had polished it with some sand Said had brought him. The beans were always good. Too long he had eaten too well. His sister Alicia and his grandmother had stuffed him with too much tamia and fried egg-plant and spaghetti. No exercise, either, ever since his old friends of the Maccabee Club and the Greek Club had outgrown in girth their interest in catch-as-catch-can. He was too fat and loose, so he had begun to do push-ups on the floor and to draw himself up on the window grille and flex his arms and to anticipate their questions which seemed to him to be amazingly the same.

They called him out again after his breakfast and they started on a new line, with a picture of Sam in British uniform, which the two policemen discussed in front of him in their office, but as if he were not there.

76

'Now look at those fine knees in British short pants,' Mahmood said to the other. Sam's knees, he said, were so round and smooth that they were indistinguishable from other parts higher up.

The other one, Hassan, drew a large upturned moustache on the picture of Sam and held it up for him to see.

'Farouk himself!' Captain Hassan said and laughed, and Sam couldn't help laughing, although he felt afraid of this development.

Then they drew an extra unit on Sam's lower half and held up the picture and said, 'That's the finest-looking English soldier I've ever seen. A two-headed monster. What a specimen.'

They were hilarious, but Sam withdrew from the vulgar joke and waited until they recovered.

'Now what about this one?' they said. 'Who is it, Sam?'

They held up a picture of Scott. It was one of many they had on the desk, this one cut from a wartime English magazine describing the exploits of the long-range desert groups with Scott the obscure hero.

'Captain Scott,' Sam said.

'Do you know him?'

'Of course I do. So do you. He is a friend of Gamal . . .'

'That's enough!' Hassan shouted savagely. 'Don't mention our Egyptian names here.' Sam had spoiled their fun. 'Anyway,' they said, '*is* Captain Scott such a friend? Eh? How do you know Scott is a friend? What makes you think you know all about this Scott?'

'I don't know all about him,' Sam said indignantly. 'You asked me if I know him, and I'm telling you I do. That's all.'

'So we did ask you. Now, listen, Sam. If you were a British soldier, and if you have English friends like this Scott, why didn't they give you a British passport? Eh? Don't they like Jews, either, these English friends of yours?'

Sam almost lost his confidence in their stupidity. This was too near the mark, and too cunningly aimed to be safe.

'I wasn't a British soldier,' he said.

'What? Are you denying this picture?'

'No!' Sam could not deny it: for four years he had worn that uniform, but the British Army denied it because he had been in Pickering's irregular unit. 'I thought I was in the British Army,' he explained, 'until I tried after the war to get a British passport. Then they showed me that I had only been on contract as a civilian to NAAFI, and that I wasn't legally a soldier in the Army . . .'

'But you were a sergeant. Look at the picture.'

Sam nodded sadly. But for this legal trick it was probable that he would not be here in this trouble now. But he had to avoid that. It was too near the truth of what they were looking for, and he began to flounder.

77

'What's that got to do with it anyway? What do you care about me in the British Army? What's it matter to you!' He was losing his temper.

'Now, now, Sam,' they said mockingly.

'Let me alone! Are you going to hang me for having been a British soldier?'

'We might,' the calmer of the two said, smiling.

Sam changed his temper.

'Simply tell us about Scott,' they said. 'Why did the English put him in prison during the war? Did they suspect him of something?'

More and more Sam did not like this. They were now interested in Scott rather than himself, and he knew it was not simply an indirect route to his own secrets.

'You must know about Scott,' Sam replied carefully, his big warm eyes watching first one, the calm one Hassan, and then the other one—the joker Mahmood. 'The English Generals got the Army into a mess, didn't they, and the young officers like Captain Scott had to get them out of it. Didn't that happen in the Egyptian Army also?'

'What else did they suspect him of then?' Hassan said encouragingly.

'Nothing.'

'Weren't you all working for the British intelligence? Weren't you all behind the Germans in the desert spying on them? Wasn't that what you were doing?'

'Yes, but we were soldiers.'

'Not spies? Are you still not spies, Sam? You, and Mister Scott and now this other one who came to visit you, Colonel Peacock, and how many others? Why are they all here? You are all now doing something. What is it?'

Sam groped for something in Arabic or English or French that would not be too harsh on them yet would say what he felt.

'Ça, c'est tellement bête,' he said weakly. 'Everything you say is.'

The joker Mahmood flushed and suddenly threw a bundle of papers and photographs from his desk at Sam, and then followed it with a box of paper-clips which scattered over Sam and the floor. In the mess Sam paled and felt himself shaking.

'Shutup! Shutup! Shutup!' Mahmood shouted at him.

'*Hosss*,' the calm Hassan said to his companion.

'Ahhhh!' The disgust suddenly burst out of Mahmood's sense of humour. 'Jews are traitors!'

For a moment Sam thought Mahmood was going to order him to pick up the mess—the papers and the paper-clips. Sam felt his stomach agree and his pale face agree; but he knew he wouldn't do it. If Mahmood told him to pick up the mess he would not do it. Even if they killed him for it.

Mahmood looked and sensed it, and he shouted: 'Said!'

78

The black-clothed peasant policeman came in.

'Clear up this mess,' Mahmood said to him contemptuously. 'And hurry up.'

Sam sighed, and Hassan offered him a cigarette.

'No, thank you,' Sam said generously, wishing to be friends again. 'I've decided to give up smoking.'

That was a mistake also. They began to taunt him with a cigarette.

'Oh, go on, Sam. Take one. Just one. It may be your last. Why do you give it up? Aren't we generous enough with you? Here, take the whole packet. Have you got any more on you, Hassan? Two more packets. Take the lot.'

Sam was tempted, but he did not give in yet.

'Of course we can't let you have matches,' Mahmood said between his small sharp teeth, and he laughed and sent Sam back to his lacerated and pink-walled room, high up in the old villa.

'Crétins!'

Sam's eyes were filled with tears at the silly inhumanity of it; although they weren't such bad fellows if they would only leave him alone.

Said locked him in, whispering: 'Don't worry, *ya effendim*, they won't hurt you. It's not they who hurt you.'

Sam was not worried about them hurting him. It was something else. They now seemed to know what they were getting at. But he did not like what they were saying about Scott. It was stupid. What would happen if they started putting things that he, Sam Hassoon, had done, on to Scott?

'I know what I will do,' Sam decided. If they ever made that mistake about Scott and blamed him, he would simply tell them what he had done.

He would confess everything.

CHAPTER THIRTEEN

GENERAL CHURCH had lived with his doubts too sadly and too long to be hurt by them now; but he had not counted on running into Scott like that.

'Some men,' he had said to General Warren after Scott's court-martial, 'are simply bad for each other and can only harm each other by even the simplest contact. I think Scott and myself are in that predicament.'

'Pity,' Warren had told him with a good friend's regret. 'Scott is really a remarkable soldier, but he simply doesn't understand what soldiering means.'

That was all they had said between them about Scott. Whatever else they had thought in those years was too faded to remember now. What ought to be remembered was that Scott, in the face of great obstacles in 1942, had been given very clear instructions, and instead of going through with them he had deliberately withdrawn his men from a very close situation, which might have been thrown wide open by such reckless action.

When he had asked Scott *Why?* the hard and contemptuous reply had seemed to Church to be very cruel without really explaining it: 'If you don't know why, General, if you don't know that you're a born butcher, then there's no point in me trying to explain it to you.'

No doubt Scott blamed him now for having ended his brilliant war-time soldiering in a military prison and finally in the ranks. He himself could certainly blame Scott for causing the whispering scandal and bad feeling which had lost him command of the Eighth Army which would have been his—with all it would have meant later on.

But long ago he had half-forgiven Scott and half-forgotten him for it. He had learned, in a lifetime of soldiering, that you must always let a disaster ride, mentally, until you rode it out. He had ridden this one out years ago, and there was nothing much left of it now. Even running into Scott like that would not have mattered so much, except that too much was at stake here. It was surely no coincidence that Scott had appeared out of the blue at the *mons claudianus* like that. Somebody must have sent him.

'You look rather worried, General. I hope we're not being too much trouble to you.'

In the shaking and shuddering of the bus Professor Maudie Gratton-Hobson was being nice to him with twinkling eyes that were famous, like Sir Arthur Evans's, for their understanding of what was there, if only you could see it. If Evans's Cretan discoveries had been indirectly the result of his short sight, confining his view of fragments to important minutae in them, then Professor Maudie Hobson's love for intimacy sometimes gave her a feeling for what ancient workman had tried to do, socially. Like Jane Harrison's discovery of the origin and social precedence of ritual over magic and religion, Professor Maudie's insight was very useful in unravelling the life and customs of ancient peoples, and because of it her colleagues considered her a generous and understanding woman, always worthy of a confidence, and a person worth speculating with because her insight could so often develop an hypothesis into a helpful line of thought.

'No trouble,' Church said to her. 'You are all very well behaved.'

'Good soldiers?' she said.

The General smiled. 'Soldiers are usually good by compulsion. You are all good by conviction.'

'But how lucky we are,' she said, 'to be in the hands of such a good organizer. Really, General, we all feel we owe you a great deal.'

The General's pink-to-red face flushed a little. 'I do like my job.'

The bus rolled through some yellow scrub country which suddenly cut itself off from the descending plateau of the limestone escarpment, which in its slope seemed to float between the grey valley below and the azure heat haze above. It was very hot country, but the scrub made it look more desolate than it really was.

'These are fairly well-watered hills,' the General remarked. 'At least they are sometimes.'

'Do you really like being in charge of these little field expeditions, General?'

He had forgotten Professor Maudie for a moment, but she was still being nice.

'Of course, my dear . . .'

'What made you take it up? Were you ever an amateur archaeologist?'

'No. Not at all. I suppose I simply couldn't stop being a soldier—bossing someone about or taking a handful of people somewhere into the field for one reason or another. I had no desire to sit in a chair before the fire in a Kentish village and die of retirement pains.'

'But quite truthfully, General, I think you have a *feeling* for this.'

81

'That's nice of you,' he said appreciatively.

'But I mean it. You've become a first-class historian of the sights yourself. So, please, General: let us have a shot at Tel el Amarna.'

Church relaxed into the shuddering dusty bus—he had learned that this was the only way to tolerate it day after day. 'It won't be very comfortable, you know. We'll have to leave the bus behind somewhere.'

'But we can rough it, just once.'

Church watched her pleasant smile rise up to the very roots of her autumnal-grey hair. 'We might try it, if you people think you are up to it.'

'Of course we're up to it. We all want to go.'

'What about Grossgudt?' Church said as quietly as he could.

Grossgudt was the Swiss professor who had caught Scott's eye at the quarry, nearly dead with the heat. He looked half a degree nearer a hot death now, after his long and wrecking bus ride across the mountain road to Qena. His clothes were drenched in buttery sweat.

'Oh, dear old Gugee is always like that, General. He's a marvellous old man. I've seen him walk fifteen miles up a Greek mountain looking like that, and he was still on his feet when we were all half-dead at the end of it.'

'Even so. We'll have to walk quite a way through the villages and then ride across the desert on donkey-back to reach the hillside. I honestly don't think he could do it.'

'Of course he can. We'll be all right.'

'Are you sure?'

Professor Maudie twinkled her eyes at him and said privately, 'You can take my word for it.'

'All right, then,' he agreed. 'We'll do it tomorrow.'

'Bravo,' she told him, and turned to the others in the bus and called to them. 'The General has agreed to take us to Tel el Amarna.'

'Ah . . . Very good . . . we should not miss it. Just to get out of this bus . . .'

They were pleased, but the General did not listen. He had been watching this country with another eye and another mind. It seemed to fascinate him: this yellowish dull gravel and pebbly groping plateau which faded off to the west in wrinkles and gashes, and rose parched behind them in the east in two great peaks, red in the afternoon sun, and then curiously gold and purple, and living in haze as everything did here, summer and winter.

'Isn't it beautiful?' Professor Maudie whispered to him.

It was lovely country, but it could be deceptive, and the General knew he must give a very clear picture of it to General Wodie Smith at the Pathfinder office they had set up in Paris. The other side of Pathfinder, the tactical side of Wallington on Cyprus, would probably be against this

82

route, even though they might be the ones to use it if they ever did decide to intervene in Egypt.

'It looks so dry,' Professor Maudie said, 'without really looking arid.'

'That's so right,' he complimented her. 'It's usually very fresh here.'

It would be child's play to cut through here, even with armour. He knew nothing about the possible Navy approach to it, but if landings were made from the Ceylon base or from Aden, then the Red Sea ports at Gimsa and Ghurdakha and even at Safaga were deep enough for TLC's and probably destroyers. The thing would be to get everything moving on this road and have it clear of the coast within twelve hours, and have the air force drop plenty of stuff ahead of them. A small armoured force could be across to Qena in a day and a half, even without parachute help. And if the Egyptians kept nothing more than the reconnaissance groups they had at Ghurdakha now, with the camel corps, there would be nothing in the way.

'What do you see, General?' Professor Maudie said with her well-known insight at work. 'Do you see the Roman legions marching in the sun with their banners tied to their lances to form an umbrella of shade?'

'Not exactly,' he said patiently. 'I was thinking of an old friend.'

He was thinking of Scott: had Nasser sent Scott down here to find out what was going on? '*I can't quite believe it,*' Church decided. But it was always a frightening thing, to see an Englishman put himself at the disposal of a foreign malcontent the way Scott had done.

Yet with all his faults, Scott did not seem to be the type for it, somehow.

There was a better-known back way to Tel el Amarna, but it was too complicated getting over onto that side of the river at Qena, and in the morning before dawn they took their bus along the green-dappled Nile from Qena and dodged the donkey carts and road-repairing trucks, and bumped over worse and dustier roads than the desert tracks, and then ran for miles along the pellucid canals which were overhung with listless, lovely eucalypts filtering the sun. They asked the way of the policeman at the road checks and bridges, and when they at last came to a turn-off from the main road, which four successive gendarmes had specified as being the correct one, they ran out of road.

They had reached a dead-end in a village which had never seen a car or a bus so close. They had crashed into it over great ditches and through the green edges of cotton fields, and when they walked through the village, leaving the bus and the truck with the drivers, they seemed to be walking not through human habitation but into piled-up stinking mud where a few women and children and babies, thick with flies, were not any more important (less so, it seemed) than the water-buffaloes lying in their own filth outside the mud huts and along the great humpy dirt paths.

83

'Oh, my God!' Professor Maudie said, when they came to the heart of it where all the children and babies had been left in a mud puddle with the beasts while the men and women worked in the fields. '*Look* at those children. Oh, look at them, General!'

Professor Jumeaux Constanza, a Brazilian who was really a Sorbonne professor, said sadly, 'We surely can't walk through this filth. These unhappy people! How do they survive in such conditions?'

'These are not so bad,' Church told them, swishing angrily at the flies with his bandanna. 'I was through here briefly when the cholera was on. Then they were lying in the streets of some of these villages, children and women, quite dead.'

'But it's worse than India!' Professor Maudie cried. 'India is not filthy like this.'

The others had marched firmly through the village, but Professor Maudie gripped Church by the arm to look at one baby, naked, lying on its stomach over some gamoossa droppings, the back of its thin curly head almost unseeable with flies and dirt, and its tiny hands, with curiously white palms, clutching its eyes. It was obviously sick; it was probably dying.

'But where's the mother?' Professor Maudie said, looking into the nearest mud hovel.

Church looked away, always heartbroken to see such poverty and wretchedness, particularly when it affected the children. 'She will be in the fields. They all must work. I suppose she had to leave the little fellow in the charge of one of these lads.'

These lads were a mixed collection of boys and girls having a very good time splitting and chewing dried water-melon seeds. They used the thin, moving stream of yellowish liquid to sail dry camel-dung from one cess-pit to the other.

'My God!' the Professor said. 'It's so awful.'

They were surrounded thereafter by the village children, who followed them from one village to the other, bringing a cloud of dust in their wake. Some villages were not so bad as the first one. And where there were adults they were met formally with delightful questions, the Egyptian determination to be happy at all costs, particularly with twelve or more soft-clad foreigners marching through their native mud.

Professor Grossgudt distributed all his lemons and oranges and packets of Swiss coughdrops as he walked with his arms around some of the children hanging onto him, breathing with difficulty, saying to them in perfect classical Arabic: 'Ah, my beloveds! Have you never seen the likes of us before? Fat old Germans and thin intellectual Englishwomen. Ah, my beloveds! Aren't you happy? Listen to me wheezing like a gamoossa. It's better to live the life of nature, here in the fields.'

84

They laughed even though they did not understand him because it was the educated Arabic, as far from their own as German was.

By the time they reached the Nile, which they would have to cross on the cattle ferry, they had collected all the children of four villages with them. The children were dancing and shouting and fighting for their favours. The professors rummaged in their pockets and bags to give each one something as a gift, even if it was only a button.

'No money!' Church warned them. 'If you start giving them even a half a piastre you'll never get free of them. Don't show money.'

He was right.

Cash, even a half-piastre, was an unseeable and almost unknowable thing to most peasants, and when they had crossed the river in the barge (which was pulled over on a steel cable) sitting on what small corners were free of the grime and scrappings of the buffalo, they had to bargain in the village through the Palestinian interpreter (whom Church brought with him) to hire twelve donkeys to cross the desert to the tombs Akhnaton had built in the higher cliff-faces. Four piastres for each donkey for a two-mile journey and back, and in the heat of the day. Two piastres for each driver, and no tipping. The price had to be decided, clearly and irrevocably, before they went. The village donkey hirer, who sent out the boys to the fields to reap the beasts in from less cash-producing work, was also the butcher. The village headman was the storekeeper. He was sent for, and when he came he unlocked his store, which looked like a packing-case, and he brought out two chairs for the two ladies, and offered them coca-cola for 5 piastres a bottle. The second woman, Professor Berebellis, who was a very quiet and watchful Greek who knew Egypt well, broke into colloquial Arabic with the storekeeper and they talked for a long time, until Professor Maudie asked her what it was about.

'He is asking me,' Professor Dr. Berebellis said in her wisp of a dark voice, 'if it's true that it's the water what causes all the sickness.'

'What water?'

Dr. Berebellis pointed her faint blue-veined first finger at the muddy canal where a gamoossa was lying and a boy was drinking. 'That water,' she said.

It was the General who explained that most Egyptians died of one kind of water-borne microbe or another.

'Half these children,' he said, pointing to the collection fighting and pushing to stand near the effrangis, 'will be dead within five years.'

Professor Maudie shook her head, unwilling to conceive it.

'Most children in Egypt die before they reach five years of age. Yes, half,' Church repeated. 'Sixty per cent, even. After that, the average life-span is twenty-five. All of these people,' he said to the sad professors who kept close to him to hear it, 'have at least one of the deadly microbe and

85

amoebic diseases slowly killing them off, usually painfully. Mostly dysentery, but also sideline diseases of filth like bilharzia and trachoma. Incidentally, keep your hands away from your eyes. Trachoma is very catching.'

Dr. Berebellis reported that the new Government (according to the storekeeper) was planning to dig an artesian well in the village to give them pure water. That was what the butcher was asking her: What will be the difference between water dug from under the ground, and this Nile water floating freely above it? It was all water. 'Do you think I ought to explain?' she asked.

'No!' Church said firmly. 'Here are the donkeys. You'll never persuade these people to abandon their beloved Nile water, Dr. Berebellis, not in a thousand years. That is their tragedy. They cling to their own destruction and nothing can change them now. Nothing at all.'

'I wonder,' the Doctor said with an instinct for painful doubt.

Crossing the desert from the village was not very difficult, except that each donkey trotted at a different pace, and each small boy running the two miles beside each donkey was faster or slower than the others.

Church was an old friend of the guardian of the Akhnaton tombs. This ghaffir lived half-way to the cliff-face in the middle of the slaty desert in a mud house with his father and wife and two children, who were both sick. One of his children was a newborn baby who couldn't take his mother's milk and would probably die in a few days' time by the look of it.

'Here you are, Mahmood,' Church said in English, giving him a photograph. 'Here's your picture, and you see—you are all in it, and your feet too, as you asked.'

Mahmood took the photograph to his wife and father; and then because el Amarna was Grossgudt's special interest, Church left them to the Professor and waved them on. He chose a separate path up the sloping cliff-face.

He preferred to do this alone because he had a fellow-feeling for Akhnaton, who was in some ways the largest of all the Pharaonic figures. Yet the Pharaoh had been a bad soldier, in fact he had not been a soldier at all, and because of it he had lost the Empire to the warlike northern tribes who had cut in on the northern borders while Akhnaton sat up on this hill, building his city and his tombs and teaching his artists to be true to life and to abandon the primitive death figures and grave-guards of the frightening old religions.

'Up here alone, General?'

Professor Maudie had found him.

'Yes,' he said. 'I like to look down over this valley.'

'And I hate to go inside tombs,' she said to explain her absence from the others. 'I simply don't get the feeling of life in them at all, although I know I have to do it. But I think I can sense this place better outside. Is that the city?'

She pointed to a few dark, rounded husks far below in the middle of the desert, between this cliff and the green Nile, all of it sugged down in the hot noonday haze.

'That's it,' the General said, wiping his hot face. 'Akhnaton's city to the sun. But it's hard to believe that once this was all flooded, right up to this cliff-face, and that the grey desert was once teeming with wild-life and domesticated game. The water has receded, of course, but even so it seems an extraordinary place to build a city.'

'Why did he?'

'He had to break away from the old religions. That meant leaving the old temples completely. He was such an extraordinary man. In his own right he was probably the first great individual in history; yet he couldn't persuade his people to follow him, walking in his own city with his wife and children—an unheard-of freedom then. But it's always the same story for the enlightened man. People drag behind and hold him back.'

They both looked across the desert in silence. They could see the Nile winding through its green wall of fields and palms, the green vein that defended Egypt from the desert, and was in fact Egypt.

'You've given me such a new view of this country,' Professor Maudie told him. 'I'm really not very good on Egypt myself. My visits here have never been much beyond the old sites. But this time, General, I feel I have seen and felt something of the people and the country. I mean of modern Egypt too. It's such an extraordinary mixture.'

'It is changing too quickly,' Church said sadly.

'But I had the feeling you thought nothing could change them.'

Church liked this friendly woman and he told her what he really felt. 'The Egyptians are a happy, generous people,' he said. 'It's a mistake to attempt to regiment them as Nasser wants to.'

'I hardly think Nasser has achieved much regimenting down there.'

Professor Maudie nodded towards the miserable villages they had left.

'He will,' the General told her. 'And when he does he will have taken away the soul of his own country. It simply isn't supposed to be a modern or a military nation. It's better left alone.'

The others were looking up and signalling to them: the three tightly-shaven Frenchmen who always stuck together, Dr. Berebellis huddled to her Greek self, Dr. Constanza with his French *barbe*, and Dr. Grossgudt sighing.

'We'd better join them,' the General said and helped her down the path.

87

'Incidentally, General, was that young man we saw at the *mons clau-dianus* an Englishman?'

'Scott? Yes, Scott is English.'

'What was he doing out there? Is he an archaeologist?'

'No. Scott works for the Egyptians.'

'Ah—a pilot.'

'I don't know what he does. There's something of a mystery about him. He works for the Egyptians, that's all we know.'

'I have a feeling that he worried you,' Professor Maudie said sympathetically.

'What on earth makes you think that, Professor?' he said. 'Well, I suppose he does worry me a little. It always worries me to see an Englishman abandoning his own country for another. It's hardly the time for that sort of behaviour, when we are being pressed so hard.'

The General supposed, thinking about it, that Scott still had a British passport. He wondered why the Embassy had not tried to call it in. It ought to have been done years ago, for his own good. Somebody ought to bring Scott to his senses. It was dangerous to have him wandering around the country, watching every move they made.

CHAPTER FOURTEEN

WHEN Helen Mamoon went from one to the other of her influential friends, she realized how old she was: old times had changed so much that her high influence in the Ministry of Interior was dead. She knew nobody important in Nasser's military regime, excepting her own cousins who were junior officers somewhere in the Sinai, and not particularly Nasser's men anyway, since they were Copts who would certainly be passed over in their next promotions—and their rank given to Moslems.

She had known the chief of the security police under Aly Maher, years ago, but he was retired, and though she went to him and he took her to the Ministry and she was received by a *Bimbashi* who was charming and invited her to meet him in the Carlton Hotel next day at 2 o'clock, she knew it was to no helpful purpose. They were polite, they were hopeful themselves about Sam, but they were powerless and she did not waste time on them.

'There must be *somebody*,' she said to Nona, never giving it up because she did not know how to give it up.

'Why don't you leave it to Scott? Let him do it. He knows them.'

'You can't leave these things to anyone,' she said, and thought what a fool her boss, Jolley, was because he had offered to talk to the British Ambassador about Sam, and perhaps the Ambassador could talk to Nasser. Knowing what she knew about Sam, that would certainly put the cap to his fate.

'You are always saving the men of the family,' Nona complained, 'but what do you ever get for it, Helen? Nothing at all? Where are your brothers now, all comfortably off in Africa somewhere, and how do they ever help you?'

'They've got their own families to fight for,' she said. 'But with Sam it's quite different. Did you ever think of what would happen to the rest of us if Sam is charged with treason or something ridiculous like that? None of us would ever be left in peace after that.'

'Oh, my God,' Nona moaned for Helen's sake. 'Is there no relief from it? Isn't there some place where papers and nationalities and religions mean nothing?'

'Now you see why I want to leave Egypt. It's so hopeless.'

'Don't you say that. Let somebody else say it's hopeless, whatever you think. I can't bear that from you, darling.'

'But how can I help thinking like that?' Helen told her angrily. 'Hanna's *laissez-passer* comes up for renewal this week. They probably won't renew it, anyway. In fact, it is even worse now than before, because of Sam. Do you think they'll ever renew it for her if they suspect her nephew of something serious?'

Helen had wanted to save her main influence in the Ministry for Hanna's papers, the *laissez-passer* the Egyptians gave to those who were technically not Egyptians although born in Egypt. It was difficult to get an Egyptian passport now, but it seemed absolutely impossible to get a *laissez-passer* renewed, even though Hanna was as Egyptian as the rest of them.

'It's really father's fault,' Nona said irreverently. 'Why didn't he register you both with the British in the Sudan when you were born, if he insisted on trying to be a European? But better still, why didn't he take out Egyptian papers, since he *was* Egyptian?'

'They didn't need papers in those days.'

'Didn't he have any foresight?'

'Don't be hard on father this time,' Helen said. 'Nobody could foresee that the British rule would change, that the Sudan would be dominated from Egypt, that the Egyptians would become so stupidly nationalistic.'

'Even so!' Nona was insisting on her own irreverence rather than her father's lack of foresight. 'Look at the trouble it's caused us . . .'

'That's because you're too young to remember the better side of it,' Helen told her. 'It wasn't always trouble.'

What Helen remembered were the black straw picture hats, always black, and each Sunday morning waiting in the worn and coffee-spattered corridors of the Ministry, trying to fight her way through two hundred years of Ottoman paperwork. That was when the good had slowly turned into the bad. Her father was dead and she had spent every Sunday morning for a year with Doctor Buelli trying to get her nationality papers. Every Sunday morning for a year at the Ministry, with Nona in bare brown sandalled feet and at an awkward age, waiting in corridors until there was simply no excuse left *not* to give them their papers. They had finally exhausted the entire supply of refusals and petty bureaucracy, and the passport was assured.

Yet suddenly the clerk at the last table, on the very brink of the last stamp on his desk, had thought of one last requirement—one final and absolute requirement, he said, if they would forgive him for even mentioning it.

'You must have,' he said, 'a signed declaration from an Omda that there is no civil conviction against you.'

Ten more Sunday mornings at the Omda's in the native quarter sitting near his boxwood counter while he conducted much yaa-salaamek business and coffee and ten thousand handshakes and touches to the forehead in his fine black robes. By God, those little waits for ten weeks! And all he needed to do was write three lines of Arabic script. But he always protested, shaking back his sleeves, that it would take time.

'Next Sunday.'

On that final next Sunday, Helen's contempt and temper had suddenly done something to her face.

Doctor Buelli saw it. He also wanted Egyptian nationality. His wife hated Egypt and had gone to Palestine to live in peace. Doctor Buelli acted quickly. He almost leapt over to the table before Helen could show her temper and he had taken the old man in a grip on his arm and he had cried out:

'I beg you, Omda, in the name of God, to put your signature to the papers. The papers! In the name of mercy, Omda!'

They could laugh themselves sick with the memory of it now, but at the time they had been on a razor's edge of failure or success. The Omda had stood up in amazement, dropping his sleeves over his hands, looking startled and helpless. Then he had let out a breath of exhaustion and signed the documents with his other hand on his heart.

'Go!' he had said, handing the papers to them. 'Go in peace. Go away.'

Their gratitude had probably been exaggerated by their unbelieving relief.

'But God almighty!' the Omda had said pityingly after them. 'What a man has to go through for a miserable piece of paper. Misqueen!'

The piece of paper made it the last of fourteen hundred others, and she and Doctor Buelli had both been given the old red Egyptian passports within a week.

Doctor Buelli had stuck it out with her, not only because he wanted a passport even more than she did but because the companionship of those years and ten Sundays had become very important to him. They were important to Helen also, because Buelli was the man she could always turn to when the money ran out.

'I want to be rich,' she had told him once, sitting in the corridors, when she had needed to borrow money from him to get Sam out of a gambling debt of a hundred pounds, which he had owed to some Greek brute who was threatening to cut Sam's throat if he didn't pay up. 'I'm tired of this work, work, work for fifty pounds a month. Argue. Argue. Argue! Tap, tap, tap! How *do* you make money, Doctor? I don't mean you, but anybody. For God's sake tell me.'

'I shall never tell you anything so stupid,' he had replied angrily.

'Why not? I need money. Then I wouldn't have to keep bothering you for the loan of twenty or thirty pounds.'

'But I like you bothering me.'

'*I* don't like it. It's wrong.'

'Let me make the money. You remain a nice woman,' he had said.

And when she had insisted beyond a joke, he had told her:

'All right. I'll tell you the only three general *règles* of money. They are quite simple. They are always the rules for making money no matter where money is made. First, you must buy it cheap, whatever it is; second, you must sell it dear, whatever it is; thirdly, you must not pay taxes or duties or high interest on the operation, under any circumstances.'

'But what do you buy and what do you sell?' Helen had begged.

'Now that,' Buelli had explained, 'is irrelevant.'

Buelli had made his fortune in illegal steel during the war, and he had made a second fortune since the war by clever trading in legal steel, anything at all from pocket-knives to hair-curlers. When Buelli's wife died, which would be soon now because she had diabetes and hated him, he would want to marry Helen, and if things went on like this she would probably think of accepting him.

They were waiting for Buelli at Nona's flat now, because he had telephoned and warned them he was coming. He had just arrived from Alexandria, where he lived most of the time now, and he wanted to see them.

'If he ever does ask me to marry him,' Helen answered Nona, who had warned her against it, 'I'll accept him . . . *comme ça!*'

'No, you won't,' Nona told her sharply.

'Why not? All very well for you . . .'

'He's twenty years older,' Nona said. 'We all love Buelli. He's generous and he has helped so much. But I think you deserve more than that.'

'Listen,' Helen said. 'You wouldn't be where you are now if it wasn't for Doctor Buelli, and you ought to remember it. I couldn't have brought you up without his help. And look at Sam. Look at Hanna and me. We all owe him a great deal. He was always there to advise me what to do . . .'

'That's all the more reason why you shouldn't marry him.'

'He's the best man I know,' Helen insisted, brushing her long hair a hundred times to bring up the lustre which she was afraid of losing; she would certainly lose it unless she ate the right kind of food and took her exercise and her vitamins regularly. 'Every Jew in this country owes him a great deal too, and the Mamoons ought to be thankful for it. I mean for Sam and Alicia. He keeps the Abraham Betesh school open, and he keeps their newspapers going. Their hospitals get half his money and their Rabbinate too. Who do you know, or what man have you ever known, who at least has gold *dans son cœur comme dans la poche*, excepting your own husband?'

'Quarts hasn't got any gold in his pocket,' Nona said frivolously, 'believe me.'

'He has it in his heart.'

'Then I wish I could get my hands on some of it,' Nona said. 'We could solve all our problems with a little cash.'

'What problems?' Helen asked cunningly.

Nona shrugged. 'A house with a garden for the children, for one thing. I mean in England.'

'But surely you have enough money for that now?'

'You need too much money to buy a house in England these days, and in one lump. Then you need a steady income to pay off the mortgages, something we shall never have, the way Quarts works.'

'But doesn't he earn enough?'

'Only in bits and pieces. With his war on everybody, you can never tell whether he can ever publish what he wants to write. Do you know where our money for this trip to Egypt came from, my darling?'

'It's all a mystery to me,' Helen said, 'how you live.'

'From Japan. They published the analysis he made of the British defeat in Singapore. But that was a bit of luck. We can't ever depend on money from England, because the English hate him because he doesn't treat everything as a polite joke. He's not restrained enough in his opinions; you know Quarts; and when he criticizes he damns outright. There's never any sweet-reasonableness about him.'

'Is he coming here?' Helen asked her. 'You should tell us, you know.'

'He might,' Nona said and closed the family door on any further questions by kissing Helen briskly as she stood up. 'Don't start worrying about Quarts and his problems. He can look after his own.'

'Ça, je le sais bien!'

Buelli was already talking to Hanna in Italian and he kissed Nona on the cheek and looked at her youthful face which never changed, the eyes that never flinched, and he felt better.

'You look happy. Thank heaven for that.'

Nona felt herself sliding instantly into Helen's view: that this small shaven-headed, ageing and argumentative and wholeheartedly willing friend was the best and most worthwhile man Helen had ever known. So much for the rest of them if Helen married him. So much for Egypt if Helen left it and went off with Buelli. He was almost twice her age and had a son in Israel as old as Nona herself, and a daughter in Italy with two children; all of them lived off him. But it would be a lesson to all men if Helen married him tomorrow, despite his bald head and startled eyes.

'And you,' she said, remembering his gold teeth and gold-banded watch and fine silk shirts and well-cut expensive suits always brown and restrained. 'And you, Doctor, haven't changed a bit.'

The Doctor was already off on a new responsibility, however.

'Now, what is this about Sam?' he asked them, as if they were to blame. 'Why is Sam in prison?'

'No one seems to know,' Nona told him, offering him a *lemoon* and a tray of sweets. 'But never mind Sam. He always has friends who get him out of trouble.'

'Have you been to the Ministry?'

'Helen has tried everything,' Nona told him, 'but there's an Englishman called Captain Scott who knows Nasser.'

'That may not be right,' Doctor Buelli said, worrying and looking for Helen who had not come in yet. 'Does Captain Scott know what they arrested Sam for?'

'I don't think so.'

'Et alors?'

Helen came in then and said, 'Did you find out anything at the Ministry?'

Doctor Buelli also had his Ministry friends, but he reported (arguing with them about it) that his friends believed it was better not to pursue the matter of Sam.

'But why?' Nona said, and Hanna went out to quieten the children on the balcony.

Buelli shrugged indignantly. 'Who knows why?'

His friends had told him nothing. But though Buelli's connections with Israel were not very firm, excepting his illegal transfer of money to his wife through Italy, it was known that he had contacts there, and it was better for Sam's chances if his name was kept out of it. They had warned him of that much.

'I'm sorry,' he said heplessly in English. 'If there's anything else I can do?'

Helen knew he had already done it. From Alexandria he had telephoned to make sure that Sam's sister Alicia was looked after. He had arranged for an allowance to be paid her while Sam was in gaol, and it was given as a grant from the Maccabee Youth Fund to which he and another wealthy supporter, Leo Lieberman, who was Françoise's cousin, were the main contributors.

Helen knew about it from Alicia herself. She had tried to persuade Alicia to move in with them here, but Alicia would not leave the flat she shared with Sam and their grandmother. She would not desert her brother. She wore black dresses and wept all day in the kitchen and comforted grandmother Hassoon, the mother of Sam's worthless Aleppo

94

father who had disappeared years ago. Alicia was determined to be as loyal to Sam as Sam was to her. Hadn't Sam refused to marry, because he knew he could not desert his unmarried sister? Now his loyalty was being rewarded in her generous tears.

'But crying won't help!' Helen had told Alicia sharply.

'What else can I do?' Alicia had answered, weeping it out.

That was when you cursed this close family instinct; and Helen could hate the family unit when she thought of it. It was another wall you had to back-up to. It was no good. That was the result of all this Semitic mother-hood, Arabic or Jewish. You boxed the children's ears and shouted at them and alienated them; and then you proved you really loved them by stuffing them with food and dressing them up in white until they became fat and revolting as Sam had. Like Sam, whose grandmother had fed him up almost to grossness to make up for her own son running off like that. A grandmother and a sister and a family duty made them all helplessly inadequate now, except for weeping. It was she who must rescue Sam, and Doctor Buelli who must support them. Thank God for the English, who brought up their children cold-bloodedly; and when Hanna brought in little Ben and little moon, here was the independent proof of it.

'But they don't look English,' Doctor Buelli said indignantly.

'That's because nobody knows who the father is,' Nona said.

That shocked Buelli rather than teased him.

'And where is their father, I might ask? Mister Quartermain!'

'Working,' Nona said. 'He is in Cyprus.'

Doctor Buelli was trying to hug the children but they shook hands politely and then they shied off, and from a cool distance little Ben asked him what sort of a car he had, and when could he drive in it. Little moon sucked his fingers and sat near his mother, who shooed him away. He stood alone for a moment and then went with Hanna to the kitchen where the servant was preparing white beans for lunch.

'You will stay for dinner,' Nona was saying to Buelli.

'Not really. I just came to see you and say *Ahlan-wasahlan* and to see about Sam. I don't like it, you know, that they've arrested him.'

But Nona was insistent that he stay. White haricot beans were not much to offer, but she knew he liked them, and damn the protocol of offering a man a feast when he preferred a plate of white beans.

'We could ring up Abu Sha'ra and ask them to send some kebab,' Hanna said quietly in the kitchen.

'Give him beans,' Nona said. 'He loves them.'

'But . . .'

Nona insisted on the beans, the fasoulya, and Buelli was more flattered by her simple English honesty than if she had secretly sent out for a meal of meat which would ruin the balanced acidity of the stomach.

'I remember,' Nona said when they sat down to the dish of beans swimming hot in olive oil and served with half a lemon each, 'when we had fasoulya at home so often that we called it pigeon to tease Hanna.'

'You were lucky to get beans,' Helen said. 'My salary at the Ministry in those days was not enough to keep the three of you, eating the way you did.'

The three of them were Nona with her younger brother and sister. The sister was teaching in Italy and the brother was a Reader in chemistry at the University of Nottingham, where Helen had paid the fees and sent him a small allowance until he had taken his degree. Nona would not speak of or to her brothers, because she blamed all her brothers for leaving Helen alone to fight the family battles.

Doctor Buelli was still trying to attract the children.

'You see my watch-band,' he said in English. 'You stretch it, *comme ça*, and it jumps back like a snake, *comme çela*.'

'Just ignore them, Doctor, and they'll soon be all over you,' Nona told him. 'In the meantime, Benjamino, just watch your shirt-sleeves. They're in the butter.'

They made a happy family with Doctor Buelli, and Nona knew that Helen was asking herself 'Why not?' They exchanged one glance which registered the question. Helen's darkened eyes said it too easily, 'Why not?' when they ought to be showing all men that she was a rare gift, difficult to get but worth the effort. 'Why not Buelli?' Where else was there manhood like that in Helen's life? Nona herself had been very lucky. Quartermain had not hesitated, and though once or twice it looked (before they were married) as though he would fade into the war and never return, he had come back and married her in the consulate as if he had never thought otherwise about it.

'Yet they behave like English boys,' the Doctor was saying as little Ben persuaded his small brother to part with a toy car Hanna had bought him. Ben had long ago lost his own and he would soon lose little moon's for him.

'Sometimes,' Nona said.

'They're so well mannered,' he said.

Now they were on him at the table, and little Ben was snapping his watch-band and little moon was watching his gold tooth flashing like a beacon, fascinated by it. The Doctor noticed it.

'Shall I take it out?' he said to little moon. 'Would you like to see me take out my tooth?'

'Oh, yes,' little Ben said. 'Can I have it?'

Little moonface was embarrassed and turned away, but he watched with a grip on Hanna, while Buelli made a flourishing extraction of his gold tooth.

96

'But doesn't it hurt?' Ben said. 'Why is it that colour?'

The Doctor put it back. 'Because it's worth a fortune,' he said, and they were all very pleased with it.

Why not? Helen was asking when she thought of the Englishman she had loved, who had lived in her house during the war and shared her life so briefly, who had lived and slept there and loved her. What was he— that Englishman who had looked such a man in his English uniform? Even the memory of him, simply pulling on his shoes in his lazy large way; his sure, thoughtful and administrative speech, his easy way in wearing his army clothes and strapping down his shoulder-straps, she could feel faint now with the desire of it again. Yet that Englishman who had been a whisky agent before the war and an intelligence Major during the war, that man who looked and grew like a man, large, clean, shoulder-sloping and so clearly unafraid, that Englishman was an infant when it came to the first steps in whatever mental courage a man had to have. The physical, visual, impressive firmness had been a fake and for nothing. He had run away from her. He had collapsed at the thought of marrying her and living properly with her because she was not English and was local and sufficiently Arab to make his English stomach quiver in racial fear. But why? What was the weakness of the man and the strength of herself that had turned him into jelly? She would never know, and now she felt disgust that she had gone so easily into such a deceptive arrangement in which he too had been generosity itself. But at the real moment of responsibility he had deserted her without a word.

'He's like his father,' Nona said to Buelli about little Ben. 'Now, the other one is just what his name says he is: a little moon. Did you ever see anyone in my family who looked like him? We don't know where he came from.' She was kissing both her sons.

'For shame,' Buelli said to her.

'He understands you,' Hanna protested, taking little moon away.

'They must be very happy,' Buelli said. 'They look so happy.'

Nona's radiant, teasing, unburdened face was good enough for him. Her cut-and-dried English manner looked too reliable on a woman, but he did not quite believe it. She was so lovely too that she deserved the luck. But she had the last-minute luck that Helen would never have. At the last moment something would always put the evil-eye on Helen, whereas at the last moment Nona would always win.

'I think I must get them each a blue bead,' he said, 'to take away envy. Such nice boys.'

'*Shhh!*' Nona said. 'Don't even talk about envy of them. Something will happen.'

Helen had taken little Ben to wash his face, and in those dark eyes like Nona's and like her own, in his small perfect teeth except for two frontal

E 97

gaps, in his generous, confiding, gracious instinct to be trusting and mischievous, so sure that he was loved, Helen saw both Nona and the strange and sometimes attractive and always independent Englishman Nona had married.

Quartermain would come. They were happy, despite whatever troubles had appeared. Quartermain would come and he could tell her what she needed to know about Scott. She wondered why Scott should worry her so much. But she knew why. She straightened up suddenly with a quick realization that she wanted not to doubt that reliable English face.

'You do it too hard,' little Ben said to her as she dried his face.

'I'm so sorry, darling,' she said, and tweaked his nose with the towel. 'I wasn't thinking.'

He butted her condescendingly in the stomach and asked for a chocolate.

CHAPTER FIFTEEN

FAHID sat on the tarmac on the green cushions that Captain Zareef would want in his plane and he watched them questioning Ali Zareef for the third or fourth time about Sam Hassoon. The policeman had walked up and down the gritty tarmac behind the planes with Zareef, reasoning with him. They wanted facts, but Fahid (laughing at their stupidity and delighted by it) knew that Zareef would simply give them arguments because he didn't know the facts.

He could hear them.

'Yes, but where does Hassoon go?' the policeman asked.

'He flies with me. You know that by now.'

'Does he fly the Army co-operation flights with you for the anti-aircraft practice? Does he ever do that?'

'Of course he does. Over the Canal zone, and sometimes over Alexandria. He has to. I need a wireless operator.'

'What could he see from the air?'

'What I see.'

'Yes, Captain, I know that. Forgive me. But what *do* you see?'

Fahid laughed out loud, but they ignored him and walked on.

'Ah, really now,' Zareef complained. 'What a question! What does a flyer see? The earth, the desert roads, the railway lines, the fields, the houses . . .'

'The houses? The house of Gamal Abd el Nasser, for instance? And Abdin Palace, for instance?'

Fahid did not hear Zareef's reply, but Zareef's expression meant a sudden halt to such silly questions. He watched them walk around a Gomhouriya. The whole school watched them promenading in the sun, and everyone kept their distance. Meanwhile, because Zareef was busy, Captain Selim was instructing. What a joke that was! Selim was holding the stick and making sure above all that the student, a Lebanese, didn't kill him—shouting loudly at all mistakes: 'Watch your direction into wind! Keep your right wing up!' It was still done in English.

99

Selim shouted when he was in an aeroplane, but he was hooded and silent and gentle out of it, with his large car. His family life was a mystery. No one knew anything about it except that his father was fat and wealthy; but Fahid looked at Selim's large car and decided that Selim had paid for it by smuggling or speculation. That was what Selim looked like. Selim's friends, who came in new Chevrolets and were gross people, were men with German instincts and bad manners: business men. Selim's family were wealthy landowners, everyone knew that much, but Selim was the younger son and that made the difference. They were all younger sons here, including the pupils, except the Lebanese and Iraqi students who were all wealthy and eldest among sons. The Lebanese were cunning, and the Iraqi were stupid.

The Group-Captain whom Nasser's air force experts had put in charge of the whole school as director was also watching their promenade.

'The policeman thinks Captain Zareef will tell him all his secrets,' Fahid said boldly to the director. 'He is trying to discover how Captain Zareef will bomb Abdin Palace.' Fahid laughed.

The Group-Captain looked at him contemptuously, but said, 'I wish they would go inside and talk.' He would like to tell Zareef to go in, but he knew that Zareef would not go inside because he hated to be in the school building.

'Poor Captain Ali!' Fahid said.

Fahid knew, everybody knew, that the Group-Captain-director favoured Selim, who would walk with him arm-in-arm, confiding and arranging affairs quietly in his secretive way and ignoring Zareef's existence.

'Why do they bother about Hassoon so much?' the director said to Fahid, because there was no one else to complain to.

'Because someone told the police silly things about him,' Fahid said knowingly.

'What are you saying? Who told them silly things?'

Fahid was deliberately watching the Auster come in, and they could see Selim in it shouting his head off. 'I wonder,' Fahid said, looking at the plane, 'who told them.'

He watched the director walk away irritably and felt sorry for him. The director knew quite well that Zareef was the better flyer and instructor. The level of instruction now was not pleasing the air force who took the advanced pupils for the 'B' tests. Which meant that the poor Group-Captain would have to improve the instructing. It wasn't like the old days. Now you had to do your job. What a joke! That should mean Zareef in charge of it. But Selim was the director's friend and Selim had some kind of a hold on him. And now a large black mark was up against Zareef because of Sam.

'*Misquin*, Captain Zareef,' a fat young man said to Fahid.

'Hello, Barmil,' Fahid said cynically. 'Are you waiting to risk your neck with Haboob Selim?'

Barmil smiled with pleasure. Usually Fahid ignored him. Today Fahid called him *barmil*, which meant barrel with something filling it up, usually (in Fahid's mind) something disgusting. Fahid was in a pitying mood today, but Barmil was always willing to be friendly.

'Do you think they suspect Captain Zareef of being in it with Hassoon?'

'Being in *what* with Hassoon?' Fahid asked.

'I don't know, Fahid. Whatever they've got Sam for.'

'Do you know what they've got him for?' Fahid asked him.

'Who? Hassoon? No. How would I know?'

'He was always lending you money, wasn't he? He always paid for your coca-cola when you hung around him. *You* ought to know.'

Barmil sighed. 'Yes, but I don't know anything. I swear it.'

'Of course you don't. Do you think Zareef knows anything?'

'Well, he might. They were friends.'

'Now you're really being stupid. How can Zareef know anything? Nobody knows anything about Sam except me, and I can guess.'

'Then why don't you tell them?' Barmil suggested.

'Me? Don't be such a silly horse manure. Firstly, they're too stupid to ask me. And when they do I shall certainly never tell them. Let them guess their own way out of it.'

It was so stupid by now that Fahid decided to save Zareef from it. He walked over to Zareef determinedly and interrupted the policeman, saying: 'Captain Zareef. It's time you checked me out. I can't wait any longer and I will not fly with Captain Haboob Selim, so please don't ask me to.'

Zareef looked annoyed, but he buttoned up his blue coat and said, 'That's right, Fahid. Well. Get into the Autocrat and be ready. I'll come.'

Fahid's intention was always to outwit the world. He thought he might succeed some day. This time he had succeeded for Zareef's sake, but when Zareef left the policeman and buckled himself into the seat with the cushions, he was too distracted to allow Fahid the controls.

'I'll taxi her,' he said as he waved to Hefney the prop-swinger, and the engine cracked into a metallic clicking and clacking.

'But it's a calm day,' Fahid said. 'Let me do it.'

It was only when they turned at a right angle to see if any other plane was approaching that Zareef relaxed into the plane itself and smiled and said to Fahid:

'You've got her.'

He had her, but he had nothing. A stiff left-handed stick. The wings dipped too easily in take-off. The Auster always bumped clumsily and the correction was too rough. But once up she was steady and hard. The tail-trimmer was on the roof, half a turn down or up, but the stick remained as if set in liquid glue.

Once around and he landed badly and that should have been his check out.

'You don't like the aeroplane,' Zareef said sadly as they waited to take off again. 'That's your trouble, Fahid.'

'What is there to like?' Fahid said. 'It's always against you.'

'*Ismaa!*' Zareef said patiently, holding him back for a minute. 'You've either got to use an aeroplane like a tool with no feelings, or you have to like it very much. Why don't you like it?' Zareef gave him a peppermint.

But Fahid would not be drawn out so softly and easily, and Zareef was wrong. Fahid liked the aeroplane, even the Auster. What stiffened him was the fear of a last-minute betrayal. He didn't trust it.

He tried, because he liked Zareef. 'It's not free . . .' he said.

'Not free? What do you mean?'

He wanted to say that there was no freedom of any kind in flying, when that should have been the very point of flying. But he had discovered that aeroplanes were not free agents at all. They did not wing around, birdlike and smooth in a turn. They looked like that from the ground, but when you flew them they edged around mechanically in a geometric ratio of very stiff pressures. That was what the pilot felt, not the free-swinging grace. The air was disturbed most of the time, and the hot vibrating roar of twenty-one hundred revolutions per minute under your feet was not disinterested enough for grace. Mechanisms interfered, air interrupted, and the grace-hungry instincts of the pilot made horrible mistakes. There was no elation in it at all.

'Do another one,' Zareef told him, 'and this time trust the plane. Don't be afraid of it.'

He *was* afraid of it, and that was probably the whole truth. It was perhaps the only thing in his life that he was completely afraid of. But he intended to outwit it sooner or later.

CHAPTER SIXTEEN

SCOTT never bothered to make conversation with Ishaak, who drove the jeep for him. Ishaak was a likeable soldier with a hot temper. Sometimes the monotony and the grit got on Ishaak's nerves and he became rude and irritable, and occasionally insubordinate and afterwards regretful.

It was too difficult anyway over this broken slate-like country. Scott pointed with three zigzagged strokes of his hand to the course: a sand track and then up over two grey hills which looked like Lancashire slag-heaps.

'Must we go over the hill?' Ishaak complained. 'We'll bog down.'

'No, we won't. Get on with it.'

Two desert strangers had been seen hiding near an unused Reqi well, according to some Reqi camel boys. The boys had passed it looking for short green fodder for the four baby camels they were nursing from a wild herd that roamed this side of the wind-washed hills.

'What sort of strangers are they?' Scott had asked them.

'Foreigners,' the boys had replied.

'Look,' Ishaak said in English now.

A small silver aeroplane was flying very low over the hot mountains. 'The American,' Scott told him.

The American was an out-of-work bush-pilot living in Cairo who flew an old Fairchild to the Red Sea to take films of sharks for American television companies. So he said, when they met him from time to time in the blue deserted bays of the Red Sea coast.

Ishaak stopped the jeep to watch the plane.

'Shouldn't he be over the coast, Capten?' he asked Scott.

'He's probably taking a short cut.'

'Why should he do that?'

Scott waited. He was being patient with Ishaak's boredom.

'We ought to report him,' Ishaak said. 'He should be two thousand feet over the coast-line and no deviations. Isn't that right?'

'It's getting too hot here,' Scott said to Ishaak. 'Start up.'

Ishaak took no notice. 'Perhaps he's looking for us.'

'Get a move on,' Scott said impatiently.

Ishaak's perfect olive eyes were insistently more interested in the vanishing plane. He kept it in view as long as he could. Then he started the jeep slowly and watched for bad patches again.

'What do you think he was doing?' he shouted at Scott.

Scott held on as they bumped over a hidden rise. 'Perhaps he was selling coca-cola,' he said.

Now they were openly annoying each other. Scott had made a mean joke at Ishaak's expense, because Ishaak had once sold coca-cola in Cairo.

'Perhaps he's a spy,' Ishaak said cynically with his pearly teeth smiling, 'for the British.'

This completed their irritation and they went on in silence.

Ishaak was not an Egyptian. He was a Palestinian who was classically and finely and pettily and sometimes savagely Arab. So un-Egyptian that he would make fun of the Egyptians, even to an Englishman.

'Egyptians are cut-throats,' Ishaak said. He used the word *attaleen* which meant killer, but since that was impossible he meant cut-throats.

He had served with the British Army as a sixteen-year-old boy in Jerusalem during the war, and there they had made Ishaak into a first-class fitter and turner and mechanic. But when the Jewish refugees and immigrants from Europe had taken Palestine by force in 1948, Ishaak was one of the million native Arabs expelled by one means or another by the new state of Israel. His mother and his sister had died of dysentery in the refugee camps in Jordan, and he liked to remind Scott of it.

'It's no use thinking I can forget my own family,' he would say through his tears to Scott, as if Scott had begged him to do just that.

Scott comforted him by saying: 'Now then, Ishaak. That's no good.'

It was nothing much to offer, but it was the best he could do and he watched Ishaak's hatred growing and doubling and redoubling itself every day. He hated the Israelis who had stolen his country, but he also distrusted the British; and distrust usually went deeper than hate.

'The British,' he would say to Scott cynically, 'will never forget a friend, will they?'

Scott could not defend the British against Ishaak. When his mother had died Ishaak had left the refugee camp in Jordan, and after firing a few qualifying shots as a *fedayi* at Israeli farmers, the Egyptian authorities at Gaza had allowed him to come to Egypt, and he had found a job as a driver for his old army friends at the British Embassy.

A very flimsy young Second Secretary with weak eyes and a strong wife had paid him well and had looked after him during the anti-British riots in 1952. The Englishman promised to look after him always because

Ishaak had not deserted his British friends when the Egyptian pressure was on him to do so: with stones and threats and torn clothes for chauffeuring the foul British who were the murderers of the Ismailia police-post defenders.

'We'll see you through, Ishaak,' that young, soft-hearted, half-blind diplomat had promised Ishaak who had sheltered the Englishman from attacks and made sure that no harm came to him in the streets with his weak eyes. 'I'll never forget this.'

'A man must look after his friends,' Ishaak had said.

'You really do understand what loyalty means,' the Englishman had responded emotionally, so that Ishaak had believed him.

He knew what Mr. Whitehead meant. He had learned from Whitehead, and from the British, how to repay loyalty with loyalty. His young weak-eyed employer still wrote loyal letters to him from the safety of Beirut. Soon after the 1952 riots he had discharged Ishaak on (he said) Embassy orders, because a Moslem and an Arab like Ishaak (even one who had served in the British Army and understood loyalty) was likely to be a security risk after the '52 troubles. Ishaak had been fired with a week's notice and 5½ days' pay, since technically he wasn't paid for holidays. His notice was operative as of 0900 hours on Monday morning to 1200 hours the following Saturday, the official dismissal said in triplicate.

Now the falconish eyes always watched to see what this other Englishman he worked for would offer. What promises, what loyalties? So far none, because Scott was too secretive to offer anything so lavishly. But who knew what sort of a man Scott was, except that he was impatient and clever and very demanding.

'Why did you leave the coca-cola business?' Scott asked him over the noonday coffee, trying to smooth off some of their irritable edges.

'Too much work,' Ishaak said, squatting on his haunches on a little knob of sandstone.

'They must have paid you better than the Frontier Department.'

'Much better.'

'Well then?'

Ishaak shrugged petulantly and did not explain.

Scott did not try again. He was used to Ishaak's bad temper, and he liked to think he had abandoned his own years ago, when he had learned that nothing was worth temper. Absolutely nothing.

But Ishaak was suddenly interested in him. 'Don't you ever get annoyed with me, Capten? Don't, sometimes, you want to kick me?'

'I certainly do,' Scott said, chewing some coffee grains and spitting them out, his usual way of ending a meal. 'I felt like kicking you this morning when you were watching that aeroplane.'

E*   105

'I guessed that. I felt I ought to be kicked. But you can't help it some-times. Have you ever kicked anybody? Hard!'

Scott thought about it. 'Yes,' he admitted. 'I once kicked a man very hard.'

'I don't believe you,' Ishaak said. 'You are English. It is well known that the English don't kick.'

'The man I kicked wasn't English,' Scott joked.

'Is that why you kicked him?'

'Not exactly.' Scott washed out his cup with sand. 'He was a good friend of mine. Still is.'

'Then you didn't mean to hurt him? I don't mean like that. I mean seriously the way Arabs do.'

'But I did mean it seriously, and I did mean to hurt him.'

'Then I don't understand.'

'It was Sam Hassoon,' Scott said. 'Sam was holding me in a foul around the neck, so I had to kick him hard to break his grip.'

Ishaak did not understand.

'Wrestling,' Scott explained.

Ishaak was disappointed. 'That's play. I meant seriously. I *know* you would not kick anybody. It's well known. Is it true though that you once shot a man who was dying?'

'Who told you that?'

'Whitehead, when I worked for him at the Embassy. He was frightened of you. He said you shot your best friend in the war and never forgave yourself. . . .'

Scott resisted the temptation to explain it with a hateful silence. This was not a joke.

'That's partly true,' he said instead, aware that he dare not avoid it. 'If a man's alive, Ishaak, he's alive; but my friend was dying. He was terribly burnt, in shocking pain, and there was no hope of getting him to any kind of help, and he begged me to shoot him, and I did so.'

'But you did it for pity, Capten,' Ishaak said, defending him.

'No. I did it because he wanted it done and it was the best thing. It was more than pity at the time. It was—like shooting myself.'

'*Ya salaam*, Capten,' Ishaak said with one green tear in an olive eye. 'Was he such a good friend?'

'We were all good friends in those days,' Scott said. 'That was a long time ago in the war. Everybody has forgotten the war. Everybody has forgotten who shot who in the war, so it's no use remembering it now.'

'They say you turned against the British.'

Scott stood up because they must go on into this heat haze which was not going to be pleasant; the sooner the better, to get it over and done with. 'A man can't turn against himself,' he said.

'Of course he can,' Ishaak told him. 'Look at me. I'm always turning

106

against myself. I even punish myself sometimes. Some men even kill themselves.'

'That's true,' Scott granted. 'But we'd better move off. We'll have to get over this slag-heap sooner or later. Pack up the stove and don't put it near the instruments. It leaks.'

'Well, where can I put it? There's no other place.'

'Put it on the floor between my legs.'

'But it smells in front, and you don't like the smell.'

'It won't hurt for a day. You can get it fixed in Ghurdakha next week.'

After driving for an hour, they bogged down on an innocent crust which was dried by the wind and looked hard, but if they had looked higher up where the wind missed the sand under the grey slag it would have been clear to them that all this side was soft underneath.

'It's your silly fault, Ishaak,' Scott said sharply, 'for not watching it. How many times must I tell you to look around and know what it's like? Don't guess.'

'But I don't guess, Capten.'

'Yes, you do. You took a chance.'

They were hot and perspiring after de-bogging the jeep and they were resting for ten minutes under the tarpaulin slung on the sand-tracks, propped over the radiator of the jeep. Scott needed the rest these days and he needed to read and to contain his life, for just ten minutes, into Frank Cowperwood's bitter conflict with Chicago society. He took out his glasses and bent his eyes away from the grey air, the grey desert, the grey mountained sky, and he looked for the page of Cowperwood's sad discovery that Aileen had tried to kill herself. He was in love with Aileen himself, but. . . .

'I must explain why I was a coca-cola man,' Ishaak was saying.

'What is there to explain?' Scott said without taking hold of it.

'You are all laughing at me because it was coca-cola. I know. But it wasn't coca-cola. It was kool-cola . . .'

'What's the difference?' Scott said, determined to read on.

'No difference,' Ishaak said in exasperation. 'In fact, that was the point. But, you know, it was hard work, Capten. I had to load my little two-cv Citroën at the factory at four o'clock in the morning, and then drive out to Shubra, which was my district, and begin my work at six o'clock every morning.'

'*Misqueen*, Ishaak,' Scott said. 'Didn't the Americans pay you well for it?'

'Yes, but that's not the point, Capten. You see, I was not delivering the stuff. No, no! I was persuading the native coffee shops and street sellers to increase their order and take another dozen bottles over what they had already ordered.'

Frank Cowperwood would not focus; poor Aileen; and Scott reluctantly closed the book to hear it out.

'Of course the poor coffee shops couldn't sell another dozen bottles, but that was all right. Men always take more than they want, by nature. And I would give them kool-cola buttons, pencils, ball-pens, and calendars.'

'So you sold them an extra dozen bottles they didn't want? That was pretty clever of you after all,' Scott said, shutting his eyes against the grey prison of space and trying out the native coffee shops of Shubra, a crowded up-quarter of Cairo where the streets smelled of donkeys and crashed with arguments. Every day hummed along in the daily fun of the *bagarres* among the street boys and the rival sellers.

'No, I didn't sell the extra dozen. You see, the rival root-kola company had started selling their drinks in larger bottles for the same price. Three glasses instead of two and in one bottle.'

'You don't say,' Scott said. 'Was that difficult for you? Did the customers really care about it?'

'Of course they did. They did in Shubra, anyway,' Ishaak said bitterly. 'You try, Capten, persuading those sharp-shooters of argument who own the Shubra coffee shops *and* the ignorant bystanders that two are better than three of the same stuff at the same price.'

'So you couldn't do it?'

'Of course I couldn't. Listen, Capten, I tried to do it until one day I broke down and wept in front of my meanest and most ignorant customer: a donkey blacksmith in a filthy black hole.'

'What was he doing with coca-cola? A donkey blacksmith?'

'*Kool*-cola, Capten. Oh, he sold it to his clients. Not to the donkey drivers, who wouldn't earn the price of one bottle in a whole week, but to the mechanics who came from a nearby workshop with machine-parts they wanted forged. "Don't insult me," the blacksmith shouted at me when I tried to persuade him that two were better than three of the same stuff. "Do you think I'm mad?" he shouted at me. "Do you want to make a fool of me in front of everybody here?" he screamed at me. "No," he said, "bring me a bigger bottle and I'll buy your syrup. Until then don't talk to me of your thieving bottles." '

'So you wept,' Scott said, taking off his glasses and watching Ishaak with appreciation. 'I know how you felt.'

'Wouldn't you?'

'Absolutely.'

'But that was not the worst of it. When I took this man's arguments back to the American supply manager, what do you think he said to me?'

'I suppose he saw the other fellow's point of view. Americans usually do.'

'What point of view, Capten? All he said was that *I must try harder.* Look what an ignorant man he was. I ask you! I couldn't tell *him* to go himself and convince the donkey-smith that two were as three of the same stuff at the same price. So I said, very simply and sensibly: "Listen, Mr. MacArthur. Why don't you make a bigger bottle for kool-cola? Then I can sell more of it." Now what do you think he said to me, Capten?'

'I've no idea, Ishaak. Maybe he said it was a great idea.'

'No. No. No! He said: "That's not the point, Ishaak." And when I asked him what the point was, he said the point was simply to sell more kool-cola, whether the bottle contained more or less, whether the smith wanted it or not, whether there was logic in their arguments or not, whether it tasted worse or better or even the same. "You simply sell more, that's the point," he said. "That's your job." '

'Well?'

Ishaak lost his temper again. 'But that man was standing on his head, Capten. Don't you see?'

'That's good business, Ishaak.'

'Yes, I know, Capten. I didn't mind the good business, but I did not like the total lack of any sense in an intelligent man like me trying to persuade an ignorant donkey-smith that two were more than three, and better, *and* of the same stuff. I couldn't do it, Capten. It was so silly.'

Scott wrapped Cowperwood in his plastic bag against the dust and agreed: 'You're absolutely right. Who wants to drink the stuff anyway? You can't beat a good gazooza. So what did you do?'

'I left,' Ishaak said, his dark eyes fading a little with the memory of it, 'and without even a courteous good-bye. That's when I went to work at the English Oil petrol station, but they fired me when they discovered I was not an Egyptian citizen. So then I came to the Frontier Department to fill out my term as a soldier so that I can get my papers as an Egyptian. Soon I will be a cut-throat Egyptian.'

'Never mind, Ishaak,' Scott said as they rolled up the tarpaulin. 'There are worse things in life than being an Egyptian.'

'I suppose so. But some day,' he said, 'we'll kill all the Jews in Palestine and then I can go back home and I shan't have to work in this cut-throat country.'

Scott expected to find that the strangers at the Reqi well were the usual de-classed nomads who had moved in from their own region, or were some of the desert beggars who sponged on any nomad tribe. When he saw these two, who were so aggressively sure of themselves, he knew they were something unusual.

'What are you doing here?' Scott asked them in Arabic.

'*Inta malaak!*' they replied. 'What's it to you?'

That was not the correct answer at all, not for any man of these deserts.

They looked like tribesmen and the younger spokesman had the proper diction; but years among them told Scott without thinking that these were not Egyptian or even Sinai Bedu.

'Where do you come from?' he asked them.

'The only place we could come from,' the younger and brisker one said.

Scott felt the edge of intellect and education cracking through this young man's careless answer. He had already measured Scott. He was not puzzled by Scott at all. He was slightly amused and very confident. The other one was older. He was lying under a rough shelter of black blankets a large, pale, loose-skinned and frightened man.

'Is he ill?' Scott asked.

'Yes,' the young one said. 'Are you a doctor?'

'No. What's the matter with him?'

'In God's name,' the young one said in his brisk voice, 'if you know anything about the sores on him, you would be doing us a service.'

This older one looked too frightened and—at close range—too urbane to be lying out here so pitifully with the insides of both his legs covered with boils. He had probably been walking too long. The sand and sweat irritation on his loose legs had produced an infection in flesh which was not used to this sort of life.

Scott sent Ishaak to get a plastic tube of penicillin powder out of the box in the jeep, and the young one watched him and thanked him: amused, quick, teasingly careful, and yet dangerously aware, and then contemptuous when he suddenly shouted at Ishaak:

'What are you doing?'

Ishaak was kicking their sacked-up belongings open, tearing angrily at a carpet-bag to open it and search it.

'Steady on,' Scott said to him in English.

Ishaak left their scattered belongings blowing about in the desert with the young one chasing them, and he walked back to the jeep with Scott.

'It's no good denying it,' he said to Scott. 'I know who they are.'

Scott also knew. 'Well, don't shout it out,' he said.

'But I *know*!' Ishaak said, almost hysterically. 'I know what they are.'

'All right, all right.'

'*You're* not worried, are you? Oh, no! You don't care. But I do.'

'Oh, be quiet, Ishaak, while I think a little.'

'What will you do with them?'

Scott kept his temper and looked very far away, anywhere at all where Ishaak was not. If he had looked far enough to the east he might have seen into the heart of the new land of Canaan, where the new men of Zion (tired, they said, of their long oppression) had taken some of their ancient people back to Zion, and had replanted them there, brutally but determinedly.

'Now listen, Ishaak, and don't get excited. You will have to stay here and watch them, and I am going to the wire near the roadway to tell Colonel Amin Fakhry at Ghurdakha to come and pick them up. Do you understand?'

'What are they doing here? Why do they come here, in the desert?'

Scott knew they were doing what he had done himself in the Western deserts for three years of the war—finding the enemy's gaps, heading as far west as you could go without being caught, counting what you could and charting what you could, and above all sending the information back as quickly as you could.

'Never mind that now,' Scott said. 'You must watch them.'

'But have they guns?'

'No,' Scott told him. Ishaak had effectively scattered all their belongings, and there was nothing near enough in which to hide a gun. Scott's own search had already made sure of that. 'Just keep up here above them.'

'*Now* you will understand,' Ishaak said to him. 'Now you know what they are like. By God! See how I'll watch them.'

'All right, all right,' Scott said and felt the hot breath of all the wars and politics and antagonisms he thought were outside him simply because he had avoided them so carefully. Now he had to make sure this hot breath, here in the desert, was neatly caught and put away. But he would not touch it himself. He could ask Amin Fakhry to come and do it for him.

'Don't get too near them,' he told Ishaak, 'and be careful.'

He got into the jeep and turned it around while Ishaak squatted down near the Sten gun they had always carried but never used. Ishaak was on a sand hill which was baked as crisp as a new-made scone, and his eyes were dramatically fixed and demonstratively hateful. But Scott saw through his drama and knew that Ishaak would relax in five minutes, and possibly in half an hour he would be down below chattering to the two Israelis without rancour and without hate and without a revengeful thought for his lost homeland and dead family.

In an hour Scott reached the telephone line. He drove along it until he found a combination of high ground and sagging wire where he could stand up in the jeep and attach the battery hand-set and cut in on the Ghurdakha military exchange which put him on to the Frontier HQ post in the Governorate.

At first his friend Colonel Amin Fakhry got the wrong picture. He became excited and told Scott not to worry. They would get out there quickly. He saw the danger to Scott in two desperate Israelis at large in the slag hills.

'One is sick, and the other is unarmed,' Scott shouted into the field phone, with the space around him sucking away the sounds on a sea wind from the coast.

'How do you know? Can you be sure?'

Amin was an old friend who had been educated at St. Cyr, the French military academy, and his good manners and rapid-fire decisions were good French training. Amin was all and only professional, which had almost been his downfall already.

'There's no danger,' Scott told him.

'Wait for me,' Amin said. 'I'll come myself.'

Scott knew it was useless telling him that there was no need to come personally. Amin wanted action. He was starved for it. Also, Scott liked to see him anyway, and they rarely had an excuse to meet.

'I'll go back to Ishaak and wait for you,' Scott told him in French and then said in Arabic, 'You can follow my tracks if you can pick them up.'

'Mais, attention!' Amin warned him again.

Scott unclipped the hand-set and left shining upon the wires in this space, two polished sparkles of sunlight, where he had cleaned them for contact, and he looked sadly at the black road running north and running south through yellow and mauve deserts. He only felt lonely in the desert when he saw this black ribbon leading to another life, although even a building or an oil-well or another truck would sometimes give him the feeling of his own isolation.

He looked over to the east, and he could see the Red Sea's white edge, then its true dark blue, then a pale and beautiful emerald green of the coral-sided shoals, and then the deeper green and marine blue in the distance of the open depths. Beyond it, out of sight, was the Sinai.

'Amin won't get here tonight,' he told himself and took Cowperwood out of his dust-proof plastic again and sat down against the jeep, the afternoon sun well hidden by the jeep's body; and he inserted himself back into the Chicago that Ishaak had robbed him of.

It was Aileen he thought of, Aileen he loved. Which meant that he could only think of that bold and spirited woman as a wronged woman. She had his sympathy. But why destroy herself for a man? Women did so. Françoise, for instance, could never quite escape the grip that Roberto Rolland still had on her, even now, no matter what he had done to deserve her hatred. Women seemed to suffer mainly from their own incredible loyalties, their own deep source of emotion which they could not cut off at the source. Look at Lucy Pickering . . .

He could read through Aileen's predicament and he could think through his own, and it was almost dark when he put the book away and got into the jeep and drove back to his own world.

As soon as he saw the scone-shaped hill and saw Ishaak, throwing his arms empty at the sky, it was clear that there was trouble. Ishaak ran down the slag side to meet him, shouting something, and Scott stopped the jeep and sat still for a second trying to hear him.

'Ah, forgive me, Capten. Come, for God's sake!'

Scott ran up the hill to meet Ishaak who was weeping, and had been weeping for a long time by the look on his wrung face.

'For heaven's sake,' Scott said in English. 'What's the matter?'

'I did a terrible thing,' Ishaak said, taking Scott's sleeve and tugging at it. 'He came too close and there he is. Look at what I did!'

Ishaak had shot the young Israeli who was lying flat out on his back with the remnants of his undershirt torn to stop his wounds. But he was dead and still bleeding, and Ishaak wept and turned away.

'What for?' Scott said, trying to get a grip on him. 'What for? What's the matter with you?'

'Don't you see what he did?' Ishaak said, losing his temper. 'He came up here to taunt me. He was teasing me and being Israeli and laughing at me. I knew what he was, Capten. I told him to get back. I ordered him back. So he sat down near me and kept it up, unbearably. If I could only explain how superior he was and how insulting to listen to—remembering my dead mother and sister. He wouldn't go down, so I got angry and I picked it up and shot him, but I didn't mean it to be like that.'

'What about the other one?' Scott looked down the hill.

'I didn't touch him. Only this young one. He was so full up with contempt. He hated me.'

Scott told him to go down to the jeep and get a shovel and bury the young one, and when Ishaak ran off he looked down at this bold young Israeli's cold grey face and hated all provocation and all pride. This one had been a little too proud, too willing to show his pride and provoke with it. Scott had felt the strength of it himself. Ishaak was also too proud and provoking, but for the Israeli's luck it was Ishaak who had held a gun with it.

'I shouldn't have left the two of them here in that sort of an impasse,' he told himself. 'I might have realized it.'

'See if he has any papers on him,' he told Ishaak.

'No. I won't touch him,' Ishaak said, horrified.

Scott would not touch him either, so he went down to the other one and shouted at him angrily:

'What made you come to Egypt?'

'But I am born in Egypt,' the older Israeli insisted wearily. He had also been weeping. 'I am born in Cairo. Believe me, I belong there, in Cairo. I live there.' He spoke the Egyptian of the mechanic and the clerk. Yet there was something not quite right about it.

'I don't believe you,' Scott said.

The Israeli brought fresh tears to his uncared and unshaven cheeks, and he was begging tiredly, as if he had begged many times before in the last hour, for his life.

'You're not going to kill me, are you?'

Scott hated him for that. 'Why did you come here at all?' he said again.

'You are English,' the Israeli said in English. 'I know you are. But you know I *am* Egyptian. I live in Cairo. You know I have my mother and my family there. I am a printer. If you don't believe me, ask anybody if they know David Hassoon. They'll know. Everybody knows me. And my son . . .'

'What is your name?'

'Hassoon, and my son was a soldier in the British Army. Ask anybody.'

He was suddenly afraid of the look in the Englishman's face.

'You are English! You are not going to kill me, are you?'

Scott shook his head and wished that he could weep as these rival Semites could weep, as the young and old and indifferent could weep, and as angry men and frightened men and lonely men could weep.

He felt like wailing and moaning, for Sam's sake.

CHAPTER SEVENTEEN

WHEN Nona wanted to tell Helen that Quartermain was finally on his way, she walked into the main entrance of British Agency House, where Helen worked with Jolley in the Oil Exploration Company, and she felt just as local and as Egyptian inside as she did outside, which was disappointing.

In the old days, before the war and during it, when you stepped in here off the crackling and jingling and dusty Cairo street, you entered an English business house carefully re-created for long survival, even though most of the people working in it were Italians, Greeks, Armenians, Maltese, Syrians, and stateless Jews.

'You won't see any of them now,' Helen had warned her. 'So many of the Europeans have gone, even the typists.'

The typists and the clerks had always done the real work; and only remotely in the executive offices were the Englishmen from Lancs and Yorks. They would come out to Egypt modest, equable and ordinary, and then something would transform them amazingly into well-born gentlemen with native servants, motor-cars, and wives who became Britannia fair, when so far, far away.

'I despised them then,' Nona had told Helen. 'But having seen the English streets and houses and obsequecies they came from themselves, having lived among them and seen what miserable toadies they are at home, I despise them even more, looking back on it.'

Helen thought her too hard. Anyway, they too had gone. But Nona could still feel their ghosts in the corridors in grey suits and small trilby hats. Her memory was revengeful, even upon ghosts, but she knew she had more than paid them back already on their home ground for their silly superiority and their hollow contempt. If only there were a few more left to punish, though.

This English memory seemed to cling, despite her antagonism to it, because the Egypt she needed to remember had been ruled and shaped entirely by the English occupation. The hours she worked had been

115

English hours—short in summer and short in winter—and the leisure had given you time to be young, to meet, to gossip, to be *sportif*, to dance, to play tennis at the sporting clubs, and to go on Sunday picnics to the desert, to the *barrage*, to the canal, and to drive back singing in the night under a white sheet of stars, the night almost liquid in their light. How lovely Egypt was at night.

She could even forget the married echo of her own English life in these corridors where she could hear the lazy tap of one old typewriter. That was herself. She could be dressed in a sailor-striped frock with short, thick, black hair and white sandals and a sense of her own loveliness and importance, so sure of herself that she smiled now with all the old pleasures of it.

They all said she hadn't changed, that she did not look a day older. She knew otherwise. Now her black hair was long and done up tight in a chignon, and she wore an English skirt, jumper and flat-heeled shoes which would have been laughably English to the girl in the striped frock.

'Sitt Mamoon, minfadlack?' she asked the white-gowned boab near the lift.

'Iowa, ya sitt,' the boab replied respectfully.

They entered the lift and here was the difference. It wasn't dull and clean, it was scratched and neglected.

The lift stopped at the second floor and an Egyptian girl got in dressed like a French copy of what the French girl thought she ought to look like, with pony-tailed hair and flat ballerina shoes.

They exchanged a look, feminine but not yet equal.

'If they must copy the French,' Nona was thinking, 'I wish they wouldn't pluck their eyebrows and use such pale lipstick. They look sick, or unfinished.'

But she knew she was looking at her replacement. One look told her that this was a Moslem girl pushing her way out of the long chrysalis of confinement. In her own day there had been no Moslem Egyptian girls as typists or clerks. The Christian Egyptians like herself or Helen might have been possible, but the rest were Europeans by origin. They were gone. Gone with so many of the Syrian and Italian and Jewish friends. Gone to other countries, or hidden away and married and plump and clinging to the Cairo life because they could not imagine any other—already predestined refugees because their European day was done.

'Are you Sitt Helen's sister?' the girl asked her in Arabic.

'Yes, I am.' Nona knew she was condescending, but she could not help it. 'Do you know her?'

'I'll take you to her,' the girl said shyly.

Nona wondered what would be her future, this girl, when she got married, anyway. It would still be the same. Moslem men had not yet changed very much. She did not question the girl, as she would have liked to, but followed her quietly and then thanked her with the same condescension which she did not like but could not help, and found Helen standing over a filing cabinet.

She was in a temper, and quite obviously it would soon become a migraine.

'This man I work for is mad,' she said in English.

'You *will* work for the English,' Nona said, the corridor ghosts still clinging to her hair.

Helen went on in Arabic because what she had to say could not get up sufficient force in English. 'The Egyptian income-tax man comes in here to see him this morning, and Jolley tells me to throw him out. Throw him out!' Helen was wondering helplessly how a man could be so insane.

'Et alors?' Nona said.

'That was all right in the old days, when the English didn't have to pay income tax and nobody could make them. But they can't act like that now.'

'Did you throw him out?'

'Of course I didn't. He came in here and was terribly rude to Jolley and me. *Fortunately*, he was rude. At least I could tell him then that Jolley was angry with him for being so impolite. He wanted to go through all our papers, and he gave us a week to produce all our bank statements and accounts. He said Jolley personally owed the government at least a thousand pounds in unpaid tax, and I thought Jolley was going to burst a blood vessel. He had to rush out of the room and lock himself in the lavatory to get over it!'

Nona burst out laughing.

Helen began to giggle. 'When he came back I said to him . . .' She could not go on but held a fist to her mouth to stop her laughter. ' . . . I said to him: "Mr. Jolley. It's no use locking yourself in there. Remember what Gaylord Hauser says!" '

'Why Gaylord Hauser?'

'That's what Jolley said! "Well," he said to me in a temper. "What has Hauser got to do with this?" '

'So?'

'So I said to him: "Gaylord Hauser says that every time you lose your temper you pump poison into your body. Go and look at your face in the mirror, Mr. Jolley," I said, "and see just how poisonous it is." '

Nona pitied Jolley, who was a fair-skinned, dark-haired, hot-tempered and energetic man who could be crushed by two blows of a woman's wit. And Nona knew the situation well enough now to know that he must have reeled from Helen's continuing blows.

'What happened to the tax man?' she asked. 'Did he hear it all?'

'Oh, that idiot left,' Helen said. 'He was really so rude. I can't blame Jolley for losing his temper. Except that now I have to get him out of the mess by going to see the head of the tax department and putting in a complaint against the official, which means that *I* make the enemy and not Jolley.'

'You *will* work for Englishmen,' Nona said again. 'You will save them their skins and their business and their troubles. Why do you baby them?'

'Because they are such babies,' Helen said with a shrug.

It was strange that after all these years Helen still admired and respected and believed in the English. Nona liked the English because she had married them; but she no longer respected or admired them. And in Egypt her contempt for them would always be difficult to hide, even now. Even when Jolley came in like a dancing master and found this cool exact copy of Helen greeting him from a supremacy in temperament, in origin, in certainty, and in physical toleration (she was taller) which Jolley's hot-and-cold temperament found difficult to come to grips with. He only tolerated it because he hated not to be liked, and because he was afraid of women.

'When's your husband coming, Nona?' he asked her, sportingly.

'I have just had a cable this morning,' Nona told him. 'He'll be here in a few days.'

'Will they let him in?' Jolley asked her.

'Why shouldn't they?'

Jolley rolled his eyes like a good actor. 'You know very well, Nona, that he is always exploding under somebody. Everybody knows it.'

'Only under the English,' she said.

Jolley sighed like a woman with a wayward son. 'That's his privilege,' he said sadly, and went back into his own office.

'You didn't tell me,' Helen said in Arabic to Nona, 'that he was coming.'

'I didn't have time,' Nona said. 'I was getting to it.'

Helen's coming migraine lifted a little. This was one problem off her mind, although she was still not sure what the situation was between Nona and her erratic husband. Nona had still not spoken of it. That in itself meant something. But at least he would be here and they could judge for themselves, although Hanna would never judge. Hanna would believe in Quartermain whatever happened, and in Nona. But Helen had to judge, and she tempted herself now with the possibility of arbitration. She knew what she would ask Nona's husband. She already knew what she would tell him for the two boys' sakes and for Nona's sake and for his own sake.

Jolley put his head in the door and said, 'Nona, when Quartermain comes, bring him to dinner one night. And isn't he a friend of that even more notorious character, Scott?'

'They're bosom friends,' Nona said.

'Oh, then you must bring him too. I know about twenty chaps longing

118

to meet Scott. Please fix it up,' Jolley said. 'I'll tell Helen what night is good for me.'

'If you don't want me any more,' Helen said to him, 'I think I'll go.'

'Off you go,' Jolley said, who was always generous. 'I'm going to the club.'

When they went out Nona asked Helen if she had told Jolley about Scott.

'Oh, he's like an old woman,' Helen said. 'He's a very decent boss, but he hates to be left out of anything, and I suppose they are always curious about Scott because he never comes out of the desert and he never mixes with them and he's so much in with these Egyptian officers. And now the English newspapers are discovering him again.'

'I can't imagine Scott running off to Jolley's for dinner.'

'Why not?' Helen said indignantly. 'It wouldn't do him any harm.'

'If he never did mix with those people at the Turf Club, why should he do so now?'

'Perhaps it's only because they never asked him to.'

Nona laughed. 'You really believe in English decency.'

'But Jolley is decent. He's curious, but he's decent.'

They had already left the office, and they were now going to part at a business building in the centre of the city, which Nona said was new and lovely and obviously Italian-designed.

'At least,' she said, 'they're getting away from those terrible imitations of English and French cities. They're so dull when you copy them.'

'This *immeuble* is Saudi Arabian,' Helen told her. 'They get all those dollars from the Americans for their oil, but there's nothing in Saudi Arabia to invest them in. So they come here, build all these modern blocks you see going up, and they drive around in big American cars like Pashas, which most of them are anyway, I suppose. Yet Nasser throws out the British and the Jews . . .'

'There's a slight difference,' Nona argued.

'What difference is there?'

'At least the Saudis are Arabs.'

'What's it matter who comes to make money on you? Whether they're Arabs or English or Jews? It's all the same, isn't it? Nasser simply lets the Saudis come and make money here because they bring in dollars.'

'I suppose he needs them. Look what the English do to get dollars. The whole of England is occupied by the Americans for dollars. All those American bombs . . .'

Helen kissed Nona at the door and said, 'I don't understand it. Why is all the world grovelling for dollars? What difference is the dollar from any other money? Why is everything being bought and sold the way the Americans want it to be?'

'Ask my husband,' Nona said provokingly. 'He'll explain to you, if you can survive the argument.'

'I'm glad he's finally coming, anyway,' Helen said. 'I was beginning to worry.'

'That's your trouble, darling,' Nona said. 'If you haven't got a worry you'll think one up.'

They had been talking at the doorway with hands, gestures, indignation in their eyes, and affection, and no one had taken any notice of them until a Greek shopkeeper in the arcade began to smile at them.

'I really must go,' Helen said and hurried towards the lift which would take her up to see Maître Mahmoud el Khony about Sam. 'If only I could discover what they actually accuse Sam of,' he had said to Nona, 'I'd know what to do. El Khony says they must tell me that much. It's still the law.'

'The law!' Would Helen never lose her faith in the weapons of the devil, in the hypocrisy of institutions?

CHAPTER EIGHTEEN

MAITRE EL KHONY was a small and ugly man who still wore a tarboush and who liked to go with Helen to the fortune-tellers. He would ring her up when he found a new one and he would pay a pound each time to have one question answered by the spirits: '*Does my wife have a lover?*'

Before the war, when they were both younger and when he was still a law student, he would have liked to marry Helen but he had been too small and ugly to ask her, and he had been too strict a Moslem to risk refusal. Long afterwards, when it was obviously hopeless, he had gone to his family village in upper Egypt, looked at all the suitably born and certified virginal girls of sixteen, chosen one, and married her and brought her to Cairo as the wife of the most successful young lawyer in the city.

He had hopes for her because she was docile and pretty and pale-skinned, and he had done his best for five years. But the only change in her as far as he could see was in her style: the dowdy little provincial girl had become chic in the European manner, and bored.

'She does nothing else,' he complained to Helen, 'except entertain silly women who giggle and eat Groppi's patisseries all day and go to the pictures.'

'She's so young,' Helen said.

But Helen knew that, being a Moslem girl and the wife of such a strict Moslem like el Khony, this young woman dare not do anything more interesting than eat cakes and go to the pictures, unless it was something as clandestine and as satisfying as having a lover.

'It's no good,' Maître el Khony said unhappily to Helen as they drove in his American car to the Ministry. 'I must accept the fact that I shall never know. That's all . . .'

'But why must you know?' Helen said.

'Of course I must know.'

'If she has someone, it's better that you don't know.'

'My dear Helen, that's the woman's point of view.'

'No,' she said. 'I'm thinking of you. Why torture yourself, Maître?'

121

'Because I'm sure she has someone else. This time that old black *nassaba* at Bulak told me in my fortune that she has an officer friend who comes every day at ten o'clock in the morning. But I sat outside all last week around the corner in a taxi and nobody came. Only those silly women.'

'Then it's obviously not true, Maître.'

'It's no good saying that, Helen. I know it's true. I feel it. I've asked her, but she won't tell me, even though I point out that I understand and won't be angry. So *she* becomes angry and actually throws her scent bottle at me. Believe me, Helen, she has ruined a suit. It was thoroughly soaked in French perfume.'

Helen giggled with him and then straightened up and said, 'It's all because she has nothing to do, Maître. Find her something . . .'

'Do you think so? I thought so myself, but look at the things I have tried to interest her in. Tennis, riding a horse, driving a car. Look how many times I have tried to bring her out to you, to see how a woman *can* behave.'

'Surely you didn't tell her that?'

'Of course I did. She must learn from others.'

'For a lawyer, Maître, you're not being clever with her. Really.'

El Khony took off his tarboush and rubbed his thin hair which he treated once a week for its tendency to fall out. The treatment always left it irritated because part of it was a friction with the Bedouin's preparation of emulsified camel-dung.

'I think it's simply because I'm so ugly,' he said.

'Ugliness is only found in the heart,' Helen said in Arabic. 'And you know quite well that you have a lovely heart. Everybody is your friend.'

'Ah, *merci*, dear Helen!' el Khony said and put his tarboush back on. 'It's my good friends who make even this excrement on my head worth while.'

They laughed because they could always share the laugh at their own expense, and he said that he hoped he could at least do something for her nephew.

'I would speak to Gamal Abd el Nasser himself,' el Khony said, 'but I think it may make it worse. Gamal would not like a lawyer trying to go around the law.'

'If they will only tell me what they think he did,' Helen said.

The traffic had held them up in the new Place of the Liberation, and they could see a wad of cars and buses jammed together behind a big truck which had lost a wheel.

'We'll be here all day,' the Maître said, and he looked quickly to the right and pulled out of the line of traffic, his small arms turning the big car with great skill. He cut across the converging traffic and went the wrong way down a one-way street and was stopped at the end of it by a policeman who threw up his hands to heaven at such idiocy.

'But!' the policeman said helplessly. 'But . . .'

'But!' the Maître said. 'There's a traffic block that will take a week to undo on the square. You want me to help block it up more? Isn't this simpler?'

'It is a one-way, *ya Bey*.'

'Of course it is. But use your head, man. If you had a head you'd be up the other end of the street filtering the traffic through here. Did God say this had to be one way and the same way for ever?'

'No. But I must take your number and name, *ya Bey*, if you will forgive my doing so.'

'If you take my number I shall take you to court and make a fool of you, *ya sidi*. Now don't be silly. Go up there and get the traffic coming this way . . .'

'I can't do that. It's not my responsibility.'

The logic went on bouncing up and down until the policeman knew what he must do. He agreed to go to the other end of the street, to redirect the traffic this way, to use his head, and to call on Maître el Khony next day in his office—which would be to his advantage.

'Really, Maître,' Helen said, 'you could win an argument with the devil.'

'Oh, policemen don't count, the poor wretches,' he said. 'What chance have they got when someone like me comes up in a big car and threatens them? What would you do, my dear, in their circumstances?'

'I'd fine you,' she said. 'I would never give in.'

'Yes, you would,' he insisted, 'if your miserable existence depends on it. How can we ever change? Yet we must. We ought to be serious and incorruptible. Look at this man we are going to see. I wouldn't trust him with my cigarette lighter, yet we ought to be sweet to him.'

'Who is he?'

'A petty official who has the ear of the special prosecutor. He may just give us what we want. But please be careful with him, Helen. He's that fellow Aboud Shakir.'

'But I know him!' Helen announced.

'Ahmed Aboud Shakir—a thin wretched man? The one whose wife tried to bite off his nose?'

'But he worked with me in the Ministry of Labour,' Helen told him. 'He used to take bribes openly from the Italians for not bothering too much with the light and air laws in the cigarette factories. I had terrible arguments with him about the tobacco dust which gave all the women skin diseases. Do you think he cared about them? Never! Never!'

'Then, *please*, Helen, be sweet to him now.'

123

'I am always sweet,' she said, 'even to the sofragis.'

'These petty officials are not even up to the level of a sofragi,' he said, 'so don't be too strong with him. In God's name be sweet.'

She said she was quite determined to be sweet, no matter what it cost.

The Ministry was new outside. Inside it, the winding circular staircase which went right up through a well in the middle of the building was called suicide's leap, because so many people (it was said) had leapt from the top of it in desperation at the impossibility of getting done what they needed done, of having papers stamped when they needed stamping, of getting a passport when they ought to have a passport. It was a very popular story.

They waited at a grubby desk, filled in a white form, behaved patiently with the man who sat bundled in a corner surrounded by yellow cards, and kept a sweet temper until it was obviously wasted. El Khony then asserted himself savagely and they were shown into a small office jammed up against a window overlooking the square. It smelled of a man who smoked bad Greek cigarettes and doused them out in a watery ashtray on his desk.

'But it's so nice of you to come,' he said. 'And Sitt Helen! Well, God willing, your family is well, *ya uztaz*,' he said, hand on heart.

'Indeed they are,' the Maître said politely.

'And yourself?'

'All right.'

'Everything is all right?'

'El humdulillah.'

'And your family? Your wife?'

El Khony took off his tarboush. 'All right, God be praised.'

He settled chairs for them in the small space near the window, and Helen took the farthest one. The man's clothes looked as if they were dry-rotting on him. His body was like an old lumpy mattress. She felt her skin grate and her teeth become dry and on edge, looking at him. He had already ordered coffee and she held hers without drinking it.

'Miss Helen would like to explain to you about her nephew,' Maître el Khony said gently, 'and to ask your help. Explain to our friend, Helen, what it's all about.'

Helen disciplined carefully all prejudice, indignation, impatience, and sourness, and she told Ahmed Aboud as sweetly as she could about Sam. The puzzle of it to her was why they had arrested Sam at all; he had done nothing wrong. Aboud listened and nodded and understood.

'But I'm not responsible for this case,' he said.

'I don't suppose you are, Aboud Bey,' Helen said, smiling with lovely teeth, 'but if I could just see whoever is responsible.'

124

'Now that's another thing,' Aboud said. 'It will be the military authorities who accuse him, if they have to accuse him. Not here, *ya sitt.*'

Maître el Khony held up the palm of his hand as if he were in court before a reluctant judge who must have things explained to him carefully.

'But there must be some kind of *procès* against him,' he said. 'That would come from your department. A *procès-verbal* would at least allow us to hear the accusations and the witnesses. At least!'

'Of course, Maître. But that's our famous lawyer who speaks. You are absolutely right.'

'Well then?'

'But surely you know that all such juridical procedures are suspended, until the new constitution comes into effect.'

'Not all, *ya Bey,*' the Maître argued patiently.

'The important procedures.'

'Then how is it,' Helen demanded, 'that the courts are so full of law cases?'

'Litigations and criminal cases only,' Aboud argued happily. 'Crimes against the State are in a different category. That is what they will probably charge your nephew with.'

'But what crime has he committed? I must know that at least,' Helen insisted.

'Wait, wait,' Maître el Khony said quickly, seeing the signs. 'Perhaps you would be able to arrange for us to see Mr. Sam Hassoon?'

'Are you representing him, *ya uztaz?*' Aboud asked in the sort of surprise which said, '*You're a fool if you get mixed up in this, and for a Jew and a Christian? What for?*'

'Not yet,' el Khony replied. 'How can I, when he hasn't been charged with anything?'

'I can't help you then,' Aboud said, offering him a cigarette.

'Who can?' Helen asked. 'You can't just shake it off like that.'

'I don't know who can help you, believe me, *ya sitt.*'

'It's your department, here in the Ministry,' Helen insisted.

'You see, Helen . . .' el Khony began urgently.

'No, it is not our department, sitt Helen,' Aboud was saying.

'But you're the special prosecutor's section. Who else can charge him?'

'The military can charge him,' Aboud said irritably. 'Go to them, *ya sitt*, if you want to insist.'

'Where have they got him?'

'I don't know.'

Helen stood up. 'Oh, but you put my teeth on edge,' she said tigerishly in Arabic. In Arabic it was *daress* which came from the word for molar, but applied to this badly rooted man it had other meanings of shape, size and cleanliness.

'Wait, *ya sidi*,' Maître el Khony said to him and simultaneously held Helen by the arm. 'Miss Helen is upset and she is worried. You will understand. Please! Now let me see Colonel Abbas, I beg you.' He nodded at the room with a grey door.

Aboud looked at Helen, dropped his cigarette into his coffee cup, remembered the days of the Italian cigarette manufacturers and thought of Colonel Abbas and himself and thought of the look on this woman's face that could threaten a man the way it did and perhaps ruin him too; one never knew . . .

'I insist,' Maître el Khony was saying, impatience beginning to sharpen his voice because the balance of authority was now at stake, 'otherwise I shall have to see him by other means. Now, please. Tell him I'm here.'

'I have done my best to spare you what he will tell you,' Aboud said, and added: 'And I mean that, Maître, for your sake.'

He went into the other room and after a while he opened the door and said, 'Colonel Abbas would like to see you alone, Maître, if Miss Helen doesn't mind. It is better this way.'

'It *is* better,' el Khony said quietly in English to Helen.

He went into the office and Helen was left with the coffee she could not drink because she could guess what happened to these coffee cups. She looked out of the window to spare her teeth, waiting with the life in the streets which flowed like a muddy river below her. She felt for a moment the isolation of all these men sitting up here in these rooms full of old paper, deciding the existence and the future of so many people down there with simply one document, one signature, one seal, one accusation.

'It's getting worse instead of better,' she thought. 'Yet it can't get much worse for people who have no papers, and for fools like Sam and the Jews like Buelli and oddities like me. It can't get worse, unless they take *my* passport away as well.'

Another undrinkable coffee was brought to her and she could hear voices. When the Maître finally appeared she could tell by his elaborate farewell at the door to the unseen Colonel Abbas that he had achieved nothing.

'You shouldn't have lost your temper with Aboud,' el Khony told her unhappily in the car, in the traffic of noonday which seemed so painfully normal. Didn't any of these people have problems? It's normalcy outside her own problems became very oppressive.

'Forgive me, Maître,' she said, controlling her bad temper.

'It's not like you, Helen.'

'But it's becoming too much to bear!' she cried out. Now she had the migraine she had been holding off all morning. 'They could have shot

126

Sam already for all I know, for all they will tell me. What did Colonel Abbas say in there?'

Maître el Khony thought for a moment, and it was clear that he was making up his mind whether to tell her the truth or not.

'I think you should spare yourself,' el Khony told her.

'Why? What did he say?'

'He said, in effect, that for your own sake you ought to leave it all alone. Not to pursue it. To keep as far out of it as you can, for your own sake. Otherwise it will not be good for you or your family.'

'But why?'

'He said you probably know why. That's why it is so bad for you too.'

'But I don't know why.'

Maître el Khony shrugged defensively. 'I'm only repeating it, Helen ...'

'I'm sorry, I'm sorry,' she said.

'But really, Helen, I think he meant it. Whatever it is' (and it was clear to her that Maître el Khony, after talking with Colonel Abbas, did not want to know what it was), 'you ought to be careful. It's not like the old days, you know. I have a certain influence. But now, with these new men, I am for them because they will save us from our own follies. But we mustn't push them too hard. You have to understand that. It's dangerous.'

Helen nodded. She could suppress the tears of exasperation, but not the tears of defeat. El Khony watched the road, knowing how useless he was to her, but wishing that he could do more.

CHAPTER NINETEEN

THE other flying students in the white school bus which took them to Cairo from the airfield were respectfully distant with Scott, but Fahid sat next to him talking about the native women they passed. They were digging in a rubbish dump abandoned years ago. They dug into it with their bare hands looking for old fragments of tins and lumps of scrap, filthy and decayed, which they sold to the scrap merchants who came to the village paying a piastre a donkeyload. Their children ran around happily in the dump. A dead dog was blown up, lying on the edge of the road, and Fahid said that every day the dog got a little bigger until one day it would burst, horribly.

'You notice these things too much,' Scott told him, trying to restrain him.

'In our country,' Fahid said cynically, 'it is usually filth and poverty that one notices least. Isn't it so, Capten Scott?'

'I suppose so,' Scott admitted, surprised by the perception of that remark. Fahid was right. How many times had Scott driven along this road himself without noticing those women, yet they were always there. There was a bad state of affairs when you stopped noticing misery.

'Look at that, Capten,' Fahid said. 'Will you eat those khaas tomorrow?'

Fahid pointed to barefooted women and children sitting beside a dirty mud pool. They washed their donkeys in the water as well as the khaas—the long lettuces which were ripe, lush and beautifully green. They shook the leaves free of the filthy water and loaded them sparkling and fresh onto a donkey cart to be taken into the Cairo shops.

'Why do you notice such things?' Scott asked him again, but more seriously this time.

'I often wonder myself,' Fahid said. 'I wonder if your friend Gamal Abd el Nasser notices these things when he drives through the city in his American limousines. Do you think he notices the stupid donkey men and the filthy street boys and the thousands of silly and childish people and says to himself: "That is us! Egyptians!" '

128

'He did once,' Scott told him. 'What else made him do what he did?'

'Do you think he sees it now?'

Scott was not sure whether this was directed against Nasser or against the poverty, or whether Fahid's mockery was making a deep joke of his own English alienation here.

'Perhaps he has other things on his mind now,' Scott said.

Fahid shrugged. 'That's right. Why should he notice us when we don't even notice ourselves? We need more than Gamal Abd el Nasser to rub our noses in our own dirt. What do you say, Capten?'

Scott reached for his Cowperwood. 'I would say that you bite, Fahid, while the others only chew.'

It was an Arabic saying really intended for a bad-tempered but astute bargainer, and in English it had no real equivalent. But Fahid had no equivalent in English either, so Scott opened his Cowperwood. Neither had these women in the eventide picking the beans and the lettuce in the fields, while the gamoossas wallowed luxuriously in the village canals and the men washed down their stinking backsides. No equivalent in English.

'Carrots,' Fahid said, nudging him.

The other students were now throwing balls of chewing-gum at each other in the bus, laughing around in high spirits. One of the balls hit Fahid and he leapt on the thrower with it and slammed the gum on his forehead and said in Arabic:

'How can you tell the child from his father, when one *baas* like a goat and the other *brays* like an ass. Ass! Donkey!'

They shouted at him, but Fahid fought them off and sat down again next to Scott feeling better.

'Tonight,' he said, out of breath, 'Captain Zareef is flying the army co-operation for the anti-aircraft practice, in the flying box. He hates it. But he won't let me go with him, even though Sam Hassoon is still away and he'll be bored all alone up there. Do you know why they arrested Sam Hassoon, Capten?'

'No, I don't know,' Scott answered quickly.

'Are you sure you don't know, Capten?'

Scott shook his head.

'Everybody thinks you know. Even Captain Zareef. Tonight,' he said, 'I shall go out on the roof of our flat and watch the green and red and white lights of the Gemini going overhead. You ought to watch it, Capten, with Zareef going back and forth like that over the city. He must be lonely without his good friend. But good friends ought not to be silly. Particularly Hassoon. Look at that . . .'

They were crossing the Embaba bridge, and what was in daytime a dirty grey prophet's-beard tree had turned at eventide into a white beauty, covered with snowy blossoms.

'You see the white ibisis,' Fahid said. 'Filthy things if you walk near them. When you see them from the air they burst off the green fields like those English thistles you blow away. At exactly five-thirty every evening, my Capten, they leave the fields, all the ibisis, and set their course exactly for Embaba bridge. If you walk around there under the trees at night the ground is snow white. The rain and splatter of their shit is something to be seen, considering that they've worked all day in the fields guzzling everything in sight.'

'You destroy things too much,' Scott said irritably, 'particularly the things you like. Why do you do it, Fahid?'

'Do you think I should deceive myself, Capten?'

'Why not? You can't live hopefully without a little self-deception.'

'Do you ever try to deceive yourself? You?'

Scott put his glasses away and tried not to be the man older and wiser and saner and gentler, because the role was annoying. Too often, though, he felt it being forced on him by the sheer violence and insistence of other men's reactions and the long memory of his own.

'We all have to deceive ourselves,' he said, 'otherwise we wouldn't believe in anything at all.'

'Well?'

'The big thing is,' Scott said as unwisely as he could make it sound, 'not to damage yourself when you're young, and when it matters. Why flay yourself alive? I suppose I did, but I don't think it got me anywhere.'

'Everybody admires you, Capten,' Fahid said cynically. 'You are honest. Captain Zareef believes in you as he believes in no one else. That's somewhere, isn't it?'

'I don't know that it is. Except that a man has good friends.'

'Yes? So what about good friends? Everybody is a good friend of Sam Hassoon, but there he is in gaol. I should think they will shoot him if they think it worthwhile. Too many things in the world bigger than good friends, Capten. Even bigger than you.'

Scott had somehow held off his misery, his suspicions of hopelessness, until now. But one shaft of insight from Fahid's casual armoury had hit him directly with the truth, and he had nothing to defend himself with.

'Not everybody realizes that,' he said to the boy.

'Ah, but everybody knows,' Fahid went on dryly, 'that Hassoon will be all right. You, Capten, will get him out. Everybody knows it.'

'You mean everybody *expects* it,' he said, 'but it's not quite so easy . . .'

Fahid did not hear. '*Ya 'osta!*' he was shouting at the driver. 'Stop here. How many times do I have to tell you to let me off here? Ah, you're a fool. Why don't you listen when you're told?'

'Nobody listens to a gamoossa swinging her backside,' the others shouted.

130

Fahid swung his backside as he went out and they pelted him with rulers, chewing-gum, papers and pencils.

'*Merci!* What a herd of goats. Good-bye, ya Capten.'

Scott had opened his book. 'Good-bye, Fahid,' he said without looking up.

He read, but he read Fahid's words: *too many things bigger than good friends, Capten.* How was he ever going to explain to old Mama Hassoon that he had unwittingly caught her own worthless son, and that he too would be thrown into prison alongside Sam himself?

CHAPTER TWENTY

AT 4 a.m. Peacock was wondering in the gloom why he had agreed to duck-shoot in the marshes of el Bindari's estate where young Bateman had brought him to impress him and plot with him, and where he had been feasted and fed on whole sheep and buckets of rice by village Omdas and given English dinners and whisky by the Bindari family in their three-storeyed French mansion. It crumbled a little, but it was lovely in the turquoise heat of barseem fields, with a hundred villagers to season the Bindaris and tender them until they became good and ripe Bindaris; father and son.

'I'm not such a good shot, you know,' he had tried.

'Well, don't admit it,' Bateman had instructed.

'What about you?'

'I never shoot anything,' Bateman had said. 'I don't believe in it, and that's understood. I fire one shot into the air every three minutes until I have used up fifty rounds, and by then our time is up.'

'It's so damned early,' Peacock had groaned.

Here he was, though, here in the motor-boat loaded with six men and ten shotguns and three thousand rounds of American 12-gauge black shells, putt-putting up a channel in the marshes. The night was damp and warm. He *was* a good shot, and now that he was here he was going to enjoy it, but he was worried that it might be spoiled.

'Is it all right?' he asked young Bindari. 'Isn't it rather warm for ducks?'

Bindari senior had his foot propped up on the ammunition. His foot was wrapped up, enveloped like a baby to protect its gout, and he was answering for his unanswerable son.

'It might be better with a little breeze,' he said, 'but we like it so in Egypt. It doesn't have to be cold and miserable like your English Norfolk shooting, my dear.'

The reeds swished along the boat. The marsh smelled of dry salt and damp fresh mist and of distant desert breezes. The night soaked up the boat because there was no track of where they were going over the marsh water.

'It's damned dark,' Peacock complained. 'What are those shadows we pass?'

'Mud hovels belonging to the fishermen,' Bateman told him.

'No. Those whitish cloths.'

Bindari senior told him they were seine nets hanging silhouetted on their large poles. The fishermen, he said, used them for catching the small mud fish, which in the light of morning you could see lying on the channel edges and you would hear them plopping back into the water when you passed them in a punt.

'Fish can't live lying in mud, old sweetheart,' his son Ramzi ridiculed. 'That's your imagination.'

'It is not. I tell you I see them jumping in.'

Peacock hoped there was not going to be another argument. Even though he couldn't understand the Arabic, he could sense violence in the language. Bindari junior was a madman. He was sitting on the gun cases drinking the coffee his friend Ali Nablis had brought for the after-effects of the shooting. He rolled little round pills from a small tin of paste and threw them into his mouth.

'What's that stuff?' Peacock whispered.

'Hashish,' Bateman said. 'Do you want some?'

'Good God no, Bateman.'

Ramzi played with a giant battery light, which he shone crazily over the marshes while he flicked hot coffee with his fingers at Ali Nablis and Bateman, until Bateman's red hair got the better of him. He scooped up a handful of water and flung it at Ramzi and growled at him in Arabic as if young Englishmen had finally learned to play the game the way they did. It bothered Peacock to see it. Ramzi replied with a handful of water full in Bateman's face, and a happy laugh.

'Enough, enough!' his father groaned.

Peacock felt like hiding, and Ramzi senior shifted his sore foot to a safer place. Then Ramzi turned upon his fair-skinned friend, Ali, the neighbouring landowner's son who spoke with an American accent.

'But this is getting dangerous,' Peacock decided.

'In the name of God,' his friend Ali said in English. 'If you don't quit it, Ramzi, I'll jump clean out of this boat and swim home. Don't push me!'

'Let's jump together,' Ramzi taunted. 'Come on!'

Bindari senior slapped him gently but decisively on the back of the head. 'I apologize for my son,' the father said proudly to Peacock. 'Ramzi is rich and spoiled and badly educated, as you can see.' The old man lifted up his giant shoulders in their French canvas jacket. He sighed contentedly as Ramzi scooped up more water and poured it over his friend's head and then at Bateman again.

'What a pig,' Bateman said freely.

133

'Enough!' Old Bindari roared at his son.

Peacock turned away from the fooling. Really, he felt as unlike an English gentleman as he would ever feel, which may not be a bad thing, but this was all too confined to be tolerable.

'Nasser hasn't changed Egypt all that much,' he had decided already. 'What a life. I wonder if, even in the days of the barons, the English ever had it as good as this. Pharaohs and poor old Gyppos. What a combination, what a life.'

'There you are, Sir Peacock. And good-bye. Hah! Do not kill yourself.'

Ramzi had put him off the motor-boat onto a punt, and now a fisherman in baggy Turkish trousers poled him through the shallows to the libda where he would shoot. A libda was an iron barrel sunk in the shallow mud, he knew that much.

'Soon, mister,' the fisherman said in English.

He was caked in mud, he was a barefooted colossus with grey hair, a slight grunt for each push of the pole, like a horse pulling a load uphill. It seemed uphill all the way, punting silently through this salt-weeded mud.

'I'd love to ask this old boy what Nasser has done for him.'

'Nothing, most likely,' Peacock had his own answer. It looked as if old Bindari and Ramzi had not been affected very much, either, although the ex-chief of Egyptian police had told him over Bateman's dinner table that if Nasser had not arrived when he did ('Even a week later!') every landlord in Egypt would have been murdered in his bed. By this sort of chap, no doubt, considering the ferocity of young Ramzi's instructions to him and old Bindari's gentle but snarling authority.

'Who could blame him?' Peacock asked.

Bindari was, in fact, lucky to have his kingdom. Ramzi (his father boasted) had ridden half-demented into the nearest town the day Nasser's officials came to announce land reform. Ramzi had rounded up the new officials with his shotgun and put them all into their car and fired a couple of shells into the back of it and sent them packing.

'So much,' Bindari had said happily, 'for that man's land distribution to the fellah.'

'And Ramzi got away with it?' Peacock had asked Bindari naïvely. 'With Nasser's men?'

The old man had laughed up from his belly. 'Of course he got away with it.'

'Then it's not so difficult. You can oppose Nasser like that?'

'Ramzi spent a few days in the local gaol and got lice, that's all. The Army came to take over the situation, but I knew the *Bimbashi* and I got him out . . .'

134

But Bateman had said privately that Ramzi was lucky to come out of it alive. If his father had not promised to restrain him and force the law down his son's throat, they would have shot Ramzi on the spot.

'How much land have they had taken away?' Peacock asked.

'Not much.'

'Then it's all a fake.'

'It's not a fake,' Bateman said. 'It's simply a trick. Nasser's reforms allow these big landowners about a hundred hectares for each person in the family. It leaves most of the estates intact, but it hands over just enough land from the Royal estates to big and middle peasants to keep them quiet. But the majority of the peasants remain landless anyway, so what's the difference?'

'Here, mister!'

The fisherman had grounded the punt near the iron tub—the libda. The tub was firmly based in the mud and camouflaged with salt-bush, but it remained an iron tub waist-high but dry.

'Rub-a-dub-dub, this British member of parliament in a tub,' Peacock said.

He tried to organize himself while the fisherman put out the decoys, but long before the old colossus had finished spreading them out in the cream water, Ramzi had started the morning's shoot by pumping a dozen shells into the first mallards and pintails that rose off the water near him, somewhere to the north.

'Get a move on, old chap!' Peacock shouted to the colossus.

Something unintelligible came back, then Peacock saw the air black about him, even in the faint dawning light, with ducks that crowded each other on the wing as far as he could see. They were already thinking of settling his end, but they were frightened off when he suddenly unfolded himself and stood up to let them have both barrels as they came over.

'Widgeons!' he whispered happily.

The driving wedge of vibrating air swung low over him and he brought down one of the fast-flyers who tumbled over and over in the air, falling with the velocity and disinterest of a dead stone.

'Oh, my God!' Peacock cried out aloud. 'What a shot. *What* a shot!'

From then on, however, the widgeons and pintails and mallards and the garganeys kept high. They knew about him. He shot at them as they zoomed upwards from him, but though one mallard took a shallow death dive from a great height, he knew they had all taken note of him. It was not going to be so easy after all.

'I need some sort of strategy,' Peacock said, and began to think about it.

When he had fought with Scott in the long-range desert treks he remembered that they had survived by the one important rule of that particular game, which was not unlike hunting ducks.

135

'Hide and anticipate,' he said. 'That's the rule. These birds have experience, particularly with that madman Ramzi down there with a pump gun.'

He broke off a piece of the salt-bush near him and stuck it into his soft hat and he crouched down and allowed the ducks to wing over him again and again, hiding with the old discipline, and carefully pouring himself a cup of coffee from the thermos and drinking it sugarless and hot and taking quick joyful disciplined looks over the edge of the libda at the washed-out, salty-grey-turning-to-desert-chalky-rose-pink dawn on the horizon, and at the decoys thirty yards off. Twice, coveys came down as if to settle near the decoys, and he kept his head down. He listened.

'Next time,' he told himself, 'I'll give it to them. No wonder old Bindari has such a dose of gout. He's stuffed with widgeons.'

He heard them wing over, wing around, and begin the beating and breaking of wings to land, but he kept himself in check and held himself down. He heard the swishing skid of their feet and tails on the water, and almost the moment they landed he stood up boldly, waited like a gentleman, and as they took off again and just as they rose clear from the water he drew his sights on one and dropped it and continued the barrel nicely onto his neighbour and ahead of him and he fired, knowing elatedly that he had hit.

'What a shot!' he cried again. 'What a marvel.'

It was heaven. But then, as he kept his head down, waiting again, he began to think about it deeply.

'Perhaps it isn't quite the thing to hit them like that as they take off.'

No, it wasn't the thing. He decided against it.

'Here they come again,' he mumbled happily. 'Ramzi sends them down from the top and I send them back from the bottom. And old Bindari catches them in the middle. Poor bloody ducks. If they had any sense they'd all fly off to Russia now, where they came from.'

He heard the next covey wing over and veer back. This time *before* they had touched the water, but when they had their feet spread out and their wings back-pedalling, he stood up and picked two together and hit them both with one shot.

'Marvellous!' he cried as he reloaded and tossed the used shells into the mud.

Yet he thought about it again. 'It's not quite right, either,' he told himself unhappily.

He didn't like it. It was still not right to catch a duck slightly off wing, in landing or in taking off. It was beautifully effective, but definitely not quite right. He was against it.

The ducks swept high again. This time, to be decent about it, he stood up to give them plenty of warning, and they winged off before they had broken their flight into flat feet and back-flowing wings.

Flamph! Flamph!

Flat, echoing, lovely, and *very* much the life. He thought he had missed both shots. Then he watched the group go high and saw one gradually glide wounded to the far edge of the lake where Ramzi was using his pump-gun like a machine-gun.

'No good,' he said. 'If I wait too long I wound them. That's much more cruel than shooting them dead on the half-wing.'

It was a dilemma. Too soon it was not right. Too late it was cruel. Both ways not quite the game.

However, there was always an exact point when enough was enough. He'd had a fair go. So had the birds. He took his hat off and put his long legs up awkwardly in a crushed and uncomfortable position, and with a sigh of relief and satisfaction, and in the sensibility of it, he dozed off. He had been up so terribly early . . .

Like that, the ducks recognized him and settled down in safety on the water near him, near his decoys. He could hear their short and clever little *crawks* as they communicated briefly. *Crawk!* Short and no complaints. Ramzi and the old man were still blowing away. *Crawk!* In his half-sleep he felt a little like a safe and contented duck himself.

Mr. Krushchev had made a speech that day, denouncing Stalin, the radio said; and over roast duck with marble-sized potatoes and orange sauce and a bottle of '47 Château Canon, Peacock felt sorry for Stalin.

'Hardly seems quite right,' he said, 'hitting at him when he's so dead. I always admired him in a frightened sort of way . . .'

'Admired him,' they said. 'Good God!'

'Yes, but you see I watched him at Potsdam with Attlee and Truman. Now that was like watching a giant crab between two little hermit crabs.'

'You wouldn't have admired him if you lived here, my dear,' old Bindari said. 'Stalin is the only name many of our peasants have heard of outside Egypt. Who won the war? *Stalin*, they say. Who will come to cut off our heads at night? Stalin! *Abu shanab*, they say, Father-of-the-moustache . . .'

'Sir Anthony Eden also has a moustache,' Peacock said, and laughed to show them that it was all a good joke.

'But it's not a joke, my dear.'

Ramzi stabbed four potatoes in one go. 'Now,' he said, 'it's our own Gamal Abd el Nasser who has the moustache.'

'His is just a little moustache,' Bateman said.

Ramzi laughed. 'He'll cut off our heads, anyway. Don't you think, Sir Peacock?'

'If you only realized it,' his American-voiced friend, Ali Nablis, said to Ramzi, 'Gamal Abd el Nasser saved your neck for you, Ramzi.'

'Then I won't spare his.'

'If Nasser and the officers hadn't thrown out Farouk,' Ali went on, 'we would have all been thrown into the Nile, and all the land grabbed hold of by the mob. You know it.'

'You think like an American,' Ramzi said contemptuously. 'Americans are ruining the world and turning us all into communists. Look at the French . . .'

Two more ducks were brought in and old Bindari complained of their slight fishy taste. 'They've been flying down from Lake Mariut and Edku, which are salty,' he explained to Peacock. 'Don't eat them.'

Three white-gowned sofragis took the ducks away from the table laden otherwise with platters of spaghetti and rice and sauces and baked apples. The table was large enough for twenty, white and clean but not luxurious, with worn modest silver and one dim light in the centre ceiling above it. It was a French country house and the tastes were worn and French bourgeois, except that there were no women present and the shutters were closed against the desert breeze. Five men ate duck and the women were elsewhere, and old Bindari tore native bread in half and asked Peacock sadly if the British had accepted their fate, had taken to the corner, had accepted world communism as inevitable.

'I'd hardly say that,' Bateman answered before Peacock could suck in his breath. 'It's simply a matter of policy. We compromise where we have to, that's all. But we don't accept communism at all, and we never will.'

'You accepted Nasser,' Ramzi said. 'Your Nutting signed the evacuation treaty with him. Look at all the others who tried to get rid of the British. Who did it this time? The British themselves, your Nutting . . .'

'Don't be rude,' his father told him.

Ramzi was not being rude, he was being sleepily amused. His eyes had drooped, and Peacock was sure the morning's drug-taking would now send Ramzi off to sleep.

'What will the British do about Nasser?' Bindari was saying. 'Will you let him eat up your Suez Canal and your oil and turn himself into a big dictator?'

'Is that how you see it?' Peacock asked.

'How else?'

'But is Egypt behind him?' Peacock asked. 'That's the question. Will Egyptians let him become their dictator?'

'Everybody hates him,' Ramzi said with a jerk of anger.

'How do you know everybody hates him?' Ali argued. 'You hate the fellow and I hate him, and probably the Copts and the Jews hate him . . .'

'The Jews . . . Ha, ha!' Ramzi coughed with laughter.

138

'But the Army and the peasants are for him; and you can't fool yourself, Ramzi, that they're not. So don't be stupid.'

'But why?' Peacock asked. 'What's he done for them?'

'Given them our land,' Bindari said.

'But you still have your land. He hasn't taken it all.'

'Never mind the land,' Ali said. 'Don't let them tell you that Nasser took the land. That's not the point. It's something else. Nasser is making every fellah into a potentially dangerous man. He's going to school the peasants and use them and flatter them, and that's what we don't like; and that's the truth of it.'

'What can you do about it?' Peacock asked. 'Is schooling so dangerous, really?'

'Very simple, Sir Peacock,' Ramzi said, spitting grape-seeds into his fruit bowl. 'We will wait until they have one of their Revolutionary Council meetings, all of them in one place, and then Ali and I will be up on a roof somewhere with the American automatics that Ali keeps hidden with his melons and then *prmppp, prrrmpp, prrrrmmmhh!*' Ramzi woke up and flicked a grape seed off his thumb straight into Ali's eye. 'Like that. I never miss. Only *he's* a bad shot . . .' Another grape seed hit Ali's nose and Ramzi collapsed in laughter.

'You really think someone will assassinate him?' Peacock asked.

'Someone!' Ramzi shouted. '*I'll* assassinate him. Won't I, Mr. Bateman?'

Bateman looked embarrassed and Ramzi laughed and Peacock wondered what there was between these two men. It seemed a strange place for a grammar-school boy to find a kindred spirit. What a curious world it was, really, when you thought about it.

'One day,' Bindari was saying to his son as he linked his arm through Peacock's, 'you'll go too far . . .'

CHAPTER TWENTY-ONE

LUCY PICKERING had flown from Israel to Cyprus, and there she had taken out a new passport clean of any Israel visa. Now she was in Cairo, walking through Gezira and reminiscing sentimentally. Pickering's death was all about her, she felt it like an old nerve which had suddenly come back to life. She had lived here happily. Up there she could dig out the very smell of the untidy but aseptic apartment they had lived in, and down here she could hear the scratching of the palm leaves in the never-never Nile wind which was the early morning sound they had always heard.

'It can't change,' she thought. 'It can only get dustier and dirtier.'

After all these years, she had become English about gardens. Before, she had never been that way. She supposed it only came now because she so rarely went back to England. These weren't English flowers in Gezira gardens, but bougainvillaeas and broom trees, with short sappy sticks instead of leaves. Pansies, yes; but bamboos and banyans with dead breasts, and acacias so old that they ought to be dead.

'I suppose the pansies are all that's left of the English,' she could say.

To whom could she say it in Cairo now? And anyway there were geraniums, roses, stocks, gladioli, lilies, and figs all tangled in dusty trunks which creaked and grimaced, and near the Nile the eucalyptus grew in clumps too high and too mighty, but too tired also.

Where was Scott in all this?

There were two kites or crows flying high in the filtered morning air.

'French crows stick to the town,' Pickering had told her. 'The desert crows stay in the desert.'

'Oh, where are you, Scotty?' she said to herself, watching the Gezira firemen in rubber boots and blue jerseys washing out their tin shed. '*Please* let me find you.'

She knew why she had walked along here—not to remember Pickering and her children playing in the garden, but to rediscover her longing for Scott. She was looking for it, but it was already unbearable that he was not really here, and she knew she would have to find him.

'If he's in the desert I'll go there,' she decided. 'This is awful, to feel like this. I didn't think I'd be like this. I think I might lose my head. I suppose he'll close up like an oyster and be terribly polite. But I shan't tolerate that!'

She took off her English summer hat. She called a taxi and hoped that Jack Church would not complicate things too much for her with Scott.

Scott had already told Hakim that he wanted to be let out of his contract, that he must resign from the last two years of it. He had had enough. There was not much sadness in it the way he did it, until Hakim began to apologize.

'But how can you leave us now?' Hakim said. He was sentimentally reluctant. 'Surely it isn't because you caught a spy. Why are you worrying so much about that?'

'Wouldn't you worry about a friend of yours, Hakim?' Scott asked indignantly. 'Do you think I am without any feelings at all?'

Hakim had the restful smile and mirror-like eyes which success had substituted for the hard resentment of the conspirator and the subaltern. But they hid him just as effectively.

'If the Hassoon father is in it, you can be sure the son is also. You yourself have proved the point.'

'I don't want to prove the point,' Scott argued, becoming angry about it. 'You may want me to, Hakim, but I'm not going to prove any point about Sam Hassoon for you.'

Hakim was hurt. 'I don't want you to do anything that is against your own feelings, or your friends. Even so, isn't there something else at stake here, bigger than friendship?'

Scott felt the jab for the second time.

'I know that,' he said, 'but I'm not up to it. I'm simply not going to be involved.'

'But you don't have to be involved. Didn't we bring you back from the Sinai when you asked? Of course you need not be involved.'

'That's nice of you. But it's a bit late to be saying that to me now,' Scott said, and they were going back and forth along the clean white mess-hall of the officers' school where Hakim had an office and taught twice a week on the character and importance of frontier defence.

'I even wanted you to come here and talk to our subalterns about the methods of infiltration—because you know them so well. You can't be serious!'

'I will not catch spies. I will not help you trap Hassoon, and I don't want my nose rubbed in some impossible trick with people like General Church, or with any of the English. I don't want to have anything to do with them.'

141

'Even with Mrs. Pickering?'

Scott was incapable of replying calmly.

Hakim stopped himself and laughed generously. 'Then forget it, old friend. Don't remember anything I have ever said or ever asked you. Of course not. I thought you would do it for your friend Hassoon.'

'No. I simply want to be out of it all.'

'Then you *are* out of it. I take it all back. If your old friends are involved in something here, then *we* must find out. It is too much to ask you. So you must forget it all.'

'What about Sam Hassoon?'

'Ah. But *we* can't forget Hassoon. You can't expect that now. Can't you leave him to us? That is the question for you.'

Scott watched the young country boys outside learning to be officers and to shoot the German and the American way—not to aim individually but to concentrate the fire-power, even of the small hand-guns and rifles, in one place. They moved in small squads over an obstacle course of sand hills, and they mimed the firing operation because there was no ammunition in their weapons.

'What chance has Sam got?' he asked Hakim, trying to think clearly, trying to be cunning.

'When we find out what is happening, he will have a good chance. Unless he has done something serious to harm us very much. But with his father at least we ought to find out something.'

'If Sam's father works for the Israelis it doesn't necessarily prove that Sam does.'

'But it's likely. Admit it, my friend, for your own sake. Don't be so blind.'

'I'll never admit it. In fact I'm sorry I couldn't let the old man go. If he hadn't been so ill I might have.'

Hakim laughed. 'And your honour? Your duty, *habibi*?'

'It may be a joke to you, Hakim. It's not to me.'

'Shhh! Don't be so angry with us. Don't you see?'

'And why did you throw me at Church like that? You knew he was at *mons claudianus.*'

'But I thought you could prove to yourself how serious this is. Please! Now don't get angry with us. Forget all I asked of you. Do what you want. Stay here, go back to the desert. Anything you like. I'll leave it to you, only please don't be angry with us.'

'I'm not angry,' Scott said tiredly. 'I've simply had enough of finding myself in situations which always lead to disaster. Not again, if I can help it. If it wasn't for Sam I would definitely go now, but I don't think I can stand aside now, Hakim, and let you put too much onto him.'

'I'm afraid that is something you can't prevent, if it's the truth.'

'Can I see Sam?'

'Of course. If you promise not to be angry, and not to leave us. They would think, you know, that you had left us because of the English newspapers.'

Scott looked at the giant greenish-coloured portrait of Gamal Abd el Nasser which hung between two republican flags and some regimental pennants which seemed rather temporary and inadequate in this modern, businesslike building. He hardly recognized the man in this over-touched photograph: the sweet almost delicate smile and the too-softened chin. But in the eyes he could recognize the original, that deep search they always made: *'Believe me, O brothers, believe me.'*

'Gamal is saying good-bye to the President of Syria today,' Hakim told him, following his eye and his silence. 'He is very busy now. Everybody from all the world comes to see him.'

Scott looked quickly at Hakim. The soft amusement and the continuous parrying echo in Hakim's inspection became very hard and sure when he talked of Gamal.

'Are you warning me in some way,' Scott asked, 'not to see Gamal?'

'What would you mean?' Hakim said, very surprised.

Scott did not try to define it.

'I'm sorry that the English newspapers are insulting you for being a good friend of ours,' Hakim said, almost overcoming for a moment the deep secrets and carefully-laid plots which allowed his eyes to look at you without seeing you. 'But you will not desert us now, will you? For our sakes . . .'

'We both know I wouldn't be much loss,' Scott said. 'But I'll stay, because what else can I do until Sam is out of trouble?'

'Good! Look! I will arrange for you to have three weeks' leave. Stay here a little while, in Cairo. You can see for yourself. Then I'll be very happy to leave Hassoon and the English to your own honourable English conscience. I'm so sure, *habibi*, it will bring us best results.'

But in the pleasant afternoon, Scott went out to Almaza airfield where Gamal Abd el Nasser was saying the official farewell to President Kuwaitly of Syria.

The official and decorated feast-day tent had green carpets laid there on the dusty airfield. Gamal sat in a gold chair and drank sherbert with two hundred visiting politicians, sheikhs, and Arab officials. Outside the tent, an Egyptian Air Force cadet force was presenting the colours, indistinguishable from the R.A.F. who had taught them how to do it.

Scott watched it sleepily, sitting on the bumper of an army car in the sun, allowing the official bustle to obscure his view, thinking about and feeling now the shift in emphasis which had affected their lives since the night he had carried Gamal into the house with a bullet in his groin. In

143

one night, perhaps in one moment, he had learned where the truth lay with himself and with this one man. They had discovered their own way to solve great young problems. Gamal had learned that it was not enough to act as one man against corrupt Egyptian politicians, and that assassination was useless; whereas Scott had learned that he *must* act as one man against Church, because there was no other way to stop Church making his blunders. Yet how mysterious it seemed, now that the truth had succeeded for Gamal, and failed for himself.

Three new Russian Migs took off, bellies well down, to escort the official Presidential plane. He saw Gamal get up, a very large man, and shake hands with a neighbour and then escort the President of Syria to the white passenger plane waiting. They all shook hands, everybody around shook hands. The band played, the Air Force flag dipped, the military shouting brought them all to the salute, and then the white plane took off and was gone with the Migs high up over it.

'Good afternoon, Captain Scott.'

One of the security officers had recognized him and was shaking his hand.

'Hello,' Scott said. 'Is it all over?'

'Yes. But don't you want to shake hands with Gamal Abd el Nasser?'

Gamal was walking slowly down two rows of officers and wives and children shaking their hands firmly, very deliberately, each man; and Scott saw him still searching as he had always searched, with the faith of a whole revolution in a handshake: '*Believe me, O brothers. Believe me! If you will only believe me!*' That was still the young Gamal, and Scott watched him go earnestly beyond the official lines and leave the Brigadier who was introducing the favoured ones and he finished up shaking hands with the straggling disorder at the end of the line which included the photographers and newspapermen and even the sofragis, and always the same hope in the same handshake: '*Believe me, brother. Please believe me.*'

'If you wish,' the security officer said again, 'you can go there.'

If he wanted to talk to Gamal it was simple now, but he said it didn't matter. The change in emphasis got in the way. It was too far, perhaps, from the day when a sudden young Gamal had leapt down from the garden wall and frightened Aunt Clothilde's tortoise, Felu, into a panic of head hiding.

'I shan't bother him,' he said to the security officer. 'Not today.'

Lucy Pickering had found him: expected, and yet unexpectedly waiting for him at the *pension*; and she took it as a matter of course that he should feel as she did, good-humoured and amused and not at all strange.

'At least it's one way of covering up old wounds and disguising any new urges,' she said when he looked confused by her matter-of-factness.

She asked him about Aunt Clothilde and inspected his room and the garden, and outside where Hakim had shot him.

'He stood so close,' she said, as if determined to remind him, always, of every detail of that day. 'I wonder why you didn't see him. Didn't you hear him coming?'

Scott shook his head.

'I was here in the old Chevrolet and I could just see you coming out of the gate. I can't *tell* you how angry I was with you that day. I wanted to do something terrible to you myself. I was going to send you to some faraway hell, for ever, for turning down Church's and General Warren's marvellous offer of the whole thing to yourself. I thought it was a car back-firing until I saw you knocked over. I just winced. In fact, I almost laughed. It wasn't until I heard you shouting that I realized someone had shot you. Dear, darling Scotty. You looked so silly, sitting there. I felt like kicking you, and when I realized you were passing out, more or less, I began to understand what had happened. I couldn't believe it. I almost fainted. I didn't know what to do. And by that time your friend Hakim had fled, which was just as well. If I'd seen or known who it was then, I do assure you there would be no Hakim today, to go on gloating and feeling sorry or whatever it is he feels.'

'How did you know I was living here?' he asked her, enticing her back inside, anywhere but out here, publicly reminiscing.

'Oh, I guessed it.'

'Did Tim Peacock tell you?'

'I haven't seen Tim, and he hasn't spoken to me for years. He never forgave me for walking out on you when I did. You're all so terribly loyal to each other, aren't you?'

She was still the pasteurized Englishwoman. Not a day had passed, not a worry had annihilated her. Her skin had a slight buttery glaze on it from the sun, and if he looked at the back of her neck as he walked behind her along the garden path, he knew it would be flawlessly clear. Her soft brown hair would turn gently in small curls there. In fact, love to a fastidious man and to a difficult and shy man could be almost alive already, if a woman was bathed and scented and absolutely fresh, as alive as Lucy was.

'In a way,' she said, 'you don't really seem surprised to see me.'

'I knew you were coming,' he told her, 'so I'm not at all surprised.'

'How could you know? You couldn't possibly have known.'

He smiled pleasantly. He could not hide it and he did not try to, and he told himself not to fight her—to go along with her. 'I had heard about it,' he said as he walked in the garden with her trying to look at her without being caught at it.

She did not bother to question him about it, she did not care, but she

145

made him explain that Aunt Clothilde's *pension* was still his actual home; that it had remained so all these years, even though the garden had not changed and Felu the silly tortoise was the same. The room was the same and the outside brick staircase was still unsafe; but Aunt Clothilde was long dead, and now there was Madame Salz . . .

'Couldn't you have got a little flat for yourself?'

'What for?' he said. 'When I was in the Sinai I had to stay away five or six months at a time without coming back to Cairo. What would have been the point?'

'But you *are* in a rut.'

He shrugged and let it happen. 'That's what I want to be in. The trouble is, though, that I'm not.'

'Anyway, I don't like it here,' she said. 'Too many bad memories. Let's get in a taxi and go somewhere else. Anywhere.'

Where could he sit with her or talk to her? That was what he needed to know. Not in the old places.

'It doesn't matter, does it,' she said appealingly, for his agreement, 'I mean—that it's been all those years? Does it? I don't feel any different, do you?'

'You never did take much notice of change,' he said, 'and you haven't changed yourself. You look exactly the same . . .'

'You're being nice,' she said, happy and holding his arm. 'I don't want to change with you, anyway. Not any more.'

He took her, for security and sanity now, to Sam's Café and Bar Helio with the tric-trac going on noisily. This was as near a place like home as he could find, and he needed it. The street boys cleaned his shoes and the old Greek waiters brought him rough-shaped sugar and tea and a whole lemon, which Lucy still approved of, and an orange squash for her which she said cheated and was tasteless and out of a bottle, sitting at ease among the old marble tops and branded chairs.

'As a matter of fact it was Jack Church who told me you were in Cairo, but I knew where I would find you,' she admitted.

'It's lucky I was in town. How did Church know?'

'Everybody knows everything in Cairo. It's still like that. He still thinks you're a terrible mystery, though. But I laughed . . .'

'Don't I look mysterious?' He could also laugh for that, coming from Church.

'You look troubled and suspicious and probably lonely,' she said tenderly. 'But I'm so excited to see you again. Only, what's happened to all those years since the war? Where have they gone? Just sitting here, I feel it, and suddenly they've gone.'

'One gets older,' he told her. 'That's all.'

'Is that really all? Oh, but it's so long. Is that really all?'

'What else, Lucy? Haven't you grown older? Haven't I?'

That was a way of defending himself, but he could not help it.

'I'm not sure if I like that,' she replied. 'It's so wretched, growing old. If anything, one gets deeper and deeper into some sort of a void, without knowing what it is. People don't simply grow old any more, darling. It's so much more complicated than that. Perhaps if Pickering had lived and if we had gone on quite normally and crazily and had more children I might simply have grown old. But it's not been that simple with me, either. I wish it had been, don't you?'

'You haven't really aged a day,' he told her. 'Not an hour . . .'

He knew that the Greek waiters wanted to ask him now about Sam, and two domino players looked at him and nodded a question, and the proprietor in his little pulpit giving out change to the waiters wanted to come over and ask him, because they knew he could get Sam out. They assumed it and they would ask it, but Lucy shut them off. She was too overwhelming for them.

'Did you know that Sam Hassoon had been arrested?' he asked her. 'Do you remember him?'

'Of course I remember him. Why? What did they arrest him for?'

He took a quick look at her English face, but he did not ask the real question which Hakim would like him to ask. 'I don't know,' he said offhandedly.

'Can't you get him out?'

'I hope so,' he said, 'by some means or other, if I can find out what he did; or even what they think he did.'

'So you really are deeply in with these Egyptian officers?' she asked.

'Why do you ask that?' he said with a resentment he did not like and could not hide. 'Everyone assumes I am in with something or somebody here. Some of them are my friends. Now even you come out of the blue and say the same thing.'

'Don't get so angry,' she said, surprised. 'I suppose it's my fault for being so inquisitive. And I was so determined not to be. But you're nice, too, when you get angry. I suppose those newspaper stories upset you. I know how you must feel about them, and what you've been going through, but sometimes, darling, you do ask for it.'

'I've been going through nothing,' he said.

'Of course you have. Those stories must have hurt. What a despicable little fellow that Mathieson must be. But all I ask myself these days,' she said with a little of the bitterness getting under her skin as if she had kept it out long enough and it must inevitably return, 'is who is to blame? Is it me? Is it you? You remember when Pickering died I thought I would kill myself out of sheer revulsion of life without him; but look what happened when I tried to save you from ruining yourself when you defied Church

147

like that. You never did understand it, really. I did what I could for you at the time, and I didn't want to walk out on you after that wretched court-martial, but I thought you were so wrong. I still think you were. So what else could I have done? You never understood that . . .'

'I understood it,' he said calmly, 'and I didn't expect anything else.'

'Yes you did. You expected me to agree with you. But you shouldn't have done what you did. It was wrong. And you hated me when I wouldn't even think of you at that stupid court-martial. But it was your own fault. I still think so, and I wish you'd understand. Tim Peacock positively insulted me for it. But I knew we would never see it the same way and I had to go, right away. If I hurt you, I'm sorry; but I felt so angry with you . . .'

'There's not much use talking about it now. I've had too long to think about it already, and I'd prefer to forget it. Why must I go on remembering something? Why do other people?'

'But I've waited so long to get up enough courage and energy to come to see you.'

'You came to Egypt to see me?'

'Of course.'

He gave up trying to keep back the balance of his restraint then. He raised his head for the waiter to come. In a few moments, in no time that would mean anything in time itself, he could be in love with this woman again, and she was stirring him and forcing him into it by the easiest attractions—being the woman who loved to give her emotion, always offering it to him if he would only see it and want it. He did see it and he did want it, and how easily he could be overcome by it. She had already cut all previous events to the bone, as if nothing had mattered or had happened to them except this casual, friendly and warm meeting at Sam's bar.

'Let's go,' he said to her anxiously.

'You can't go,' she told him teasingly, as if she knew he was trying to escape her. 'The boy is still cleaning your shoes.'

He looked down and greeted the wreck of a boy who usually fought with the magazine sellers on the street outside and was usually chased out of the café by the sofragi or by the other boot-blacks.

'What an evil-looking little boy,' she said to him.

He was not a pleasant-faced boy, this one, by any means, and you could not be sentimental about the look of him. Scott waited impatiently for him to finish. Ever since this boy had discovered Scott with Sam a year ago, he had been a nuisance. Sam usually shooed him away and threatened to smack his backside hard if he ever bothered them again.

'He's the one who stole my pants,' Sam had said. Possibly he was, with his small hunting eyes. That day Sam had been taking home a pair of trousers from the American Express Cleaners and he had put them on the neighbouring table because they had smelled of petrol. When this boy had cleaned Scott's shoes and then disappeared, the trousers could not be found.

'Where's the big sweetheart?' the boy asked him now, cut off from news by the other boys who would not tolerate him, for some internal reason.

'He's away,' Scott said.

'Is he still angry with me, Capten? Does he still want to beat me?'

'I should think so.'

'I didn't steal his trousers. It was a taxi-driver who took them.'

'All right. I'll tell him. Hurry it up, please.'

'I kiss your hand, Capten.'

Knowing the possibility of it, Scott folded his arms quickly and looked up at Lucy Pickering and caught in one second her inspection of him, her right to their old intimacy which he had been steadily killing off for so many years, and which he ought to destroy again now before it went too far.

'Your hair is going a little bit grey,' she said to him. 'I like it.'

She was reviving it all deliberately, nursing and stirring up old biologies so that he blushed.

'Now we can go. He's finished. How much, Alex?' he asked the waiter.

He had given the boot-black boy five piastres. That was far outside his usual exactness in generosity and the boy ran off quickly so that his mistake could not be corrected. Alex, the waiter, also gained an extra five piastres. Then Scott touched Lucy's bare, enticing arm as they went down the tiled and broken steps, but she seized his arm impulsively and held it tight, as if she would not let him go this time.

He felt guilty, because he had forgotten to tell Alex the waiter about Sam, so that he could tell the others.

CHAPTER TWENTY-TWO

WHAT did Hakim think of Scott, having once tried to kill him in 1942 as a British spy who had betrayed Gamal to the police, when they were plotting the end of Farouk?

'You can't help being English. But we must forget you are English, old friend, because we simply can't help hating the English.'

That was now. But Scott always felt the remembrance in Hakim, not the forgetting. Hakim had far too much to remember; and an old friend full of such bad memories could not be depended on to be too generous.

Gamal himself, the young revolutionary under the flinty slope of Mount el Cherif in 1939, had been the only man among the six officers stationed there who could get the primus to work. Hakim had often told the story. Servants could not be trusted, so they had shouted all night on Mount Cherif about the British, above the noise of the little yellow Swedish stove which made them coffee.

They had argued then that if the British and the Germans were about to fight a war, it could be the salvation of Egypt. That was something to plot about in 1939. But in plotting revolutions there was always some sort of mental primus going on dully and stupidly in the background, making shouting necessary. Hakim had always told them how unnecessary it was to shout. If need be you could always act without having to talk at all; and that night on the Saidi hill-slopes even Gamal the selfconscious thinker had shouted. They had gone on shouting at each other until Hakim had put a stop to it. Didn't they all think the same things, and say the same words? So why shout at each other while that idiotic primus made coffee and made more shouting necessary?

'Turn it off, Gamal,' Hakim had said at last. 'That one noise turns us all into bellowing idiots with each other. Open the tap.'

Even then, too young and too fresh from the Abassia academy to be holding disloyal opinions too loudly in the desert hills, Gamal had been the republican among them.

150

'The trouble is,' Gamal had said, 'if we stop the thing, it's the devil to start it up again. The pricker's broken and the hole is too big.'

The others had mocked Hakim's fear of the desert hearing their secrets, but none of them knew, not even Amin Fakhry and the other Hakim—Hakim Amer, and stodgy Anwar who were both clever plotters and good patriots, that the best secrets were those made quietly in a man's own brain, and kept there to be nurtured but never displayed.

So they went on plotting like wildflowers.

'Chaos,' Anwar had said, 'is the way of advantage.'

They had sworn on it—secret death to the British and secret salvations for the Egyptian people, who knew nothing of these twenty-year-old soldiers just privileged enough to be officers and therefore privileged enough to be plotting an end to Egypt's sorrows in the name of the future.

They had sworn for it all night, back and forth, but they had never recognized the one political weapon that Hakim had always understood best through his thin body and his hopeful moustache.

'One man's life,' he insisted, 'is worth no more than anyone else's. We might as well begin with that. Our own people are dying with poverty, but the British are always polite and they never shout except when impressing themselves. Let's start on the British, but silently, silently.'

They had laughed at him and they went on arguing noisily.

'*Maganeen!* The English will outwit you with their silence,' he had warned them angrily.

But they did not listen. They were too young. That was 1939 when Nahas Pasha's watery eyes were as big as the opal ring on his fat fingers. Who had ever heard of Gamal then? The King was in the casinos with twenty thousand peasants digging up the money for him in beans and barseem; the parliament was self-elected by its own junkerdom in its own provinces for its own privileges; and Gamal had shouted at him one day:

'For God's sake stop plotting and let me *think*, Hakim.'

They had quarrelled. Gamal did not want to silently cut the King's throat on the way to his Friday mosque the day after the Italians had invaded Egypt.

'Don't precipitate,' Gamal had cried. 'What's the point of it?'

'If you want republicanism, why not precipitate it? How else can you get it? Now!'

'You'll only precipitate the British, and what then?'

'All right. Let's start with the British. But let us start. You and me.'

'Not yet. Not yet,' Gamal had begged.

There was no point arguing it, even with Gamal. Gamal had always said *Not yet!* and there was no use shouting about it. Better to let Mussolini come in, the victor over the British on his silly white charger, the patron of Islam (profanity on God!). That was better and more ridiculous than the English fly-whisk, and their suede boots in Cairo, and Sir Miles Lampson telling Aly Maher to get out of power because he wouldn't break off relations with the Italians.

What was Lampson's weapon with the King that day? Why, his moral indignation. How could Egypt *think* of an Italian being as valuable and disinterested a ruler as the British who had given their all to Egypt these eighty years.

'All!'

Hakim that day had been taking the Army ciphers to the King, who still had an interest in collecting stamps and unravelling puzzles—and what fascinating games you could play with an army's ciphers system. Hakim had looked that day on the face of the enemy at Abdin, that heart-hidden English face which knew nothing, registered nothing, admired nothing, was impenetrable to nothing, but was terribly steadfast with its righteousness. It was frightening.

'God give me patience!' he had cried aloud in the royal courtyard.

After that, feeling sick to his soul, he had gone with Gamal down the back streets of Shubra on the Prophet's birthday, not with the usual sugar dolls and coloured clothes for the children, but to see the hero of the Moslem Brothers in his red cloak, in the long corridors where they had talked of shock battalions and supreme guidance.

'Not yet,' Gamal had insisted again.

'Not yet? Why not?' This was the Supreme Guide's own answer. 'Any time you like, and the sooner the better.'

'What about the British?' Gamal had asked in his caution.

'These two boxes,' the Supreme Guide had said of the shell-cases at his feet, 'are filled with the secrets of the British. If you can carry them between you I will tell you where to take them, where they will be of most use to help defeat the British.'

That had begun it.

Why tutor or why even murder the King away from English ways when England was on her knees and the Germans were in Libya and the revolution was not a committee with Gamal still saying '*Not yet! Not yet!*' but growing bitter because the *Not yet* was becoming *For ever*. The world war went on very clumsily, but in 1940 Rashid Aly with German help had tried to revolt in Iraq, and even Gamal had said excitedly:

'It might be done . . .'

This time the plot might have meant bombs, with the Germans also assisting it. But that too was a postponement. The Germans had sent their messengers, but so had the British. The aeroplane the Germans had sent with their officers to plot it all had taken off and flown away from the rendezvous when the right man had failed to turn up. The right Egyptian . . .

There were no right Egyptians.

Only Gamal saying *Not yet* and listening and understanding, at last, how necessary it was not to talk.

'The problem is to conceive it before you talk about it,' Gamal had said.

'The problem is to act,' Hakim had argued. 'Never mind the perfect conception.'

They had argued again. Conception or action, first or last?

They had quarrelled and gone different ways. Gamal was a full Lieutenant and Hakim remained the Subaltern until Rommel was at El Alamein and almost in the streets of Cairo.

That had been picnic day. Chaos day. *The* day!

The British had turned out Hussein Sirry that day, and Sir Miles Lampson had again walked through Abdin Palace with his South African bodyguard pushing the Egyptians aside and shouting: 'I know my way!' and giving Farouk the ultimatum to take out one Prime Minister and put in another. That was just like an Englishman changing his hat, changing an Egyptian Prime Minister. But that was the last real day of the King's life, the beginning of the long way to his purgatory and exile to the casinos of the world. That day, the British had abandoned their care and their silence. They had displayed their true contempt for Farouk and it hurt; even those who hated Farouk were hurt. Even Gamal had changed his ideas that day, although he had already shot at Hussein Pasha and had been wounded by the Pasha's grandson.

Captain Scott had found him on the street wounded, that night. An Englishman had found him! Scott had carried him into his house and had then betrayed him—Hakim had thought so, anyway, at the time. Hakim had fired six bullets into Scott one evening, but they had not killed him, because he had used copper-nosed bullets and they simply went through him and Hakim had learned that night how perfect an assassination must be to succeed; how absolutely perfect.

But it was Gamal's luck that Sir Miles Lampson had insulted Farouk that day, because the Palace, in a pique at the British insult, had released everybody who had been arrested for anti-British behaviour, which had included Gamal.

But Gamal had been very angry about Scott.

'You mistrust too much,' Gamal had accused Hakim bitterly when the Englishman had survived and had returned to his war.

'Should I trust an Englishman ever? How can I, Gamal?'

'You should trust your friends and hate your enemies.'

'The English are our only enemies, who else?'

'Aren't there men among them too? Don't be so narrow and harsh.'

'Like Sir Lampson?' Hakim had cried angrily.

'You remember the face of Sir Lampson too much, that's your trouble.

153

Why blame Scott for Lampson's face that day in Abdin? Forget Lampson . . .'

'You wouldn't forget him if you had been there.'

That was too long ago now to be important. Now Gamal was in Abdin, not Lampson and not Farouk.

But who knew why a silent man acted the way he did? Particularly an Englishman. Who knew what he planned and plotted and played with? Quiet men were always hollowed through with secret tunnels. He knew, because he was a quiet man himself and so was Gamal. So was Scott.

'If it hadn't been for him, where would I be?' Gamal reminded him as they left Abdin and rode together in the Frontier Department's green Chevrolet. 'Lying dead in the street, perhaps.'

'True, true!' Hakim said gently. 'But it's a pity, Gamal, that you still don't understand about the English. You never will.'

'What don't I understand about them? What do you mean?'

'You forget,' Hakim accused, 'that they always have that unpredictable conscience about being English.'

Gamal shrugged calmly and laughed. 'No. I'm not going to quarrel with you about it,' he said. 'Even for Scott's sake. Even for something so important or unimportant. Let's, for God's sake, get over this quarrelling.'

'It's only the English who want to quarrel with us.'

'I know that, but why think of Scott like that?'

'I don't think of Scott like that. I simply think—I only ask myself— can an Englishman ever be loyal to anything except being English?'

'Why should it matter to us now? Leave him alone.'

'It may matter very much,' Hakim said with his knowing smile, 'if they ever try to murder you. They would love to do that.'

Gamal saluted the guards at the gateway of the officers' club, which was decked out in official coloured canvas. They were celebrating in the freshly sanded and watered Gezira compound what they had plotted so noisily that night on the slopes of Mount el Cherif.

But Hakim had still not learned the habit of noise, even in victory, and he knew he never would.

'I don't think they'll murder me,' Gamal said calmly as they prepared to get out of the car, to receive an ovation. But Hakim let him go ahead and sat still and listened to the applause and the shouts for Gamal and said nothing, knowing it must depend on him and only him, to see that no one did try to murder Gamal.

CHAPTER TWENTY-THREE

QUARTERMAIN, Nona's English husband, walked through attendants and British counsellors and secretaries in the Cairo Airport building, looking at each man very carefully—particularly the ones who carried conspicuous-inconspicuous red despatch boxes marked *George VI*.

He was looking for someone he knew among them, hoping he wouldn't find anyone because it might be unpleasant; yet he needed someone like Taylor at least, who was one of the Foreign Office public relations officials, or Jupp.

Outside, in the hot isolation of politeness and respect, British Embassy wives waited in Embassy cars, having come twenty miles from town to catch a glimpse of the Foreign Minister, Mr. Selwyn Lloyd, on his way to Bahrein after seeing Gamal Abd el Nasser. Outside on the tarmac the Minister's special plane beat off the rising heat, and the plane Quartermain had travelled on from Cyprus that morning was already loaded with petrol and ready to go on. He tried again, failing all else, to get by the Egyptian soldier under the sign DOUANE, beyond which was the glass-fronted lounge where a press conference was awaiting the Minister.

'*Carnet*,' the Egyptian soldier said brusquely, his body in the door.

'I haven't got one,' Quartermain said conversationally. 'But I must see Mr. . . . uhh . . . Let me through.'

'No *carnet*?' the soldier said, and shook his head in refusal.

'You're being *too* independent,' Quartermain complained. 'And you're as blind as a bat if you can't see that I'm a close friend of the Minister's. Doesn't that impress you?'

'*Mafeesh carnet*? Not in!'

'I wish you'd say that to Selwyn Lloyd himself,' Quartermain grumbled. 'He's the man to say it to.'

Quartermain felt that his suitcase and typewriter were worth abandoning in the lounge if necessary, and he went outside again, around the front of the main airport building and down a TWA freight ramp through the back of the passport control.

'This ought to do it,' he said.

He was looking as much like an official old friend of the Foreign Secretary's as he could, allowing for his sad, grey distinction which looked easy enough and very friendly, but not enough (he decided) like servant, stockbroker or hee-hawing soldier to be in the official entourage. He bared his teeth in a slight grimace and decided that was better.

He passed an Egyptian passport officer who looked up at him, but he walked on. At the door of the press conference a pleasant-faced Englishman greeted him with a friendly handshake.'

'My name's Jobson,' he said. 'The Foreign Minister will be along for the press conference any minute now, if you can find a seat. If you're interested, the Minister's plane is the one that brought the Queen home from Kenya when George VI died, and there's a plaque to that effect somewhere at the back.'

'Actually,' Quartermain said, 'I'm here on false pretences.'

'Really?' Jobson looked hard at him and then smiled cheerfully.

'I hope you don't mind,' Quartermain said.

'I don't think so. Not unless you intend to take a quick shot at someone.'

'Oh, I don't think I'll do that.'

'Are you English by any chance?'

'I'm afraid so.'

'Well, that's all right. The Minister won't mind this once. Just take a seat quietly.'

'That's decent of you,' Quartermain said, knowing he ought to go before Jobson, who was a decent fellow, discovered that Quartermain could never keep hidden long enough, which was the refusal of his voice to be taken seriously or to take itself seriously when face to face with official importance.

'That's all right,' Jobson said obligingly.

Quartermain could not resist the temptation. 'Incidentally, Jobson, is Colonel Taylor with you?'

'Yes he is. You know him?'

'Old friends,' Quartermain said into his grey moustache and sat down before the look on Jobson's face could be turned into that usual question: *Who the devil are you?*

Quartermain liked people to arrive at the question and he liked very much not answering it. It was all a matter of timing and officialdom, particularly if Jobson asked Colonel Taylor about him. Taylor might be friendly or he might not be, depending on how successful or how guilty he felt. It was a long time since he, Quartermain, and Sam Hassoon had delivered Major Taylor to besieged Tobruk with no real point to doing so except for Taylor to be able to say twenty years later (now!) that he had been through the wire, which he had been, but barely so. Only Quartermain and Sam knew the rest of it. No doubt Taylor could put up a ribbon for that exploit, if he happened to be here in uniform.

Jobson had been greeting other arrivals, but he could not resist a temptation either, and he came over quickly and said to Quartermain:

'Who are you for?'

'You probably mean who am I *against*,' Quartermain said, feeling discovered.

'No. I mean what papers are you here for?'

'Oh, the Northern Allied Agency,' he said, naming a Canadian agency.

'I see. And?'

'My name is Quartermain, and if you see Taylor you can give him my regards.'

His name was enough. Jobson's friendly smile was friendly, but there was difficulty and surprise in it. Quartermain thought then that he should have done it the simple and decent way, instead of the complicated way. They didn't like him being here, perhaps. But there was no reason why he shouldn't be there.

'There's Taylor out there,' Jobson said before returning to the door.

Outside, near the plane (far off from that dim, low, dusty line of palm horizons) and standing in a little group were the red-banded caps and gold-braided left shoulders of the Generals, and likewise a perfect R.A.F. officer. The permanent F.O. officials of high rank and untidy clothes looked so amused at all this that one knew they might burst into their little laughs at any minute, particularly the Army man with his slapping little leather stick.

'The Minister is coming!' Jobson announced excitedly.

The Minister, followed by five men, walked briskly into the room to the table near the windows; he slapped down his soft hat and sat down while a young official at the table, Jupp not Jobson, announced that the Minister would use his political meeting voice because the acoustics were bad and forty newsmen were not tightly packed enough around the table. He would start off, Jupp said, with a statement for the Egyptian State Broadcasting and the B.B.C. recorder, and Jupp would ask people holding the microphones to keep their heads down so that the rest could see.

'When the Minister has finished here,' Jupp said, 'he will go out and around the corridor, and I would ask you *not* to follow him onto the tarmac, so that his departure is reasonably seemly.'

The Minister, in his black badly-knotted tie, made his statement as the doors creaked. Jobson whispered for someone outside to be quiet.

'Full and frank exchange of views,' the Minister said. 'Full and frank discussions with Colonel Nasser.'

A baby cried in the outside lounge and Quartermain's overdeveloped

157

sense of the significance put the baby down into his memory. A short note—*Baby cries.*

'All British ministers,' he wrote hurriedly, 'have variation of baby face. Why is that? Probably result of school, or what Nanny did. What did school or Nanny do, anyway, to make them all turn out this way?'

An Egyptian asked the Minister, 'Had you heard, sir, that Glubb Pasha, the British officer, had been dismissed this morning by King Hussein of Jordan?'

The Minister lifted his head. His bottom lip came up a little over his top one, hesitatingly. 'No,' he said. 'I did not know.'

Quartermain sucked in his moustache and wrote, 'Didn't know Glubb gone.'

'Any comment, sir?'

'No. No comment,' the Minister said, unruffled, 'excepting that General Glubb had served the Jordanian Government faithfully for many years.'

'Sir!' Quartermain, looking at Jobson regretfully, was preparing himself to ask: 'You mean to say that you did not know, at 10 o'clock this morning, that the last direct control the Foreign Office has in any Arab country was broken this morning? This very morning. Even I heard it on the local news before I left Cyprus. Didn't any of your officials this morning hear the news? Didn't Nasser tell you? He would have known. Everything you don't know here, Nasser will tell you about.'

'A decent fellow,' he thought of Jobson and changed his mind because someone would say, '*Who let that disorder in? Who allowed that disrespecter, that unreasonable debunker and anarchist Quartermain to get in here with his questions? You, Jobson?*'

The conference was continuing successfully without it. Nobody had asked it in a stunned voice because nobody else had any sense of the significant.

'I hope no Government in this area will attempt to use force,' the Minister said.

Quartermain put that down in black to be remembered later.

'If there is an aggression there is a procedure laid down,' the Minister said.

Quartermain asked: 'What procedure?'

The Minister looked friendly. 'We are bound under the tripartite agreement, outside the U.N., but in the spirit of the U.N.'

The red boxes of George VI gleamed in the sun, the Egyptian police officers hovered in dark glasses in the sun, and the Minister regarded Britain as primarily looking north, as a protection against attack from the north.

'What do you mean *the north*, Mr. Foreign Minister?'

But he wanted to break it up. It was in his blue eyes.

'One more question, sir. About the Baghdad Pact . . .'

158

The greying hair and grey suit of the Minister had no comment on the extension of the Baghdad Pact. All he wanted was peace and quiet on the armistice line between Israel and Egypt. Britain had no *idea* of sending contingents.

'Contingents where?'

But the Minister had not heard, and Quartermain wished sometimes that he had an insignificant mind which would take insignificant answers and be very happy with them, or simply not hear them.

The Minister had already gone politely. The departure was seemly. Behind him followed the officials: bow-tied, permanent-voiced, and some with round scholarly glasses and suede shoes. *Bon Voyage* and *No Smoking* the sign said in English and Arabic. The officials managed to suppress their amusement until the last. They boarded the plane after the Minister and the door closed with a bang.

'Did they laugh in there under the Queen's plaque?' Quartermain asked himself as he watched it while the rest of the newspapermen rushed away. 'Did they just manage to close the door in time before the laughter and the guffaws were too much to hold in any longer?'

What a joke it was—that plane load of foreign office laughter.

'Hah *hah!* They got the joke!' he said when he read about it in *La Bourse Egyptienne* next day in the arms of his family.

Selwyn Lloyd had arrived in Bahrein safely. But: *Manifestation hostile de la part de la population* at Bahrein, it said. More than a thousand persons were massed in different parts of the *unique* route which leads from the aerodrome to the residence of Sir Bernard Burrows. It was *bloquéd* for more than four hours. Tomatoes were thrown.

'They must have found that very, very funny,' Quartermain told his wife happily.

'*La foule devient houleuse* and cried "Go home Selly-lloyd!"' he read out

'Did they hurt him?' Nona asked.

'The Minister's car was not touched, but the vehicles of the high functionaries who accompanied him were *lapidéed*.'

'They ought not to be so violent,' Nona complained. 'What good does it do?'

'What's *lapidéed* mean?' he asked her, waiting for coffee.

'It's untranslatable,' she said, pouring it out.

'Why is it,' he complained, 'that whenever I want a significant word it's always untranslatable?'

'I suppose that's what makes it significant,' she said.

'I'm serious,' he insisted.

'Then get a dictionary. I don't know what it means.'

'Very well,' he said grimly. 'I shall.'

CHAPTER TWENTY-FOUR

IF they both wanted to be sentimental about it (and Nona was willing, because she liked Sam) they could say that Sam Hassoon had brought them together during the war when Nona was a voluntary tea-server at Y.M.C.A. garden-parties for soldiers. Sam was a non-Christian invitee who had been fond of his Christian cousin Nona; there, when he should have been packing stores at No. 1 Workshop. Quartermain had finally discovered him, with Nona bossing Armenian girls and tea tables, and polishing her short black hair. Once, in his earlier gambling days when she was still a schoolgirl, Sam had taken her to the Heliopolis races, and when she had become bored with it he had bought her a bicycle with all his winnings and had sat with her under the mud verandah of a native coffee shop eating prickly pear, freshly peeled and iced from a street seller, trying to teach her to ride, all in one afternoon.

'You don't remember it,' she told Quartermain, now that he ought to remember these things, 'but when I had to get the permission of the Bishopric to marry you, and the clerk wouldn't find any record of me because I was born in the Sudan, I had to call Sam as the witness. You should have seen that! The British consulate wanted proof from the Bishopric that I was not bound by contract in marriage. The clerk wouldn't give me any written proof, so Sam arrived in his mechanic's clothes and stood there over him and said *he* was witness that I was un-contracted and pure.'

'How would Sam know?' Quartermain asked her.

'That's exactly what the clerk said.' Nona's eyes were joyful, paying out the price of the clerk on her husband without her realizing it. 'Sam just looked at him. He was standing there half-dressed and half-willing to wring the man's neck . . .'

'You didn't tell me . . .'

'. . . The clerk sank into the floor in terror and wrote it out so quickly, the letter of my purity, that I was sorry for him. But how I laughed. Sam

160

didn't even have his shirt on, only a greasy singlet under his overalls, and I laughed all the way home, although Sam was so indignant.'

'It's a wonder he hasn't smashed down the gaol long ago,' Quartermain said sadly.

'What good will that do?' Helen said, joining them at the table, having just arrived. 'They would catch him.'

'All my friends seem to go to gaol,' Quartermain complained, eating frozen *bateekh* (watermelon) with a fork and routing out the seeds violently so that he could think around Sam. 'I don't always see the point to it.'

'Neither does Sam see the point to it,' Helen told him.

'He will, Helen. Sam's *in* the gaol.'

'But what did he do wrong? Nothing. It's because he's Jewish. Look what men do to each other, and your friend Nasser does, now that he's in power. They always pick on the weakest men.'

'Never mind, Helen,' he said, finding the watermelon seeds impossible to control and giving up. 'Nasser gave the women the vote, didn't he? That's more than the civilized women of Switzerland have.'

'What good does that do Sam? Or us for that matter?'

'No good at all,' Quartermain agreed. 'Absolutely none.'

They sat at the oval dinner-table in the apartment, and the servant Ali had cleared off the dishes and left them with the *bateekh* on the damp tablecloth. Outside in the evening a tame goat tied to the boiler-house of the next block of flats *baaed* to itself, waiting to be slaughtered on a feast day.

'Does that thing baa all night?' he asked them.

'You won't hear anything in the bedroom,' Nona assured him.

'I need lots of sleep.' He looked at his wife. 'Are the boys sleeping well?'

'Now that you're here, they'll be waking up all night.'

The boys were in trouble with their mother, particularly the elder boy, little Ben, who had this evening talked Ali into giving him the whole second-joint of a chicken, which had shocked his mother.

'Are you still worrying about that chicken?' he said to her.

'They get out of hand the moment you come and spoil them.'

'No, they don't. It's your own fault,' he told her. 'You give them a taste for good food, you encourage them not to eat good English boiled cabbage; so accept the consequences.'

Hanna gave Quartermain the last of the *bateekh* which she had been saving for him and he thanked her, while Helen diverted them from their quarrelling by continuing a minor quarrel of her own with Quartermain, a disagreement they had already discovered yesterday.

'Why are you all for Nasser?' she asked him.

'Who, me?' he said innocently.

'Yes. You've only been here a day, and yet you are already on his side.'

'Dear Helen. It's all a matter of ending old privileges,' he told her. 'You know that. It's obvious.'

'We haven't got any privileges left,' she said.

'But you had all the privileges before the war. The rich Moslems, the rich Copts, the British, the Jewish families who were rich, the Greeks who were rich, the Italians who were rich, the French, the Belgians, even the Armenians. You lived like kings, while most of the Egyptians lived like pigs.'

'That's all very well,' she said bitterly. 'But we couldn't help it. And why does he punish us for it? Today,' she informed them, 'Nasser's government sent around a form for everybody to fill in to prove our qualifications for the job we are doing. They could decide tomorrow that some Moslem was better at it than I am. They're such hypocrites. Why don't they come out in the open and say only Moslems may work, and all the rest of us can starve? Every day now there's something new . . .'

It had turned into a sad evening, because Helen had taken her quarrel with Nasser to heart, and she had quickly become miserable and frustrated about it.

'She takes it too personally,' Quartermain complained when he lay awake, never sleeping but making his own stubbornness the problem of his thinking. He could not deceive himself, and he could not ever escape the truth, the significance—however painful. How safe and easy it seemed sometimes, though, to see everything without its real point. Some day he would have a holiday from significance. Then he would grow young again and his hair would turn a healthy, rich black colour. 'Helen will never understand her own predicament if she sees it all personally. It's a dead loss, that way, sweetheart. You ought to tell her.'

'So would you see it personally,' Nona said, 'if you had to keep a family together as Helen does. You don't even understand.'

'If she understood what she was up against, she could cope with it; but she only sees it all as a personal affront. It disarms her . . .'

'So only you know what's happening then?'

'That's right. Yes, I'm afraid that's right.'

'Well, that must make you perfectly satisfied with yourself,' she said.

'Oh, heavens,' he groaned suddenly. 'What are we arguing about now?'

Little moon coughed in the next room, and the impersonal father was out of bed in a second listening to Hilal's breathing beneath his coughing. Little moon was an infantile asthmatic, and a long night would be spent crouched over his bed if he had an attack now.

But he was still asleep, still all right, and he looked like a perfect little apple which had just arrived on the ground where it was meant to fall. Quartermain knew his son. Quartermain looked at him, and pushed his moustache up hopefully from his lips and sat on the bed watching his two sons thoughtfully. Then he went out onto the balcony and looked at the Cairo night above the white night dust and the mango trees. He wondered where impersonal truth went to sometimes, when men (Oh God, and women!) treated truth as a personal affront, to be resented and fought down. What was the use of that?

'If my wife kept as much patience and understanding for her own children as she does for two perfectly normal adult unharmed human beings it wouldn't be so bad,' he had decided, over and above the impersonal truth of it.

If Nona would only come out here for one second, now, onto the balcony, and simply say, 'Come on in, old truthful, and forget it!' their lives would have been simple. But Nona had also learned all the best lessons against men, the first one being never to bend your knee in that sort of compromise with a man; any man. In fact, she would probably be impersonal with him for two or three days now as a punishment.

He knew she was lying in there, building up a wall of contempt for him as a defence against his moods and his impersonal and irritating truths. She would go on indefinitely if he didn't go in now and stop it before it began.

'He's all right,' he said about little moon.

She pretended sleep. The contempt was working, and he was already too late. He tightened his nerves, and lay down unhappily beside her.

CHAPTER TWENTY-FIVE

IN gaol, seeing Scott, Sam's tears were the tears of welcome and appreciation, whereas Scott's restraint was the restraint of wanting Sam to keep all his secrets. Well, almost all of them. The worst of them, anyway. He only wanted to know what would help, and no more.

'Let me tell you something interesting about Hassoon,' Hakim had said at the barracks, giving Scott the official Chevrolet and a captain to take him to the villa gaol. 'We know this much: the man who told us about your friend Sam, and about your other friends, was an Englishman.'

'Which Englishman?'

'We don't know that either, but we *will* know it.'

'But what are you suspecting?' Scott asked. 'What are you accusing Sam Hassoon of doing, anyway? You've never said what he did.'

'There is a plot to murder Gamal,' Hakim said casually.

'You told me that before,' Scott said. 'Is that all you know about it? Do you know for sure that Sam is mixed up in it?'

'I'm not at all sure,' Hakim admitted. 'But even a suspicion is enough. Or do you think we should take a chance?'

'Of course it ought to be prevented, if it's true . . .'

'Perhaps you don't believe in the possibility, eh?'

'I don't believe that Sam would do such a thing.'

Hakim shrugged. 'Ask him, then. Ask him yourself.'

He had sent Scott here in his own car to see Sam.

Sam was trying to be businesslike when he walked so urgently into the police-officers' room saying, 'Hello, Capten,' with the *largesse* and very deep concern expected of him. He felt all right as long as he was making sure that his sister Alicia and grandmother Hassoon were safe and cared for. He only came to tears when the family responsibility was over and he had to think of himself. But this urgent man of affairs was almost a broken man.

'Can we go outside?' Scott asked Mahmood the policeman.

'By all means,' Mahmood said, 'but not over the wall, Capten.'

They left the good jokes and went into the rose garden of the villa, which had been transformed. It was now a prison garden by the medium of whitewash. Scott knew very well the main problem of prison life: how to occupy wastefully a man's time. He himself had painted railway sleepers and navy boxes at Abu Suwair. Sam had probably painted these sandstone rocks.

But no, Sam said, it was not like that. This was not a real prison, Sam complained. If it were, he could have had fresh clothes and permission to buy extra food and sardines at the canteen, Said told him, assuming of course that he had the money. Instead, this was a special prison for enemies of the republic, and the only guards were four Frontier Force soldiers at the wooden gates with German Smeissers, talking to the Captain who had brought Scott; while over the high wooden gates and through the gap down the middle they could see and hear the metros clattering back and forth to Heliopolis and the donkey-carts and the water-sellers shouting *Tamr hindi*. The water, they swore, flavoured with the flowers of India.

'It's Campbell Pasha's villa, isn't it?' Sam asked him.

'It must be,' Scott answered. 'It's the only one here with such a high wall.'

'I thought so,' Sam said, relieved at last to have Scott's confirmation to know for sure where he was.

Where was he? Campbell Pasha had been the Englishman in charge of the Egyptian Security Police when the British ruled Egypt. Who else would have brought roses to a desert, built a mansion to become a prison?

Sam was reassured; but what had Sam done?

'Believe me, I swear, Capten, I don't know what I've done,' he told Scott miserably. 'If I did I wouldn't involve you, anyway, and I'm not going to do it. You shouldn't come here.'

'Don't be like that,' Scott told him. 'I've got to know what you did, Sam.'

They sat in the sun leaning their hands forward on their knees.

'I admit I'm often stupid,' Sam said in reply, 'but this time if I've been stupid I must pay for it myself. But, anyway, they're wrong. I swear they're wrong. Please believe me . . .'

'If they're wrong, then someone must be able to tell them so, Sam.'

'But I do tell them, only they're so silly . . .'

'Why? What do they accuse you of? Tell me that much. What do they say?'

Sam dropped his voice by bending his big head down. 'They don't accuse me, they only ask me if I want to kill Gamal Abd el Nasser, because I'm a Jew and because I fly over Abdin with Ali Zareef. But how would I kill him? Isn't that stupid?'

165

'I know it's stupid,' Scott told him, 'but listen, Sam, there is one problem . . .'

Sam put his fist down quickly on Scott's knee to stop him, to warn him.

'Did you know that I had picked up your father near the Reqi well?'

'Ayee, that!' Sam said grimly. 'Said told me and I didn't quite believe it, and then Mahmood made jokes about it all the time. Where is he? Have they shot him? They wouldn't do that, would they?'

'He's all right, he's in the military hospital.'

'God be praised.'

'You know that I didn't realize it was your father.'

Sam was holding back an unhappy break in his face. 'Of course I know. I forgive you, Capten, in God's name I do. But what was he doing there? Why was he near the Reqi well?'

'I wouldn't have taken him in but he was too sick to leave out there. I had to. Ishaak shot the young one with him . . .'

'Yes, yes, don't worry. I know you would not have hurt him. But what was he doing there?'

'He told them himself who he was. You see . . .'

'Shush!' Sam said, his hand in Scott's for a moment. 'But I know! I understand. What could I have done myself if I'd been there? I ask you. But they haven't shot him, have they? They couldn't do that, surely.'

'Why should they shoot him?' Scott said, hating the question. 'What for?'

'They knew he was living in Israel and that's enough. I know. I can guess.' Sam was in tears again now.

'Had you seen him lately?'

'How could I see him when he was in Israel? But we all knew he was there, because my cousins were always writing to one another in Italy and telling us he was there. But what did we care, except that he was alive. Why was he at the Reqi well, anyway? I don't understand at all.'

'He was probably cutting across to reach the Qena road.'

'But what for?'

'They'll probably find that out,' Scott said unhappily, 'and no doubt if they think you've got something to do with it, Sam, they'll find that out too, so . . .'

'I've got nothing to do with my own father, Capten, I swear it. You do believe me?'

'Of course I do. And that is all I wanted to know. But what *have* you got to do with, Sam? Perhaps I should ask you that too, although I don't want to.'

'I don't know what I've done. Honestly, I swear. I don't know *exactly* what I've done wrong,' he said erratically and tearfully. 'But it's hopeless for a man here now, you know that. What hope have I got in Egypt without papers? And who would give me nationality or a passport? Do you know what it is like to be a man of nothing, nothing at all? How long could I stay working without papers when they will not even give me a *laissez-passer*? I haven't got a thing, and never will have. It's a terrible thing being a Jew now, and I'm tired of it, Capten. But I can't help it. And if it is so terrible, who can blame the Israelis for wanting to fight everybody? I don't want to fight anybody myself. Who can I fight that will change what I am? Nobody, ya Capten, nobody. Nobody cares about us, you *know* that. I was born here and I've lived here, and if some Jews have hated the place, I haven't. It's my home. Why can't a man simply work? Why must he have a piece of paper which says he is this or that before he can work? It wasn't like that before. What's happening to the world when it comes so far down to punishing innocent people like me for not having a piece of paper? That's what made me so angry when I thought about it.'

'I know,' Scott said. 'I know what you've had to suffer.'

'The director at Gedida had been asking me every day for my documents,' Sam said. 'What documents? Why should I have documents? I thought, Capten: "What do I owe him? What do I owe the world? What do I owe anyone?" Pardon me, but what do I owe the British? They owe me something.'

'I know,' Scott said again, helplessly.

'I was in their army for four years,' he went on, almost dispassionately, but with the tears running quietly down his cheeks, 'but even when I asked for a British passport they cheated me. Even the English, who are so strong and to whom it would have been no loss to have me. And if it hadn't been for Ali Zareef, and you, the Gemini company would have fired me long ago. But you'll stop them, Capten, if they blame Ali Zareef for anything I have done. He knows nothing about it.'

'About what? Are you sure I shouldn't know?'

'About nothing. All I wanted were some documents, an identity paper, anything, so that I could go on working without all this trouble every day.'

Sam was becoming angry and more hysterical now, crushing his big hands on his knees, stirring himself into a tension to fight an opponent with every muscle ready for it. He would crush his enemies. But he had to weep instead, because the opponent was invisible. His strength which he had never used hatefully against anyone, except in a temper, was useless now that it came to a fight in which there was plenty of hate but no knowable, breakable, touchable enemy.

'Who is it I must fight?' Sam groaned now, holding his head.

167

'God knows,' Scott told him.

'Who am I supposed to be for, who must I be against?'

'As long as you weren't anything to do with the Israelis. That's what they will think now.'

'I swear I don't even know any Israelis.'

'And nothing else?'

'Nothing else! But I must have done something, Capten, otherwise I wouldn't be here. But I'm going to be cunning, so that I don't hurt myself and make it worse. That's all I will say. Believe me, that's all I'll say. They can shoot me, but I won't say anything else.'

'The trouble is,' Scott said sadly as the Captain at the gate waved to indicate that he must leave, 'I have a feeling you don't know who you have helped or *what* you've helped.'

'That's right, Capten, that is the trouble.'

'It doesn't give me much, does it?'

Sam shook hands dramatically and sentimentally with him, and as they stood up he pointed out the King's barber sitting under a rose pergola weeping and waiting for his prison customers. 'He has wept all the time for two years, can you imagine that? Misqueen! He's done nothing. They ought to let him out, but they say he dealt in drugs and killed four men. Can you believe it? I can't. He shaves me every day now.'

Sam's heavy face and thick hair were closely shaved, and he looked as if the small room in Campbell Pasha's villa had sweated off the fat which had grown too thick on his arms and legs and neck, since he had abandoned the Maccabee halterophile to follow as a spectator the basketball season with the young Maccabees who were this week playing the Egyptian Army in the second round of the season.

'Go and see the match if you can,' Sam urged him at the gate, 'and you can tell me how it was. If the Egyptian Army is losing, you'll see: they'll make a lot of trouble to gain penalty time. They always do, and then they turn the lights out and score a goal.'

'That's in the game,' Scott said. 'They all do it.'

'Does everybody know that I've been arrested?'

'No,' Scott lied. 'Only your family and your friends at the aerodrome.'

'And they know all about my father. Do they know that too?'

'Nobody knows about him except your own family.'

Sam was greatly relieved, and he was already feeling better when the Frontier Corps guard opened the gate and Scott left him standing there in the rose garden.

But he knew he had given Sam the evil eye. In the Cairo newspapers next morning, in *La Bourse* and the *Egyptian Gazette*, as well as in the Arabic papers, the Frontier Department announced that a patrol, under one of its vigilant officers, Mr. I. N. Scott, had captured an Israeli agent, David Israel Hassoon, and killed another, Mordecai Kanaan, who had tried to escape.

'Yeskhatak, ya Hakim!' Scott said savagely when he read it. May God animalize you, Hakim.

CHAPTER TWENTY-SIX

NONA QUARTERMAIN'S picnic at the *Barrages*, where the Nile was dammed for the last time before it rushed out into the Delta, was arranged for the children and her husband, and for her own matter-of-fact sentimentality about a place where she had enjoyed schoolgirl picnics, then girl-guide picnics, and in her teens picnics with Helen's boss, Barker-Danderson, on his expense account with food supplied by Groppi's.

Barker-Danderson had played hide-and-seek with them, sitting up on a tree-crotch smoking his pipe refusing to be found and refusing to come down until he had been found, so that they had to start eating the hot pigeons without him, until Helen called: '*You've won, B.-D. They really can't find you. Please come and eat.*' He would complain that they had started eating without him, and when he had eaten vastly he would go off in a huff to inspect the pumping-house which he maintained. They would have to go and get him again at dark to make sure he took them home in the four taxis he had hired.

She knew what Helen meant when she regretted other days.

'Do you remember,' she said to Helen while Hanna unpacked the wicker baskets on the hilly lawns under a ficus tree that was too large to be considered a normal tree, 'how I used to stand on the breakwater in Port Said with my Italian friends and sing *Giovinezza* to the Italian troops who were going through the canal on their way to fight in Abyssinia? When I tell that to Quarts he goes mad. When I tell him I was only a schoolgirl, he blames you for being ignorant. *Don't you know*, he says, *they were on their way to use mustard gas on the Abyssinians, those same Italians?*'

'I suppose he's right. It was awful, but how could we know?'

'Never say that to Quarts. But I can't help laughing, even though it's terrible to think of it.'

'Shush!' Hanna said. 'It *is* awful!'

'I mean at myself in sandals waving them on. One forgets that they did use gas,' she said sadly. 'One forgets so much.'

170

'The Americans used an atom bomb,' Helen said, 'and Jolley even boasted when the English sprayed burning petrol on the Greeks after the war. Don't criticize the Italians.'

'The trouble is,' Nona teased, 'you admire the Italians and the English so much.'

'At least the Italians are gentle and polite,' Helen said. 'And so are the English, on the whole.'

'But you have never seen the English as they are. You've only seen them out here as they are not. When I think of all those silly Englishwomen lording it over us before the war! Then I see what they are in their own country and it makes me want to laugh.'

'Don't worry. Even before you went to England,' Helen pointed out, 'you were quite able to cope with the English. I remember, for instance, that the Egyptian girls broke up the English guide companies . . .'

'Well, why not? Do you remember how they insulted Sara Tewfik for setting up the Sea Rangers without the permission of the English commissioner, simply because she was Egyptian, and the Egyptians were not supposed to take the initiative? If it hadn't been for Sara and a few of us Egyptians, there wouldn't have been any Egyptian guides at all, except for a few little fools being condescended to by the English.'

'You didn't do too badly,' Helen reminded her.

'Of course we didn't. Sara was the Captain of the best company in Egypt, including the one at Helmieh barracks which the English padre (who was a nice man) asked her to form, but the Englishwomen were in an uproar when they heard of it. That woman who was married to the whisky importer, Mrs. MacMillan, rang me from Gezira that day and said that Sara had already broken the fifth, eighth and tenth guide laws. She didn't even know what the laws were. So we all resigned for Sara.'

'I don't remember that,' Hanna said.

'I didn't tell you, darling, because I knew it would upset you. But when I told her that we didn't want anything done and that Sara was our Captain or no one, she accused us of breaking the fourth, eleventh and third guide laws by flirting with boys at our local concert, which was the only one that was ever gay enough and successful enough to make money, which the English hated.'

'But you had the best time, anyway,' Helen told her, 'so you shouldn't complain.'

'Don't worry, darling. I know we had the best times. When Sara took us camping, one night, the cook—a big, fat Sudanese soldier—walked in his sleep and bent over Doria in bed. She couldn't even scream. When she did we all rushed off and hid behind the cook who had caused it all.'

They laughed helplessly now.

'There was always something to laugh about. When I think of the energy

I had in those days. After all, I did work all day, and at night I was supposed to be instructing the girls in how to tie knots; but do you think I ever learned to tie those silly knots? But we did put on the best concerts, you remember, and we didn't need the English to envy us the best and happiest companies. We were all friends because we were all Egyptians or locals. That's what the English resented. We were supposed to hang on to their condescension. Poof!'

'You were *never* condescended to,' Helen said firmly. 'I wouldn't allow you . . .'

'Did I allow myself?'

'Not you, my darling. What was that song you used to sing?'

They laughed over it and Nona sang the marching song of the 3rd Cairo Company.

'Old King Cole was a merry old soul and a merry old soul was he, he sent for his pipe and he sent for his bowl, and he sent for his tenderfoots three. Now every tenderfoot had a fine badge, and a very fine badge had she; we will keep this badge, said the tenderfoots, we won't stand at ease. Oh, there's none so rare as can compare with the 3rd Cairo Company . . .'

When they had recovered, Helen begged her to go on.

'It's too long,' Nona said. 'It goes up right through the seconds, the leaders, the Lieutenant, the Captain, the Commissioner, until it gets up to Lady BP.' But Nona gave them the last verse. 'Old King Cole was a merry old soul and a merry old soul was he, he called for his pipe and he called for his bowl, and he called for his Lady BP; now Lady BP had a very sweet smile and a very sweet smile had she; *this* is a fine company, said the Lady; what was the last command said the Captain, move to the right in four said the Lieuters . . .'

'Did Lady BP ever come to Cairo?'

'Not in my time, but she did eventually. But by that time the Egyptians had broken away. The Egyptians! We weren't allowed to be an Egyptian Company. We were the Third International Company, but when we sang that song about the King's Highway and marched down the Pyramid road, it was the Union Jack we had to carry. There wasn't an Egyptian flag allowed in those days . . . until the Egyptians in the company broke away.'

'You still had the best times,' Helen repeated. 'I knew a lot of those English girls, and they didn't know how to enjoy themselves half as well, poor devils.'

'They were all too dull. No wonder. They all had mothers trying to be something they were not. They should have all been at home in England, sitting in their little houses, sewn safely together along the by-passes, instead of sitting out in the hot deserts of Egypt marrying the British soldiers and thinking they ruled the world. They hadn't enough spunk to say boo -to -a -goose, let alone bah to a guide commissioner.'

172

Nona sighed and bent her long arms upwards at the sunny gardens where the Egyptian conscript soldiers, peasant boys, were arriving in their best uniforms and changing into pyjamas and taking their boots off so that they could have fun on the grass.

'Oh, my God!' she said. 'The picnics we had here . . .'

'Don't! I feel old enough,' Helen said.

Nona began another song, singing lightly through her nose.

'How sweet is the pleasure of May's lovely morning, la-la-la-la-la-la, la-la-la-la-la-la. There's pleasure in freedom, whatever the season; that makes every object look lovely and fair; then surely for pleasure we'll have a good season; for freedom has blessed us, and freed us from care.' She sighed. 'That was originally yours, Hanna,' she said.

'Believe it or not,' Hanna told her. 'It was the English missionaries who taught me that song in the Sudan.'

'May is so lovely in England,' Nona said. 'When the English stick to that, it's all right. But they become awful when they leave it for another country.'

'Where are the children?' Hanna asked.

'Watching the boats,' Nona said, and pointed, 'with their mad English father.'

'Don't!' Hanna protested sharply, her hidden, secret temper emerging for a moment. 'Don't say that.'

'But he is mad, darling.'

'Even so, you are too free with your tongue,' Hanna said firmly. 'It's annoying.'

Nona had pointed to the slope where the gardens joined the bridge over the giant weir. Little Ben and Hilal were standing near a lock with their father, watching the feluccas laden with stone and sand and cotton bales waiting their turn to broach the higher levels of the Nile.

'So long as he's holding the children tight,' Hanna said. 'I hate those locks.'

'He is,' Nona said. 'That's one thing at least he's sane about.'

She unfolded a parcel of warm native bread. 'He calls *me* mad because I won't be casual about having his friends in—just asking them in without a thing prepared for them. Well, I can't do it that way. I'm too Egyptian. But when I do ask him to bring home his friend Scott, he loses his temper and says, "Leave it alone. Don't touch it." '

'Don't touch what?'

'Who knows? I suppose his friendship with Scott. Call them for lunch,' she told Hanna, 'before they disappear half-way up the river.'

CHAPTER TWENTY-SEVEN

ALICIA, Sam's sister, could not help weeping when Scott told her that Sam was all right, although she was really sobbed out long ago. She wanted to send the kitchen boy for her Aunt Helen Mamoon and have her understand it, but Scott said he would tell Helen Mamoon himself. It was the first real news they had heard of Sam from someone who had actually seen him.

'I don't know what questions to ask you, Alicia,' he said when they had finished talking about Sam, and when Alicia's gently blown body and face were like a becalmed shipwreck. Her grandmother swayed back and forth silently in black watching him, making him feel like an accused man. Or was he the accuser? 'If you know about Sam, then you ought to tell me.'

'If I did know,' she said, and repeated it. 'If I *did* know.'

'I understand. It doesn't matter,' he said to keep her calm. 'I know you'd tell me anything you knew.'

She poured him out a little Greek cognac where they sat in the compacted living-room where Sam's remnants were in the cupboards and on the walls, not only his pictures in British uniform and the few souvenirs of the desert he had not given away, but the baubles of far-away childhood, a stuffed dog and a flat punching ball hung on a wire in the hall.

'Sam will not tell me anything,' he said, 'and I can't ask him too many questions where he is now. But I can't help him the way I think I can, not unless I can understand what he did. Had he been seeing anyone?'

'Only friends.'

'Who are his friends?'

'The Greeks and the Maccabees,' she told him. 'The gambling clubs and sometimes Captain Zareef. But you know who his friends are. He didn't tell me. Why do you ask me?'

'I don't like to ask you, Alicia,' he went on carefully, 'but did he see his father? Had Sam seen him at all?'

'Mamma!' Alicia said. 'Swear to Captain Scott that we didn't see papa.

174

We didn't know about my father, and we don't know now. Why did you put him in gaol with Sam?'

'I didn't put him in gaol,' Scott told them wearily. 'I didn't even know he was your father. If I had known I would probably have sent him away, but it was too late. He would have died out there if I'd left him in the desert.'

'But what did he do?'

'I don't know yet.'

'Why did they put him with Sam?'

'He's not with Sam. He's in the military hospital.'

Mamma Hassoon, still swaying on the distant shores of much older sorrows, dropped a sighing little groan for her son, for Sam's father. Scott felt spared by that, because she would not talk. He knew they spoke Arabic at home and she could speak English, but she sat now as if they had no language in common, refusing to understand what was being said. That one small groan would at least spare him from any more accusation. She moaned gently once; but he felt as if he would throw it all away if she ever broke her silence to ask one question about her own son.

'I'm sorry, Mamma Hassoon,' he said to her.

She did not hear it.

'We only worry about my brother,' Alicia warned him so that he would not forget Sam. 'I don't care about my father. You'll have to help Sam because he hasn't hurt anyone, not a soul, whatever he did. Why should they hurt him?'

'But they haven't hurt him,' Scott said. 'They will not hurt him.'

'They took him away because he has no papers,' Alicia said. 'I know it.'

Her white soft face had wept itself out, so she plucked angrily at the table-cloth without hearing what Scott said in exasperation about Sam: *What had Sam been doing about a passport? Whom had he seen about documents?*

'I think it's the English who ought to help him,' she said. 'He always helped them. Now they ought to make the Egyptians let Sam alone.'

Mamma Hassoon got up and used the table to help her, arthritically, to the curtained door behind them.

'She doesn't understand,' Alicia told Scott. 'Sometimes she thinks Sam has deliberately run away and deserted us, like our father did. She gets him mixed up with father.'

'What about money?' Scott said and took out an envelope he had carefully prepared. 'They gave me Sam's wages at the aerodrome.'

'It's not the money we worry about,' she said, taking it and folding it nervously. 'The Maccabee Youth Fund gives us enough. But what will we do—Mamma and me—if they keep Sam? I'll tell the Egyptians to take me as well, I'm not going to wait. I shall kill myself if we are left like this.'

'That's no way to feel, Alicia,' he said unhappily. 'It won't help your brother.'

'I *will* say it,' she said. 'And you can tell them so. I don't care.'

She was not hysterical, she was talking to herself as if she had said it many times before, and Scott was confounded by their strange removal (both of these women). Sam was gone, that was real enough. But nothing else was. They had already gone to the wall. The cries were low and monotonous and defeated, but they were thought to be helpful for Sam—these cries against fate.

Even Alicia sat quietly now as if Scott were no longer there.

'I don't know what I can do yet,' he said helplessly to her so that he could go, 'but I'll see Sam again. He's not worried.'

'If my brother is not here there's no use us being here, either,' she cried. 'Tell them that.'

She let him out. In the hall Mamma Hassoon held herself up lumpily on the hat-stand and hall-mirror and gave Scott a bundle of Sam's clothes wrapped in brown paper. Because her old teeth were loose, the words she forced through them nearly disintegrated over the difficult course of her lips.

'My son likes to be clean,' she said in French. 'Give him these.'

He knew that she meant Sam rather than her son, but he looked at Alicia to clarify it (for Sam or Sam's father?). Alicia did not seem to care nor even to follow what it was about. He took the bundle from Mamma Hassoon as he went out, wondering if it was now a dual and indefinable Sam—father and son—he must feel responsible for.

If so, it was already becoming too much for him.

Françoise had telephoned from Port Said to tell him, next day, that she would be coming to Cairo on the Friday for her son's seventh birthday, and she wanted Scott to come to her cousin's house. Her cousin was a tubercular jeweller and goldsmith named Leo Lieberman, a popular man among many people in Cairo, but Françoise had never invited him there before.

'Sans blague,' he said to her, determinedly amused about it. 'Am I getting to be respectable, Françoise?'

To be revealed to her family at last? Something must be stirring.

'You are only trying to hurt me, saying a thing like that,' her voice told him seriously.

He apologized. 'I'm in a bad humour,' he said. 'But I was joking, truly I was.'

'Come if you want to,' she said. 'You know where it is.'

He remembered that he had once taken her as far as the door to Leo Lieberman's flat when she had been to Cairo to see her aunts and uncles,

176

and the cousin in business she should have married if she had had a decent dowry instead of a French Gymnasium schooling which had made her just dissatisfied enough to expect more. Leo had not been rich enough or perhaps he had not known her well enough in those days to help her.

'I'll try to be there,' he said, 'but I must see someone first. What did you want me for, anything in particular?'

It was a slender simple French voice which replied, not the teasing intellectual one. She seemed to be forgiving him for something, or perhaps for everything.

'Soyez gentil,' she pleaded.

'But I'm always nice when you give me the chance,' he protested. 'I'll be there, don't worry.'

That was the normal edge to their talk, but he was already feeling depressed, and when he put up the telephone in Madame Salz's front hall, he withdrew a letter from his pocket which he had received that morning and read it again.

It was an anonymous letter, addressed to him and signed 'An English Friend', telling him that he must be aware that he was disgracing himself once more, and that the memory of his father and his own background should surely have some call on him. A balance of loyalties was at stake, the writer said, not only in Egypt but in the whole area. Couldn't he see what he was doing when he embarked on a course of helping the very forces which opposed his own country's most vital interests? Couldn't he change his attitude and forget his old resentments before it was too late?

It was not a crank letter, and when he first read it he had not minded it so much. But now he was beginning to think about it, and he began to feel some responsible hand behind it, and he felt the anger growing as he folded it up and stuffed it back in his pocket, determined to ignore it.

Also, two more newspapermen had found him and he realized that pressure was coming from somewhere. But where? One of them was an Australian whose open and natural voice seemed to make a mockery of anything in high places, particularly an Englishman with motives. (Could there be anything more suspect?) The other one was a Frenchman whose questions curled away mystically like smoke from his perfectly slouched cigarette. He had not resisted them, he had simply let them both slide in on his defenceless moment, one after the other, within an hour of each other, knocking at his door.

'Do you feel that all this spiritual deceit of Nasser in calling all Moslems a *sommation* of the Arabs is a worthy cause for any true Arab, let alone an Englishman who looks so much like an Englishman? What would you say to that, Captain Scott?'

'I'd say I'm an Englishman,' Scott answered, standing at his door, trying boldly to argue with that letter. He had to argue with someone about it. 'Let it go at that,' he added.

'I thought that might be your answer,' the Frenchman said. 'You may *think* you remain an Englishman, Captain Scott, but is that possible these days? Don't you fear that your rather free-minded support of Arab ideas, coming from a Westerner, might suggest to the Arabs that we are as spiritually bankrupt as they are, and will only encourage them in this folly of self-determination and drag you in, personally, as a sort of temporary traitor? I mean, that after-thoughts then will be too late?'

'Yes,' Scott said.

'Yes?' the Frenchman said, taken aback. 'But what sort of yes do you mean?'

'The only kind I know,' Scott said. 'The opposite to No.'

'I suppose, therefore, that one can assume that you also hate the Jews.'

'Why should I hate the Jews?'

'After all, you do capture them rather neatly for the Egyptians. Don't you think that matters?'

He no longer understood the Frenchman, nor his face, nor his language, nor his heart. That smoke curled away too wistfully. It was a curious post-script to that letter, however. Why had he arrived that morning also? And why had the Australian followed him: with that rebellious voice but with such deeply loyal questions. Not intellectual smoke, but cheek. Was Scott training Egyptian commandos, fedayeen, to filter across the Israel borders to commit acts of sabotage and murder, and was he advising Nasser on his policy towards the British? The cheek had become a whine, a very suspicious one. He had closed the door on that one, and he began to doubt their authenticity as newspapermen. It was not quite in their manner; not quite in their hearts. He understood men like de Brazio, whatever else he thought of them. These men were not true.

Who had sent them? Who had written that letter?

'You are violating all sense of decency and honour,' it said, 'when you set out to help a man like Colonel Nasser against your own country's very real interests, and I hope that you will realize it before it becomes disastrous for you . . .'

'I haven't really helped a man like Gamal Abd el Nasser,' he said, entirely on the defensive by now. 'I have simply understood what he is trying to do. I suppose that's the crime. I'm only sorry now,' he said aloud, defiantly, to his unknown correspondent, 'that I did not try to help him a little more than I did.'

He had not heard Madame Salz coming up the stairs with his tea.

'Can I come in with your tea? Have you a guest?' Madame Salz said at the door, knocking discreetly.

'No. No. There's no one here,' he said, embarrassed but opening the door. To talk to yourself in a desert was normal, to do it here was odd. 'Come in.'

She put the tray on a round table among his undarned socks and his books.

'I have come to visit you,' Madame Salz told him, 'to talk about my daughter. May I sit down, and I'll pour the tea. Do you mind me?'

'But, please,' he said. 'We never have a chance to talk. What's the matter with Becky . . .'

'Oh, it's not Becky. Becky is a model, a perfect sweetheart. If she can only find a good and kind husband. No, it's about my eldest daughter in Italy.'

'Ah.'

'Dear friend,' Madame Salz said appreciatively, 'you are the only person I know who I can talk to honestly about my own family, because I know you don't tell anyone and I can always trust you. Everyone talks terrible scandal in Cairo. But I need your advice because my daughter in Italy wants to divorce her husband and marry a Pole with a British passport, but I wonder if I can trust such a man? What would you think?'

'That depends,' he said weightily, sipping the tea she gave him.

She sat near him with her confiding Viennese eyes, and he nodded understandingly. Madame Salz had two daughters, the elder, Grazia, was married to a man with an Italian passport and she lived in Ravenna and was unhappy; whereas the younger, Becky, lived in the *pension* and worked in the office of Cicurel's, the department store, to which she went every day and came back every day as inconspicuously as possible. Scott had watched Becky grow up from a freckle-faced little girl with reddish hair into a tiny freckled young woman, barely twenty; and whenever he looked at her, whenever he managed to see her, he would always wonder if it were possible for someone with that face and that manner to have an evil thought about anything. She still dropped her eyes when she passed him, the way a good Jewish girl should.

'Children,' Madame Salz went on, 'make all the *bêtises* for you, even when they are grown up and married.'

He took a piece of cake. 'It's the *bêtises* that make a family,' he said wisely. He had to be wise with Madame Salz because she expected it of him and she needed it. 'You know the saying in Arabic,' he went on: 'A man without troubles is a man without family.'

'True, true,' she agreed. 'But daughters are too much trouble. They go on being *la plus grande responsabilité pour la mère*. A boy becomes a man, they say in Yiddish, but a girl remains a daughter for ever.'

He sighed for her. 'Never mind. At least Becky is near you and not far away in another country.'

179

'I'd die,' she said, 'if I didn't have one of my family near me. I thank God every day for Becky. That's something the English don't usually understand. Only Jews and Arabs understand what the family means, because it's such a part of our religion. But you *do* understand it because you've lived here so long.'

She would give him an example, though, of a friend who was married to an Englishman, and she was astonished to find when she went to live in Liverpool with her husband that he had cousins and relatives in the same quarter, almost in the same street, whom he didn't call on and never did know.

'Why are the English like that?' Madame Salz asked him. 'It's one of the mysteries of my life.'

'Not all English are like that,' he told her.

'But I think they are,' she insisted, buttering and jamming a piece of bread for him. 'Where are your aunts and uncles and cousins and brothers, Captain Scott? They never come to see you, and you're such a nice man.'

'I don't know them,' he said. 'They don't know me.'

'What difference does that make?' she replied indignantly, and she was accusing his aunts, uncles and cousins of neglecting him. 'If you were my nephew and if I could not reach you I'd write to friends and tell them to call on you.'

More tea, more sugary fig jam pushed into native bread (delicious), and told Madame Salz that it was a matter of regret and distance rather than he neglect which caused an Englishman like him to have no family and no relatives. He had never really lived in England. It was the price you paid for the work you did, for being the Englishman in Egypt or India or Timbuctoo.

'England is so far away for us,' he explained.

'But will you never go back to England?' she asked him.

'I doubt it.'

'Pauvre ami, sans famille,' she said.

Madame Salz rescued him and reinforced him; and he suspected she did it for him—for his own good, for his sad lack of family of his own. Every day she had some small problem for him to solve: some need for advice which concerned the condition of the house, or the storage of the paraffin for the primuses, or the dreadful state of the garden because it was impossible to find a gardener. He gave good advice; and he was fortified by his own advice by the time he went to see Lucy Pickering, who took him to the Gezira Sporting Club to see if she could play tennis there on the strength of her wartime club membership. But he stopped her at the gates of the Club.

She had been away, rather mysteriously he thought, on business, and now she was suddenly there, wanting to play tennis, with his help.

'It won't work,' he told her. 'You can't just go in there like that.'

'Why not?'

'You can't just walk into Gezira these days as an Englishwoman,' he said, 'and get what you like. It's all Egyptian now.'

'What's the matter with that? I'm not going to insult them.'

'You may be insulting them, even by imagining that they'll accept you. After all, it's supposed to be a very exclusive club.'

'Don't be silly. I'll just remind them that I was once a member and ask them if I can play tennis here occasionally. They can't object to that.'

'Can't they? Would the English have tolerated a stray Egyptian wandering in here like this during the war?' he said rather irritably, her sudden need of him making him suspicious. 'I don't think they'll be very pleasant about it.'

'What an attitude. What silly revenge,' she groaned and took him by the arm. 'You are absolutely on the defensive about being English. That's what you get for living out here as a half-and-half. Well, I'm not . . .'

'I'm simply trying to warn you not to expect too much.'

'If they refuse me, I'll point out that I'm a friend of yours, and that you are a friend of Nasser's.'

'Oh, no you won't,' he said. 'I'm not even going in.'

'Do come on,' she insisted. 'You're their hero, aren't you? You capture poor Jewish spies, don't you? And you're a good friend of their horrible assassins, aren't you? I need you, darling.'

She could joke, and he went in with her under the acacias and by the flower-beds and lawns which were English laid. There were dark-skinned boys on the paths because the English nannies and their English children, playing on the grass under the eucalypts and laughing in the tenderest of evening suns, were only a memory now. He had never been in here himself as a child, he had only passed by it and occasionally watched the polo ponies galloping to short biting stops on the training pitch and he had heard, from beyond the tennis courts, the ringing crack of a cricket ball in what the English always longed for: the perpetual long summer days, every day and always long, and the quiet waste of time that led up to tea or the long pale drinks that made these Englishmen look like ripe oranges. It was a feeling rather than a memory, but he knew he missed it because you lived backwards as well as forwards and the regrets like this were all English in him.

'Look at that!' Lucy said to him.

She had stopped near a gardener and she asked him in halting Arabic *why* he was watering the azaleas so much. When she did not understand his reply she turned back on Scott.

'They're so lazy about hoeing, that's all it is. They live in a water-starved country so they overwater. If they hoed up the top earth so that it didn't cake, they'd grow much better flowers. These beds are much too hard. You tell him that.'

'You tell him,' he laughed. 'I don't want to be hosed for interfering.'

'Oh, dear,' she said. 'It's so like old times. It hasn't changed. I haven't changed. Nothing has . . .'

'Yes, you have,' he told her. 'You're turning into one of these no-nonsense gardening Englishwomen. You'd better watch out.'

'But I believe in no-nonsense. What's the matter with that?'

'Too many Englishwomen like that here already,' he warned her. 'They always like to impose their no-nonsense on the locals. They wouldn't get away with it for long in England, because somebody would hit them with an umbrella, so they all end up out here in Egypt: no-nonsense for the natives!'

'Then I'll be sweet and nice,' she told him, 'and full of nonsense. There's the club-house. It is a little suburban-looking, isn't it? And they really ought to clean it up. Come along.'

'Don't take me in tow,' he said. 'I'll get there.'

'You are too much on the defensive these days,' she said sadly.

The club secretary was not back from lunch and the Egyptian telephone girl, swathed like a fashionable Frenchwoman at the cocktail hour, told them he wouldn't be long and they might like to sit near the pool and wait? They would do that, and they could argue beside the empty pool where, during the war, Lucy remembered every important affair which had ripened between the high-voiced officers, too quickly gentlemaned by rank, and the silly English secretaries too easily impressed by their own shadows in the hot Egyptian sun. They were nice-looking willowy men; Davids and Peters and Philips: Boo-boos and Binkies and Bunnies if you knew them that well. Someone as diffident and workmanlike as Scott, or a carnivorous aristocrat like Pickering, had built the thing these Bunnies and Binkies had lived on. They couldn't have built a thing themselves, but they could sit beside the pool in the war like icing on a cake, in fact they became the cake. It served Scott and her dead husband right. They were to blame, being too disinterested or too contemptuous to gobble up the Bunnies and Binkies in one bite and claim the whole lot for themselves and to run it properly. That was all she had ever asked of them or expected of them; but now it was too late.

'Some day,' she said, 'your diffidence will strangle you.'

'I'm not that diffident,' he resisted, trying to avoid this common-sense talk. 'In fact, you once said I was too intense or something like that. The very opposite to diffident, anyway.'

'Only when you're doing something quite destructive, mostly to yourself. Otherwise you are just too removed, and you ought not to be.'

'You're not going to no-nonsense me, are you, sitting here in Gezira?' he appealed.

'Don't mind it, darling. I need someone to scold. That's why I need you, I suppose. But I'll take you anyway you like to be, did you know that? Except unpleasant. I don't want you ever to be sour. You're a little sour today. What made you start acting like a madman, though, picking up that miserable Israeli in the desert—and Sam's father too?'

He knew there was something behind her own mood and now it was coming out, but he would not get too involved. Let it go, he warned himself.

'If I'd known he was Sam's father I'd have let him go.'

'Would you? But why should you capture an Israeli spy for them at all?' She was serious and worried.

'I had no choice,' he said. He shrugged defensively so that he did not take any responsibility for it at all. 'He would have been dead in the desert if I'd left him there.'

'Don't shrug,' she told him, suddenly fierce but shifting her chair out of the sun as if to discipline herself. Her eyes were not quite as soft, and her hard, capable fingers were putting on her sunglasses. 'I don't think you should shrug at such things.'

'I've got to shrug at something,' he told her.

'Must you? Then tell me if you will also shrug when there is a real showdown between the British and Nasser here. It's bound to happen sooner or later. What will you be then, that's what I'd like to know? Will you be this sort of diffident man with the shrug you are affecting? Good friends of Nasser's to the last?'

'I'll wait and see,' he told her.

He had pushed aside an ashtray so that the sofragi could put down the drinks they had ordered, and when the sofragi said: 'Are you a member?' before presenting the chit, Lucy said 'Yes' irritably, and Scott said 'No' and explained carefully that they were waiting for the secretary.

'Then you must pay at the desk,' the sofragi said in English, and Scott gave him two careful piastres for the service.

'Why did you say that?' she said. 'Surely we don't have to explain to sofragis? Surely we can just sit here as members?'

'Why should we?' he argued, and tried to explain it to her. 'Don't you understand that it has all changed? You have to be very careful these days. The old times have gone, Lucy.'

'I know that. But I'm not trying to restore British rule to Egypt by asking to be treated decently. You're so self-effacing and so defeated. I *do* mean defeated.'

Scott put his large hand over the chit which she would have suddenly torn up. It was a square printed card still marked in English because it didn't pay the club to install a new cash register with Arabic numerals and letters on it.

'Perhaps so,' he said, 'perhaps so.'

'Oh, well, I suppose you and I can't ever help finding ourselves on opposite sides,' she said, and then told him, for no apparent reason, why she would always prefer the Jews to the Arabs, and why she had gone often to live in Israel rather than Egypt.

He listened, but he would not argue.

Not a day had touched her. She still looked like any Englishwoman who had four children away at boarding-school and was probably ripe and ready for another. It was in her body, in her flushed cheeks and in her sensible, rounded perfection.

'I don't really care about this argument between the Arabs and the Jews,' she was saying. 'I only went to Israel in 1954 because I needed something that was already clear and determined and sure of itself. I simply *had* to have something with conviction in it, enough to carry itself along, and me with it. Otherwise I would have been quite suicidal. Oh, it's so hellish, being a woman.'

He looked down at the empty swimming-pool in embarrassment.

She laughed at him. 'Don't be so solemn,' she said. 'I'm much too dull and frightened to kill myself, anyway. But now that the girls have grown up and gone their own foolish and ridiculous ways, I can't see that I have any more use left—even to myself. That's what you think too. I'm simply no use to anyone, as I am.'

'I don't think that at all,' he said to her, eyes down, still deeply avoiding her.

'Oh, if you only *knew*,' she said, almost in a temper. 'Why aren't there crusades or causes or wars or something that one can be absorbed in without all this waste? A man always has a chance. But a woman has none, absolutely none, unless she finds a man who can do it all for her, as Pickering did. Or as it looked like you would do, until you threw it all away on some notion that you would sooner abandon yourself to these Egyptians than be a good English soldier. That's all it ever amounted to. But then what? You tell me! Then what? You let everything go to pieces. You were so determined, weren't you, to take your punishment like a man and run away?'

'No,' he said, stung by that. 'I simply learned my lesson.'

'What possible lesson could you have learned by running away?'

'That you can never oppose any real authority if you happen to be British. It's always been too strong. And you can never oppose what is wrong, because it is always in power. I never did it again.'

184

'So you wasted yourself for thirteen years, never trying again,' she said contemptuously.

'No.'

'You should have gone on,' she cried. 'Even though the Army did punish you and lock you up. You should have gone on, even if you had ended up throwing bombs at the Prime Minister like your Egyptian friends. I hated them. But that would have been more admirable than drifting off into nothing as you did here.'

The tiles of the empty pool were blue and white, and two half-naked Egyptian boys were getting into it now to clear the silt from the deep end.

'And, anyway,' she said, 'where did all that deadly conscience get you? I ask you.'

'Nowhere,' he admitted, retreating again, refusing to argue with her—never about motives and never about conscience. 'Except that I have had good friends . . .'

She took that personally. 'Not me, you mean? That miraculous friend Nasser?'

He said nothing, and though she saw that the club secretary had arrived she obviously did not want to break this intimate grip she had on him, something that she seemed to be stringing up around them like barbed wire at a crossroads of their lives.

'Are you even helping Sam,' she wanted to know, 'or are you really trying to save your friend Nasser?'

'That's going too far,' he protested angrily, but he repeated grimly to himself his own admonition: *Don't argue. Don't fight her.* 'I'm not going to let anyone hurt Sam, so don't say that.'

She threw a small cork beer-mat into the empty pool and it hit the side of it with a loud smack and the boys laughed. 'I don't suppose I should have said it; but I do hate Nasser, and what he did to you.'

'Why did you come to Egypt then?' he said sharply.

'For you,' she told him.

He laughed in puzzled embarrassment, but then he suppressed it quickly.

'Don't you laugh at me like that,' she said. 'I *did* come here for you. I decided that it didn't matter much what I did, the only thing of any value I ever had in my life was Pickering, and then you. I thought I'd come and get you back. I don't care much whether I agree with you or not. At least you have the strength, even now, to make it worthwhile to be with you. For what it's worth, I want to be with you.'

'Did you ever stop to think?' he said, resenting the savagery of her bitterness and remembering again her original desertion, feeling in it her old contempt rather than any new affection she was trying to give him. 'Did you ever think that I might have found other ways and other people in all these years?'

'Of course,' she said matter-of-factly, 'but since I don't know them, and since I can't see them or hear them, I don't even consider them. Why should I? This time I shan't walk away in a huff. Couldn't I persuade you to leave this wretched country?' she appealed.

'What for?'

'You should get out of it. It doesn't do you any good any more. Look at you. We could both leave and go anywhere you liked, anywhere but here. Oh, if you would only think of it, Scotty, I know it would be better for both of us.'

'I'm not even listening,' he said in amazement.

The secretary, a smiling young Egyptian with English clubman's manners, brought them a repetition of their drinks with the sofragi and asked if he could sit down, saying *What* could he do?

'Anything,' he said in Oxford English, 'to help. How nice it is to see old friends again.'

'In that case,' Lucy said to him, 'it should be simple.'

But when she asked if she could play tennis, he said she must be a member. She *had* been a member. Ah, but the membership lists had been revised many times since the war. Couldn't she find two friends to nominate her? There were three or four English families still listed as members. No, she wouldn't know them.

'Then it's simple,' the secretary said. 'You must go to the Government Tourist Office, and they will give you a card which will allow you to be accepted into any club in Egypt for three months. It is specially for tourists.'

'For tourists?' Lucy said. 'Do I have to be a tourist?'

'But it's a formality,' the secretary said effusively. 'Please.'

She got up. 'I don't think it's come to that,' she told him. 'Thank you very much, anyway, but I shan't bother. Good-bye,' she said, and took Scott's arm to walk away.

Scott held back for a moment and thanked the secretary carefully in Arabic, and when they walked down the path again she clung to his arm and refused to talk until they were out on the street.

'I'm sorry for what I said about Sam,' she said to him then. 'I know you are trying to help Sam, but the only man who can probably help you undo Sam's trouble is Peter Dukes. Go to him. He'll help you.'

'I doubt it,' he told her ruefully. 'Not that fellow.'

'How do you know until you try?'

'Peter Dukes is deep in it himself,' Scott argued. 'He's been a British political agent in Egypt for heaven knows how many years. He doesn't like me and I'm sure he's not going to do me any favours.'

'Don't be silly,' she said. 'You must go to him if you want to help Sam.

186

Don't ask me why. I don't know why. Just do it. I won't provoke you about it any more if you promise to try.'

'If you say he can help, I'll have to try.'

'That's all right then,' she said happily, as if this were all a normal hour in her life. 'And now I want you to remember to take me to that pigeon restaurant for dinner on Friday. That's my only free night this week. I want to see if that place is still the same.'

It was still the same, he said, but he could not go on Friday because he had to see someone else. She asked 'Who?' But he did not tell her that he was about to be presented to the family of Françoise—to her merchant cousins, and to the jeweller Leo Lieberman—her other cousin to whom Françoise was very attached, and who often made many important decisions for her.

CHAPTER TWENTY-EIGHT

FRIDAYS now were crowded with prayer all over the footpaths of Cairo. Nasser's compromise with the Azharites and even with the Moslem Brotherhood had resulted in a decree allowing any man to break work for prayer on Fridays. Every sensible man took the opportunity to undo his shoes and bend over the footpaths and office corridors and warm garden lawns for five minutes and say to God: 'There is only you, God; and there is only your prophet Mohammed.'

Litanies were litanies—on the knees in cathedrals or noses to the street pavement. Only a Christian (it was said) could detect any difference and think it funny to see backsides a little higher in the air than their own.

Zareef was a religious Moslem, but he walked distastefully through the khaki servants in the Civil Air Authority offices, prostrate in prayer in front of the lifts on the second floor opposite the *Agence de Bière d'Alsace*.

'God seems to have subdivided us,' Fahid said to Zareef in a sharp whisper, 'into those who can believe in him standing up, those who can believe in him sitting down, and those who can only believe in him bashing their heads on the floor.'

'That's a shocking thing to say,' Zareef said angrily. 'Don't say it to me.'

Fahid looked hurt, a mockery of hurt. 'Nothing is sacred, Captain,' he said sadly. 'Not even God can make it so. If they haven't got my Intelligence clearance through for my "A" licence today, I'll insult their religion.'

Fahid might very well insult their religion—his own—but there was still no suggestion implied in anything he said that God was not there, or that Mohammed was not his prophet. Who could be that irresponsible, even Fahid?

In the office, a dark-moustached friend, Shukri, held Zareef's hand affectionately and begged him to come around from the old blotting-paper on the counter and sit down near him. What a lot of decent things friends can say to each other in Arabic. Fahid listened cynically to the greetings, the protestations, the re-protestations and re-greetings, and he was disappointed that Zareef fell in with it so effusively. Fahid was left behind the old blotter, outside it. 'Coffee, Captain Ali?' 'No, no, Habibi.' 'Ah, but I insist!' Shukri the functionary insisted, and Zareef the pilot resisted. Insist, resist.

'Captain Zareef,' Fahid said impatiently in English across the counter. 'Please ask Mister-Shukri Bey if my Intelligence clearance is through.'

'But he is here,' Zareef said in Arabic. 'Ask him yourself.'

Fahid sighed. 'But he'll never tell me. I'll be here all day waiting.'

'It's through. It's here, *mon ami*,' Shukri said. 'Be patient. Wait.'

Everything must be said thrice. Fahid showed a moment's happy satisfaction for Zareef's sake, but Zareef was already being called into the inside office.

The best navigator in Egypt, Captain Latif el Mansour, wearing a large beard, was now the CAA under-director, and he wanted to tell Zareef that his licence—Zareef's highly rated commercial and instructor's licence, in fact his entire flying licence—had not been renewed and would not be renewed for the time being.

The heavens had just fallen in on Zareef.

'But why, why, why?'

It was almost noon and the muezzin from the mosque behind the electricity company's building could be heard in the under-director's room over the tram bells and city noises that padded down over the streets like dust in the autumn.

'God is great! God is great! God is great! I bear witness that there is no God but God! I bear witness that Mohammed is the apostle of God. I bear witness to God. Come to prayers. Come to prayers. Oh, come to salvation.'

'You'll have to have a medical test,' Captain Latef was telling Zareef quietly beneath the muezzin's cries. 'Perhaps it's that, Ali. But I don't really know.'

There was no other God but God, that seemed sure; but Ali Zareef wondered what he had done for God suddenly to do this to him.

The law announced in the morning's newspapers, as part of the new constitution, established that crimes against the State were the only ones now punishable by death.

Murder remained, in a semi-legal way, a religious crime so long as it wasn't political. As far as the religion was concerned, an ordinary everyday murder could be forgiven by the murderer paying a fine or releasing a slave. But the Egyptian slave-owning class didn't often commit murders, and the lower classes and peasants who might commit murder in the violence and tragedy of their lives would be too poor to pay a fine, so they would still have to pay for it with a lifetime in prison.

That left spying and treason as the only sure way that Sam could be condemned to death and executed under the new constitution of the republic, and there seemed to be every possibility that he could be accused of both, if they ever found out what he had done.

Scott fed Felu on the paper when he had finished reading it, and he wondered if sitting under this mango tree feeding the dusty-walled tortoise, which had grown very bold over the years, was the best way of deciding what he must do. To take tea and sit it out for years to come? He had enough money saved to do it. The cheek he got from the sparrows, however, as they tried to steal the crumbs from under Felu's nose, was not the sort of company a man could stand for long.

'Get away with it,' he said to them. 'Go and get your own crumbs.'

He shook the newspaper and they flew away.

All right! Hakim had refused his resignation, and he had as much leave as he wanted; but it all had to end somewhere. It was coming to an end and he ought to face it.

The first logical thing to do was to go back to the desert and collect his belongings and his instruments which he had left at *mons claudianus castellum* and in the Frontier Department's villa at Ghurdakha where he had a trunk in Amin Fakhry's storehouse. But he already suspected that scheme himself. Logically he couldn't leave his things there, but beware of excuses to go back to the desert. Do not deceive yourself . . .

'Someone is calling you,' Madame Salz said from the house, 'on the telephone.'

'Merci, madame,' he said and went inside.

Peacock was back. 'What a country,' his voice groaned. 'In two weeks I've seen more horrors on this earth than God ever did dream of, and if I haven't got dysentery now I'll never have it. Furthermore, Scott, what I'm really telephoning about is that Eileen sent me a letter from the Cambridge Antarctic Committee for the Geophysical Year. They're the people responsible, or some sort of special committee is, for this expedition to the antarctic, and they've heard of you and your work because I wrote and reminded them about you, and they will be quite willing to submit your name and qualifications to the committee if you'll oblige. Will you oblige? I mean, if you're interested. Does it interest you?'

'Very much.'

'Then it ought to be easy.'

'You don't think they read the English newspapers?'

'Of course they do. But don't be so sensitive. Not everybody in England lies down and dies when the newspapers say something. Anyway, I'm going to a party tonight, in fact, I'm giving it. I know you're going to a jeweller's named Lieberman's at six o'clock, but afterwards you can come to us.'

'How did you know I was going to Lieberman's?'

'Spies all over the bloody place. You ought to know that.'

'It may be too late; after dinner, anyway.'

'We'll be going on all night I hope. After that journey I need some good sophisticated understated-looking people, healthy and red-faced if possible, just for one night. If you come we can talk, because I've simply got to answer this letter. Being an M.P. I can't set things going and then let them slip by unanswered, you know. It gives you a reputation for not-following-through.'

'All right, all right,' he said and told Peacock that Quartermain was in Cairo, but Peacock already knew.

'Have you seen him yet?' he asked Scott.

'No. I thought I'd give him a while to settle down.'

'He'll be here tonight,' Peacock said. 'What we ought to do before all the arguing sets in—since Quarts is probably going to despise me and is going to work himself up to debunking me—is to get all the reminiscing done we possibly can, the three of us. After that, it won't matter.'

'Old times are as good as any,' Scott said. He also needed English company; and old times, strangely enough, were always English, never Egyptian. 'I'll try to get there for the reminiscing part of it,' he said.

'Come to Bateman's place,' Peacock told him and gave him the address.

At Leo Lieberman's he could anticipate the children, because they would be the same. Although, if Françoise wanted finally to produce him, in public, as a friend, he ought to be able to anticipate something better. But he had learned doubt from her also.

'Don't be so suspicious,' Françoise had said in her invitation. But she had said that she too had read about him in the Egyptian newspapers—about that vigilant catcher of Israeli spies, Mr. I. N. Scott. Wasn't that a shameful thing for him to have done; and to his friend's own father?

He would have to face her for that, but he would depend on the presence of the children to make it easier. He would be all right if he saw her being confidently overpowered by her own children. He liked to watch her on the defensive before them, because she was always more reachable after she had been thoroughly upset by her own son, André.

André was irrepressible, but the girl, Mireille, who was nine, was more adaptable and was always willing to have him for a father, leaning against his knee and saying nothing. But André the boy was a French boy. His hair was clipped to a *longue-brosse*, and the intellectual shape was already decided. *Mon vieux* was the same at seven years of age to André as it would be at fifty-seven, with or without a father; Françoise would have no say in it.

'Mon vieux,' Scott had tried on André when he had last seen him in

191

Port Said; but the boy had looked up with his mother's careful and knowing eyes and ignored him.

'Tu sais,' the boy had begun familiarly when he did finally get around to Monsieur Scott. 'Mireille doit apprendre . . .'

'*Vous* savez,' his mother corrected sharply. 'Say *vous*, always *vous* to adults, André. You imagine you're already a man?'

The boy shrugged. What was the difference? child, boy, man and *mon vieux*? Scott had laughed.

'You mustn't laugh,' Françoise had said. 'He must be *respectueux* to adults. Go and take your bath and finish your *devoirs*.' *Devoirs* would be another half-hour's homework. At seven the Lycée also had them well in hand, but not André.

'*Tu* sais,' he said to Scott calmly as he went out, 'Mireille has to learn Arabic this year. *N'est ce pas idiot? Eh?*'

'Comme *tu* dis,' Scott had replied, '*mon vieux.*'

Françoise had slapped André on the warm bare legs and he had gone to his bath without feeling it. *Je m'en fous* was not far off in André's fatherless French life.

'It's silly,' Françoise was saying. 'The Egyptian government are making the children learn Arabic at school. It's a French school. Why should they learn to speak like an Arab?'

'Because they live here,' he said to her. 'They live in an Arab country.'

'But the children are not Arabs.'

'No, *mon vieux*, they are not,' he teased, but he had no real argument against the logical lilt to every word in the French language.

The children would help perhaps; he hoped so; but what of her family of aunts and uncles and *commerçant* cousins? He worried unnecessarily. They were not there. The children were not there either, and where was Françoise?

'Putting the children to bed,' Leo Lieberman told him.

He took Scott's arm in the hallway and spoke English slowly over a large-bowled pipe he smoked. He looked very healthy in the face for a sick man. Everybody knew he was dying of a kidney disease. He held Scott's arm and did not move, his feet had to be firmly planted otherwise with his double limp he would fall over. He held Scott there as if to gain time to gird himself. The twinkle of his German blue eyes said Scott was safe here, and Scott liked him for it and knew that his new reputation as a catcher of Israeli spies had not affected Leo.

'Françoise thought you might like to meet some friends,' Leo said. 'Cairo is a village. You will probably know most of them by sight, anyway.'

'I met you before,' Scott told him, 'at the Maccabee club.'

'Yes, I remember,' Leo said. 'Do you still wrestle there?'

192

'Not since Sam Hassoon grew fat.'

'Wait here,' Leo told him, beginning the tremendous effort to move, 'and I'll get Françoise.'

He waited in a formal little room with a plate-glass window, and he looked out of it from this high platform of a modern block of flats. The city was going to sleep, spread out below and clumped up in the middle with monolithic white blocks in concrete and steel. Far off, the veiled Mokattam hills crumbled down to the desert's edge with a red light on the top of each sandy peak to safeguard Zareef and Co. who flew over the gay city at night.

'*Voilà*, Monsieur Scott,' Françoise said, as if she were teasing herself.

She was the flushed mother fresh from bathing her children.

'Are the children in bed?' he said, giving her the toy electric car he had brought for André's birthday.

She nodded, taking the present and then taking one of his thumbs in her fingers and squeezing it hard.

'Is that all I get?' he asked. 'After all this time?'

'You talk!' She slapped his hand kittenishly and dropped it. 'Look at this beautiful city,' she said, huddling near the glass. 'When it is like this I hate leaving it.'

'You don't have to leave it,' he told her. 'You can easily get a job in Cairo. Or there are other ways, if you would only consider them.'

'You know very well I couldn't get a good job in Cairo without better English. French language in Cairo is only for the worst-paid jobs with the *commerçants*. I couldn't live . . .'

'There are other ways. Plenty of them.'

'There are not other ways. Don't talk about them, please. Not now. Let's go into the other room. In any case I only like Cairo from up here. Down there it's too troubled and frightening now.'

'Wait a moment,' he said, holding her back so that she leaned gently by him for a moment with not very much restraint. 'Who are you friends? Shouldn't I know about them?'

'Nobody important. Just friends,' she said. 'You'll probably know some of them.'

'What am I supposed to say to them?'

'Nothing. Nothing. Be nice, that's all.'

It meant be restrained, and somewhere here was the reason for it.

Leo struggled into the room and interrupted them, and she said to Scott in her sudden embarrassment:

'Tu connais Leo déjà, n'est ce pas? Mon cousin.'

Thou knowest Leo already, not so?

She had *tu*'d him unthinkingly, and when she realized it she did not know how to erase it. She was upset. She had implied the only thing that wasn't true—the flesh in French. It was a mistake and a lie.

'You must be more *respectueuse* to adults,' he said to her.

In the library four men were arguing in English about pre-Arab Egyptian songs, on which Leo was an expert. Leo was a wealthy man from trading in gold and selling watches and jewels on Emad el Din, and now he employed an Egyptian student to hunt out the remnants of the pre-Arab Egyptian songs in the village folk-music which seemed to be all Arab, yet must have kept in it a remnant of the original Pharaonic tradition. Only a Moslem could really sift it out, though, and Leo's student was a young Moslem from the university who had been singing some of the songs on the radio a few moments ago.

They were four middle-aged, respectable men. Scott had been at the English school with the youngest of them, Jack Santos, who was now an English teacher there. Jack was wondering these days when they would replace him with a Moslem under the new educational laws.

'I'm an Italian Jew who's never been to Italy,' he said to Scott ruefully, 'but I can't see myself teaching English to little Italians. Do you think I could get a job teaching in England, even though I've never been there either ?'

They all lived with the same problem—each one of the four men, sitting in Leo's well-used library with pre-Hitler abstract art on the walls. Leo and Françoise kept out of it a little, in the corner over Leo's records, where they came to grips, Scott supposed, over the sensitive French culture which excluded all others, perhaps even Leo's German culture, excepting that Beethoven was hard to exclude. The others were subdividing themselves into those who had somewhere to go when and if they left Egypt, and those who didn't; those who would get out of Egypt and those who couldn't. Some had papers, some had no papers, and Phillip Lieberman, Leo's younger brother, who dressed and looked like an Englishman, was the only safe one. He had a British passport. He had been sent by Leo after the war to be educated at the London School of Economics, after he had served very successfully in the British Army in Normandy. Phillip told them the joke about David Gaster who had owned a plastics factory in Alexandria. David had escaped Egypt six months ago with his money, by getting permission to go abroad with foreign credits to buy more machinery, which the industrial-minded republic fell for, particularly for plastics. So he had taken fifty thousand pounds in foreign credits and gone off to Zürich and left everything else in Alexandria— house, limousine, furniture, clothes, factory and bank balance, everything as if he would come back. But he never would, and that was a good joke.

They were obviously men who hated Nasser, and they turned to the more serious aspects of it. The young Egyptian officers, they said, were now taking over all the businesses they could get their hands on, forcing the foreigners to sell. Nasser had even put his own brother-in-law into the department-store business at the top.

'Why complain?' Phillip Lieberman said philosophically. 'We should be used to it by now. The day always comes, no matter what country it is.'

'They're going too far this time,' the surgeon of the Jewish hospital said, 'even in the hospitals it's Arabic now.'

'It's their country,' Jack Santos said, 'and they are Arabs, aren't they?'

All very true, but when Nasser threw out all the foreigners, the country would go to the dogs—collapse. The factories wouldn't work, the commerce wouldn't flow, banks would stagger when Europe withdrew all the money they had invested here, and the big oil companies would fizzle out in a state of helpless Egyptian confusion and corruption when the foreigners left.

'What do you think, Captain Scott?' Phillip asked him. 'I mean, how do you see it?'

'I try not to think about it,' Scott admitted. 'It's so confusing, anyway.'

'I suppose it is a big problem for you,' Phillip Lieberman agreed. 'You must wonder about it; but I suppose you only feel the impersonal edges of the problem, not being a Jew yourself.'

'Why should the country fall to pieces because a few foreigners leave?' Jack Santos insisted. 'What use are we, anyway?'

'At least we're efficient,' Phillip argued. 'Nasser studied Hitler and the Nazis very closely. That's all very well. But what the fellow didn't take into account was the fact that the Germans are efficient and the Egyptians are hopelessly inefficient, as a race. How could he hope to make the same thing work here? All very well to admire Hitler . . .'

Scott looked up at Françoise and knew now that she had invited him here for his own good, to have Phillip Lieberman explain Nasser to him. He sat on a Moroccan pouf, elbows on knees and head down, listening without trying to listen, but failing.

'I don't think Gamal Abd el Nasser admires Hitler,' he said.

'But it's in his book,' Phillip Lieberman insisted gently.

'Is it? I remember him mentioning the Germans at one time, but not Hitler. That would make it quite different.'

'Not if you're a dictator anyway,' Phillip said with his gentle laugh. Like Leo he was a non-violent-looking man, and likeable for it. 'In any case, people like Colonel Anwar Sadat, his close friend, collaborated with the Nazis during the war.'

Scott shrugged. 'Most Egyptians don't see anything worse in the Germans than they do in the English.'

'Was that a reason to side with the Nazis?'

'No. But I still think there's a difference. It's wrong to compare Nasser with Hitler.'

'Why is it? He has the same impulses.'

'I think it's wrong,' he insisted.

'Nasser says he is nationalist and a socialist, which is all Hitler was. Hitler tried to take the people's mind off what he was doing by persecuting the Jews, which is what Nasser is doing. Hitler smashed the old German parliament, which is what Nasser is doing. The comparison is too close, Captain, not to be serious.'

Scott regretted the *Captain*. An Englishman ought to call him Scott and be done with it. Phillip Lieberman's English, like his clothes, was impeccable. Scott felt like a foreigner in comparison, an ignorant and a local one. The *Captain* was only an old intimacy he had with Sam and his Egyptian friends.

'Hitler wanted to conquer the world,' Scott argued, 'but I doubt if Nasser can have that idea.'

'Almost,' Phillip said, handing Scott a cigarette which Scott shook his head over. 'He talks about the whole Moslem world as being a unit. Even the Afro-Arab-Moslem world is an ambition with him. That would include more people and more countries than Hitler ever dreamed of.'

'He talks of Arab unity because he's an Arab, what's the matter with that?'

Phillip patted Scott's knee affectionately. 'I see you have that strange English mystique about the Arabs, which is such a deadly disease once it gets hold of you. What is it, I wonder?' he asked himself blowing a thoughtful cloud at the ceiling. 'Is it their so-called racial nobility? Is it their tribal customs which still have in them the old medieval noblesse and high-worded heroics? Brotherhood? It's such a myth, you know . . .'

'I suppose it is,' Scott said, knowing that the myths and mystiques didn't touch him. 'But Egypt is a country like any other, and no doubt it wants to rule itself and be itself. That is probably what Nasser wants . . .'

'Ahhh!' one of the others said, and blew his nose in relief.

'Can it rule itself and be itself?' Phillip asked. 'Can Egypt be itself in the way Nasser wants it to be? Is that the way?'

Four other men listened to them and Françoise and Leo were very busy with their record exchange. Françoise would not look at him and he knew he was becoming angry when he ought not to argue or be angry.

'It depends,' he said as a last resort. 'It depends . . .'

'On what?'

He knew he was in some kind of an enclave here, and that Phillip Lieberman's persuasive English voice was the voice of them all.

'I suppose it depends on whether the Egyptians want Nasser or not,' Scott said.

'Do you think they do?'

'Not all, but most,' he said impatiently.

'The Germans probably wanted Hitler. Do you think that makes a man valid or desirable? In any case the Egyptian people can't want him, because they're too ignorant and wretched to know what they want. They'll need a great deal more help and tutelage from more advanced countries before they will ever be able to choose wisely . . .'

'That's a rather old-fashioned English view,' Scott said. 'More English than the English. It's what the Israelis are also beginning to say, and it is silly. *Know-how* they call it.'

He regretted saying that to Lieberman, and he folded his hands not in argument, but in the nature of a man listening to advice. Françoise had brought him up here to listen to the voice of reason. So he was being reasoned with. All right! Accept it! But then he decided recklessly that he ought to argue, because he knew Gamal as these men did not know him. But why argue? Why?

'A dictator,' Phillip told him, 'must always rule entirely in his own interests. That's the tragedy of it. Egypt will not be ruled wisely by a dictator, but more and more cruelly, because Nasser is too ambitious and therefore needs violence and persecution to sustain him. But you know, Captain Scott, his days are already numbered. Someone from his own entourage will probably become more ambitious than he is, and one day they'll cut his throat. Then you'll have a situation here like South America, where one military junta takes over after another. But what a tragedy for these people . . .'

'But you don't understand,' Scott interrupted. 'Gamal Abd el Nasser has only one test for anything he does, and that is whether it is any good for his own people. That is all he cares about. You can't understand him unless you understand that.'

'Oh, come along, Captain Scott,' Professor Halliday from the American University said. 'You're a reasonable man. Lieberman is trying to persuade you that it's not a nice thing to help Nasser. How can you sympathize with him? Surely you can see that Colonel Nasser is using you. Let him hear it, Phillip! Surely, Scott, it's time you took some sort of a stand to relieve at least your friends the Hassoon family, for instance, of this silly persecution. In all conscience.'

'That's not the point,' Phillip Lieberman pointed out sharply to the Professor.

'It *is* the point . . .'

'You mean you people are asking me to save Sam Hassoon?' said Scott.

'Of course we are.'

197

'But you must know that Sam Hassoon is my close friend.'

'That statement doesn't mean much to a Jew, and in any case we were beginning to wonder about it,' the Professor said. 'You ought to realize that you're doing everyone, including your own people, a disservice by letting Nasser use you.'

'Don't listen to him,' Phillip Lieberman said calmly to Scott.

But they all listened when Scott wetted his lips and looked at them.

'I don't mind listening to him,' Scott said, 'but what has my disservice got to do with Sam Hassoon? Who are you trying to save?'

'You're a Nasser man,' the Professor said. 'If Hassoon is your friend . . .'

'If I'm a Nasser man,' Scott interrupted, 'it's very courageous of you to bring me here, into your little enclave, and try to persuade me to turn on my master.'

'We don't mean that,' Phillip said. 'It was not meant that way. Harold always has a weird idea that everything is black or white.'

'Everything ought to be set down clearly,' the Professor said, his whitish hair flopping over his healthy face, a no-nonsense man like Lucy, who was not cruel against lies, but simply ruthless with the truth.

'You couldn't have put it any clearer, Professor,' Scott said sarcastically.

'Good, then we all know where we are.'

'Aren't you afraid that I'll go back and report this to my superiors?' Scott said contemptuously.

'No,' said the Professor, 'because whatever else you are, we know that you're an honourable man . . .'

'So are we all honourable men,' Jack Santos the teacher of English said. 'Leave off, Harold. What bites for one, bites for all. Scott's been bitten enough. We're not all straight-from-the-shoulder men. We haven't all been in the U.S. Navy.'

But it was Leo who saved him with his uninvolved eyes which refused to allow conflicts to poison what was left of his life, because he and Scott knew that Professor Halliday was about to mention another straight-from-the-shoulder truth. He would say that it was not a nice thing to be catching Sam's father and calling him an Israeli spy. What sort of a man did a thing like that to his close friend, eh?

'Harold,' Leo said to the Professor. 'I'm going to put on the record you brought me last year from the States. You remember you said then it was the rage of New York, the funniest thing you'd ever heard in your life. Now, just to prove that there are two sides to everything: are you ready?'

The Professor got up in quick defence. 'Oh no, Leo. Not that,' he begged. 'I couldn't stand it.'

'Then sit down,' Leo said and put on the record.

It was the old song 'Jingle-bells' sung by a dog, which barked rhythmically through the tune: whoof-whoof-whoof, whoof-whoof-whoof, whoof-whoof-whoof-whoof-whoof!

They had to be reasonable men, and though Scott allowed the argument to lapse and though there was no more pressure on him to do his duty by his friends, there was a feeling on both sides already that any further discussion was pointless. Scott left as soon as he could politely do so, but before he left he made a date with Leo Lieberman for lunch to smooth over all bad feeling. The enclave was closed. Françoise went down in the lift with him and held his arm, but it was she who could not allow it to simmer off in silence.

'So you are angry,' she said indignantly.

He hesitated, but then it got the better of him again. 'Of course I'm angry,' he said harshly to her.

'But why, *chéri*?'

'Do you think I need to be told by your Jewish friends that I ought to do something for Sam Hassoon?'

'It was not that.'

'What was it then? Were they explaining Nasser to me?'

She was neat and lovely. On the street, under the peppercorn trees, her French was winning. He looked up, remembering Fahid's warnings about the overcrowded ibises coming in from the fields to roost in the city trees.

'Why shouldn't they explain?' she said. 'Do you think they should agree with you? Are you frightened to hear the other side of it?'

'Do they think I have no conscience about Sam at all?' he said. 'Don't even say a word about Sam to me, you haven't the right. Not even you . . .'

'We all have consciences,' she argued firmly, 'and they tell us to do different things. Don't you think those men worry about Hassoon also?'

'They worry about themselves.'

'They wouldn't be here if they did. They could leave. We all worry about each other, and that means your friend Hassoon too.'

'Then you get him out of gaol. Go ahead.'

'We can't, you know that. But you might. Anyway, it wasn't for that.'

'What was it for, then? To warn me?'

'You are childish (*vous etes puéril*) and it's silly talking to you. I thought you were a reasonable person.'

Raisonable was not a fire-brand word in French, but when his mind transmuted it into English *reasonableness* he flared up against Phillip Lieberman's reasonable English characteristic of seeing the other-man's-point-of-view, this English absorbent of all resistance. Be reasonable! It lit old fires never quite dead, never quite silent.

'I'm not reasonable,' he said. 'You can't even shame me into being reasonable. Anyway, it was a mean trick, getting me into it.'

'Into what?'

'I don't know. But you're all so confident,' he said bitterly, 'and so sure that you're superior to the Arabs. Do you want to hate Nasser? Go ahead and hate him. But don't try to shame me into the same point of view. I won't listen to it any more.'

'Chéri . . .'

He threw it all away and stripped a sticky leaf of peppercorn through his fingers, a hopeless thing. 'Ah, it doesn't matter,' he said. 'Forget it, Françoise. Let us forget it. It will only hurt us if we quarrel about it. I don't care what they think.'

'I'm sorry too,' she said. 'I didn't know you would take it like this. When you want to know something, you talk about it. You should, anyway.'

'I know, I know,' he said. 'Forget all about it. I don't want to quarrel about it. I quarrel with everybody about it, but I don't want it with you. I don't even know how it all starts, because I do nothing to provoke it. I only try to keep out of such discussions and disagreements.'

'Then you must forget it. Please.'

'Yes, all right. Yes, let's not even talk it.'

'I'm going back to Port Said tomorrow,' she told him. 'Will you come soon?'

'I'll try to come down next week,' he told her, wanting to leave her now. 'But I have to go back to the desert and get my affairs there, and bring them out.'

'Why? Are you leaving the desert?'

'I've already left it,' he said, and he felt that she knew that too.

'You're not going to leave Egypt, are you?'

'I might,' he said. 'Yes, I'm thinking of going.'

'But not soon?'

He knew he was saying it to annoy her or to worry her, but once said the words could not be unsaid. 'I don't know. I've been offered another job. I don't think I know yet.'

She clung and teased him. 'Some day you must simply say *Yes* or *No* like the French do. Not "*I theen so*" and "*I don' theen so*" like the English.'

She had said it in English to give in to him, intellectually. Her English was bad. But she knew he liked to hear her atrocious accent, which usually made him ruffle her lightly with sudden desire.

He had not heard it, and they parted abruptly under the peppercorn tree.

He went on to Bateman's and found Quartermain already at bay, even before the reminiscing had begun. Bateman's tape-recorder was playing rolls of battering trumpets. Peacock was dancing with one of the Ambassador's secretary's secretaries. Young official Englishmen and pencil-shaped women in wide skirts and fashionable nylon petticoats rustled and tinkled ice in long glasses and danced or sat on the floor playing the children's card game 'Snap' with hilarious fights over each victory. On the refectory table two native servants filled fresh glasses very seriously with punches and cocktails and served them perfectly.

Once, it might have been typical and very common to see this. Now it looked like the concentration of all the English left in Cairo, combining their forces in one determined effort. Quartermain was obviously trying to hold his own in the face of it, saying cynically to Bateman:

'When I talked to the Minister at the airport the other day, he was saying . . .'

It was a shock to see Quartermain greyer than himself, even though he was not yet forty; and he was lanker and drier, but still a self-mocking man. But he looked dry now instead of being darkly elegant. His moustaches did not look like polished black shoes but were silvery, and they dropped casually over the cheerful snarl which had once been a hateless, good-natured laugh at all things, mostly at himself.

'Here he is,' Bateman said. 'It's the notorious Captain Scott.'

They were curious, but the noise did not stop. Quartermain interrupted his point and Peacock danced the Ambassador's fifth secretary over and said, 'Scotty! Here at last.'

'I didn't think you'd be seen dead in this lot,' Quartermain told him.

'Peacock told me you'd be here,' Scott said.

They were shaking hands on it, nostalgically, after thirteen years.

Peacock was anxious about the girl. 'Look at this young and lovely thing,' he said to them. She was gay and young, twenty-six, lovely, and very polite to Scott. 'Who do you think she is?' Peacock asked. 'Who? Guess!'

'The Prince of Wales,' Quartermain said.

'She's my aunt. Honestly! I didn't know she was here, but I came back yesterday and went to the Embassy and there she was.'

That was a joke, and Bateman nudged Scott.

'Honestly,' Peacock insisted. 'My mother had a young stepbrother born after me: my uncle. He was killed with the Royal Navy in the Korean War, and this is his widow.'

'Peacock,' Bateman said, 'that's not nearly clever enough.'

'It's true, isn't it, Marigold? She's Marigold Maycock.'

'It's simpler to say it isn't true,' Marigold said, 'and then they won't bother us. Come along.' She took his arm.

'Please stop arguing, old chap,' Peacock told Quartermain, 'and look after Scott while I finish this. I've got to learn it sooner or later.'

He knocked over a drink and said, 'Sorry, Bateman,' and danced on

H*   201

and said that a slow jive was really at heart only a hill-billy gavotte. 'It's all in the knees, like ski-ing,' he said to his aunt, whose nylon petticoats flew out when she held one damp arm over her head with Peacock's and swung from side to side.

'This is what you started on at Lieberman's,' Bateman said to Scott and put a whisky into his hand. When Scott looked surprised he said, 'Oh, don't worry, I could smell it, old boy. No spies necessary.'

'It's amazing,' Quartermain sighed. 'We're all alive, Scotty. Fancy that.'

'You haven't changed,' Scott told him, 'except that you look a bit pepper-and-salty.' He thought Quartermain had changed a great deal, but he couldn't fathom it yet.

'You think so?' Quartermain said. 'My wife will be pleased. She thinks I change every day, from one man into another. After twelve years of it she's probably getting fed up.'

'Is she here?'

'Good God, no. She hates the English, once they leave England.'

He saw Lucy Pickering, but she ignored him, sitting in a window-seat with an Englishman who talked to her earnestly while she stared outside without apparently listening.

They all knew Quartermain's reputation as the debunker of generals and statesmen and colossal blunders, and they did not spare him. It was a lark to have him. Had he come to Egypt to do a job on Nasser?

'He's probably come to de-bag me and you,' Bateman said to Peacock. 'British M.P. dances till dawn while Nasser plots to blot out the thin red line.'

'Sometimes I feel like debunking myself,' Peacock said, drinking his punch determinedly.

'But you do, from time to time.'

'. . . but,' Peacock concluded, ignoring Bateman, 'I think Quarts can probably do a better job of it. We're all fools, anyway.'

'If you ever do get to Nasser,' Bateman told Quartermain, 'he'll tell you what foul beasts we all are. You can write it all down. You won't have to look for another thing.'

Why didn't men dance and forget Nasser for a while?

But Bateman, like Quartermain, never let anything go either. 'Anyway,' he said, 'the only man here who has any right to talk about it won't say a word. Captain Scott probably knows all the secrets, but what are they? What is Nasser really up to?'

Scott flushed. 'If I could tell you . . .'

'Oh, come on, Captain Scott,' Bateman said. 'Give us a chance. What happens next? Is he going to sell the canal to the Russians for 600 million roubles, or is he planning to abolish the word *khara* from the Arabic language?'

202

Scott tried to play the game. 'He doesn't usually tell me these things.'

'Then you ought to ask him. You could make your fortune on the stock exchange speculating on canal shares. Since you're a friend of Nasser's, though, can't you at least tell him how an Englishman ought to think? I mean a died-in-the-wool, back-to-the-wall type like me.'

'I could tell him,' Scott said, irritated now, 'but he wouldn't believe me.'

Bateman went on ignoring all discomforts. 'Peacock and I have decided that the only way for Nasser to survive is to have a plebiscite on union with Israel. That's the only way he'll ever avoid being absorbed by the Israel Army. If he absorbs them first, by a clever trick like that, he'll save his reputation, get the Egyptian Army out of ever having to fight a battle, and be in the nice position of letting the Israelis run the country for him while he gets the credit.'

Scott could not advise on this, he said as dryly as he could manage. 'If he *is* your friend . . .'

'Oh, leave a man alone with his friends,' Lucy Pickering said to Bateman.

'Don't interfere, Lucy,' Bateman answered. 'Scott can look after himself!'

'No, he can't,' she said. 'He's been long years in the desert talking to desert rats. He doesn't know how to cope with any other kind. So leave him alone,' she said and left as she had come, dancing with the white-haired Englishman who grinned from ear to ear at everything she said and stood behind her when she said it and went with her when she had finished it.

Bateman laughed and patted Scott's shoulder.

'Never saw a man with so many protectors. Never saw a man who needed them less. Only a brave soldier could have hoed your row. God, yes! Although I think you ought to tell them to let your friend Sam Hassoon go. He's quite innocent. I know he is. It seems very cynical to me the way you are all treating him seriously as some kind of horrible menace. Sam? It's a fantastic joke. And now they've picked up his friend Zareef the pilot . . .'

'Who has?' Scott asked.

'Ah hah! So they don't tell you. Your boss, Hakim. He's had Zareef's flying licence called in, and I think he's about to be arrested and sent off to the criminal prison at Abu Za'bal until he confesses how he helped Sam Hassoon plot the assassination of Gamal Abd el Nasser.'

Quartermain took it mercifully out of his hands.

'You hate too much,' he said to Bateman, 'and you laugh too much. That's bad, you know.'

'Do I?' Bateman said, shifting to another target quite happily. 'What about you, Quartermain? I could say the same of you.'

'But I do it in a different way,' Quartermain went on academically. 'You hate the facts, whereas I hate the results.'

203

'I prefer my way,' Bateman said. 'For instance—is there any reason why I shouldn't hate you, and you're a fact?'

'None at all, only it's bound to have a horrible effect on you.'

Scott could withdraw at this stage, but he could feel already—simply standing between these two men—how much both men hated. In half an hour they had recognized something in each other worth hating. But what was it? Once, Quartermain had never hated anything; even Pickering had complained of that. Now he seemed happy to put a thin sharp blade into anything, particularly into Bateman.

'People shouldn't argue,' Peacock told Scott sadly, joining him. 'That's what I've learned out here. I suppose it's always been like that in this part of the world. But why?'

'At the moment it's politics, politics, politics,' Scott said.

'But why should they hate? I'm a politician and I don't hate anything except boiled artichokes. And even that's a love-hate relationship with me. Do you hate? I mean, you have reason to—I suppose. But do you?'

'No, I gave that up years ago. Too hard on the nerves.'

Peacock drew him into a quieter corner then and said, 'I've been thinking, Scotty, I don't know how you'll take this, but you do know that Church is in Egypt?'

'I saw him in the desert,' Scott replied.

'I'd heard about that. But do you think it would do any good if I brought you and Church together?'

Scott was not interested in Church. He was thinking about Zareef and saying to himself, 'Someone must be behind it all. Why Zareef? What is it coming to when they start taking in people like Zareef? It's impossible.'

'What's Church in Egypt for?' he asked Peacock.

'I don't know. Some archaeological expedition. Does it matter?'

'Isn't Church likely to be the head of British intelligence in Egypt?' Scott said, suspicious now that he was looking for explanations.

'He might be,' Peacock said casually.

'Is that why you want me to see him?'

Peacock was deeply hurt. 'Nothing like that, Scotty. What made you think of a thing like that? I don't care a tuppeny-damn about Jack Church or what he does. I wasn't thinking of that. I was only feeling the other day that it was time you tried to settle this business with him somehow. And if you don't want me to get your court-martial reviewed or appealed, I thought you might be able to settle with Jack Church personally. That's all I meant.'

'I know. I'm always far too suspicious,' Scott said apologetically. 'I was thinking about Zareef.'

'I heard about that too,' Peacock said. 'It's terrible. He's obviously such a harmless fellow. It wasn't because of me, was it?'

'No,' Scott assured him. 'It must be more serious than that.'

'Oh, damn this whole idiotic world,' Peacock said. 'How could anyone be afraid of people like Sam and that pilot? What for?'

Scott looked closely at him. 'They're very worried here about a plot to kill Nasser,' he told Peacock.

'With Zareef and Sam? Oh, but that's crazy!' Peacock protested. 'Only a madman would think up a thing like that. Anyway, let's talk about something else. I'm depressed enough as it is, after looking at the misery of this country. I also wanted to give you this . . .'

Peacock handed him the letter Eileen had sent on from the Royal Geographical Society inviting Scott to give them some particulars about himself if he wished to be considered for one of Dr. Fuchs' antarctic parties.

'Not here,' Scott said, taking it. 'Let's discuss it in some quieter pla e.'

'All right, but please write to them, will you?'

'I will,' Scott promised and saw Lucy Pickering approaching them.

'And incidentally,' Peacock added, 'I wrote such an insulting letter to that fellow Mathieson that I wouldn't be surprised if he sued me for libel. In fact, I hope he does, then I'd really tell him what I thought of him in public. I'll never get over it.'

Lucy had listened to it and had taken Scott's arm lightly in hers as she stood with them for a moment. Then she turned to Scott and said, 'Will you take me home, Scotty, if Tim will ever forgive you for doing it?'

'Why me?' Peacock asked in his innocence.

'Because you know I came here uninvited.'

'That's silly,' Peacock told her. 'If Scotty's made it up with you, so have I. I would have invited you if I'd known where you were. Anyway I'll forgive you anything, Lucy, as long as you *don't* write home to Eileen and say that *he seems to be having a very gay time*. I'm not. I have an awful stomach-ache.'

'May we go?' Lucy asked him.

'Oh, all right, take her home,' Peacock said graciously.

'But I haven't had a chance to talk to Quartermain,' Scott said.

'You'll never talk to him here,' she told him. 'He's too busy fighting the class war with Bateman.'

It was true. Nobody could interrupt that reckless debate which had passed beyond personalities and was sailing at a pace into economics and even into hydrology. Quartermain was asking why, in eighty years of occupation, the British had sunk only eight artesian wells to give pure water to the Egyptian villages, when it was the foul water of the Nile which killed off millions of fellaheen over the years; whereas in four years Nasser had sunk eighty wells.

'A fat lot of good eighty artesian wells are going to do,' Bateman said cheerfully, 'when you have over ten thousand villages along the Nile. What's he going to do? Sink ten thousand more?'

Who could interrupt? But Scott listened for a while and tried not to hear the bouncing music, the throbbing dance and the hard voices, and he chose a moment to say to Quartermain, quickly, that he was going home.

'Wait. I'll come with you,' Quartermain said.

'I was about to take Lucy Pickering home,' Scott said in embarrassment.

'Oh! I don't suppose you can help that,' Quartermain told him cynically. 'Then I'll see you Wednesday.'

'I was wondering about that also. I think I'll be going back to the desert for a few days to collect my belongings.'

'Whenever you like then. How long will you be away?'

Scott said he didn't know. He did not know because there was already something ominous in this news about Zareef, so much worse, that he felt it was all hopeless now; and he could not shake the feeling off as it took hold of him.

'I had hoped to go down by air,' he explained to Quartermain, 'but the pilot is in trouble. You knew about Sam . . .'

'I hear about nothing else,' Quartermain said.

'Then I'll have to see you when I come back,' he told Quartermain as he said good-bye to Bateman, who walked to the door with his hand on Scott's shoulder, hoping he had had a good time—such a rare bird for other Englishmen to see. Peacock told him to take no notice of Bateman and they shook hands at the door to prove that anything said was unimportant, and then he left with Lucy clinging to his arm, feeling that he had already had too much for one day.

He sat back in the taxi and felt Lucy's arm in his and felt her willingness to be gentle with him, and he did not object; he knew he could not go on being disciplined like this.

'You know, I really did go to that party uninvited,' she said.

'Did you?'

'Yes, just to find you. I always tell you that. I love to say it to you, even if you don't really think I mean it. But I do! So please don't leave me this time.' She was holding his hand warmly and firmly and keeping close to him. 'Don't just turn on your heel at the door. Please come and be nice to me. I do need you, darling. All I ever wanted was to see you again, even to *see* you. I can't tell you how I felt sometimes. I could imagine you so clearly, and I just wanted to be like this with you. But now I want you near me for a little while longer, and I don't ask anything else . . .'

He kept a firm grip on her arm and nodded quietly, knowing that there was little else he wanted himself, except to be near her for just a little while longer.

206

Lucy could always be generous, but she knew about Françoise and she said she could not help asking what she was like.

How did she know about Françoise?

'You can't start an affair like that,' she said, as if truth was no longer anything that need stand between them, 'without everybody knowing it. Particularly you and particularly in Egypt. But why do you always choose ready-made women?' she asked tolerantly. 'First me, with two children. Then this little French girl with a ready-made family. Are you so desperate for a family of your own?'

'I shouldn't even be here with you,' he said, 'so don't talk about it.'

'Too late,' she said triumphantly and teasingly. 'What's done is very much done.' She sighed deeply in contentment. 'Thank God, oh, thank everything and everyone!'

He could not feel happy in a paper-walled hotel room in the middle of a Cairo night discussing his guilt. His happiness, even his brief need of it, had gone. He could only feel disappointed with himself and with Lucy because they had failed themselves so long ago and were trying again now, without any right to try again. It was not the same and could never be the same.

'We should have felt thankful years ago,' he told her. 'Now it's too late.'

'Please don't recriminate about it, not tonight,' she begged.

'When do I recriminate then?' he said without real bitterness, making a gentle recollection of it. 'It's the first chance I've had since you simply left me like that. Years later you come back, and look what happens. Do you think it's that simple?'

'It is if you want it to be,' she told him.

'I don't think I want it to be. I only know I shouldn't be here.'

'Because of your silly little French girl? Oh, really, Scott.'

'She's not silly, nor French. Don't talk like that. She's a Jewish girl.'

'Good for you,' she said sleepily and snuggled into his shoulder. 'Mustn't be prejudiced, you know.'

He realized suddenly, for no apparent reason, that however much he had forgotten the war, he had completely forgotten the day when Church's blunder had blown up Lucy's husband and his own best friend, 'Moses' Brodie, whom he had shot dead over a jeep tyre with a pistol to spare him a torturous terrible death from his atrocious burns. The real, physical, painful memory had completely gone, even if the results had not; because over the years he had remembered it so often and with such pain that he had worn off the memory a long time ago. It did not hurt any more, and it did not even revive a hurt. In one day, the combination of Peacock and Quartermain and Lucy had revived it a little, but it still did not hurt. Too far away, too faint. Only Atiya's death hurt, the most wasteful of all. That would never leave him, no matter how much the memory tried to scour it away. Atiya aroused a vision walking over the desert, stumbling about in sloppy boots without any real reason for being there, except that Pickering had picked him up as a freak, as he had picked up Sam and Quartermain and no doubt Scott himself, to make it a unit of freaks, to ridicule the English awe of normalcy which Pickering himself had made fun of every day, simply by looking at himself in the mirror. They were all a denial of something . . .

But some men were not supposed to be in a war. Violence ought to be set apart from them, and Atiya the poor Egyptian was one, just as Sam was another and Ali Zareef a third. He was already finding it difficult to separate them.

'Shh!' Lucy said softly as he tensed his body. 'Put your terrible conscience to sleep.'

'I'm cold,' he said.

Cold in this warm-nighted city? But if it was not his conscience, what was it?

'Whatever do you go on worrying about?' she said. 'Is it really worth it?'

'Mostly I'm a fool,' he admitted, 'but you're right. I don't want to worry about anything now. Why should I?'

'Being right is such bliss,' she murmured, 'and I do feel quite blissful. It's so perfect to be with you.'

It was perfect because she could make it perfect simply by saying so.

'Do you think I've grown fat?' she asked. 'I mean thickened. I'd hate that. It's the thickening that makes age so horrible, worse than anything else, worse than the skin drying or the teeth falling out.'

'You needn't worry,' he told her. 'You probably look younger now than your own daughters. Where are they, anyway? Are they married yet?'

'I'm not sure. I don't think so. One of them is married to horses. That's Hester. Do you realize that she's almost twenty-two? She went mad on horses at the age of sixteen and now she breeds them and jumps them in

208

Berkshire with some Guardee, but I don't think they've ever legally married.'

'Where is little Joanna?'

'Oh, you'd like Joanna. You always did, I know. She's twenty and in love at the moment with an Italian she picked up on holiday in Sienna. He swallowed a bee. It's quite true! He swallowed a bee while he was drinking an aperitif, and she was the only one in the restaurant with the presence of mind to get up and hit him hard on the back, a perfect stranger.'

He laughed. 'That's exactly how Joanna would grow up.'

'She's a practical English girl, and the Italian said she had saved his life and his career. Think, he said, of the catastrophe if that bee had stung him in his throat. He's a singer at the Milan opera and twice her age and so fat, but I don't worry about Joanna. If she marries him she will turn him into a sound, practical, English husband drying the dishes.'

'You're very lucky,' he told her. 'At least you've had your family.'

'That's envy,' she said, 'but you really ought to console me.'

'What for?'

She held his hand for a moment. 'It was never a family. Didn't you realize that? They needed a father. I always had to push them away, so that they didn't grow up to be mummy's little girls. English girls can be horrible with their mummy complexes. I didn't want that. But if they'd had a father it wouldn't have been necessary. They needed Pickering, or you. They would have been such fun then. Instead, it's been too unsentimental to be very valuable now.'

'Why didn't you marry again? Try again, anyway.'

'I was *gatéed* early in life,' she said, 'by two such unusual men, ever to find anyone else worth marrying.'

'Nobody ever *gatéed* you.'

But he was glad of her tender hand now, and he did not stop its affections, its search for his heart. He had no way of responding to her tenderness, but he responded by trusting her completely.

'I didn't mean spoiled in that way,' she said gently. 'I really meant it was all my own fault.'

'Even now,' he said, 'you look like a nice healthy happy Englishwoman with three or four children who have everything English and normal about them. It would still seem very natural if you had two or three more.'

'At my age?'

'Why not?'

'Let us not play with fire, my sweet, nor with children asking to be born. I couldn't bear that . . .'

Once, the passion would have risen quickly; now it simmered quietly at peace.

'Anyway,' she said, 'you're the one who needs the family, not me. You'd probably be such a good father. Although sometimes you're such a dour type. What makes you like that? Was it your Scots mother?'

'Am I that dour?'

'Oh, just a little, old chap. Just a little,' she said, touching his chin.

Coming out of the desert he had always been conscious of the city noises. Now he heard the city strays, the toll of some Christian sounding bell inexplicable in the Cairo night, and the laughter of native taxi-drivers across the street chewing hasheesh.

'What do we do now?' she said.

'I don't know,' he said sleepily. 'I'm not even thinking about it. I'm far too tired to care.'

'Good.'

'I shouldn't be here,' he repeated. 'That's as much as I know. But I don't care about that any more, either.'

'Now *that*,' she said, mooning down roundly and softly over his sleepy face, 'is the part of your conscience I don't want to know about. There's no future in it. You think of me, and I'll think of you. Let the rest go hang —just for once. That's called love, darling. And believe it or not (but please, please believe it and seriously too), I would still love you in any way you wanted me to.'

'Too many other things in the way,' he said lazily.

'But I'd ignore everything else this time. Really, I would. I don't care what it is. If you could only do the same. You're such a wonderful man. Don't you think we'd have a chance, particularly if we just up and went away, just like that . . .'

He ran his fingers thoughtfully through her soft English hair, as soft and unspoiled and as well-washed as a girl's, and he wondered if tenderness and love were really the same thing when you were nearly forty and not in your twenties as they had been thirteen years before.

'I don't know,' he said. 'I'm not in a fit state to decide anything.'

'I can wait,' she said. 'I just want to love you now. I won't spoil it. I don't ask for anything else yet. Not now. Not yet . . .'

CHAPTER THIRTY

HAKIM telephoned him urgently at Madame Salz's to tell him to come to the new Fertilizer Building near the Square of the Republic, near Abdin Palace, where Farouk had lived. It was now the Presidential Palace of the Republic. He must be there at eleven-thirty, Hakim said, and he was sorry it was such short notice, but he would see something today which had to be seen to be believed.

'If it's so important,' Scott asked, 'what is it?'

'You'll see. It's something for you and for me and also for Gamal. It might be very important for you,' Hakim said, although he sounded gay. 'You will see.'

The new Fertilizer Building was not a Saudi Arabian speculation like so many of the new buildings in Cairo, but one of the mammoths built by the landowners after the land reform, to save their money and still get back the usual thirty or forty per cent on the investment. One man had built it for that sort of investment. He also had half the monopoly of Egypt's biggest import—fertilizers. He had built it on fertilizer profits. Everybody knew that Bindari Pasha and his son Ramzi were very astute that way, and Scott wondered what Hakim was doing sitting in the grey lift of the Bindari Fertilizer Building waiting for him, while other visitors to the building took the other lift or walked. They did not go to the top floor, but only to the eighth floor, as high as the level of the older buildings surrounding this new block.

'I wanted to save you the walk up,' Hakim said, 'and my heart . . .'

Hakim was afraid of his heart collapsing before the republic had been satisfactorily established, so he had borrowed the Bindari's lift.

'Out on the roofs,' Hakim said. 'But we must hurry.'

They left the Captain (the same adjutant who had taken Scott to see Sam) and went out of a window on a staircase landing and crossed over the crumbling old roofs, which were littered with filth and rubbish and badly erected tin huts and clothes-lines and hen-houses and even a goat.

'I know all the roofs of Cairo, did you know that?' Hakim said to him while they negotiated the gaps from one building to another. 'Only a conspirator appreciates the fact that a city has two thoroughfares: one down below and another one up here—much more private.'

'Slow down,' Scott told him. 'I'm much heavier than you are.'

Hakim was nimble over the roofs, but sometimes Scott felt his weight threatening the flat mud and plaster with collapse and Hakim laughed to see him trying to walk like an overweight cat.

'You'd be a poor conspirator, my friend,' he said. 'You'd be like Gamal.'

Hakim kept his uniform clean and passed through dim passages and huts to a corner overlooking the palace itself, the side entrance of the Abdin Palace. On this dirty rooftop two Frontier Corps Sudanese were standing guard outside a little hut made of boxes which had once housed Glennifer Diesel engines; the name was stencilled across the door. Hakim raised his leather stick to the overwhelming salute of the dark Sudanese and told them to open the door and he went in, turning on a light which flooded the box and made it a tiny room with a bed and a stack of arms and a pair of field-glasses on a tripod.

'You look through the binoculars at what you will see,' Hakim told him.

Scott put on his own glasses and bent down, and he saw through the port-hole in the box (which Hakim had opened) the side entrance to the Abdin Palace where the Republican guards controlled the passage, and the big gate would swing open for limousines to come out.

'A nice view?' Hakim said, joking through it happily.

'Is that where Gamal comes out?' Scott asked him.

'You'll see in five minutes. Look at these.'

There were two light machine-guns and a box of round, greasy drums, fully loaded, as well as two or three rifles still in their grease wrappings. They were lying carelessly under a bunk which was covered in army blankets and crumpled with recent occupancy.

'What would you say the range was?' Hakim asked him.

'Oh, four or five hundred yards.'

'Would that,' he pointed to the mounted long-barrelled machine-gun, 'cover the range accurately, you think?'

'Of course,' Scott said.

'No, it wouldn't. It would reach the car all right, but would be unlikely to kill anyone in it because the only way to kill a man in a car, for sure, is to throw a bomb in it from two paces with an instantaneous fuse, and even then it will probably fail for some reason or other, or kill the thrower. This is all very nice, but it would have succeeded only by a great deal of luck. Too much luck.'

'Who put it up here?'

'Ah hah!' Hakim sat on the bed. 'We only suspect, we don't know. I'll tell you the truth, we don't know.'

'Then how did you find it?'

'Unfortunately, my dear, by accident. Unfortunately . . .'

'When?'

'Two days ago. By accident,' Hakim repeated sadly.

'What does it matter, as long as you found it? It's such a stupid idea, anyway. They would have been caught.'

Hakim spread his hands. 'Well, we haven't caught him. We should have caught him, though, because the man is always more important than the gun,' he said. 'So where is the man? Where are the men? You can see that this isn't one man, but a whole conspiracy. It's very crude, not at all clever; but it might have worked, and if it can be tried from here it can be tried from anywhere else, don't you see?'

Scott saw. 'How did you find it? It couldn't have been an accident.'

'Old conspirators know the roofs very well,' Hakim said. 'I send out someone to look at our city roofs from time to time, and one of my soldiers discovers this without the man in it. We waited for him, but he must have seen the soldiers who were not very clever. It is almost twelve o'clock, and you must look through the binoculars.'

Scott kneeled in the space and Hakim turned the light out so that Scott could see better, then he lit a cigarette and watched quietly while Scott adjusted the vision.

'He will be on time today,' Hakim said. 'I have told him.'

Gamal was on time. The black American limousine turned out of the gate with plenty of warning from the guards who had saluted, a thirty-second preparation for anyone firing the gun. Then the car came out and even from this rather high but long angle Gamal was visible in the back, sitting with the other Hakim, General Abdul Hakim Amer, the Chief of Staff, and an officer who was reading letters to them. Gamal looked up in their direction, laughed, and waved.

'Gamal,' Hakim said, 'likes to eat his lunch at a regular time. His wife is very fussy about that, otherwise he'll ruin his health, and he would miss seeing his children. Doesn't he look fit? He plays tennis every Saturday and swims on his holidays.'

Gamal looked very fit, and the view was close enough to be a valuable one for an old friend.

Hakim sighed. 'So there you are,' he said.

They sat in the darkness.

'Couldn't you find out anything?' Scott asked. 'Even from the rifle, or the hut or the binoculars?'

'The binoculars are German, so are the machine-guns, but the rifles are British. They could come from anywhere. They mean nothing.'

'What about the people in the building below?'

Scott sensed Hakim's slight-shouldered shrug. 'Assassins wouldn't come up that way. They would come here through a hundred other buildings. I myself picked the Bindari's Fertilizer Building because it had a lift, but whoever it was could have been on these roofs from anywhere, anywhere at all.'

'They must have been ready to do it,' Scott said. 'In fact, it looks as if it's been ready a long time.'

'Exactly! They must have been waiting for orders to do it, only that. Somebody's order . . .' Hakim turned on the light again.

'The fact is,' he said, 'we can never discover who it is, not from anything here. We will have to go on uncovering the conspirators by other means. We'll have to find out from other men, whom we do know are involved—if we catch them. Perhaps we have caught some of them already, and several more yesterday.'

'That isn't why you arrested Ali Zareef, is it? I hope to God, Hakim, you don't suspect someone like Zareef.'

'Zareef?'

'The pilot.'

'Ah, yes. Has he been arrested? I didn't think we had done that yet, but he will be, I suppose. How did you know? Never mind, I suppose it is logical.'

'It's not logical at all,' Scott argued, putting his glasses away carefully, storing up his care, using a little of it only. 'Zareef couldn't be involved in a thing like this.'

'Perhaps not,' Hakim agreed.

'Then why do they arrest him?'

The laughter had left Hakim, who now seemed resigned to a sad world. 'Do you think we should take risks, even with innocent men, when you see this?' It was always Hakim's defence. 'The men doing this look innocent enough when you meet them in the street, or have business dealings with them, or work with them. All conspirators look innocent. I looked innocent enough, didn't I?'

'I can't believe Zareef or Hassoon had anything to do with this.'

'Neither do I,' Hakim said as they went out. 'But this is only one little corner of a conspiracy. If traitors plan little things like this, they can plan a bigger and more dangerous scheme. And that's the one I worry about. Come over here.'

Hakim led him to a higher building which he seemed to know intimately, walking around a huge water-tank to find an iron ladder up it. He jumped a foot or two from the tank to the next roof which was flat and long, and then crumbling as it joined another. It was a clever maze, and Hakim took him this time to a roof-top laundry room, stinking with filth now and unbearable for more than a few seconds.

214

'That was the worst part of the roofs always,' Hakim said. 'The filth. We chose this one because we could keep it clean, there is running water. We had this one when the British were keeping Farouk in Abdin. Do you remember in February 1942? I was here the very day that Sir Lampson marched his men into Abdin to order Farouk to change the Prime Minister. We watched Farouk from up here every day, because we were going to kill him one Friday as he went to Mosque, since that seemed to be a merciful enough end for such a Godless man. From up here we could have dropped a dozen bombs right on him, you see. That's much cleverer than a machine-gun.'

The drop was direct over a narrow corner of the main street of what was now Republic Street.

'One morning,' Hakim said, 'I was sitting up here watching with my friends to see who came and went, timing all the King's exits and entrances ready to drop the bomb on his car. Then, in the afternoon of the very same day, as a soldier, I was actually sent to the King, into the palace, with the Army codes. You can imagine how my own friends must have laughed to see the conspirator going into the palace itself, where I could have shot the King if it had not been senseless to do so without certainty of success. I learned a great deal, my dear, sitting up here on these roofs and watching the men come and go through the palace gates, and the women too, and sometimes the men we trusted as well as those we hated. I could sit here and learn the lesson of the government of our country by that ugly building, by that one man, by all those men; and instead of government and power being such unobtainable and mysterious and unknown things, they suddenly became very simple things to me. Simply men! A group of men; a gathering of men; one man. You see? In that one place they came and went. I gained more heart for our revolution sitting up here watching that sink of corruption down there, filing by, than I ever did from conspiring to kill the King. It's true, my dear. It was up here that I learned that the power is still simply flesh, and the men of it were comparatively few, while down there on the streets the people very many. And when I went back to my duties at the barracks, the soldiers were also plentiful and disciplined and removed from the King and the corrupters. What an idea! They were nearer to us, I realized, and nearer to our hopes than anyone else, if only they could be properly directed. That was the understanding I reached up here. The King was only one man, and he didn't matter. In a revolution it was the Army that would matter even more than the King, and also more than the hungry, undisciplined mob.'

'Did Gamal ever sit up here?' Scott asked.

'Never. He didn't have to. He knew what we knew by being born to it. My own family was well off. Gamal's were always poor and he was poor.

215

I learned by observation and hatred. Gamal learned by the life he had led which has never left him. But he knew it would have to be the Army too, because he knew that the rest of our people were too vast and undisciplined to do what had to be done.'

There was nothing left of Hakim's joke.

'Now other men watch, other men plot. But what are their motives, my friend?' Hakim asked. 'Are they doing it for their own hopes and ambitions? Or for someone else who would gain by seeing Gamal dead and bloody in the street—the whole life he has given us smashed into confusion? Who gains by our confusion? That is the question.'

Scott watched the palace gates close. The Republican guards were the old Royal guards, but instead of the fez they now wore purple berets; instead of the crown their penants were embossed with the Republican eagle.

'Who *does* gain?' Scott said. 'What possible good does it do anyone to murder Gamal and create confusion? I know that you mean the British. You usually do. But surely it's too late for the British, Hakim, and they must know it. Aren't you getting the British Army out of the Canal zone peacefully enough? In a few weeks the last British soldier will leave Egypt for ever . . .'

Hakim found his sense of humour again.

'You can only think with English logic,' he said, 'because you're a logical Englishman. I think with Egyptian logic. I ask, who will gain by Gamal's death? There is only one answer: why, the very corrupters and foreign rulers Gamal threw out. Who else? Of course the Jews also. That's the only logic worth considering. I live by it, my friend. I must know my enemies, *all* of them.'

'You really think the British sit up here on these rooftops the way you did?'

'No. They send other men up on these rooftops. Stupid, evil and perhaps partly innocent men.'

'If it's not the innocents you're worrying about,' Scott told him, 'you ought at least to spare them, and find the guilty ones.'

'First, we must find the guilty ones,' Hakim answered, and the like and dislike of their friendship and their enmity had settled down again to the humour that Hakim spread on everything like a fertile top-soil over such barren ground. 'Have you ever been into Abdin?' he asked Scott. 'I mean the Royal part of it where the museum is?'

'No,' Scott said. 'I saw Kubbeh Palace and that was quite enough.'

'Kubbeh was too big a monument to appreciate. There, Farouk might as well have been Nero, it seemed unbelievable. Abdin is more intimate. If you want to know Farouk, you must see Abdin. Come along and we will look.'

216

'It will be closed, it's lunch-time.'

'Then we will open it,' Hakim said, wagging his stick a little.

They went down again, this time through the sad squalor and dirt of the building they stood on, where native children sat on the wooden landings and Scott wondered how they did not fall off into the abyss below.

'You can see also,' Hakim told him, 'how we climbed up through this misery to reach our roof. It became heaven up there, particularly at night. We learned our best lessons, we hardened our hearts on the way up to heaven.' He laughed, and they walked across the main road to the main gate of Abdin, the Royal Gate, where the Royal guard were now museum-minders. Hakim told one of them to go ahead and see that the main door of the palace was open so that they could get into it.

'I've been here many times,' he said. 'I don't ever like to forget what we've won. It reminds me of what remains to be destroyed.'

'You always know what to destroy,' Scott told him slyly.

'So I did. So I do,' Hakim admitted.

The palace was the palace of any King gone out of business. The carpets were thick, the furniture was French, the receiving room was red, and the corridors were long. The intimate apartments were like any old and rich French villa with the occupants gone off for the winter somewhere. It was old-fashioned, it was sadly like something to let, and Scott knew what Hakim meant about the power being only a man after all when they went into the bathroom and saw the Macleans tooth-powder in the stuffed medicine chest, and out on the verandah the dove perches strung up under the eaves where a boy King had had them erected because he had been passionately interested in the homing variety. They were still at home up there messing on the verandah, which disgusted Hakim—not for the filth, he said, but because he remembered the pudgy young boy coming home from his school in England, a King, even though an Albanian or a Turk, but a boy King, and only a little older than Hakim had been himself. In those days, Farouk had shown a great deal of hope in his dark eyes and in his fat little hands. But how soon the boy had become the man, and how soon the man became an obese ruler whom one could not love but only despise. The King's swimming-pool was empty, it was now a public pool and a night club; but even that seemed a healthy reflection of a younger man, not the man who had eaten himself out of ordinary manhood into . . .

Hakim used a word that was unpleasant to hear.

'It's not palatial,' Scott said, 'it's not even luxurious.'

'That's why it's so sad,' Hakim said. 'It should have been a simple thing for a King to live here, in the middle of his city. The mistake Farouk

217

made was at heart only one thing: self-indulgence. If he had ever disciplined his appetite he might have served us well. We did not hate him at first, we only hated his corruption. Just as we don't hate the British, we only hate their interference.'

Scott knew a hard joke when he heard one. 'You have to hate the British,' he said to Hakim. 'They're the one sure enemy you have.'

'I suppose so,' Hakim agreed. 'The trouble is, the British never give me any reasons to love them. Now if they would only . . .'

Hakim was looking up at the roof across the square and he pointed now with his leather stick to the view he once had of everyone that went in and out of this Royal Gate.

Such an education for a revolutionary. Scott looked appreciatively at Hakim and felt as Hakim had once felt: power was nothing more than men after all. Here was the conspirator standing in the palace grounds of the very power he had conspired against. Hakim had come down from the rooftops. And he was no more than a man, just as Farouk had been. It was true. It took away the awe and any of the mysterious unknowability of all rulers and governments. They were only men.

But in Hakim's case and in Scott's it created another puzzle, a private one. Hakim might be right. If someone were trying to shoot Gamal, everything ought to be done to prevent it, no matter who was doing it. Zareef and Sam meant nothing when you considered the forces at work plotting here now from the city roofs to the palace gates.

The forces were tremendous. The power in them was awesome after all. It must mean more than Hakim or Sam or Zareef, probably much more even than Gamal himself. But where did it begin and end, that idea of it, when the innocent men who might be involved were the men you also believed in? Did you ever abandon an innocent man simply because the weight of the world was against him?

But Scott knew he would never abandon Sam. He could not.

'It's lunch-time,' Hakim was saying pleasantly, 'and if you like, *habibi*, I'll drive you home. I'd hate to keep you from your lunch.'

218

IF you had betrayed something yourself, it was often too easy to believe afterwards that all life was betrayal and cheating.

That was part of the ordinary pathogenic process of the conscience. But Scott was not sure yet that he had really betrayed Françoise. He defended himself bitterly against the thought. He fed Felu her breakfast crumbs and he asked himself how he could have betrayed her, when she had never promised him a thing. She would not even fix any part of her life to meet his, even half-way. She would not promise, and therefore he was held to no promise.

'Nevertheless, you've cheated!'

He had to accuse himself, but it was tempting to go back a long way and decide that any wrong he had committed could be resolved by declaring the whole bloody business of life to be nothing but cruelty and cheating anyway. Who were you to avoid the inevitable deceptions?

'You can arrange a little self-justification on that idea,' he warned himself, 'but not much; because whatever you say, a man's mistakes are his own. Nobody else's.'

He had tried to avoid it, but the moral weight would not shift, and he swore to himself he would not betray Françoise again.

'Aren't you going away today?' Madame Salz asked him at breakfast.

'No. Friday,' he told her.

Friday he would go back to the Red Sea. Today he would go to see Church. That seemed to be the only way. Never mind Peter Dukes, never mind Hakim even; somewhere in all this it must be Church who mattered most.

'I don't know that I'm surprised to see you,' Church told him, sitting in his office in the Immobilia building where the International Archaeological Society's headquarters looked like a tourist agency. It showed counters and folders and a clerk outside, but deep inside and behind the glass partition Church sat with his wire baskets. He stared at Scott with an old burden of seniority, over half-mooned spectacles.

'Leave us, will you, Mrs. Jobert?'

Mrs. Jobert left promptly with her notebook, and Scott remembered that generals always took their generalship with them, everywhere. Why? Because the wars they fought were never over. That was Pickering's thought: 'You should kill off all generals promptly the moment peace is declared, because the war stops but the generals don't. They'll reminisce in print. They'll fight it twice over again. And most likely they'll start another war with someone else to prove they were right in the first place. All generals ought to be shot the day the war ends,' he had suggested, only a few days before Church's blunder had murdered him instead.

'Nevertheless, I am quite surprised to find myself here,' Scott told Church rather stiffly, as a warning that this might not be pleasant. It seemed fair at least to warn him that he was not going to be friendly.

'Are you, really? But you're here, that's the important thing. Would you like a coffee? I was about to have one myself.'

'All right,' Scott relented. 'Thank you, I will.'

'Give me your hat.'

Scott had brought along his large-brimmed hat for protection, and he gripped it firmly in his lap. But Church took it away from him and walked around his desk to hang it on a hat-stand behind Scott.

'I don't suppose you recognize it, do you?' Church asked.

'What's that?'

'The hat-stand. It's the one we brought out of Fort Capuzzo in that first push we gave the Italians. Years ago I gave it to the Turf Club as a memento, when I left Egypt. Someone recovered it from the ruins of the old Turf Club when the Cairo mob burned it down a few years ago. I found it in their new place in the Shell building, so I jolly well borrowed it back.'

'You see what I mean?' Pickering would say if he were still alive.

'Achmed,' Church called to the servant. '*Etneen cafe. Sada?*' he asked Scott.

'No, I'll have it sweet.'

'*Sukar ziyada*, Achmed,' Church instructed over the partition. 'Now. Are you well? You look very well indeed. This remote life of yours must suit you. I understand you went on mapping all the eastern regions for the Egyptians, is that right? I must say that all our own maps of that sector are hopelessly inaccurate. We had a few expeditions over there in the Sinai looking for early Biblical or Christian remnants, but it's too difficult now because of the strained situation on the Israeli border. I wish they'd all settle down so that we could get on with our searches. Did you follow the discovery of the Dead Sea scrolls?'

220

'I read the American book about them,' Scott told him.

'That's only a beginning. There's another excellent book you ought to read, by an Englishman named Farringdon, called the *Origins of Christianity*. He takes the rational and historical view which is the only one to take. It's a fascinating beginning to this business of finding out where all the actual social function of our moral system began. It's extraordinary, when you think of it: the social system itself has changed over the years, is even dead, but not the moral system it gave birth to. It hasn't changed substantially, that is. It's such an anomaly, really, that it's worth a study in itself, don't you think?'

But Scott had come to ask the General as simply as he could to give up whatever he was doing which might make Sam's predicament even worse, and Zareef's also. It was the only way—to persuade him to stop it, to let Sam get out of this mess at least, since the heart of the trouble must be the cause of it also; and didn't it begin somewhere with Church? Wasn't that obvious? If Church went on with his schemes, whatever they were, it would be Sam who was hanged for them.

'You would be an ideal man for us,' Church was saying crisply now. 'I told Peacock so. We have the clues and the experts, but you know the country and how to survive in it. If we ever set up a Sinai Archaeological expedition again, if things quieten down, I hope we can approach you about it.'

'Do you mean that you told Peacock you wanted to see me?' Scott asked him incredulously.

'Yes, I did. And I'm very glad he persuaded you to come.'

'But he didn't persuade me, General. I assure you I came for my own reasons.'

'That's even better then.'

Achmed brought the coffee and Church took off his glasses and rubbed his blue eyes, and Scott realized that Church had also talked through it in embarrassment. Church was not happy at all. He was in difficulty, just as Scott himself was finding it hard to make this easy. Did Church really have so much interest and conviction in all that archaeological talk?

'What did you want to see me about?' Scott asked him. 'The Sinai?'

'No. No. That's part of the future, perhaps. Frankly, I wanted to see you for more personal reasons. You don't smoke, do you?' He pushed a box of cigarettes towards Scott.

'No, thanks.'

'I remember that. Neither do I. I suppose that's what keeps us both looking so healthy. It's a wretched habit. I'm sure these stories of cancer are absolutely true.' The General could not continue without getting up, and he sat on the corner of his desk, aligning the crease of his spotless gabardine trousers so that they had no more character of their own in them.

'What *can* I say to you, Scott,' he said appealingly, 'talking to you as a man who never had any but your own interests at heart? You know that, don't you? I never did consider anything but the real duty behind our actions, and the values we both were trying to serve. Do you understand me that far?'

Scott knew the past too well, and he had not come here to have it talked about like this. Church ought to know that. Yet he let it settle, as if in front of Church he were determined to show no reluctance of any kind concerning the past which lay between them.

'I think I follow you,' Scott said. 'It wasn't ever your motives I quarrelled with,' he added calmly.

'That gives me courage, then. You see, I too have reviewed quite often the campaigns from the very beginning of '39 right up until Alamein, and I have even made something of a study of the possibilities we missed, mainly to see where we went wrong. Yes, we did go terribly wrong, I know that quite well. I went wrong as much as any man. But one of the incidental things that always keeps coming back to me—when I wonder at our failure to go on with the early Wavell ideas of daring deception— one of the tragedies to me has been to realize how much we lost of a brilliant soldier, in that line, when you turned down the offer we made you . . .'

'This is old history, General. You've said it all before, and I didn't . . .'

'Yes, I know I've said it, but not as forcefully as I feel like saying it now.'

'I think it's better forgotten,' Scott insisted. 'I didn't come to talk about that.'

'Perhaps you didn't, but I have always wanted to tell you what I felt.'

The General had the freedom of movement. He got up restlessly again and leaned against the window, and Scott sat still, watching the old seniority working on him. He felt it succeeding. The soldier was always the soldier. And whatever contempt he had felt for Church, the General remained the General, even this one whom he had once called a bloody butcher to his face for slaughtering Pickering and 'Moses' Brodie and the rest, and on whom he had broken most of his own life.

'Is it true,' Church asked him, 'that you've given up your Egyptian Frontier Department job? Peacock thought you had.'

'He's quite wrong,' Scott replied. 'I'm on a few weeks' leave.'

'What a pity. I'd thought you'd finished with all that.'

'What do you mean, finished with all that? With all what?'

'I don't know. I just don't know. Everything you do seems to turn to trouble and bad luck for you, Scott. I thought it was time you had better luck. I thought you might like to come and work for us, as I have said . . .'

'For whom? Who is us, General?' Scott asked in surprise.

'Why! This society.'

'Archaeology?'

'Of course. I suppose it does seem odd to find a retired General running archaeological field expeditions and tours, but it's purely organizational on my part. I'm not an expert, I'm an enthusiast. That carries me a long way. But I'm getting too old and too occupied with other details to go bouncing across the deserts in rickety buses and finding ways and means of getting our experts into inaccessible places. But you're the ideal fellow for that sort of thing. Would you consider it? That is, if you can pry yourself loose from your Egyptian commitments.'

'You already have a wrong notion of my Egyptian commitments,' Scott told him, trying to get away from this investigation of himself, but failing to because there was an older argument in it which had never been finished between them.

Church's precision sharpened a little. 'I don't think I am misunderstanding your problem,' he said firmly. 'I know that you couldn't get work with the British oil companies after the war, because of your court-martial. If I had known that at the time I would have written them myself and told them you were court-martialled for military disobedience and stubbornness and not for inefficiency. I suppose you had no choice but to go to the Egyptians. Isn't that so?'

'Partly so,' Scott admitted.

'I think you've paid your price, then. I was rather worried when I suddenly saw you that day at the *mons claudianus* ruins. I thought then—how sad it is when Englishmen serve rival interests. But I've had time to think of it, and I realized after a few inquiries that you had very little choice. So I thought—in view of old feelings, Scott, and your bad luck, that someone ought to give you the better choice. However, you must have your own ideas about that.'

'You mean about the choice of working for you?' Scott asked, wondering why he prolonged it. It was not only ridiculous, it was an ironic and bad joke.

'You wouldn't be working for me exactly,' Church said seriously. 'But you'd be working for an organization that does not throw you into perpetual conflict with your own background.'

'Thank you,' Scott said more cynically. 'But what *I* am already wondering is—what it really means. You may be an archaeological specialist now, General, but is that all it is? Is that really all?'

'My offer to you is absolutely genuine, with nothing hidden in it. I admit that I'd prefer to have you with us, rather than with these Egyptian officers. My conscience dictates that much.'

223

'Your conscience,' Scott said loudly and grimly, 'has nothing to do with me being here.'

'Don't be like that. Don't lose your temper, I beg you, Scott. Not here . . .'

'I'm not losing my temper. And if you want to talk of it somewhere else, then by all means . . .'

Church dropped his voice. 'No, no. You can say anything you wish here. I simply dislike shouting.'

'Then let us not shout,' Scott agreed, resting on the immobility he had learned in years of silence and sometimes in years of loneliness. He felt them in his gorge, because Church could not feel them, and because Church believed in what he was saying. That was what did the damage.

'I simply feel that you are misguided about your Egyptian friends. They may be honest men, but it is wrong when soldiers take over governments by force, breaking up the ordinary rule of law . . .'

'You are quite wrong,' Scott told him. 'There was no rule and no law in Egypt. This country under Farouk was ruled by corruption and cruelty.'

'Then there were other means of ending the evil. Soldiers should obey, Scott; they should not interfere in Government, I don't care what the reasons. But if it worries you so much . . .'

'It doesn't worry me at all,' Scott insisted. 'But let me say, General, that I may also have been wrong in the past. I too can admit that. I *was* wrong! The need in a war to keep one line of action clear forces a certain amount of blind mistake. I accept that. But there is no war now. That is why I can't accept anything you are doing out here.'

'Steady, lad. What can't you accept?'

'I came to ask you, General, to give up whatever you are doing so that it doesn't all fall dangerously on people like Sam Hassoon. I can accept that you have to go on being a soldier, but it is a terribly cruel business to drag in people like Sam, and others you probably don't even know about, because they're going to get the worst of it.'

'Hassoon? The Greek?'

'The Jew, General. Hassoon the Jew.'

'But what have I got to do with him?'

'Hassoon has been arrested by the Egyptians.'

'I know that.'

'They believe he's involved in some sort of a plot against Nasser . . .'

'Well, then?'

'Whatever you are doing here, I would say you ought to give it up as a failure, and a cruel mistake which will only fall on people like Sam.'

'Ought to give what up? What are you referring to?'

They faced each other gently and calmly over the truth they longed to tell each other and could not. Yet they almost had, so that the ferocity sighed away almost audibly in their calm English voices.

'What exactly are you asking me to abandon?' Church asked.

'I don't know,' Scott told him, 'and I don't think I want to know. I am simply trying to save Sam Hassoon from the results of it, because they'll hang Sam if . . .'

'Aren't you assuming a little too much?'

'I don't think so.'

'Is it Hassoon you are worried about, or some plot you imagine is afoot against Nasser? Really!'

That was what Lucy had said, but he didn't care about that now.

'Both. They are both my friends,' he said recklessly.

'And what about your own countrymen? Don't you feel any sense of duty or friendship towards them?'

'We all see our duty and our friendship differently, General. I'm not going to argue about that.'

'I suppose we do, and I'll be honest with you, Scott. A soldier's duty is never done. My duty will never be finished until I'm dead. I don't expect you to be impressed by that, because you don't understand what it means. That was always your trouble. I can't blame you, I can only regret it. But whatever my duty brings me to do here, I swear it does not involve your friend Hassoon. That much I think I owe you, but no more. Do you believe me?'

The old passion against Church had gone too easily. Perhaps it had gone long ago without him ever realizing it before. He only knew it was not there now. The disbelief in Church, which might have come quickly when he was younger and angrier, simply did not rise in his eyes; and though he tried to stir it up again, he knew in the limpness of his nerves and in his sense of failure here that Church was telling the truth. He waited a moment longer for a denial from his own heart, but it would not come, and he finally had to admit it.

'Yes. If you put it so positively I must believe you.'

He was already standing up to leave.

'Then please don't go,' Church said. 'Sit down. Can't we discuss this other plan, which I'm sure will help you in the long run?'

'I only came to see you,' Scott said stubbornly, 'to ask you about Sam Hassoon. If you can't help me there, then I'd better go. But I don't think you are here quite so innocently as you imply, General, and I think I owe it to *you* to say that.'

'Perhaps not,' Church said, 'but if you are going to worry about my presence in Egypt, do you think it wise of me to allow you to go on being here yourself?'

Scott smiled faintly. 'Can you throw me out of Egypt?'

'No, but there are other ways. If you oppose me, I must oppose you.'

'That's all right,' Scott said with more determination than he really felt about it. 'You can't damage me any more than you have already, General.'

'I'm sorry you think that way, Scott.'

'So am I, General,' Scott agreed, leaving. 'So am I.'

CHAPTER THIRTY-TWO

WHEN Fahid heard of Zareef's suspension (Zareef had stayed at home with his six children and his wife from the villages whom no one had ever seen) he was beginning the first flight he would ever make with his 'A' licence held in his hand, with no one there to pity him for his bad landings and no one to watch with any affection at all, even for the aeroplane in the air regardless of who was flying it.

'They wouldn't pass Zareef's medical,' Barmeel told him. 'Captain Zareef still has a rupture.'

Zareef had ruptured himself a long time ago shouting into the voice-tubes of Tiger Moths to students who had to be instructed half in Arabic and half in technical English they didn't always understand.

'Who said it was his rupture?' Fahid asked. 'You?'

'No. Captain Selim.'

'What does the Haboob know? Or you . . .'

'Don't you think it's the medical, Fahid? Don't you believe it?'

'It's horse-shit.'

Fahid took off without the good wishes of the control tower—those irritable men with Very pistols and telephones who could not believe he had finally been cleared or that he had come back safely from a cross-country test or that he had finally satisfied the engineers that he knew the fuel system backwards, or that he had even satisfied the control officers themselves that the rules and restraints of air navigation were worth studying, if worth obeying. They could not find an excuse to stop him. The slip was signed for local flying. The students lined up to give him a mocking cheer as he thumbed his nose at them from the Autocrat, rocking it around in a dangerous down-wind turn and taxiing it too fast for safety.

'That's the last of our dear friend Fahid,' the successful Lebanese sighed. 'When he gets off the ground he'll simply disappear. We'll never hear of him again.'

'That's what you think. He'll come back in an hour asking to fly the Gemini, now that Zareef's out of action.'

The sad thought of Zareef spoiled their fun, but when the wheels of Fahid's Autocrat bounced too long on the stubble they recovered and groaned happily.

'He'll hit the ditch.'

'No, no. He's holding it down. Watch him.'

Fahid knew the value of their cynical interest. He held the plane too long on the ground and then just skimmed the grass; and when the air speed was just over eighty he lifted the nose up quickly in a forbidden and lurching steep climb so that the plane hung on the top of it with a frightening pause. There, in terror, he opened the throttle and levelled out in safe flight with too much engine.

'If Zareef had seen that one,' he said, shivering with a cold recovery of fear and hatred of the plane this time, 'he'd ground me for a month. Oh, my God, I wish he would.'

If Captain Haboob Selim grounded him for it he'd insult the Haboob with a few long-needed truths. What had he done to put Zareef out of action? Let the Haboob answer that.

He looked down sadly on Zareef's world of the yellow Shell wagons and the met cage with its brown copper rain-trap. The train to Aswan wiggled along the track under the smoke of the single sugar-beet factory in the fields, and below on the beginnings of the dry stubble the round hangars hunched down suspiciously over their cement edges. By raising his eyes he could see the desert, and he could feel what he saw: the smell of aeroplanes in the heat, the tick of them, the cough of hot engines. An Auster taxiing below was like a man puffing and running, out of breath. He was hot. He saw the dust rise, as always, behind the propeller wash of the Auster. One never saw the dust settle, but it did settle—imperceptibly.

Zareef's world, there on the ground, had begun before the war at Almaza, when the British R.A.F. had been flying Hawker Harts and Gladiators from the far side of the old pebbled airfield. The British had given one corner of Almaza to the Cairo Flying School, which an R.A.F. officer instructed in Gypsy Moths and Hornets when they started in the cool atmosphere over the desert before 8 o'clock in the morning, testing and holding the still air without the slightest tilt of a wing. By ten o'clock the flying would be hot and bumpy.

Zareef had never doubted an aeroplane in his life. The only men who had ever counted in his life were the men who made flying possible, those who took it seriously and who served it well and did not vulgarize it, those who taught it truthfully without frills and pretences. That made a man a good pilot. Before the war it had been the English who instructed like that.

Zareef was lying on his old bed now, looking at the ceiling of his father's

228

house (where he had come for refuge from his catastrophe), wondering if it had been better before the war, when the distractions in Egypt under the British were unimportant and each day nearly perfect, although— being a good and strict Moslem and needing to be a good Egyptian—it was not always easy to like the Englishmen you admired as pilots.

'Ali,' his father said outside the door, shuffling by in his turned-up slippers. 'What's the matter? Why are you lying in there?'

'*Mafeesh kef*,' Zareef said. No gusto!

'Shall I come in?'

'No. I'll be all right, father.'

His father shuffled away and Zareef also remembered the very good Egyptian pilots before the war: Captain Aziz the best of them all. Aziz had opened up the Cairo Airlines for Egyptian pilots with old DH Rapides which he never crashed, never force-landed, and never minded sharing with the students from the other corner of Almaza who might have been laughed at, in a country like Egypt where men laughed easily at each other. Captain Louca, Captain Hafiz el Alfi, Captain Mourad, Captain Latif the navigator, who now sat in the C.A.A. office and had taken away Zareef's licence with tears in his eyes. Latif had become the best navigator in Egypt, but once (strangely enough) he had also been the worst pilot.

It was sometimes possible to remember the bad ones, even though they did not count. A bad pilot could not help it, that was all. A man must be a man to be good at it, and the bad pilots simply lacked something. Lacked what? The young men now at Gedida lacked it because they had no conviction in it. There was something wrong with them. If they did have conviction it was nervous and dangerous, like Fahid Rahman's. In 1940 Zareef had not felt like that. He had grown a beard in loyalty to Farouk. He had taken his commercial licence with the highest marks under Captain Aziz and he had flown the Alexandria service with Mahmood, a rich man's son.

The flying school then had also been a club for rich younger sons. Some of them were good pilots and some were not. Mahmood was not. Mahmood had been an instructor until he had tried to give a nervous student confidence by waving his spare control stick in the air from the front seat of a Gypsy as his nervous student was landing. The boy had frozen on the controls, and by the time Mahmood had pushed his stick back into its socket they had stalled thirty feet off the ground and smashed the under-carriage, the tail and the propeller. Mahmood had been sent to the airlines as punishment; and the day they had flown a Rapide to Alexandria in a dust-storm, a khamsin—with Zareef as second pilot—Mahmood had said he hated all khamsins. In anger he had lost his bearings, and not being a genuine pilot he had lost his grip on himself as a man. He had forced-landed the plane-load of passengers near Ras el Tin on the desert, over Zareef's agonized protests. Mahmood had escaped his second punishment by giving up in disgust and going back to his father's large property; but Zareef could not give up in disgust. He had been forced to bear the mark of Mahmood's shame ever since. They had to punish someone, so they had punished Zareef. He had been sent back to the school as a junior instructor. That was in 1944, as long ago as that.

'But don't you know that you're the best instructor in the world?' Fahid the uncrushable son of Maître Rahman would tell him in 1956, twelve years afterwards.

What would the ceiling of his merchant father's house do with that statement? He had often been lying here as a boy dreaming. But what could he say to that now, except that a good pilot could not help being a good instructor? A half-mad and very nervous young man like Fahid would not understand that about flying, because he did not understand the ease he could get out of it if he would only trust it and trust himself. A pilot must trust the thing he was doing. Even so, it was this same young fool Fahid Rahman who knew all his secrets. He could feel the boy's eyes sucking out the truths he hardly knew himself, then tossing them back carelessly with his mocking tricks; revelations to Zareef himself.

'Why should you be an airline pilot?' Fahid had teased. 'You, Captain Ali! What a waste. They're stupid men, quite ordinary men.'

Zareef did not think so. If a man was good enough, he ought to fly the largest planes the longest distances. Beneath, twenty thousand feet below, the seas and the coastlines and green fuzz of forest should be an unfolding right-of-way for pilots: all pilots. That was the view of all views, the right use of space. The pilot ought to have it as a universal right.

'Why should you want to go back to Cairo Airlines, simply because they now have British Viscounts and fly all over the place in turbo-jets?' Fahid had said when they had watched the new Viscount coming down over the edges of Cairo International Airport. Zareef had gone there, specially, to see it arriving. Who had he taken with him, without knowing why, but this mockery in Fahid's strange eyes? 'You would become another ignorant airline captain. No imagination needed. Just another Captain Ali, with the earphones on his ears.'

How could you hide things from a boy like that? Why become an airline pilot?

He could look down, lying on his bed now, at his girth—rounded like a barrel and happy. *Ayee!* the kitchen was a menace. But there were rounder and fatter pilots than he was, and that was not the reason. He could remember the face of every man he had instructed, although not long after Mahmood's catastrophe in '44 he had abandoned the flying school in disgust for the air force. But he had soon escaped that disciplined routine to buy a Fairchild with money from his father and almost achieved it —perfect flying. But he had flown newspapers and fish. Fish!

The rest was better forgotten.

The last days of Farouk had ruined flying in Egypt: no school, no pupils, and for himself no parts for the Fairchild from America. He had not flown at all, only spent the time trying to fly in any way he could, even instructing, until Gamal Abd el Nasser had come to power and taken over the airlines and subsidized the school and given them planes and pilots, even if Captain Selim was the chief instructor.

'Captain Haboob is even more frightened than I am,' the boy had said.

'Don't say that to me,' he had reprimanded Fahid. 'Don't ever say it to me.'

Yet, despite Selim's hooded cunning, and despite the desire to go to the airlines, despite the knowledge that it was too late now to fly Viscounts, and that he would never fly a jet (it was incredible to think that there were actually planes he would never fly: how could life be so short and so singular and so finite?)—despite the unhappiness of not being the chief instructor, they had been the happiest and the best flying days he had ever known, despite even the Gemini.

'You don't really hate this stupid Gemini, you love it,' Fahid had said when he had come back from the Red Sea, air-sick from the hot bumps and glad to be down on the ground in Zareef's car going home. 'Do you know why, Captain Ali? Because only you are sentimental enough to fly it like that. Do you think the Haboob would land it where you do, or get it off again without hitting the sides of the wadis? You *like* doing it in that flying donkey-cart. You love it, by God, you do.'

It was true.

When Sam Hassoon had become his wireless operator and they had set up the Red Sea patrols with Scott, he had enjoyed all the sensations of perfect flying, which he had always felt himself deprived of.

'Let me know if you're ever sick, Ali,' Sam had said. 'Ring me up, for God's sake, because I intend to be ill that day myself. No Ali Zareef, no flying for Sam Hassoon.'

Sam was a frightened man, he hated aeroplanes. But he would go anywhere at all in an aeroplane if Zareef asked him to: to the sand sea, to Kuwait, across Arabia Deserta, or even over the sea where there were no landmarks or visual flight rules to help. Sam was frightened, but he would trust Zareef with it, absolutely and without fear. Sam was the passenger of all the world's passengers, because he gave the pilot the trust and confidence the pilot deserved.

With Scott, what a trio they made. *What* a trio! What a flying trio when Scott gave him—deliberately—the most difficult flying, near enough

231

to the impossible when you had to land downhill on a sand slope and take off again downhill on the same slope inclined twenty degrees.

'What about that corner of the slag-heap, Ali?' Scott would shout.

What was there? What did it matter what was there. If Scott wanted to land there it was not going to be a Bedu trap to murder them. Scott gave him dangerous landings and take-offs, and Sam had no fear at all—a frightened man with no fear. They were the two men who had made it happy and worthwhile. It was, after all, the fulfilment of a lifetime of flying: a salvation from the anguish and frustration of never flying the far distances, never navigating in the old style like J. P. Mermoz, and never knowing how it would be when the cockpit of a jet became a most beautiful and precise instrument in itself. He would never know it, but he had known this other kind with Scott and Sam. He was satisfied to have lived when flying was still a man's work, and not the pure science of calculating machines and self-deciding instruments.

'Are you ill, Ali?' his wife called through the door.

'No, *el humdulillah*!'

'It's dinner-time and your father is waiting.'

'Are the children washed, or must we wait half an hour for them too?'

'No. They are waiting.'

'All right. I'm coming . . .'

A wife could spoil a dream you dreamt; but what was the dream? It had come to an end when they took Sam away. That was the truth. He was no good without the man who trusted him. But why should they stop him flying because of Sam Hassoon?

It didn't matter.

Did Sam really want to kill Nasser? He thought not and hoped not; and he decided it was very necessary to trust Sam, because he knew quite well that their idea of Sam was completely wrong. If only he could tell them so.

But Zareef had already been arrested and sent to Abu Za'bal, the criminal prison, by the time Scott went to his merchant father's house in Gezira. The old man, who was not so old but was breathless with over-eating and a tight kuftan, was weeping when he took Scott by the hand into his son's room to show, to prove, that they had taken him away. He wept and cursed them.

'What could he do? He didn't steal money. What money? Ali doesn't touch money. He's a pilot, always up in the air. What can he steal up there? When does he ever see money to steal? And even if he didn't steal money, what did he steal? Are you his friend? If you are, you ought to know that. Why do they shame him and me? Ah, it's a stupid mistake and I told them so, but if you're a friend of my innocent son's why don't you tell them, curse them? He is innocent.' He wept helplessly.

232

Scott found the right answer coming too quickly and repetitively to his mind: the obvious answer to all questions of guilt and innocence.

'If Ali is innocent, someone must be guilty. But who? If it's not Sam and Ali Zareef, then who *is* it?'

But old men like this were not consolable with the world's riddles. He did not see Zareef's wife who was still sick with shock, but he heard the children playing in the garden counting black men on their toes.

'Of course Ali didn't steal,' Scott said. 'Everybody knows that, *ya effendim.*'

'What is it, then?'

'Wala haga!' he consoled. 'Nothing! A mistake. It will be all right. Don't worry, *ya sidi.* Ali is in no danger. He is innocent.'

'Then send him home,' the sidi moaned. 'I beg you.'

The old man had already confused him with the two polite policemen who had taken Ali away. He held his heart under his kuftan and swore that they'd kill Ali if they kept him in prison. He would not be used to it.

'God will send us the truth,' Scott said, having no other recourse.

But God was forgotten, even as a Moslem provider of the truth, when your son was in gaol, although he ought to be invoked, just in case: and the sidi held Scott's hand in the sadness and misery of his own: plump, affectionate, and anxious to do business with men who would not trick him in the trade—dried mish-mish and sudani from Khartoum and figs from Siwa unpacked and sold loose to the exporters who sent them to Italy and Greece, which it still paid to do, even though the discount rate on foreign exchange under the officer's government was 25 per cent. The Egyptian pound was still stable, God be praised, and the discount rate was still high enough or low enough to encourage the exporters. Business, thank God, was fairly good through the exporters; yet what could bring on this sudden blight, this bolt from heaven? In God's name! What was a man's life coming to when a boy as innocent as Ali was arrested? For what? How could a father help weeping?

'Don't worry. Don't worry!' Scott said, squeezing his hand. 'Please don't worry. We will see that Ali is all right.'

'Curse them!' the old man cried.

'He'll be all right!' Scott repeated and one of the sidi's tears splashed on their joined hands. There was probably a meaning in the native religion to that omen, for a thing like that happening, but he had to say good-bye and go. He could not bear the old man crying.

'Good-bye,' the sidi said. 'But I *curse* them! I curse the day they came. I curse their own mothers . . .'

Scott found the servant waiting to open the shuttered doors to pass him through to the garden under the trees. Three of Zareef's children and probably the neighbour's were making fun of a small boy, almost a baby, who had misbehaved himself.

'Fassia fassengi; 'araba hindi; tsha maha; allazi afsaaha!'

Who was going to laugh at their innocence, when in their innocence their rhyme was so rude to English ears? Scott found himself laughing painfully at it anyway:

'Fart, farter; Indian scorpion; you're the farter!'

He remembered, as a boy, the Sudanese son of the cook, a little younger than he had been, exchanging a tooth with the sun, throwing the lost and rotten tooth at the sun and chanting to *ya shams, ya shamoose*! Thou sun, thou silly sun, take this old tooth and give me a new one. Or, when you had lost something and couldn't find it, you called on *ya iblis, ya addiendi waadeck*! Devil, devil, I will exchange with you a hen for a rooster, if you will only find me what I have lost.

There was a rational point in throwing your tooth at the sun. The sun blinded you, impossible to see where the tooth went to; as far as the thrower was concerned the sun had snatched it away. The devil, however, did not always find what you had lost . . . You could not always persuade him to accept a rooster for a hen. *Ya iblis!* The problem with the devil was to find what you had never ever had in the first place. Find out if you could what made men innocent or guilty. In whose eyes? And for what? Who was to blame, and what was it for?

CHAPTER THIRTY-THREE

'I'D sooner you had not told me,' Quartermain said to Scott when Scott had unburdened himself of every detail without knowing why, except that Quartermain was the only man he was sure was not involved in it.

'Why do you say that?'

Quartermain pulled his son Hilal away from the edge of the footpath, while they walked through the Cairo streets, so that the boy would not run his hand along the car doors and either get cut or pick up a disease of some sort.

Ironically, Quartermain could think, it was his wife Nona who was born and bred here who had not wanted her tender English children to come to Egypt and thus be exposed to the ten thousand local diseases that could kill them. It was he who had said impatiently: 'They've got to be exposed to more than that in their lives. Your first instinct is always fear. You're so bold in everything else. Let them take a chance.' Nona was bold in the face of any man or any tongue that matched hers; but frightened in the face of riots, violence and disease. But to be fair, he knew that her fear was on behalf of everyone in the family itself, and not only for the children.

But now that the children were here, it was he who was afraid they would catch something. Knowing the deadliness of one touch of the fingers, one diseased cup to the lips of a child, he must at least try to reduce their exposure. But it became ridiculous when you looked at the servant Ali preparing the meals in the kitchen. Did he ever wash his hands after going to the toilet? And almost certainly he was one of the 98 per cent of all Egyptians suffering from some kind of dysentery. And what happened to Benjamin at school, at the Lycée? Or to this little moon-face when he played in the dirt in the gardens and then sucked his fingers?

'Don't drag your hand on the cars,' he said irritably to Hilal.

Hilal put his fingers in his mouth to console himself.

'And take your fingers out of your mouth,' his father said.

The result was foregone. When his father pulled his fingers out, the

235

large mouth softened into rose-like putty, the lips broke and the eyes reddened. In a moment it would be a wail.

'All right, darling,' Quartermain said to his son. 'I'm sorry. We'll go into a shop up here and have a lemonade. But only if you behave . . .'

Hilal got his fingers back in his mouth and sucked away all indignation.

'He doesn't look like you,' Scott said.

'No. He's temperamental, like his mother.'

'You mean like his father.'

'I am calm by nature,' Quartermain said goodnaturedly, 'and only temperamental by circumstance. Marriage and children ruin a man's real character.'

'It certainly changed you,' Scott said as Quartermain took them into Groppi's to satisfy the finger-sucker and take away all punishments and irritations from life, in family life, anyway, by buying quick forgiveness.

'I remember bringing Lucy Pickering here once during the war,' Quartermain said over the sfogliatella which he ate dripping through his grey moustache, 'when she tried to persuade me to let you be "discovered" by General Warren. Recognized, I mean. You don't know how near you were to becoming one of the war's greatest and deadest heroes, with Lucy's help.'

'She told me about it.'

'She did?'

'Yes. But as I remember it she said that *you* brought her here and tried to persuade her not to corrupt me, nor snatch me away from Tracks and Survey. Was I that helpless?'

Quartermain thought about it over the poised spoon of ice-cream. He interrupted Hilal's efforts to drink the second bottle of coca-cola out of the bottle direct.

'You were quite helpless,' he said. 'I did try. I admit I did. I wanted to get her out of your way, push her off a cliff if necessary.'

'Do you think you succeeded? Do you think you influenced her or me at all?'

'I'm not sure. I think your friend Gamal persuaded you to see reason where I failed to. Do you know why?'

'No. I've forgotten why.'

'Because you're such an empirical bastard, and you don't know how to think.'

'Ah . . .'

'If you see someone doing the right thing, you can understand it. But I never met a man as reluctant as you are to investigate human behaviour. Why?'

'That's not true at all,' Scott argued lightly.

236

'Isn't it? Let me put it another way. If I—with my knowledge of what Church and Lucy Pickering are and always will be—if I had taken a pistol and blown their brains out in 1942, you would have agreed with me and probably admired me and followed my example. You would have become a simple-minded assassin yourself overnight, simply by seeing an obvious example.'

'That's because I'm a practical man,' Scott said, and held the bottle of coca-cola for Quartermain's son while he sucked at the stuff with a straw from a kneeling position on the chair. Hilal's eyes were on Scott. Scott tried smiling at him, but the large brown eyes dropped in concentration to the business of pumping up short jerks of frothy liquid.

'You'd probably be amazed,' Scott told his father, watching the boy working hard at the liquid, 'if I told you that I once thought the most practical thing to do was to shoot Church.'

'Not at all. In fact, I thought you might do something like that. Why didn't you, anyway?'

'They say Englishmen never shoot Englishmen. It was Tim Peacock who pointed that out to me, I think.'

'That's brilliant,' Quartermain said dryly.

Hilal had finally sucked up the last drop of coca-cola and he put up his eyes to demand a third bottle. His father shook his head sternly. In his sudden indignation Hilal accidentally knocked over Scott's glass, so that the beer ran over the marble table, and Quartermain had it in his lap and over Scott's shirt.

Quartermain slapped down his handkerchief in a show of bad temper.

'That's the sort of thing that begins in my family at 8 o'clock in the morning when they both get into my bed,' Quartermain snarled happily, wiping it with his handkerchief while Scott called the sofragi for a cloth. 'It goes on until 7 o'clock at night. I shan't bring you here again,' he said to his son.

Hilal knew better than to take that statement seriously, and he sat quietly and cunningly, sucking his fingers again, watching the sofragi wipe up the mess and loan Scott a clean towel to dry his khaki shirt with.

'Don't you ever get out of that soldier's uniform?' Quartermain asked him.

'When the laundry allows me to. You can't wear anything else in this country and keep it clean.'

'Are you any relation to the Scott who went to the South Pole, by any chance?' Quartermain asked, removing all bottles from Hilal's area.

'No. Why?'

'You're beginning to look like him. Squat, remote and frustrated. What exactly are you frustrated about, anyway?'

'About everything I've just been telling you. Sam and Zareef, mainly.'

237

Quartermain had heard, but he still did not want to hear.

'What would *you* do about it, Quarts?' Scott asked.

'About what?'

'About this idiocy around Sam.'

'I don't know. You know this country better than I do. Why don't you go to your friend Nasser and tell him that Sam and the pilot are absolutely innocent, and that he ought to set them free?'

'But I can't do it like that.'

'Why not?'

'It's almost the one thing I can't do. You have to have lived in this country to know why. It used to be like that. You could always find someone high enough to interfere, but that's the very thing Nasser has been trying to do away with. I can't go to him and say here are a couple of my friends who are innocent, so let them off. It's not the way it can be done any more, and I can't do it because he wouldn't listen to me, anyway. He'd say he couldn't interfere himself . . .'

'All right, all right. Don't ask him.'

Quartermain was counting up the bill carefully so that he would not be cheated by Messrs. Groppi, who never cheated, so must therefore be trusted even less. Service was compris, the ticket said.

'Do I leave the boy something extra for the mess?' he asked Scott.

'Oh, two piastres,' Scott said impatiently.

Quartermain looked at him quickly over the impatience. Scott saw again the eyes that heard but refused to hear, the sudden cut-out from involvement or astonishment or even indignation at anything Scott could say.

'Merci,' Quartermain said to the sofragi and gave him five piastres.

'That's too much,' Scott told him.

'Never mind. It might remind him of the good old days.'

'Anyway,' Scott said to him on the street with little moon dragging them along the cars again, 'it's not only Sam and Zareef. If someone is trying to put a bullet into Gamal's back, should I just sit and watch it happen?'

'You said Hakim could attend to that.'

'Of course he can. He won't let anything happen to Gamal. But he obviously counts on my help, because he suspects that Church and the others are here for some evil reason. I told you. Hakim more or less expects me to watch them or—to put it crudely—spy on them.'

'Well?'

'Can I do a thing like that?'

'Do you think they're involved?'

'I don't know, and I don't want to know.'

Quartermain shrugged.

238

'You don't seem to be very impressed,' Scott complained.

'With what?'

'With anything I've told you.'

'You think I should be impressed with Church and Lucy Pickering and Peacock doing what they're supposed to be doing? It's an old geometric law. If you can't corrupt a native, treat him as a wild beast. They'll treat Nasser as a wild beast if they have to. Or rather they'll get someone else to get rid of the beast for them, like that chap sitting up on the roofs with his sights on Abdin Palace. All very geometrical and logical . . .'

'You make it sound just too matter-of-fact.'

'It *is* matter of fact.'

'You talk like Hakim.'

'I don't think I like Hakim, he's a bit too machiavellian for me; but this time he's quite right.'

'Then you think I should do what he asks?'

'I can't answer that for you,' Quartermain said, and shrugged it off again and looked at his watch. Old watchmakers carried pocket-watches not wrist-watches, but apart from this sentiment, how lucky you were to have escaped the fates of Clerkenwell where the cemetery of St. Bride's was full of Quartermains, all guildsmen and clock-makers since 1496. He put it away. It was almost midday, the religious hour for the Mamoon family to eat, and he was late.

'Come on,' he said to Hilal. 'Don't drag. Your mother will be waiting out on the street for us.'

'I really came to you for advice,' Scott appealed.

'Me? Why me, Scotty?'

'I can't work it out myself. I'm hopeless at this sort of thing. Plots . . .'

'Hah! I'm not such an expert myself,' Quartermain said quickly.

'I didn't mean that. At least you seem to know what it's all about, which is more than I know. You get involved in politics. It's an everyday thing to you. But it's all confusion to me.'

'Better keep out of it, then.'

'But why? You know I can't, anyway.'

'Haven't you had enough trouble in your life?'

'What about Sam?'

'I'm not thinking of Sam, I'm thinking of you.'

'You don't understand,' Scott said irritably. 'I've been working with Sam and Zareef for a long time. I don't know what Hakim suspects them of, except that it's part of this plot to kill Gamal. Hakim is simply holding them to see what happens. Or he's trying to discover if Sam is tied up with the Israelis. If he ever does find any link, then Sam has had it. If I can just prove to him that Sam has nothing to do with the Israelis or with Church.'

239

'Can you prove it?'

'No, I can't . . .'

'Then that's your answer,' Quartermain told him, calling a taxi to the kerb. 'There's nothing much you can do, is there? Don't you know that once the machinery of plot and counter-plot starts grinding, it takes a brave man to jump into the wheels all by himself in some mad attempt to stop it? I know that much about it. Keep out of it, Scotty, for your own sake.'

'I'm already in it, don't you see?'

'Then heaven help you,' Quartermain said, lifting Hilal into the old taxi. 'Are you coming to dinner tomorrow night or not? First you say you are coming, and then you change your mind.'

'I'm going back to the Red Sea. I can't delay that much longer.'

'When?'

'Tomorrow or the next day. I don't know.'

'We'll have to leave it until you come back, then,' Quartermain said, and left him with a last warning of his self-protecting eyes: *keep me away from it*. In cold blood Quartermain was running away from something he did not want to speak about, and did not want to hear. He was hurrying home because he would be late for dinner, and only then did Scott realize that Quartermain was as much afraid of involvement in this as he was himself.

Fahid thought that something ought to be done about Zareef, but he was up in the air where the laws on flying over anti-aircraft sites were strict and stupid. Wasn't Zareef a perfect example of the stupidity and ignorance of all the people who made laws? Good laws for aeroplanes, bad laws for men.

In any case, he had a friend in charge of the Rod-el-Farag A.A. battery, and a little ground-to-air practice might do them some good. If they wanted to practise on an Israeli, he would serve as one.

Also, if Zareef were worth arresting, he, Fahid, was worth making a fool of them.

It was very simple to dive an Autocrat. All he had to do was to increase the glide a little, and the nose dropped. He cut back the engine and began the glide as the nose dropped lower and lower. Then he suddenly pushed the nose well down towards the sandbagged perimeter of the A.A. battery and kept it there in the roaring vertigo of a dive, until he was too frightened to hold it down any longer.

'Even if it kills me!'

He was deciding to hold this roaring, shuddering path, and he held it until it might have killed him, because he found that the stick was harder to wrench back than he thought. There was little more than ten feet to spare by the time he had wrenched it back and climbed in a vertical and confusing rise, because only the sky was visible and he was afraid of going over in a spin. He pumped the stick forward and opened the engine until the plane staggered and bumped and levelled-out noisily by itself, and he saw the horizon straightening out mercifully from its crazy tilting.

'Once more for Zareef,' he decided savagely, almost in tears because he was shivering and sweating and wanting not to do it against his own terror.

He turned slowly and saw the soldiers standing in the A.A. perimeter looking up at him in delight.

'Go on!' he cried.

In a moment a red Very ball would go up from the airfield telling him to land immediately, because the control-tower officers would see him breaking every law they considered valuable—these good laws for aeroplanes. He would be disqualified for it anyway, so he might as well make it worthwhile for Zareef's sake.

He tried a frightening steep turn. Then he took the plane on into a dive before he had quite finished it. He held the nose down until he felt his cheeks puffing out. Then he pulled out of it suddenly on one wing with a few more feet to spare.

Tears of fear and anger and other emotions he did not understand were running down his cheeks when he came out on top again.

He saw the red ball go up from the airfield near by, and he did not even laugh as he turned around to face their stupid condemnations and their good laws for aeroplanes.

Peter Dukes seemed to know what Scott wanted, but he let the point escape him for a little while. Instead Peter wanted to explain why he always sat in a dark shuttered room in his deserted office, so still and muffled and so inactive that he looked like an old man going sadly out of some sad business. But Scott remembered him ten or twelve years ago, the day when (as a favour to Peacock) Peter had arranged a forbidden visit to Gamal in gaol. During the war Peter was very much in business, but what had happened to him now?

'Would you have a brandy with me?' Peter asked him.

'If you make it a small one.'

'I never bother to wash my cups. Plastic. Are you squeamish?'

'If it's brandy it probably purifies itself.'

Peter smiled, a little dissipated and swollen and ageing and sallow. His face had wrinkled up like a cheese-cake.

'I never work on that sterile theory myself,' Peter argued, 'If the disease is bred in the dirt, then you ought to make a friend of it, get it into your stomach while you're still healthy enough to tolerate it. That's a better theory than the prophylactic, don't you think?'

Peter was not going to pretend.

'Of all people I might like to deceive,' his calm knowing voice and manner were implying, 'I won't bother deceiving you. We are old hands in this, so let's talk like men who know what we are and what it's all about.'

Yet who was this particular Peter Dukes, this man with such self-effacing honesty?

Everybody in Egypt knew that Peter was a British political agent. A long time ago Peter had earned a bad reputation for drinking too much with Collins the wire-cable importer who had died of apoplexy, who had also been a British agent. Neither of them had seemed very interested in politics, and they were always cotton brokers in Alexandria or cable company representatives or whisky salesmen. Peter also had a bad reputation for not paying his debts, and his intellectual standing at the Turf Club was low because, apart from his money-owing, he had chosen the card players and brandy drinkers and horse betters, rather than the local-colour enthusiasts and whisky drinkers and good-talk professionals. His best friend had once been the R.F.C. quartermaster who had opened a bar over the Metropole cinema in 1926, and a lot of the drinking went on there, the best of it in the days before the second war when they had served mezee of chips, olives, anchovies, shrimps, radishes and pickles free with every drink you ordered, and in the late part of the hot afternoons on the balcony under the potted trees and canvas roof you settled down to serious drinking and gambling and well-told stories, and also, when the racing was on, out to Heliopolis for the day if you could stand the heat.

Peter could never survive a day in that heat, so his betting had mostly been done through his friend Hollins, who could stand it, and inevitably a situation had arisen when there was a misunderstanding about how much had been put out on which horse. Hollins and Peter had fallen out so bitterly over it that Hollins had brought a *procès* against him for a written IOU which said that Peter Dukes owed Hollins a thousand pounds. Only the delaying tactics of a clever local lawyer, Maître Rahman—a delay that lasted brilliantly until the closing down of the Tribunaux Mixtes—saved Peter from serious trouble. Hollins had died a rich man with his money invested in local cinemas and no one to leave it to except the People's Dispensary for Sick Animals; which had made Peter pass the savage judgment that Hollins, red-faced and alcoholic and evil, had ended up like the sex-frustrated spinsters who leave their fortunes to homes for stray cats. Peter should have had that money; half of it had been won from him over thirty years of good sport, and the least Hollins could have done was leave him half. But a pique was a pique, whether you had an alcoholic temper or not.

This was all well-known Cairo incident, it was part of this village, part of the pre-war and the few post-war years in Cairo when British life had dragged out sadly to its end. Now, Peter was one of the very few remaining survivors of it, as was Scott also. There were generations and chasms dividing these two, but it was no use either man pretending to be anything but what he was. Scott was a stiff, shy man who had always been rigidly stubborn and professional, the son of a stubborn but ticklish father who had been better company than his son; and Peter was another sort of man, a rascal who knew everybody in Egypt without liking or disliking them, excepting that he had needed some sort of professional knowledge of every friendly politician and of every useful enemy. Yet no one had ever seen him working at his real profession, not even his best friends.

They were not likely to have anything in common now, sitting in Peter's dark room sipping brandy, excepting that they had both lived in Egypt a long time and knew the truth of each other and must therefore behave as the other one thought he should behave. They thus gave each other their respective roles; Scott must be still and shy and difficult, and Peter must be an underhanded rascal.

Yet a wary respect for each other made it easier than that.

'Another?'

'Very little. I start putting on weight if I drink too much alcohol.'

'Good and bad brandy,' Peter said, as if repeating the apologetic explanation of the drunkard to a sober man, 'has kept me going through a damned dark world. It opens up the shutters . . .'

Scott felt again that he was being lightly persuaded of their intimacy—old hands together who ought to come to some arrangement after all these years.

Perhaps Peter was old and lonely without all his cronies at the Turf Club. The Turf Club still existed, but not in its quiet brick mansion with a garden. That one was now a ruin, now a petrol station, and the Club had re-established itself above an oil company which you reached by lift and stayed there once you got there. The luncheon companionship was not the same. The only friends left—those who had not been frightened home by Cairo burning or had not been thrown out of the windows that Black Friday and torn to pieces, those remaining were inclined to be the more intellectual clubists who kept their drinking steady but dull, and compiled small volumes of quaint Arabic sayings and Goha jokes from the fellah, which they printed privately and circulated, with each man's name after each contribution. You sat with them if you had to, and with any visiting politician or general or old curiosity, but that was not the same. The only genuine old hands remaining in Egypt were oddities like Scott, or powdery old school-teachers who flitted around as if they were still schoolgirls, and still occupied themselves with the same mad frivolities. They came occasionally and adventurously to the Club, giggling and wriggling, to collect a contribution to the Y.M.C.A. tea fund for the boys still left on the canal.

'Are you going to stay on in Egypt?' Peter asked him.

'As long as my job lasts,' Scott replied, hating the kind of question and hating the kind of answer.

'When is your contract up?'

'Two more years.'

'You'll be all right,' Peter said. 'If we can get over the next two years in safety you'll be able to stick it out here for ever, if you want to.'

'I wonder,' Scott said. 'What do you think is going to happen?'

'I ought to ask you that,' Peter said. 'You know this crowd better than I do.'

'I meant the British,' Scott said. 'It's very peaceful at the moment. Will it stay that way?'

'That may be the problem—to keep it this way,' Peter said. But he was quickly disinterested, or he had not yet finished confiding and attracting Scott's sympathy.

'Did you know old Gillespie died yesterday?' he said.

'Old Gillespie!' Scott felt an age and a shock reach him, and he knew that they did meet here. Gillespie was a fat old English doctor who had been here for ever, as far back as anyone could remember. 'I didn't know,' he said. 'Gillespie must have been well over eighty, wasn't he? In fact, I'd forgotten he was still alive.'

'Died like a pauper,' Peter said. 'Nobody had cleaned his house for God knows how long. The servants had abandoned him. He must have been rotting in his house for days. I'm glad the Egyptians got there before I did. I'd hate to have seen it.'

Scott felt sick with a loss he knew was not a loss at all, but a shaky bridge for this intimacy Peter was putting over them. Every echo of the old days had its meaning, even the death of a man he had hardly known but who was part of the old life that was quickly disappearing. Another familiar face gone.

'If Gillespie had had his way,' Peter reminisced, 'I'd never have stayed in Egypt more than a month. When I first came out here, even before your father, the sun almost killed me. I went to old Gillespie one day, writhing like a tortured snake. I was crawling around the carpet of his office with an irritation all over my body. Nothing could soothe it, even getting decently drunk, and I was quite often drunk in those days as a result. But I felt as if ten thousand fleas were feeding on me, and old Gillespie looked down at me on his carpet and said: "Ah hah! Eczema, eh? Crapuleuse dose of eczema." He thought it very funny. He told me to go home and sit in a hot magnesium bath until it went away, and then to get the first boat back to England and never for God's sweet sake to come back to any hot country ever again.'

'They always said he was a bit behind the times,' Scott commented.

244

'But he was decent enough. He would always come out in an emergency.'

It was Gillespie who had presided over the death of his own parents.

'He was too far behind the bloody times in my case,' Peter went on. 'I crawled out of his office that day and got into a chemist's shop, and took a sleeping powder. I hadn't slept for three days, writhing and itching on the floor, and the moment I drank the draft in the chemist's shop, right outside the old Continental Hotel, I fell into a drugged sleep in the dark, right in the gutter, and I would have been killed by a gharry if the horse hadn't shied at my luminous wrist-watch, or so they say.'

Scott said 'Ttt!' in sympathy and interest.

Peter held up his white-gloved hands, fingers spread out. 'It still comes back from time to time, when things get bad. It took an Austrian Jew, you remember Sternberger who used to drive himself around to his patients in a gharry, it took Sternberger to tell me that it was a failing of the natural pigment, a mistaken combination of genes, "a logical Nordic mutation" he called it, that somehow accumulated in *me*, so that most of my skin cells were defenceless if exposed to a few hours of bright sun. That's why I have lived like this . . .'

No wonder Peter lived in darkness and no wonder they were suddenly intimate: the darkened room, the sound-proofed voices that confined them so close, the half-seen faces. All Peter Dukes had to do was get any man in here and probably he would spill out the entire secrets of a nation. Yet it wasn't like that at all. Peter still did not look nor behave like the type, and no one saw him at it except when he might pick up the phone and talk to someone here or there, very simply and by-the-way. In the old days that was open sesame, close sesame.

'It hasn't been much of a joke. Even getting across the street to eat my lunch has often been hell,' Peter said grimly, sipping a new supply of brandy in his plastic cup. 'Early morning and late evening is about all I can tolerate, and it gets worse as I get older. So when I say that brandy has let the sun in a little, I mean it literally. But it's not enough these days. Sternberger used to laugh every time he saw me, being a Jew, and he used to say that if nature was any guide the pure Nordic type, the so-called Aryan, ought to stay strictly at home and mind its own business and not go off building empires in hot places, because I was a sort of freak perfection of the type: pale and perfect and useless. One blink of the sun and I would burst out into a painful eruption. He would roar his head off. Not many other people ever knew about it. I don't suppose you did?'

'No. But everybody knew something was wrong with you.'

Peter spat into his handkerchief. 'When I was a young chap I didn't like people to know. I'm not sure why.' He shrugged. 'Nobody likes being too close to a man who is odd in any way. I suppose that's it. Anyway, perhaps Sternberger was right. It will probably take a better pigmented race than

245

we are to stick it out in Africa, in the long run, although you're not such a bad example of Nordic resistance. But you were practically born here. Have some more, just a drop.'

'No, thanks. I've had enough.' Scott put down the dirty plastic glass.

'It's not catchy, don't worry,' Peter said, giving him more anyway.

'I'm not worried,' Scott said with an embarrassed laugh. 'Like you, I've learned to live with the germs.'

'Nevertheless, we're a dying race, you and me.'

They shared the role, anyway. It was as much a part of Scott as it was of Peter, or old Gillespie, or any one of these Englishmen who would soon pass out of Egyptian life altogether. Peter, in ten minutes, had carefully wrecked one picture of himself also. This plotter—this drying stick of a man who was always hiding in his lair, covering his real activities with his roué behaviour and his drinking companionship which had always seemed more like a disguise than the real thing. His thin, sallow face and known reputation were obviously more real than that other dissolute man he pretended to be. But this one, half-way between both, was more difficult to dislike or contest or demand something of, now that the disguise had been gently peeled away by the man himself, as if to show himself defenceless, begging for understanding of his suffering. Pity, regret for things past, and a feeling of mistaken judgment about Peter were going to make it difficult. The dissolute man might be true, and worth pity; but nevertheless, the cunning man was still somewhere hiding in the shadows, wanting something else.

'You know that I came to see you about Sam Hassoon,' Scott said.

'I could guess that without too much effort. I wondered when you'd come to me.'

'And I wondered if you knew how he'd got tangled up in something political.'

Peter smiled. 'I hope you're not going to blame me for that.'

'No. No. I don't want to blame anybody,' Scott said apologetically. 'I simply want to know.'

'If you don't want to blame anybody, you won't get far. So go ahead.'

'I want to get Sam out of trouble and leave it at that,' Scott said in an attempt at disinterested non-interference: *just Sam; I'm not interested in anything else you're doing.*

'I might be able to help you,' Peter told him.

'I'd be very grateful.'

'You might also be able to help me,' Peter added.

'Fair enough.'

'You're not too sure, are you?' Peter said, amused, the guilty to the innocent. 'How much do you know of what's going on here these days?'

'I can guess that it's not all as peaceful as it looks,' Scott said, trying to

246

pretend as best he could that everything was above-board and matter-of-fact, when the truth was otherwise. 'There's always some sort of under-hand work going on, I suppose, but that's normal out here.'

'So you came to me about it?'

'As a matter of fact it was Lucy Pickering who said you might be able to help; that is, help Sam.'

'Lucy Pickering? That's very interesting.'

'I suppose you knew.'

'Not at all. Did Mrs. Pickering also tell you she was sending you into the enemy's camp, so to speak?'

'She didn't say that.' Scott hesitated. 'What does it mean, anyway? Are you supposed to be enemies?'

'Didn't you know?'

'No. Why should you be enemies? I can't follow that part of it.'

'That's because you are lucky enough to be stuck out on the Red Sea all the time. But it's very simple; and if you want to save your friend Hassoon you might as well understand what it's all about.'

'Is Sam caught up in politics?'

'Wait a minute. Never mind Hassoon for the moment, perhaps he's not really important—yet.'

'It's mostly Sam that's important to me,' Scott insisted. 'The rest of it doesn't interest me. I know nothing about politics.'

'More fool you,' Peter said calmly and then added forgivingly, 'in this case. But you can be very important.'

Scott shook his head. 'I don't want to be important, thanks. Just Sam.'

'Unfortunately, it's not that simple,' Peter said, undiverted and leaning back in the dim corner he occupied. 'If you want to get Sam out of trouble you're going to have to play politics in one way or another. Unless you want to leave him to the Egyptian military courts, and they'll almost certainly shoot him eventually, if they ever try him.'

'I'm not afraid of what the courts will do to him,' Scott lied. 'In fact, the Egyptians don't know what he's done either, so . . .'

'They'll soon find out. A lot of people do know.'

'Do you?'

'I've an idea. But don't ask me. It'll do you no good. And it will all come out in the wash, anyway. What you really need to know, Scott, is what is at stake here, and that *should* interest you.'

'I hate politics, and I can do without them, if you don't mind.'

'Can you? Then put it on another level, a much simpler one. Are you interested?' Peter said, carefully taking off his white gloves.

'No, but go ahead.'

'I intend to, for your own good,' Peter said sharply. 'You see, there's a rather silly war going on at the moment between two points of view about

247

your friend Nasser. That is—two strictly British points of view. One side wants to get rid of him as quickly as possible, violently if necessary, while the other wants to butter him up a little and make good as best we can that way. Mostly it's the young idiots who want to rush in and have a crack at Nasser. But it's also some of those old public-school types at home who go to work every morning and do *The Times* crossword puzzle sitting in front of the Colonial Office fireplace before getting down to work on the new constitution for Bechuanaland. If you want to put it higher than that, there are probably some British ministers, so very famous for their knowledge of how to run the Empire (mostly learned at the Eton wall-game which they go on playing at home and abroad); there are probably quite a few of them who also think they can bring down Nasser with one quick tackle. That's one side of it; and you can imagine what's going to happen out here if that lot ever get their way, or can you?'

'I can imagine it, because it's happened before.'

'That's why other men, who have sunk a lifetime into knowing what this country is all about, are getting worried. They think there's no choice now, much as we dislike it, but to get along with Nasser and the junta. Otherwise . . . well, never mind the otherwise yet. Needless to say, since I do know what will happen and I do know what's at stake, I belong to the second group. I don't like your friend Nasser at all. I've never liked soldiers because they can never see farther than the regimental rules for good discipline which simply won't do in local politics. But I knew he was inevitable. You know that and I know it; anybody who has any brains knows it. But at the moment, if I might warn you, we are in the minority.'

'That's a minority I've always been in, anyway,' Scott reminded him.

'And without politics,' Peter said cynically.

'Why not? I don't have to know about politics to know that Nasser is right. It's obvious.'

Peter chuckled. 'What happens to you some day is going to be your own bloody fault. Anyway, that's not important unless I can persuade you . . .'

'I said no thanks,' Scott repeated. 'I don't want to have anything to do with either British side.'

'All right, all right; if you feel so strongly about it. But if you admire Nasser you can play a very good hand in saving his neck.'

'I came to see you about Sam.'

'You can save Sam too, if you want to. Do you know what happened to your friend Sam? You do know, I suppose, that he wanted a British passport?'

'That's a long time ago. I knew he had tried and failed.'

'That's right. So he wrote to Mrs. Pickering, the silly chump. Do you know what she did?'

Scott shook his head, hating this dim, yellow, smiling face now.

'She put your friend Sam in touch with one of her friends here, who put him onto another friend, young Mr. Bateman, who got your friend Sam into the trouble he's in now.'

'That makes Bateman the man who knows. At least that's something.'

'He knows. But if you're thinking of rushing off to that young idiot and insisting on a reckoning, you'd be more stupid than I think you are. Don't do it.'

'What am I supposed to do then? Sit by once more and watch it?'

'Do you think it will help, going to Bateman? Now honestly, Scott? Will he do anything for you or for Sam?'

'I suppose not. Oh, all right . . .'

'But since there is more at stake here than Sam, it might help, don't you think, if we could prevail upon friend Bateman in other ways?'

'Your way?'

'Now, listen, Scott,' Peter said coldly but very patiently. 'I'm talking to you very simply and clearly, because I know that's the only way your brain will ever accept something like this. You don't seem to grasp anything that isn't as cut and dried as a dead fish. All right. I'll admit it's not a particular habit of mine, and I'm not very good at it, but I must make you see that Hassoon is not the problem. Even in your own interests, and in the interest of the men you admire, you must grasp that.'

'I don't even know what you're getting at.'

'Never mind the trickery you imagine is behind it—British self-interest and all that nonsense. Don't think of all that stuff, because *I'll* think of that. That's why I don't intend to see a lifetime's work laid waste here, simply because young bastards like Bateman come out here with football minds, or because some stupid cabinet ministers (though twice his age) are just as infantile. And the soldiers!' Peter groaned. 'I'm too old now to tolerate stupidity and interference like that. But that's my affair. For you it ought to be clear that your friend Nasser will only have a chance if he's left strictly alone. And believe me, he will not be left alone for long if a few of our drastic decisions are not influenced now, very quickly.'

'You don't think I could have any influence on the British, do you?' Scott said incredulously. 'You know what they think of me. Even the newspapers in England are still attacking me for working for Nasser when every other decent Englishman has left . . .'

'Oh, that's nothing. I'm not talking in those terms.'

'What terms do you mean then?'

'My own terms! I do these things my own way, not the newspaper way or the schoolboy way or the Embassy way. Anything valuable that's done in this country is done despite that trio of mummies. Forget the lot.'

'Well? What is it you want?'

'Two things, Scott. Two very simple things if you keep them simple,
249

and I'll keep them simple for your sake. Firstly, I need your help against Bateman and the schoolboys. And secondly, I need your influence and your help with Nasser or Hakim or whoever else among your friends is not too prejudiced to take advice from someone like me.'

'Do you want to see them? Do you think you can explain this to Hakim?' Scott laughed into this yellow-faced dimness.

'No, no, no! I want nothing to do with them. You can do that.'

'What about Sam?'

'Don't you realize that you're not going to get your friend out of trouble unless you play a strong hand in this? Even when you're facing up to the Egyptians. You're not going to get him out by begging and pleading. Nasser and his junta are not in business to be soft-hearted about local Jews like Hassoon, or even with you, whatever you feel about them. They lock up Sam Hassoon; but don't you realize they are using him to chase up something much bigger than he is, something potentially tremendous? Don't be a fool, Scott. You know they're determined to keep what they've got, and if some fool like Hassoon, guilty or innocent, is caught up in the slightest lick from the other side, they'll make short work of him. And can you blame them?'

'No. But you and I see it differently,' Scott insisted.

'Does that matter, as long as the result is the same?'

'All I'm thinking of at the moment is one man,' Scott said. 'I dare not think of anything else. It's too complex, and I don't want any more trouble; and I'd make a mess of being cunning, anyway. I just want Sam out.'

'Just that idiot Hassoon?'

'That's right, and his friend Zareef.'

'You're refining it, aren't you?'

'I have to. I don't know how else to do it,' Scott said frankly and desperately now.

'You really think it's possible to rescue one man from all this hulla-baloo?'

'That's what I must do.'

'You haven't a hope in hell, old chap.'

Scott could not shrug, because the truth seemed too near and too dangerous. The dark room drew it so near that he knew it was not quite real to be settling Sam's fate here. Yet Peter could make it very real.

'Perhaps I haven't a hope,' Scott admitted, 'but I'm not going to make it worse, and that is what your schemes would mean.'

Peter sighed heavily in disgust. 'People go around so much these days talking of the individual, don't they? The only thing that most of them do for the individual, caught up in a mess like this, is to pity him or weep over him or go to church and pray for him or set up a committee for him, or write books about him. The result—the world is full of refugees all moaning about the individual. The intellectuals are so happily sick over them that it's disgusting to see it. I thought that you at least would have a more practical approach than that.'

'I would have, if I could find the practical approach. You tell me. But I'm not going to be dragged into political scheming. That would not help anyone, because I'm no good at it.'

Scott stood up to go, shaking his head, trying to get out of it before it was too late. He hated this dark room now.

'Don't go,' Peter said simply. 'Sit down just a minute and tell me one thing. Did Church talk to you at all?'

'I went to see him,' Scott replied, remaining on his feet, 'but how did you know that? Do you work with him?'

'That's a silly question. Church is a soldier, and I told you—soldiers have a barrack-square mind when they meddle in politics. To me Church is that other point of view, soldier or no. Did he offer you a job?'

'He did.'

Peter laughed. 'What did he want you to do? Find out the weapon strength of a first-class Egyptian battalion?'

'He offered me a job with his archaeological survey.'

Peter did not laugh. 'Was that also Mrs. Pickering's idea?'

'I don't think so. She only suggested coming to see you.'

'They're playing a pretty close game, aren't they?' Peter said thoughtfully. 'Anyway, both sides see that you are very useful, placed as you are. You ought to be flattered. You're in a very nice position at the moment, don't you see that?'

'I don't want to see it.'

'What will you do, then? Go to Nasser and beg?' Peter sneered a little at that possibility.

'I don't know yet,' Scott said, definitely leaving now.

'You know that he won't help you.'

'Perhaps not.'

'Did it ever occur to you that Church was here as a soldier,' Peter said without getting up, 'and a rotten one at that?'

'A soldier doing what?'

'You want the answers, old chap, without doing anything for them.'

'No. I don't care about the answers.'

'One way or the other, they're after Nasser, you know. Someone is . . .'

'I suppose they are,' Scott said. 'Hakim knows that, but I can't help it.'

'Not even for Hassoon?'

'Can you actually get Sam out of this dirty business safely?'

'Me? I might. But only with your help, your influence with Hakim.'

Scott shook his head. 'I only want Sam and Zareef out, nothing else.'

251

'Sorry,' Peter said, putting his cups away, resting in the corner where his life was so close and so protected from the dangers of exposure. 'It isn't all *that* simple. If you can't help me, though, I can't help you. Not for lack of sympathy, mind you, but in sheer practical necessity.'

Peter laughed as Scott closed the door on him.

CHAPTER THIRTY-FOUR

At the villa gaol, Sam did not mind the questioning so much, because it was not very dangerous, but it seemed unfair to him that some of the prisoners in the garden should not be allowed to talk to each other, and he brought this up with Said the gaoler, who said,

' I know, *ya hawaga*, but it's nothing to do with me. They order me not to let certain political prisoners talk.'

'Why shouldn't they?' Sam said indignantly. 'We're no different from anybody else. It's wrong.'

'You'll have to talk to Captain Mahmood about it.'

Sam knew better than that, and though he hated Mahmood for silencing him, and though he was often bored and frightened and upset, he had begun to adapt himself to it by living with outside sounds. Every noise which filtered over the wall was a revelation because it was all so familiar, and yet he could not remember ever feeling their separate impressions on him so acutely. He could not only hear the metro coming and passing and going, but he could count the wheel combinations on it by its race over a culvert near the road bridge. He could hear the slap of its loose brakes, and the blinding screech of the bogies on the curves. He heard children, birds, motor-bike engines, and even bicycles and milkmen and the far-away rumble of the city, and the near rush of all warm traffic outside.

Every street-seller, every donkey braying, every raised voice was an old time, sadly remembered. He cursed his fate most formally and most often when he lay still, listening; and when it became too much, he begged Said to let him go back into the garden, even though there was no work to do. When Said told him sadly that it was impossible, he would begin to sing Egyptian songs to stop the world filtering in on him through the huge cracks in his isolation.

It was not unpleasant. But life was so still and so complete in itself that he almost felt safe, until they came one day to take away Mohamed Khalil the King's fourth barber who had wept every day for years, even when they had allowed him to cut hair under the trellised rose pergola which Sam had painted white, even under the leaves and thorns.

He heard a cry of terror from the garden below and he sat up.

Below, through the window, he saw two of the soldiers, who normally guarded the gates with carbines, dragging poor Mohamed the barber across the garden paths. Mohamed was kicking and trying to hook his feet into the stones and bricks, screaming and begging for mercy as they dragged him shoeless to the gate.

'In the name of Allah, in God's name, don't kill me,' he cried. 'I swear I'm innocent. I beg you on your own mother's honour don't murder an innocent man. I beseech you, brothers. I kiss your feet. I swear on my father's tomb. Don't be cruel. Don't take me away to shoot me now. I'm an old man. Look. *Look* at me . . .'

Mohamed was dragged through the dust until they picked him up; the gates opened and they carried him out in a dead faint, a pitiful and wretched remnant of Farouk's barber shop.

'Said! Said!' Sam called out angrily, and kept it up until the old man came.

'Ah, but you're impossible. Don't keep calling me,' Said said, unlocking the ordinary door of the room and complaining bitterly of Sam's demands. 'Not the W.C. again. Oh, no . . .'

'Why are they doing that to Mohamed Khalil? Why are they going to shoot a miserable wretch like that?'

'But they're not, *hawaga*. They came to let him go free, but he didn't believe them. They came to take him to his sister's house.'

'But did you hear him?'

'He's an old man.'

'But they dragged him out.'

'They did that to let him go. They didn't want him any more.'

'How can I believe that?' Sam shouted. 'If they shoot a poor old man like that, what will they do to the rest of us? You know all about it, but you won't say. You don't care what happens to us.'

Sam had been stamping up and down in the small space of his room where there was an enamel basin on a stand, and he wrenched it fiercely out of his way and dumped it on the cot, as Said begged him to calm down.

'Captain Mahmood is below in the bureau, and if he hears you walking up and down making a noise like this, he'll blame me. *Ya sidi!* Please. For my sake. Don't put your feet so heavily on the floor. Don't make so much racket. I'll get into trouble.'

'All right, all right,' Sam said bitterly, dropping heavily on the cot.

'And I swear he was set free.'

'This place is full of innocent men,' Sam protested once more, 'and I suppose they'll start torturing us next. Oh, my God . . .'

Said left him crying out against injustice and fate. And Sam also announced to the world that if they ever came to get him out of here he would hold onto the bed and the iron-barred window with a grip which a hundred of those miserable soldiers could never break. They wouldn't get him out so easily, and if they did break his grip he would break a few heads before they put him up against a wall and shot him, because everybody knew that they had shot people and tortured them also. And they *always* told you that they were taking you home.

Even Said admitted that.

In fact, they had probably done that today expressly to frighten him, and Sam knew that he was very frightened and admitted it and felt bitter, because everybody had forgotten him—all his friends and family, and even his good friend Captain Scott.

They came to take him away in the afternoon, not Said his friend nor Captain Mahmood or Captain Hussein, but two other guards he had never seen before, and Sam knew what his fate would be if he allowed them to take him.

'No!' he roared when they told him curtly to come. 'I shall never move from here. Kill me here, but I shan't move.'

'Don't be silly,' they said. 'We are taking you to a hospital.'

'To poison me. To cut me up. I shan't budge. Kill me here.'

Sam had braced himself with his arms through the iron bars of his windows, and he wished he had not been lying down before they arrived, because he had his shoes off and he could do much damage to these pigs with his bare feet. One of the guards unlatched a carbine from his shoulder and pointed it threateningly at Sam.

'You must come without trouble, otherwise I shall wing you. Believe me . . .'

'Go ahead!' Sam cried. 'Touch me and I'll break every bone in your body. Call them all to witness what you are doing. Let them see what you are . . .'

'Come!' they said appealingly then. 'We are not going to hurt you. We have orders, that's all. We have to take you to the hospital in Abassia.'

'Never!'

'Said!' one of them called, and when the old gaoler came they told him to send for Captain Mahmood and some men.

'*Ya sidi*,' Said told Sam. 'It's all right, I swear it is. Go with them . . .'

'I'll break their backs first,' Sam roared with his great chest heaving, and his temper flying about the room now in tremendous rushes. Touch him if they dared.

255

Yet they dared. Captain Mahmood failed to convince him, Captain Hussein failed to persuade. Said also. They could not move him. Then one man stood guard while five others grasped Sam's flaying legs and tried to hold him still while they prised his arms loose, but Sam let one arm go and wiped them all off him across the floor, bellowing threats of death and destruction to their families and their religion and their whole nation. He would kill or be killed, let them take their choice.

Two more guards were sent for, and Sam heard them running up the stairs as he breathed heavily and fiercely and braced his huge arms so tight that he could feel the iron bars cutting into his muscles and flesh.

'Ahhh!' he growled as they came in, making seven in all. 'Now I will show you. You will see now!' he cried in a voice which made every man step back one pace but did not prevent Sam committing the one daring mistake which made it easier for them. He would die bravely with his whole body, and he launched himself at the collected opposition and flung one man at another and became berserk with strength and desperation until bones cracked and blood flowed and the mêlée was an anarchy of pain and flaying limbs. But a double attack on the rear, a blanket over his head from the bed, a push, a trip, a terrible blow in the stomach, a body in his back, and Sam was down and helplessly tangled in blankets and mattresses, and their shouting had defeated him. He lay still and exhausted and let them bundle him up and lead him downstairs, outside into the garden, stumbling blindly in the hot rough darkness of the blankets until he was put in a truck and driven away, his stunned body resigned, his fate sealed, his heart contracted against humanity for this terrible thing they would do to him. Let them do it! It was fitting . . .

They unbundled him again, and he walked between them as they told him to be careful of stairs, to go up, to go down. He could smell a hospital, and he could feel the cool air of corridors, and then whispered consolations. Their grip on him remained firm, but he could see their feet near his. He would wait. If they were going to shoot him bundled up like this he would break free. But they weren't going to shoot him in a hospital. They were going to torture him. He would wait. When they started . . .

They took off the blankets when someone told them to.

'Don't be afraid,' someone said to him.

He saw a dozen soldiers surrounding him with guns, and two of them were torn and bloody, but the rest were new. There was a general and a man in a white coat, a male nurse.

'Go on,' one of the soldiers told him.

When he hesitated, the General himself said, 'Go on, Sam. Nothing will happen to you. You will be taken back to the villa in a few moments. Go on, I swear nothing will be done to you. Don't cause trouble, otherwise we will have to hurt you. Now go on.'

Sam did not believe him, but he moved on with the soldiers and they took him through a double door and then left him in a small room with a male nurse in a white jacket and someone lying prostrate and pale in a bed. Sam only needed to see him once, however, to glance at that distorted mirror of himself lying there, and he knew it was his father.

'Ah . . .' He moved forward with the cry itself.

Eyes knew nothing, words lacked life, recognition struck up the oldest chords of sorrow and guilt and dismay and sentiment.

'He is your father,' the male nurse said in Arabic.

'Oui, oui, je le sais,' Sam said, and stood there and dropped down carefully beside the bed and took the sick man's hand in his and kissed it through his tears and cried gently: 'Mon père, mon père.'

'C'est toi, Sammi?' the father said weakly.

'It's your own son,' Sam cried in French, speaking the language he spoke at home with Alicia, although he had always spoken Arabic with his father. He had forgotten. The male nurse said something to him, and Sam did not understand it. Did he hear? What was that? What did it matter? He was kissing his father's hand and sobbing in relief and feeling his body dropping into the chasm of relief and pain. 'Oh, mon père.'

'Shhhh!' his father said. 'Don't weep, I am all right.'

Sam looked then and realized that his father was a thin streak of what had been a large man, with the flesh hanging loose and the jowl sagged and the eyes lost in deep cavities of loose flesh.

Again the male nurse spoke in a foreign tongue, and Sam suddenly realized that it was Hebrew. He could guess it, even though he didn't understand a word. He looked up at the nurse in a puzzled way, but his father nodded.

'They promised me I might see you,' the father said in his loose, hanging voice. 'God is good. God has been merciful.'

'He asked to see you,' the male nurse said in Arabic to Sam then. 'He says he has something to tell you . . .'

'Everybody is all right,' Sam told his father in Arabic. 'Don't worry, papa,' he said tearfully with his father's hand held tight in both of his. 'Everything is all right. Do not worry. It's all right . . .'

'He has something to tell you,' the nurse said and prompted the old man again in Hebrew and then leaned over the bed to catch what was said.

'God curse the day,' the old man said weakly in Arabic, 'that I left my family. Forgive me, forgive me. God will forgive me. I must say to you, dear Sammi, that I beg your forgiveness, and I beg you to tell my mother that her own son has been on his knees to beg forgiveness, and that I did not do it because I was cruel. I was weak. But God has punished me. God has punished me now, and I only beg you to forgive your father . . .'

Sam kissed his father's hand and sobbed again.

K 257

'I am a poor weak man,' his father cried then. 'They should never have sent me here. I did not want to come. What could I have done? And look how you see me now . . .'

'What did you have to say to Sammi?' the male nurse said to him. 'You must speak quickly, because he must go. You must tell him why you came.'

'You know why I came. I told you. I did not come to do anything wrong. I did not want to come. I wanted only to see my family before I died. I swear it . . .'

'Ah, yes, papa. Don't worry. Don't be upset. God curse the day when things like this happen. I thank God I saw you. I . . . I . . .'

Sam could not go on and his father had turned his head aside and was dropping off to sleep in exhaustion, so that Sam looked horrified for a moment, fearing the worst, but then the male nurse said he had gone to sleep, he was very ill, and Sam would be allowed to see him again.

'He was trying to tell you something,' the nurse said.

Sam had no emotional room for suspicion yet, neither for what his father might be trying to tell him, nor for this dark, lean, harsh-eyed man who spoke Hebrew over his sick father.

He stood up and he suddenly found the pain in his own body, in his broken nerves and overstrained muscles and badly scratched face, and he allowed them to lead him back to the truck with twelve soldiers to guard him and a general to watch over him and to promise him a further visit, when his father was feeling better.

Scott had seen Lucy Pickering almost every day, but he had still spared his conscience any investigation which suggested that it could be wrong. She had already given him so much of what a woman usually seemed to hold back either in self-defence or in terrible moral fear of the consequences.

She would lie near him and say, 'But you're so beautiful; so perfect.'

A shy, selfconscious man could not understand it. His body was not beautiful at all. He knew that his legs were too short, his calves too thick, and his chest and shoulders far too vast for any kind of aesthetic admiration. And anyway, a man's body was an awkward thing to expose or discuss or allow freedom to.

'Oh, my darling,' she would say sometimes in a helpless, delighted ecstasy. 'Why can't it be so perfect always? Isn't it perfect?'

He would try to agree. He wanted to unleash one word, any word which would explain the emotion exploding in his whole body; but he knew he would fail if he tried. 'Don't try,' he warned himself desperately. 'Don't even say a word to her.'

He kept such a frightened silence that she begged him to say something, anything.

258

'Don't ask me,' he would answer unhappily. 'I can't say anything wonderful to you, Lucy. I honestly don't know how to . . .'

But Lucy poured out ecstasies and mooned down over him tenderly. She could live out long moments on this exalted feeling, which astonished and exhausted and overwhelmed her. He was grateful and in love with her then. But when he had recovered his mind from passionate involvement, he began in a more tranquil way to long for constancy—for a way to the daily life of love, to have it every day in other ways. And if it wasn't Françoise now—with her long-promised hope and postponement of it, then it would have to be Lucy Pickering. Or someone. He needed help for himself now.

She guessed it intuitively.

'If we don't make this permanent very soon,' she told him, sitting out on the sand one night near the large pyramid in a lavender-coloured light, 'I'd prefer to stop it all now so that it doesn't get the better of me.'

'Don't say that yet,' he appealed to her.

'But I must. You may think you owe that girl something, but do you, really?'

'You can't know what I owe Françoise,' he told her. 'I can't even discuss her like that.'

He could not explain that once Françoise had also saved him from utter loneliness, that in the beginning their feelings had held all the same promise of fulfilment, and that they had nurtured a different kind of affection carefully until it had also needed to go further; and only then had Françoise leapt back. The first time he had touched Françoise she had invited it by all her powers, all her longing, but then she had pushed him away so violently that he had tried to hold her to prevent himself from falling. Then she had struggled desperately, as if he were trying out some sort of violence on her as the horrible satisfaction of love. She had been in a frenzy. Brute that he was! He had hated himself, not her. But then he had suddenly felt like breaking down such stupid pretences, and denouncing them as lies and coarse untruths. But he never had, even though she seemed to have expected it in her poised, nervous panic. Why hadn't he pierced her reluctance with a terrible blow? That was all that they had lacked. The promise of tenderness had always been there, the constancy of affection too. Only this last-minute discovery of another need had made it difficult between them. She had loved him very much up to that point, but she was afraid to go beyond it. But he still knew she would give him a great deal more, some day, when she could cross her own moral barrier, the reluctance which made it impossible for her to give herself freely to him as long as she was still married to Roberto.

It had been too easy for Lucy Pickering to step into this void. Not to fuss, not to doubt, not to hesitate; when Lucy offered that kind of love it had been too much for that other long-held promise to withstand.

'It's not much use talking about Françoise,' he told her.

'All right,' she agreed, 'but you're thinking only of yourself, and not of me. You're being selfish. You want you and me to go on like this for a little while, I suppose, and then what? Am I supposed to drift obligingly away, having filled in the gap of your waiting time for this French girl, who receives all at absolutely no cost?'

'The more you talk about it, the worse it becomes,' he tried to warn her, begging her for time to postpone answering and to solve his unhappy apostacy. 'It was always wrong.'

'Why did you love me, then?' she said, as if he had been the instigator of it in the first place.

He could not tell her why; but he was accusing himself now of weakness and inconstancy, bad faith, bad character; and he could never tell her why he had needed her.

'You are always the same person to me,' he said. 'I can't help feeling that.'

'Then why don't we get married and make it useful and permanent?'

He felt every shaft, every demand, every weakness and every possibility —but he dare not try to explain. The tiny café on the sand near the pyramids was glowing like a blue fiend—a monster in the shadow of the moon; and he could feel his own shame tempting him into sudden indulging decisions.

'You owe *me* something too,' she was saying.

If she could only have understood the whole truth of it for him instead of simply her own intense fragment of it, he knew he could have abandoned Françoise in a second. But even now she was demanding too much and he resisted.

'I don't feel that I owe you anything,' he said stubbornly. 'You knew that I couldn't promise you anything. I told you . . .'

'I don't care about promises,' she cried angrily. 'I only care about feelings. Has your French girl given you this sort of love? I'll bet she hasn't. I know she hasn't. You wouldn't be able to love me the way you do if she had. You can't even deceive me.'

'Don't ever talk about it like that,' he insisted. 'If you understood, if only you knew, you wouldn't be so sure about it. I'm not sure about anything, except that I'm wrong, and that I can't turn my back on Françoise, no matter what you say about feelings. I don't even want to. I can't.'

'But you're deceiving yourself and her.'

He felt now that his only hope was simply to hold out grimly against promising her anything, against abandoning himself, against her desire, her will, her claims. And he was not thinking of Françoise now, but of himself. He could not turn himself over to Lucy so easily. There was too much of an old threat in it—her strong grip on him.

'I mean it,' she said calmly now. 'If we can't actually get married, I don't want to see you again.'

He lay back on the sand where they had been eating sandwiches from Groppi's and he shook his head and said he couldn't do it, he couldn't possibly do it.

'Then go back to your French girl, and good luck to you,' she said, because they had reached the moment when they both knew they would have to end it.

They said no more about it but walked down the hill to the taxi which was waiting for them near Mena House, and they drove home in silence. At the door of her hotel, on the footpath, she made it very clear again.

'I'm going to go away . . .' she said.

'Where to ?'

'. . . but if you do change your mind, you can always write to me here. Then *I'll* think about making up my mind.'

'Are you leaving Egypt ?' he said, knowing he could weaken now.

'No. To the country,' she said. 'But I won't tell you where. You'll just have to write to me here.'

If she had said then, 'Yes, I am leaving Egypt,' he knew that he would have sworn to go with her. But she had saved him with that one promise of modest travelling. She was sniffing gently and perhaps she was crying a little, but he could not feel that it was over, by any means.

He said, 'All right.' He agreed that if he changed his mind he would write to her. It was a formal quarrel now, but he wondered, as he walked away, if this time he had not made a terrible mistake, leaving her as casually as that.

CHAPTER THIRTY-FIVE

IF the Egyptians had arrested your wife's nephew, Sam, for plotting to murder Nasser, what would their security police do with your request for a press pass? That was a nice bureaucratic puzzle. They had already sent their plain-clothes men to talk to the boabs who sat below the lifts and they had checked up on the whole family.

'They'll probably tell me to get out,' Quartermain decided on the way up to the Egyptian press department. 'Or they might let me stay on, and keep an eye on me to see how I'm involved. That will be very nice.'

'Good morning, Mr. Quartermain,' the school teacher in the Press Office said to him.

'Good morning, Mr. Aboud. Are you well? Is my press pass through yet?'

'Ah . . . I'm afraid not.'

Nasser's new regime had filled this Egyptian press department in this insurance company's modern building with former school teachers of English who knew the language very well, but what else could they possibly know? Aboud was a young round-faced man with a schoolmaster's slightly superior detachment from his pupils. He banged his knees together and tore the corner off a dry blotting-paper to chew on, and he looked outwards, through his spectacles, with a schoolmaster's private inquisition against all doubters.

'Why didn't you come into Egypt as a regular correspondent, instead of getting a tourist visa?' Aboud asked. 'It wasn't the right way, you see.'

'A correspondent's visa would have taken too long,' Quartermain told him. 'You know that, Mr. Aboud.'

'And who is this Northern Allied Agency? We've never heard of it.'

'Do you read English literature, Mr. Aboud?'

'Of course.'

'You must know of Steinbeck, Hemingway, Graham Greene?'

'Of course.'

'They have all worked for the Northern Allied Agency during the war.

Perhaps it was before you took an interest in foreign newspapers,' he said charitably.

Mr. Aboud knocked his knees together and did not hear the clever pupil cheeking him. 'Ahhh!' Aboud said happily as a hand shot right over Quartermain's shoulder and into Aboud's with a slap.

The new visitor had blue-tinted glasses and a thin religious beard, a white silk shirt and a gold-banded watch, and he had this good old method of bureau visiting. The protests and greetings began over Quartermain's ignored head, and when he had watched it politely enough and long enough, he got up to go because this sort of treatment did not do your pride any good at all.

'What about my request to see Colonel Nasser?' he flung out suddenly. 'Have you done anything about that?'

Aboud tilted back his chair. 'We have put your request into the bag for Gamal Abd el Nasser. If he is interested he will see you.'

'What if there's a press conference of some kind in the meantime? Can I get into it?'

'When you have your press card, Mr. Quartermain.'

'Surely you can help me in some way,' he protested. 'Or don't you care?'

Aboud pointed through the door. 'You may like to study our publications, Mr. Quartermain. They're all there. Take what you like. Have you read Gamal Abd el Nasser's *Philosophy of the Revolution*?'

'I read it probably before you did,' Quartermain said rudely.

'There are many other publications on the new labour laws, the land reforms, the economic plans. You will find them very interesting.'

'I've already found them interesting. Is that all you can offer me?'

'Come back tomorrow, Mr. Quartermain. Or you can give me a ring on the phone. It would be easier.'

'Bukra fil mish mish!' Quartermain said cynically. Tomorrow there would be apricots. Mr. Aboud, being a good schoolmaster, didn't bother to hear it, but the bearded bureau visitor laughed as Quartermain allowed the swing-doors to slap behind him.

Mr. Aboud must have looked up a file, or he had asked questions. Perhaps he had been stung into action. When Quartermain went determinedly back the next day to force the issue of his press card, the questions were different and the answers were not so pleasantly evasive.

'We know about you,' Mr. Aboud said mysteriously. 'We know you are an English communist, Mr. Quartermain.'

Quartermain felt cantankerous. Denying communism or denying that one was a member of the communist party had lately stamped such a fine seal of validity on political grovelling that he refused to join such abject

263

company, and anyway he *ought* to be a communist, only he wasn't up to it.

'Even if I was a communist, why should that worry you?' he said to Aboud.

'Have you come to Egypt for political reasons?' Mr. Aboud demanded.

Quartermain always felt happier when the real issue came out in the open, because he could cope with it as cynically as he liked.

'What sort of political reasons do you mean?' he asked.

'That's what I must ask you,' Aboud told him, worried by the sudden good-natured willingness of what was surely an unwilling man. 'It's forbidden for foreigners to interfere in Egyptian affairs.'

'I haven't interfered,' he said. 'Who says I have?'

'Communists are illegal in Egypt,' Mr. Aboud warned him. 'It's well known that you spoke and wrote about communists in Malaya and Indo-China and other countries. You can't do that here, because there are laws against it. Even talking to communists is considered to be a conspiracy . . .'

'I didn't realize that you had any communists left,' Quartermain answered. 'I thought they were all in prison. Aren't they the only political people you keep in prison these days?'

Mr. Aboud gave him an angry look. 'There are some in prison.'

'Anyway,' Quartermain said, 'I came to see Egypt, not Egyptian communists. I won't see much of it, though, if you don't give me a press pass!'

'But you are not a real newspaperman.'

'Who said so?'

'You write books which are opposed to what we think.'

'Have you read them?'

'No, but you are well known for your extreme views.'

'That's true,' Quartermain admitted. 'But why should you worry, Mr. Aboud? My extreme views at the moment are quite in sympathy with Gamal Abd el Nasser's extreme views.'

'We would also like to know if you are here to see any relatives.'

Quartermain almost lost his temper then, but he knew better than to permit an indulgence like that. 'Naturally. My wife is Egyptian.'

'Egyptian?'

'As Egyptian as you are, Mr. Aboud, even if she isn't a Moslem.'

'I didn't mean your wife. Perhaps you have friends . . .'

'Perhaps you mean my nephew by marriage, Sam Hassoon, who is in gaol?'

'Please, Mr. Quartermain!' Aboud said sharply, as if to snatch away this reckless use of forbidden subjects. 'What countries, may I ask, have you visited lately?'

'Not Israel, anyway.'

Mr. Aboud's habit of jiggling his knees between questions was beginning to annoy. He was so bad at this sort of investigation that the wit and pleasure had gone out of the contest. They were now irritating each other.

'You see!' Mr. Aboud complained. 'You don't even answer my questions properly. You seem to be hiding something.'

'On the contrary, I'm not hiding anything. That's what upsets you. Do you want me to be more evasive? If so, let's start all over again.'

'I don't mean that. Other correspondents who come here don't join in with politics, even though they report our politics. They are not political . . .'

'Then how do they know what's happening in Egypt?'

'They *report* what is happening.'

'Once upon a time, Gamal Abd el Nasser's superiors in the Army told him he shouldn't be political,' Quartermain said joyfully.

But Mr. Aboud stood up resentfully, hearing Nasser's name mentioned so boldly a second time. 'You can have your press pass,' he said, handing over the little green book, 'but only if you agree not to mix in Egyptian politics.'

'How can I avoid mixing in Egyptian politics? It's part of my job,' Quartermain insisted.

'As part of your work, yes. To observe is all right. But if you are ever found trying to contact illegal organizations, Mr. Quartermain, like Zionist and communist political agents, you must know what will happen to you.'

'Terrible things,' Quartermain said wearily.

But he consoled himself, as he went down in the high-speed lift with his stomach shrinking in dismay, that he would some day go to a far-away country, another world even, where he would not have to fight the world's Abouds, and his stomach at least could live in harmony with the surroundings.

He was too tense to go home, it wouldn't be a good idea. He must change atmospheres; and he crossed Cairo on foot, remembering as he headed towards the old Muski how the beige dust always lay over the city, undigested dynasties of it. But Cairo looked very different without British soldiers in it. Where were all those British officers with their suede boots and fly-whisks now? Well tucked away into the nine-to-six of English life, mortals after all.

'Nice bint, George?' one of the beggar-boys said to him when he reached the very edge of the native quarter.

The streets here looked like a world's junk shop: the surplus mess left behind by a dozen armies. Take anything conceivable—say ten thousand miles of army signal wire coiled up in little lengths, for sale very cheap. To whom? Down the crowded streets came jingling donkey-bells, and on the sidewalk the black women squatted with their knees up in their black gellabiyas, living on the pavements. He walked deeper into it where the tinsmiths, who hammered and laughed like gods, could turn you into an expatriate overnight.

Think of the Englishmen—engineers and pump salesmen and oil company clerks and retired officers and missionaries—who had been sucked into exile by these same donkey-bells and a tinker's hammer. There were still Englishwomen driving around Gezira in their pre-war baby Austins, grey-haired school teachers and god-knows-what, who lived it out without knowing why. They had sunk their lives into this cloying attraction which returned them nothing at all except daily doses of atmosphere, noises, happinesses, and a swelling, ignorant humanity. Could they ever leave it? Could they ever go home again to black pavements and to buses which carried men, not gods and devils on donkey-back?

'Nice bint with no squint, George?' the boy insisted.

Where the dickens had he learned that? He must have been born at least ten years after the war, this boy. He looked about six years of age, the same age as Benjamino who was now sitting at his desk at the Lycée in a white (maybe) tablier chanting *La mère Michele a perdu son chat*.

'No, thanks,' he said into this hard-driven, dirty face which laughed and mocked him. 'Not today,' he said and turned off towards the tram-stop to go home.

But he couldn't quite escape it, even at home.

Mr. Aboud had bothered his stomach, and the unpleasant taste remained.

'If they keep watching me and making it difficult for me, I won't be staying long,' he told Nona when he went into the kitchen to inspect a marsh duck which Ali had cooked. 'What would this be?' he asked, prodding it.

'A wild duck,' Nona said. 'Perfectly fresh.'

'It smells like fish.'

'Don't let Benjamino hear that. He'll complain and make a fuss.'

Benjamino was learning to make a fuss, and his mother would not tolerate it—not the smallest fuss or the larger ones. The result, he decided, was an Egyptian household. Mother quarrelled with children on their own level so that all English reasonableness was overcome by childish bickering and nagging. If she would only learn to keep her tongue still and punish without that annoying moral: *you must learn!*

'Ben wouldn't make a fuss,' he said to her, 'if you didn't listen to him make it.'

'Somebody has to listen to him. He'll get out of hand.'

'You're an adult. You ought to reason with him.'

'With a child?' she said.

266

'You get too irritated with him. Then you carry it over onto everyone else.'

'Do I? Then there's no use arguing about it.'

'Why do we fight about them?' he wanted to know in his sudden anguish. 'I suppose we concentrate too much attention on them.'

'You do, I don't,' she said. 'Why don't you forget your children?'

'They won't let me forget them. I hear them all day, from morn till night. If I'd been a bank-clerk I could have walked out of the house at nine o'clock in the morning and come home at six o'clock in the evening. That would be better, I suppose.'

Nona's shrug was always the shrug of disinterested victory. 'Much better, if you think so. But remember—you're the one who thinks like that.'

Benjamino and Hilal had arrived with Hanna from the gardens and they had their muddy hands all over his shirt, until their mother sent them to wash, quickly now, if they wanted to eat lunch with their father. They half-listened and half-obeyed, and Quartermain picked them both up in his long arms and brought the obedience quickly up to standard, so that the nagging and bickering he alone heard would not go on. Perhaps she was right. Benjamino was not ever willingly obedient, and Hilal sucked his fingers and wailed when he did not want to do what he had to do. He had to persuade them into it with quick diversionary stories which were exhausting. He could not remember where he left off the invention of one detail or another, which they insisted on keeping exact and consistent.

'Now that's enough. I'll finish it after lunch,' he said as he dried their hands. 'But only if you behave at table and don't make a fuss.'

But he knew before the meal began that Ben would ask for more than he could have, and Hilal would eat nothing: one to be restrained and the other persuaded. Tears were certain, and his stomach nerves were already braced for the contest between mother and children.

Who would win it? The children, of course. Who would lose? The father; only the father, because the father felt that a battle against children was a waste and disciplining them painfully unnecessary.

But Nona had bought them ice-cream and there was peace after all.

'You've got it all in your moustache,' Nona told him. 'Use your serviette.'

'That's what moustaches are for,' he said, licking it. 'Filters.'

The dry moustache, dry eyes, and dry hair looked out at the world of his wife, who did not appear to be any older now than on the day they had married. What subdued him when he needed not to be subdued? Was it that clear skin and unwrinkled forehead? Nona lived as if she had stepped into the world naked and adult, and she walked through it boldly and didn't notice and didn't care what *they* thought, whoever *they* were.

'I hope Nasser will appreciate the trouble I'm taking when I finally get it all written down so that the English can understand it.'

'I never heard you worry about appreciation before,' she said.

'I'm getting old,' he told her. 'Too long without it and the fountain of confidence dries up.'

'Not yours.'

'Even mine. I think I'm tired of bashing my head in. I'm getting lonely. Sometimes now I feel like calling it a day.'

'Let's go home then, if it's so hopeless.'

He looked suspicious and troubled.

'Honestly,' she said. 'If it's better.'

He nodded pacifically. She meant it.

'Never mind, darling,' she told him, suddenly coming around to kiss him when she knew that the mockery had died away and left him quite defenceless. She had won, anyway. He was leaning back on his chair looking at the ceiling, avoiding her eyes. 'I don't think it's all that hopeless,' she said. 'It's always like this at the beginning.'

'I suppose it is,' he agreed reluctantly.

CHAPTER THIRTY-SIX

THE mounted Egyptian lancers flew their striped pennants and trotted around the gymkhana field, doing their best to avoid the peasants and ditch-diggers from Ismailia who swarmed around, dancing and hopping like children and stirring up a choking dust. Shouts of command made it almost military, but the peasant cries and the tooting passage of the Egyptian army jeeps spoiled the tattoo atmosphere.

The British were handing over, officially, the eighty-year-old occupation of the Suez Canal zone to the Egyptian Army. The last British soldiers were leaving Egypt for ever: the evacuation treaty was finally coming into effect. It was very significant. A British guards' officer and a brigadier carried off the ceremony with careful modesty, as other soldiers had once carried off the far-away frontiers; at the Pathan gate, down the valleys of the Imchin.

'I suppose it is sad,' Peacock said, 'but somehow, everything that happens to us these days seems inevitable. That's all I can summon up in the way of a feeling. It's inevitable. It's all so inevitable.'

'You're growing up, Timothy,' Lucy told him. 'I wish you wouldn't.'

'I keep getting maudlin. Perhaps I ought to go home. I know we still *own* the canal, but I hate to see this happen. This place is really beginning to get me down.'

'Why have you stayed out here so long then?' she asked.

They would go over and say good-bye to the Colonel and to some of the men. *Something* had to be done to make this significant among them. Here was Lucy in a picture-hat, and the dusty disorder getting the better of them in this happy peasant confusion, so it ought to be done as well as a man could do it. Shake hands with Phillpotts and make the heartache felt in some silent arena of the past; let Lucy's hat memorize for ever all the other gymkhanas on the white-pegged parade grounds of Moascar and Ismailia and Abbasia, where the dresses were long and floral, the days so pleasantly hot, the evenings golden, and women carried garden-party parasols and walked on the carpets laid on the sand among the tents and tables set out for the other ranks to have beer and mugs of tea and Y.M.C.A. sandwiches in the shade.

'Secretly,' he told her, 'I thought I ought to specialize a little, that's why I stayed out here so long.'

'On Egypt?'

'On the Canal, at least. I do my best for my west-country farmers, but as long as the Government keeps up the subsidy arrangements I'm stuck with my committees and fighting the potato board. But that can't go on for ever. I was brought up on this, after all.'

'They ought to make you an under-secretary,' she said.

'Don't joke. Look at this. Handing over the Canal zone. Really, it is quite significant. Yet there's nobody here that matters to see it, excepting the obvious officials and you and me. When you realize what is drawing to its end here . . .'

'Don't,' she said. 'I hate it as much as you do.'

Peacock sighed as the bugle blew, very well blown too by an Egyptian soldier mounted on a nice dapple-grey Arab, beautifully kept. A drummer with two ceremonial drums in leopard skin (the Blues?) banged across his saddle in a roll call, and Peacock felt his eyes getting the better of him. It was a shame that no Minister was here. It was being done so decently, and there was no ill-feeling. It was, in fact, a loss that ought to be turned into a gain. It was a graceful retreat, and the white-haired Egyptian brigadier who looked like any British soldier on the eve of retirement told them that it was a happy thing for everybody. Prime Minister Nehru of India had once said that Britain should sail off nobly into the bay of Bengal as an enemy, and then turn around and come back nobly as a friend. Why not? Peacock said.

'We hope so,' the Brigadier answered softly, and bowed to Madame with such seductive grace that Peacock said he must have learned that in the old Turkish Army where the manners were better on this level than the soldiering.

'They all look terribly British to me,' Lucy said.

'That's the sad part of it,' Peacock told her. 'We have it all here. What we have given them is, after all, what we have left them. They look British. They must still half-think British. That's what makes me feel so sad. Why can't it go on, even on other levels?'

'With Nasser?'

'Oh, never mind him. Not everybody here is Nasser.'

It was time to leave the dais and shake hands with Phillpotts, who had marched like a Greek god across the polo pitch with a lieutenant holding the sword at dressed position, shining in the dust-laden Egyptian sunlight and breaking up the ceremony into a going-home, a going-away from this dusty place.

'And what about Scott?' he asked her. 'How did you find him?'

270

'Oh, he's hopeless,' she said on the way home in the official green car the Egyptian Army had provided for them with a standard flying—not a Union Jack but the pennant of General Hakim's frontier force.

'He just up and disappeared again,' Peacock told her, 'and I had to write on his behalf to the Royal Geographical Society saying he would take any job they'd give him, and filling in as many details as I could. Something must be done, somehow, to get rid of these terrible stigmata he still carries. It ought to be cleared up. It's always on my conscience.'

She slumped a little tiredly. 'It's gone to his soul by now,' she said. 'Oh, look! Look at those water-buffaloes all covered with white birds.'

Peacock ignored nature.

'People haven't been very kind to Scott,' he persisted. 'I mean specific people who should have known better.'

'You mean me, I suppose.'

'No, of course I don't. I would not say that to your face, Lucy, even if I thought it. Even though we do disagree about the whole thing.'

'Even if it's true,' she said, 'why can't he simply get over it?'

'He's such an unlucky sort of chap,' Peacock informed her. 'He doesn't ever quite get hold of what's happening. As a matter of fact I don't think he was ever meant to be in all this trouble he gets into. What sort of Englishman do we breed now? I don't know,' he said sadly, 'but not Scotty's sort, anyway. He's out of date. He should have been cutting his way through a continent for us, like Stanley or was it Livingstone? I can't remember which one really made the tracks and which was the American. Anyway, he's that sort. What's happened to us, really? It's that Calvinist conscience of his that gets him into depths way beyond him, that's all it is. That's why I'd like to get him onto this antarctic expedition. It would be very good for him and it's absolutely his line of work, without complications. There's nothing at the South Pole he can get his crazy conscience involved with. No Sam Hassoon, no Church, no silly bloody politics.'

'You don't know anything about him,' Lucy said suddenly, as if she had listened too patiently to a lot of nonsense.

'What do you mean? I feel I know him very well.'

'You don't even know the first thing that matters.'

'Don't I? What is it, then?'

'He's weak,' she said vehemently. 'He may know his job, or what he does; but he's so ignorant of everything else that it turns him into a helpless baby when he has to face other people. He doesn't know anything about himself at all, and he doesn't know anything about other people. That's what's wrong with him.'

'He can't help that.'

She pulled a wry face as if everything she was saying was a very poor

271

expression of what she meant. 'Oh, he needs someone all the time to prod him, and to *tell* him what is right and wrong for him. He doesn't know, he simply doesn't know.'

'Why don't you take him in hand again,' Peacock suggested, forgiving Lucy all her past mistakes. Why shouldn't he, since Scott had forgiven Lucy himself?

Lucy knew how innocent a man Peacock was, and she did not hesitate now to tell him the truth, because it would hurt less than a lie.

'How can I take him in hand,' she said, 'when he won't let me do what I can for him?'

'I know. He's a hard man to help,' Peacock said understandingly.

A military convoy was passing them along the sweet-water canal from the Cairo direction, and he leaned forward because he thought he ought to take a good look at it. Think of all this Russian equipment in Egypt which no one ever sees, except in the Liberation Day parade when, from the dais, you got a fair view of the Stalin tanks and the Czech armoured cars, and even a few self-propelled guns; but nothing new worth seeing except the Migs which shot overhead in a very hot fly-past, so low and in such good formation that quite obviously they were piloted by experts, if one only knew who the experts were. Probably not Egyptians.

'I don't know,' he sighed. 'I suppose Scott is still a bit of a mystery to all of us.'

'Sam!' he said to her at dinner. 'Something ought to be done for Sam too.'

They were eating in the badly lit annexe of the pigeon restaurant—a whole pigeon each, eaten with the fingers and wiped around in the gravy with native bread while the frogs croaked coarsely on the Nile bank at their feet.

'Oh, I don't think they'll hurt Sam,' she said. 'They probably want someone else rather than Sam himself.'

'Even so, it's a pity old Scotty just disappeared like that,' he said, and watched the fresh hot pigeon come apart, flesh from bone, as he took it delicately in his fingers. 'I wanted to talk to him.'

'Oh, damnation to him!' Lucy said irritably. 'Don't let's think about him.'

'Sorry,' Peacock said and sat back, sucking his fingers. 'Listen to those bull-frogs on the river,' he told her. 'Can you imagine it? Those bull-frogs probably have ancestors going back to Pharaoh. The same breed was probably croaking down there when Cheops was building the pyramids and even before that. *Crawwk!*' Peacock made a skilful copy of a frog and she laughed. 'My children would love that,' he said. 'I'm very good at it. You know, Lucy, *that's* the only sort of continuation there really is. Look

272

at all the empires in history. Not one of them ever left more than a mockery of itself behind. Look at the Romans. Every time I go to Italy I feel like laughing at the Romans for coming to that! And the French. Do you imagine it will happen to us? I've been thinking about it all day. The fact is, you know, that *time* is not what passes, Lucy, it's really what continues.'

'You're such a very nice man, Timothy. Profound too.'

'I think better when I'm well fed. I only hope my gyppy tummy doesn't come back.'

'I shall write to Eileen tomorrow and tell her how lucky she is.'

'I hope we're both lucky,' he said generously. 'It would be nice if you finally got around Scotty after all. Would you like another pigeon?' he asked her when she laughed and kissed him lightly with the pleasure of restored friendship and their mutual hopes for the future.

CHAPTER THIRTY-SEVEN

JACK DE BRAZIO was an old friend, if you counted as old friends the ones you almost forgot about until you saw them again.

Americans were frightened to talk, and that could be hard on Quartermain's friends. If you talked to an American who had even been suspected of having un-American sympathies, as de Brazio must have been because of his support for the Spanish republic and Roosevelt and Harry Hopkins, who had been a close friend, you had to go mincing around every subject with elaborate qualifications so that you did not embarrass him with the need for direct answers and forthright opinions.

Good-bye to all those blind, exhilarating free-for-alls, to the prejudiced repugnance for the obvious. Praise for the un-obvious was absolutely out of the question and would be dangerous. It meant that you could not talk to a man like Jack for fear of insulting him or his country. You might also put him into a situation where he might say something joyfully outrageous (he'd be just getting into the swing of it) when he would suddenly realize it was forbidden fun. He ought to keep his mouth shut.

Was de Brazio like that now? he wondered. Was his pretty and outspoken and normal-looking wife with dark curls like that? This was Jack's second wife. His first had been a smart woman with a shy frightened face. This one, Ella, looked very pretty and unfrightened, which meant that Jack did not look frightened either. That was hopeful.

'What do you think of the English these days, Jack?' Quartermain asked him, because Jack had always admired the British.

'What English do you mean?'

'I don't care,' Quartermain said. 'Take your pick.'

'You mean the English type in general; or the particular chap?'

'What's the difference?'

'It's always the chap that's nice,' de Brazio said. 'It's the type that's the bastard. You know I never thought Eden was capable of being much more than a clothes-horse. Didn't we all admire him? When I first saw him, here in Cairo during the war when Churchill sent him for something or

274

other, I thought then: is this the chap or is this the type? He giggled a bit instead of answering our questions. I never made up my mind about him after that. What do you think of him?'

'Don't ask me.'

'I guess it's too obvious,' Jack agreed.

They were walking up Garden City after a good lunch and a bottle of heart-firing Greek *Zibib* to visit the British and American press attachés, with Jack's small wife Ella running between them to keep up. Since lunch they had been arguing, edgily and flushed, about men; the world's men.

'Do you want to tell me,' Jack said graciously, 'what you think of Dulles?'

'I don't think so,' Quartermain said obligingly. 'I would only have to qualify anything I say.'

'Not necessarily,' Jack urged. 'I can take anything. Go ahead, old man.'

'You know that I'm an independent thinker . . .'

'Okay!'

'. . . and that I've got a water-tight case against Dulles.'

'You don't say. I suppose you shot Dulles in self-defence yesterday.'

'No, no!' Quartermain said reasonably. 'It's just that John Foster Dulles is a well-known communist.'

'You poor sick chap. What's water-tight about that?'

'All right. You argue with me. I say Dulles is a well-known communist. Well—go on—deny it, if you can.'

'I do deny it! I know he isn't,' Jack said firmly.

'Are you defending a well-known communist, Mr. de Brazio?'

'No, I'm not. But I don't believe this of Mr. Dulles!'

'Ah haha! So you are putting yourself on the same side as a well-known communist.'

'But after all, he's . . .'

'No *buts*. No *after-alls*. Be careful, de Brazio. You'll end up on the stand on a perjury charge.'

'I still don't think Mr. Dulles is a communist,' Jack said heatedly, 'and a man's entitled to his opinions.'

'Not when it means supporting a well-known communist like John Foster Dulles. Will you come out openly and deny that you support this communist or will you not?'

'If you put it like that. I didn't know . . .'

'I'm waiting.'

'Since that's the situation you put me into, and under protest, I deny all association with John Foster Dulles, and I swear I have no sympathy with him at all. I never did have. I'll do all in my power, furthermore, to expose him at all times, and hereafter I'll even refrain from thinking of him.'

275

'Then you're cleared,' Quartermain told him with a sigh. 'You're okay.'

'Now, listen,' Ella complained then. 'I'm not going another step until you both shut up. You've both had too much *Zibib* to be trusted, and I'm not walking into any U.S. Embassy with this sort of talk going on.'

'We're only kidding,' Jack explained.

'I know you are, and you might just forget yourself and go on kidding when you're talking to Morrison. So please call it off. Please . . .'

Jack bit his tongue and Quartermain took Ella's arm and they lifted her up the steps of the American information office between them, refusing to say a word to her. Morrison the attaché looked puzzled and amused when he opened the door for them.

'Come on in, you guys,' he said. 'What's the matter? Is Ella sick?'

'No, no,' Jack explained quickly. 'She's been drinking that Greek *Zibib*,' he said, and he introduced his friend, Quartermain.

When Jack was more serious, eating the dinner that Scott should have had weeks ago at the Quartermain's flat, and while Nona and Ella estimated the best and the worst that was foreign in each other, he regretted the good old days. Not the drunken days, Jack said, but simply the good old days when newspapermen behaved like Red Knickerbocker and Red Sheehan and Red Casey—none of whom were reds at all, but that wasn't the point in those days. They simply had red hair.

'The last time I was at the UN in Paris,' Jack recalled sadly, 'there were all those agency men and *Time* and *Life* men and *New York Times* men sitting around in dark grey two-button flannel suits, looking more like diplomats than the diplomats, terrified the tone of the place was getting too low. Some of them were taking hand-outs like a post-office sorting machine. One day a tall thin guy from the Quai d'Orsay came into the Palais de Chaillot and ran down the corridors of the press section shouting that the French Prime Minister had just shot his mistress at the metro station at Pont Neuf. You know what those *New York Times* guys in the grey suits said when they finally stopped him jumping out of the window of the fifth floor: "Could you give us an official statement on that, sir?"

'It's not true,' they said.

'Honest! They took the wrong man to the looney-bin that day. It's no joke, I'm telling you. The next time I saw the Prime Minister coming out of the Ministry of Marine after a dinner for someone or other; no, I'm telling a lie, it was the opening of the oyster season; anyway, I asked him very politely, very politely, mind you: "Is it true, Mr. Prime Minister, that you recently had a problem on your hands in the Pont Neuf metro station?" So what do you think happened?'

'He knocked you down with one of the Gardes Republicains,' Quartermain said, eating a chocolate.

'No. The *New York Express* man hit me hard in the stomach with his grey-flannel elbow and said I'd be expelled from the Foreign Press Association for life if I ever ever asked a dirty question like that again. I tell you, men have changed.'

'But it's not true,' Nona said. 'Surely?'

She had appealed to Ella because it was not for her.

'Partly,' Ella said sympathetically. 'I think your husband is a bad influence on mine, Mrs. Quartermain. He only gets like this when he meets a fellow-feeling.'

'I'm partly used to it myself,' Nona said. 'But is it true?'

'Of course it's true,' Quartermain told her. 'If you don't believe it, then it's pointless. You must believe it.'

'The funny thing is,' Jack went on indignantly, 'the Prime Minister *had* shot his mistress, though not at the Pont Neuf metro station. She was grazed under the right eye outside a villa at Chamonix. But she'd already been shot at before, so she took it like a veteran. I mean she was a veteran to some extent. She'd been shot at by another Prime Minister in 1938 or 1939, before or after the Popular Front. Same mistress, different Prime Minister, that's all. I think that's right. It's like the chicken or the egg: which comes first, the Prime Minister or the mistress? You know, some day de Gaulle is going to come to power and clean up French politics of all these indiscriminate layabouts . . .'

'That's enough, Jack,' Ella said. 'Not everybody likes mistresses in the conversation.'

'I'm terribly sorry,' Jack said, turning wide-eyed to Nona. 'I didn't mean . . .'

Nona looked forbidding and prudish, then she threw back her head and laughed and said, 'It's really very funny.'

'See!' Jack said to his wife.

But they knew it was meant for no one. When Jack de Brazio walked into your house and out of it again it did not remain a special house with special people in it. Jack was too universal-minded for that. It was simply some house Jack had been to, with some sort of interesting people in it: good company, but sometimes hard to remember until the next time. He loved good company, he over-ate, he loved the moment. He looked at Mrs. Quartermain, trying to see her through her own barriers, but she remained unseeable. He must try though to be nice, and to make a solid impression. He was a serious man.

'That was a nice dinner, Mrs. Quartermain,' he said.

'You must come again,' she told him, also trying.

'I will.'

That was all they could manage, and the failure was obvious. He was not embarrassed but he turned quickly to ask her husband if he would go down to the Red Sea with him to find Captain Scott in his hideaway.

'There was a report from Tel Aviv yesterday that your friend Scott was training Egyptian commandos in the Gaza strip, but when I got hold of his boss, General Hakim, he laughed and said it was premature. That's an official way of saying it might be true. But then he said Scott was on duty at Ghurdakha on the Red Sea coast, so I thought I'd go down there for a couple of days in my hired Chevrolet and check up on it. And if he's there we could see what else he's doing.'

'Will the Egyptians let you go down there?' Quartermain asked.

'All you need is a desert pass, and I can get that in a day. You simply have to show your passport. I don't have to tell them I'm going after Scott. What about it? You're a friend of his.'

'I don't know,' Quartermain replied. 'I'm inclined to leave Scotty where he is. He's been away a couple of weeks now, so he probably intends staying there for ever.'

'But why? What turns that guy into a hairy anchorite every now and then? That's what I'd like to know. What for? What does he really do down there?'

Quartermain didn't know why Scott was so mysterious. 'Nobody knows, least of all Scott himself.'

'That's why I thought I'd go and find out,' de Brazio said. 'That Israeli he caught in the desert, a while back, died in the military hospital this morning, according to the Tel Aviv radio at noon, and they usually know everything that goes on here. They say he was beaten to death. I wonder how Scott feels about that?'

'You mean Sam Hassoon's father died?' Nona asked.

'The one Scott picked up. The Egyptians say he was a sick old man . . .'

'But that's terrible,' Nona said, and excused herself to go into the other room to telephone Helen, who must go to Alicia at once. Someone must tell her, and the grandmother, if she did not already know that Alicia's father, her son, was dead.

When she was out of the room, Quartermain said he had changed his mind. Perhaps he would go down to the Red Sea to see Scott after all.

'I hope Sam doesn't do anything foolish,' Quartermain said to Nona as they calmed themselves down for the night.

'What do you mean?'

'He's quite capable of jumping out of the window when he hears about his father,' her husband told her.

'What a thing to tell me when we're going to bed. I shan't sleep.'

She went into the children's room to see that they were safe and that

278

they were asleep. Cover the children when the world's dangers were pressing too hard on you.

'When will it all stop?' she said dejectedly when she came back. 'Why should Jews and Arabs kill each other? They never did before. Not until the British set them at each others' throats in Palestine. Even I can remember when there was no antagonism at all. Now, even my school friends among the Jews are suddenly hating the Egyptians. They're frightened, and they're just waiting to be thrown out, and they don't want to go. They don't want to be Israelis. It's so bestial . . .'

'Once,' he pointed out again, 'they had all the privileges.'

'That doesn't make any difference,' she insisted. 'What could they do? They were born the way they were born. They couldn't help being Jews in a community where the Jews were well-off. Do you think they could give it up and live like the fellah? Or abandon what they were, simply because they ought to be miserable in order to be Egyptian?'

'You can never be what you are not,' he agreed, 'but it might have helped if they hadn't been so stupidly and contemptuously exclusive, or if they had learned the language of the country they were born and brought up in, the Arabic language, or if they had tried to be a little more semitic among semites, and not be European and despise *les sales Arabes*.'

'Tell that to a sixteen-year-old schoolgirl when her mother and father and uncles and friends all say the opposite.'

'Too late now, anyway,' he said. 'They're done for.'

'Sam never despised the Egyptians, and Sam learned the language. But where is he now?'

'I wonder how he'll feel when he hears that Zareef the pilot has been arrested, as well as his father being dead. No wonder Scotty ran away . . .'

CHAPTER THIRTY-EIGHT

HELEN, swinging her leg from the floor, brought it up high enough for Nona to see while she lay still waiting sleepily for the alarm to wake her, no longer necessary now that Helen's leg was going up and down. Up, down. Nona closed her eyes.

Quartermain was away. They had made it too difficult for him to go to the Red Sea, simply by delaying his desert pass. He had gone with Jack de Brazio instead to see one of the model agricultural villages that Nasser had set up in the Liberation Province, off the Alexandria road. Perhaps that would persuade Mr. Aboud of his good will, his genuine interest in Egypt.

He would only be away one night, but who knew what the noises were in the floors and ceilings at night? Nona had never slept alone in her life, and she did not want to try it now. The devils and evil spirits of any good Arab story were very mean practical jokers as a rule, and however much reason and disbelief thinned them out in daytime, at night, alone, the well-equipped Arab imagination brought them back again in droves. She was then afraid to believe in her own disbelief. One never knew. That was the only safe system with unnatural sounds, and a second presence was necessary to dispose of them safely.

'Benjamino will be late for school,' Helen told her. 'It's after six.'

Helen moved to the window, stretching a towel around the air above her head, gripping it firmly between her outstretched arms as she exercised her stomach.

'You're making me giddy,' Nona told her. 'Stop it.'

'You should do this every morning yourself,' Helen said.

'I'd have palpitations.'

'You only have palpitations if your liver is out of order, and this is what makes it work better. It's all digestive.'

Nona laughed. 'The way your stomach goes in and out, I should think your liver must be fed up by now.'

'I can't stop. At my age I'd sag like a Chinese peasant.'

When Helen walked like a younger goddess through her city, it was all done with exercise and respect for the liver and with a will that would never give in. But anyone who saw her knew that it was worthwhile, however she did it. Women didn't walk like that any more by nature, excepting peasants in the villages with old oil-drums on their heads coming from the water-hole. What a regret to lie married here for a moment and watch it. Not for Helen, but for the fools of men who did not know what they were losing. What a stupid loss it was that she did not share it with someone, anyone decent enough to give her a chance to be herself.

'It's a pity English Christians don't allow their men to have two wives,' Nona told her.

'Don't say that! Why? Are you so tired of being one wife? You shouldn't say such a thing.'

'No. I'm thinking how much better Quarts would be for you. After all, he started off admiring you first. Honestly. I'd share him with you, if I could.'

Helen slapped the bedclothes over her backside. 'I'm too old now for that kind of *plaisanterie*. Anyway, one of us is enough for any man. Particularly an Englishman, and I'm older than he is. Why did you think he chose you?'

Nona got up, her long legs and dishevelled limbs looking much too thin for a moment, and Helen was worried about her. She did not eat the right foods, and she wore herself out. Nona had always been a tall girl, and at fourteen she had already been fully developed and beautifully made, but to see her now, the mother of children, was hardly the same thing. Did one ever forget the adolescent girl? Did one always expect her to remain that way, without the troubles of life bending the nerves and the muscles a little more each year? It was horrifying to think of someone like Nona growing older at all.

'Your posture,' Helen said to her, as if to ward off the process that way.

'After two children, what do you expect?' Nona answered, unbothered by it.

'You ought to look after yourself more.'

'It's my liver, darling,' Nona teased. 'And you'll have to resign yourself to it.'

Helen had seen Sam in his prison, for five minutes, and it was better to joke now rather than turn it into something serious. She had seen Sam's father safely buried, and now that Hanna had gone to Alicia's to help them over their rivers of sorrow, it left Helen and Nona alone to be at peace for a little while, even though they knew it was impossible.

Helen could begin to say now (safely because it was daylight) what she had been forbidden to say last night when they were about to sleep—when Nona had objected: 'Don't talk about the dead now, or about Sam.

281

I couldn't stand it. Night makes everything so much worse. And none of you liked him, and I don't even remember him. Leave it till morning, darling.'

But Helen had a right to unburden herself of it now.

'Sam was clinging to me like a child,' Helen told her, scrubbing her face with a loofah in the bathroom. 'I had to get angry with him when I didn't want to. I felt like weeping myself, though. But Sam wept so much at Abbasia that I *had* to stop him. He was so miserable and guilty. Oh, I know what you think. But why does he always turn into butter like that?'

'After all, it was his father.'

'I know!' Helen soaped her face and began to douse cold water on it. 'But I saw my own father and mother buried within a month, and I didn't let that happen. What cruel idiocy, anyway,' she groaned. 'Why do orientals have to prove death? I don't mind the Moslems slaughtering something at the door as the body leaves it, but this moaning and crying! The English behave so much better. You've got to have some restraint, even in Sam's case.'

'I suppose it's more the prison with Sam than his father. And he hasn't even seen anyone, darling. He must be frightened all the time.'

'He has seen Scott, and he had seen his father. I wouldn't mind it so much if I thought it was only loneliness and fear. But he was getting hysterical about his father. He hardly knew him. His father never gave that family anything but trouble. Sam was sobbing "Mon père, mon père!"'

Nona found her own tears suddenly there, inexplicable and unwanted.

'Did he seem all right otherwise? Is he sick?'

'He looked ten years younger. He's lost all that fat which Alicia and the grandmother pushed into him with the *pâté* and risottos and macaronis. He said they were letting him do the garden now.'

'Did he know about his pilot friend, Zareef?'

'Of course he did. I thought he would take that hard. But he just treated it as a sort of passing error. That was a silly mistake, he said, and he was sure they would let Zareef out. After all, Zareef's a Moslem and Zareef is innocent. He seemed to have a lot of confidence in the Egyptian security police realizing that. "Ali will explain," he kept saying. It didn't worry him as much as I thought, knowing how sentimental he is.'

'But what did he say about Scott?' Nona asked, watching Helen closely.

'He just shrugged when I told him Captain Scott had gone back to the Red Sea and left him there. As a matter of fact he seemed to have resigned himself to being left there—in prison. Poor Sam! I suspect he'd got over his fear of being beaten, and he was almost willing to give up everything and feel that he was being punished, and that was that. He was almost secure in a way.' She shuddered a little.

Nona had dressed herself and was doing up her sensible English shoes, which, on her large feet, looked too deliberately dull. Helen turned away so as not to see them. She ought to wear good shoes made to measure by an Armenian.

'Perhaps it's just as well Sam feels like that,' Nona said. 'The only way he can survive is to accept it.'

'What are you saying? Accept what? What right have the Egyptians to keep him there just because he's a Jew—without a trial, without even a *procès*?'

'Listen, darling,' Nona said. 'Are you sure that it might not be worse for him if there is a *procès*? I don't know what he did, but they still might shoot him or do something just as terrible.'

'No, they won't.'

'How do you know they won't? Be realistic, Helen.'

'I'm very realistic. That's why I felt so angry and helpless yesterday. I wrote an angry letter to the famous Captain Scott last night and told him he ought to do something.'

'Quarts says he has his own problems . . .'

'You are always trying to find excuses,' Helen said on the two-hundredth stroke of the hairbrush through her long hair. 'If you give up so easily in this country you might as well lie down and die. You've forgotten.'

'No, I haven't.'

'Then why are you so defeatist?'

'Because I know that in helping Sam you're going to get the worst of it yourself.'

'I'm not going to let them frighten me!' she said sharply. 'Even Jolley is frightened now . . .'

'Because of Sam?'

'No. No. He's afraid they'll close him up.'

'Who will? The Egyptians?'

'The Egyptians and the London office, both.'

'Does that mean you'll be out of a job?'

'Of course. And there aren't any others going, as you jolly well know. Not for someone like me. Unless I want to be a miserable typist . . .'

'There he is,' Nona said, rushing out. 'He's going to break the springs.'

Benjamino was awake and was taking off in high jumps from Hilal's bed and landing heavily on his own so that the springs hit the floor and threw him up into the air.

'Nothing seems to penetrate,' Nona said, shaking Ben.

'Oh, he's a child,' Helen protested. 'Let him have his fun.'

'And if he breaks the bed?'

'Worry about that when it happens,' Helen said.

Helen was going to be angry about it, but when she saw little Ben winding his legs around his mother's waist, and when she noticed that Nona held him tightly around the neck, she knew it was not the bed that Nona was worried about, but that precious neck. Nor was Benjamino worried about his threatening mother. Threats? Those confident young eyes knew what the world did not know—that all things were there for his own protection, even his mother's discipline which was the safe rock of his life. Benjamino would always be stretching life to its limits, that was clear; but where would he be without this limit, which he reached in safety because he expected it to be there?

'My sweetheart,' Nona said to him and forgave him.

But then she reminded him, nonetheless, that he had torn the bed-clothes two days ago, and that he had eaten too many sweets at Aunt Hanna's on Saturday, and that he had dirtied his tablier at school and was never sensible . . .

'If you'd only learn to keep it to the particular complaint in hand,' Helen said, but she knew it did not really matter. The children knew their mother's secrets, and they would never believe her complaints.

Helen kissed Hilal, who had come for his share of it, and she went out to the kitchen to make sure that Ali had taken the yoghurt out of the ice-box so that it was not too cold to eat, since anything frozen was ruinous to the kidneys.

But they must finish with it over breakfast.

'After all,' Helen said, 'under the English, at least a woman like me had something useful to do. When the English ran the Ministries they didn't confine women to the fields, to the kitchen and to Groppi's pastries, like the Egyptians. The Moslem girls can be typists, that's all.'

'Then it's the Egyptian women's own fault if they accept it.'

'That doesn't help me,' Helen said.

'But you were born before your time, sweetheart,' Nona said, kissing Helen on the top of her head and realizing that Quartermain was right: Helen would never see the true situation she was in, and why. 'You should have married an Englishman,' Nona teased, 'and showed them how to save their skins here, instead of throwing everything away by their silly snobbery and their ignorance and contempt for everything Egyptian'.

Even so, it was going to be much worse for Helen if her office did close up.

CHAPTER THIRTY-NINE

PEACOCK had said to the Ambassador, 'I must see Nasser again, alone, before I leave,' and the Ambassador had made the appointment and suggested, breathing protocol lightly, that he'd come along himself as well.

'If you don't mind, I'd prefer not,' Peacock said apologetically. 'I know protocol requires it, but I'd like to talk to him, just once, on his own level. It's got to be done somehow, don't you think?'

The Ambassador thought so. They leaned against the Ambassador's window in the Ambassador's long, graceless bureau.

'I do miss the Residency, though,' Peacock said. The half-moon of modern grey offices in one corner of the Embassy gardens was not a decent atmosphere. It was an office; an office-of-works High Holborn office with glass water-coolers from America crested and ensigned Elizabeth IIR and a red steel lift to three floors. 'When did they build this horror?' he asked.

'A couple of years ago,' the Ambassador sighed, too used to the question.

'And the Residency?'

'It's finally a residency,' the Ambassador joked.

Even finding your man was different. Lampson had been more like a Viceroy, the last of them, living in largesse in his colonial mansion. Business and diplomacies and government were elsewhere, and the crooked old wooden floors and good furniture and Persian rugs and wire-screens opening with a squeak onto the watered lawns and rose paths kept the air of a reception house waiting for Kitchener, Lord Lloyd, and Gordon in his elaborate and sweaty uniforms. They arrived from up-country, usually dead and dying and too late.

'I hate to see it go,' Peacock said, 'and yet that is what I've been watching here, you know. That's the feeling I'm going home with.'

'Oh, I wouldn't say that.'

Below the window were a dozen cars with CD plates. Below he could hear Wilson the press attaché talking to some newspaper on the phone, and the voice wafted out into the rose garden.

285

'I'll look at the diary,' Wilson was saying. 'Yes. The Ambassador returns the visit of Prince So-and-so of Kuwait. Where? At the Semiramis, I think. Nothing much. The canal? Oh, yes, you'll have to get in touch with Major Digby at Navy House in Port Said. But it's all being run from Cyprus now. We don't do anything about the canal here any more.'

'You see!' Peacock left the window and paced the faded green carpet. 'We don't do anything about the canal here any more,' he echoed out of Wilson's voice two floors below. 'What a terrible thing to hear, don't you think?'

'Don't blame us for that,' the Ambassador said, trying to cheer him up, amused as they were all amused at the intensity of Peacock's recent sadness. Try as he might, Peacock's good nature could not convince them that he was feeling as tragic as he said he was. It wasn't in him, it simply wasn't in him.

'Oh, I don't blame you chaps,' Peacock said. 'Not really. You know that.'

'In fact we are doing very well at the moment,' the Ambassador pointed out. 'The British are more popular in Egypt now than they've been for years.'

'Because we are getting out gracefully?'

The Ambassador shrugged, which was not typical of him. He had a large dent in his chin, a slight scar on his cheek, and Peacock liked him because he was a strong-faced self-achieved man with a curious way of fighting you off with hard-mouthed answers, like a stubborn pony. It made him feel like a junior officer asking a very senior officer to reveal his mind. It was a strictly business mind too.

'I must be off,' he said.

'I'll send for a car.' The Ambassador pushed a professional button.

'No. No. I'm going to walk to the corner and get in a taxi. I'll get there myself.'

'In a taxi?'

'I don't even want CD plates tailing me there. I've got a feeling now that we've simply got to make up our mind about Nasser one way or the other, and I want to do it without outside influence of any kind.'

Peacock was looking for his hat and the Ambassador found it on the mantelpiece of the fireplace and gave it to him, and Peacock looked and asked what the devil did they want a mantelpiece in this business office in Egypt for?

'I don't think a couple of CD plates will influence you,' the Ambassador said, still smiling, 'and they'll give you a more comfortable ride.'

'No. I'm going to do this the hard way.'

'You may find the going very hard indeed,' the Ambassador warned. 'It looks as if the World Bank experts have definitely abandoned any idea of financing the Aswan Dam.'

'Well, surely Nasser will not blame us for that?'

'He doesn't even know it officially yet, but he has probably guessed it.'

'What will he feel about that? Is it so important?'

'It's very important,' the Ambassador replied thoughtfully. 'The Aswan Dam is the Colonel's pet project. He is planning his whole idea for the future of his industrialized Egypt on the power and irrigation of that dam. You may arrive for the worst of it.'

'You think he'll browbeat me! I hope it's not going to be unpleasant.'

'He never browbeats anybody. He may not be responsive, that's all.'

The Ambassador tried again to persuade him to take someone, at least a translator from the Embassy, because it was rather better protocol. It would also be a safeguard against ever being misquoted later. As a politician he ought to take that much precaution.

'I'm not quite that professional-minded,' Peacock said. 'I'll take a chance.'

In leaving, Peacock took a drink of cold water from the gurgler marked ElizabethIIR which fascinated him. 'Marvellous gadget. Gurgle, gurgle! You know, I have a feeling that there are two Nassers. One the newspapers write about at home, and the other one you make up your mind about yourself. I really haven't made up my mind at the moment, that's the trouble.'

'You must have some notion of what he's like.'

'Oh, I have. But I keep thinking about my old friend Scott. I simply can't imagine him ever trusting a man who wasn't worth it. That's what sticks on the wrong side, even though Scotty is quite naïve sometimes. It's quite confusing at the moment. It used to be so simple and straightforward in the old days. He *is* a dictator, I suppose. *That* can't be swallowed. Professional too, and a pretty cool customer. Oh, well . . .'

The Ambassador smiled and closed the lift door and Peacock went down, talking to himself. As he went out he waved an absent-minded acknowledgment at the Egyptian guard who saluted him stiffly at the Embassy gate.

He discovered in the formal, workless, pristineness, in the objectless atmosphere of the President's receiving room, and in the spotless carpet and cream walls and unused red chairs, that Nasser was not interested in what he, Peacock, had done in Egypt since he had arrived with the other M.P.s—now all gone back home long ago.

Wasn't it really interesting that a British M.P. showed such a desire to see so much of his Egypt? If it was, the President was not going to reveal his fascination.

Peacock had to jog his own memory to throw in, every now and then in his narrative, a *Mr. President* the way the Americans did. After all, Nasser was the elected President now, even though there was no Parliament or elected body of any kind to ratify or even justify the existence of a President.

The President ran a pencil through his large opposing hands, hunched, listening and looking up occasionally without giving anything away.

'I'm going to be babbling on for ever at this rate,' Peacock warned himself, and gave the President a frankly puzzled and hurt look. '*Is this the way he works? Just sits there and says nothing. But what the devil's he thinking?*'

To stir this massive, mysterious, dark-eyed Egyptian out of the trick of listening, Peacock said, 'And of course, I did take a look at Aswan, where you wanted to put your dam. What bad luck that you might not be able to build the dam after all.'

The President looked up, nodded, and smiled slightly, perhaps artificially.

'Ah, Mr. President. I'm so glad you can smile,' Peacock said cheerfully. 'Only this morning someone said to me that you'd be angry because the World Bank might not give you the money to build the dam.'

'There's no use being angry,' Nasser said to him in English, 'when you are trying to get something done. We'll get the money somehow.'

'Of course it wasn't our fault, you know,' Peacock pointed out. 'I'm sure we would have given you the money if we had it to give. But I don't need to tell you, Mr. President, that Britain isn't a rich nation any more, not from the point of view of lending capital to that extent. Although I think our capital investment in Egypt has always been very high, hasn't it?'

'Your returns have been even higher,' the President argued. 'That's partly the trouble . . .' Nasser seemed to stop himself there, as if he had decided beforehand not to say anything unpleasant, and yet here was one man in the world already taking Peacock seriously. Peacock felt it and sat up straight.

'But that's the nature of capital, don't you think?' Peacock said. 'After all, capital can't reproduce itself unless its returns are high.'

The President concentrated on his pencil. 'The returns are high for one country and very low for another,' he pointed out. 'They have been too high for you and too low for us. That's what I meant.'

'I'm sure you are absolutely right,' Peacock conceded. 'But to be fair— we did leave many good things for you in Egypt: your entire irrigation system, your roads, railways, ports, power-stations, cities even. And look at all your doctors and technicians who came to England to learn. You can't shrug those off, you know.'

The President looked very doubtful for a moment, gauging something, estimating, guessing, not believing and yet struggling to believe. He looked hard at Peacock as if to ask himself: 'What sort of an Englishman is this one?'

'Would you like to come home to lunch with me, perhaps?' he said to Peacock. 'If it is not too early for you.'

Peacock flushed. How extraordinary. He hesitated for no more than a second and then he said, 'That's very nice of you, Mr. President. Of course I would be delighted.'

'Good. Then let's go now. It's a long drive in the noonday traffic.'

The President was the president. He could not help behaving in the role also. Lunch was political, with General Hakim of the Frontier Department and a Moslem priest who spoke perfect English.

'My English Professor,' the President said.

The President appeared to be so deliberate in all things that he ate deliberately and politically, and he would pause for ten, fifteen, thirty seconds before he replied to any question. It was this little pause, this wait that gave Nasser his strongest characteristic of being a man who waited for all things to affect him before he responded to them. Nothing was going to panic him.

Peacock ate the fish course and longed to ask the President what he really did. What sort of a man was he? Had he ever put a ball to a bat or swung a mallet to a lump of leather? Did he have no games?

He didn't look as if he did, but only the English had games in that sense, and the more time you spent away from home the more you realized why there was no exact equivalent to 'fair-play' in any other language—German, Italian, French and most certainly not in Arabic. At the very most there was something for foreigners called *noblesse*, which was not really a sporting term at all, and was only admirable on another level.

'Do you play any sport?' Peacock asked, anyway, biting asparagus tips from his fingers and sending them delightfully down his throat. 'You look so fit, I'm sure you are *sportif*, Mr. President.'

The President had shaken his head. 'No sport,' he said, amused and cutting up his asparagus before eating it.

'He swims like a fish,' General Hakim told Peacock slyly. 'He's very good.'

'Ah . . . swimming,' Peacock said.

The President swam? In that case he probably got his athletic posture from his military background: good health and discipline. That seemed to be adequate. The trouble was that one always thought of a President as the President of France. There he was, with a red sash around his stout stomach, and a red rosette in his buttonhole, holding a top-hat and looking

L   289

plump and gallic and childishly solemn as he stood to attention for flags and anthems.

This President wore a white shirt and an American businessman's tie and a militarily shaved face which organized his appearance so well that it was hard to deny that he was a successful man. Also, that calm habit of waiting before he answered a question gave him a right to say what he was saying, and it worried Peacock a little. There was something poised about it.

Ice-cream filled with crystallized fruit allowed them to escape the dullness of the polite conversation. It would be all right, however, when they could start chatting more casually over small coffees.

They shifted to another white room and the President sat on a couch and asked Peacock why the British Government was being so unfriendly about the blocked Egyptian credits in the Bank of England.

'You mustn't think it's unfriendliness on our part,' Peacock said.

'But I'm afraid we *must* consider it unfriendly,' the President argued, a little more earnestly. Egypt, he pointed out, needed every penny she could get, now that she wanted to create industry of her own. She would immediately buy machine-tools and whole factories to help create Egypt's new industrial future, if she could use those blocked millions.

'It's not easy to understand the British attitude,' Nasser said.

'But do you really think you can make Egypt industrial?' Peacock asked simply. 'Is it possible?'

Nasser's pause weighed it all up, and his strange smile showed that he had an answer. 'There is absolutely no other way of raising the standard of life in Egypt,' he said. 'We *must* have industry.'

'But it takes years, Mr. President, to create a skilled working population.'

'It didn't take the Russians or the Chinese very long,' Nasser replied.

'Ah . . . but will you use their methods? In fact, to be frank, that's what everybody worries about.'

'We don't want communism, if that worries you, Mr. Peacock. It has no value for Egypt. None at all. I don't believe it will ever be useful here. In fact, we oppose it vigorously because we have to have a single purpose. We can't allow class wars and other diversions like that to divide us.'

'But your people are so backward, Mr. President. How will you train them?'

'Their backwardness is only the fault of the past,' Nasser corrected pointedly. 'You, in the west, always imagine that the Arab *will* and the Arab intelligence are very low. Why do you think that? I don't understand you. Our history is as long and as rich and as continuous as yours. Our *will* is just as great, even though we don't have modern techniques yet. But we shall have them. In five years we will even have a heavy industry . . .'

'You mean, surely, a manufacturing industry.'

'We will have our own steel works and chemical works. We will be building our own locomotives, certainly our own motor-cars, certainly our own fertilizers. In two years we will finish building our fertilizer factories. Even nylons and plastics. When we have the Aswan Dam, our electric power will be plentiful enough and cheap enough to supply the whole Middle East with electricity. It will not only be Egypt, but all the Arabs who begin to live much better.'

'But I simply can't see it,' Peacock said incredulously. 'Will your people accept it? I do think that everything you do to raise them out of their misery is worthwhile. Oh, yes! But you know—people who don't know machines don't like them as a rule. I hate them myself. Look at the English people. During the industrial revolution they started smashing the new machines . . .'

'Because the machines threw them out of work. That's not true in Egypt. Even the poorest fellah wants his sons educated and skilful.'

General Hakim and the Moslem priest had tactfully left them alone, and Nasser's English improved with the subject because he talked with his hands and his brow and his intense desire to convince. He had to convince this Englishman somehow. That was the point.

There was not another sound in the house. There wasn't a sound in all Egypt, perhaps, at this time in the afternoon when the thick walls soaked away the sun and feet shuffled. In the noonday warmth of July the days always sagged sleepily in the middle. No kitchen noises, no children, even though it was a small white villa with a garden and a street gate. Yet it was, after all, a presidential house. Peacock felt the importance of it—of their concentration on the business in hand. Nasser was very good at that. But it must be hard on his wife and children. He had two. What could they excite in this man's cool one-mindedness? If he had been a harder or louder or less normal man it would amount to a fanaticism. But Nasser in a business suit with his little pause before talking and his tricky way of listening a long time had removed the fanaticism from himself and put it into . . .

'Into what?' Peacock wondered, puzzled. Did he really feel so passionately about the Arabs? Did he kiss his wife when he came home for lunch? And where was she now? Moslems didn't show their wives in public life. But after all, this was his home. Was she an ignorant peasant girl?

Peacock took his eyes off Nasser and disciplined himself again. He really mustn't wander off like that. He must keep his thinking clear.

'Can you convince the Egyptian women, Mr. President? That's your problem,' he said.

Nasser looked surprised by this sudden arrival of women.

'It is a problem,' he admitted. 'But everything is a problem, Mr. Peacock,' he said, and showed his teeth and looked restless.

Peacock sighed and stood up.

It was time to leave, the exact moment which Peacock could recognize anywhere.

'Well, then, Mr. President, it was very kind of you to have me,' Peacock said, pleased and grateful, but still wondering what it amounted to.

The President shook his hand too firmly, too convincingly. It was over. Why had he come here? What an odd experience. It was neither here nor there; it was over with before it had begun. The President was shaking his hand, though, as if his life depended on it, like a speechless man trying to be friends yet incapable of doing much about it except to put feeling into his grip. Nasser would not let him go.

'Ah, but one more thing,' the President said.

'I do wish you success, Mr. President,' Peacock interrupted without waiting for it—quickly catching up with the formal courtesies which he had nearly forgotten in this curious atmosphere. 'After all,' he went on, 'we have always had very close ties with Egypt—for a very long time. We can't easily forget our old friends.'

Nasser nodded over the double-sided truth of that, and stopped smiling and came to his own point.

'But we must also understand each other,' he said in his short-lipped English, in his demand to be understood. 'We would only ask you to remember one thing, Mr. Peacock, to remember that we *did* ask Britain and America for their help to build the Aswan Dam. We even counted on their help. You must remember that. However, they have decided to say *No* to us, as you mentioned yourself.'

'Yes, I had heard about it,' Peacock said sadly.

'That can be very bad for us, Mr. Peacock, and for you also.'

'I'm sure you are right.'

'So, I would only like to say this before you leave us: if you are going to make it so impossible for us to do things *with* your help, then we will have to find ways of doing it without your help. Will you blame us then?'

'No,' Peacock said. 'I hardly think we could blame you at all.'

'Then I hope you will not be angry when we do what we have to do.'

'But what will you do?'

The President smiled again and was evasive and then firm. 'That depends. But whatever we do, remember it is the Aswan Dam that means life or death to Egypt. We have the most densely populated land in the world. In less than ten years, in 1965, we will have 35 million people living on land which can only support 10 million at the most, and even then on a starvation level. If we build the Aswan Dam we can irrigate and reclaim over two million more acres of land—the difference between starvation and survival for us. As well, ten thousand kilowatts an hour of electricity will revolutionize our economy overnight. If you can understand that in England, Mr. Peacock, you will understand why we do what we must do. Why we must take the most drastic measures immediately. And you must not be angry with us if we get the money for it by any means we can. We *must* have it.'

Peacock spread his hands and shoulders obligingly. He was willing to understand. Well, he *did* understand. 'Of course I see your point,' he told Nasser.

'Then I hope that your Government will think the same way,' Nasser said.

'Oh, I dare not speak for the Government. Heavens, no . . .'

'Never mind,' Nasser said encouragingly. 'Everybody must speak for himself. But you must understand what we will do. That's all we ask.'

'We'll try,' Peacock said generously, and after shaking hands again, firmly, he went with General Hakim to the door.

Apart from wondering how Nasser knew that Britain and America would not lend Egypt the money, since it had not yet been announced, he was already asking himself how the devil anything was ever achieved in politics. It was all done by such inconclusive and intangible means. Was Nasser telling him something important?

Furthermore, here was the very man—Hakim (General Hakim Abdul Sarwat)—who had shot Scott in the chest in 1942; here he was, the same Hakim, showing him out of President Nasser's home. Hakim took him right to the car, and he realized only then that he had forgotten, in the whole business, in the sudden end, even to mention Scott or Sam. Sam was impossible. You might be able to mention Sam to the President of the French Republic while watching fireworks over the Champs Elysées in a moment of *entente*, but this was not the same. He would have felt too exposed, too much on dangerous ground, because this man would think of it as an interference, and probably react accordingly. But he might have said a word about Scott to remind them.

'What an extraordinary experience,' Peacock said aloud as the Chevrolet turned out of the gate and the guard saluted. He turned to wave to General Hakim, but Hakim had already turned around and was walking (nay—slouching fragilely) into the President's villa.

'And why did he ask me to lunch?' Peacock wanted to know, hunting for his sunglasses against the dry empty glare of the streets under the dusty jacarandas.

His only possible conclusion, forced slowly and good-naturedly from

293

the memory of the handshake (which would be all he would ever remember, he felt sure), was that this man was terribly anxious about something. To be friends? Was that it?

'I suppose that's it,' Peacock decided, 'unless he was trying to warn me about something. But about what?' Peacock decided he would never know.

It was, in fact, not until the thirteenth of the month that the United States (and a day later the British) officially and publicly withdrew their offer of financial assistance for the construction of the Aswan High Dam, and Peacock felt very sad.

He was already at home in England, feeling as if he had never left the warm, wet, sunless summer. But he still had the same strange feeling of an inconclusive puzzle about his lunch with Nasser, as if there was more to come.

What could it mean?

He could not imagine; and he did not puzzle about it too much because anything to do with politics was always an inconclusive puzzle, anyway.

On the twenty-fifth of the same month the Italian liner *Andrea Doria* sank off Nantucket and Peacock thought it was a sad and terrible tragedy, even though many of the passengers were saved. But where lay safety if such large liners could come to disaster? Was there no certainty left at all?

Another regret, another doubt. Life was suddenly full of the strangest feelings. But the long English summer days were lovely in the high-grown grass of his west-country farm. The neighbour had loaned Eileen his wood acreage in which to browse and exercise the ponies for the girls, and above it in the green jelly of leaves the wood-pigeons hid themselves in a ravaging vantage point, raiding the young crops in the spring and avoiding now, in the summer, the number 10 cartridges in a Purdy which Peacock carried about in the early mornings, trying to knock over a brace or two for a nostalgic pigeon dinner.

Unlike the ducks of Bindari Pasha, English wood-pigeons could not be fooled into thinking he was salt-bush and marsh. They stayed high, and they hid in the oaks and beeches. They would burst out when he had turned his back to walk home through the stubble for breakfast.

As he crossed the stalky field, the earth crumbling and sucking under foot, he found the remains of two dead wood-pigeons and a rook in the furrows. They had chosen the same place to lie down and die, and by some miracle they had not been caught in the act of death by an owl or a fox, or even by a farm cat.

He was looking at them when the farmer's son came by with a gun on his shoulder, and Peacock pointed to the birds in dismay.

'It's that Dieldrin stuff you use for dressing the grain,' he told the farmer. 'You don't plant the seed deep enough, and these pigeons come and rout it out, even in the summer, and they die of poison. You're going to kill half the bird population of England if you keep using all that DDT stuff so offhandedly.'

'They're a pest, anyway,' the farmer's son said, defensive but respectful.

'I know, but let's kill them properly. Why poison them?'

'You wouldn't say that if you were a farmer, sir,' the young man said and went off.

'Perhaps not,' Peacock thought, digging a hole with his heel and burying the carcasses. 'But what a wretched way to kill anything.'

If you were a farmer, sir . . .

'I suppose that's what I get for being a tax-loss farmer and not the real thing,' Peacock sighed. 'Which is fair enough, I daresay.'

But how lovely England was, when the west country awakened with the bees and took acres of poppies in the grass to make even a few ounces of summer honey.

Wet to the knees in the higher grass, happy, he did have a nostalgic preference, though, for the dry hot past of Egypt where there were also good friends and something more, some enticement to the English hunger for being there, because all the eastern plains seemed to be waiting for Englishmen (his sort, anyway) to come there and administer in the afternoons by simple pleasures and to die under cool latticed verandahs among cheerful dark-eyed people who did really need them. What a pity it had all gone.

'What a bloody mess,' he said about the world, watching some clever pigeons disappear over his own house where the girls would be feeding the new dogs, and Eileen would be getting ready to go to London for his 1950 Committee in which Cyprus and Malta were supposed to take up all the time, but he felt now that Egypt would be the principal subject and Eileen would also want him to lunch at some unpolitical restaurant, as far removed from the House as possible where, instead of talking, they would have to watch smart women greeting each other like schoolgirls and talking about silly asses. They dyed their hair in the most amazing colours. Eileen didn't even like the place herself, but she had to see her friends somewhere, no matter what they did to their hair. But it seemed pretty dull like that, compared with one lost day of Cairo life.

CHAPTER FORTY

THE summer was so hot that Nona and Hanna, walking the Cairo streets in mid-morning, went from one large store to another to cool off, so that they could progress and survive.

'I've lost the habit,' Nona complained, breathless. 'Did I ever live through this heat?'

'But this year is unusually hot,' Hanna told her.

'It's the atomic bombs,' Nona said. 'They have ruined the world.'

She did remember Cairo being just as hot. But then it was youth that survived heat, an impatience to do what had to be done. There was nothing to do here now, except see it out for Quartermain's sake and stay with Hanna and Helen as long as she could. Otherwise it was over.

'I don't know how I'll get through the summer,' she said.

'You should go to Alexandria or Port Said with the children.'

'No money, my darling.'

'Will you stay in Cairo all summer then?'

'If he wants to,' Nona said. 'He's got to finish his work.'

That was the mystery of it: how and when would Quartermain finish what he came here to do. Quartermain's work was simply to say to the English: 'Look what the world is doing.' It was not a very definable kind of work. Men in politics in England preached it where they could: in parliament or committees or congresses or on street corners or in the long lines of a million written words. But what did that achieve? His theory was that the English were crumbling at the far-away edges, and they ought to know what the crumbling process looked like. It was almost a gleeful process, holding up one sample of it or another for them to see. There may be strikes in Coventry and a by-election in Swaffham, but they weren't the battle of English life. English life was facing its end where most people didn't recognize it: on the Nile, on the mountain plains of Kenya, over the domes of oil in Persian deserts, in Tanganyika, and on the sad high roads of retreat from anywhere east of Calais.

'Do the Egyptians make it so difficult for him?' Hanna asked.

'Of course they do. That's the irony of it. They still won't even give him a pass to go to the Red Sea.'

'Couldn't you help him with them?'

Hanna was not projecting her favourite dream of harmony again, she was suggesting a reasonable solution. Nona could help, if she tried to. But Nona could not avoid replying irritably to it for its sentimentality.

'How can I help him?' she said. 'What can I do for him?'

'I don't know,' Hanna said, 'but you do know the language and the country.'

'The Egyptians suspect him too much for me to help,' she said. 'It serves him right in a way. He doesn't see the advantages of his own country. He won't live in England. We only really tried once, after the war, when we bought a cottage in the country near London and converted it.'

'I always wondered why you didn't keep it. Did he hate it so much?'

'Who knows? There weren't any children then, but he gave it up just the same. Although I suppose it was horrible. I hated it too. There was a stockbroker who lived next door, and when the kitchen was still only half-finished, he rode into it one day on his horse, right into the kitchen. I don't think I would have believed it if I hadn't seen it.'

Nona laughed now, and Hanna smiled.

'What did you do?'

'Quarts looked as if he would blow up in smoke. The stockbroker was playing the role of the local squire. I didn't understand all that then, but I do now. I suppose he made a genuine mistake. He must have expected us to touch our hats. He blew his nose and asked me who owned the house. All I could do—I was so stunned and terrified of the horse anyway—was point to Q who was carting away a barrow-load of old bricks from the garden.'

'It would have been so nice to have a garden with the children,' Hanna said. 'They need a place to run around in.'

'This garden was only a heartbreak—stones, ashes and clay. If you could have seen that stockbroker's face when Q walked up to him with a large broom in his hand and said: "Out of my kitchen with that horse." '

Nona was fumbling for a handkerchief to stop any flood of laughter and giggling in the street. It was too hot to laugh, and she sighed to exhaustion as they stood in a doorway while heat palpitations pounded up her wet neck to her face.

'What did the man want?' Hanna asked. 'The one on the horse?'

'That's what we asked. He said he wanted manure. One side of the cottage was a coachhouse and the other stables, before we converted them. He used to send his gardener, he said, to get the cow manure from the stables for his garden, because someone had been keeping cows in there.'

'Keeping cows inside?'

'It's cold in winter, my darling,' Nona reminded her. 'But when he asked for manure, at that precise moment his horse chose to deposit some on the kitchen doorstep.'

'It's not true,' Hanna said. She refused to laugh in the street.

'But it is. Quarts thinks all Egyptian humour sooner or later ends up with manure, so he won't exaggerate. Ask him. It did happen. When the stockbroker said manure, and the horse did that, my darling husband said to him, "You seem to be in the manure business yourself." '

Hanna laughed helplessly. 'What a terrible thing for the horse to do,' she said.

'The stockbroker didn't think so. He tried to ride out of the garden, but Q locked the gate and got a spade and simply put the manure back on the horse, and then he said he would return the call next week with a cow or something.'

'Are they really like that in England?' Hanna asked. 'You exaggerate.'

'Not quite like that, but almost,' Nona admitted. 'Oh, it's an exaggeration, I know, but everything in England is an exaggeration. They're too polite or too rude, or too decent or too beastly. Then they say they are reasonable. I suppose they are, but only to themselves. But I like living there, even though Quarts doesn't. You always know where you are, once you treat them with the right amount of contempt which they deserve. That's what is hardest to learn. All these class differences among themselves are terribly rigid and important, but to a foreigner like me it's simply silly.'

When something was silly to Nona it was not something unimportant. Silliness was worth despising, and she usually made the word mean something. But today it was a limp word, too far away from England to bother about. They moved heavily into *à l'Américaine* near the Tribunaux Mixtes, and the cotton-wool coolness under the canvas awnings was a dry buffer against the continuing clanging and waving of the heat on the street outside.

They ordered hot tea because an iced drink would make them hotter and thirstier. Discipline was essential.

'Where is he today?' Hanna asked.

'He's gone to see one of those chemical factories the Germans are building in the Delta somewhere for Nasser. He goes about with that American and his wife, the ones he knew after the war in Singapore, Jack de Brazio. He usually gets on better with Americans like that.'

'Won't he ever settle down in England? Doesn't he like his own country?'

'I suppose he does. But, like most Englishmen, he loves it best only when he can spend half his time out of it.'

'But why?'

'*How does one explain that to Hanna?*' she asked herself suddenly. '*How does one explain his distaste for that English life?*'

She could picture Hanna's other view of the world, which was mostly the dead and regretted past, her parents, and the stability of life in the Sudan which had been prosperous, thoroughly established, and blossoming in the security of family ties until their mother and father had suddenly been snapped off like plucked flowers by a casual and unthinking God. God's will always seemed to be unthinkingly cruel to Nona, and she blamed God for her parents' death and would not forgive or forget. On the other hand, Hanna had learned to accept God as a terrible necessity. She had understood the look in God's eye when he did it—taking not one parent, like that, but both. Yet Hanna also had a sudden rebellion within her somewhere. Nona could see it sometimes when she almost lost her temper. Then her whole body seemed to rebel against her moral restraint on it—as if it would burst out with violence, if it were ever given the chance. It was never given the chance, and the rebellion of her life had therefore never emerged, because it was too frightening to imagine the consequences. But perhaps she would understand Quartermain's kind of revolt after all.

'The English are an odd people,' she told Hanna. 'And Quarts is still very English, whatever he says. But he believes that they are so hopelessly tied to their rigid class system that nothing short of a catastrophe will ever change them.'

'But why should they change?'

'Ah . . . my darling, if he could explain his theories on that, mine too. If you could live in England a little while you would understand. He is quite right. It does ruin the English. They simply don't understand how it is ruining them slowly. That's why they will go on accepting everything —the terrible things they do in the world, the Americans, and I suppose the Germans again, and everything else their worst people do. The English have all been neutralized, somehow, by this terrible feeling of every man knowing his place. They really act that way. They can't help it. They are absolutely educated like that and you have to be a foreigner like me to see how deep it goes. They don't see it themselves, ever. That's why he sends the boys to a French school, because he says that whatever else they learn, they won't learn this English class mentality, not on any level.' Nona sighed. 'I argue with him, but I suppose he's right about that too. He's always right when you stop to think about it, but he always makes it so difficult for anyone to agree with him.'

'But the English are always so calm and polite,' Hanna argued, 'and clever.'

'And hypocrites as well,' Nona added, sipping her tea.

'You have an honest husband,' Hanna told her loyally. 'He is never a hypocrite.'

That was true, and nice to hear. But Quartermain had always treated Hanna with more patience and respect than he did anyone else. He never teased Hanna or hurried her, and he respected her opinions, however naïve they seemed to others. For a moment, in the recollection of it, Nona felt her heart rush off somewhere to her husband's side in admiration and affection, knowing why she had loved him and would never change. He was never cruel, he would not hurt anyone close to him, and he valued sensitivity. If he hated his enemies it was with the same sort of hate that a man could have for an act of brutality or for repulsive behaviour. One *had* to have some strong feeling of right and wrong in life.

'I'm the mean one,' she said to Hanna. 'I know I can be so vindictive. But he isn't. I only wish I'd known him before he changed, though. They say he used to laugh at everything and was never serious at all. I wonder what did change him.'

'You must love him as he is,' Hanna said, and Nona laughed happily at Hanna's simple cures for all emotional disturbances. But perhaps she was right after all . . .

Quartermain shouted out, that night, after hearing the B.B.C. news, that Dulles had just refused Egypt the money to build the Aswan Dam.

'Something's going to happen now,' he called out ominously from his room; but Nona was reminding Helen again and again that discipline was necessary for the children. Little moon had given his aunt terrible trouble all afternoon.

'I didn't have enough myself,' Nona said. 'I was only given one good hiding by Mother, and I should have had many more.'

'When?' Hanna asked indignantly. 'You can't remember Mother smacking you.'

'Don't you think she did?'

'*I* don't remember it. Father might have given you a slap, but Mother always used her tongue. And you were quite spoiled.'

'This time she slapped me on the bare legs,' Nona insisted. 'And very hard.'

'What for?' Hanna asked, still not believing it.

'You weren't there,' Nona said. 'But when Grandmother was ill, she and Aunt used to share the same room in the Matarieh house. I always hated to go in there because they had all those Sudanese smells. Grandmother would be sitting up in bed chewing *miswack* like the Sudanese women and spitting it out . . .'

'That's how they cleaned their teeth,' Helen said. 'And they didn't spit.'

'Oh, yes they did. Grandmother and Aunt Sophie would sit there chewing and gossiping and laughing all day. When Mother asked me that day to take some oranges into them, I simply couldn't go into their room because of the smell of that other stuff they ate. So I stood at the door' (Nona folded up and giggled) 'and simply threw the oranges in and said, "*Mother sent you these.*" Aunt Sophie and Grandmother laughed their heads off, but Mother didn't. She caught me, and when she asked me what I did that for, I said, *Because I hate that horrible Sudanese smell in there.* She gave me a hiding for being so rude. I suppose I was seven and Grandmother and Aunt giggled all day about it, but Mother was very angry. I can still smell that stuff they chewed, just like Sudanese peasants sitting up on their haunches. They used to hitch up their nightgowns as if they were galabiehs and tell stories and laugh all day.'

Quartermain sat down with them.

'You left the radio on,' Nona told him.

'I'm half-listening to it,' he said.

There had been riots in Poland a week before and the B.B.C.'s special correspondent was now describing how he had seen the well-starved Polish students marching down the street with a bloodstained flag shouting *chleba, chleba* and: *Tell the world what we are doing.*

'Students,' Nona said.

'God protect me from them,' Quartermain told her. 'Go on.'

In the contest of worlds, Nona's version seemed much better.

'You were such a devil to Aunt Sophie,' Helen said to her.

'But we weren't *really* cruel. We only played mild jokes.'

'If you had been cruel I'd have whipped you,' Helen told her.

'Was your aunt completely blind?' Quartermain asked.

'She was, all my life, anyway,' Nona said. 'But that didn't make much difference. She always knew what dress she had on, and what dresses we were wearing. She walked around the Matarieh house in *ship-ships* without a stick and she never bumped into anything, except at the end.'

'She was so old and frail by then,' Helen said. 'She really was old.'

'But she didn't have a wrinkle on her face. Not a one. She simply shrank into old age. You couldn't tell how old she was, except that she walked with her shoulders hunched. In those days . . .' Nona told her husband, who seemed anxious to avoid the other voice in the other room and was calmly studying his wife's face in its fluidity and mockery and intemperance and picturing it then when she was eight or nine, realizing that the little white devil in her hadn't changed much either . . .

'In those days,' she was saying, 'we used to buy all the household supplies a year at a time; all the sugar, rice, soap, flour, even beans. Aunt Sophie kept them in big sacks in her big cupboards in her bedroom. Whenever rice or sugar was needed for meals the servants were sent to get it, but she would always put her hands on her hips and say to them: "More rice, eh? What for? What will be left for the rest of the year if I give you a whole rotle of rice now?" They used to call her a Sudanese cupboard behind her back, but they were always joking with her. It was Mother who used to get angry with her when she wouldn't open up the cupboard. She had all the keys and she'd never let anyone else near the supplies, not even Mother herself.'

'Why didn't you steal them when she did open up,' Quartermain said, 'if she couldn't see?'

'That's just like you,' Nona said. 'We used to try, but she was too cunning. She even got angry if something spilled on the floor. If she ever walked over anything gritty she would squat down and put her finger in it and taste it and then say: "Ah! So you're throwing the sugar onto the floor now. Don't think you can come to me for more sugar." But my brother David, who was always the favourite, would teach me to play tricks on her, and he'd tell me to pour a little salt on the floor. When she squatted down to taste it, we would hide until she spat it out. We'd laugh so much. Poor David . . .'

'I was only thinking the other day,' Helen said, 'that Sam is so like him. He might have been Sam's father instead of his uncle. Who could ever really get angry with David, any more than you can with Sam? They are so much alike.'

'Was he built like Sam?' Quartermain asked. 'With all the weight on top?'

'He was even bigger,' Nona said. 'Before he got fat he was the strongest man in the Nile dockyards. When he and my other brother Tom got into trouble at a Greek restaurant, they fought off twenty Italians who were attacking them with chairs. David simply tore the chairs apart. Poor David! My father couldn't do anything with him. He only wanted to be with his low friends. In fact, David was always with Greeks, the way Sam is. He liked everybody. Hundreds of people we'd never heard of came to his funeral. He was closest to Aunt Sophie, too. He'd bring home packets of sweets for her, and she would lock them up in her cupboard. They were all there when she died. She wouldn't part with them when we wanted one, and she wouldn't even eat them herself. The funny thing is they died almost on the same day. Aunt Sophie died at midnight one day, and poor David died at 11 o'clock the next morning. They didn't have penicillin in those days, and pneumonia in summer in Egypt was certain death. That's when I met you, my darling,' she said to Quartermain.

He remembered her dressed in black: white-faced with short, ebony-soaked hair which was always washed, oiled and curled back from her transparent face in rich waves, glistening and close. Her rounded young body had not looked very unhappy in that black dress, because it had been too short at the knees to be taken seriously, and her pale face had not really kept a sad memory for long. She had been in love with him then without doubts or disturbances, but she had remained in mourning for David until they had married, and he still regretted never knowing the one brother who had stuck so close to the family. The other brothers had gone off on their own somewhere.

This deep thrust of love for his wife, from the memory, was riper now in recollection than it had been then. He had realized very little of it then. She had surrendered all she had needed to surrender—innocently and with an impatient generosity which did not question the moral of it. That would have been silly. And marriage had been the result rather than the aim. Love had not been difficult then.

'What was on the news?' Helen was asking him.

He told them again that the Americans had refused the Egyptians money to build the Aswan Dam.

'Why did they do that?' Nona asked. 'I remember only a month ago they had half-promised it.'

'They're all putting their heads together,' he said.

'Who is?'

'Everybody who wants to get rid of Nasser,' Quartermain said mysteriously.

'*Can* they get rid of him?' Helen asked.

'If they don't do it now, they'll never do it. All of Nasser's plans and hopes for Egypt are based on that dam.'

'They'll blackmail Egypt, the way they always do,' Nona said bitterly.

Quartermain turned the other B.B.C. world off—that perfect world of restraint where you had the right to think as you pleased in that sane voice, providing (he said) you didn't question the right of others to starve as they pleased.

'If only they keep the mob in check this time,' Helen said when she was leaving, remembering the burning of Cairo because she knew it might happen again. In fact it would probably happen every time the balance of Egypt's future was being weighed, as it had been weighed so often lately.

'Don't start worrying about that now,' Quartermain comforted her. 'Not yet.'

'But what will Nasser do? Can he make trouble for the Americans?'

'I'll tell you tomorrow,' Quartermain told her as they went to the lift.

He kissed Helen good night. He had always admired Helen, except when she panicked like Nona; and he looked at his wife with secret eyes and a bemused moustache.

'But why tomorrow?' Helen said, turning back, still worrying about the streets.

'I'm going out to the airport to see Nasser coming back from Jugoslavia. He's been talking positive neutralism to Tito and Nehru. But if he

303

wants to get out of this situation he'll have to show he's positive about something more than being neutral.'

'As long as they don't go wild on the streets again.'

Helen (very worried now) took the lift and left them alone with their own secrets, which were harder to find in each other these days, although by no means lost.

'You ought to put oil on your hair,' he said to Nona.

It was not so black as it had been, and now she wore it in a bun, but it was still as rich and abundant as it had been the first day he had seen her in her black dress and black stockings.

'In those days,' she said, knowing his memory, 'you used to tell me it was too oily.'

'Did I? Well, you've finally convinced me. Oil it . . .'

'You know,' she said. 'Sam *is* like David. I suppose that's why we baby Sam so much. It's a pity you didn't know my brother. You would have liked him. He was such a simple man. He was always a working man, the way Sam is. He didn't want to be anything else. You would have approved.'

'Perhaps he wouldn't have approved of me,' Quartermain said modestly.

They behaved carefully. They went in to make sure the children slept, and they tried to make sure that they did not break this heavenly ring of good feeling which had bound them together again, even though they knew it was unlikely to last.

CHAPTER FORTY-ONE

QUARTERMAIN went with Jack in his station-wagon to the Cairo airport, where Nasser’s plane came down in the sort of perfected, concentrated landing which one expects of planes carrying important people. The pilots were always so good, and they looked so sure of what they were doing. It was an atmosphere for Presidents, even on a sticky, mauve day with the sun baking the planes like hot silver potatoes, cracking and spitting on the tarmac.

‘It’s the biggest disappointment of his life,’ Jack said, ‘so he ought to say something.’

He had his Greek cameraman and his black tape-recorder.

‘He won’t say anything,’ Quartermain argued. ‘He always waits.’

‘You’re always so right, aren’t you? But what’s he going to wait for this time?’

‘He’s going to decide what he’ll do before he says anything. He won’t talk.’

‘Maybe he’ll lose his temper,’ Jack said hopefully.

The President appeared, ducking his wavy head to get out of the plane. The salutes smothered him, and he stepped down the gangway and walked straight to the black Packard waiting for him, refusing to hear questions shouted at him by the Syrians, Americans, British, and French-men who claimed his attention. His political secretary, in reluctant dispensation, made a tired joke and said he would answer questions, if they didn’t mind. The President was in a hurry. After all, he had just come back from a busy meeting with Nehru and Tito, and he had other business . . .

‘What about the Aswan Dam?’ they said.

‘What about it?’ the secretary, Ali Sabri, answered.

‘Has Mr. Dulles’s refusal upset your plans?’

‘Of course,’ Ali Sabri said. ‘The American withdrawal of help has completely upset our plans.’

‘What does President Nasser do now?’

'I can't answer that,' the secretary said. It was a grim little joke.

'Who do you blame?' Jack bellowed.

'Ah, Mr. de Brazio. We blame the enemies who want to undermine our future. Old enemies, and now it seems like some new enemies.'

'All right, but what do you do now?'

'We'll build the dam, anyway,' Ali Sabri said rather formally, quite without indignation, and then he too was urged away by officers and attendants.

When he had gone there was nothing left, no real story of any kind, and Jack grumbled, 'That's not much to work on, is it? So what? They don't even give you a clue to their real reaction.'

But Quartermain insisted again (knowing he must be right because he understood the significance of it and wasn't so dependent on *the facts*) that it was too soon. 'What we ought to do is to see if the British or the American Embassies have any answer,' he told Jack. 'And before the others get there, too.'

'That's right,' Jack said urgently. 'Let's go.'

'I suppose it was the cotton lobby or the Israeli lobby putting pressure on the Senate,' Jack suggested, driving like a desperado along the Heliopolis road to get to the Embassies before the others thought of it. If you got there first you got the unthought-out fresh answers, not the thought-out stale ones.

'More likely the British lobby,' Quartermain said.

'The British haven't got any influence left in Congress,' Jack said. 'It's the one sure influence that doesn't count.'

Jack had missed the point. Quartermain was tempted to argue, but Jack was too set on getting the facts, and they went into the assistant press officer's room at the American Embassy where the girls drank coca-cola all day and a ticker machine was so congested with the facts that it coughed them out in long white rolls, non-stop. There was nothing new on the record, Morrison, the assistant attaché said, except that it was Mr. Dulles's own idea, and not the Senate Appropriations Committee.

'Did Dulles do this to Nasser because Nasser wouldn't join the Baghdad Pact?' Jack asked.

'You can't get me to say a thing like that, Jack.'

'I don't want it officially, I want it privately. Give me a lead.'

'All I can give you are the facts,' Morrison said and looked suspiciously at Quartermain, who was laughing. Quartermain was not really paying attention to the facts when he ought to be, and that seemed suspicious. He was reading the ticker news.

'You might recollect that the Egyptian Ambassador to Washington was recalled to Cairo in June,' Morrison was saying. 'He warned Nasser then

—we have it on good authority—that unless Congress voted credits by July 1, they would probably miss the bus this year on any credits they wanted. That's why the Egyptians suddenly announced that they would agree to American help, after they'd been playing a very cagey game with us for months. The trouble is that Nasser was talking to Shepilov at the same time, asking the Russians for help, but Shepilov said *Nyet* . . .'

'So Dulles, knowing the Russians had refused, said *Nyet* out of spite?'

'What else could he say? That's a lot of dollars: two hundred million!'

'Has the State Department finally decided that Nasser is a communist?'

'That's not the reason, Jack. We're still giving money to Tito, and isn't he a communist?'

'Then why do you give it to Tito and not to Nasser?'

'Nasser is no longer a good risk, Jack, but don't quote me. Who knows whether he will last or not? And, anyway, the Egyptians have already mortgaged five years of cotton crops to get Russian arms. There's nothing much left to pay us back with, even at $3\frac{1}{2}$ per cent over twenty years. Anyway, Nasser can't build the dam without consent of other Nile countries, like the Sudan and Ethiopia, and they won't give it to Nasser for sure.'

'Won't this send him back to the Russians for help?' Jack insisted.

'Too late, Jack,' the American said cunningly, smiling blandly. 'The Russians have already said No, and they rarely change their minds.'

Jack went on arguing and extracting facts as best he could, and Quartermain stopped feeling like an interloper and stopped pretending to be disinterested and listened to this battle for facts which Jack loved so much. When Jack had fought for all he could get he said, 'Okay. Let's go over and see what the British say.'

This was different. The American Embassy had been choked with activity, with posters and typewriters and pretty local girls working over long drafts of thick Jeffersonian documents for propagation to unhappy peasants. The British did it behind locked, pale-grey doors, and with one solitary counsellor, who wore his hair rather long over his pale face and half-apologized for everything.

'Britain hasn't withdrawn her offer of a loan to Egypt yet. But I tell you, off the record, that she will do so today. The International Bank will logically follow suit.'

'Why?'

'I don't think I need answer that. I mean, surely, you know.'

'No, I don't.'

'Oh, come on, old chap. Let's not be naïve.'

'I'm very naïve,' Jack insisted. 'I need to know.'

'Because it's not good policy at the moment.'

Jack went on asking why, but the answers were apologetically unrevealing. Jack ought to know, he ought to guess, he ought to sense the basic position that Britain must still maintain in Middle East affairs.

'What do you think Nasser will do?' Jack asked.

'I should think he'll find it hard to do anything.'

'But he set so much store on this,' Jack said. 'His whole plan for Egypt.' The counsellor shrugged a little.

'What if he gets help from the Russians?' Jack tried.

'We don't think he will be able to. They've already said *Nyet*.'

'They may change their minds.'

'We don't think they will,' the counsellor said.

'Don't you think this will produce a crisis here?' Jack asked.

'Probably,' the counsellor said, 'but that's off the record,' he added, and refused anything more.

'They don't think anything and they don't know anything,' Jack complained bitterly. 'When they say "off the record" like that I think of all the ships' bores who, when they hear you're a newspaperman, immediately start talking to you "off the record". It must be the only phrase in any language that can turn an everyday idiot into a prime minister in two seconds. It was the smart way Roosevelt had of letting out unwanted secrets, but now it's the babbling echo of all morons and chorus girls.'

'What do you care, as long as you got your facts?' Quartermain teased.

'What facts? There aren't any,' Jack bellowed.

'Let's start looking for reasons then,' Quartermain said dryly.

He took Jack to see Bateman. Bateman would know everything, and Bateman would spill it. Bateman was young and clever and up to his neck, and he would tell them what was really in the British mind at least.

'How do you know?' Jack asked.

'Because he's a schoolboy plotter. And he's silly enough to boast of it.'

'Can you believe him? Is he an Embassy man?'

Quartermain dragged on his moustache. 'I don't know. He's somebody's man. But at least he likes open warfare, and he likes showing off the dark side of his own manœuvres. He's your man, Jack.'

'They asked Peacock's Aunt Marigold, the secretary in nylon petticoats who was twenty-six and lovely and Bateman's friend. She worked at the Embassy and remembered Quartermain very well, but she told them Bateman wasn't in Cairo.

'Has he very suddenly left the country, by any chance?' Quartermain asked.

'Not at all. He's gone duck-shooting.'

'You don't duck-shoot in midsummer here,' Jack told her.

She coquetted Jack a little, as Englishwomen often do with Americans.

308

'Don't they?' she said. 'Then they must be shooting something else. He's gone to his friends in the country, the Bindaris, with Lucy Pickering.'

'He's getting on,' Quartermain told her.

She laughed knowingly and said, 'What are you doing here, Mr. Quartermain? Are you going to expose a hotbed of plots in the British Embassy?'

Quartermain pointed to her knees and said, 'Your petticoat is showing.'

'It's supposed to,' she said as they left.

'The French,' Quartermain complained downrightly, 'don't have enough intellect or sense to understand Saint-Saëns. They treat him as a joke. Berlioz sounds like melting ice-water, Poulenc and "Les Six" and Satie and Ravel soak up Berlioz with a dishcloth. Whereas Saint-Saëns . . .'

They told him to keep quiet so that they could listen to Saint-Saëns. Ella was back from Aswan, where she had gone to report on the site of the dam that would never be built. They were listening in the de Brazio's hotel suite to his lovely donkey-bells and to the soft mud of the Nile flowing like molten fire. Saint-Saëns had seen Egypt with khaki soldiers in black moustaches and cities crowded on white ponies, festive women warbling the zagharit, and sudden alarums of outlined figures on dusty horizons; he had found the pashas dressed like Turks listening to older songs of the night, and sometimes the Turkish military bands playing the brass and pipes that could bring out a whole parade of Ottoman pleasures. He had romanticized Turkish Egypt, not British or French Egypt.

'Whereas Saint-Saëns is what?' Ella asked, turning it off.

'Proust said he was a good pianist,' Quartermain replied resentfully, damning the French for their hollow intellect. 'That's all he is to the French.'

Ella had found Saint-Saëns in a Cairo bookshop, but the record itself came from Russia. The finest pianist in the world, she said: Richter. There were Russian magazines and books everywhere these days. Soon the Russians would also come dancing and singing in one of those eastern dialects. The Egyptians would go mad with delight.

'I've seen them,' Ella said. 'They know how to talk to these people, because they've got one of everything themselves: Armenians, Arabs (or Moslems anyway), Tajiks, Persians, Turks. They're all eastern brothers under the skin.'

Jack disagreed. 'Nasser is frightened of having hundreds of Russians in Egypt, even building dams. He won't go to them for help.'

'He'll go anywhere,' Quartermain said.

'I'd still like to know what really made Dulles turn them down,' Jack was still complaining.

'It's simple. They're after Nasser,' Quartermain pointed out.

'That's only a wild guess. You're always going off half-cocked on things like that. You don't know . . .'

'Then it's a wild certainty,' Quartermain said impatiently. 'Ben Gurion gets rid of Moshe Sharret his Foreign Minister who was trying to talk to Nasser. Half the Africa Department of the Foreign Office goes to Washington. Monsieur Pineau goes from Paris to see Dulles. They've all suddenly decided to do something, and it's my guess that they're after Nasser—to pull him down by the boots if they can.'

'Oh, they don't plot like that any more,' Jack mocked. 'It's not that clumsy.'

'You're crazy!' Quartermain said. 'You explain it then.'

'I can't. Why should they suddenly want to get rid of Nasser now? They didn't think it up just like that. They had even intended lending him the money . . .'

'They were going to lend it to him if he allowed them to move back in. That's the only thing Nasser won't do. If he doesn't do it, though, he's no good to them. In fact, he's a terrifying monstrosity, because he's setting a very bad example to the rest of these run-down Arab autocracies. If he can stay independent and survive, think of Iraq or Kuwait or Syria or Saudi Arabia where the oil flows. Oil! No wonder Dulles and Eden are terrified. They'll all be following Nasser soon. Revolutions all over the place. Nasser will have to go.'

'Maybe,' Jack admitted reluctantly. 'But I'd love to know what he's going to do in the meantime. If he takes this lying down they'll simply laugh him out of power.'

'Like you,' Quartermain said, 'Nasser reacts to facts. In a few days he'll react somehow. It's simple. Just wait.'

'Did you cable that valuable clue to your backwoods agency?'

The Northern Allied Agency had finally asked Quartermain to send them some kind of story on the crisis, eight hundred words at a time. It was financial salvation at one hundred dollars a time, and he had sent them two short despatches during the day.

'I told them it was a test for Nasser,' he told Jack. 'I sent them all those facts, remember? I said that what happens here in the next week will not only decide the future of Nasser, but also of the western powers in the Middle East, and of the Middle East itself.'

'You really believe that wild stuff?'

'Absolutely. And if they don't print it they'll be sorry.'

'You just guess all over the place,' Jack groaned. 'You're in the wrong profession.'

'But I never guess,' Quartermain insisted. 'I know . . .'

He was leaving. He called out good night to Ella who was already going to bed in the other room. She asked him, from there, to bring his wife to dinner sometimes, but Quartermain said Nona was very busy these days, spending as much time with her family as she could, in case they were forced by coming events to get out of Egypt in a hurry.

It was an excuse, and they both knew it. But it was not quite a lie.

'Do you think something like that will happen?' Jack said seriously at the door, not quite sure, not quite satisfied with anything he had heard today.

'Anything can happen now, Jack,' Quartermain answered triumphantly. 'You'll see.'

He walked towards his home along the Nile which had turned electric blue where it scooped up the neon lights on Shubra bridge. It was midnight. Street children still played on the lawns along the river. Peasants, riding staggering old bicycles, were delivering milk in cans strapped over the back wheels. They rode in a rattling convoy of four, but a policeman saw them and began to chase them on foot, probably because they were selling contaminated milk and were now being driven off the streets with their rackish trade.

He wondered why he was going home so unsatisfied on this significant night. He felt as if it were actually wrong, as if he were being robbed of something.

'I can't go home yet,' he told himself on the dark side of the river.

He turned back then and walked the other way, crossing the night-blown city through the deserted squares towards Abdin Palace.

He was a lone night-walker now, looking hungrily for significance, even though he knew he would only find it in his own eyes, through a veil of his own intelligence, and in his own dialectic appetite—that sense of a place, of a people about to erupt with some sort of historical event.

'What did I expect to find here?' he asked himself outside the Palace.

Abdin Palace bore no apparent significance at all. It looked deserted and its atmosphere was architectural. Its empty square looked like a giant black baking-dish cooking up sparse bubbles of electric light, an artist's atmosphere not a politician's. No candle burned in some single window. There were no presidents, no chancellors, no generals, and no dark-hatted secretaries hurrying in pairs through the iron gates.

'Even so,' he said, 'they're definitely after him. I suppose he knows it.'

But he knew now that Nasser was probably at home, safely asleep in his suburban villa.

He went back along the river to Gezira, knowing that he was the only man walking through this city who understood the pressures and calculations which were working to bring Nasser down. He alone in this city was still awake with the drama of motivations, significance, history and personal danger. It might be a romantic view for which Saint-Saëns could be partly blamed, but it was a fact that only an Englishman was here to hunt down these dangers in a tired metropolis which should not be asleep.

Yet nothing happened.

They waited for events to prove a tremendous reaction. Jack's cables from New York told him to see Nasser immediately—to get any kind of statements on his reactions.

'Baghdad reports say that Nasser is on the skids,' Jack said. 'There's some Arab diplomat in Beirut who claims that Egyptian officers have already arrested Nasser and replaced him by Neguib.'

Where was Nasser? Nobody had seen or heard of him for a week.

'He's making a speech at the opening of the new refinery this afternoon,' the press department said. 'You can go there, but he won't talk to you.'

Jack pummelled the lumpy river road with the Chevrolet and Ella brought along a Syrian girl with blonde hair and French eyes who could translate.

Jack held up his microphone over the heads of the refinery engineers, while the President wiped his forehead with his folded handkerchief. When he spoke, Jack whispered anxiously to the Syrian girl. 'What's he saying? Don't miss anything.'

She said 'Shh!' to Jack and translated what President Nasser was saying. 'The President said: "I tell the Americans to choke to death on their fury. Because we'll find a way, somehow, of building the dam, even if it kills you."'

'Kills who?' Jack asked.

'The Americans,' she said.

'Is that all?' Jack complained, disappointed when it was over and when nothing else was said, nothing of any significance.

'That's all,' the Syrian girl told them.

Where could they rush to now?

'Insults don't impress anybody any more,' Jack grumbled on the way back. 'If that's all he can do, it's a let-down.'

'What else can he do?' Quartermain asked, puzzled himself by now.

'I don't know,' Jack said. 'But I'd like to see him do something. You said he would react. I thought he might blow up. I took your word for it,' he said to Quartermain. 'It was you who got me steamed up for something drastic.'

Quartermain sighed. 'I was wrong,' he admitted, not hiding his own disappointment, not in Nasser but in his own judgment. 'So far I'm completely wrong,' he said. 'Perhaps Nasser is licked.'

But the twenty-sixth of July, four days later, was the fourth anniversary of the revolution—the fourth year of Farouk's expulsion, and President Nasser would speak in Mohamed Ali square in Alexandria to celebrate it.

312

'This is his last chance,' Jack said.

They went down to Alexandria and felt the sea blowing cool funnels of air up the garden streets of the Place Saad Zaghloul, the rue de l'Ancienne Bourse, and the rue de la Poste. Two hundred thousand Egyptians waited in the square. The sandstone walls of the English church, the Bourse, and the Palais de Justice had cooled off quickly in the damp velvet air which they soaked off the old bay of the Grand port des Anciens. The names were all French, but everyone knew that the city was really Greek, not only ancient Greek but modern Greek, and Alexander the Great himself was still buried under it somewhere. The old British Navy basins were full of dirty barges and dredgers and coal-hulks, and that was about all that was left of the British.

From the balcony, which the press department had reserved for them overlooking the faces of two hundred thousand Egyptians, Mr. Aboud leaned forward and said to them: 'There, from just there, the Moslem brother Abdel Latif tried to kill Gamal Abd el Nasser two years ago. He fired all eight shots at Gamal Abd el Nasser, and none of them hit him.'

'Say that again,' Jack said, holding up his microphone.

Mr. Aboud repeated it like a schoolmaster, and Ella signalled to the Greek cameraman, who was on the other side of the balcony, to photograph the very spot where the assassin had stood.

'Maybe someone will try it again today,' Jack whispered to Quartermain.

It was getting too dark to shoot good pictures and Jack was getting impatient with Nasser who had not arrived. The faces below were shifting recklessly and they felt as if all Egypt was doing just that. For a week now the Egyptian people had waited restlessly in a tight compact of expectancy. Something had to happen today.

'He will come at the very hour that Farouk left Egypt. Seven o'clock,' Mr. Aboud told them, and Jack complained again about the light, although it was too late to bother now. He hoped his Greek was using HP³ which would film anything almost in total darkness, but there would be lights.

'Voilà!' the Syrian girl said.

Voilà, it was the President. He had mounted the little platform from behind, and he stood at the microphones waving to the shouts and the exultations of his countrymen.

'Now,' said the President, holding one of the microphones and preparing to joke—it was going to be a joke because the idea of it was simply conveyed in the forward mystique of all joke-telling. 'Now, brothers, I'm going to give you the low-down on my adventures with the American diplomats.'

When the soft mass below laughed it was like a finally arrived wave.

Jack said to his Syrian girl: 'What was that? What's he saying?'

'He's talking like a peasant,' she said. 'He's never done that before. It's *balladi*, Egyptian argot . . .'

'The President is talking like a peasant,' Jack whispered into his microphone.

'Well,' the President was saying, his fine teeth biting off each word in rapid *balladi*, 'it was like this: one day an American official came to me and said, "If a Mr. Allen comes to see you with a note from the State Department complaining about Czech armaments in Egypt, just throw him out of your office. You see (this American diplomat told me) if this Mr. Allen goes back to Dulles empty-handed, then Dulles will toss *him* out." Now what could I do with poor Mr. Allen when he came to see me?'

'Et alors?' the Syrian girl said, laughing.

The laughter was raving around the Christian cathedrals and the banks and the palm trees.

'What is it?' Jack begged. 'For God's sake translate it.'

'You can't,' the Syrian girl said. 'It's the way he says it . . .'

'Oh, my God!' Jack said. 'Give me the gist of it.'

'He's attacking the Americans,' the Syrian girl said over the cheers.

'Saying what? What's he saying?'

'He's attacking Israel and the British too.'

Jack waited desperately for excerpts, until the President began to speak of Eugene Black, representing the World Bank, who had come to see him. That's where it had all begun, the President said.

'Every time Black spoke to me about money,' the President was shouting bitterly now, 'I kept thinking of the year 1854 when Ferdinand de Lesseps told the Khedive that he wanted to dig the Suez Canal. "It will bring you untold riches," de Lesseps told the Khedive, who believed him. So Egypt gave him twelve million pounds to build the canal, and gave him the labour to dig it. A hundred and twenty thousand Egyptians died digging the Suez Canal. That's what I remembered when Mr. Black talked of money. I also remembered that the British stole our forty-four per cent of the shares, by using a confidence trick on a stupid old man like the Khedive. Everything was filched from us. Everything! And instead of Egypt owning the canal, the canal company owned Egypt. Isn't that true, brothers? You all know. It was a state within a state. It grew rich and full of profits, richer and richer, while Egyptians got poorer and poorer and died of hunger . . .'

The Syrian girl had run out of translatable words.

'Go on,' Jack insisted sharply. 'For God's sake don't stop now.'

'But it's so fast . . .'

She had lost the thread. But the whole cloth was suddenly rent by a volcanic effect. The entire population before them became insane, throwing caps, newspapers, shoes and sticks in the air. Around them all the

314

Egyptians were jumping on their chairs and shouting at the tops of their voices, while President Nasser, in the uproar, was laughing and Jack was cursing and Mr. Aboud was screaming.

'What did he say?' Quartermain begged in the ear of the girl.

'He said,' the Syrian girl shouted at them, 'that he has just nationalized the Suez Canal.'

Jack held his head and groaned and looked at Quartermain, while the uproar went on and on. Across the square the two hundred thousand voices rose and fell with every word like an Atlantic swell rolling a thousand miles across the ocean and then suddenly thundering down on some surprised but African shore.

'We shall rely on our own strength, our own muscle, our own funds,' the President was shouting, whirling his hands in the air over the waves. 'It will be run by Egyptians! Egyptians! Egyptians!'

The rollers rolled on, and Jack lifted his microphone around the sky to catch the echoes, standing on the chair and holding on to Quartermain's plentiful hair so that he could not fall over.

'What did he say then?' Jack asked his Syrian voice.

'He just said,' the Syrian girl told them, stumbling excitedly with her French aspirates, her long blonde hair flowing across her eyes, 'he just said that the canal will pay for the Aswan Dam.'

'You heard that,' Jack said with his lips to the microphone, whispering to his American public under the uproar of two hundred thousand Arabs. 'President Nasser has just said that this is how they'll pay for building the Aswan Dam . . . The President is now leaving the steps, he is waving, you can hear the fantastic ovation, and if the smile on his face shows how happy he is, it doesn't say much of what he's up against now. France, Britain and the United States will probably have something to say to President Nasser about this *coup*. It's anybody's guess now what will happen . . .'

CHAPTER FORTY-TWO

THE longer Quartermain watched Scott doing the thing he claimed he knew best—this remote map-making—the more he felt it was all self-deception, if it were possible for a man to live this sort of life for so long only to deceive himself.

Scott had, in fact, remained an outpost soldier without knowing it.

Sitting under the tarpaulin in the hot and dead afternoon he could go on for ever reducing and working out the details of ten years' surveying. It could probably occupy him for another ten years. His steel-rimmed glasses had settled on his hard-boned nose, his black notebooks were neat on the card-table, and a large bundle of quarto maps on tracing paper, clipped together and frayed crisply around the edges, stained and baked by the sun, dusty and worn, looked like just another pigeon-hole where life was being put away.

'Couldn't you do all this in Cairo?' he asked Scott.

'I can't sit in an office all day,' Scott told him. 'I tried it in 1949 and gave up after three months. Anyway, I always work better in the field itself, and more accurately too.'

Why did he do it?—sitting out here at the foot of the Red Sea mountains in the late summer when the heat almost floated you off the ground, and the sun would never dry up the moist blanket stretching across the desert at night, at noon, at eventide, and even when the fresh winds came in after sunset from the sea? Quartermain longed for a gulp of cool dry air.

'I have two more years to serve in the Frontier Department,' Scott said.

'Doing this sort of thing?'

'I might as well go on doing it. They'll begin a new geodetic survey out here soon, and I can prepare a great deal of the ground for it. Why sit in a dusty Cairo office? In the meantime I finish this Sinai stuff.' He was insisting on his right to do it. Dare Quartermain argue?

'But why all this effort on the Sinai?' Quartermain did argue, flicking a hand at the maps. 'You haven't been in the Sinai for years.'

'It takes years,' Scott insisted. 'It's partly a collative map of resources.

316

It requires great detail. We made the original survey comparative and geological, even hygroscopic; so that it comes in very useful now when they are looking for everything they can find.'

'But you're no geologist,' Quartermain said. 'What are you fiddling with that sort of stuff for?'

'I had a geologist with me for two years. In fact, he's still there.' Scott took off his steel spectacles and put them away. 'He couldn't make a map worth reading, but he was a good field man. Between us we mapped enough possible coal deposits in the Sinai to supply some of the steel industry they hope to set up in Egypt, if they ever set up anything now,' he added gloomily. 'Everybody out here seems to think that the British and the French will try to take back the canal by force. What do you think? What's it like in Cairo?'

President Nasser had announced on the radio that day the formation of an Egyptian Liberation Army, a people's army to defend Egypt, and in London twenty-two nations were meeting to form an international Suez Canal Board to operate the canal in the interests of the users, if they could ever get it back from the Egyptians.

'They'll do anything they can to get it back,' Quartermain said. 'That's pretty obvious to everyone.'

'God almighty,' Scott complained. 'It goes on for ever.'

It looked as if Scott's life in these deserts would also go on for ever, now that he had persuaded the Egyptians to let both Sam and Zareef out of prison.

'What did you write to Nasser?' Quartermain asked him, lying back on the camp-bed and watching him. He had come a long way to see Scott. Mr. Aboud had obviously been so encouraged by the nationalization of the canal that he had arranged for Quartermain to have a desert permit, and Quartermain had come here with Jack de Brazio to see how well the Egyptian borders were guarded in case of military action against Egypt. That was a good enough excuse to see Scott, although Jack had already gone back to Cairo in disgust.

'What did you say that decided Nasser?' Quartermain asked. 'Did you beg him for old times' sake? Did you swear they were innocent? Did you appeal to his sense of humanity?'

Scott began to put away his maps with a deliberate precision, pressing each one carefully into its frayed folder. 'I simply told him the truth,' he replied reluctantly. 'I said that Sam had probably done something silly but not dangerous, and only in desperation, and because he had no nationality papers. That's all. I said I was sure that Zareef must be innocent also. That's all I said.'

'If it was so simple . . .'

'It was not simple at all,' Scott answered sharply. 'I should never have asked Nasser that sort of favour. But what else could I do? I had tried everything else.'

'Why shouldn't you ask him a favour? He's an old friend, isn't he? Or has he forgotten you out here?'

'Friendship is one thing,' Scott said, 'but this goes deeper than friendship. It's not like the old regime.'

'Puritanical . . .'

'They don't like using it for privileges. I should have had some belief in what they're trying to do. Why should I claim a favour?'

'Was it such a favour—asking them to let Sam out?'

'Of course it was. I know Sam is mixed up in some way with the British. The Egyptians know it too. They want their new laws to apply to everyone, so it's not easy to ask them to get around their hard-won principles, simply for the sake of a friend. Would you?'

'Depends on which I thought more valuable,' Quartermain said lazily, 'my friend Sam, or my revolutionary principles.'

'There was no other way,' Scott repeated. 'I had to do it.'

'Then leave it at that.'

'Yes. Sam's out,' Scott said as if a grim battle had been won and was therefore better forgotten (wasn't it always better to forget the past?). 'That's all I really care about.'

It was Peacock who had pointed out how helpless Scott was in protecting his own interests. Peacock had begged Quartermain on the phone to look after Scott. 'He's as helpless as a babe,' Peacock had said the day before he left for England. 'I can't get down there to see him again. I tried. But you talk to him, Quarts. Get him out of that idiotic private desert. He's not going to look after himself at all. He simply doesn't know how to. He'll go on doing everything except the right thing for himself. He's been hiding out there too long, so beg him to reply to that antarctic letter.'

It seemed to be an extraordinary discovery, even now.

Over the years, whenever Quartermain had given more than a passing thought to his old friend, he had pictured Scott doing what had to be done and doing it well: behaving with such sanity and self-possession (no wasteful intellectual torture) that one could be sure that of all the men in the world, Scott at least was not spoiling or failing himself.

'He's been fooling himself all these years,' Peacock had insisted when Quartermain had scoffed. Quartermain claimed that he knew Scott too well to think of him as being all that helpless, whatever this trouble about Sam had done to him.

'You don't know him now, Quarts. He never did get over that court-martial.'

It was true. Scott sat hiding at his field table, busy with fragments. No

318

matter how valuable and useful they were, they were now no more than fragments of his life.

'But I'll miss Sam out here,' Scott said now, and that was almost an admission of a final resignation to his isolation.

'Maybe Nasser released Sam for political reasons,' Quartermain told him cunningly, as if to stir him a little. 'Just to prove he is not the brutal dictator everybody is now saying he is.'

'Sam's release was decided before the Suez Canal business. It was a favour to me,' Scott insisted unhappily.

It seemed strange, this distaste for the favour; but Quartermain knew why he was burdened by it. He had seen his own wife Nona weighed down by the burdensome Egyptian idea of favours, which usually involved an exchange of exaggerated but inviolable duties. One had to repay them twicefold and without question when asked, otherwise you betrayed the friendship and the favour you had counted on yourself.

'What happens now?' he asked Scott. 'Can Sam get his job back?'

'I doubt it.'

'Will they kick him out of Egypt?'

'I don't know. I hope not. They could spare him that. But I can't help him even if they do, you know. I can only do so much . . .'

'Perhaps they let him out of gaol to see where it will lead them. What about that? Is it possible?'

'Of course it's possible, if Hakim is behind it,' Scott said, as if it had already occurred to him. 'Hakim wants to find out who might be trying to murder Gamal, and Hakim never gives up.'

'Is he still so sure about it?'

'He's very sure,' Scott said. 'Can you blame him?'

'No, not after that business on the roofs.'

'And now that they've taken over the canal,' Scott went on, 'Hakim will think Gamal is even more of a target. And if he thinks Sam is going to help him discover who is behind it, then Hakim would let him out, anyway. But I can't quite believe it. I can't believe it.'

'Someone ought to warn Sam about it.'

'I wrote to your sister-in-law, Helen Mamoon, and told her to make sure that Sam keeps away from the British Embassy, and from anybody suspected of being a Zionist. He had been to the British some time ago, trying to get a British passport. You ought to tell him to keep away, when you go back. It's very important.'

'If he has no papers, the poor bastard, what can he do but go to the British or someone and try again?'

'He'll be in more trouble if he does. If Sam goes to the British, moreover, they'll try to use him again. I can't do much about that from this distance.'

319

'Don't worry about it then. I'll talk to him.'

'There's absolutely nothing more I can do,' Scott said miserably. 'Nothing.'

Jack de Brazio had already gone back to Cairo in a Shell Company station-wagon. Cairo was still staggering with sensation and reaction to the canal nationalization, and Ella might not be able to handle it on her own. Anyway, he had found nothing down here to justify the idea that Scott was interested in the fedayeen, or that the British might invade Egypt from the Red Sea coast.

But he had tried to get other passing answers from Scott. Jack was willing (he said) to try once more to justify this lonely world of Captain Scott.

'Justify?' Scott had been angry. 'Justify what? Why do Americans always look for sensation?'

'I didn't ask you to be sensational,' Jack said. 'But you can't hide out here in these deserts any more, Scott, and pretend you're out of it. The world is collapsing on your ears. Why do you go on kidding yourself?'

'Isn't that my affair?' Scott had replied resentfully.

Jack had taken his revenge in one question. 'Have you been training Egyptian commandos out here?'

'Yes,' Scott said. 'I've trained my Egyptian driver how to cook.'

Jack had turned on his tape switches. 'No commandos?' he asked. 'No fedayeen for raiding Israel? No lessons in infiltration from the famous Scott of the western desert?'

'If I want to, I will train them, don't worry about that.'

'What happens if the British Army comes marching down that road to retake Suez?' Jack asked. 'Are you going to fight your own brothers?'

'That's not likely, and it's my own business.'

'Don't you know that the British Navy has already sent every available ship to the Eastern Mediterranean? The French too.'

'I don't care about that.'

'Would you fight the Israelis?'

'I told you. I'm not in the Egyptian Army,' Scott said angrily. 'I don't want to fight anybody. I've finished with fighting. Now leave me alone.'

Jack had turned off his switches, and Quartermain had felt sad. Two fine fellows had failed to understand or like each other, and he felt guilty for not setting them right. But how could he? Scott had fallen too easily into the sort of indignation which Americans often provoked, and Jack had been too easily hurt by a man who was always defending himself against a forgotten crime.

'That stubborn bastard deserves all he's going to get,' Jack had said in parting. 'The United News office in London says he's probably advising

320

Nasser on canal defences. What a mockery. That's the old story of Nasser's Englishman.'

Jack had left Scott the newspaper cutting which Ella had posted to him at the Shell Rest House at Ghurdakha. But when Scott saw the newspaper cutting he had screwed it up and thrown it away without looking at it.

'Jack could have helped you straighten out all that stupid sort of mis-information,' Quartermain said to Scott. 'Why did you antagonize him?'

But Quartermain did not go further, knowing at a glance that it was private, silent, lonely ground that Scott guarded so well.

Hakim arrived urgently in an Air Force Fairchild, which Scott thought was very badly landed. Zareef and Sam would never arrive like that on Thursdays again, but here was Hakim himself. What the devil could he want?

'I was in Ismailia,' Hakim explained, 'where our English and French friends, the canal pilots, are already running away. Did you hear? They think we're going to make a mess of the canal without them, so they are going to resign. Don't they understand how Gamal works? Did they think he would take over the canal without first knowing whether we could work it ourselves or not? You can see their stupidity. "*Lazy, ignorant Egyptians,*" they say. Hah!'

Hakim was happy, and he was allowing the gaiety to fall where it may. His greeting had been perfunctory. Who was this Englishman with Scott? He knew, but he did not care, and in his handshake he had looked at Quartermain and laughed contemptuously under the skin. Scott gave him the best canvas chair under the tarpaulin and called in the pilot. But Hakim told the pilot to wait—he would not be staying long.

'Now we have to watch out for the English,' he said to Scott in Arabic, and it obviously gave him pleasure to watch out for the English. 'They are all furious! They can't *think* of the British Empire without the canal.'

'Is that why you came down to the Red Sea? Do you think they will attack Egypt?'

Hakim loosened his jacket and let out a hot thin breath as if he were exhausted, but he looked quite cool and not at all tired.

'I thought I would ask you what you thought, *habibi*,' Hakim said to Scott in English now. 'Do you think Sir Eden will actually use force to take back what he could not even hold by force?'

'If he remembers what happened at the Ismailia Police Post a few years ago, he won't,' Scott said.

'But *does* he remember?' Hakim asked. 'Do men like Sir Eden ever remember anything?'

'I don't know,' Scott said. But he knew he had a means now to defend himself with, because he was not going to let Hakim tease him about the canal and Eden. That could lead to unpleasantness. 'I don't know about Eden, but my friend Quartermain probably does. Ask him.'

Hakim looked at Quartermain as an adult would look at an unwanted child suddenly thrust upon him. He did not ask Quartermain the question but simply waited for the comment, anyway.

'I don't suppose Eden is going to let you get away with it if he can help it,' Quartermain said obligingly. 'That's certain.'

'Is it certain?' Hakim said, turning back to Scott, ignoring Quartermain. 'But what can Sir Eden actually do about it? You tell me.'

Scott shrugged. 'Nothing, I should think.'

'But he must do something,' Hakim insisted. 'If I were the English I would fight for the canal.'

'The English have already done too much fighting for it,' Scott said. 'You couldn't get them to attack Egypt so recklessly, not just for the canal.'

'Is that true?' Hakim said to Quartermain directly—an opportunist who needed an answer.

Quartermain answered slowly. 'The English could probably be persuaded to do anything,' he said, 'even that. They may not like it, but they'd do it.'

'You see,' Hakim said triumphantly to Scott. 'The English are always obedient. You will all fight. Yet you are both wrong. First, Sir Eden will try other methods . . . very old methods.'

'Diplomacy?' Scott said.

'Oh, yes—that is also for Sir Eden.' Hakim laughed at Sir Eden's diplomacy—a chit-chat world for Sir Eden. 'But that will mean nothing. Now they will try to punish us, and' (Hakim looked provocatively at both of them) 'how could they best do that?'

'There's nothing much more they can do,' Quartermain said, 'short of going to war. They've already blocked your money.'

Hakim waved that aside. 'Don't you think they would like to put an end to Gamal Abd el Nasser? Wouldn't Sir Eden be very happy to see that?'

'He's already said so,' Quartermain agreed. 'But he can't do much about that either, can he?'

'Ahhh,' Hakim said mysteriously and perhaps bitterly. 'Sir Eden would do anything to get rid of our Gamal Abd el Nasser.'

But he said no more about it, and simply slumped in his canvas chair and called in the pilot.

The pilot brought up a fat thermos of iced fruit-juice, and Ishaak— impressed and also obedient—brought in a kanaka of coffee and served it as if he did it like that for Scott every day, with a valet's politeness.

'If you stay for dinner I can offer you fattah,' Scott said to Hakim.

322

Fattah was rice cooked in mutton broth and served on fried bread soaked in vinegar.

'La-a!' Hakim said, and after protests and insistences he stood up and said he must go. But first he took Scott outside, the Egyptian way, arm-in-arm. Where could they walk to? There was another tarpaulin over the jeep jutting out from the old Roman quarry, and they sat under it on the pillar signed by Annius Rufus, a centurion of the XVth Legion, who had once been in charge of the quarry here.

'I must be in Ismailia before nightfall,' Hakim told him in Arabic. 'Tomorrow I will go up to Mersa Matruh. Let us see what they might do to us there.'

Hakim was obviously looking after the frontiers of his country, and Scott suddenly suspected that he was about to be given a role in it himself. Hakim was not here for a friendly call. Hakim held his arm, cast a little net of brotherliness over them, and said he was pleased that Scott's friend, Sam Hassoon, was free. Yes, yes, it was finished. Let there be no more thought of it. There would be more important things to think about now.

'Why,' Hakim asked, 'would your friend General Church want to take his archaeological expedition to see the western deserts at this time? There are no serious archaeological remains there. Why should he suddenly want to do that?'

'Now?'

'At this very moment.'

'I couldn't even guess.'

'But there must be some reason, eh?' Hakim insisted.

'Perhaps they want to see what remains of the Roman villas at Mersa Matruh,' Scott suggested, 'or find a few of the old Roman wells in the desert.'

'No, no,' Hakim said, abandoning his customary search for the hidden joke. 'Church has asked permission to take his bus to the desert battle-fields.'

'When was this? Before the canal news?'

'Oh, no, habibi. After . . .'

'Then he probably wants to show his professors where he won the war,' Scott said. 'Did you let him go?'

'Of course.'

'Why did you do that, if you're worried about him?'

'But I'm interested,' Hakim replied in surprise. 'I thought you might be also. Are you? I told Colonel Mukri, who is there, to warn them how dangerous it is.'

'Which dangers do you mean, Hakim?' Scott knew that this joke meant a real danger.

'Mines,' Hakim told him.

'Is Church taking his bus into the open desert?'

'Of course. I told you—the battlefields.'

The savagery in the pleasure of his own mockery never pleased Scott, particularly when it showed up in front of Hakim. But he could not resist it. 'He'll finally blow himself up on one of his own minefields,' he said. 'After all these years.'

'And the professors also?'

'Is that what worries you?' Scott asked.

'I don't think so. General Church must have a very good idea of where to go and where not to go, not so? He must have good maps. Oh, very good maps. Wasn't he a general staff officer? Wouldn't he have all the details (more than we have) of where the minefields are?'

Scott tried not to be cynical about it. 'If I were you, Hakim, I'd call him back.'

'But then I wouldn't know what he was doing.'

'He'll kill his professors,' Scott said. 'Call him back for their sake.'

'Why don't *you* go and see what he is doing?' Hakim suggested.

'Me? What for? Why me?' Scott said, rejecting it quickly and fearfully.

'You know all the tracks and landing fields and whatever else he is looking for in the western desert. What *is* he looking for? I want to know that, *habibi*. I need to know.'

'Why should he be looking for anything in particular?' Scott asked. 'If the British are going to attack Egypt they won't come that way—if they have any sense.'

'Won't they? But do you *know* they won't? Do you know what the British are thinking?'

Scott shrugged.

'You don't know. Nor do I. But I must know. Would you go, *habibi*? *Argouk!*'

'But why me, Hakim?' Scott repeated. 'I've forgotten all that part of the western desert. I haven't been back there since the war. What can I do that one of your own officers can't do?'

Why me? What do I owe? How far, one could ask, were these new debts of his deepest honour to be repaid or refused? Was this going to be the price of Sam's release after all? Was that why Hakim or Gamal had released him? *'But they owed me Sam!'* he told himself angrily and bitterly.

But Hakim had cancelled out all duties and debts with the contempt in his eyes. He seemed to be standing there now challenging one Englishman to disprove that he remained for ever English, whatever else he pretended to be.

'Well, *habibi*?' Hakim said firmly.

324

'But what the devil can I do?' Scott said again, trying to cry out against an unfair advantage, but knowing he was helpless. 'If you insist, of course, I'll do it. But I don't honestly know what I could do.'

Hakim slapped Annius Rufus's column. 'That,' he said, relieved to find the hidden joke again, 'I would leave to you. You're the expert. Find out what your General is up to. That's all. Ah, *habibi*, you are always a good friend, and you know we are very proud of how you help us. Believe me . . .'

There was nothing more to be said, and when Hakim walked them back to the plane, arm-in-arm, and got into the Fairchild to fly away he said he had already arranged everything.

'Au revoir, mon vieux,' he said cheerfully. 'Je ne demande rien que votre amabilité.'

When Hakim spoke French he was trying to think like a Frenchman (how else could you understand an enemy?) because he was on his way to Ismailia to talk to the French pilots again.

'We'll offer them more money to stay on,' he went on in French from the plane. 'That ought to make them feel sick when they desert us—as they will. But they'll spend the rest of their French lives counting all the money they left behind them—*leur joli souvenir de l'Egypte et des sales Arabes*. All that money they refused. Oh, how it will freeze their French souls.'

The plane started up and they saw Hakim laughing as he closed the door.

The evening softened and dampened again when Hakim was gone, and Quartermain went on looking for the man he thought he knew. But the complexities of self-deception were too great to fathom.

'Do you have to go?' he asked Scott. 'Does his word count?'

'I don't have to, but I will,' Scott replied moodily.

'Do you think I could go with you?' Quartermain asked him. 'I'd like to see all the old NAAFI dumps again.'

Scott hesitated only a moment, but then he looked grateful and said, 'Why not? If you want to . . .'

'Will they give me a permit? Your Egyptian friends don't like me very much. They say I'm a communist, so they can't trust me.'

'Are you?'

'Am I what—trustworthy?'

'No. Are you a communist?'

Quartermain wondered about naïveté. Was that the sort of question people asked so simply any more? Probably it was the only question in the world which could never be asked without giving it a particular feeling, yet Scott was doing so.

'I ought to be,' he said to Scott, 'but I could never quite overcome my sense of doing it all by myself. I'm no good at discipline of any sort, you know that. No. That's not true. The only reason I'm not a communist is that, if I was, I'd have to go the whole way, and what good would that do? I couldn't do it. Not now. Children and wives are such valuable things. That's what beats me. You know, I never forgot what they did to you. I learned a terrible lesson that day—just how vulnerable a man is, if he ever tries to correct a great wrong. I have tried to avoid giving them any cause to do the same thing to me.'

'But you're always attacking something,' Scott said. 'Peacock told me. He said it was a wonder they hadn't locked you up years ago over something you wrote about Malaya or Korea.'

'Did he say that?' Quartermain said happily. 'That's all right. That's what they can *say*, so long as they don't actually do it, the way they locked you up. You've got better nerves and a whole stomach. I couldn't survive it the way you did.'

'Do you think I survived it?' Scott asked suddenly of an old friend.

'I don't suppose you did,' Quartermain admitted carefully, 'so you can see my point.'

'I can see your point very well, and I can tell you that you're absolutely right. Never oppose authority, Quarts. It's not worth it.'

'I didn't mean that at all,' Quartermain corrected quickly. 'I think it was worth it, if you can take the results. I simply don't think I could take the punishment. It would kill me to be cut up the way you were. I hate even to think about it.'

Scott did not want to remember it either: nor hear anything so near the very edge of his real feelings. He did not want to put his head inside his heart, only to listen to its troubles.

'Anyway,' he said quickly, 'why do the Egyptians suspect you? Why should they care what you think?'

Quartermain shifted his position because the sun had crept around cleverly and was under the tarpaulin on his feet. 'Everybody cares,' he said. 'Make no mistake about that. No matter where I go, they all care.'

'But why?'

'I still believe in the old upheaval. But now I can't wait for the white man to save the world for his black brothers to wonder at. The white man never will. So I've joined up with the black man to see what he can do. He'll do it, I think. But even the Egyptians don't like it to be that clear, that advanced. Nobody likes the idea of an upheaval against society itself. Can't have that! So they watch me, you see?'

Yes, Scott saw. But he also said, in his present mood, that he didn't care about all that. Let them watch him. 'I don't know anything about politics,' he said, 'but I don't think you've changed much after all. In the army they were always after you. I'm amazed you got through the war yourself without getting into trouble.'

'I *was* in trouble,' Quartermain reminded him indignantly. 'Why do you think they had exiled me to those NAAFI dumps, where Pickering found me?'

'I meant real trouble,' Scott said.

That was the inequality showing; because Scott, in those days, had been the one in serious trouble and Quartermain had not been. That was the difference. Whatever the reasons, the moral of a man's action was always strong for men like Quartermain, who had the sort of conscience which tried to tell him what he ought and ought not to do about the world. It would always trouble him. But that did not bring him up to his own estimation of Scott, who, while boasting of no politics and denying real intentions, had nevertheless challenged authority with a motivation which was of the very highest and was impossible to deny.

Why else did men admire Scott, even though they thought him a fool sometimes, and even though he boasted of his political ignorance; even though he had hidden himself out here in pain from a world which had punished him too harshly for his deep concern for it?

But Scott was elsewhere.

'I wonder what Church is looking for,' Scott said then, obviously pre-occupied already with this unpleasant task Hakim had set him. 'Landing fields, do you think? Open ground for parachutists?'

'In the western desert? Are they that mad?'

'They must be.'

'If they're going to invade Egypt they ought to do it from Israel. They could probably take the Sinai in a week.'

Scott said that was impossible. 'German engineers have been building concrete defences all along the coast.'

'Concrete in the desert,' Quartermain pointed out cynically, 'is always put there to be abandoned. Look at Tobruk and Benghazi. A few days, a week at most, and any good army could have all that side of the canal. Nothing could stop them.'

'You're forgetting that the Egyptians have finally got a proper air force.'

'Poof! They'll never get off the ground. They'll be wiped out.'

'Even so—even the British Army couldn't finish it off in a week. I don't believe it.'

'If they do attack Egypt,' Quartermain said, 'it will probably end up in a horrible mess like Korea.'

Scott unfolded his maps to begin his work. 'I begin to understand Hakim's theory about Nasser,' he said dismally. 'I suppose the easiest way

327

for the British or the French to solve it would be to get rid of Nasser some-how. But how?'

In the cooler evening, when they were preparing their supper over a primus, they saw a jeep approaching them at a reckless pace in the far distance. It was running erratically in its own dust, up a dried-out river-bed.

'That's Amin Fakhry,' Scott told Quartermain in surprise. 'Only Amin would tear up the old road like that. He must have cut clean across from Safaga or somewhere.'

'Is he one of your geologists?' Quartermain asked as they watched the dust spiral, and as Ishaak pointed excitedly to it and called out: 'It's Colonel Fakhry.'

Scott smiled a little, obviously pleased by this arrival. 'Amin is a soldier,' he told Quartermain. 'He and I have been exiles out here to-gether.'

'A soldier?'

'The most professional of them all,' Scott said affectionately. 'That's how he got into trouble with Hakim after the revolution.'

Amin Fakhry's jeep was still a mile away, but from their height they could see it taking everything in its course—plunging up slopes and over them as if the driver cared little about the desert hazards.

'What do you mean, he was exiled out here?' Quartermain asked. 'In disgrace?'

'Not quite exile or disgrace,' Scott said, 'although it amounts to the same thing. Amin Fakhry thinks that Hakim plots too much for a soldier. He wanted a forceful, intelligent, professional army that would keep out of politics, or at least hand the Government over to someone they could trust—anyone but the army itself. He thinks it ought to be a means of control, but no more, because he says that politics corrupt the soldier. And in that I've always agreed with him.'

'Did they take his opinions that seriously—enough to send him out here?'

They walked down the slope to their own jeep where Amin would eventually arrive. 'Amin is probably the best professional they've got,' Scott said. 'That's all he is. But he was very popular, so they had to take him seriously. I suppose his opposition to Hakim at the time worried the rest of them enough to want him out of the way. They wanted to get rid of him completely, but I think Gamal saved him. They took him out of the Army and put him in the Frontier Department, which is more in-nocuous; and anyway Hakim can keep an eye on him.'

'And is he any good?'

Scott laughed a little. 'A little too professional for you, but he's hard

328

to beat, even out here. He gets around everywhere. He's a passionate administrator too, and fussy. He won't even allow the Camel Corps to scatter its bales of hay all over the place. He makes them stack it up. Everything has to be organized and he practically turns everything into a little fort. He's very exact as a soldier, but he's probably too contemptuous of some of his fellow-officers to get the best out of them.'

'That's nice,' Quartermain said, recognizing a fellow-feeling.

'No, it's not. He doesn't quite mean it in the same way as you do,' Scott corrected. 'Amin thinks that all the young Egyptian officers are weak, inefficient and boastful. But the senior officers are his brothers, even with all his contempt for politics. So don't expect him to agree with you. He likes these black Sudanese professionals he's got under him out here, and he leans more and more on them, because he thinks that the rest of the army is too miserably equipped at birth to stand up to much or to his requirement of them. He's an aristocrat at heart, the French kind. That's where he got his military education.'

Scott obviously considered this to be a friendship worth explaining, and when Colonel Amin Fakhry did arrive and leapt out of the jeep in a happy and exploding burst of energy, Quartermain stood aside and watched Scott's usually restrained expression break openly into pleasure and good humour.

'You're going to tip over that jeep and break your back one day, driving alone like that across the hills,' Scott said. 'You shouldn't do it.'

'I can always jump before it rolls on me,' Amin said, speaking French like a Frenchman. 'I was trained on horses, *mon ami*. I know how to get clear of the beast.'

When Scott introduced Quartermain, as an old friend in the western desert during the war, Amin Fakhry did not avoid him or ignore him the way Hakim had done, but gave Quartermain his complete good-mannered attention, asking him in French where he had come from, what was he doing, how long was it since he had seen Scott, and was he still a soldier.

'Not me,' Quartermain answered in French. 'Never again.'

That was a slight disappointment, but Amin forgave him. He was a tall, attractive man in the Egyptian manner, not unlike Gamal Abd el Nasser to look at, but shaped by some more erratic force which seemed to push him to the limit all the time, everything he did and said, as if the power of it could not be switched off.

'Hakim est parti ?' he said to Scott.

Scott nodded. 'How did you know he was here ?'

'I heard from Ghurdakha, and I knew he would come here, so I came straight from the old signal station to see him.'

'He was in a hurry.'

'Isn't he always ?'

When Scott laughed at the pot calling the kettle black, Amin went on seriously, not bothering to spare Hakim because of Quartermain's presence. It had to come out, it couldn't wait. Or perhaps in trusting Scott so much he trusted his friends equally.

'He's afraid to see me,' Amin said. 'That's all it is. Why didn't he come down at Ghurdakha, or where I was, even for five minutes? I can't even go to Cairo to talk to him. *No, no*, he says, *you can't leave there yet, habibi.* What does he expect me to do, *mon ami*? Spend the rest of my life in the Frontier Department with the camels. Now it's becoming silly. All right —I don't agree with him, but I'm wasting my time. Look what everyone is saying now. I listened to the French radio. Oh, my God, what they cry about now. I'm sure they're going to send the Foreign Legion and the *paras* to this end of the Mediterranean, perhaps to the Lebanon. And what will Hakim be doing except looking for plots? That's not what counts now. It's quite serious.'

Who could take it seriously? Or at least—who could listen and not feel indulgent about Amin's enthusiasm for the seriousness of it.

He was gone again almost before they could persuade him to eat some sausages. He ate, wiped his fingers delicately on his clean handkerchief, and got into the jeep which Ishaak (at a shout of firm command from Amin) had refilled with petrol.

'Good-bye,' he said to Quartermain, quite completely, and shook hands. His hands were still clean. He wore an American Army green overall with his insignia on the epaulettes. The overalls were also clean and uncreased, and the only apparent sign of his desert ride was the line which his cap had made on his forehead. He had taken it off for a moment to wipe his glistening hair.

'I will have to see Gamal,' he shouted in French as he revved the jeep and put it in gear. 'This is becoming too ridiculous to put up with any longer.'

He was gone and they watched him racing away in the dusk.

Scott shook his head. 'Hakim will never let him get anywhere near Gamal,' he said almost to himself. 'But they'll have to have a showdown some time.'

Amin had already turned on the powerful headlights of the jeep, and these two startled eyes wiggled and swam across the horizon.

'How does he hope to get back across such difficult country at night, like that?' Quartermain said. 'He must be off his head.'

'Amin could set out for Cairo, right now, just like that, and get there. They say in Arabic that God patted his head when he was born; and it does seem as if something looks after him.'

Now it was night, and Quartermain had already lost his taste for the

330

desert, lying on the low camp-bed under the tarpaulin, reading, surrounded by nothing. He longed to be in a city with sparkling window lights and wasteful noise, or on a vibrating ship with a moist deck. It was too empty under this black-starred sky, in this place without doorways. The smell of garlic from Scott's fattah cooking stuck stale to the tarpaulin and seemed almost too human, but the hissing petrol lamp was a wretched, lonely noise. Better to turn it off and sleep. Asleep at eight and awake in the pre-dawn darkness of half past four: what kind of a life was that for a man, every day?

'Why do you fiddle with those maps?' Quartermain asked sadly. 'An aeroplane could survey in a week what you've done in years.'

Scott bristled more than seemed necessary. 'An aeroplane can map topographically but it can't do a proper job of it. In fact, what do you think I'm doing with this particular chart?'

'God knows. But is it worth it?'

'Of course it is,' Scott said impatiently. 'They had a plane over here a year ago making a photogrammetry survey along the Qena road, but half these features aren't even visible in the photographs, and even the distances can't be measured accurately enough from the air—not yet anyway. When they start using electronic devices, like *Loran* or *Gee* or some of these hyperbolic navigational devices, they'll be better off. But even now they can't measure true directions or azimuths . . .'

'And so?' Quartermain said, ignorant of its point.

'So, it just took Ishaak and me a week to check the errors of detail in one small feature alone. But that's not the point. The big need here, some day, will be for a good and accurate geodetic survey which they can rely on if they start to develop these areas. Everything will depend then on a good geodetic base, which is what I am trying to prepare the way for.'

'Even so,' Quartermain insisted, 'it's too lonely out here to do a man any good. You ought to get out of it.'

'The moment I get out of it, something worse happens to me,' Scott pointed out. 'I'm happy out here; so don't worry me about it. I'm all right.'

'Hakim did you a favour, anyway,' Quartermain growled stubbornly, 'sending you after Church. That ought to do your soul a lot of good . . .'

331

A STUDENT flying an Auster from Cairo to Alexandria had noticed a stream of petrol running down the cabin floor, vibrating and dancing on the sand-grained alloy and smelling dangerous. He had force-landed in the desert near the half-way house, the cockpit explosive, and he had jumped out the moment he could get the door open, knowing it was his only chance of escape.

When he had not arrived in Alexandria an hour after his estimated time of arrival, the Air Force were sent up to look for him, but before they found him he had reached the half-way house on foot and telephoned from there.

'I'm safe,' he said to Captain Selim. 'Don't worry.'

'The plane, the plane,' Captain Selim cried. 'Is it all right?'

'Kwayis, kwayis owi, ya Captain.'

'Did you turn all the petrol cocks off?'

'Yes, but petrol is pouring out onto the sand anyway.'

Captain Selim took off in a Tiger Moth with a mechanic, and when he found the Auster he landed near it to be sure a landing could be made. He left the mechanic there and returned to Gedida with the student, and twenty other students crowded around the Tiger Moth asking the news. Selim said nothing to them. When he saw Captain Zareef wâiting, but not yet asking, he went over to him and said that he had taken off in the Tiger and landed near the Auster to see if he, Captain Ali Zareef, would be able to land near it.

'Thank you,' Zareef said in English. 'Thank you very much, Captain.' Selim did not understand the sarcasm.

'Do you think if a student can force-land a plane that I can't, Captain?' Zareef said.

'Ya Captain!' Selim replied sadly, walking away.

'Many, many Captains this morning,' Fahid the cynic said in English to Zareef, knowing that Zareef was losing a moral supremacy. They had freed him from prison, they had even given him back his licence and his job, and what had happened did not worry him. It was a mistake, and Zareef could forgive it and forget it in the relief of being able to fly again. What worried him here was his loss of moral supremacy over the Haboob. Zareef was almost in tears: that Selim could do a thing like this to him.

'I think I'll leave the school,' he said. 'I'm going.'

The students saved him by arriving *en masse* to tell him what had happened, and he had to listen to them.

'Are you ready, Captain?' Selim called out to him. 'The Auster is waiting. I will come with you, and Wing-Commander Izaat also.'

'Ah well,' Zareef said to escape the students. 'I must go.'

Captain Selim had two new fuel pipes for the mechanic, and the promoted Wing-Commander director told Zareef to fly the plane, not Selim. Yes, that would be better all round. They got into it, with Selim in the seat behind and the director next to Zareef who taxied to the wind-sock. As they turned into wind the director felt how heavy they were and changed his mind.

'The civil aviation officer should go,' he said. 'Taxi over to the control tower and let me out. I'll call him down.'

Zareef gave the Auster a burst and taxied it so fast that he almost took off, but they reached the tarmac and he let the tail come down gently and stopped under the staircase of the control tower.

'Mahmood,' the director called up to the tower officer. 'Send down Captain el Baghdady and tell him he ought to go with Zareef instead of me.'

'Then I'll move to the front,' Selim said to Zareef.

Captain Mahmood el Baghdady, the C.A.A. official, was very large and a little idle and happy. He was pleased to be with his friends and offered them chewing-gum, though he did not look forward to a bumpy ride in the hot morning over the desert. When he got in the back Captain Selim sat in the front and they turned down-wind again, but as they were about to face up to take off Selim also felt the heavy reluctance of the plane.

'Wait,' Selim shouted.

'What's the matter now?' Zareef said.

'We're overloaded,' Selim told him.

'La, ya Captain,' Zareef said. 'Not that much.' He adjusted the tail trimmer.

'Wait. You might get off,' Selim said, 'but you'll be too heavy coming down in the desert in that loose sand.'

'If I get off I can get down,' Zareef insisted.

'No,' Selim argued. 'We're overloaded. You'd better let me or Baghdady out.'

'In the name of God,' Zareef protested. 'Sit still.'

'I tell you there's not enough surface on the desert to fly on carefully

333

with this weight,' Selim insisted, and they began then their rival protests
which ended in anger.

'It's going to be your responsibility then,' Selim said.

'I'm flying the plane,' Zareef shouted. 'Of course it's my responsibility.
You won't take it, then I'm happy to take it.'

'Then it's your responsibility,' Selim repeated.

But Selim insisted that they go back to the tarmac where the engineer
could pull on the wings and look at the wheels while they argued.

'These planes will take weight as long as they're flown on,' Zareef said.

But Selim was still not convinced. The students had collected again,
and Zareef got out of the plane and said once more, 'I'm disgusted. I'm
leaving the school.'

'Ttt, ttt, Captain,' Fahid said to him.

The director arrived and took Zareef aside and said, 'Why, *habibi*?
Why?'

'Why! Why!' Zareef complained. 'He wants me to fly it, yet he's afraid
of the responsibility. What sort of a man is that?'

The students' bus arrived and disgorged fifty schoolboys who had been
brought from an elementary technical school to be shown the possibilities
of flying for their technical education, their future. They had already taken
over the Auster and were taking pictures of each other in front of the
planes, combing their hair. The firemen sat and watched, and the engine-
driver's little boy, Mish-mish (little apricot), played hop-scotch on the
tarmac. The control-tower staff leaned out of the windows in the sun,
watching in snobbish isolation. Two sparrows came and sat on the rudder
of the Auster, as they loved to do, in the middle of Zareef's protests,
while a sparrow-hawk winged around with very ragged-looking wing-tips
waiting for them.

'It's my turn to spin today,' Barmeel told Fahid. 'I wish they'd get this
over and done with. I'm nervous.'

'Ahhhh!' Fahid said in disgust. 'Let's all go home in protest.'

The other students were politely keeping away again and playing the
fool with bottles of coca-cola, and the engineer shunted the schoolboys
out of the way and the teacher as well.

'Let's all walk out,' Fahid shouted to the others.

They carefully took no notice of him.

'Always joking,' Fahid complained, watching the others splashing each
other with the coca-cola. 'What can anyone do here? Where's the director?
He can't even settle an argument. He's gone back to his office. What's
the use, anyway? Even if you become a pilot here and you go to the airlines
you have to sign up for ten years. Then they have you for ever and pay
you nothing. And what do you do in ten years' flying for Cairo Air Lines?
Ahh . . . they've settled it. They're taking the Gemini instead. They

334

don't know what they're doing. What do you care, Barmeel? You'll never be a pilot anyway. If you ever spin a plane it will fall down dead. Now watch Zareef with the Gemini. He can put it down anywhere. Selim was scared, now he isn't.'

The argument was settled. Zareef had offered to fly the Gemini instead of the smaller Auster. Hadn't he landed the Gemini with its two engines and sharp approach and wide wheels on every strip of sand on the Red Sea coast? Selim was satisfied.

Fahid laughed. 'Zareef won after all,' he said to Barmeel. 'Thank God somebody wins sometimes.'

'Wins what?' the barrel-shaped boy asked.

'Oh, never mind. It's all over. You wouldn't understand.'

Zareef had won back all moral superiority, and he was talking like an old friend to Captain Selim who sat next to him in the bigger Gemini with its twin engines, its boxlike frame which Zareef said he hated, while el Baghdady of the C.A.A. was sitting in the back offering them chewing-gum.

They all watched the Gemini start. Captain Zareef called down to Hefney the prop-swinger for his cushions. When he taxied past the firemen he leaned out and waved to them, and to Mish-mish, the driver's little boy, as if he hadn't seen them for weeks. They waved back. The black caps of the wind-recorder gathered speed in the back-wash, and he took off in two spiral tails of dust which became one and smothered the whole tarmac, students, schoolboys, so that the firemen pulled their black jerseys up over their faces.

Thus it was settled and the weather man was brushing the dust off his charts when his old friend Sam Hassoon came in and said 'Et alors!'

'Et alors!' the weather man said and embraced him.

Nobody else greeted Sam, mainly because Sam was feeling embarrassed to be here. It was bad luck for him that Zareef had just flown away, because Ali was not here to show the way to the others.

Fahid laughed slyly at Sam and offered him a coca-cola which was accepted.

'Where has Captain Ali gone?' Sam asked.

'He's teaching the Haboob how to fly the Gemini,' Fahid said.

'When will he be back? Did he say?'

Fahid looked at the taxi which had brought Sam, then at the English-woman trying to talk to the urchin son of the guardian who slept under the planes at night in the hangar with his donkeys and his wife and four children. Who was she? What did Sam want? *Ah, Sam! It is not going to be so easy for thee. Thou hast none of Zareef's moral supremacy because thy morality isn't like Zareef's.* Zareef had won by the morality of good

335

flying. What other morality in the whole world could there possibly be?

'If Zareef had any sense he would keep flying and never come back,' Fahid said. 'He's wasting his time here.'

Sam was about to drink the coca-cola before going into the workshop hangar to see Bambo the mechanic, when he remembered Lucy Pickering, who had come out in the taxi with him. He gave her the bottle.

'Would you like a cold drink?' he asked her. 'Nobody's touched it.'

'No thanks, Sam. Where's your friend the pilot?'

'He just took off.'

'Then where is the director's office?' she asked, smoothing her skirt.

'In that little house by itself.'

'I'll go and talk to him,' she said, and Sam rubbed his hand over his shaven head and wondered how Bambo and Hefney the prop-swinger would greet him in the workshop. He ought to see the director first, but he needed his friends first and he went over to test their friendship.

336

Nona, driving through the fields, realized why she would hate all her life the smell of the fresh *barseem*. A lucern field ought to be a refreshing relief after the concentration of Cairo heat, but these cool green fields would always remind her of going home to Matarieh every evening and leaving the best part of her youthful life in Cairo. To be the girl guide, amateur dramatic, young-Christian-woman, and a student at the British Institute—these had been good excuses to be with one's friends.

At the sandwich bars, where for breakfast every morning before work she had eaten an anchovy sandwich with olives and pickles and a cup of cocoa, there she would always hear the parquet clatter of Greek waiters and dishes and the anchovy taste of Cairo. In the afternoon-tea time they had met for a glass of *limoon* and cakes at Locques' which had eventually become a small and almost private meeting-place for her friends who had been at the English Mission College with her (girl guides all), and in the Heliopolis Sporting Club, at tennis, at dinner parties, on picnics to the canal, to Port Said in the summer-time, and in the winter the Cairo night full of young women's life which looked for a brim to fill itself up to. But then, when it was over, she would get on the train and rush home through the cool evening, through these damp perfumed fields—a journey away from the fun of living in that *imago* of life.

It would never be easy, ever again, to appreciate the countryside, even the English. It flanked the way out of life. Whereas the city was the street where life went on, although Quartermain hated it and did not believe in it at all.

'I suppose he's happy, now that he's back with Scott,' she told Helen.

'In the desert? What do they see in it?'

They were riding in a horse-drawn gharry (becoming rarer in Cairo now) along the Pyramid road, and the *barseem* fields were beginning to depress Nona.

'He needed to get out of it all for a while.'

'Out of what?' Helen asked. 'Cairo?'

'I suppose so.'

The old gharry driver clicked at his high-boned beast.

'Look how most people waste their lives,' Nona said, the *barseem* getting the better of her at last, its sweet green coolness weighing on her. 'People go on from day to day all through their lives never having done anything they really, in their hearts, want to do. In their hearts do most people ever feel useful?'

'What's that got to do with your husband?'

'I don't know, except that Quarts for one does do what he wants to do, and what he thinks is right and worthwhile. At least it ought to be useful, but where does it get him? I mean himself?'

'He ought to be happy,' Helen said, 'with two such children. And you don't look a day older than the day he married you.'

'There's more than that to it, as you ought to know,' Nona argued.

'What should I know?'

Nona brushed irritably at the flies which had abandoned the gharry horse to settle on her nose, her eyes, her long fingers. 'The trouble is that he is absolutely alone. He keeps himself alone. That's why I'm glad he went off with Scott. Perhaps they see eye-to-eye.'

'Do you really think it was the stolid Captain Scott who got Sam out?'

'Who else?'

'It may be a trick.'

'Oh, don't talk like that, darling. Even though you don't like Nasser you know very well that most Egyptians can be much more humane than anyone else you've ever known. Even under Nasser you can probably find human beings in the Ministries. But try to find anyone in the British Home Office who will stretch a law to fit a human being when you want something out of them. Look how the British tricked Sam, after he had served them so well.'

'I know. I know. Anyway, here's the house.'

They had come out along the Pyramid road to see the villa of Princess Farida, the first, lovely, divorced wife of King Farouk. The villa lay on the wide green belt where the eye fell down from the pyramids to the irrigated fields.

'They say sometimes you can see her working in the garden. *Elle est devenue rustique,*' Helen said. 'She wears floppy hats and trousers like Greta Garbo, and they say she's still absolutely young and beautiful. She doesn't see anybody and she only goes out with her father in his car.'

The villa was a large white mansion surrounded by a high wall, and about once a month photographers would climb the eucalyptus trees near by to take pictures of her in the garden, using telescopic lenses to discover her, hiding under her floppy hat.

Nona guessed what it meant. 'You can imagine,' she said sadly. 'I

338

suppose Farouk was tragic enough as a husband. You can imagine that. But to have your children taken away when they were just four or five years of age, by your own husband.'

Nona would not allow herself to weep for an ex-Queen out of luck, but she could always feel, painfully, the young mother suffering. It was too much to think about in these *barseem* fields.

'To know that her children would be growing up like that,' she said. 'Have you seen pictures of them? They look like their father . . .'

'It's a risk she took when she married him,' Helen said.

'How can you say that? She was only seventeen or eighteen. I remember . . .'

What she remembered was the strange feeling then of every flower-bud of a Moslem or even a Coptic girl. This eighteen-year-old Farida—so transparent and so innocent—could have been any one of them. That was an ecstasy of her youth. The only pity of it then was that Farouk had changed her name from Safi-naz, which meant 'white rose' to something as dull as Farida, which meant little more in Arabic than a limit to something. But what had that old Persian aristocrat Zulficar been doing to permit the marriage? Yet who could have blamed him at the time, even though his daughter was only eighteen? They had said since then that old Zulficar, who was more aristocratic in any case than the Mohamed Ali family who begot Farouk, had insisted, after the tragedies she had suffered, that Farouk divorce her. Her father had kept some power and influence in the Arab world. But think of the marriage scars left on this young girl. They were so terrible that she had cut herself off like this from everything. The Mohamed Ali family were vulgarians, they had always been crude and self-indulgent rulers, whereas this old Persian aristocracy had always been in command of itself, and Farida was now paying out her life as the price of it—a sad act of nobility for a gross mistake.

Unless, of course, you imagined the truth. One could imagine horrible bedroom scenes; brutality perhaps, and the shattering attack on virtues by coarse behaviour. Moslem girls were still innocent and sheltered at eighteen; and what (thinking of any Moslem marriage of this sort) one fat hand could do to an innocent girl was horrible to think of.

'I remember people saying, when Farida gave birth to her first daughter, that she had borne a girl simply to avert the evil eye, because every mother envied her marrying the king. That was one way of forgiving her for not having a son, I suppose. But after three daughters, what chance did she have? Can you imagine,' Nona said to Helen, 'what she suffered to get those children born?'

'But the whole country was like that at the end,' Helen said. 'During the last days of Farouk, nothing was safe. Nobody was respected.'

'Then why do you complain now?'

'I don't complain. But why did Nasser have to throw Neguib out, for instance?'

'Perhaps Neguib wanted the old days back again.'

'Everybody respected Mohamed Neguib. He would have been much better than these young officers, who want everything for themselves.'

'Too late now,' Nona said. 'Nasser is here to stay, and you might as well accept it. He's got the canal, which is more than Egypt ever dreamed of having in our lifetime. Admit it, darling. I don't think Neguib could have done better than that.'

The white villa was a cold white jewel on this green field. But the real pain, the real coldness, had surely passed, now that the old days were gone for ever.

CHAPTER FORTY-FIVE

To please his expedition, Church brewed tea in the old way where Alamein was marked on the map. On the desert itself Alamein was no more than a flat view of the tufted plain, a hard-based blue sea, coiled and limping lines of old and rusted barbed-wire, and faint car tracks which still radiated nervously in all directions. He avoided the official cemeteries.

'It's strange, isn't it?' he told them. 'Twelve years later and our tracks are still here.'

'And where are the men who made them?' Professor Maudie asked with her searching insight. She had thus filled the desert for them all, but with shadows.

Church was almost overcome. 'What wonderful lads they were!'

The haze might have dimmed his view of the silent horizons, but he would hear all his life the din of the half-tracks squealing and rumbling like a load of pots and pans across the umber plain, and he could smell the foul smell of petrol smoke stewing in the heat, and cordite smoke.

He had his own burning insight too, usually of a British soldier in khaki shorts and black boots carrying a shovel, walking and whistling from nowhere to nowhere across the desert. He often wondered where he imagined that visionary soldier was going.

'I didn't really mean those who were killed, General,' Professor Maudie said, realizing his sudden unhappiness. 'I meant, where are the ones who survived it? The ones who are back at home in brick houses, in such badly pressed suits, white-faced now, and not at all like soldiers, and certainly not high-spirited lads any more. When I go back,' she said, 'I can look at them and say to myself: *I know where you once were—on those spidery tracks across the hard sand, brewing tea like this*. But,' she said, looking at the tracks and squatting down to feel one of them—a faded, crusty tyre mark, 'it might just as well have been twenty thousand years ago. That's what is so extraordinary. There's no difference in time really between a year and a day, not once it's happened. This could have been ten years ago or a millennium.'

341

The General lifted the pot off the primus and poured the black brew into their mugs.

'It is not tea,' the Frenchman in his exclusion said, 'it's po-i-zon. It's a vicious drug, and now I can't do without it.'

René Harcourt could make everything sound a little absurd, but the General was pleased. 'You can see what a good brew-up meant to us when there was a lull, or when the sun got low enough for us to start cooling off.'

They sat in the shade of the bus and Professor Grossgudt asked the General if this very spot of Alamein was where the battle was fought.

'No. The Australians had pushed the line up the Ruweisat ridge, which you can see, I think, if you drop your eye-level low enough and look almost due west. But it would be best,' he told them, 'if we did Alamein on the way back.'

'Oh, but we're here now, General,' Professor Maudie protested.

'I know we're here. But our retreat back to Alamein was in some ways more significant and interesting than the advance from it. As you know, we had to fall back so often, but that last retreat was our best.'

'Ah, we were very cynical in Zürich,' Professor Grossgudt puffed, 'when we heard of British going forward and British going back.'

'Let's get on tomorrow to Mersa Matruh and the Libyan border,' the General went on. 'I can show you where Wavell fought his best battle. Then we can come back along the coast over all the old ground, and we can halt here at Alamein for a day or so, and that way you'll understand it better.'

They agreed and stayed the night on Alamein, near the sea, shooing off the Bedouins begging money or food while they sat talking under the white acres of starlight packed across the top of them like an upside-down city.

'I don't ever ask for anything more,' Professor Maudie sighed, 'than the night sky.'

But there would be more. The Greek bus driver had found Radio Athens.

'Yes, yes,' Professor Grossgudt said quickly, hearing snatches of some warm-hearted Marschallin singing *Schatz du, mein junger Schatz*. 'Oh, do leave it there.'

Her darling, darling Octavian.

'Du bist Mein Bub, du bist Mein Schatz, Ich hab Dich lieb!'

The cavalier of the silver rose in German voices. Oh, how the Professor was happy. Strauss had not written his music for deserts, but the auditorium was boundless and the desert pealed with little bells when the servant in a golden dress hung with tiny silver bells ran into the bedroom to give the Marschallin her morning chocolate.

342

Professor Grossgudt was unashamedly in tears.

The Frenchman, Professor René Harcourt (whose name was pronounced correctly by all but Church who knew that *ar-cour* would sound silly coming out of his mouth, even when he spoke French, and he spoke it well), and Dr. Berebellis who carried her sad Greek world with her, and Professor Maudie and Grossgudt were good company, compact and interested. The others had stayed in Alexandria because they were not interested in modern battlefields, and now everybody thought the others foolish.

'I think they were a little afraid,' Professor Maudie whispered to Church when they stood on the Libyan border at noon the next day, looking down on the naked bay of Sollum sheltering under the escarpment.

'Of what?' Church asked.

'Oh, I don't know. The Bedouins, the mines, even the Egyptians—since the canal crisis.'

'Mines? Perhaps! But the Egyptians have been very decent to us, considering.'

'I suppose among soldiers,' she said, 'there is always a certain natural sympathy, even if they don't like us these days. But what silly-billies they were, Ménard and the others, not to come and see this. How nice of the Egyptians to have built their own border fort at the end of the Roman road up on the cliff.'

'I'm afraid we built it,' Church told her, 'when we guarded the frontier here. The Egyptians built the barracks below it.'

'But it's so ridiculous to draw a frontier line across the desert like this —with barbed wire,' Professor Maudie said. 'It's unnatural.'

They discussed silly frontiers. Weren't they all silly?

'I don't think so,' Church said.

He had a theory on frontiers which he outlined for them while they used his field-glasses to see how far the barbed-wire border went, how blue the sea was, how white the sandy bay. He believed, he said, that there was nothing arbitrary about frontier lines, even those drawn by idiotic peace or treaty commissions.

'In general,' he said, 'most frontiers have fallen naturally where the group of people behind them is best able, at maximum effort, to defend them. They are usually the true outline of a natural nation at any given time, and are absolutely correct.'

'That may be all right in Western Europe,' Dr. Berebellis said in her gloomy dark-faced way, 'where nations are small and populous; but how true is it in vast areas like Russia and China, or in tribal lands in Africa, or even in deserts like this?'

'It still applies,' Church insisted. 'African tribes define their frontiers

343

not by calculation or treaty, but simply by certain knowledge that they can hold that much terrain against interlopers. Even the hunting tribes have their boundaries outlined by their maximum hunting and defensive limits.'

The French mind, looking for absurdity, turned to the space about them again. 'But, General,' René Harcourt said, 'where there are deserts like this there is no natural population to defend the natural frontiers.'

'That's true,' the General agreed, 'but desert frontiers fall at about the exact physical distance that each group, or nation, so widely separated, can cope with.'

Professor Maudie had thought about it and she began to agree. 'It's as good a theory as any, General. It might even be brilliant. I've always been rather against frontiers, probably because I never thought of them as natural and useful delineations.'

'They are not natural,' Dr. Berebellis argued dryly, 'and they are only useful to soldiers.'

René Harcourt laughed.

'She didn't like the City states either because they were too military minded,' Harcourt said.

Professor Grossgudt offered them barley sweets and wiped away the sweat and said, 'Anyway, without soldiers there would never have been any rapid changes in history. Without wars and destruction we would not now be students of dead and dying civilization. Not so?'

'Just so,' Dr. Berebellis said contritely, and they said no more about it.

'Mines,' the General told them when he came to them, 'are only dangerous if you don't know where they are.'

Nobody laughed, but the General felt like laughing at the absurdity of his own deduction. How else could they be dangerous? Would a man willingly drive across a known minefield?

His party was on the edge of one now in the bus. The Egyptian Colonel at Mersa Matruh, Colonel Mukri, with huge moustaches and large popping eyes, had given them permission to move down the wire to Gherba on the tracks, giving them a pass without hesitation, even with a sense of humour and the loan of three or four extra sand mats in case they got bogged. If they were not back by Wednesday night, he said, he would send out a car to look for them. The General was very grateful. He wanted to show them where Wavell had begun, in June 1940, to fight the best battles they had ever fought in the western desert.

'Of course, by the end of 1941 there had been so much reckless mine-laying in the deserts that no one really knew (neither side) where they all were. They eventually became a thorough nuisance for both sides, no matter who laid them.'

'But didn't anyone make maps of their mine-fields?' René Harcourt said. 'Could English *and* Germans be so inefficient about killing themselves?'

The General's silk handkerchief swished the flies away. 'Laying mines over the desert,' he explained to Harcourt, 'is like setting a lot of small boys loose in Hyde Park on a paper-chase with bags of carpet tacks, scattering them anywhere they feel like it. Then you try asking them, when they come home exhausted at night, exactly where they had scattered the wretched things.'

'It must have been awful,' Professor Maudie said. 'More so because the desert looks clean and innocent.'

What an insight she had, the General felt. *Innocence* was exactly the word for the desert itself; but what could be greater deceit than a virgin surface hiding all sorts of horrible, mangling death?

'You are so right,' he said admiringly. 'I think I hated mines in the desert more than I hated any other weapon in the war. Even more than gas in the first war. A man firing a gun at you, any gun, is one thing. But death that simply lurks, simply waits there silently for a soldier to put his foot on: that is very dirty war and very unmanageable too. We had far too many tragedies.'

The minefield here was simply marked with the usual warnings of mines, a hand-printed board in English and Arabic set up beside the Gherba track and the wire. The old Gherba battlefield itself was simply a gap in the rusty barbed-wire fence, and beyond it there was not a sign of life or movement between the lemon-coloured hot horizons.

'It was here,' the General told them, as they leaned on the front of the bus, 'that the first tank battle of the war took place. It was really only a skirmish. Twelve Italian tanks and some motorized infantry were caught here by a mixed tank squadron of the 7th Hussars and thoroughly smashed at absolutely no cost to ourselves. It was a clean, straightforward fight: the kind soldiers dream about, but the kind we very rarely get. Most of Wavell's victories were like that. That's why I think his were the greatest and the finest battles of the war, and why this whole desert has much more valuable memories for his campaigns than for any other in the war—even the Normandy victories.'

Professor Maudie, feeling the atmosphere now, and knowing better than the others what could best give them the real feeling of this desert war, persuaded the General to take them through the whole first battle of General Wavell, to move as they had moved, to know how they had known where the enemy was, and to see how they had fired their guns at him.

'Did you just see a tank or a soldier in the distance and simply fire at him? How was it done, General?'

It was a very exciting idea, and Church had studied closely his latest and most carefully compiled War Office 1 to 100,000 maps to see if he could safely take them along the top of the escarpment and follow exactly the battle of Sidi Barrani, the first and perhaps the best all-out tactical victory won by the British Army in the entire war.

'I think it can be done,' he said over his maps.

'Oh, please!' Maudie said. 'It will be such a unique experience.'

So it would be for them all. 'But I don't want to blow you all up on some uncharted minefield.'

He took them back to the top of the escarpment south of Mersa Matruh, finding the best and most used tracks, sometimes driving the bus himself, often lost, but eventually finding what he felt was the concentration area of the nights of December 6 and 8, 1940.

'From here,' he said, pointing to the desert which showed no sign of anything alive or dead, only the perpetual haze, 'we will go just the way the division moved. But first you must know the dispositions. You might remember how the Italians first advanced into Egypt in 1940 as far as Sidi Barrani. West of here, just below Sidi Barrani, below the little apex of the escarpment I showed you yesterday, just under that, the Italians had set up their main camps in Egypt. Three of them. But what we discovered, which was most important, was that two of their camps were not linked by any kind of defences at all. There was a gap between them . . .'

'Ah, yes,' René Harcourt said quickly. 'There is always a gap.'

'But what sorts of camps were they, General?' Professor Maudie asked. 'One hardly thinks of camps in the desert. Tents? Dug-outs?'

'Tents here and there, yes. But let me tell you this much: the Italian camps surprised us, and perhaps you would like to wait and find out, the way we did, just what they were like.'

They agreed it would be fascinating.

'There were seventy-five thousand Italians, two hundred guns, and about a hundred and twenty tanks spread out in these three camps.'

'How many tanks did you have?' René Harcourt asked.

'Almost three hundred.'

'More than the Italians?'

'One of the few times we had the advantage. But we had far fewer men and trucks; in fact, we were less than a third the Italian strength.'

He instructed them very carefully in the problem of tanks: they could only travel about 1,500 miles, total, before they wore out; replacements did not exist, petrol in those days was carried in tin cans, and after 500 miles of desert two-thirds of it evaporated.

'It's very important to understand all this, because when we decided to attack the three main camps of the Italians we had to count on getting up very close to them without detection, which is a very difficult thing to do in the desert. So every tank had to work well, because we could not afford to manoeuvre about too much.

346

'Now,' the General went on carefully, 'we picked that little apex on the escarpment' (he outlined the bump on the map) 'because with that we would be able to dominate his three camps. But first we had to move our main force, the infantry and the 7th Armoured Division, from here to there—about a hundred miles—without being detected. That's how we stood on December 8 and 9, lying out here in full kit in these little spinifex tufts waiting to move up to the little knob overlooking their positions, to launch our first real attack of the war.'

'Then let us go just the way you did,' Maudie said.

'That would mean making the last march by night,' the General told her. 'And that might be dangerous.'

'We're game. Aren't we?' she said to the others.

Of course they were game. The experience was unique. He had caught their interest, even that of Dr. Berebellis, who had entered this expedition as if painful, wretched time had to be filled somehow, but she was now (the General detected it) very ready to watch his maps closely, to follow his instructions when he pointed out the landmarks, and to wait patiently through René Harcourt's absurd jokes.

How to live through old wars over reddish, grey, waterless, sightless country? Down the escarpment after the night march (only an hour and safely done) in a bus they rolled along at dawn in dust over fold after fold of hard sand which rose and flew along with them, catching them, passing them, disappearing.

'We would fire about now, at that.'

At what?

Looking out of the bus windows they could, if they wished, imagine flashes on the rise.

'I think it was that rise,' the General said. 'Can you imagine the dust and the bedlam as we raced across here, the dust of the vehicles, the dust of the heavy "I" tanks? We won this battle because they didn't know we had the new "I" tanks in the desert. They were terribly slow tanks, but they were so heavily armoured that the Italian guns couldn't puncture them. They just rolled on.'

Thus, they stormed over the Italian camp.

'We couldn't imagine the camp, even when we saw it,' the General told them. 'Extraordinary how the desert has covered it.'

'But what was it you saw here?' Professor Maudie pressed.

'A most luxurious encampment, built for an army that was incapable of fighting a war of movement but was trying to squat for ever in this hellish place, hoping to make it civilized. They dug beautiful little palaces under the sand. They built mess huts, bath-houses. When our "I" tanks and artillery had smashed their defences we came in here laughing in amaze-

347

ment, although it was a horrible mess. Normal battle scenes, yes: tanks burning, dying and dead men sprawled out of these little dug-outs, and General Meletti, the Italian Commander, covered with his jacket and his medals, dead in bed in his tent with a machine-gun beside him. But when we went into the dug-outs to rout out those hiding there we found their incredible life of luxuries: sheets on the beds, furniture, mirrors, scents, magnificent clothes. And the food: crystallized fruits, hams, wines, champagnes, fresh bread, and the *cheeses*; and suddenly hand-grenades abandoned everywhere. Extraordinary how they wanted to get rid of their pretty little hand-grenades. But the capes and the swords and the silver hairbrushes—can you imagine how we felt when even officers in the British Army lived on bacon and bully and tea most of the time, and a mug of water to shave in? These Italians actually had bathrooms . . .'

'And you had tanks,' René Harcourt said and sighed.

'But surely there must be something left,' Grossgudt asked.

He had done very well, not counting the sand he had accumulated in his sloppy shoes and the stains of sweat all over his stout body, even down his trouser legs. But he had climbed into the old sanded dug-outs to find out how it had looked from the Italian side of things—sitting up here with a machine-gun and watching these fat yellow British tanks roaring across the desert. He sat in the outline of a collapsed dug-out, being an Italian. But firing at what? The tanks?

'At anything that moved, I suppose,' the General said. 'But the Italians abandoned these gun-sites rather soon, and we found most of them hiding below in their beautiful dug-outs.'

'Poor things,' Professor Maudie said.

'Italians should be builders, never soldiers,' Grossgudt said. 'Romans were one thing, but Italians! It is sad to think of them here, very sad.'

'I suppose God made a mistake with the Italians. He probably meant them all to be women,' René Harcourt said. 'Not so, mesdames?'

'Nonsense,' Professor Maudie argued. 'Most women who go to Italy think the men are terribly manly and charming.'

'They never behaved much like men here,' the General said regretfully. 'They ran as fast as they could. Although they did try to make a stand at Buq Buq. We had to race across the desert to try to cut them off.'

'Then let us race across the desert,' Professor Maudie suggested. 'Where next?'

'You must all be tired.'

'Of course we're tired, General, but it's only a little of how *you* must have felt, after all.'

The others did not have Professor Maudie's hunger for the feel and the experience of the partaker, and they voted to wait a day. 'Good!' the General said, and explained how they had heard reports on their wireless of a big Italian column moving across from the south-west to attack their flank.

'*Did* they attack your flank?'

The General smiled. 'Let's leave that for the march to Buq Buq. We kept getting these reports as we turned north-west to the coast: big enemy forces to the south-west. Tomorrow we'll cover the ground if we can. I must look at the maps. It might be risky because of the mines. In fact, no one should move too far off this high ground tonight,' he warned. 'Let's make camp on the north side. They never mined that part at all . . .'

Only once after that did Dr. Berebellis let her gloomy world get the better of her, and she returned to the General's theory on the natural frontier, the natural delineation of a nation.

'What happens to your theory, General,' she said over the coffee when the General's instinct for camp management had made them comfortable in canvas chairs before the desert got too cold and before they all went through the embarrassing business of going out into the desert for their evening toilette before crawling into their camp-beds, 'what happens to your theory here, General, when you take into account that the British did not belong in these deserts, nor the Italians? You were fighting over national frontiers that were not yours.'

'Empires have their secondary frontiers also,' the General explained.

'Do you think the English soldiers and the Italians wanted to die out here for secondary frontiers? Is that what was in their minds?'

The General gave it a little thought. 'I think it would be presumptuous to speak on this ground for the dead under it. I dare not say what was in each man's heart when he died out here.'

'Would they feel it was worthwhile, if they could arise and see the world how it is now, in 1956?'

'I don't think we should ask that,' the General said politely and the stillness depressed him because they were all still, like the night itself, listening. 'A man dies for his duty, and it's unfair on him to project that into the future to see if it was worthwhile dying for. He does his duty as he sees it at the time; not for what it will be like twenty years hence . . .'

'Then why die?' Dr. Berebellis asked. 'You are saying a man ought to die for the past and the present, but not for the future. Why die for the past and the present only? Why die for what you have already had, and probably found wanting?'

'Because we can only live in the past and the present, not in the future,' the General said. 'Our duty is partly inherited, partly our own creation. How on earth can the future influence it? Of course,' the General pointed out, 'they made the future possible. Isn't that enough?'

'I personally don't think men die for duty or the future. Not really,'

Professor Maudie put in. 'They die for intangibles. They don't know themselves . . .'

'Would you die for an intangible ?' Dr. Berebellis asked her.

'No. But I'm an educated person,' Professor Maudie argued.

If that was a bombshell explaining humanity nobody had reacted to it.

Dr. Berebellis sounded gloomier than ever, and a little harder. 'We are all being nicely abstract,' she said. 'There ought to be a very good reason in human affairs if one man is going to kill another.'

'A very good reason,' the General agreed.

'Do you think the English will go to war for the Suez Canal ?' the Doctor asked. 'Is that good enough reason, General ?'

'It might be,' the General said, reluctant to discuss it.

They had already listened to the B.B.C. news; they had silently agreed not to open any discussion on the situation, which was nervous and worrying if one thought about it—being so isolated out here while both sides growled bitterly at each other across the continents.

'England has called up all its reserve soldiers,' Dr. Berebellis said. 'Monsieur Mollet says that he will use the French Navy and the Army to impose a solution on the Egyptians . . .'

'That is politics,' the General said. 'That's nothing to do with a soldier !'

'When does it concern the soldier then ?' Dr. Berebellis asked.

'When the politics break down,' the General told her.

'Politics always break down,' René Harcourt said.

'I do hope they don't this time,' Professor Maudie said. 'It would be terrible.'

Professor Grossgudt sighed, and Dr. Berebellis seemed unsatisfied.

'Would you fight another war, unquestioning, for a duty, General ?' she asked Church.

'I believe so,' he replied. 'Yes. Of course, but . . .'

'Without asking yourself what the war was about ?'

'If there is a war, and we are involved in it, then I don't think I need ask. The duty should always be clear to a soldier : he must obey. Or rather, he must serve as he has sworn to serve. These aren't intangibles, you know.'

Dr. Berebellis rose to go into the desert before the others, taking a spade with her and saying in a friendly and almost affectionate tone to the General, as if she were patting him gently on the head :

'Then there's no hope for the world, General, if people *will* go on killing each other for no better reason than that.'

'Don't go off the plateau,' the General told her discreetly as she walked away, 'and *please* take my electric torch with you.'

She usually refused the torch because she said it blinded her, and she refused again, saying 'No, thank you,' and she went off (she said) to do *her* duty. They laughed to overcome this little embarrassment which occurred every night in the desert where there were no bathrooms, no doors, no water systems, and (as René Harcourt had said) 'no little latches on the door saying *libre* or *occupé*'.

CHAPTER FORTY-SIX

FRANÇOISE had a right to be told that someone called Lucy Pickering existed. 'You cannot,' Scott warned himself, 'go on pretending that it did not happen. It did happen, and it will never do any good if you try to hide it now. You can't even hide it from yourself. Tell her, tell her, tell her . . .'

He would have to tell her because he made up his mind to do so, to explain carefully about Lucy, to show how it had happened, and to swear that it would not happen again, because he had said *No* finally—not simply to seeing Lucy, but to the woman herself—to that whole person. He would feel miserable and deprived by his decision and yet he was determined that it would be so.

To go through Port Said was not the quickest way to Alexandria and the western desert, but they had to stop overnight somewhere, and he left Quartermain in the small Greek hotel telephoning his wife, and he walked along the canal, jarred with the green mercury lights which he hated, into the city, to Françoise's apartment, wondering as he went why he had never moved himself to Port Said to live. The thought was absurd, even as he considered it. She would not have liked it; she would have worried about the scandal, the children and Monsieur Beauvoir. She felt much better when he appeared suddenly, stayed as long and as safely as he could, and then departed without leaving any real trace of himself in her French life.

It was after 10 o'clock at night, and he knew he ought to telephone her first, but surely the children would be asleep and it wouldn't matter. She would let him in and they would talk.

He rang the bell, but he knew already that he had made a mistake.

He heard music and voices. She must have guests. He retreated to a dark corner of the landing. She opened the door a little and said, 'Who is it?' and he did not say anything, but stepped forward.

Her face was sufficient—all surprise and reprimand.

'You can't come in now,' she said. 'Gisele and Marie-Thérèse and their husbands are here listening to music.'

'I'm only in Port Said for one night,' he told her.

'Come in the morning, early.'

'I can't. I must leave before dawn. When will they go?'

They were now shouting at each other angrily in whispers.

'They always stay very late.'

'I wanted to see you.'

'All right. Shhhh! Please go. I'll come downstairs and meet you near the little garden, but not yet.'

She had closed the door; and this terror she had—of her marriage vow being publicly betrayed before her friends and enemies by one small public acknowledgment of his existence—was turning him into a wanton. He was angry as he stamped downstairs, yet he understood. Roberto, her husband, had left enough talk battering about her ears without him adding another clap of thunder to it.

'Effendi . . .'

The night boab in his fine black robes stood up silently from his bench at the foot of the stairs.

'Good night, Ismail,' Scott said as he passed, amused despite himself.

To wait: and to wait a very long time through the green electric night, standing, walking, confined to a few yards of street and garden for fear of missing her. He could not sit down. He avoided the black-clothed policemen on night patrol who might see him. He leaned against a hairy palm tree in the little deserted square wondering why he had brought his life to Françoise in the first place.

That was not difficult to answer. She had been there when no one else had been there, and she too had needed him. That had instantly been true, from their first brief meeting at breakfast in the Ghurdakha resthouse, where she had come with her friends for a few days' holiday. He had needed to be grateful for her existence, for someone's existence. At that time in the eastern desert, having just shifted there from Sinai, he had no reason at all ever to leave the place until she had suddenly appeared. He could remember, in amazement now, all his long journeys to Port Said simply to see her, to sit with her in her clean flat for a few hours on Saturday or Sunday night (if her friends were not there) and then his long journey back. He had sometimes travelled a whole day simply to spend a few hours with her.

Where had love begun?

He was not sure. He could not trace it because it was confused with an overwhelming sense of gratitude that she existed at all, and a memory of how excitedly he had made those journeys, and with what heartfelt joy he had written her day after day from the desert and sent off his letters with Amin or Zareef or Sam.

The first warm embrace had been the mutual joy of his arrival after an unusually long absence; but the slow burning of temperament into passion had been the beginning of her difficulty which had forced her to barricade herself the way she did. Of course he had asked her to make it permanent and she had agreed, but in her agreement she had clung even more fearfully to the pretences of this deserted, respectable life she led with the children.

What good would it do now, to tell her about a moment's impatience? Was it only a moment, or had it been a desperate extension of his old desire to have someone, somewhere, he could give his heart to?

How could she keep him out here like this? He began to walk away. He went down by the old shops, the booths which were called Woolworths, Johnny Walker, and Marshall & Smallingrove. They were shuttered up for the night. He looked up at her windows. They were dark. She had forgotten him. It was after one o'clock. But he went back to the garden . . .

When she did come, tying up her hair with a scarf, it was almost two o'clock. She was not apologetic, but worried and upset.

'Why do you always come without telephoning first?' she said.

'I thought I'd be here earlier, but we were delayed at Gimsa.'

'And just for one night? Can't you stay until lunch-time tomorrow? I could come home early. The children could have lunch at the club without me.'

They were walking back towards her flat and he shook his head tiredly: 'I must leave here in another three or four hours. I have to be in Mersa Matruh by noon.'

'Will you come back this way, at least?'

'Yes.' He was holding her arm and feeling all resolution flowing out of his fingers. 'And if you have your friends?'

'I couldn't help them, you know that. I couldn't send them away.'

'Why . . .' he began. He wanted to say why couldn't she have invited him in and made a public confession of his existence, since they must know of it anyway. But the past was the strong past, and he knew too well how Roberto's behaviour had hurt her and frightened her, and he could not blame her.

'What are you saying?' she asked when he let the complaint die away.

'I don't know,' he said. 'Can't I come up for a few moments?'

'Not now,' she said quickly. 'It's after two o'clock.'

He knew then that he would not tell her anything. Was it resentment or anger, or the fear in his own harsh world that he would actually lose her if he exposed himself so stupidly to her unknown and unhappy response? It would hurt her very much if he told her the truth; and her reaction would certainly be bitter and final. Wouldn't it prove that all men were alike?

'I'll come to see you when I get back,' he promised.

'*Please* telephone me,' she begged.

He promised that too and she clung to him for a moment before she ran inside so that the sleeping boab did not see her.

'Effendi . . .' the boab said to him when she had gone.

'Good night, Ismail,' he said again.

Scott was well aware, when he was driving deep into the western desert, that he was wasting his time searching here for Church.

He looked around the horizons of the west, the east, the south and then he put down his field-glasses and knew that Hakim was making a fool of him.

'This is a hopeless business,' he said. 'I don't even know why I agreed to do it.'

'Then let's go into Libya and forget Church,' Quartermain suggested. 'We can take a look at Tobruk and Benghazi, and perhaps even Jalo.'

'What for?'

'Don't you want to see the old places?'

Scott looked at him to see how cynical Quartermain could be. 'I prefer to forget the old places,' he said. 'So ought you.'

'Why? I could even think up a very sentimental story about old battle-fields,' Quartermain told him. 'Don't you realize that every soldier who ever crawled back and forth across these deserts, the way we did, wants to know what the old place looks like now?'

'Are they that sentimental about it?'

'The best years of their lives, they say. They keep telling themselves they were free men out here. Remember the old hump-back ride after Fuka? Did they ever rebuild Mersa Matruh? That sort of thing. Nothing like old battlefields to bring back lost youth.'

'I don't feel any lost youth coming back,' Scott objected. 'On the contrary, it seems so long ago—that war.'

'I know. I feel old and grey and wasted myself.'

'We ought to go back,' Scott said. 'There's no point to this.'

'Don't give up so easily,' Quartermain told him. 'There must be a reason somewhere. Hakim wants something out of you, doesn't he?'

'I'm beginning to wonder. Hakim's reasons can be a little too obscure sometimes.'

They had brought their Frontier Force jeep south from Mersa Matruh after the Colonel there had told them what Church and his party had asked for in the way of permissions and tracks. Church's party had not been reported since.

'We'll wander down the Siwa track and cut across the escarpment,' Scott told the Colonel. He knew that Church would probably be fighting Alamein over again. It was the most likely memory Church would have. Didn't he want to show them how he had won the war?

355

'Too easy,' Quartermain had groaned in disappointment when they had found fresh tracks compressed over ten thousand old ones: four heavy tyres, certainly a bus.

But it turned out to be two Egyptians in an old army truck licensed to scour the desert for lumps of old tanks, trucks, guns, shells; the scrap iron which fetched a high price in Egypt now.

'It's a nice holiday. Let's forget Church for a while and enjoy it,' Quartermain suggested when they had waved the truck on, when they had had their cynical jokes about it, about Church, about puffs of dust that could easily be the dust of four old professors going up in smoke. The dust clouds were in fact whirligigs snatched up by one puff of wind which stirred around the desert like a mischievous finger searching and whirling and then suddenly snatching up a whole column of dust, away up into the sky.

What disturbed them was the report from the scrap-iron truck that they were the last of three such trucks in business. The other two had long ago been blown up on the mines; and in the back of the scavenging sand-coloured Ford, which still had Royal Engineers Base Depot insignia on it, in the back were the remnants of one of their brother trucks, now scrap for the maw they had been serving themselves.

'I wonder if he'll ever lose his self-confidence,' Scott said, nursing the horizons again. 'That absolute bloody certainty that he's right.'

'Who? Hakim?'

'No. Church.'

'Your friend Hakim shouldn't have allowed an idiot like Church to come out here. That's also being a bit over-confident.'

The day was done and they went about their camp-making with old habits. But Scott had his own routine, and Quartermain was only now learning it over again. The water-can out of the jeep first and buried in the sand, the light lit before dark to make sure it would light, and then the beds unrolled, and finally the primus to cook dinner—eggs and bacon every night, fried bread, cheese, boiled coffee.

'I don't know!' Scott was still complaining. 'Any sergeant in the Frontier Force at Matruh or Sollum must know these deserts now better than I do, and they would probably know where the mines are, which I don't. They should have kept Church under observation themselves.'

'You needn't fool yourself,' Quartermain said, rinsing out his cup with a grain of sand and a few coffee grounds, wiping it carefully before he put it away. 'You're more a soldier than you think. They probably know it, even if you don't.'

'There's absolutely nothing of the soldier left in me,' Scott insisted. 'Don't you start imagining it. I shall never be a soldier again, I can tell you that. I don't care what the reason.'

356

Quartermain shrugged and put a pot of water on the primus to boil so that he could shave now, at night. Scott's early starts, his pre-dawn awakenings and his impatience to move with the sun (for no good reason because they were not really in a great hurry), his set habits in this sort of life were too hard on a man who was out of practice. Five extra minutes gained for early-morning leisure in the sleeping-bag were worth the difficulty of shaving the night before by the light of a petrol lamp, which Scott hung very low because he liked to read, lying on his camp-bed, glasses on his nose, a woollen sweater over his pyjamas to keep out the cold, a beret against the night air, and his large pocket-watch ticking and clicking on a petrol can beside him.

'You turn the desert into a suburban bedroom,' Quartermain complained.

'Why not?' Scott answered. 'I have to get up early and go to work in the morning, just like anybody else. What's the difference between me and a bank-clerk?'

Scott was reading Balzac's tragic tale of Colonel Chabert, but he knew before it was half-way told what the fate of that old Napoleonic hero would be. Brave soldiers returning from the grave could hardly expect a welcome from a society which had forgotten them. They were a bad memory. It was not very good bedroom reading, either, because now that he was out here in these western deserts he did not want to be reminded that he too had been reviled, punished and imprisoned. Old Chabert was happier when he eventually threw it all away and pretended to be an idiot. That was better than pretending it was all perfectly normal and forgotten and even forgiven. It was not forgotten or forgiven or normal; it was very fresh and unhappy, because Church was dragging him back through the memory of it here.

'Good night,' he said to Quartermain.

He turned off the valve of the petrol lamp, not noticing that Quartermain was still shaving. He said, 'What are you grumbling about?' when he heard Quartermain muttering and trying to re-light the lantern.

'I don't mind the desert in the daytime,' Quartermain told him, 'but at night I begin to wonder whether there is any other living thing in existence besides you and me. Is that the way you like to feel?'

'Not at all, and I don't feel that way.'

'How do you feel?' Quartermain asked.

'Good night,' Scott said again.

'I'm homesick,' Quartermain said miserably, and Scott laughed to himself.

357

CHAPTER FORTY-SEVEN

GENERAL CHURCH had never seen, even as a soldier, the victim of a booby-trap, and Professor Maudie was not a good beginning to the experience. To see and hear her in terrible pain and being so brave about it was the worst thing that had ever happened to him, even though she kept reassuring him that it was not his fault but her own fault for picking up the confounded thing.

'I'm so sorry,' she kept repeating childishly, groaning and clutching at herself in pain.

She was perfectly coherent, even though one hand was shattered to the wrist and her left hip and side were mangled and bloody. They did not know yet if she had internal injuries, but it was terrible to see even the superficial damage to her gentle body.

Church worked like a madman with Dr. Berebellis. The thing had blown up in her hand the moment she had picked it up, stooping over it on the desert where the Italian armoured cars had once tried to ambush them. He was telling them about it. The old booby-trap had looked like a little leather tool-bag dried up in the sun, and it had cracked up with a tremendous explosion, retching white smoke the moment she touched it.

'Please . . . don't worry,' she begged him, gasping a little. 'Just get me back as best you can, but please don't worry.'

Church worked frantically at first-aid. He applied the tourniquet Dr. Berebellis had made, and he bound up her mangled hand as best he could with a strip of cloth, trying to judge just how bad it was without panicking and being sickened—not so much by the sight of the wounds as by her pain, which upset him so much that he had to avoid looking at her white, transformed face.

'It's all right, it's all right,' Dr. Berebellis kept saying to Professor Maudie as she worked.

One reassuring the other. It was all reassurance while they did what they could. He must not lose his nerve or his sense of proportion, but this was terrible, terrible.

'I should have warned you not to touch anything.'

'But you did warn me,' Professor Maudie moaned. 'I remember . . . oh, it's my side . . .'

'You'll be all right,' he said. 'You'll be quite all right!' He was simply echoing Dr. Berebellis.

'I know,' Professor Maudie said, but she was now weeping with pain. 'I'm not really frightened, so please don't worry. It's my side, not my arm. Oh . . .'

The sun glowed. How ridiculous, Professor Maudie's tortured eyes with their insight were saying, to be lying here near this bus in the barren sunlight with this happening. Dr. Berebellis had cut her cotton dress to ribbons, and something was under her head, whisky on her lips, and Grossgudt and the driver were arguing in Greek. What about?

'Poor General,' she said, wondering how much hotter the pain could get, fighting it off by her concern for him. It was the burning heat of it that hurt. 'You mustn't be upset. You mustn't.'

The General's red healthy face, small and usually crisp, seemed already to have shrunk to the size of a dry orange, crinkled and aged. She saw it happen.

'My God, I'll never be able to forgive myself,' he said in anguish. 'But you will be all right. You *will* be.'

He knew she had some sort of internal injury but that could not help it, and Dr. Berebellis was whispering soothingly to her as Grossgudt finally came up with a blanket which he and René Harcourt held up to make shade.

'Now we'll get you to a hospital,' he told her. 'Just hang on.'

It was all perfectly normal and they got her into the bus after taking out the luggage in the back so that they could open the double doors and hand her up into the long seat at the back, padded with blankets.

She fainted with pain when they put her down clumsily. It was not wide enough to take her comfortably or even safely, and Church ordered the suitcases and anything else they could find to be packed up on the floor near her to hold her in, and then he told the Greek to start up. He would come forward and direct him. It would be quickest to go back along the escarpment, and then up to Mersa Matruh, because that way would be better going and there was sure to be a military hospital and doctors at Matruh.

'Let me know,' he told Dr. Berebellis, 'how she's taking it.'

'Yes, but go quickly,' Dr. Berebellis told him.

They all looked sick and worried. Dr. Berebellis's English thickened, and her dark face seemed to have retreated deeper into that underlining of black sadness—those dark-minded eyes. Grossgudt was suddenly argumentative with Harcourt and the driver, as if he had to feel angry with

359

someone for such a tragedy. Professor Maudie's homely and pleasant face was more alive than dead, bursting suddenly with a pained and reassuring smile when it normally burst forth with sudden enthusiasm and insight. Her insight was at work now, and she looked mainly at the General, and worried about him, and whispered weakly to Dr. Berebellis:

'Don't let him blame himself.'

'You'll be all right,' the Doctor told her.

'Of course I'll be all right.'

But it seemed doubtful when she went white and unconscious before they were half-way to Mersa Matruh.

Under the circumstances Church was not surprised, ultimately, to see Scott, to be caught by him. That was how he felt, sitting in the medical officers' quarters in the barrack hospital at Mersa Matruh where the nurses were thick-booted peasant soldiers in round, soft, khaki caps. The young army doctors on national service were patching her up as best they could, and the startled-eyed Colonel was bellowing Arabic into a phone to get a plane to take her to Alexandria. They would do everything.

'A helicopter, perhaps?' Church had begged.

He knew the Egyptians had one or two, but the Colonel said it was too slow, it was in Cairo, its range was too short. The Air Force had a small ambulance plane somewhere. It would come. Church had been told to wait in this antiseptic room with one cracked glass cabinet with ear syringes, and one desk and one window. A soldiers' dispensary, an Egyptian soldiers' complaint dispensary. When Scott opened the door on him the General looked upset and exasperated.

'I suppose they sent you after me,' he said.

'They most certainly did.'

'It is unethical, unworthy!' the General complained.

'Do you remember Quartermain?' Scott asked him without worrying the ethics.

The General nodded. 'Yes. Of course I do.' And then he regained his authority, although it was only with effort, because he was ill and badly shaken.

'I'm sorry it happened,' Scott told him sympathetically. 'But how *did* it happen?'

'She picked the thing up—a little leather bag. I didn't even see it, and it simply went off as those things do. They always were the most horrible and filthy things.'

'Is there anything you want me to do?' Scott asked. 'They say they are patching her up.'

The General inspected Scott to determine his motives. But no one ever doubted the motives of a man who planted himself like that,

360

like a restful bull, frowning gravely over his troubled eyes to hide himself.

'There is a great deal you can do, Scott. We must get her to Alexandria or Cairo quickly.'

'They said they were arranging that,' Quartermain told him.

'Then we'll have to get the very best available surgeons,' Church went on urgently.

'Of course. They'll do everything, General. They understand.'

'Who would be the man to see in Alexandria? You must help there.' Then he faced Scott with whatever it was that tied them and bound them, smashed them together and parted them, made them good and bad for each other. 'Anything you can do to help her, Scott, to speed it up,' he appealed, 'I would be personally most grateful for. I've asked to talk to our Embassy on the phone, but they don't seem to like that idea.'

'They'll do everything they can,' Scott assured him. 'Don't worry, General. I don't think I'd put the Embassy into it yet. Not from here. They'll get her off soon.'

'Please go and make sure. Talk to the Colonel. Don't let them slack off or mess it up. I can't impress them any more than I have, but you might. If you want me to come along . . .'

'You had better let me do it,' Scott told him quickly.

The Egyptian Colonel understood Scott (as they all did) at a glance (*Iowa, ya effendim*) establishing so quickly that curiosity and friendliness and yet intangible withdrawal which Quartermain had seen every Egyptian show towards Scott. (They usually ignored Quartermain himself or simply accepted him because he happened to be with Scott.) The Colonel seemed always to bubble up happily and then prick his own jollity with a long sigh. He simply could not abandon his jollity for this situation until he suddenly said, 'Misqueena!' with real pity for Professor Maudie.

'But she is all right so far, *el hamdul lillah*,' he said cheerfully to comfort them.

'Which one of them was it?' Scott asked him.

'The Englishwoman,' he said.

Scott asked in Arabic if there was a plane available. The Colonel told him it would be here from Alexandria in half an hour, or an hour at the latest. There would be an ambulance waiting in Alexandria to take her to the European hospital. Scott thanked him profusely on behalf of Church and went with Quartermain to see if the others were all right in the bus— Grossgudt and Harcourt and the driver, who were familiar faces from their first meeting at *mons claudianus*. Dr. Berebellis was still with Professor Maudie, holding her hand.

'It is the pilot,' Grossgudt said to him, remembering the plane, shaking

N*   361

his hand gratefully. 'The English pilot, not so!' It was probably Scott's large hat he remembered.

'Yes,' Scott said without bothering to correct him. 'You'd better get ready to go on to Alexandria tonight,' he told them. 'Your injured friend will be taken off by plane in a half-hour or so.'

'And will she live?' René Harcourt asked. 'Is it very bad?'

'I don't know. Apparently they can't do much here.'

The plane arrived while they waited for it in silence. They saw it circling. The young doctors were barely finished, and Professor Maudie was still unconscious. She was better that way, they said, it would be easier to get her in and out of the plane. They had given her blood and morphia and sewn her up as best they could. The rest would require real surgery. Was it bad, dangerous, fatal? These two dark-eyed young doctors liked to use the English medical word 'satisfactory' which could mean life or death and still remain stupidly non-committal to either.

'I think I must go with her,' Church said to the Colonel. 'If I may.'

'Not necessary,' the Colonel said. 'The Greek lady will go with her.'

'Isn't there room for both of us?' Church asked. 'I really must go.'

The Colonel asked the pilot, who said it might be risky, but it could be done, excepting that he had orders to pick up only the patient. Who was the Englishman? Her husband?

'No,' Scott told him in Arabic, 'but he feels responsible. If you can take him it would be much better. It will save a lot of trouble later.'

'But what will he say when he gets there? Will he blame us—the Egyptians?' the Colonel asked. 'I have been told to get a statement from him here first. I waited until he felt better, to do it. If he goes now it will be too late.'

'Let him go,' Scott insisted gently. 'I'll make sure you get the statement, and I'll certainly make sure he doesn't blame you or any Egyptian.'

The Colonel agreed reluctantly. 'Kwayis,' he said to the pilot.

'We're really wasting time,' the General told them. 'What do they say?'

'You can go with her,' Scott told him, 'but you must make a statement about all this as soon as you can to the Egyptian authorities.'

'Of course. If they wish, I'll leave them my passport.'

The polite Colonel said, 'La-a!' like a bear. He was insulted. 'Not necessary,' he said. 'Not at all necessary. Go.'

The pilot had to get into the little Czech plane first so that they could put Professor Maudie in the back, with Dr. Berebellis and Church each side of her. Professor Maudie reeked of their surgery and drugs, and they had covered her face lightly with the brown army blanket to keep the flies off. The orderlies lifted her in, and Church ordered the Greek driver to bring the bus as soon as possible to Alexandria, and to report at the European hospital after taking the Professors to their *pension*.

362

'And I would be grateful,' Church said, turning to Scott, 'if you could also follow as soon as you can. I'm sure I'm going to need help to get everything done that should be done. As you know, things are not so easy for us these days.'

'We'll leave immediately in your bus,' Scott told him.

'I can't begin to thank you . . .'

'That's all right,' Scott said. 'It was bad luck, anyway. Accidents will happen . . .'

It was Quartermain the onlooker who could stagger at this piece of casual forgiveness. Accidents happen! He had watched Scott and Church fall into their mutual pacification so easily, so anxiously, that he wondered if they realized themselves how desperately concerned they were not to be enemies, not to hate, not to obstruct or to blame. Quartermain put it down insignificantly in his black-covered memory: 'Two blame-weary Englishmen have finally collided in the same forgotten grove, and out it comes: *So sorry*. And the answer: *Quite all right*.'

'You might thank these people here for me, too,' the General said as he got in.

'I'll settle all that,' Scott reassured him, urging him in.

'Good-bye, Scott,' the General said. 'Please come as soon as you can.'

'Good-bye, General,' Scott said. 'We'll be along.'

Scott looked for a moment as if he might make a wry joke of it, but he did not; and Quartermain knew for sure then that he had seen the end of something—of a very long war and of a wasteful and weary attrition, as if both had realized suddenly that nothing in the whole world was worth the misery they had caused each other, particularly in the face of a new misery like this one.

'Poor bloody Church,' Quartermain snarled sadly as the plane flew off.

'Do you think he found his landing fields ?' Quartermain asked.

'I'm not going to worry about that now,' Scott told him as they walked towards the bus. 'I doubt if he was looking for anything so stupid anyway, even Church. Hakim's ideas are always like that.'

He was obviously going to be angry with Hakim now for provoking this silly chase.

Scott asked the Greek driver if the bus was ready, and the Greek said they needed petrol. Could they get it from the Egyptian Army ? Scott decided that the permits would take too long, so they went with the Greek to the civilian pump which was housed beside an old beach hut, where an old man and a boy used a hand-pump pushed into a large drum. Scott paid for the petrol out of his own pocket and told the Greek to go back and get the others while he and Quartermain left the jeep, which had blown a gasket, with the Frontier Department's transport officer. They would travel back in the bus to Alexandria, and they would wait to be picked up by the bus near the main-road check-point.

They had delivered the jeep, but the bus was delayed; and as they waited by the roadside they felt as if they were very near home, sitting on their kit waiting for transport to take them somewhere in this familiar desert.

Men did not always have the opportunity to glance back on their lives and remember what it was like, and it was too tempting for Quartermain to resist making a point of it. He therefore spurred it on with a relentless purpose before it faded out. What was Scott intending to do about Church?

'I simply don't believe he was reconnoitring anything,' Scott said.

'You may not want to believe it,' Quartermain argued, 'but can you think of Church *not* doing what he should be doing? Can you imagine him not getting the lay of the land, if that was what he was sent here for?'

'It's so unlikely, considering where he actually went to out here.'

'Why did he go along the top of the escarpment?'

'I don't know. Do you want me to denounce him for that?'

'Not me. I'd sooner kill a man than denounce him. But I hate to be simple-minded. What do you suppose Church was doing out here, then?'

'I don't think it matters any more,' Scott insisted, standing up on the roadway to look for the bus which should have been here by now. 'Oh, to hell with Church and Hakim.'

'I wonder if you'll say that when a British assault force lands along this coast somewhere?'

Scott sat down and got up again. 'I don't know what I'll say if that happens. I don't even ask myself. I simply don't know what the devil to think of all this conniving. First of all Hakim thinks they want to kill Nasser; and now this. I only want to get right out of it.'

'You can't get out of it,' Quartermain said dryly, 'because you are already sitting in the middle of it.'

Quartermain watched him walking up and down the road looking towards the sea for the bus, and he thought: 'He's trying to evade this one too. But I don't think I should let him. No more burning up the old secrets with internal fires. Let him burn them out in the open this time and he might liberate himself. Just once.'

'History does repeat itself,' he said ruefully to Scott, 'but the second time it's a joke, like this one.'

But Scott refused to consider it a repetition of anything, even as a joke. 'I pity Church, that's all. Even if he's plotting or doing his job out here,

364

he is so incompetent at it that he'll bungle it. I can only feel sorry for him. He must have been born unlucky, or born wrong. Like me. But I can't blame him for that now. What's it matter what he is, anyway?'

'Have you forgotten the damage his bungling did to you?'

'I don't need to be reminded of that,' Scott said docilely, very dispirited now.

But he looked, now, to where he could find the worst memory of his life—to the west, to the south, to the deserts where the war had been won. But by whom? Not by Church the blunderer; only in spite of Church.

'Don't let him fool you because he's in trouble,' Quartermain was saying dramatically. 'Do you want your Egyptian friends to go crashing down in the dust because of Church?'

'They don't need me to defend them, and they won't go crashing down in any dust, and I'm not going to get mixed up in it any further. I've honestly had it this time.'

'That's no good,' Quartermain pointed out impatiently. 'You can't ignore what's happening here, so don't try to, for your own sake.'

He picked up the first bundle, ready to throw it into the bus which had stopped by them on the road.

'You don't know Hakim as well as I do,' Scott said then. 'He always exaggerates these things, particularly for my benefit. I don't believe Church was doing anything at all.'

There was trouble. An Egyptian sergeant was standing over the Greek driver with a rifle, bayonet fixed. The Greek driver threw up his hands in despair when Scott boarded the bus.

'He won't let us go,' he said to Scott.

'Why not?'

'General Church left with all our passes and permits in his pocket,' the Greek said.

'We tried to persuade him to see the officer,' René Harcourt told Scott, 'but he won't do it.'

'What did you stop them for?' Scott asked the sergeant in Arabic.

'I must stop every vehicle I see,' he told Scott.

'Who are you?'

'Field security,' the sergeant answered.

He had the eyes of all sergeants in all armies when dealing with superiors—half-resentment and half-fear, or perhaps half-threatening and half-ready to retreat. He was not sure of Scott, but Scott made very sure of him.

'You can go,' he said. 'Leave them alone.'

'I order you to go back,' the sergeant said to the driver.

'Slowly, slowly!' Scott said to him and produced his green pass, which he showed to the sergeant. 'I will take charge of this bus. You can go back to Colonel Mukri.'

The sergeant looked at the Frontier Corps pass and then at Scott and recognized the Englishman they all recognized. He saluted Scott for the oddity he was. 'Yes, *ya effendim*,' he said resentfully but obediently.

'Tell Colonel Mukri to please telephone the other check-points between here and Alexandria to let us through.'

'Yes, *ya effendim*.'

As he got down, the others expressed their relief and Quartermain sighed for the role of a friend. Scott was still the soldier. It was amazing. He still behaved like one, except that when he did it in Arabic he was more like an Egyptian than a British officer, but all the same values of decision and purpose were still there.

'He doesn't look unhappy and he doesn't look at all sorry for himself,' Quartermain admitted, 'so what am I worried about?'

Nevertheless, he felt guilty and decided that a man ought to take his eyes off the significant sometimes, and travel across the world, if he could, to help a friend. There may be a risk of sentimentality in that idea, but Scott had carried the burden they should all have carried, and he had deserved better of his friends over the years than they had given him.

CHAPTER FORTY-EIGHT

FRANÇOISE felt like a widow at times.

She wept alone on the divan, reading a passage in Stefan Zweig's *Marie Antoinette*. It was not Marie's fate or reflected self-pity for her own predicament (husbandless yet not a widow, two children, the Suez Canal nationalized and her job at stake and where could she go?), it had no particular point at all. The tears fell. She wiped them away, curled up her feet, sipped her very white coffee and went on reading.

'It's simply because a woman in this country is so helpless,' she said bitterly to herself.

Sans défenses. She got up and walked about restlessly in her stockinged feet.

'How helpless and futureless and thoroughly without roots I am,' she complained. 'Is this supposed to be my home—this neat, silly apartment not far from the sea, not far from the canal, not far from my bureau? It's not far from anywhere, yet it's too far from everything. Is that what I must live for? Oh, I don't want to cry . . . .'

She wept a little more and wiped her eyes and nose carefully.

'I ought to commit suicide,' she decided, her practical French education getting the better of her. But she would not say it aloud, even to herself. 'All Jews want to commit suicide,' she went on miserably. 'Every Jew. All educated Jews. Every intellectual Jew. Even Leo who is dying would like to. What is there for a Jew in the world? Nothing, nothing, nothing!' She sniffed her coffee, trying to find its appeal. 'My children will have nothing, either. Only by pretending to be French will they have something. And why? Who can really tell me why? But they'll have nothing at all, because they will really be Jews. They'll know! There's nothing for them. No wonder we all want to be dead.'

She knew what would happen when she washed her coffee cup in the kitchen sink. When the gas heater would shake the room with a frightening roar the moment she turned on the hot-water tap, and she would ask herself a question.

367

'Would you,' she would ask, 'like to have died in the gas chamber?'

She would shudder. She would feel as no other human being but a Jew could feel, teetering on the abyss of horror, not terrified by murder, but undermined by the method of civilized preparation for it. First starve you, dirty you, turn you into a hollowed-eyed beast (wasn't that enough for them?) and then they say, 'Look at this animal. Let's kill him.' So they gas a Jew to death in damp cement walls in countryside with muddy paths, horrible wet landscapes, and dirty little fields with the ashes of Jews fertilizing grim and ugly cabbages, forgotten by the entire world. It was all true.

'So much for your suicide,' she would say, forgetting everything French and knowing that she could not be practical about it. A Jew should not, never, commit suicide. A Jew was superior anyway; in the heart he knew it. It was therefore a moral duty never to contemplate it, even so revenge-fully and frivolously.

But what would she do? What could she do if they turned out all the foreigners from the canal, particularly now that the French canal pilots were deserting, and the French and English newspapers were talking of terrible things, while the Egyptians threatened them all with arrest for treason if they left their work. The Egyptians were bringing in Russian and American pilots, and Monsieur Beauvoir had said that French troops were already on their way to Cyprus to take the canal back again.

'How can they,' she asked herself, 'without a terrible war?'

Nobody believed that possible, excepting Monsieur Beauvoir.

'And in any case,' she decided, 'I should go to France now. I should divorce Roberto and finish with him. Then I should marry *l'anglais* and be safe for ever. Oh, if only that would be possible now.'

With her mind firmly made up she prepared him Red Sea shrimps. He had already telephoned her at her office that he would come, but wet eyes and muddy cheeks would not impress him. And there would have to be much more to it than simply impressing him.

How much could she tell him without quarrelling?

She must do it so carefully, and here she was too upset and worried to be clever now.

'You know that they arrested Phillip Lieberman,' she said.

'No, I didn't.'

'Phillip was simply walking into Leo's office in Emad el Dine and they took him away, right off the street.'

Scott turned away as if he would prefer not to hear any of it. 'Did they take Leo as well?' he asked.

'No, but they asked him questions about his business and about Phillip, and they took away all his books, or some of them. Leo has an Egyptian

368

partner, but that day Leo couldn't find him at all. So he must have known the police were going to do something to Leo and Phillip. It's horrible. Leo asked me where you were.'

'What for?'

'I suppose he wants you to help.'

'Oh, no!' Scott moaned to himself, but she simply saw him hunch his shoulders up and draw in his head a little, like a tortoise trying to hide from terrible noises.

'I don't know if that's what he wants. He simply asked for you.'

'But what does he say? He must have told you more than that.'

'He won't say anything more on the phone when I ring; but I'm worried about him because he is so ill. Everybody must know that, even the Egyptians. Why do they pick on a dying man? He wrote me yesterday that they're probably accusing Phillip of smuggling money out of the country, or something silly like that.'

'Phillip Lieberman was probably doing exactly that.'

'Allons donc,' she said accusingly. 'On cherche les excuses, on les trouve toujours.'

'They don't need excuses to arrest Phillip Lieberman,' Scott said calmly. 'But if he's done nothing wrong, he's got nothing to worry about.'

'You make me angry when you say that. You forgive the Egyptians anything.'

Now he had spoiled the carefully prepared hors-d'œuvre which they were eating. He was sitting on the couch and she on a chair in the semi-darkness of the room, under the green mercury glare that lit the horizon from the port above the oil tankers and the passenger ships waiting off the crowded roadstead to form a convoy and enter the canal. It still worked, despite the world of doubts.

'Nevertheless,' he said, losing his appetite, 'it's probably true about Lieberman smuggling money out.'

'Of course it's true!' she said and dropped her voice a little. 'If it had not been for Leo and Phillip, how many Jews would have left this country penniless, with nothing at all to take out except the fifty pounds the Egyptians allow them? What could people do in Europe or anywhere on fifty pounds? Of course it's true. They helped so many people.'

'Then I don't even want to hear about it,' he said wearily.

'Shh!' she said. 'You will wake the children.'

There was too much to quarrel about now and they fell silent because they did not want to quarrel. But her tears were too fresh to wash away so easily, and she had already dissolved from the petite Françoise with the diamond-bright eyes into the simpler girl with an old luminous film of sorrow. She was worried and frightened.

'J'ai peur toujours maintenant,' she told him. 'Now they'll find excuses to arrest us all.'

'Why should they arrest you? They don't want to do that.'

'If they arrest me what will happen to the children? That's all I think about. What will happen to them? I don't care about me any more. It's my children. They at least ought to be safe.'

'But they won't arrest you! Why torture yourself, Françoise?' he said gently, trying to tease her. 'It's not quite so bad.'

He was not trying to comfort her, he was arguing with her because he knew already that he could not cope with Françoise melting into a natural state. He had exhausted his understanding and his pity of that process on Church and on himself.

Church had been grateful at the hospital, grateful at the telephone, grateful at the caracol where he had gone voluntarily with his statement, grateful at the Frontier Corps where they had sent him with it, grateful at the hospital again where they had returned to find the surgeons still working on Professor Maudie. She might or might not be all right, depending on an absolutely secondary matter—anaemia which had been aggravated by a month of gyppy tummy. Professor Maudie's chances of surviving would depend now on the effect of the blood transfusions and the injections they were giving her every few hours. The wounds themselves were bad but not necessarily fatal, except that she would be a cripple all her life and she would never use her left hand again—she had no fingers left on it.

'Somewhere, sometimes,' he said to Françoise sadly, 'I suppose it has to stop.'

'It never stops for us,' she said. 'They want to get rid of all the Jews now. Poor Phillip.'

'That's too much,' he groaned, finally angry. 'Phillip Lieberman was probably breaking the currency laws. You admit it. So don't pity him. He knew what he was doing.'

'You are like the others,' she cried.

'Oh, don't say that. Say something else.'

'But it's true. To you we are all spies and enemies—*tricheurs*.'

'Sometimes it's your own fault,' he complained, going further than he meant to, 'because that's what you make yourselves. Do you want to say there aren't Israeli spies in Egypt? You know very well that Ben Gurion despises the Egyptians the way you used to; and you still do. *Les sales Arabes*. Do you think there aren't spies among you now, doing what they can to kill Nasser or blow up the canal, or do whatever they can?'

'You see?' she wept. 'Now you say it like the others.'

'It is true, none the less.'

'Was Sam Hassoon a spy? Your own friend?'

'I don't know, and I don't want to know. People like Sam get caught up in contests which are nothing to do with them. I don't care if he's a spy or not. Sam is different, and he's nothing to do with Lieberman. I won't even talk about Sam.'

She came around to his side of the table, onto the couch near him, and she sat down and put her arm through his and held him very close.

'I know,' she said. 'I know you are right too. But something is wrong.'

She went back to the French to show him what was wrong; not to Racine and the Lycée poets she admired—not to Paul Harel the Catholic or Madame de Regnier who wrote about nothing so lyrically; lately she had remembered Edmond Fleg, the French Israelite who had re-sung the old psalmodic songs. She said only a Jew could write how a Jew could feel now.

'*Isaac! Isaac,*' she said, '*pourquoi nous as-tu mis au monde?*
Nous allons, sans abri;
Nous n'avons point de part et la terre feconde,
Et sur le sol natal nous sommes des proscrits.
Le faible nous insulte, le poltron nous brave,
L'enfant siffle contre nous;
Et nous avons pris des âmes d'esclaves,
A force d'user nos genoux.'

He did not like it. 'I'd sooner Mr. Ben Gurion than that,' he said.

He thought it self-pity, but she said he would never understand because he was not Jewish.

She told him then that the Egyptians had already started interfering with the canal staff.

'The Egyptian officers came today and took all my books away, with all the staff appointments and grades. I had to help Beauvoir give them all the information they want, although they know it already. They seem to know everything. One of the officers took every scrap of paper out of my drawer and Beauvoir's also, every morsel of it. I asked him what for, but he simply smiled and shrugged. All Beauvoir does is walk around with a knowing smile on his face as if they're all fools. He doesn't care what they do. He just laughs to himself. He thinks the French will take it all back, with the help of the British, but that's silly. Isn't it? How can they?'

'Have they dismissed anybody yet?' he asked her.

'No, but the Greek accountant says they've taken all his books also. What they want to see is how much we are being paid, but they probably know that too. Everybody says it will be the Jews and the French who go first, and I'm both, so I suppose I can count the days now.' She was talking about it calmly, however, as if she still did not quite believe it.

'You'd better come down to Cairo,' he told her. 'It will be safer there.'

'I don't think so,' she said with the teasing voice which never quite left them in peace sometimes. It would always annoy him. Now she was pushing her small mouth forward in a very French *bouderie*, something an Englishwoman could never quite do. She was sulking a little.

'I think,' she said, 'that I will go to France and finish with Roberto.'

'If you go to France, the Egyptians will not allow you back in.'

'Then I will stay in France.'

'If you go to France,' he told her, 'I'll leave here and go with you. I swear it . . .'

'*Bien*,' she said offhandedly. 'Let us go together.'

But she did not take him seriously, nor herself. It was simply a *plaisanterie* which had no meaning yet, and he was too tired to pursue it seriously.

'Now it's all right,' she said, seeing how tired he was. 'Nobody but us.'

If she could only go on being the pale-faced girl brought up by her Jewish family with the old prejudices and the carefully nurtured sorrows. Never mind the Françoise who had been educated at the Lycée among the Armenians, Greeks, Italians, and the other local girls who had all tried to acquire some sort of insouciance française.

She had only acquired enough to hide the frightened Cairo girl who had once been taught religious truths, not rational ones. The old truths made little provision for sex or franchise; they meant marriage within the old family circle and sex within the Hebraic laws: birth rather than passion, and obedience rather than abandon. Put that kind of girl into the hands of a passionate young Frenchman and it ought to be liberating. It had been brutal, because what was normal to Roberto had been an aberration to her. Disgust had made her a woman, and it was not a very easy way to become a woman.

'I don't think I want to live in France,' she told him. 'The French are so stupid with their vanity and their meanness. All the Englishmen I have ever met have had *le bon air*. Frenchmen brush their hair too much and think of their shirts and even their eyebrows.' She giggled a little pleasantly, forgiving the French none the less. 'Monsieur Beauvoir trims his eyebrows, but sometimes he forgets for months at a time, and suddenly they fall down over his eyes and he tries to brush them away like flies. Then he borrows my nail scissors and my mirror and trims them. I want to tell him he ought to pull them out; cutting is what makes them grow so quickly. I'd love to see you cutting your eyebrows, *mon gros joli anglais*. But I don't want to live in France. When I have finished with Roberto I'll go to England, if you like. If I can support the weather and the fogs. Could we live there? What would you do?'

Allowing for all the reality they had held at bay recently, it did not shock her to discover that *l'anglais* should have fallen asleep.

'Tant mieux,' she decided, touching him affectionately to be sure.

Now she would not have to worry about the hard desire that sometimes came over him and transformed him from a shy man into an angry but helpless one in the face of her unwillingness.

'Soon now,' she could promise him quietly and safely, but secretly.

She had a few clear visions of the prospects. She wandered secretly over them. She would not have to work any more when she married *l'anglais*. She could dress decently, perhaps *à l'anglaise*, and he could help her manage young André, who was getting beyond her control with his boyish eyes which never saw her any more, or when they did see her they seemed to be mocking and contemptuous of her. How could a child be like that? Yet he was. *L'anglais* would be firm with him, but wouldn't shout. Mireille would be very loving. They would live in a flat somewhere, and she would keep it neat and perfect.

The rest would be simple. He could have her then, and it would honestly be simple, because all she expected of a man was already there: shyness and tenderness and consideration and trust. And when the moment did come it would not be sordid, because it could be . . .

'It will come then,' she told herself, 'when we are married. It will come.'

The only detail she could not settle was what country it would be in. She tried to picture herself in England, but she could not really believe it. It could not be England.

'He will decide,' she said generously. 'I will go wherever he likes.'

She caught sight of her shrimps.

'Oh, my shrimps,' she said. 'Sixty whole piastres' worth.'

She shrugged resignedly, and she settled down under his arm and decided to wait for him to finish his sleep. Look how beautifully he slept. She loved him. Let him sleep. Then he would wake up and she would tease him. Then he would eat the shrimps, and they would not be wasted.

'I will make him a good Jewish wife,' she said to herself.

It was such a relief to be able to think that way. It had never been possible with Roberto and his hateful *vanité*. She wondered if Roberto was still in Algiers, and how she would go about divorcing him. She would ask Leo. Leo had always offered to pay her fare and expenses if she ever decided to divorce Roberto Rolland in the French courts, the only place where it would be legal now.

CHAPTER FORTY-NINE

As a rule, Helen Mamoon did not like helping her employer, Jolley, with his parties at home, but this time it wouldn't matter. Her job was finished. Jolley was secretly closing up the office. Soon she would be out of a job, and then what?

It was almost a relief to help him with this party, therefore, and it wasn't as bad as some. Usually, Jolley spent his evenings with the well-established group of travelling Englishmen who drank whisky all night and played noisy and sometimes violent practical jokes on each other and kept all conversation well inside the coterie of their professional habits. They were men who sold motor-cars or machinery or cement-bags or electric cables, even crockery; not in retail bits and pieces, but in large enough quantities to make their lavish spending on their self-indulgences an unimportant detail in the total. Although Jolley was not strictly a salesman, he lived their kind of life, and they lived cash lives. Their drinking and their clothes and apartments and travel and hotel bills formed a perfect circle of conviction, tightly enclosing them and completing them, drunk or sober. An outsider had very little means of penetrating, unless he wrapped himself up in the same life and rolled along with them in their cash and their drinking and their good-fellowship; but Helen Mamoon thought them all childish, and though she did not hesitate to call them all by their first names in Jolley's living-room, she would not do so in their offices. She would listen and laugh at their horseplay and pretend to drink a little whisky, but her interest and her drinking were too thinly disguised to convince anyone, and they all felt her contempt, which was mainly feminine because she did not think much of them as men.

Jolley easily saw through her camaraderie, but he never dared press her or make fun of her attitude. His boldest efforts at personal riposte were his jokes about her crazy brother-in-law, Quartermain. Why did he write such violent books denouncing British mistakes or British politicians.

condemning the British for defending themselves in Malaya or Africa? Why did he hate Churchill for instance?

'He's a raving Bolshevik,' Jolley said teasingly. 'Somebody ought to put a stop to him.'

'I thought Englishmen didn't mind other people having different political views,' she said, but her eyes also said to Jolley: '*He's twice the man you are, anyway.*'

'Elle m'a eu,' Jolley said and roared with laughter.

He knew a little French and a little Arabic, and he loved to use what he could of both.

Tonight was his farewell dinner for his local foreign contacts, however, and though they didn't know he was going away, they could guess it. It was little more than a noisy dinner, well-served by Groppi's with magnificent salads, Russian salads, hors-d'œuvre of lavish Continental tastes, and kebab and cooked meats which were served hot from their containers; then high ice-cream cakes and jellied fruits soaked in kirsch and cherry-brandy.

These were his business friends: one Armenian and one Greek and two Syrians. No fellow-countrymen, not friends in the real sense, but temporary local copies of his English colleagues, with the same carefully acquired sportive habits, although Jolley considered every man here to be much sharper and more cunning in business affairs than any Englishman alive.

The Greek ran lorries for crude oil from Suez to the power stations in Cairo, the Armenian re-refined oils for the Egyptian Army, and the two Syrian brothers with their wives were Levantine or Syrian Jewish, probably original Palestinian, who distributed detergents for the big petrol companies. They all had their own wealth and their own way with it, but when they were with Jolley they did what the English did: they drank his whisky and joked noisily in English and became familiar and talked money.

But they were all on edge tonight.

'If the oil tankers stop coming,' Karamanlis the Greek complained, 'my wagons are going to be kept in the siding at Suez and I'll have to pay the railways a fortune in line rental. That's how the Egyptian Railways make money whether the oil comes or not.'

He had been a poor man and now he was a rich man, and he only damned the Egyptians when they cheated him, otherwise he got on well with them, he said.

The Armenian who re-refined used oils and saved the Egyptian Army thousands of pounds in lubricants every year did not mind the air of crisis so much as the uncertainty of Army payments. If the Egyptian Army reneged on paying him for work done, as they very well could do,

375

then his whole business would be threatened for lack of liquid cash. He had put so much money into his new equipment that he needed the regular Army payments to meet his own wages bill.

'They know they can put me out of business when they want to,' he said in sad Armenian-English, 'and my Egyptian partner is waiting for that to happen so that he can buy the business back from the wreckage, and pay nothing for it.'

Their complaints were not petty, they were real. The Egyptian Government forced them all to have Egyptian partners, who took half the profits and did little of the work. Helen knew it was true in every case among them. The Syrian-Jewish brothers, with their plump, simple wives, were the only two who did not complain, because they were used to it. Uncertainty was deep in the long tradition of their sort or trading.

Opposition and tricky-business had always been used against them; and they were themselves accused of smart practices in supplying industrial detergents cheaper by a considerable amount than any other distributing agency in Egypt. How did they do it? They sat together eating pineapple cake and allowing their wives to talk and play the social games which Jolley's good nature tried to drag out of them, with Helen's help. He had begged her to come along and help him with this social evening, but at the last moment he never needed help. He was a good, happy host and he was getting on with his local contacts as if he enjoyed it.

But the nervousness was not easily hidden.

Foreigners in Egypt were already beginning to feel the familiar signs of tension. They were careful about displaying themselves too much on the streets. The Egyptian radio was at it, night and day: Egyptianizing the Egyptians, going over and over the salt of their victory. The canal was Egyptian; Egyptians would run it; Egyptians would soon control all the wealth which was rightfully Egyptian. Egypt would soon build the Aswan Dam, now that they had the canal dues to pay for it, and then what would the west say when Egypt achieved everything they said she couldn't do? What a shock they had felt in their comfortable club-rooms in London when Gamal Abd el Nasser had nationalized the canal for Egypt. Egypt! The radio was saturated with *Masr*, *Masr*, *Masr*!

They all knew what would happen, so they talked about getting their money out of Egypt, and ultimately themselves; but it was not quite that urgent yet.

'Jewels,' Mrs. Karamanlis the Greek's wife said, 'are the best way. You can easily buy good old jewels and they don't know it. If you go to the *sagha* and have new real gems set in gold, they must record it in the Government book, but not the old jewels.'

'Where do you hide them?' Jolley asked roguishly.

'You mustn't ask,' Mrs. Karamanlis said, coquetting him.

It was not serious. If they had means of getting money out of the country illegally (and assuredly, Helen knew, they all had means) they would not bandy it about here as a joke.

They simply argued about it to relieve the air of urgency which they felt breathing fearfully on them the moment they talked of their situation in Egypt. Cameras? Motor-cars? Buying sterling notes or French francs for twice what they were worth from an Egyptian who never delivered them to the boat when you were leaving as he promised to do. *Ah, no!* Libya, the Lebanon and Syria—all the other Arab countries offered safer routes because all kinds of speculators there did semi-legal foreign transfer business in millions. That was undoubtedly the best and safest method. The moment Jolley mentioned this method deliberately, however, they stopped talking about money.

'Ah hah!' he said, whispering to Helen. 'I put my finger on it that time.'

She wanted to go because he did not need her here.

'Why do you ask me to come?' she said. 'You don't need me now.'

'But I do. You keep them all in their places.'

She knew what he meant. The locals could get so familiar but no more. The difference between them had nothing to do with snobbery, it was simply one of mental attitude. Jolley was afraid of being bored and at the same time he was afraid of inspiring any sudden gust of familiarity in case it got out of hand and went beyond the line of demarcation between them. 'They're all nice people,' she told him. 'I really must go.'

'You despise them,' he whispered as they prepared the coffee which Jolley made a fetish of preparing himself, because no native servant knew anything about wines or coffee. 'Your nose gets longer and longer.'

It was not true.

She did not despise them, any more than he did. She had no link with them, that was all. They had made their money on petty levels, and that was what they talked about. It was this that she despised. They had nothing else but money—unlike Buelli, for instance, with whom she could discuss Italian and talk in Italian and feel the pleasure of something more aesthetic than money manipulation. Buelli had also made his fortune speculating, but he refused to allow it to ruin his mind and his sensibilities. Even Jolley's English friends didn't make it as much of a religion. They probably didn't have to, being English, but one could sit with them and joke with them without feeling like an un-moneyed outsider. The strange thing was that most of these Greeks and Armenians and Syrians knew as many languages as she did herself, but they never tasted the languages they knew, they never looked for the pleasures of good Italian or good Arabic. They had no culture, not even in their indigenous Greek or Armenian or Jewish culture. They had lost it, which surprised her. In

377

Jewish communities in any part of the world there was usually the most cultured life in the country. But in Egypt the middle-class Jewish families had not developed their culture at all, on any level, neither music nor art nor literature nor even intellectualism. The easy well-served eating life had corrupted even the Jews away from their deeply mined talents. It was such a pity. Only the Armenians in Egypt had kept some part of their culture intact.

'I don't know what to talk to them about,' she said to Jolley. 'You can make jokes with them, and tease the ladies. I can't. So I shall go.'

'I wish you'd stay a little longer,' he begged.

She shook her head. It was getting late. She said she did not want to walk through the streets late at night. Anyway, she did not drink coffee, it was bad for the heart and the stomach. If she slipped out quietly now it would not be noticed and she would not force polite departures upon the remainder.

'Don't forget to get my plane tickets first thing in the morning,' he said to her at the front door. 'Don't do it on the phone. Go yourself.'

'I know, I know,' she told him. 'It's all arranged.'

'Good. I don't want the Egyptians to have any forewarning,' he said.

Jolley was trying to leave as quietly as possible. Only she knew that he was closing down the Anglo-Egyptian Oil Exploration office for good, taking with him as much of the capital as he could safely get out, and leaving Helen to close up the office and dismiss herself.

He had been very decent about it. Helen would have a month to close down the business, and for the termination of services she would have three months' salary as indemnity.

Jolley himself would leave quietly in a few days' time, as if he intended coming back, but the moment he had gone she would sell up, little by little, his apartment, his car, cameras, tape-recorders, crockery, radio— all his viable world of cash wealth. Then she would keep the office ostensibly open, although in fact her work was at an end.

'You knew it had to come sooner or later,' he had consoled her.

'That doesn't help much,' she told him bitterly.

'But you can't expect any British firm to stay here now.'

'If you run away,' she told him, 'Nasser will never let you back.'

'If we don't run away Nasser will take everything we've got.'

She had never known how much capital the Anglo-Egyptian Oil Exploration company had kept in Egypt. Not much anyway; so that fear of losing it was not the real reason. The real money was in the hands of the big English and French oil companies which did the actual exploring, and their capital was not kept in Egypt. This subsidiary which Jolley had

378

managed was mainly for negotiating the concessions to explore for oil, and to keep the rights intact through the changing governments and decrees which had threatened them for forty years, but had never yet removed them, even under Nasser. Now it was done. Technically the exploration concessions would remain theirs for certain areas, until Nasser cancelled them. They were not even giving up their concessions, they weren't even saving their non-existent capital, they were simply transferring themselves out of Egypt to safety. They (she admitted to Nona sadly) managed to protect themselves, without losing anything.

'I don't think Nasser will ever let you back in again,' she said again to Jolley, not hiding her disgust that they should run away the first chance they got.

'Perhaps the Egyptians will start prospecting for a dome of oil themselves,' Jolley replied, and thought it a huge joke, 'with a divining rod . . .'

'Don't be silly,' Helen said to him. 'If the Egyptians want to be as clever as you are, they can be. It's only a matter of money and equipment.'

'That's true, but where will they get it?'

'The Russians perhaps.'

'That would start a war,' Jolley replied indignantly. 'If the Russians try to move in on our concessions here, do you think we'd sit by and let them do it? The canal is one thing, dear Helen, but oil is another . . .'

She shrugged and did not argue. She never talked politics with him, and she had only mentioned the Russians to punish him for his silly joke about the Egyptians. He often forgot that she was Egyptian, and he ought to be reminded occasionally that the English weren't the only pebbles on the beach.

When she told the family at dinner that Jolley was going, and that her job was finished, she turned to Nona and said, 'Now you know why I want to leave also.'

'Because Jolley is running away?'

'It's not only that,' she said angrily, the finality of it getting the better of her. 'You tell me who else wants my Ministry experience now? If I stay on in Egypt I'll have to become a shorthand typist. Is that what you want me to do? Do you want me to end up like poor Miss Wren who is dying like a pauper in Kasr-el-Aini hospital among the natives? How could I live on the sort of salary they pay those Egyptian girls?'

Nona came around and kissed her and said perhaps she was right.

'I suppose we've all got to go,' Nona said sadly.

Quartermain had already told her that she ought to prepare to leave Egypt with the boys, because the British would probably try something dangerous, sooner or later, and he did not want his wife and children caught in Egypt if there was going to be a war.

'I think he wants to book a passage on a P. & O. boat,' she told Helen, 'so you and Hanna could come with us.'

'Yes, but how?'

'Can't you come to Europe for a holiday?' she told Helen. 'Then you could come back to Egypt if things don't work out, or if there is no war.'

Helen was about to reply that she did not think she could get an exit permit to leave Egypt, and that she could not afford a 'holiday' anyway. But Ali, the servant, came in and she knew she must be careful of what she said to Nona. Furthermore, she could not leave Egypt for at least six weeks, not until she had closed up the Anglo-Egyptian Oil Exploration Company, once and for all.

CHAPTER FIFTY

'POOR Miss Wren' who (Helen had said) 'was dying like a pauper in Kasr-el-Aini hospital among the natives' was such a sad woman to re-discover, that she became for Nona a proof of the decency of pity, and a further proof of never ever turning away from the down-trodden simply because they were sometimes grotesque, and of *never* behaving the way the English did with each other.

She had discovered Miss Wren by accident, having heard casually from old school friends that she was in the Kasr-el-Aini hospital—the hospital for poor Egyptians only.

'But that's awful,' had been Nona's angry comment.

'Les anglais sont toujours les anglais,' her friends had replied.

So they were, and Nona had decided then and there to visit poor Miss Wren, in order to justify the better emotional values of Egyptian life, which the English in Cairo had never had. But she begged her husband to go with her, even though they were hardly on speaking terms because he had commented a little too dryly on her queen-like behaviour with some visiting Coptic cousins. But she asked him as nicely as she could, under the circumstances, would he come?

'What for?' Quartermain complained, exasperated. 'I've never even heard of Miss Wren.'

'Yes, you have,' Nona told him. 'I often talked about her. She was the Englishwoman who said, when we were engaged, that I ought to marry you quickly before you ran away and left me with a baby.'

'Why should I want to see anyone who said that?'

'Because she's dying in misery and poverty and forgotten by all of her famous Cairo English, who liked to stick together against the natives. She was always decent to me.'

Remembering Scott, he could no longer denounce the higher morality of a good friendship, and though he grumbled about it, and though he had a risky and perhaps dangerous rendezvous later on, he took her in a taxi to Kasr-el-Aini hospital which was not really for Europeans but for peasants and Arabs only.

381

It was a disgrace for an Englishwoman to be dying there in the public ward.

'You won't remember her to look at,' Nona said, 'but you did see her once during the war. She used to wear her dresses inside out, and some say she wore a wig. It was either a dirty wig or she simply never brushed her hair from one year to the next. She admitted to Hanna once that she never washed her face or her body. She simply put on white powder until, I swear, you could have peeled away the layers of sweat and powder mixed like a skin. Surely you remember her.'

'Why should I remember a woman like that?' he said again, although it was too late to retreat now.

'Don't be cruel,' she told him. 'That's the way the English used to treat her. She didn't know how she looked, because she used to think it didn't matter, because it was enough in this world to be born English. But it was terrible to be with her. You can imagine what it was like to be near her on a hot summer's day. It must have been something biological, because nobody could be so unclean and not know it. The funny thing is that all the so-called dirty oriental countries like Egypt have strict rules about feminine cleanliness written into their religion: even the Arabs. It's only the Christians who forgot about it. The English particularly. Next to the French they are probably the most unwashed women in the world. I don't mean their faces. At least the French have *bidets* which the English have never even heard of. Although how they manage to keep their lovely hair and complexion is a mystery to me. I suppose that's all they wash.'

The taxi had stopped under a great propaganda arch being built over the end of Soliman Pasha street. It showed a bold-faced Egyptian soldier digging a bayonet into the backside of John Bull astride the canal, and John Bull was shrieking in pain and fleeing for his life.

'No doubt he stopped here so we could have a good look at that,' Quartermain said. 'I've seen it,' he said to the driver in English. 'Drive on . . .'

The taxi driver grinned and they went on.

'You shouldn't be so familiar with them,' Nona told him in a whisper. 'What do you think would happen to us if he made a fuss? These days . . .?'

'We'd end up in prison,' he told her, 'like Sam did.'

'You can joke,' she whispered, 'but it's true. And look how difficult it was to get Sam out; so don't be so sure of yourself.'

He was not sure of himself, he said. He was simply provoked by the thought in every Egyptian head that all Englishmen were the same.

'How can he tell one kind from the other?' she said.

She was right, but he felt that he could not help being irritated and dry-witted about it. But she did not punish him too much for his silliness. She was anxious that he tolerate what he would see when he got to Kasr-

382

el-Aini, knowing that he might as well be prepared for it. He hated wretchedness and he hated death—the misfortunes one felt most helpless about. The after-effects of misery always remained with him longer than they did with her.

'Before the war,' she said, 'Miss Wren was a rare thing.'

'You mean,' he said cynically, 'that there were other Englishwomen even dirtier than she was?'

'I didn't mean that at all. I meant that she was an English shorthand typist. That was long before the local European girls took it up, and there were more secretarial jobs than women to fill them. She used to live in hotels then, that's how much money she was earning. All the English used to say that she drank; the English were always so ashamed of her that they used to accuse her of anything.'

'Why should the English be ashamed of eccentrics? Look at Pickering.'

'Oh, but she was different. If she'd only known what she looked like perhaps she might have been all right. But when Hanna once told her that her dress had a big hole down the back of it and her slip, which was filthy, was showing through it, she said: "Oh, my dear, we English don't have to fuss with such things." That was all very well until she began to lose one job after the other, simply because people couldn't even sit in the same room with her. So she simply began to slip farther down. The last time Helen saw her she was actually living in one of those roof-top slum huts which the native servants have. Helen got her out of there, and put her in a boarding-house until she found her a job as a housekeeper, but by the end of the war it was rather hopeless trying to keep track of her. She came to Hanna once after the war and asked if Hanna would explain to one of our Egyptian friends, who was the son of a rich landowner and one of the old aristocratic Copt families, that she was willing to marry him. The fact that she was English was enough. When Sobhi, who was a third her age, heard it, he started to describe and imitate what life would be like with Miss Wren with her false teeth slipping off her gums and her wig and her terrible shoes. It was so cruel that Hanna got angry. But could you blame him?'

'What made you so patient with her?' Quartermain asked.

'I don't know. She was never stupidly prejudiced against the Egyptians like the other English, and the more badly the English treated her, the more sorry we felt for her. She once told Helen that she could probably find her an English sergeant who would be quite willing to marry her. That was supposed to be the end-all for us—marrying any Englishman, even a sergeant. But she wasn't really cruel or condescending about it. She was simply ignorant and pitiful . . .'

Quartermain was beginning to be depressed about the whole expedition and he sank back into the taxi and pictured that pre-war Cairo when the

English were what they were, and if there were any innocents among them they had to be ignorant and pitiful and filthy in order to be even tolerable.

'Poor Miss Wren,' Nona was saying. 'She must be eighty now. I wonder how she's hung on this long. I'm sure the Cairo English didn't help her. If it hadn't been for Helen and Hanna, dozens of times, she would have died of sheer starvation.'

It was obviously going to be a gruesome sight, this piece of wreckage the English had left behind them in Egypt, and when the taxi left them at the grim stone steps in that vast hall of sadness which took incurable natives in and sent incurable natives out, the prospect was more than the fruit and flowers could possibly counterbalance, or the friendship either.

Hanna and Helen had already arranged to come in the afternoon, which meant that there he was—the pioneer searching for poor Miss Wren. Nona found out where she was from the inquiry desk and they walked up the staircase around the hobbling patients and into the women's wing, where the smell of carbolic was too strong for normal nostrils to breathe without revulsion. Though everything was scrubbed dull and clean, the air itself seemed rotten with the real misery of sickness and poverty.

'Oh, my God!' Nona said. 'I'm glad you came.'

With the hustle of a few more visitors—peasants—they went into the free ward which was an echo-less hangar with a bare stone floor and fifty iron beds in chipped white paint. It was spotlessly, carbolically clean. Fifty women patients were being visited by their families, and thus the carbolic was suddenly lost. It didn't matter. The pandemonium was full of high-pitched Arabic, and when they looked down the rows at the men and women and children and aunts and friends over the bedsides, the daylight seemed like daylight and the sickness didn't matter. In here the peasants were peasants, the poor were the poor, the miserable were the miserable; but the families were also the families and the whole place looked like a peasant village moved into town.

Where was poor Miss Wren the Englishwoman?

'There she is,' the Egyptian nurse at the swing-doors told Nona.

Because of their European clothes and their alien appearance all Egyptian interest followed them, and tongues whispered.

Miss Wren was at the very end. Two native women were putting a small copper pot of food on the table near her, where there was also part of a chicken and some flat bread wrapped in newspaper.

Miss Wren was almost sitting up, a long leafless figure with white hair. 'So her hair is real,' Nona thought with her first plunging thoughts. 'And it's so clean and so white.' She could see the pink scalp through the thin fuzz. Miss Wren herself was dressed like the other women in a rough

384

nightgown, and her eighty-year-old face looked a healthy seventy. She was not powdered white, and her cheeks were clean and transparent. She had an old woman's firm English complexion. She was talking to her two native friends in thin-scaled Arabic.

'Miss Wren,' Nona said. 'Do you remember me? My sisters wrote to you . . .'

Miss Wren's face had shrunk at the jaws with the loss of her false teeth or their absence for the moment, but her eyes were bright enough to respond almost gaily.

'Of course I do, my dear,' she said. 'Oh, of course.'

She remembered very well, so well! Where were Helen and Hanna? When would they come? When Nona bent down to kiss her Miss Wren did not make too much fuss except to flutter a little, and when she looked at Quartermain and saw a tall gangling Englishman with a grey English moustache, even if it drooped a little, he was, after all, obviously English. She recognized him instantly.

'Fancy that,' she said to Nona. 'You left England and came back to Egypt.'

She was quite well, she said. It was only her gall-bladder. The family of her neighbour in the next bed, a young peasant girl almost blind with trachoma but in here for other reasons, had brought her extra food, because there was never enough in the hospitals. The doctor, who was a *charming* young Egyptian with an F.R.C.P. degree from England, had offered to send her to the French or to the old Anglo-Egyptian hospital to be among Europeans if she wanted to, but why should she? She was quite comfortable here, and the European hospitals had been spoiled since the English left.

Was Nona's husband an author? She had never heard of his books.

'That's because I never take any interest in serious things,' she said dreamily. 'I was always too Bohemian. I come from Tenby. You know? Augustus John and Nina Hamnett came from there too. During the first world war I knew all those artists and they were so gay, and once I went to stay with Nina Hamnett under the arches near Putney Bridge.'

'Would you like some books?' Quartermain asked her.

'I'm much too lazy,' she said. 'And it's too noisy here to read. Everybody comes into it. And nobody is very clean. But I don't think I mind any more. I suppose I've become acclimatized to Egyptian habits after all the years I've lived here.'

She patted Nona's hand and repeated odd disjointed stories of how everything had changed for the worse since the English left, and Nona shook her head and *suk-sukked* and agreed, listening with a puzzled resignation, seeing that she was quite happy, that she was clean because someone else (Egyptians) had washed her, that she was with friends because no peasant woman in this room would see her alone and they would pity her and help her with a little of their own existence, and that she was happy simply because she was not sad. What more could you ask?

'It's so odd, seeing her like that,' she said to Quartermain on the way out. He had sat on the end of the bed and said little except when Miss Wren had addressed him as one Englishman to another, in which case he had replied for the vast simplicity of it. 'She even looks younger and healthier now than she did twenty years ago. I suppose she'll die there. Where are all her English friends now, when she's dying like a pauper in a native ward?'

'She doesn't mind it, so why should you?' Quartermain said.

'I don't mind it,' Nona said passively, 'but it seems terrible that she should finish up among the peasant women. What an awful life she must have led. Poor Miss Wren. I only begin to feel how old I am when I think back on her in those dirty rayon frocks she used to wear.'

Nona did not feel old at all, Quartermain decided, but she could be very frightened by poverty. Perhaps that was the only state of life she was thoroughly frightened of. She was also afraid of side-issues like violence, potential violence, street mobs, and those arrogant cold-eyed youths who pinched women on the buttocks, or on the arms as they walked in the Cairo streets.

'I was brought up comfortably and I have always been well-fed and I've never had to worry, and I don't enjoy the thought of ever being poor,' she had said before now. She had often rubbed into him the logic of her Egyptian feelings about poverty when she had looked at English poverty, which had depressed her and frightened her more than the Egyptian sort. 'Marie Antoinette couldn't scrub floors and I couldn't even face being miserably poor—not in England. I'd die . . .'

She probably would not die, he decided, slumped down in the Cairo taxi. She would probably disintegrate, which was worse. The years when they had been very near to hard times had proved it. She had slipped too easily and quickly into bitter and rankling despair. So far he had managed to be well enough off. But anyone with his politics . . . sooner or later there would be dark days. That was inevitable. Then she would be a problem, particularly now with the children growing up.

'You're not going to let Miss Wren depress you, are you?' she asked him now.

He realized he had been slumped down, involved in the unhappy *if* of the future.

'I was thinking she might have depressed you, sweetheart,' he said to her.

'Why should I be depressed? I'm not Miss Wren and never will be.

386

'Not with your sense of hygiene,' he said.

It was a fair joke, but she did not laugh.

'Anyway,' he said to her, 'it's never the poverty that depresses me. It's how people react to it.'

'You can't romanticize poverty to me by talking about courage in the face of it,' she said, 'so don't try. I hate it. I will never be poor. I will jump into the river first.'

'That's a clean way to die,' he said.

She would not do that, either.

'Where are you going now?' she asked when he stopped the taxi and got out near the Metro cinema.

'I want to see Jack de Brazio,' he lied. 'Jack's going to visit the new steel works tomorrow and I want to see if I can get permission to go with him.'

'Don't be late,' she said, kissing him suddenly. 'I've got kuftah for lunch.'

He closed the taxi door, and she went on home.

He watched her out of sight and then he looked up at the Metro cinema and down at the café below it where they served the best sandwiches in Cairo, and where he was supposed to meet not Jack de Brazio, but some Egyptian communists, who were illegal and very much underground, and very dangerous to meet if he were caught—according to Mr. Aboud.

He hoped now that it was not a trick.

He had been walking out of the press department the day before when a young man had touched him on the shoulder and asked him if he was Mr. Quartermain.

'Yes? What do you want?' Quartermain had replied impatiently.

This young man had not replied immediately, but he had gone down in the lift with him and had then accompanied him along the street telling him quickly that he had read his books and that he had some friends who would like to meet him.

'What for?' Quartermain had asked suspiciously. 'Who are you?'

He was a slim, Europeanized Egyptian, he wore his clothes like a Frenchman and cut his hair like one. His white, clean, silk collar and long narrow tie were near enough the well-dressed young man about town in Cairo, of university age and intellectual age and political age. His face was very solemn.

'Will you please come and see my friends?' the youth repeated.

'But what for? Why do you ask like this?'

'We thought you would like to help us.'

Quartermain had shrugged. 'I don't know who you are,' he had insisted.

'Don't be angry,' the stranger had said. 'We are Egyptian communists.

387

That's illegal, as you know. But we know about you and we know we can trust you. We would like to talk to you, if it's possible.'

There was nothing frightening or conspiratorial about it when said so simply then. But when he looked up now at the café sign which said *Excelsior* he knew the Greeks who ran it would never consent to known communists eating their expensive sandwiches. And what about the too-casual police informers who infested the place? Perhaps that was why they had chosen this obviously dangerous rendezvous.

If, in fact, it was not a press department trick inspired by Mr. Aboud to trap him into the illegal activities which could bring about his expulsion. Was that what they wanted?

'I hope I know what I'm doing,' he said as he walked in, enjoying the aroma of pickles which wafted off the bar over the coffee urns and the freshly cut bread on the clean wooden platters.

But the young Egyptian was clearly not there, even though Quartermain waited until noon, when there was still no sign of him.

'You want something more?' the Greek waiter said to him in English. 'No,' Quartermain said and paid for his coffee and looked around him as he stood at the sandwich bar for a moment before leaving. The business men were making their deals over coffee, and the idle were telling their beads. There wasn't a man in the café under fifty, excepting himself and all those secret young policemen waiting for customers.

'Something must have gone wrong,' he decided, but he was not sure yet that it had not been a test arranged by Mr. Aboud.

If so, he had something else to worry about now, if he felt like worrying.

CHAPTER FIFTY-ONE

SAM was getting married, now that he was free, because there seemed to be nothing else he could do. His grandmother had complained that there would be no son after him, no boy with the family name, nothing to be proud of in his undone duty as a man.

He chose the youngest daughter of Madame Salz, Becky, whom he had seen many times but never noticed, and in the pre-marriage contract it was agreed that the *pension* should be Becky's, should be Sam's that is, when Madame Salz died. It was a long-term investment dowry, not particularly good in these troubled times, considering that Madame Salz herself was not very old and was in good health, but Sam said *What would I want with a pension anyway?* Sam had taken a job with a Lebanese who had just set up a business in Cairo importing German radios, of which he knew nothing technically. Sam had no work papers, but he was employed as an expert, which he would be when he learned enough about transistor circuits to cope with tape-recorders and new sorts of radio sets and high-fidelity equipment.

Sam had finally made up his mind, the contract had been signed, and now it must be done. His grandmother, who was happier than she had been since the death of her son, went about smiling blindly with no teeth, as if losing Sam was not going to be sad at all. But his sister, Alicia, wept every day in the kitchen and announced that Sam would forget them and leave them. What would they do? He tried to reassure her, in tears himself, that he would bring his bride home to live with them. But when Alicia went on doubting and doubting and weeping, he became angry and shouted at her to be quiet.

Sam took his betrothed a gift every day, because the marriage had been arranged for only two weeks ahead. Sam bought eau-de-cologne, large boxes of chocolates from Groppi's, silk scarves, and once quite daringly silk stockings which brought love to Sam himself without any warning. To hand a woman a pair of silk stockings, even in a box, seemed to Sam to be a most erotic thing to do, and he saw little Becky Salz in a new way. She blushed.

That convinced him. He loved her. So much so, that Sam became formal and polite. Becky laughed nervously when she opened the box. That took the conviction deeper, and thereafter he did not doubt that he loved her, although he knew it might very well be an excuse, since it was his duty now to love her.

He remembered painfully that he had once fled Becky, when Madame Salz had tried to press him into marriage by indignation. Now he was ashamed to think about it. He could only forgive himself by deciding that he had fled from Madame Salz and her forceful match-making rather than from Becky herself. That was definitely the explanation.

Becky, who had always noticed Sam, had also decided to love him—partly as a duty also. But Sam was such a big baby, and his attempts at formal behaviour were so serious and solemn that she could not help herself, giggling and loving him at the same time. She did not think it ridiculous and she did not mind that she looked tiny and red-haired and child-like beside him, when he was dark, huge and Greekish and almost twice her age.

They were very happy together and spoke in a mixture of French and English which helped to make talk (after all—the neutral ground of love) unembarrassing. Both languages were theirs and yet not theirs. They had none of their own, except perhaps Arabic which Becky barely spoke at all. But they settled the awkwardness of awkward moments by simply changing from one language into another when a moment got beyond them, doing it also when shyness got the better of them. It worked very well.

They were both shy. Sam not so much, because he had such a firm belief in largesse (it must be a big ring, everybody must come to the reception, she must have a good car to bring her to the synagogue, a black one, not a taxi), in a largesse that was deeply formal and proud and often child-like perhaps, but always generous; and though she would laugh in a small cheerful twitter at some of his noblesse, she too was shy and never did place her freckled hand in his black paw until the day he put the ring on her first finger in the synagogue.

She did think about the need to be kissed. But to be kissed by that large, pale face with deeply embedded dark-stubbled beard seemed nearly impossible. She knew she might want it. She felt her pink face shrink with frightened pleasure at the possibility. More than that, more than the likely miracle of one kiss, she knew it was impossible to take love much farther than that—if for nothing else than the imbalance of their different sizes. Yet she knew that she would come to that sort of love also.

At the synagogue in Adly Pasha, which was flanked by the Credit Lyonnais on one side and by a dirty little lane on the other, Sam arrived late with Scott in a Chrysler driven by one of his Greek friends who had put on a black peaked cap as a gesture to Sam. Some of Sam's other Greek friends were already there in two more Chryslers, having brought Becky, who was too early, and her family, who were waiting in the anteroom for Sam to unveil her.

'Haven't you any Jewish friends at all?' Scott asked him, teasing.

'Of course I have,' Sam said, but he was too preoccupied with his new hat—and his bearing, which became soldierly and true at the first steps of his wedding.

His Egyptian friend Captain Ali Zareef was standing at the top of the steps like a barrel that might topple and roll down any minute, beaming so widely that Sam's serious approach to marriage could make no real impression on such a delighted face. Zareef was not going to be solemn.

'Ahlan wahsahalan! Mabrouk! Mabrouk!' Zareef said, welcoming him and congratulating him with an embrace. Sam had to stoop to receive it.

'Ali,' Scott said, not having seen him since he had been freed from prison, but finding a sudden relief in Zareef's rotund good nature. 'You didn't expect this,' Scott told him. 'Admit you didn't expect Sam to marry. Isn't it amazing?'

'But why not?' Ali Zareef said. 'Look how happy he is.'

Becky's cousin, a photographer named Levy, was taking a picture of Sam in his hat, while Sam made the pose worthwhile for his children-to-be.

'That's for his children,' Scott said, knowing Sam.

Sam insisted that the cousin take a photograph of himself with his two friends, who were (if the Jewish ceremony permitted such things) his best men.

'Closer,' said the photographer.

Sam stood in the middle and Scott and Zareef posed either side of him, hats on. Sam told Levy to hurry up because Becky would be waiting; and it was Sam who should be waiting.

'The last of the old days,' Scott said. 'Today and tomorrow you will be a married man, like Ali Zareef.'

'That's true,' Sam admitted solemnly. 'Only *you* are not married,' he told Scott sadly.

Sam felt it his duty not to crack jokes yet.

'Cheer up!' Scott told him. 'You look marvellous.'

'We will always be friends,' Sam said. 'Here we are, like old times.'

But old times were gone. No more would they sit in the same aeroplane waiting for Zareef to put them down in some difficult wadi. They were aware of it, and they must stick closer than ever. When Sam, in his solemnity for the occasion, shook hands with each of them before going in, they suddenly found themselves agreeing with him, having no sort of

391

fun left. It must be serious. They followed him into the synagogue and sat together with the relatives—Becky's, with Madame Salz, uncles, cousins, and friends. And on Sam's side, his mother and sister and all his Greek friends.

Scott was embarrassed by religion. He kept his eyes fixed forward on the canopy, the black tent which was hung with flowers and the initials S and R (for Rebecca).

'How do you do, Captain Scott?' someone said behind him.

It was Helen Mamoon, who sat with Nona Quartermain and her other sister, as Sam's relatives. They were goys, but aunts none the less.

'Hello,' Scott said as if he had been caught at something illegal.

'My loving husband refused to come,' Nona whispered to him, 'but he'll be at the reception.'

'Yes, I know.'

'Don't you have strong objections to religion also?' Helen asked him.

'No. I don't think so. Not for weddings, anyway.'

He had heard that Quartermain, on one of his principles, would not put foot in church or temple, nor allow his children to do so, but Quarts obviously had no control over his wife. Nona looked very lovely and very young and very sure of herself, and when Scott's eyes met Helen's briefly, both of them seemed to admire Nona at the same time, and Helen forgave him a great deal for that admiring glance at her sister.

Becky was a tiny and startled bride, but when she walked in from the side aisle, followed by her bridesmaids on the arms of her top-hatted cousins to meet Sam under the canopy, she looked at her guests with a sly, shy, amusement. Then she would look ahead. It was too embarrassing watching her relatives and her friends weep, although they wept not so much for Becky but under the influence of the cantor who sang twanging sad songs for the racial memories of almost everyone present. Madame Salz could not stop weeping, and Scott felt Zareef wiping away a tear, although these sad songs had nothing to do with him.

'He's different already,' Helen whispered to Nona.

Scott heard and agreed. Sam's solemnity marked a new man.

'Oh, he's still a big baby,' Nona argued. 'He takes it all so seriously. Even little Becky is laughing.'

Becky's lively pink face, freckled and provoking, made the most of it; not laughing at Sam, but up to him. He stood almost seven feet tall in his top hat.

'Voilà, Madame Salz,' Helen said, as Madame Salz sobbed again.

'Mais pourquoi donc?' Nona said. 'It's supposed to be happy.'

'After all these years,' Helen said, 'she finally got Sam.'

It did not matter. Sam and Becky faced the east, the Rabbi spoke in

Hebrew which neither understood, not even Sam's memorized spoken answer announcing that Becky was married unto him by the ring and by the laws of Moses and Israel. They drank the wine, they crushed the glass underfoot to remind everyone present that the Temple in Jerusalem still lay in ruins, and after the vows and the signing of the Kesubah and the last sad song of the cantor, Sam took off his praying shawl and gave it to Scott as he passed by him in the aisle.

They passed out into the hot sunlight, where Sam's cousin arrested them at the steps and took photographs, while the Egyptian taxi drivers and beggar boys clapped their hands and called out to Sam—with the instinct of generations before them: *haboob!* big sweetheart.

The reception at Madame Salz's *pension* had been in preparation for days. The cantor broke the bread and sang the grace and everybody took a good grip on the roast chickens, roast ducks, pigeons, rice, macaronis, and a seven-tiered cake which melted under the candelabra, among the gifts, the wine, and Sam's speeches in French, with the help of the cantor, saying that all were his friends and would remain so. He meant the shaven-headed Greeks in borrowed skull-caps sitting with each other at Sam's request, and those sitting near him—Ali Zareef, Capten Scott (also in paper skull-caps), his aunts, and his new uncles and all his cousins by marriage. Even Alicia his sister looked happy, and his grandmother was nodding at everything said.

Sam began the impossible with little Becky, dancing around the table when the four Armenian musicians played a Viennese waltz. Becky was laughing now because they had never danced before, and once more because of their difference in height. She would never get over it. They were forced to hold each other at arm's length, swaying a little while everyone clapped. Sam said: 'Et alors!' and that was his only protest.

Scott drank the wine, became very happy, and argued teasingly with Quartermain about religion. Why hadn't he come to the synagogue?

'Why would I want to go back to the Stone Age?' Quartermain said, loudly enough for his wife Nona to hear and understand, as if it were a long argument going on.

'What's the Stone Age got to do with it?' Scott demanded.

'Why go down on your knees in this day and age in some dark cave simply because our ancestors were half-beasts who were afraid of the dark . . .'

'It was a wedding,' Scott said. 'You're taking it too seriously.'

'*I* don't. You do. God was probably the only possible explanation of life for the tribes of Israel, but he isn't mine.'

'But the religious part of it wasn't important.'

'Some people don't like going to lunatic asylums,' Quartermain went on, arguing insistently. 'I don't like going to religion. They both poke

o* 393

around in the same dark recesses of the mind to no purpose, as far as I'm concerned, and I don't want to have recourse to it. I won't even contribute to it. I certainly don't want to throw my children into the snake-pit with the lunatics and the priests.'

'You're a lunatic, my darling,' his wife said.

Quartermain looked as if he would argue, he was in an argumentative mood. Scott watched husband and wife regretfully to find out how much of it was a real dispute. He could not tell. He hoped it was not real. There was always battle in Quartermain's grey face and in his sharp eyes and in his dry complaining moustache. But what had changed him from the man who had never taken anything seriously into this one who might be taking everything in deadly earnest? You couldn't quite tell, either. Almost a month with him had revealed nothing to Scott. He knew very little of this Quartermain who was ready for argument with anyone, yet not quite seriously. He must have his reasons; but who knew what they were?

'Everybody must dance,' Sam was insisting.

It was quite correct to be gay now, and Sam's gaiety came in large gusts. He sang songs dragged up from the deep of some ocean with the Greeks, who had also been sailors on the onion boats, briefly, with Sam in his very young days.

'Here,' Sam said, bringing Helen Mamoon to Scott. 'Dance.'

'I'm no good at it,' Scott panicked. 'I can't dance at all.'

'That doesn't matter,' Sam insisted. 'Go on.'

Scott folded up his black skull-cap with a careful man's care, but his flushed cheek had suddenly changed the man. He was apologetic. Was Helen Mamoon willing to forgive him? She watched him calmly. The relatives were dancing, the Greeks were drinking Greek brandy, the cantor sang, and Ali Zareef was relieved to be talking Arabic to Nona Mamoon who coquetted him gently: '*La-a ya*, Captain!' Zareef blushed. There were no responsibilities left.

'Why don't we go into the garden?' Helen offered Scott.

'All right,' he said thankfully.

He needed Felu. 'Felu, Felu, Felu,' he called elaborately in the garden.

'Is that silly tortoise still alive?' Helen asked indignantly.

'Felu goes on for ever,' Scott said.

How hard the garden paths were in years of stamping down the dust, of neglect. The old lawn was dusty, the dusty mangoes were too high to be useful, and the spidery tree they called a pine was simply a dust scatterer, even when there was no breeze to waft over it. A minah or a flock of fussy sparrows shook the scraggy needles and down came the Egyptian dust of ten years, twenty years, a few lifetimes.

'I think if we all blew to pieces tomorrow,' Scott said as Felu came boldly across the path, 'the dust and Felu would still be here.'

394

'Does she really come because you call?'

'No. She comes because we tap this shell under the water-tap. It used to be Aunt Clothilde's way of announcing her dinner-time.'

It was almost evening, it was cool enough to sit on the rickety cane-chairs and listen to the summer day fading away: the birds began to cluster in all the gardens about, and the haze of eventide deadened the street sounds outside, which seemed to thin out as the light thinned, or darken as the light darkened. The sky turned yellow and faded pink, then washed down to a pale grey, and a donkey braying seemed to do likewise: a strange muffled protest. 'Must be the moisture beginning to precipitate off the ground already,' he decided. The air seemed dead. 'It's amazing,' he thought, 'how quickly the condensation begins out here.'

'You're very quiet,' she said. 'Do you like to keep so quiet, or is it something the matter with me?'

'No, no!' he apologized. 'I've had too much of that Greek wine, I think.'

'Captain Scott!' Helen Mamoon said in the firm voice of a woman determined to admit a mistake, although not yet willing to give in. 'Why did they release Sam? Do you know why?'

He was surprised but not bothered by it. 'Why shouldn't they?' he answered. 'Sam had done nothing terribly wrong.'

'Do you believe that?'

'Not quite. But he's out. That's what matters, isn't it?'

'I wonder if it does,' she said thoughtfully, as if she had given it some thought and must discuss it. 'Don't you think they may be playing a trick with him? They may have let him out of prison to see what he does, so that they can catch him and put him back in again, only worse.'

'Catch him at what?'

'I don't know,' she said. 'Don't you know? Isn't that why you wrote to me?'

He had the feeling that he was being interviewed. It was her upright manner, as if she had won her world by interviews, or held the family together by them or won her passport with them. There was always someone who must be talked to, approached, pinned down. She was pinning him down now.

'If Sam did something the Egyptians dislike, I don't want to know what it is,' he told her quickly. 'He must have had his reasons. To begin with, he's stateless.'

'I don't need to be reminded of that,' Helen told him. 'I've been breaking my heart for years to get Sam an Egyptian passport. That's how all this trouble started.'

He knew that could mean many things; but it seemed to mean that she

395

knew what Sam had done. She was even tempting him to ask, as if she were willing (perhaps anxious) to tell him. But he would not ask her. Nor did she mention Sam's father, although he was afraid now that she had wanted to face him with that. If she did, how could he defend himself against it?

'Do you *think* they will arrest Sam again?' she went on.

He doubted it. 'Once they've let him out . . .'

'But you don't really know.'

'How could I know? They don't tell me.'

'I thought you understood these people,' she said. 'What they are doing.'

He got up impatiently, but she remained sitting, so he sat down again. 'I don't understand any of it, frankly. Lately I've given up trying to. I think I'm about ready to give it all up and get out myself. You see . . .' He had told nobody this because it was not quite sure, not quite settled in his own mind, and he didn't know why he should suddenly tell it to her: 'I'm thinking of leaving Egypt.'

'But I thought you were a Nasser man?' she said simply.

'Perhaps I am. But I'm not much use here now.'

'Don't they want you either? Do you mean they are making it difficult for you too, because of all this talk about the British and the French wanting to take the canal back?'

'It's not that.'

She waited, but he could not tell her what it was. There was nothing more he could say. He could have this same argument every moment of the day and still get no further with it.

What had decided him? He did not know. What had cut him off? He did not know. He could easily blame Hakim for trying to involve him in their dirty business, but it wasn't that. How could he tell her that Egypt was gradually slipping away from him? Perhaps the desert had sucked him dry. Perhaps his own restraint had finally ruined his best emotions. Furthermore, he could never sit in this garden without thinking of Gamal's achievements and his own failures. He could look up and see where the young Egyptian Lieutenant had once frightened Felu in the morning. By the same evening Lieutenant Gamal had shot Husein Amer Pasaha and was a different man, already solving a difficult human problem.

But she was asking his help now, and that was really what she wanted of him. 'What I wanted to ask you about Sam is . . .'

'I'll go on doing what I can,' he interrupted hastily. 'Sam will be all right.'

'Not that,' she said. 'I wanted to ask you to get Sam out of Egypt.'

Dark eyes were normal in Egypt, but Helen Mamoon's unblinking, confident, shaitan eyes were unique. When they wanted something they seemed to put you down and hold you down. Deny her if you could.

'I doubt if Sam wants to leave Egypt,' he replied.

'But he ought to leave Egypt, Captain Scott. He's married now. He's happy. Wouldn't it be terrible if they arrested him again? And I *know* it's not over.'

'Where could he go?' Scott asked.

'That's where I thought you might help,' she said. 'If we can get him out of Egypt, at least he'll be safe. You can feel everything worsening every day now, since the canal was nationalized.'

'But he has no papers, no passport.'

'Thanks to the British,' she said with calm bitterness.

'I can't help Sam with the British, you know that. I only wished I could.'

'Yesterday,' she told him, 'I wrote to Colonel Peacock. If he can get Sam into England, would you persuade Sam to go?'

'What could Sam do in England? He'd hate it there.'

'It would have to be England or Israel, nobody else would take him.'

'Israel?' Scott flushed angrily. 'That would be worse.'

'Oh, I know you hate Israel.'

'I don't,' he said, controlling his temper. 'I honestly don't. But what would Sam do there either? I know him too well to believe it.'

'Of course you hate Israel,' she insisted, also keeping calm. 'But I don't care about Israel one way or the other. I only care about Sam.'

'Why should Sam leave Egypt at all?' he said. 'Have you talked to him?'

'No. But all the Jews will have to leave,' she reminded him. 'Even I'll have to leave, even though I'm not Jewish and I'm as much an Egyptian as any Moslem. But now it's all Moslem or nothing. For being a Christian or a fraction of something else, and I suppose because of my links with the British, I shan't get work again, or even be sure that I'll be able to keep my Egyptian passport. My office is closing up. We'll all have to leave.'

'If you know you're Egyptian, why give in?'

'Because I still have a sister to support, and I can't do it here. Now that the company is closing up it will be the last job I'll ever get. The Egyptians are not going to give real work to a non-Moslem and a woman.'

'I suppose not,' he admitted. 'That's the pity of it.'

'And everyone knows I've worked all my life for the British.'

Everybody in Cairo also knew that Helen Mamoon had worked when women in Egypt did not work. He knew that. She also had a look in her eyes which claimed a great deal for women. In a country where women were still bundled up and hidden in black melayas or were decked out in plump silk finery with dark rich hair and oval faces and painted eyes, this

397

one had always been too noticeably different to escape notice. She behaved like a European and yet was clearly not one. Englishwomen had once walked the streets of Cairo trying hard to be memsahibs among the natives. What pale and spineless failures they had looked beside this one, who was well aware of herself but did not care what others thought of her.

'Why not try to stick it out here, anyway?' he said to her. 'It's your home. Where else could you be happy?'

He had coaxed Felu's head out and was stroking her reptilic jaws.

'I might ask you the same question,' she said. 'Why don't you stay?'

'Very simple. I'm not Egyptian, and I never can be.'

'You've spent most of your life here, which is almost the same thing.'

'I wish it were. Now I know it isn't the same thing.'

How could he reveal to her the jigsaw of a lost identity? Who was he? Why was he here? The only memories he had of any country, of any value, were probably the same as hers—of another time in Egypt which had been good for foreigners and for educated Egyptians like her. Nothing remained of it, excepting these same summer evenings, the same street sounds, and the same clattering, ragged, noisy habits which never changed because the people did not seem to change. But what had thirty years of it done with the rest of him? Delivered him to Church? To Hakim? Or to Peter Dukes the British agent who was slowly perishing with his back to the sun?—all of them at work in this dangerous and confusing and ruthless world of politics, fighting some last desperate battle over the bones of the past.

'It's not the same,' he said. 'You know how it has changed.' He spread his hands helplessly. 'I'm not a part of it any more, I suppose.'

The past had simply shifted the whole country away from under his feet, and only lately did he realize how lonely he was for that other Egypt, however much worse it was than the present one.

'What will you do when you go to England?' she asked him.

'I'm not sure. Perhaps I might go to France. I might then go to Antarctica with the Royal Geographical Society's expedition.'

She did not say that it would be exciting. 'Surely that will be worse than Egypt,' she told him. 'Ice and snow, and nothing else. Why that place?'

'Not much choice,' he said. 'I simply can't stay here much longer.'

'It seems so unfair . . .'

She was complaining on her own behalf as well as his, but what could she tell *him* of those happy years in Cairo offices when uniqueness was possible for a woman like her? Life had always seemed about to ripen in those pre-war days, waiting for something culminating to happen to it, some sort of fruition to youth. Now, at her age, it was slowly slipping away without fruition, and the mystery remained. Each day shrank; the city changed, life changed, time changed, the friends had gone, work was work and nothing more—no pride, no worthwhile sense of place, no pleasure in being what you had fought all religions and black customs to become.

'If only I'd been born a Moslem,' she was tempted to say now, in a second's misery. But if she had been born a Moslem she would probably have married a fat doctor or a lawyer like el Khony and lived a dull and silly life like el Khony's wife, ending up in the arms of an officer in sheer boredom.

'We seem to have something in common,' she said, recovering her sense of humour and standing up, because the music in the house had stopped and it would soon be time to go.

'What do you mean?' he asked her.

'We have lived our lives here at the same time,' she said, 'and now we have to face the same problem.'

'That's true,' he said, sorry that this brief encounter in the Cairo evening, on Sam's wedding day, was over—probably once and for all.

CHAPTER FIFTY-TWO

It was impossible not to be infected with the atmosphere of crisis in Cairo now. He was restless anyway. Hakim had told him to wait in Cairo, not to go back to *mons claudianus* yet.

'Something's afoot this time,' Hakim had told him on the phone after he had reported so negatively what he thought about Church and his tragedy, 'and we may need your help.'

Was it still Church he worried about now, or some new plot which he would uncover, in this fear that someone would try to kill Gamal Abd el Nasser?

'Why can't I wait in *mons claudianus*? I can get back to Cairo in a day if necessary. I want to finish my work there,' he had complained. He wanted to say to Hakim: 'Oh, come on, Hakim. Don't play about with me.' But what use was indignation here? Hakim would be only too delighted by it.

'Your work can wait,' Hakim was saying. 'Patience, *habibi*. It's all for a good reason. You'll understand some day soon. It's not yet so simple.' Hakim always had his mysterious phrases.

It seemed almost like an act of explosive anger and protest, therefore, to find himself in a shipping office, inquiring about a passage on any boat leaving Egypt for France or for Britain.

The Armenian shipping clerk, who was excitable and indignant, laughed: 'You'll be lucky, Captain. Have you seen the news today, this week? Look at that.'

He handed Scott an open copy of an American magazine which said that the Ministry of Defence in France had appointed General André Beaufre—an expert on airborne operations—to command a new Mediterranean force which was being built up outside Paris, while armour and paratroop forces were massing in Algeria.

'And look at *that*,' the clerk said, amazed, jabbing a finger on another item, as if this was what Scott had come into a shipping office for; or per-

haps it was all proof that the shipping company could not be held responsible for the world. 'If *that* happens, there'll be a very big war. If the
Russians come here . . .'

He was obviously terrified of Mr. Kruschev's warning that the Arabs
would not stand alone, and that if the Arabs fought, it would be a just war
against imperialism and there would be Russian volunteers in it.

'Volunteers!' the clerk moaned. 'Whole Russian divisions, he means.'
He knew Scott by sight. 'Then it will be awful, don't you think, Captain
Scott? Is that why you want to go away also? Even you?'

'Not at all,' Scott said sharply. 'I don't believe any of it. Is it possible
to get a passage—or several rather—to France, that's all I would like to
know.'

'There's the Egyptian ship, the *Mahroussa*, sailing in eight weeks' time.
If you pay a ten per cent deposit now I can get you two or three berths on
that, I think.'

'How late can I leave it?' Scott asked him, already made nervous,
infected with Armenian panic, and ready to book immediately under the
influence of this excitable Armenian face.

'Not too long, please, Captain. Not too long. It is only possible now
because exit permits are hard to get, but in a week . . .' He threw up his
hands as if the whole situation would explode wide open in a week's time.
'And your passport, what about that?'

'When will you want it?'

'Two weeks before sailing date, but you must have an exit permit when
you pay your deposit, otherwise we can't book. Eh? We can't book without
an exit permit.'

'All right,' Scott said defensively, promising everything as if it were
settled.

'I'll be expecting you.'

The clerk seemed to have settled it for him. Obviously he must go
through with it now. No doubt about it. It was urgent. Those flying hands
made it imperative. And money? Money had such decision in it. Once he
paid his deposit he knew it would be irrevocable. He had not paid any yet
so he fled from this infectious clerk as quickly as he could.

'All you have to do,' he told himself cynically, 'is to get an exit visa out
of Hakim.'

But at least it seemed settled, if Françoise could be persuaded. Although he still had no idea what had made the final decision for him; only
those flying Armenian hands—up in the air like that. An explosion in a
week's time.

'I wonder how she'll feel, the day she definitely decides to leave?' he
asked himself.

He was not thinking of Françoise, but of Helen Mamoon, because she

401

would probably feel the way he did—walking now down Soliman Pasha with new eyes, the eyes of farewell, a farewell without a heart in it.

Every jingling sound and face told him it was wrong.

'Most likely she'll feel it even more than I do,' he decided. 'But how can I ever leave? How?'

He could already dread, also, the sort of reception he could expect in England. And, in any case (he told himself hopefully), it was by no means sure, despite Peacock's letters, that the antarctic committee of the Geophysical Year would have him on their expedition.

He stopped for a moment and bought a half-piastre's worth of *dora* from a street seller who wrapped the roasted maize in fresh green leaves from his hand-cart, shouting: 'Ya dura neely, ya mashwiyya; Zei el ssal hilwa tariyya; Yalli zabainik matu fiyya; Bahawaat wi affandiyya.'

'May your blessings be increased,' Scott said to him, a work-a-day thank-you in Egyptian.

'And yours tenfold,' the old man replied, a little surprised.

It was usual to take the corn and go without a word. Scott felt a little foolish and sentimental. He remembered that this old man had looked old twenty years ago, and he was still here.

'Oh, Nile dora,' he went on singing in his nasal voice, 'Oh, roast dora. Like honey, you are so sweet and tender. All the clients are dead set on me. Beys and effendis alike. Ya Dora Ni—eee-lll.'

On he sang throughout a lifetime, the same few words over and over again.

He went, the next day, to Leo Lieberman. Leo had not asked him to help his brother Phillip, who was still under arrest, and Scott did not want to offer help. He wanted to talk about Françoise. Something had to be done. Françoise ought to leave. It was true now, there might be violence. But he had no means of actually deciding her departure, any more than he could seriously finalize his own.

'Am I panicking like the rest of them?' he asked himself.

It was nothing to do with panic. Although everybody felt the mounting tension, Françoise herself was living with it in that important corner building where she could watch the ships putting their noses south and waiting in long queues for the canal pilots, who did not come. The French and English pilots had already left. Hakim had failed to persuade them to stay, because the Suez Canal Company in Paris had offered them much more money if they would stick by the company, which they had done, and the canal was temporarily at a standstill. Françoise must be quivering in local fears for herself, her children, her job, and her future.

Perhaps Leo would decide what would be best for her.

Leo begged his pardon for not getting up. 'These days,' he said, 'I get wedged down like a piece of wood. I can't get up because it takes me five minutes of massage to return my legs to flesh.'

Scott was not embarrassed by it. He already felt that Leo had less sense of self-pity than any man he had ever known. He remained heavily anchored in his thick chair behind the desk, backed by a big safe, in his jeweller's shop in Emad el Dine. He worked here in the decor that he and Françoise had admired in the French magazines. Stacked in the safe behind him were large green ledgers, and Leo was working on one of them with a gold pencil.

'I'm not disturbing you?' Scott said. 'I could come back.'

'No. Sit down,' Leo said in his cheerful way. 'I'm hunting for all the genuine mistakes in our books, the sort that might look like cheating. Tax problems. They come after me so often these days. And because I don't cheat, and because I keep very honest books, they don't quite believe me.' He chuckled. 'They go over and over them.'

'That sounds as if it doesn't always pay to be honest,' Scott said, sitting in the only chair which seemed big enough for him.

'Oh, we're not all that honest. But if we are ever dishonest, we're certainly not going to do it by tricky book-keeping. That would be silly.'

'I thought it was better regulated now than it used to be—the tax demands.'

'You mean since Nasser came to power? It's better for them, but worse for us. It was very simple once. We always kept honest books, but we simply paid the inspectors a regular sum each month and got on with our business. Now we still keep honest books, and we still pay some of the inspectors, but they don't let us get on with our business. They make it very difficult for us. Although I can't blame them, because we deal mostly in gold or gold imports, or watches which cost Egypt hard currency, which they're getting short of. Particularly now.'

Scott realized why he liked Leo and could talk to him. He spoke the truth without resentment, and one had to believe every word Leo said in his thick, calm, German voice. It was the kind of calm, resourceful temperament he wished he had himself. He admired it, because discipline was not a necessity to it.

'Achmed,' Leo said in Arabic without looking anywhere in particular. 'Bring us two coffees and a little brandy.'

When Scott looked around to see where the servant was, Leo smiled.

'You can't see him,' he told Scott. 'Achmed sits in his own room through there, and looks in on me when someone comes, in case of thieves. Sometimes we get people in from the provinces whom we don't know. Once, one of them tried to hit me on the head and take away a tray of diamond rings I was showing him. After that Achmed and I thought it would be best if he watched.'

403

'What happens if someone does try to rob you?' Scott asked. 'Does Achmed have a pistol?'

'Oh, no. He simply slams and bolts that door. He has a lever.'

That was the door Scott had come in by. That would leave Leo locked in this room with a thief who might very well murder him.

Leo shrugged. 'I would talk him out of it.'

Leo was obviously so used to being locked in with death by now, that another version of it did not seem ridiculous. Was he still dying? He did not look worse, but day by day it seemed to happen. His legs were so much more useless now than they had been, and the relentless process of being eaten to death by disease was far advanced.

'Is there any news of your brother?' Scott asked him, which had not been his intention at all. But he felt sorry for Leo.

'Yes. He's being kept in a house near Cairo. That's all we know.'

'Why did they arrest him?'

Leo did not stop talking when Achmed came in with the coffee and the brandy, although he looked out of the open door once as if to see who else might be near.

'Apparently a Lebanese said that Phillip had paid him money to evade the currency laws. But how and for what reason they don't know.'

'Is it true?' Scott said, and then apologized. 'I don't mean that, exactly. What I mean is—why should the Lebanese have said that?'

Leo handed him the brandy. 'Perhaps there is some truth in it.'

Scott did not ask him why Phillip was evading the currency regulations. He knew why.

'It's never a wise thing to avoid the currency regulations,' Leo observed. 'The English are even stiffer about their laws than the Egyptians. But of course the English haven't got a refugee problem. My brother was really sent here to help. If he was avoiding the currency regulations it was a sort of deliberate risk he was taking. He was not doing it for himself.'

'Did he tell them that?'

Leo smiled. 'Phillip could hardly tell them that, because it would have involved others.' He was proud of his brother and his pride had probably kept his nerves intact. Wasn't racial noblesse a value worth paying for? Although there was also a hint that he did not agree with Phillip's activities.

'Phillip is a British subject,' Leo said. 'And as long as they don't accuse him of being a spy he will be all right. I don't think they will call him a spy.'

'But what's the punishment for trying to smuggle money out of Egypt? Surely it's just a fine?'

'Not any more. Too much of it is going on. Now they can give you a year in gaol or even two years. They gave another acquaintance of mine

404

thirteen months' prison for trying to board an aeroplane with five hundred English pounds in a tube of toothpaste, the silly idiot.'

'But Phillip is a British subject.'

'They are even stricter with foreigners now,' Leo said and shrugged. 'But that is better than being accused of spying. I don't think they'll accuse him of that. I don't think so.'

'I hope not,' Scott said. He knew he meant it, even though he did not like Phillip Lieberman and did not trust him. He still resented Phillip Lieberman for his interference over Sam. But that had been Françoise's attempt to educate him, and he could hardly blame the man entirely.

'I was talking to Françoise on the phone,' Leo told him. 'She said she will go to France to divorce Roberto. Did you know that?'

Scott nodded. 'I wondered if she was absolutely definite about going. That's what I came to see you about.'

'I would like to make it definite,' Leo said, eyeing Scott over his coffee, over the brandy, over the sympathies between them. 'But she is very difficult.'

'Did she say when she wanted to go?'

'Perhaps she is waiting for you to decide that for her,' Leo said.

'Is that what she said?'

'No, but I guess it, old man.'

That sounded like his brother Phillip, but in Leo's heavy accent it did not sound so bad, in fact it might be comforting.

'Can't she go to France alone?' Scott asked him. 'She doesn't tell me much, either. Is there someone she can go to?'

'Of course. I have a sister in Paris, her aunt. I can arrange all that, and her passage. I also have a cousin in Lyons who is a lawyer. He will help her. It shouldn't be difficult, unless Roberto Rolland himself turns up and makes trouble.'

'That's always possible,' Scott said. 'Don't you think?'

'Oh, yes, indeed it is. That boy Roberto has such a natural vanity about himself that he may make it difficult for Françoise whatever she does. But I hope not.'

'And you can arrange her passage when she wants to leave?' Scott asked.

'Yes. I'll try to hurry her now, because of the situation. But she is reluctant.' Leo shrugged. 'I don't know why.'

But Scott felt relieved. Leo would look after it. He did not have to make that decision yet—for himself or for Françoise; although it was obviously only a temporary relief.

'I don't suppose there's anything I can do about your brother,' he said, knowing that Leo would not ask, and knowing that he could not help.

'I don't think so. The British Embassy is doing everything it can. I know you helped Sam Hassoon out of trouble, but I don't honestly think you can help Phillip.'

405

'I'm afraid not,' Scott agreed.

'I think Françoise is all you need worry about,' Leo told him as they shook hands. 'Please let me know what you decide, or even what she decides. If you can persuade her to hurry, I'll arrange everything.'

But Scott knew already that he could decide nothing yet. He only knew that he could talk to Leo Lieberman more intimately than he could talk to anybody else. Why was that? They had met only two or three times. The only other person he felt like that about was Lucy Pickering, but he did not want to remind himself of Lucy now. That could be a most dangerous influence.

'Don't go near her,' he warned himself, even as he left Leo and even as the thought occurred to him—this uncontrollable desire to talk to her. Only to talk to her—he swore. He could not help it. He did need to see her.

He went to her hotel. Was Mrs. Lucy Pickering in—or even in Cairo? The porter looked at him and then shook his head as if it were a secret between them. No, Mrs. Pickering was still away; in Alexandria, he thought.

He walked out again, rescued by the sort of luck he did not like.

He was still tense with his own desire and weakness, and he sat down heavily in the Café and Bar Helio and ordered an aperitif, and he bought a newspaper to take his mind off himself.

The bootblack, one of the respectable boys and not the outcast, banged his brushes together to demand custom. Scott put his foot up and read the front page of the *Egyptian Gazette*.

How could you escape yourself in this world, he wondered, when you read what Sir Anthony Eden had told the British people the night before, over television and radio?

'Some people say,' Sir Anthony had declared, 'that Colonel Nasser has promised not to interfere with shipping passing through the canal. Why therefore don't we trust him? The answer is simple. Look at his record. Our quarrel is not with Egypt, still less with the Arab world. *It is with Colonel Nasser.*'

The boy slapped his shoe to change work from one foot to the other.

'No wonder Hakim thinks the way he does,' Scott said silently and indignantly to the Prime Minister, to the top of this bootblack's curly head. 'You prove his point for him. And that's the way to ruin the world.'

It seemed a very ominous thing for a Prime Minister to say. It also made a man feel very guilty in the face of Hakim's arguments. What could he ever say now when Hakim asked him to wait, to be patient, to be useful to help—because, Hakim said, there was this ever-present danger that someone might try to kill Gamal?

How could he ever argue with Hakim now?

406

CHAPTER FIFTY-THREE

WHILE he waited grimly for Hakim to utilize him, he helped Sam in the garden.

Sam had lost his temporary job. The Lebanese radio dealer had been trying to avoid import controls on his German radios by bringing them in illegally through the Lebanon. He had been using an insurance agency as a cover for the export of Egyptian pounds to Beirut in payment for his illegal imports. It was one of a thousand dangerous leaks in the Egyptian pound, and unwittingly Sam's presence in his shop had pointed authority towards him. They had caught him and closed him up, and Sam was out of work.

'But everybody in business in Egypt is doing something illegal,' Sam complained miserably to Scott, 'so nobody wants to give me a job, because they know the police will come around looking for me and discover them.'

'What about all your Greek friends?' Scott asked him.

'Ah, no!' Sam argued firmly. 'I don't intend to get them into trouble. One of my friends offered me a job remaking Army instruments, but if I go there the officials will start looking at his tax account, so why should I do that to him?'

It left Sam digging the garden at Madame Salz's where he now lived.

His gardening was a taste (almost a passion) which he had acquired during the worst days in the prison villa. Just to be out in that garden! Now he could indulge in its freedom, and he began to think of planting the same English roses under the banyans and the mangoes. 'That's all they need,' he said. 'Some shade, and plenty of manure, and insect spray. It's the midges that kill roses, not the weather.'

Sam was not afraid of getting down to peasant work to dabble in the mud. He had also taken to walking around the streets looking for the peasant gardeners in big villas, asking them questions about planting and seeding and watering. He had gone to the Botanical Gardens by the zoo, where he had sat down near the gardeners, offering cigarettes, to discover the secrets of pruning, manuring and plant-names from the barefooted

fellaheen who had generated themselves in this rich Nile silt for thousands
of years.

He now had a large scheme afoot for Madame Salz's back garden to
bloom in season with ranunculus, flags, zinnias, roses, daisies, lilies, and
perhaps a few exotic flowering shrubs if he could afford to buy them. He
had asked the peasant gardeners for a clipping or two from the Botanical
Gardens selection, but they had laughed and refused. It was strictly forbidden. But Sam knew that he could go back when he wanted them, give
Ali or Mohamed or Said five piastres each, and get what he wanted. They
were already his friends.

Becky had gone on working after marriage, in the department store,
which was disappointing to Sam, although she did not mind. But it was
encouraging to hear Sam explain the future of their back garden to Becky,
to see her delighted and amused interest, her eyes naïvely teasing her
husband with a sort of love-lorn disbelief and admiration mixed. She was
in love with his solemn plans, and in love with his solemn love. She walked
with him in the dry old garden before breakfast while he explained how he
would remake it, and her upward looks made tender fun around each
word, each idea, each hope; but she never let him fear anyone else's
ridicule. Oh, no. That would have been cruel, and anyway it was all a
loving sideline to his manly strength, of which she was already very proud.

But Sam also had his own means of persuasion.

Scott found himself actually digging along the back mud-wall of the
n in a pre-breakfast late summer's morn, with his shirt off, while
Madame Salz looked out of the upstairs balcony window and admired their
massive backs, their golden skins, their strength.

She was happily but respectably in love with both of them. She noticed
that Sam's skin was whiter than Scott's because Sam usually kept his
shirt on (or at least his vest) when he worked outside, whereas Scott had
been burned through vest, shirt and all else, and he emanated bronze knots
of muscles as he bent over the dirt. She could not understand how Scott
had escaped marriage. She thought briefly that she must do something
about it, and began to think of cousins. There were always cousins. But it
was well known that Scott was in love with the local Lieberman girl who
had married a Frenchman who had deserted her. What was the point to
that?

'You should have been married long ago with six children.'

She had coquetted Scott one night when she had caught him talking to
one of her new boarders—an Italian, a Rabinowitz girl who had married a
small merchant in Alexandria who was a distant relative of Madame
Salz's. She had come to Cairo to be near her sick mother. She could not
live in the mother's house because two other brothers and sisters were
already there, and they could not tolerate children because the mother

408

was mad, off her head completely. So Madame Salz had reduced the rent and put the girl in the upstairs room with her baby who was four, and quite pretty but badly dressed. She had caught Scott talking to mother and daughter on the way home along the hot, dusty street, the little girl clinging tiredly to Scott who had carried her from the bus stop. Scott must be the only Englishman in Cairo who did not own a car, and though it seemed silly that he should take the bus into Cairo when he could easily afford a small car, she admired his frugality and wondered what woman would eventually enjoy the prospects he offered.

Would the Lieberman girl ever divorce the Frenchman and marry him? Some people said she was doing so already, but nobody knew. With her rich cousin Leo Lieberman in trouble, and the other one arrested, it would be difficult for her to leave Egypt. But everybody said that the English were going to come back to Egypt and everybody wanted them back. Then all these difficulties would be solved, even her own. In the meantime, Captain Scott ought to get married and have children and never mind the Lieberman girl. That was a waste.

'I'll wait for Sam and Becky's children,' Scott had said in reply to her little joke.

'La! A ce moment je deviendrai grandmère,' she protested.

'That's very nice too,' he said, enjoying their respectful counter-play about parenthood and love and age and match-making.

She had thought about Scott for a long time. 'Honnêteté!' she decided was his real value, and *gentillesse* too.

She looked out and watched him digging the mud with her son-in-law and she wondered what they talked about. She admired their friendship; but why didn't they let a barefooted Egyptian dig up the garden? It would only cost them a few piastres.

CHAPTER FIFTY-FOUR

THIS time it was Peter Dukes who wanted to see Scott, and he came to the *pension* when the sun was still up.

'I told you I'd come,' he said.

Scott had ignored repeated telephone messages that Mr. Dukes wanted to see him urgently. Scott had other reasons to be occupied, trying not to think of Hakim and working over the last survey he had ever made of Wadi Kerim below Kusseir, which he had corrected for the Survey several times already. But Survey had also found him, and they had asked him to check it again, because they had decided to try, some day soon, to exploit the magnetic ore which was deposited there in large quantities. He had been sure, so far, that they would never get the silica out of it economi-cally, because it was twenty-five per cent of the content, unless they used a more advanced process than those available in Egypt. He had already spoken with the mining engineers about it, and they thought that the Russians or the Americans would help, if the Council of Production agreed. Anyway, it was worth trying, he thought, even though the geologists' own maps had been so narrow in their self-interest that all of it would have to be re-done.

'Yes,' Peter said. 'The mountain comes to Mohammed.'

Madame Salz had brought him up and Scott had opened the door, dressed in trousers and singlet in the late but hot afternoon for this indoor concentration over his gritty maps and notes.

'Come in,' Scott said, embarrassed to see Peter Dukes at all, taking off his spectacles.

He began apologizing for not coming to see Peter Dukes, realizing what an effort Peter must have made to come out here with the sun still up— that burning pain still in the sky.

'Don't apologize,' Peter said. 'I didn't expect you to come to me. I sup-pose you thought when I telephoned that I wanted something of you. Well, even if I had, you might have paid me a friendly call.'

Scott felt rude and cruel. Peter was dressed in fresh white trousers and shirt, so well starched that they crackled when he moved, although it sounded more like the creaking of his thin body. His arms were sticks. He was growing older every day now, but he was in a cheerful mood.

'I came to do something for you,' Peter told him.

Scott put on his shirt and made sure that the shutters were closed sufficiently for Peter Dukes's comfort, although Peter waved his hand to say it didn't matter. He looked unashamedly at Scott's maps, at his room, at the photographs of a schoolboy Scott standing with his mother and father against a bougainvillaea wall of the house in Matarieh, each one of them squinting into the sun. His mother and father were both wearing tussore dustcoats.

'How old were you there?' Peter asked him.

'About seven or eight, I suppose,' Scott said, glancing at it.

'Just a grinning schoolboy.' Peter laughed. Scott the schoolboy was not grinning. He was looking serious and selfconscious. 'I'd hate to be re-minded of my boyhood,' Peter said. 'It was all so full of doing what I didn't want to do.'

'I keep that one to remind me of a picnic we had that day,' Scott told him. 'We had just arrived in Egypt.'

'To the pyramids, no doubt.'

'No. To the Barrage. I fell in the Nile from one of the locks. My mother thought I was drowned. Then she was afraid that I'd get bilharzia from the mud when I scrambled out. My father thought it very funny and gave me that dustcoat he's wearing, because he refused to go home and spoil a good picnic, and anyway he was inspecting the water levels.'

'Your old man was a strange character,' Peter told him. 'I don't think I ever saw your mother. She must have kept very much to herself.'

Scott did not say that his mother had died within a few months of the photograph and the picnic, nor that the photograph reminded him of his grief rather than his happiness. Why did he keep it, when he hardly glanced at it any more? He could not think of the reasons any more. He only remembered now that grief was always the price of love, because you could never have one (even in a family sense) without the other. Sentimen-tality aside, the most painful thing that had ever happened to him was the death of his mother, when he was still a boy but old enough to feel what it meant. He remembered the disbelief, and the end of boyhood. His mother's death had wiped out all that went before it, his entire boyhood existence, and he had understood then that emotionally a man must stand alone. It was therefore never wise to trust anything emotional too far, it was too easily snatched away by death, or by betrayal, or by confusion. And even the emotional memory itself died eventually. His only view of his mother now was a series of sharp outlines, which were quite clear but really no more than sad snapshots of a small woman at a kitchen table,

411

unlatching a back door, baking currant scones, holding a pair of pruning scissors, and her daily refusal to lie down in the heat. Lying down in the daytime had seemed too indulgent. She had hated the barrenness and the heat; she had hated the things in Egypt which he was now wondering if he could do without.

'And that's Pickering,' Peter said dryly, watching him closely.

That was another photograph—of all his dead companions in the desert.

'I was only wondering the other day,' Peter went on thoughtfully, 'what would have happened to you if you had never met that crank, Pickering.'

'He wasn't such a crank,' Scott said, wondering why Peter had disliked Pickering so intensely, even his memory. 'You didn't know him, did you?'

'I didn't have to know him,' Peter said. 'But every man who ever served with him during the war was left with bits of Pickering stuck to him. And I suspect he left more of himself on you than on anybody else. You shouldn't have been so gullible, Scott. He was just a crank.'

Scott took no notice of the insult. He knew that Madame Salz would soon bring tea with bread and slightly rancid butter—her enthusiastic service for the arrival of a friend. She would be pleased for his sake, and he did not want to disappoint her by arguing with Peter Dukes now.

'I suppose there was some reason for all that admiration of Pickering,' Peter went on reminiscently, 'though God knows what it was. Anyway, he's thoroughly dead now,' Peter decided, satisfied.

But Peter's rather coarse voice was almost muffled with a wistful air of resentment. Perhaps Peter had also wanted to be admired. Men had probably liked him, but they certainly had never admired him; and now at his age he was aware of Scott's pity rather than of any real respect, and perhaps a man of his age wanted respect above all else. Peter took out a long cigarette holder and fitted a cigarette into it with his parchment fingers and said something so calmly and obscenely about Pickering that any frustration about being admired was thus disposed of.

'But he left us Mrs. Lucy Pickering,' Peter added casually. 'And she's still Mrs. Pickering, I notice.'

When Scott refused to be goaded or insulted, Peter laughed.

'Don't worry, Scott. I didn't come out here to tease you,' he said. 'I came to warn you . . .'

Madame Salz arrived with the tea. She turned the light on.

'Why are you sitting in the dark?' she asked.

Scott was sitting on the window-sill with his feet on an old trunk, and Peter Dukes sat at Scott's desk going through the mysteries of a pile of rough sketch-maps and a host of neat figures tabulated carefully on a large white board. He picked up a slide-rule and shook his head over it when Madame Salz went out.

'You know, it's impossible for a man who uses a slide-rule ever to understand politics,' he said, still making his point. 'There's something in the approach to one which excludes the other. Mathematics, for instance, are ruled by logical sequences. Isn't that so?'

'More or less.'

'Whereas politics are the result of illogical contradictions. That's why people like you are duffers when you start dividing up your loyalties. It's an illogical impossibility for you. You get into a mess, and then you want a simple formula to solve everything. And when you can't find it—all becomes blackness. Well, there isn't any simple formula . . .'

'I know that,' Scott agreed. 'Do you want tea?'

'Very weak,' Peter said. He took out a little box of saccharine tablets and dropped two into the cup Scott had poured for him. When Scott told him to help himself to the bread he shook his head and said, 'I seem to have developed an allergy to bread lately. I don't know why.'

'That's bad luck,' Scott said sympathetically.

Peter was still inspecting him and he smiled a little. 'Well,' he said, 'since you obviously won't ask me why I came, perhaps I'd better tell you. Are you interested?'

'Of course.'

'I'm really doing you and your friend a favour.'

Had Scott heard, he went on, that last night the Egyptian police had arrested two well-known local Englishmen and eight or nine Egyptians as British spies? One of them was Jamie Swinburne who ran the Arab News Agency, and the other was Pittuch who was something-or-other in the Marconi Radio. The Egyptians didn't matter.

'How could I avoid hearing about it?' Scott said. 'Everybody knows.'

'I suppose it worries you.'

'No. I don't even know them.'

'It ought to worry you,' Peter said sharply. 'What about your friend Sam Hassoon?'

'Don't tell me that all this is something to do with Sam, because . . .'

'I didn't say that, did I? It's nothing to do with Sam Hassoon. Furthermore, I doubt if either Swinburne or Pittuch are anything like spies. There are plenty of people floating around Cairo whom the Egyptians could justifiably arrest as British agents, but they seem to have picked the wrong men. In fact, you ought to tell them so for me.'

'Is that the favour?'

'No. It's nothing to do with that. If the Egyptians want to arrest two casual bystanders, that's their problem. What your friends don't know is that the real effort hasn't yet been made.'

'What effort?'

'Somebody,' Peter said, 'is about to knock-off Nasser, if they can.'

413

Scott let it remain a calm conversation. 'How do you know?' he asked.

Peter was delighted with the question. 'If I answered that, Scott, I'd probably be arrested myself as a British spy.'

'Then what do you want me to do?' Scott asked irritably. 'Convince the Egyptians of something you're saying—just like that?'

Peter used his saucer as an ash-tray and said he would try to explain it.

'If you knew anything about politics, you'd know that there's a real political point to killing Nasser just now. The canal trouble has made it really worthwhile, and timely too.'

'Worthwhile for whom?' Scott demanded. 'Do they want Nasser, or do they want the canal?'

'Both,' Peter answered.

'Killing Gamal Abd el Nasser wouldn't change anything.'

Peter shrugged. 'Some people seriously believe that if Nasser disappears the whole regime will collapse. In comes Neguib, or somebody like that, and the canal comes back to us. It's not talk, it's a serious policy. It's a stupid one, but that doesn't make it less dangerous.'

'You told me something like that before,' Scott reminded him.

'Did I?' Peter answered complacently. 'Then I'm telling you again, because within the next week or so, someone is sure to kill Nasser if he can.'

'But who is? How do you know?'

'Perhaps I don't know, for sure. But I do know the symptoms for sure.'

'Am I supposed to tell the Egyptians the symptoms? What on earth are you suggesting?' It was Scott's turn now to inspect his visitor very closely, but he could not see him well enough in this light, not enough to see what the colourless face or the hidden mind registered.

'If I knew the details, I'd tell the Egyptians myself,' Peter said patiently. 'Don't get bothered. I thought I ought to tell you, because it's becoming a nuisance. It's absolutely against logic, what is happening, and it ought to be stopped.'

'I don't see why you come to me with it.'

'All I can tell you, Scott, is that Bateman and your friend Lucy Pickering keep on seeing the wrong people. It's very foolish of them, and they have been behaving very badly. Something is sure to happen. Bateman has already got his exit visa on a diplomatic passport, and your friend Mrs. Pickering is in Alexandria talking to Church. She is also very anxious to leave, they tell me.'

'All the English are anxious to leave Egypt,' Scott pointed out. 'They all expect a war.'

'That's not why Bateman and Lucy Pickering are leaving. Believe me, they know something. You ought to grasp that.'

'How can I? What sort of proof are you offering me?'

'None, old chap, except that I *know*. You warn Hakim about it. That's all I'm suggesting. He can do the rest.'

'But warn Hakim of what?' Scott said, exasperated now. 'That Bateman and Lucy Pickering are leaving Egypt? He probably knows that.'

'Then tell him what you like,' Peter said with a shrug, 'but tell him.'

Scott longed for space now, and for daylight; not this shuttered intimacy which Peter lived his weird life in, and infected others with. It became real. It was real now, and he looked out of the crack in the shutters to watch Sam replastering the old garden wall with fresh mud from the garden.

'You don't think much of Nasser yourself,' Scott reminded Peter suspiciously. 'So how can I know that you're not playing some game yourself?'

'I don't think much of anybody,' Peter agreed. 'But for me Nasser isn't much of an issue, not yet. It isn't even the Suez Canal. Oh, let him have the canal. The funny thing is, though, you're the man who works for the Egyptians, not me. You're the man who sticks by them, not me. If you thought Gamal Abd el Nasser was right when he threw out the British, why do you quibble now? I don't understand you. If you want to do your stuff by the Egyptians, then do it! Don't fiddle about with it. Are you going to worry about a bitch like Lucy Pickering when something more important is at stake? What are your values, anyway, I'd like to know? Eh? Don't you care any more what happens here?'

Scott took his punishment in silence, and Peter was already putting out his cigarette in the saucer and standing up and leaving, apparently in disgust.

'Well?' Peter said finally at the door. 'What about it?'

'I don't know,' Scott said. 'You're too clever for me.'

'Do you think I'd come out here to have a little joke with you—and at my own expense? Don't you think it's serious?'

'I'm sure it is.'

'Then let me give you a little more advice. Everybody knows that Gamal Abd el Nasser goes swimming on Fridays. Today is Sunday. That gives you about a week.'

'Why are you telling me that?'

'Let's say I'm only guessing. Or let's say that I know you don't want to see your friend Nasser dead. Perhaps I don't want to see him dead either, because if anybody kills him now it will take away the only man who will ever be any good to us, in the long run, in this part of the world. If only those silly bloody idiots in London could realize it . . .'

'I CAN'T wait much longer,' Quartermain warned Helen when they sat alone in her office, where he had come to see her outside all the family temper. 'Nona won't leave without you. But I'll have to book your passage now. There's a queue of people trying to get passage out of Egypt. They're all talking in London about the canal, but they won't talk for long and I don't want to leave it too late for the children.'

'I know she worries about Hanna and me,' Helen said. 'But she can't help that.'

'I'm not blaming her,' he told her. 'But do you want to leave Egypt, Helen? Have you made up your mind?'

'I intend to leave,' she said, 'even for a holiday. What else can I do? It's becoming too stupid and unpleasant now—too much like a prison. I feel it every day. Even the street urchins outside our flat are beginning to behave the way they do when somebody has been getting at them.'

'Then why don't you do something about it?'

'I can't get exit visas,' she told him. 'I've already tried through Makram at the Ministry, but no Egyptian is allowed to leave Egypt.'

He sat down, disconsolate. That was the first he had heard of this problem.

'Why didn't you tell Nona that?' he asked. 'She blames me, you know.'

'I didn't want to worry her and Hanna.'

'But she punishes me for it,' he complained. He got up again restlessly and said he ought to book passages for them anyway, whether they had exit visas or not.

'I've already tried,' she said, trying to calm him by speaking calmly. 'They'll do it for British subjects, but not for Egyptians. I got Jolley's passage straight away, but I have a friend in the travel agency who told me that it was impossible even to book a place for an Egyptian.'

'Nona won't go without you, or until she knows you can get out somehow.'

'I know,' she said. 'I've tried to talk to her. But what can I do?'

They were like business partners who kept to business and kept personal likes and dislikes out of it. But they were limited by the shadow of Nona, who could not be betrayed by either of them, though for different reasons. And Nona was right.

'Can't you bribe someone in the travel agency to hold two places on a ship for you?' he asked.

She shrugged. 'They're too afraid. And they want ten per cent down, anyway.'

'I have a little money now,' he said. 'I've been writing a despatch a day.'

'I have enough money,' she said. 'You go ahead and book for Nona and the boys.'

'I've already done it,' he said. 'But what's the use of that if she won't go without you?'

'She'll go when the time comes,' Helen assured him. 'Don't worry. It's the children she will always be most worried about.'

Helen felt the coldness and the difficulty between Nona and Quartermain overflowing into his better nature. He acted as if Nona's loyalty to her sisters was a closure against him, particularly when he tried to make the decision for all of them. Nona had always felt resentful that the world had given nothing to her sisters, therefore her family demands on their behalf were probably being overstated too loudly and too clearly. But surely he could forgive Nona for that, and understand it.

'I don't know what I can do about the tickets though,' she told him.

'Neither do I,' he said and left her with a helpless, dried-up shrug.

She had not told him that she must also worry about Sam. She would not leave Sam to the reckless mercies of the Egyptian police; Sam without papers, and Sam unable to look after himself in the crush of events which might imprison him again and punish him, and Sam who was still guilty.

'First things first,' she decided and thought of Hanna and Nona and the children: the children must come first.

She went immediately, fired with the need, to the Ministry to see her second cousin on her mother's side, Makram, who had once wanted to marry her, but had been forbidden to do so because she was poor and dowryless. He had married the daughter of a rich neighbour instead, who brought in enough cash by her dowry for his father and brother to build a new and expensive pumping-house on their land in upper Egypt where they were the principal family of a town, of an estate, for which his brother had been the deputy in the old house of parliament.

'My dear! My dear, dear Helen!' Makram said enthusiastically.

He was a likeable man who clowned unconsciously, and he could mimic the world. He sat in his office at the Ministry looking as important and forbidding as his large eyes and funny, bird-like movements permitted.

'You look so well, Makram,' she told him.

'Do I?' he said. 'I swim every morning now with Gamal Abd el Nasser at the pool. I see him every day.'

He didn't. Makram was a Copt, and no Copt was that close to Nasser.

'I am training under Mohamed Ahwaz who won the Olympic back-stroke in 1933,' Makram said, with his large eyes proving it to her. 'He thinks I'm very good.'

'Oh, Makram,' she said. 'At your age you'll damage your heart.'

'But I'm fit,' he insisted. He was. It was nice to see a healthy face and a cheerful one, a *punchinello* perhaps but the most generous and innocently unconvincing man in her life.

They went to sit in Groppi's garden. The place was full of German tourists in green suits and she wondered if these fat, shameless men were the same ones the British had fought to keep out of Egypt. Nona would say: 'What would have been the difference between the Germans and the English, anyway?' She didn't really believe it. But to see the Germans sitting in their tourists' clothes, with their tourist wives and their horrible talk—it was unpleasant. She considered them all murderers of Jews and Poles and Russians and how many other millions of innocents? Did they have no shame?

'But I can't tell them apart from the English,' Makram said. 'Are they Germans?'

He had been educated in France, not England. His attitude to the English was usually a funny imitation of Winston Churchill hopping around the room like a bullfrog or a kangaroo with a cigar and a scowl and other things less polite, depending on the company.

In G'afra where Makram's brother now ran the estate, the family lived in two large French villas in a formal dusty garden by the river. Two servants sat in primitive sentry-boxes at the iron gateway, and the mud-walled town grew up behind them, and their fields wavered away along the Nile, a mysterious little continent of poor village life and hard peasant life which they had ruled and goaded into a diseased continuation—the sad ebb and flow of such an ancient people. She had once been made love to by Makram in one of the cotton sheds, and they had come home full of fleas, which seemed funny and not revolting. But within a month under pressure from his family and almost in tears he had married his neighbour and he had done his duty to his father, his brother, and his property.

Now it was like eventide in Groppi's, when the noise of the hot city was cooling down like a gently muffled drum. They drank tea.

'When will you come to see us at G'afra?' Makram begged her.

She never would. She was not supposed to. But they talked about their families, and remembered friends, and asked after children. Life flowed up to them again by the back door, which they opened, to look back on a pleasant relationship in an azure past. The front door of their lives led to places they did not want to look at together. Their ways were now different. The mistakes had already been made. Makram might still admire her, even prefer her to the country girl who had become a plump, white-faced wife; but all the habits of their different upbringing were against them in anything they tried to see of their present existence. She was a free and impoverished and lovely and educated woman. He was an un-free, under-developed man, firmly bound to the convention of his class and his wealth —however clownish he made it out to be. She could understand him quite easily and see herself in his eyes, but she knew he would never understand her.

But Makram had always helped her whenever he could.

'Can I get my exit permit?' she asked him. 'And Hanna's. Did they give it to you?'

He shook his head sadly. 'Not even *I* can get one for myself,' he told her. 'Gamal Abd el Nasser has said, personally, that nobody must leave Egypt now. If there is a war we will need everybody. We can't do anything about it.'

That must be true.

'Will you get me back my passport then?' she asked. 'And Hanna's *laissez-passer*?'

'Of course.'

'Can you do anything for Sam?'

'If only he had not been in trouble,' Makram said unhappily. 'Why didn't the British give him a passport?'

'You know why. They said he wasn't really in the British Army.'

'Pity!' Makram said, cocking his head with his bird-like look at life. 'But I'll keep trying, my dear. I swear I won't give up.'

He would try, innocently and with no particular thought of caution. He was fearless by childish exaggeration. Makram swore to his friends that he had been on the King's yacht, the *Mahrousa*, during the King's last hours in Egypt. He said he had been present when General Mohamed Neguib came aboard, and when Farouk made that equivocal and strange statement about the revolution which had just dethroned and exiled him: 'I would have done the same thing myself,' the King had said. Makram had once been all for the King and for the Parliament and for General Neguib, and now he was all for Gamal Abd el Nasser. He was always hopeful, and he still boasted naïvely of a world of influence which other men would have smothered in fear long ago.

'Come next week, my dear. I'll try to help Sam again,' he said and told his chauffeur to drive Helen home, and then to come straight back to the Ministry without stopping for coffee with all those friends of his in Boulac.

CHAPTER FIFTY-SIX

QUARTERMAIN did not know what to expect of these illegal Egyptian communists, who had put a note under his door apologizing for their failure to attend the rendezvous. Would he come again, to the same place on Thursday? They would be there; they would make themselves known. 'Can anybody be that naïve?' he asked himself.

He shook off any further suspicions of a trap and decided that he would be there, although he was doubtful now if he could ever believe in their serious communism, in that young man's communism, or this note-under-the-door communism, or of any communism in Egypt for that matter.

He remembered that during the war he had met the only Egyptian communists ever known to exist at that time, not among the peasants and workers of Egypt where they belonged, but on the top floor of the most luxurious block of flats in Cairo where a Frenchman had placed his intellect at the disposal of the Egyptian people with whom he had no contact, excepting theoretically and sympathetically from his penthouse. He was the son of a wealthy French father, and though he had devoted himself to the only cause which could save the Egyptians from the terrible misery they lived in, and paid for his cause with regular gaol sentences, he had kept his French intellect intact. A strange British officer, brought in casually from a nearby bookshop to see him (simply because he had been buying the right political and philosophical books), was too suspicious a subject to be treated seriously. Quartermain had been casually snubbed, and all the penthouse conversations of communism had continued in French without him.

That had been communism in Egypt during the war.

After the war, during Farouk's reign, during Nasser's, there was no apparent record of it, no history at all of communism, and Nona would say:

'How could Egyptian fellaheen be communists when they don't read or write, and can't even understand written Arabic?'

Who could turn an ignorant Egyptian peasant into a communist when the peasant had no idea at all of the simplest politics in life, never even hearing of alternatives to disease, poverty, death, and the soothing word of God?

There had been pre-war trade unions. But Helen Mamoon had told him too many stories of the poor lawyers in those days who had become the trade-union secretaries for the tramwaymen and the bus drivers and the factory workers. These men had been abject intellectual paupers who had simply wanted to enter politics or marry a rich politician's daughter. When they invited you to visit their houses, they offered you nothing more than a glass of water, not from poverty, Helen said, but from *meanness*. When Abdul Wahab (the textile machine-workers' president) had married a prosperous merchant's daughter they had refused to give the wedding guests more than a bowl of rice and five chickens among fifty people. That was one of Helen's jokes, because Abdul Wahab had eventually become a rich dealer in chickens himself. Where could communism take root in that sort of hopeless vacuum of the spirit which had characterized Egypt for so long, before Nasser, before Farouk even?

But he went to the café, hopeful anyway, sure that they would be there, these new Egyptian communists, whoever they were. What could they be?

It was not the young man who awaited him now at the Excelsior's cold table but a young girl and an old man who wore a tarboush, the Turkish headpiece which was now out of favour. The girl beckoned to him in the Egyptian way, not with the fingers curled upwards, but downwards. 'Come, come!' the gesture said to him.

'I'm Sophie Mourad,' she told him quietly. 'This is my friend, Mohamed Osman Pasha.'

Quartermain shook hands with them both and the waiter stood near while Sophie asked Quartermain what he wanted. Something to eat, perhaps? He said he would have a glass of orange juice for his daily vitamins.

From the moment he sat down the old man seemed to lose interest in him. He was stout and old and heavily Egyptian, a merchant or a doctor or a politician-Egyptian of the old school. His thick yellow walking-stick was almost a trade-mark for the old manipulators who had gathered every other week in the Assembly to argue volubly against each other, with no evil intent except to survive and prosper.

It was the girl who occupied him, until he had finished his orange juice.

He had been here long? she asked. Would he stay long? Was he going to write a book about Egypt? Had he travelled? Had he talked to Egyptians? Had he seen the peasants, or the new projects in the Liberation province?

421

He answered yes or no and studied the girl.

'I must be getting middle-aged,' he decided, admiring her chestnut eyes and her rich, loosely coiffured hair, the same colour exactly as the eyebrows and eyelashes and even the eyes themselves. She was as well dressed as the young man had been, and she was so young that he doubted if serious Egyptian politics could have already captured her so completely. But the impersonal way the girl treated him, and her natural innocence breathing out through her fresh ideas so freshly come-by were very convincing.

They left the Excelsior and got into Mohamed Osman Pasha's car and drove away into the outskirts of Cairo, and Quartermain had already forgotten that this might be a primitive trap to catch him conspiring with enemies of the new Egyptian republic.

'Where are we going?' he asked the girl.

'To find a friend,' the girl answered.

Friend seemed to be a very useful word among these people, he decided. It covered almost everybody.

He thought they were going to stop at one of the villas on the outskirts of Abassia, but they picked up a dark, short-sighted, round and jovial Egyptian from one of the buildings in the suburbs which looked like a laboratory.

'This is our Mr. Pickwick,' Sophie said in introduction.

'That's a joke,' the Egyptian said pleasantly.

His name was Rushdi and though he was dark-skinned he did have the naïve and benign appearance of Mr. Pickwick, even if it meant an Egyptian Pickwick.

They turned around and drove into Cairo again, into the back streets where the driver let them out at a printer's shop in the heart of Sayeda Zenab—the poorest section in the centre of the city where there were small hovels of workshops and lathes, panel-beating shops for dented cars, paint shops for metals, ramshackle garages, native laundries, and native provision shops with bags of dry beans stacked on their counters.

'This is where we print our newspaper,' Sophie told him.

He could hear the press smack-smacking on the flat-bed inside, but they went into a large, dingy office looking like a print shop anywhere, with its large glass window which was painted over, and the damp smell of proofs and ink and oil. Though it backed up to the press which was working inside on a dirt floor, the office was more or less self-contained, although it contained nobody at all.

'Sit down,' Sophie told him, 'and we will call our other friend.'

Their quiet Pickwick from the laboratory went out to talk with a small intent man who would obviously be the real communist among them because he looked the role: a small, thoughtful, intense man with dark-rimmed glasses, busy with a printing machine, pouring out propaganda. Wasn't it typical enough?

Quartermain looked around the walls and guessed that they printed Arabic calendars. The wet proofs in the communist's hands when he came in to be introduced as Ali (he could not shake hands, they were too black, so he offered his wrist politely) were of complicated Arabic hieroglyphics which surrounded all Arabic calendars: stern religious exhortations and helpful rules for daily use in accepting one's fate as Allah had willed it.

'Now we are all here,' Mr. Pickwick said, and they sat down on greasy chairs.

Quartermain had already thought of the questions he would ask them. He must first find out (remembering his war-time experience) what sort of communists they were.

Mr. Rushdi, Pickwick himself, had not stopped smiling; so much so that his face looked very muscular but unimportant, and a serious question asked of him would seem ridiculous. Rushdi spoke English with a slight Yorkshire accent and Quartermain could not help asking him how he got it.

'I was living up in Bradford for four years,' he said. 'Can you tell?'

The 'up' was not quite 'oop' but it was near enough.

'What were you doing up there?' Quartermain asked him. 'Were you a printer?'

No. Rushdi had been studying wool dyeing, which was his profession. When Quartermain asked him if he now dyed Egyptian cottons, he said, 'No. I am still a wool dyer.'

'In Egypt?'

'What do you think Egypt's biggest import from Britain is?' he asked, as if he were full of such valuable information.

'I'd have thought it was machinery or motor-cars,' Quartermain replied.

'No,' said Rushdi, beaming. 'Wool-tops. We import inferior raw wool from England, then we make up large quantities of cheap woollen cloth which we export, even to India.'

'Is that how you became a communist?' Quartermain asked. 'Dyeing wool in Bradford?'

'No, no,' Rushdi said. He dropped his voice. 'You mustn't say things like that. It was here, in my own country.'

It was Rushdi and the girl who spoke. Ali the printer was simply the printer, perhaps fanatically a printer with that face and nothing more. He obviously did not speak English and he sat still ordering coffee and holding his proofs tightly gripped in his inky hands, as if he were impatient to get on with his work. Mohamed Osman Pasha sat apart in the biggest chair in the office, breathing asthmatically, nodding occasionally,

423

and reading proofs of an Arabic broadsheet. He was no more interested in Quartermain than he had been from the beginning.

'Do the Egyptians know you exist?' Quartermain asked Rushdi. 'I mean the Egyptian police.'

'Of course,' Rushdi said. 'But they don't know who we are.'

'Why did you trust me then?'

'But we know very well that we could trust you,' Rushdi said in surprise.

'That seems foolish to me,' Quartermain told him.

Rushdi went on looking surprised. 'But we felt that anyone who thought so well of Asians and Africans would understand us.'

'Don't you believe it,' Quartermain told him. 'Plenty of people have sympathy for Asians and Africans who don't like communists.'

'They must be very silly then,' Sophie Mourad said.

That, too, seemed to be such a complete answer that Quartermain did not laugh or argue with it.

'What about Nasser?' Quartermain asked. 'Are you for him or against him?'

Rushdi pointed to a picture of Nasser on the wall. 'We are for him as far as he goes,' he said, smiling about it to himself, 'but we know he'll never go far enough.'

'In what sense?'

'He has not really done away with capitalism or exploitation in Egypt. He has not taken away even a third of the land from the landowners to give to the peasants or the co-operatives. And he has not undertaken the social reform of Egypt the way we would.'

'Why do you support him at all then?' Quartermain asked, still fascinated with this benign simplicity which concerned itself so tenderly with complex politics.

'Nasser is a bourgeois man,' Rushdi said with his hands entwined together on his stomach, 'and his officers have made a bourgeois revolution. It's quite simple, Mr. Quartermain. They have done away with feudalism and introduced capitalism, which is correct; but it can't go much further. You see?'

Quartermain said that all this might sound correct, theoretically; but what did the Egyptians themselves think? Weren't the peasants and workers for Nasser?

'True, true,' Rushdi said, with a more contemplative look, a slightly worried frown, a mere flicker perhaps; but even that small break in his face seemed like a surge of pessimism. 'They support Gamal Abd el Nasser because he has made them Egyptians. He threw the British out, which everyone wanted. He keeps the British out, which we all want. And now he has nationalized the canal and will build the Aswan Dam, and he will have everybody supporting him for that too. Even us. Oh, yes! But he is only creating his real problem, rather than solving it. He's a clever man, but he doesn't understand that.'

'Why? Don't you think he can build the Dam?'

'Some day, yes, with Russian help. Only the Russians will ever help him. But he is beginning to create an industrial Egypt, not so? That is his dream—we all know that. Nasser understands that much about the future. But when he has done that he will also have created a working class, you follow, who will ask for much more than he will be willing to give them. It will be true of peasants also, when we begin to irrigate new lands and change the peasants' lives. Nasser will also do that. The country children are already going to school in the villages. Imagine! In Egypt all our children will go to school. It's undreamt of. But then Nasser will face his real problem.'

Though this seemed to be the happiest and simplest theoretical discussion he had ever had in his life, Quartermain interrupted it now, because he wanted to know more specifically what they wanted him for.

'You see,' Sophie Mourad explained to him, 'we print a newspaper here.'

But it was not what he imagined it to be—an illegal communist broadsheet. It was a perfectly legal weekly on agricultural matters which also publicized what the Russians and the Chinese were doing on their collective farms and communes, as well as news of Egyptian agriculture in transition. The communism in it must have been well hidden, and cleverly enough to escape the censor or the security police. But was that all?

'We can't print a newspaper for the peasants,' Sophie explained, 'because they can't read. We want to do it the way the Chinese do it—with pictures. We will have to teach them that way, until their children can read, and only then can we think about printing a newspaper for them— for the next generation. This one hasn't even reached the level of the printed word yet . . .' Her brown eyes were so pretty and her eyes were so sure.

He decided then that she must be devoted to someone, some other student, perhaps the one who had involved him in this. He asked her if there were others. Yes, of course there were. Was she a Moslem? They all laughed at him. No, she was a Copt. But all the men were Moslems. It would be very hard, even now, for a Moslem girl to be doing what she was doing.

'We wanted to ask you if you could help us,' she said. '*I* thought about you,' she said proudly and Quartermain lost his heart to her in this wonderful but rare world of appreciation. 'I knew you would help us.'

'In what way?'

'Will you be going back to England soon?' Sophie asked.

'I suppose so,' Quartermain said. 'Why? What do you want me to do there?'

It was very simple, Rushdi explained cheerfully.

'You see,' he said, 'as Sophie tells you, we need to print a sort of picture propaganda for the peasants. But here we have only a small flatbed press and type. We need good equipment for producing real line and half-tone blocks. What we need here is a good photo-engraving camera for making good blocks of both line drawings and photographs. We can pay you here in Egyptian money, but we have no money in England.'

Was Sophie a rich man's daughter? 'Could you, Mr. Quartermain, pay for it in England, say, and have it shipped to us, if we give you Egyptian money here?' she asked.

'How much will it cost?' he wanted to know quickly.

'About a thousand pounds to begin with,' Rushdi said. 'But that includes shipping and insurance and all other costs.'

'I haven't got a thousand pounds,' Quartermain said. 'Nothing like it.'

'We would give you fifteen hundred Egyptian pounds,' Sophie told him enticingly.

He laughed, he marvelled at them, because he knew he needed to alert all his humours, otherwise he would begin to be upset by this simple approach to revolution, and by this brown hair and those chestnut eyes.

'I might have done it if I had a thousand pounds in England,' he said. 'But I honestly haven't.'

'But you would do it?' Rushdi said.

'I might,' he said, retreating a little. 'But I can't.'

'If we can give you one thousand pounds in English money here, could you take it out with you to England and arrange it for us?'

'Take it out illegally?'

Rushdi nodded cheerfully, but he blushed at his own suggestion, at his evil thought of breaking the currency laws.

'Can't you find anyone else to do a thing like that? An Egyptian?'

'No Egyptians are allowed to leave the country now. We had an Iraqi friend who tried to take four hundred English pounds to England as a deposit. He was discovered not by Egyptians but by the English. They put him in prison and took his money. If you are a foreigner you are not allowed to take that much English money into England.'

'You're not allowed to do it even if you're an Englishman,' Quartermain pointed out. 'Ten English pounds is the limit. And what would I do with all that money, assuming I got it out of Egypt illegally and into England illegally?'

Ali, the printer, was asked to hand over a folder. The glossily illustrated photo-engraving equipment was listed there, with the name of the firm and the various prices.

'You simply go to this firm and order it for us and pay the money and tell them to send it,' Rushdi said. 'It's very simple.'

Ali, the printer, began to explain in hurried Arabic the points of the folder, which was printed in English and French. What was required was the photo-engraving camera with a corrected (process) lens with diaphragms and prisms and screen. All the rest of the equipment, the whirlers, vacuum printing frames, and the etching and routing equipment was already in existence here in Egypt.

He knew he admired practical men. How could you help it? Here were two practical men, Ali a printer and Rushdi a wool-dyer, who operated their politics on practicalities and were matter-of-fact about it.

But did they dream? Did they ever burn with desire for the long-promised future of equality and sanity? At the moment they simply wanted a processing camera and a monthly journal. Perhaps therefore it was Sophie Mourad and old Mohamed Osman Pasha (almost asleep at the desk) who were dreamers. He looked at Osman Pasha and realized that he was not asleep at all but was watching him now between those heavy breaths. But the Pasha was no dreamer. He was too old. That left Sophie who was too young to do anything else except dream. A sly glance at Sophie, and a man could be in love with her youth in a second.

But it all seemed too simple and practical here; not dangerous at all and by no means romantic or conspiratorial.

'What will you propagate to the peasants with your pictures?' he asked them. 'Revolution against Nasser?'

'No,' Rushdi answered. 'We don't want that. We would show the Egyptians why communism is the only way to end their misery and transform their lives, because no one else will really free them. We will show them what the Chinese and the Russians are doing for their peasants and workers, particularly the Chinese. They'll understand. They'll know.'

'With simple pictures?'

'Very simple pictures.'

They were silent for a moment. Quartermain got up restlessly to watch the flatbed machine waving its wire arms. In a moment like this, he was telling himself, his western sophistication got in the way of his understanding. Was it all so simple? Out of where, for instance, among the Nihilists and Decembrists and Narodniks had the Russians produced their complex and successful Bolshevik revolution? Or, what was the beginning of the Chinese communist revolution, of their famous Eighth Route Army march—that desperate evacuation across China which was by no means simple or naïve. Had they begun in the same way—so credulously? Was this how the beginnings were begun? Obviously these four Egyptians were not the full strength of the communists in Egypt.

427

There must be others somewhere. But were they all like this strange quartet?

'Weren't there any communists among the Army officers?' he asked them.

Rushdi folded his hands and thought. 'They say one of the Moheddin brothers was a communist. But we don't know whether he was or not. He was banished from Egypt and then came back; but he is nothing to do with us.'

'What about the workers? What do they know about communism?'

'Our two heroes,' Rushdi said, muting his good nature to admit the occasional but regretful cruelty of the world, 'are two workers who tried to organize a strike in the Beida Dyeing Company.'

'A wool-dyeing company?'

'Yes, in Alexandria. The workers had just formed a union for the first time in their history and they had begun to make demands on the owners when there was provocation and riots and ten people were killed, including some policemen. This was just after the revolution. General Neguib was the president of the officers' Revolutionary Council then, and he ordered the arrest of two workers at the factory—Mustafa Khamis and Mohamed Hassan el Bakhari who was a guard. They were tried by the Army and sentenced to death for high treason.'

'Neguib was still in power?'

'Yes. Neguib personally, in his own office, offered to save Khamis from death if he named the principal communists in the factory, but Khamis refused to denounce his friends and they were both hanged.'

Quartermain nodded. 'I remember . . .'

'You see,' Rushdi went on sadly, 'only a few soldiers were killed in the actual fighting of the officers' revolution, a few only, and neither Neguib nor Nasser ever hanged a landlord, nor any of the men who had committed terrible crimes against Egypt during Farouk's reign. The only two people who were hanged in our national revolution were two workers, two Egyptian workers.'

'So you became a communist at the Beida Dyeing Company of Alexandria?' Quartermain said to him.

'I was already a communist. Mustafa Khamis had not betrayed me. He had spared me,' Rushdi said sadly, 'but I could not save him. There was nothing I could do.'

Quartermain knew he could go on asking more details, they were quite willing. But it was almost lunch-time and they must all go home. The flatbed had stopped, the print-shop workers—who did not wear shoes and walked along valleyed tracks in the dirt floor of their workshop—had stopped work. It was noon.

428

He stood up, saying he must go. They stood up reluctantly. They agreed it was lunch-time, and Sophie Mourad asked if they could take him home.

'I prefer not,' he said.

They insisted, he resisted. He knew what they did not know about Mr. Aboud's hopeful suspicions of him, but he was not going to bother them with that.

'But will you take the money for us to England?' Sophie asked him anxiously.

'Before I go to England I'll try to see you again,' he said, evading a promise or a denial of it. 'If you find someone else in the meantime, let me know.'

They did not think they would find anyone, they said. They waited for a promise, but he simply gave Sophie his telephone number and told her to talk to him and to no one else. That was all he could do. Osman Pasha rose from his proofs and Ali the printer came in from closing the main doors which the workers had used. Quartermain shook hands with each of them and said he would see them again for sure. He dried his moustache with his handkerchief, embarrassed now because they were obviously disappointed in him, as if they had been sure that he would solve their requirements as simply as they had hoped for, and believed possible.

'If only everything could be that simple,' he thought, as he left them.

Over lunch he asked Helen Mamoon if she had ever heard of Mohamed Osman Pasha.

'Everybody has,' Helen told him. 'He is one of the Red Pashas.'

'Is he rich?'

'He was once quite rich. I think the Government sent him to Russia during Farouk's reign to see if he could exchange Egyptian cotton for Russian fertilizers, because that's what Egypt is always paying out all her foreign currency for. They say he travelled all over Russia and saw the big farms they have there. They say he used to weep when he saw the Russian peasants working in the fields, singing and looking very healthy and happy, and he came back saying that Russia was just like Egypt, and that some day the Egyptian peasants would also be singing happily in the fields like the Russian peasants. I think they took all his land away from him and he doesn't have much money any more. Why? Did you see him?'

'I saw him but I didn't talk to him.'

'You ought to be careful. Everybody knows who he is.'

'I gathered that,' he said. 'Have you ever heard of someone called Rushdi?'

Helen was only half-listening. She was reading an Arabic paper which

429

came to her from the Lebanon. It proposed a new religion which coalesced the saints of eight faiths into five, the gods of five religions into three, and the prophets of three religions into one: into *He* who had not yet come. The symbolic numbers were therefore 531, which was the name of the new faith itself.

'Rushdi?' she repeated. 'There are thousands of Rushdis. It's a very common name. It means lucid, from the word Rashid.'

'This one is a wool-dyer.'

She shook her head.

'Mustafa Khamis, then. Do you know of him?'

Helen's connections were not necessary here.

'Of course,' she said. 'He was one of the communists Nasser hanged during the revolution.'

'Neguib hanged him,' he told her.

'It wasn't even Neguib,' she said. 'As a matter of fact it was Gamal Salem, who was then the principal judge of the military tribunal. He would have loved to have hanged everybody, but they stopped him. Neguib merely did what Gamal Salem told him to do. They wanted to make an example of Khamis.'

'They wanted Khamis to betray his friends.'

'That was not Neguib,' she insisted.

'But Neguib says so himself, in his own autobiography.'

She would not turn on Mohamed Neguib, he had been tolerant and well-loved by everybody. He had not only visited the mosques, but the Christian and Coptic churches and even the synagogues, and he had tried to get on with the British, and even with Israel. 'He was never a cruel man.'

'Except with communists,' Quartermain insisted.

'But they *all* hate communists,' she said. 'And Neguib was the most humane of the officers. That's why they keep him locked in his villa. If they ever let him out, even now, the whole country will greet him like a father.'

'Was Khamis also a hero at that time? Do the Egyptians talk of him?'

'How could Khamis be a hero? He was a communist. Everybody felt sorry for him, that's all. Egyptians always feel sorry for anyone who is going to be hurt or hanged or punished. We weep so easily. Nobody wanted the communists hanged. The name Khamis means Thursday, so they hanged him on Thursday. I thought that was cruel; and think of how his family felt; and anyway they knew they were not hanging the ringleader. The real communist leaders in the Beida works were never discovered. Everybody knows that.'

Who (he asked himself) had been the real communist leader in the

Beida works? Had it been a wool-dyer whose life had been spared because a man named Khamis had refused to betray him?

Quartermain was very affected by it, by all of it.

'What do you think has happened to our simplicity?' he asked his wife, later that night, as if asking her forgiveness for many years of pointless complexity. 'We're all so afraid of being artless. That's been our terrible mistake.'

'Whose mistake?' she asked.

'I wish I could go back a dozen years,' he went on, 'and do it all over again. I would learn to do everything as simply as possible—whatever was in my head or my heart.'

'Don't imagine you *don't* do whatever is in your head now?' Nona told him.

'That's only because I think I'm usually right. But one needs also to be simple and honest and unsophisticated, even if, sometimes, one may be wrong. Being right is not everything.'

'Oh, my God!' Nona said in stunned agreement.

CHAPTER FIFTY-SEVEN

ALL the way to Alexandria in the train Scott tried to look at Egypt with the eyes he knew he had lost. Peter Dukes had asked him for his values but hadn't he been trying for years not to give himself values, because they had always brought him pain and punishment and isolation?

Now (he thought guiltily) it was only when murder and war were beginning to interfere that he was looking again for the means to think with. Peter Dukes was right. How was disinterest possible, when the British and the French politicians were already calling Gamal Abd el Nasser another Hitler, presumably so that they could safely destroy him, and thus save the world?

On the other hand, here was Peter Dukes trying to save Gamal Abd el Nasser, while insisting that he was just a stupid soldier who had not fundamentally changed Egypt. Could that be true?

He had witnessed an example of its possible truth at the Cairo station before the train had pulled out. The native porters had fought theatrically among themselves over who ought to be paid, and how much, for carrying the passengers' luggage. The moment the train began to move, however, peace had settled all over the place, and the barefooted porters had gone back to their old fellowship. But an interloper—a beggar or a servant who had found his way onto the platform somehow—had encroached in some way on their territory and they were all suddenly beating him and hounding him out of the station as the train left.

Had Gamal Abd el Nasser actually taken on their lot and changed it?

Had Nasser, truthfully, given them a way out of their inhuman degradation?

'I'm too ignorant even to guess,' he concluded bitterly. 'What do I know about it?' He resented his ignorance, but he resisted it also. 'All I know is that it's infinitely better now than it was before. Isn't that enough?'

He looked out at the fields, dissolved so easily by the speed of the train. It was always the same landscape of rich green poverty, the same planted fields of diseased men and women, the same mud-compounded communities of ignorance, near-starvation, happiness, good fun, and calamitous bolts from a reckless heaven.

But one rode through Egypt on a train and never really saw it. One simply rode the same train every day of one's life. That was the only way that you could bear it—by rushing through the misery sightless, safe, and curtained off by these moving glass walls from any reality which threatened the conscience with the pain of discovery or response.

'It will take more than Gamal to change all this,' he thought sadly, not in a critical sense, but in an overwhelming sense. How could anything ever lift these people out of the filth and the festering vigour of their endless misery?

He knew where to find Church in Alexandria, which seemed to be the best place to find Lucy Pickering. After the accident, when he had settled Professor Maudie in the hospital, he had left Church in an unusual pension-hotel run by Austrians. It sat on top of one of the modern office buildings near the Cricket Club on the Promenade.

A few potted palms and a clean carpet were all that suggested the *pension* at the lift door, but once inside the passage the furniture was Jacobean polished oak from Maples, and a Greek in a black tie sat behind a small desk in a windowless hall. It was lit by electric light, although it was noonday, but it was cool. It was clean and cheap, probably Swiss, and the sort of place he might have picked for himself, and it did smell of the sea, even in its clustered, clean darkness.

He asked for General Church, who was eating lunch.

'Go in,' the Greek told him. He remembered Scott from that tragic day.

Scott stood at the restaurant door and saw the General at his table near a window, with Lucy opposite him. They were very busy eating, and they were also deep in earnest conversation. He hesitated to interrupt a pleasant and intimate preoccupation, but he told the sofragi to tell the General that someone wanted to speak to him. Even before he had finished saying it, however, he could see Lucy Pickering looking towards him in surprise.

She poised herself, about to drink from a glass of water, a round clear goblet half-way to her lips. Her skin shone with a polish which would have looked olive or almost oily on a darker woman, but on Lucy it was a nut-brown caramel colour, glazed with a fine English perspiration.

Church got up to meet him, napkin in hand.

'Come and sit down,' he said. 'Have you had your lunch?'

'Yes, I have, thank you,' Scott told him, although he had not.

'You're not here to catch a boat, are you?' Lucy asked him, holding out her hand and her bare arm, to be touched at least. He knew that the touch would overwhelm him instantly, as it must. It was not simply a touch, it was an intimate, illicit meeting of the flesh, already.

433

'A boat?' he said weakly. 'Where to?'

'Oh, anywhere,' she said in disgust.

That covered almost everything. He sat down and nursed his hat, and watched her with too-easy admiration. They finished their stewed pears and asked him what he was doing here. He said he was passing through. He asked them how Professor Maudie was. Church said she was much better, but she could not be moved from the hospital yet.

'Where are the rest of the Professors?' Scott asked, looking around. The last time he had been here the *pension* had been full of them: Grossgudt, René Harcourt, Dr. Berebellis, and the others he had not known so well.

'They've gone off to Beirut,' Church told him. 'I sent them off, in case . . .'

Lucy looked from one to the other and suddenly laughed.

'Do you realize,' she said, 'that this is the first time I've seen you two together since the war? Don't you feel odd, somehow, as if everything is repeating itself the wrong way?'

Scott put his hat under the chair, and Church handed him coffee. Everything was perfectly normal with them. Weren't they both Englishmen of that characteristic civilization and good order? Was there anything to feel odd about?

'Have you heard any news, Scott?' Church asked him carefully.

'I haven't seen a newspaper since yesterday,' Scott told him.

'The London conference on the canal has decided to send a mission to Cairo to persuade Nasser to hand it over,' she told them. 'I just read it upside-down in French in that man's paper.'

'I suppose you're keeping in touch with the Embassy,' the General said to him.

'I don't follow,' Scott said. 'Why should I be in touch with the Embassy?'

'You ought to, you know,' Church told him. 'They have to keep track on everybody, if there's any kind of a disturbance.'

Lucy was still amused. 'I hardly think that's exactly apt—in his case,' she said. 'But I'd love to see him queueing up with all those old schoolmistresses and missionaries, getting ready for evacuation.'

Church defended his point. 'The problem is to know who is safe and who isn't, that's all,' he said. 'Five hundred people have already left.'

'Oh, they'll all come back again in a month wishing they'd never listened to the Embassy,' Lucy said. She had been following someone with her eyes and Scott looked up to see who it was.

A self-confident young Egyptian with a rich black moustache had entered the restaurant, and Scott recognized a trademark—a leather patch on the right armpit of his jacket. He also recognized the man.

'That man,' Lucy told Scott, her eyes already trying to make love to

434

him, 'is the world champion clay-pigeon shot. I read about him in the paper yesterday. He's going to show all the Egyptian schoolteachers how to shoot the British.'

As the young Egyptian passed near the table, Scott looked up and wondered. These days all Egyptians were trying hard to be loyally Egyptian, to forget foreigners, even friends.

But the world champion put out his hand and clapped Scott on the shoulder and held his hand at full length in a proper grip.

'Hello, Shakir,' Scott said. 'Are you really world champion now?'

'Hello, Capten!' Shakir said, almost respectfully. Then he remembered that he was almost world champion and became very jolly and conceited. 'Not quite,' he said, 'but near enough, you know. How are you? *What* are you doing here?'

Scott introduced him to Lucy and to the General, and Shakir begged himself away from their invitations to coffee with polite heart-searchings. He held Scott's hand in farewell as his companions arrived, wearing blue blazers with emblazoned pockets. One wore the Olympic Games circles, and the other wore shooting-club mottoes. Shakir pulled Scott away a little and said,

'*Habibi!* How are you? I haven't seen you for so long. How is Amin? Is he still at Ghurdakha? Why don't you come and see me more often? Come to the Cairo club and we will do a little gambling together on your shooting, not mine.'

What a delightful chap he was.

Scott promised to meet him and Shakir made a date for the following week; a promise, an absolutely certain hour, which he swore (didn't he?) to keep.

'Of course I'll come,' Scott said, knowing he would get a phone message the day before saying that Shakir Bey had regretfully left Cairo and gone to his country house along the river.

'Tomorrow you'll see me at my best if you come at five o'clock to the Ras-el-Tin Club,' Shakir said. Then he went over to his companions who were also young and wealthy and handsome, and in good, forceful cheer. They were knocking each other on the knuckles with table-knives to see whose reflexes were fast enough to snatch his hand away in time.

'How do you know him?' Lucy asked in surprise when Scott sat down again. She had obviously been taken by his physique, his *présence*.

'Shakir? I used to shoot clay pigeons at the Sporting Club in Cairo,' he told her. He would not look at Lucy because he was jealous. He did not like to see her looking at other men like that. 'You can sit in the club-house and gamble on the shooters,' he said, 'the way you do at the race-course. They are all dead shots, like Shakir.'

'You must know his family?' the General asked him.

'I knew the father and the uncle. I think you know his other uncle—one of the Bindaris.'

He looked at Lucy and wondered what she would do, what she would say.

'I know the Bindaris,' she said informatively, tauntingly.

'Weren't you at their estate with Bateman?' he asked.

'For two lovely weeks.' She leaned her elbows on the table and cupped her face in her hands. 'I'd never leave this country if I could live that sort of life. It's like something out of a Russian novel. Do you know what I mean? Do you know the Bindaris' house?'

'No,' Scott replied, 'I only know of them.'

Lucy seemed to laugh at him, to his face, but he could not be sure.

He remembered, though, what this *pension* was.

All the duck-shooters and sharpshooters of Egypt came here in the spring when the duck season opened. They would usually spend the night here before they set out in the early-morning darkness to reach the neighbouring marshes and lakes.

These rich young men would shoot away a small fortune every year in expensive American cartridges; and they used this *pension* as their sportive dormitory. But what were Lucy and Church doing here, living in the same *pension* as such people?

'Isn't Bindari's son here too?' Scott said. 'He's also one of the famous marksmen of Egypt.' He looked around.

'I don't see him,' Lucy said teasingly. 'But I do know him.'

'Is he as mad as they say he is?' Scott asked.

'Yes. But he's such fun.'

They were playing at what they knew, and at what they ought not to know. Church was already unimportant. The world had already gone beyond Church, quite suddenly, and he seemed to know it. The General sat for a little while raking up a few crumbs of bread on the tablecloth into a neat small pile, big enough for a neat sparrow to make a dinner of. He was such neat man, and his reverie over the crumbs seemed to be small and self-contained and worried, perhaps.

The General looked at Lucy and said nothing. He looked at Scott and smiled. The General was obviously tired. His pink face looked faded and his eyes seemed old and quite uncertain of the world. He scooped up his neat little pile of crumbs with a cheese-knife and put them carefully on his small plate. Then he rose to go.

'I'll leave you two, if you don't mind,' he said. 'I'm rather tired. Will I be seeing you tomorrow, Scott? That is—would you come and see me? I'd like to ask you a few things.'

'I'm going back tomorrow morning,' Scott said.

'Try and drop in for a few moments beforehand,' Church told him.

436

'Good night, then. Good night, Lucy. I'll leave a message with Andreas if there's anything new from the hospital. Don't be too late.'

Left alone, Lucy said quickly to Scott: 'I don't want to stay in here. Could we go to a cinema or something? I feel as if I'd already spent half my life in this place, and I'm terrified I might have to spend the other half as well.'

'Why? When are you leaving Egypt?' he asked her, getting his hat out. 'Isn't that why you're here?'

'I suppose I'll leave when I get my exit permit,' she said.

The eyes of every marksman were on them as they left the dining-room; and she took his arm, as if to make a point of it.

Outside, it depended on Lucy whether they would quarrel or not. He was careful, but he was ready to be angry with her, perhaps in self-defence, or in a contest with his own conscience about her. But he was also willing not to be angry if she would be pleasant.

They walked slowly and quietly and they seemed to be safe.

He had not realized how impressed he could be with her soft and intelligent English face, and how sensible her English manners were, how pleasing it was; how alike. It was already too easy to be in love with a woman who promised to forget the failures, who adapted herself to hope, who took his arm and held it as if she needed it, and who made sense out of their being together.

But when would she say to him: 'Have you come this time to make it permanent?' because that had been the silent, angry agreement between them, the only reason left for ever seeing her again.

'Where's that famous old *phare* in the port?' she said to him in the street. 'Let's go and look at that.'

'I wouldn't know where it is,' he told her. 'I don't know Alexandria that well.'

'Never mind, let's walk towards the sea. That's why I love warm countries. Everybody uses the nights to stroll. Have you ever been in Sienna? I don't suppose you have, but at night the whole town emerges into the streets and squares, just strolling around between those bright little cafés jammed together in the cobbled streets. The whole place smells of coffee and vermouth and is coloured a sort of bright vermilion by the neon lights. All those Italian men, too, dressed more beautifully than the women. They're so spotless. And their shoes! I often wonder why the Italian women do it—ironing and washing the men's clothes all day so that their husbands can go out at night looking smart and ogling the girls.'

'I passed through Sienna during the war,' he told her, 'but it wasn't like that. We had to sleep to windward of it, in the valley below.'

437

'Oh, smells,' she said with a shrug. 'Have you been to Europe since the war? I meant to ask you. I need to ask you so many things.'

'I've only been to Greece since the war.'

'Didn't you ever have leave? Holidays?'

'Of course, but I usually spent my leave sailing at Port Said, when I was in the Sinai; or I went into Syria skiing.'

Port Said meant Françoise, and they moved on silently until Lucy put her fingers into his and squeezed them as hard as she could, digging into his bones.

'I wonder if I should let you go,' she said, almost threateningly, and then, appealingly, 'I wish you hadn't come here at all, because I know you haven't come to ask me to go with you. I know it. *Why* did you come? Couldn't you have left it as it was?'

'I don't know,' he said. 'I was passing through . . .'

'Oh, don't say that.'

'All right. I was told something which worried me, and I didn't stop to think about it much.'

'Told what?' she asked.

'Were you . . .' he looked for the word . . . 'rather close to Bateman?'

'Oh, terribly close,' she said frivolously.

'No. I'm very serious, Lucy.'

'So am I serious,' she insisted. 'I can hardly say that I don't know Bateman, can I? He invited me to the Bindaris', so I went, and I had a marvellous time.'

'Is that all?'

'Oh, come out with it, darling. Don't try to be so cunning.'

'I'm not trying to be cunning,' he told her.

'Then say what you want to say, for heaven's sake.'

They were walking along the sea-front; the olive-green water shifted glassily under the street lights as if the whole sea was being gently taken away and then replaced and then taken away again.

'There's a rumour about that there is some kind of a move in hand to do something to Nasser,' he told her obscurely. 'Some people think Bateman is involved. And you know Bateman, so . . .'

'So, good for me!' she said. 'You know quite well that I'm anxious to see your friend Nasser get what he deserves or something, my darling Captain Scott. I have hated him ever since *you* were misguided about him, years ago.'

'This is nothing to do with me,' he said. 'That's not the point of this . . .'

'Then what are you worried about? Me? Or your friend Nasser?'

'All I can tell you is that the Egyptians know about it.'

'You are such a nice person,' she said, squeezing his fingers tighter and tighter so that she hurt her own but hardly indented his. 'What if some-one does do something to Nasser? Will you blame me?'

'You seem to know all about it. Please, for heaven's sake, be serious.'

'How do you know I'm joking? What have I said?'

'Does it matter what you've said . . .'

'All right. If Nasser is—er—removed,' she insisted, going on with her frivolity, and confusing him and making him feel like a fool now, 'what would happen to me? Would they shoot me? A woman?'

'Don't be so cynical,' he said in appeal. 'And don't tease me all the time. I'm no good at it.'

She laughed affectionately then and the night smothered his other doubts. Who could walk the calm promenades of the Mediterranean and think seriously of a threat like that to one man, to any man? Or was this the conflict for the sea itself: canals, oil-wells, and men who worked hard to possess the natural world? All of it, if possible. Was it true?

'Hakim also knows, incidentally, that you came here from Israel,' he warned her. 'In fact, it was he who told me.'

'Did he?' she said teasingly. 'Well, if someone is going to hurt Nasser it won't be because of Israel. So you jolly well think of your friends here, and I'll think of my friends there. But don't let's start blaming each other for our friends.'

She still held her grip on him, but he lost his temper. 'What did you come here for in the first place?' he growled at her, feeling the uncontrol-lable rise of it swamping his discipline. 'You can really go to hell as far as I'm concerned. All right, Nasser is my friend. I'm not going to desert him. And if one of your friends wants him dead, then I would be quite willing to kill off a few people myself. I mean it. What right have you to come here and meddle the way you have? I know you too well, Lucy . . .'

'You don't know me at all.'

'Oh, yes I do! There's always a reason with you.' He was trying to pull his arm away from her, but she held it and refused to let it go. 'Look at what you've done here. Look at Sam. You can't tell me you don't know all about Sam. You do! Don't you care what happens to other people? After all these years you drag me into it too, and then you joke about it. How do I get into these situations with you? Why don't you just go away and leave people alone? And don't try to tease me. I'm fed up with this cat-and-mouse game anyway . . .'

'Shhh!' she said to him pleasantly. 'Don't be so upset.'

'I'm not upset,' he almost shouted. 'I'm trying not to lose my temper.'

'*That* would be worse,' she said soothingly. 'And we were being so nice.'

'I don't feel like being nice,' he said, but his temper had not really risen at all. He had found it useless even before it had got the better of him, and he could allow her amused toleration of it to calm him down into a boorish sullenness which made it even more ridiculous. But he would not give in. 'At least tell me honestly,' he said, 'if you're involved in any of this. You must know something.'

'I can't help knowing what I know, can I? You can't blame me for that.'

'What do you know? You must tell me.'

'I know nothing that can help you,' she said in her perfect humour.

'I could walk away from you, right now, and never see or care a hang about you again, Lucy, and I'd be better off.'

'Of course you would be. Do you really care that much?'

'Oh, come on!' he begged. 'Don't be so hard. I can't help what I am, either. Don't take it out on me.'

'But I like to, darling. I like you when you lose your temper a little bit. So long as you don't do silly things. You're so much older and wiser. But you ought to be *yourself*.' She kept her grip very tight and lowered her voice and mimicked him. 'But don't hold yourself back like this, with your eyes down and your voice locked up in a cage with a snarling lion. Why can't you be gay with me sometimes?'

'Because I don't feel too gay.'

'Oh, my darling, that is such a lovely understatement.'

'I know you think all this talk is fantastic,' he told her, 'but I also know that it's true. Sam was put in prison, that's true, isn't it? So don't think it's as ridiculous as you try to make out.'

'But I don't think it's ridiculous,' she protested. 'I'm sure someone is trying to kill Nasser. Didn't someone shoot at him a couple of years ago?'

'Oh, let's leave it alone,' he said finally. 'Let's forget it. If only I could forget it.'

The discipline was coming back. Doubly so. He would regret his outburst now and feel how foolish he had been, how ineffectual it had made him, and how wretched afterwards.

'Never mind,' she said, as if it had all been a light interlude for his sake. 'Look!' She pointed to a beacon. 'Is that the *phare*?'

'I don't think there is a *phare*. What *phare* do you keep talking about? Why don't you leave Egypt?' he suggested, the appeal anxious and the reasons obvious.

'I told you. I'll leave when they give me an exit permit.'

He did not believe her. 'Why haven't they already given you one?'

'I should ask you that. They say there's a long queue waiting for them. Over three thousand British subjects are trying to leave Cairo alone.'

Was this also one of Hakim's devices? Was he keeping Lucy here?

'Where are you staying?' she asked. 'Because *now* I would like to be nice to you.'

'At the old Montana Hotel.'

440

'Are you? I can remember Pickering telephoning me from there. Why do you always go back to the same places? I suppose they're old friends of yours by now.'

'They've all gone,' he told her. 'It's owned by a Czech refugee now, and it's full of Germans. I simply go there from habit.'

'Let's go there now,' she said.

What did she want? Love? Did she want to play more of those profound jokes on him, with her smooth almost plump arms which caressed his shirt with every step and forged a little flow for the heart and the lungs and their feathery clusters of hungry nerves? She had not for one minute let go the very tight grip on his fingers, and they were both cramped to the wrist, but she did not seem to notice. She would not let him go now. 'Oh, never!' she said, and clung.

But when they arrived at the door of his hotel she stopped him and nuzzled him a little and held his coat and kissed him and cried out that she had been too nice, too forgiving, and that he had been unfair.

'You don't know,' she said, clinging to him, 'what you do to a woman's heart.'

'Don't stand out here . . . ' he began.

But she pulled away from him. 'I can't go on punishing myself like this. I simply can't. Go away. Please! Go on upstairs . . .'

'What about you?' he said, helplessly agreeing and disagreeing with her, wanting and not wanting her; oh, resisting her and himself and thankful that she did it for him.

'I can get back alone. Go on!' she insisted. 'Quickly. I don't want you. And anyway I'm coming back to Cairo with you. Now go inside.'

He went in and closed the large wooden door behind him, but he knew before he had gone a step that she was still standing outside. It was only his harsh feeling of resentment, his anger that she actually waited there expecting him to come back, that made him go on up without thinking, without asking, without allowing himself the indulgence of a moment's joy.

But hunger and love could outdo the soul every time, and his lost discipline was somehow waiting on Lucy in the morning. While she packed her suitcase, he went to see Church, who had been writing letters. Church looked at him over his half-moon spectacles and then shook his hand. It was a surprising gesture. Or was it simply a local habit easily acquired?

'I would still like you to join our Professors Unlimited,' Church told him, smiling. 'We're going to move a new party into the Lebanon and Turkey and Iraq next month. We're trying to start off from Antioch or Edessa, and then go down the Euphrates to Babylon. Couldn't I interest you, even now?'

'I'm afraid it's not my field,' Scott told him apologetically. 'You need an archaeological expert . . .'

'No, no,' Church argued. 'You would be ideal. You see, I can't leave Egypt for the moment, not until Professor Maudie is much better. It may take some time. If you went instead of me you would be the responsible person, and I'm sure it would be useful to you.'

'You probably didn't know,' Scott told him, 'but Peacock arranged for me to have an interview in London for this antarctic expedition for the Geophysical Year.'

'No, I didn't know. But I'm terribly glad, Scott. I'm very relieved. I admit you've been on my conscience. Very much so, lately. But I feel much better to hear that. You should get out of here, you know. Egypt is no place for an Englishman now, despite your feeling for these people. If you stay here I think you might be put into a strange position—of helping Nasser against your own countrymen, perhaps. That would be very unfortunate.'

'Why do you say that?' he asked Church. 'What's happened?'

'Nothing in particular, but you must know what will happen.'

'No, I don't.'

Church took off his glasses. 'I don't see how we can avoid taking military action to restore the canal,' he said. 'It's only a matter of time, I should think.'

'Force?' Scott said, still refusing to believe it possible.

The General moved his head just a little, quite sadly. 'There will always be force, as long as there are men to use it. Remember that, Scott. Remember that very well . . .'

'Surely you should leave Egypt also,' Scott told him. 'It won't be very pleasant for someone like you in the streets of Egypt, if there's British military action.'

'I'll leave when Professor Maudie is able to travel,' he said. 'But I'm glad Lucy is going with you to Cairo. She'll be safe with you. But please try to get her away soon.'

Scott promised to do that, and they shook hands in a strange farewell, for whatever Hakim or Peter Dukes might think, he knew that Church remained a soldier, not an assassin. And Lucy . . .

He did not believe it.

Lucy Pickering was many things in her life, but not that.

CHAPTER FIFTY-EIGHT

EVERYBODY in Paris was laughing; not because Marshal Juin had changed his military mind from *Algérie! c'est la France* to *Algérie! nous devions, peutêtre, avoir une fédération*; but because the Suez Canal Company had been caught sending 'help' money to the Paris newspapers.

The editor of *Libération* had opened his mail one morning and found a cheque and a mimeographed letter from the Canal Company saying that this was for the paper's 'expenses' for the month of August, and added that the payment might be renewed. The editor of *Libération* had published the letter on the front page, and asked other newspapers what they thought.

Every other newspaper suddenly thought it shocking, and admitted that they had also received money from the Suez Canal Company, who denied that it was corruption.

'How could we bribe anyone with such small sums?' they said. 'It was all a mistake. We picked on the wrong newspaper. We sent out one cheque too many.'

Mr. Aboud was very pleased to show these reports, in the local French press, to the correspondents of *Le Monde* and *Le Figaro* and *Paris Match*.

'What would you think of us if we were caught doing that?' Mr. Aboud said. 'Wouldn't you say we Egyptians were corrupt? But *we* haven't tried to bribe you. They have.'

But nobody laughed, because no one was very pleased with Mr. Aboud.

The Egyptians had just expelled four newspapermen, two of them women. They had taken Stevenson of the *Toronto Star* out of his hotel room and sent him off to Rome at twenty-four hours' notice, and the police had told Anne Sharpley of the London *Evening Standard* and Eileen Travis of the London *Daily Mail* to leave, because, Mr. Aboud said, 'they have been spreading falsehoods and fabrications to mislead public opinion.' Two other newspapermen had already been expelled weeks before, and when two plain-clothes policemen knocked on Jack de

Brazio's door at the Semiramis Hotel, he thought he knew what they wanted.

'I know, I know!' Jack said to them. 'You're after me.'

'Please, Mr. de Brazio,' one of them said seriously. They were so neat, so clean, so naïve. He invited them in, and they stepped inside and carefully closed the door behind them.

'Ella!' Jack called. 'We have some visitors.' He asked them if they would have a drink: a *limoon* of course, nothing alcoholic because it would be against their religion.

'No, thank you,' they said.

'Well?' Jack said, suspecting the worst. 'What is it this time?'

'It's nothing personal,' one of them said. They were so polite that they would not smile, they would not sit, they would not disturb. It was something quite unimportant. 'Why did you take Mr. Quartermain with you to the Red Sea last month?' the spokesman of them asked.

'What do you want to know that for?' Jack said. 'I didn't take him. He simply came with me. He had a desert pass.'

'But you paid for the car?'

'That's my business.'

'Of course it is,' the other one said. He was older and wiser, but he still looked too regretful to be doing this, Jack thought. 'Please forgive us, but we have to ask you. You needn't answer if you don't want to.'

'I certainly don't want to,' Jack said. 'Why? What's Quartermain done?'

'Nothing, Mr. de Brazio. Nothing at all.'

'Then what are you asking questions about him for?' Ella said. She joined them from the bedroom holding a length of gold brocade over her arms. She had bought it in the *muski* to have it made up into something Chinese-looking. She had just rearranged her black Italian hair into a thick high bun, and Jack looked surprised to see his wife's Italian face so suddenly Chinese. The policemen were in retreat already.

'We know that you do not tell unnecessary tales on your friend,' the older one said to Jack, 'but we are not going to hurt Mr. Quartermain. We are a little worried, that's all.'

'Who is? Are you from the press department?'

'No, of course not. It's something quite apart from the press department.'

'Do they know you're here?'

They smiled and looked doubtful. Apparently they had not expected it to be so difficult. Were they simply trying it on? If so, why hadn't they tried it more cunningly—by asking for a passport or making a small mistake so that they could ask their questions more casually?

'But it's really a simple question we would like to ask,' they said. 'Is Mr. Quartermain a well-known English communist?'

444

Jack laughed. 'Is that all?'

Ah yes, that was all.

'He's a firm supporter of Gamal Abd el Nasser,' Jack said. 'I'm not, for instance; but he is—if you want to know. Does that satisfy you? You don't have to worry about him. He's not going to help the British, you can be sure of that.'

'Thank you very much,' they said, and left with polite gentility.

The door closed and Jack was already wondering if he had given them the right answers.

'That was too naïve to be pleasant,' Ella said. 'Do you think they were really asking about Quarts?'

'We'll soon know. Maybe one of them saw me this morning, and he's just checking up to see if it was me.'

That morning Jack de Brazio had gone out of Cairo to the villa where General Mohamed Neguib was under permanent house arrest. Jack had tried to throw a microphone over the neighbouring wall, wrapping it in a towel and allowing it plenty of wire. He had spent half an hour throwing notes over the wall wrapped up in stones, telling Neguib to pick up the microphone and give the world his view of the crisis. Nothing had happened. He had failed. He had been lucky to get the microphone back over the wall undetected.

While he had been trying the back way, Stevenson of the *Toronto Star* had been trying noisily the front way. Stevenson had tried twice in the same day and had been arrested twice for trying to reach Neguib. That was the reason why they had expelled him. Jack had been luckier, not to be caught.

'I'd better warn Quarts, anyway,' Jack said.

445

CHAPTER FIFTY-NINE

HAVING finally written to the Cambridge Antarctic Committee agreeing to be in England for an interview not later than mid-November, Scott felt that he could ask Hakim for two things: first to see Gamal personally, and then to let him go free of all the commitments—personal or professional—which Hakim would want to hold him to.

'But do you want to leave us now, *habibi*?' Hakim complained.

Although Peter Dukes's question of values had been bothering him, like an accusation of moral cowardice, he still had no truthful answer to that question. Why did he want to leave now? It might have been easier to answer if he had been resigning from the Egyptian Survey Department, or even from the Frontier Department itself. But he knew he really had to resign from Hakim, and Hakim was not going to make it easy. Why should he desert Egypt now?

'I want to go on this antarctic survey,' he said, 'so don't make it too hard on me, Hakim. Let me go.'

Hakim gave him back his letter from Cambridge, and gave him back the second letter—his resignation from the Frontier Department, addressed to Hakim himself.

'Don't give it to me now,' Hakim said disinterestedly. 'Not yet.'

'You might as well accept it now as later.'

'This is not nice,' Hakim said casually in French.

They would have gone on arguing over Hakim's official glass-covered desk, but it was very glaring to sit there under the windows. Hakim got up. He was at his second office, at the Military Academy where the road made an L-turn before it crossed the desert towards the Cairo airport. Out of the window, Scott could see a restaurant left isolated between two ragged roads, and beyond it the new apartment houses of Heliopolis. Once, this restaurant had been considered a pleasant place for an outing on a summer's night because it was isolated out here in the cool desert breeze. Now it was grown over with Heliopolis suburbia, and it looked ramshackle and forgotten.

446

'To begin with,' Hakim said, pulling in the shutters a little, 'Gamal would never forgive me if I let you go like that. What do you want to go to the South Pole for? What a terrible place, *habibi*!'

'Let me see Gamal.'

'Oh, he's much too busy. You heard that they have sent a committee from London to see him, led by a bushman—Menzies. Look what they do to us now. The English always send bushmen to talk for them when they are too frightened to talk for themselves, in case they are soundly beaten at it. What are they afraid of? Why didn't Sir Eden come himself? It will be Mr. Menzies the bushman who will be beaten, not Mr. Selly Lloyd or Mr. Eden. Just a bushman, you see. I even remembered during the war it was General Smutz, whom we thought of assassinating one day with Sir Lampson when they went to see the King. But Gamal would not listen to that. They weren't really important, he said, so they weren't even worth killing. But they are always ignorant and sly men, nevertheless. This bushman tries to look like Churchill. He comes in red-faced like a lion, but Gamal will send him home white-faced like a lamb.'

Hakim was still being gay with the certainty of his kind of victory, in his kind of contest with bushmen.

'When could I see Gamal?' Scott asked him.

'Oh, not for a week. It would not be fair now, *habibi*. He is too busy.'

That was probably true. But Scott knew he could not tell Hakim what he knew or what he was supposed to know. He would have to find another way of seeing Gamal and telling him to keep away from beaches, to watch out for a strike against him. But he was not even sure how much he would tell Gamal, because he was not sure how much of Peter Dukes's warning he could believe. Couldn't it all be a trick to unnerve Nasser while he was negotiating with Menzies? Anything was possible, and Peter Dukes was not a man to be simple-minded about. One thing was certain—he was not going to tell Hakim.

'Did you know that your friend Mrs. Pickering has asked for her exit permit? Why do so many English want to leave Egypt? One thousand two hundred British, all in a hurry to leave us,' Hakim said.

'They always go, but they always come back,' Scott answered. 'If you'll let them back this time.'

'Do you think I should let them go? Perhaps I will let one thousand one hundred and ninety-five go and the rest can wait. Don't you think that's fair?'

Scott did not want to juggle with Hakim for the jokes of revenge. He would not ask who were the five British he would not allow to leave.

'The trouble is they've all been reading the American magazines,' Hakim said and picked up an American weekly and looked over at Scott before he read aloud from it with bland humour. '*The British and French continue to build up pressures to make sure that Nasser takes no new action against their vital interests in the area.*' He looked at Scott and threw up his hands. 'What about our vital interests? Don't they ever think of that?' He went on reading. '*The British announced that they had underestimated the deterrent value of the parachute battalions they posted to Cyprus last winter, and were accordingly beefing-up the eastern Mediterranean garrison to three division strength.*' He looked hard and repeated the phrase: 'What does beefing-up mean?' he asked.

'They mean building up,' Scott explained.

'Ah, a mistake,' Hakim said loftily. 'The Americans speak terrible English.' He read on. '*Gibraltar was stripped of its infantry, Malta's harbour and airfield were jammed with Cyprus-bound ships and planes.*'

Hakim pulled a face of sardonic fright for that summation. 'And now the French,' he said. '*Le Monde* says it isn't time yet for the cannons to speak, it is simply being shown that they are ready to do so.' Hakim laughed. 'The French put everything backwards,' he said. 'It's the woman-ish nature of their language. Have you noticed?'

'Perhaps it's all a bluff,' Scott said. 'Newspapers talk a lot.'

'They all want to smash us,' Hakim said offhandedly and contemptu-ously.

It was not so much Hakim's logic but his disgust with the intention: it was this that made it possible for Scott to agree with him. Were they going to smash Egypt? Were the British and French going to bomb the cities and send tanks through the streets of Cairo?

'I'll tell you a secret,' Hakim said. 'It is really Gamal they are after.'

'That's hardly a secret,' Scott told him. 'All the English politicians and newspapers are saying it . . .'

'Yes, yes. But I mean that we *know*. We know all about it.'

'What do you know?' Scott asked, suddenly drawn out of the helpless fatalism which always took hold of him when he was locked up in the same world with Hakim's mysteries.

Hakim shrugged. 'We know that the real criminals will escape us. Some have already. We let some go deliberately. I dare not tell you the worst, my friend,' Hakim said with a sudden tantalizing glance at Scott's alert eyes. 'Not even to you. Today is Monday. Come to see me on Saturday or Sunday or even Monday, but not on Friday.'

'Friday is a religious holiday, anyway,' Scott pointed out. 'I wouldn't come on Friday.'

'Of course,' Hakim answered. 'But this Friday I'm going with Gamal to Alexandria to the seaside. Perhaps you'd like to come too. Then you could talk to Gamal.'

Scott wondered now if Peter Dukes had done his job for him.

'That's exactly what I would like,' Scott said. 'If I could talk to Gamal.'

448

'Friday is not too late?' Hakim said.

'I don't think so,' Scott answered.

'Good. Where is that friend of yours, Hassoon, these days?'

'He's living in the same *pension* as I am,' Scott said. 'Why?'

'He wants a *laissez-passer*. I think he wants to leave Egypt also. Should I let him go, *habibi*? Before Friday?'

'I didn't know he wanted to leave so soon.'

'Perhaps he doesn't,' Hakim said. 'I hope not. I really hope not.'

Scott felt as if he were locked up in Abu Suweir again, but this time with a world that did not exist outside Hakim's brain and Hakim's obsessions. Yet so many others seemed to share his world. It was not so fantastic after all, except that it was a dangerous world, whatever way you looked at it—that dangerous part of human affairs which no one ever saw when they were walking the streets of their cities, accepting the news of all events at their face value, or at newspaper value at least.

'How do you know they want to hurt Gamal?' Scott asked out of the darkness.

'Of course they do, *habibi*,' Hakim said calmly. 'They'll try that first.'

Hakim was leading him to the door, his arm affectionately over Scott's shoulder to signify an end to this. Why speculate? Why worry? Why doubt the worst motivations of politics and men? Everything was possible, normal and logical.

'When Governments start the killing they call it war. But who will draw the line between killing one man, and killing thousands? Isn't war a continuation of assassination by other means? The only point, therefore, to worry about is which side is right. Or, rather, which side are you on. That's all a man can ever ask of a friend or of a politician or even of an assassin, *habibi*. That's all, really.'

Scott needed to walk a long way home after this visit to Hakim's normal world, postponing arrival as long as possible. By now he felt as if he never wanted to arrive anywhere. There was no reason to arrive.

He walked down the Heliopolis avenues of thin acacias, dried out by the dry end of summer. It was still too hot to be doing this, but he went on by the palatial and arid monkey-house of Baron Empain, the Belgian who had built the whole of Heliopolis and still owned it. He was still walking another four miles away, almost into Cairo itself, at Ghamra, where the conglomeration of Cairo life started in earnest. He was crossing the noisy road when an Egyptian Army van stopped on the other side, and the driver shouted at him.

'Capten, Capten! Why are you walking? Get in. I'll take you.'

It was Ishaak, and Scott crossed the road and said, 'What's this, Ishaak? This isn't a Frontier Corps truck. It looks like an ambulance.'

'That's so, Capten. I borrowed it. They transferred me.'

'They did?' So he had lost Ishaak in his absence. Although, perhaps it was not such a surprise, because Ishaak had been appealing for a long time to be taken out of the Frontier Corps and sent to the Medical services; and here he was. Which meant that he would be alone in the desert now, if he ever went back there for sure; and that was always possible, even probable.

'Mabrouk!' he congratulated Ishaak.

'And I'm not a driver any more,' Ishaak told him.

'Good for you,' Scott said. 'How did you manage it?'

'They want me to be a *Feldscher*.' He used the German word. Scott knew there were German army officers reshaping that part of the Egyptian Army Medical Corps which trained the medical technicians they called *Feldschers*, who were really medical orderlies in the field. That was a big step up for Ishaak.

'But they're mad,' Ishaak said with his natural amazement at the Egyptians. 'They think because I speak and write English that I can understand German, or ought to.'

'You can learn it. That's probably what they mean.'

'But why should I, when they teach me the work in English anyway?'

'Heaven knows,' Scott said. 'But if they ask, you ought to do it.'

'Oh, I'll do it,' Ishaak said as he almost drove down a handful of native boys chasing each other across the street. He braked, shouted, and lurched the ambulance forward. 'They pay me a shilling a week extra for learning German, and I can become a sergeant very quickly if . . .' (he dropped his voice) '. . . I go back with the fedayeen into Palestine at night. On commando raids.'

'You be careful,' Scott warned him. 'I thought you'd had enough of being a fedayi.'

'Yes, but even I get angry sometimes, Capten, when I think of what I have to do in order to be something; to be anything. Who will remember us, from Palestine, if we don't remember ourselves?' he said bitterly with a few tears rising already. 'I don't want to live here all my life. I'm not Egyptian. I'm a Palestinian, and when I think of those Jews there, where I lived, and when I think of where they come from, I could murder them. Why should Germans steal all my land and live on it? I'm glad I killed that one. I swear I'm glad.'

'You be careful,' Scott warned him again, knowing that Ishaak had never owned a fedahn of land to be stolen by anyone; but he could call it his home. 'Killing can hurt both ways,' Scott said sadly.

'Aren't we all in God's hands?' Ishaak said piously and dramatically. 'Even when we kill for what is right.'

450

HAKIM had watched Mr. Menzies closely during his arrival at the airport, and he was thinking now: 'If someone does succeed in killing Gamal, I'll kill this bushman, personally, with my own hands.'

But he was worried, wondering if what he already knew might simply be a deception for another and more dangerous attempt on Gamal's life —one he might not know about. It was possible. But its probability was difficult to estimate, and the only thing he could do now (if such a thing happened) was to calculate a revenge. And there was the object of it— Mr. Menzies who surely knew nothing about anything.

When Hakim's green Chevrolet arrived at the villa on the Nile, he tried to think himself into the mentality of Mr. Menzies arriving to trick Gamal if he could. But how did a bushman think? The only possible arguments Menzies could present to Gamal were so crude that the man ought to feel a fool to try them.

'Keep the cars away from the entrance, far away,' he told the guards.

He sat in the villa's garden in a wicker chair, watching them arrive: Menzies, and Henderson the American, the Swede with curious eyes, and the Persian who ran a long way behind them. An Ethiopian was a joke. What was he doing for the African world in Gamal's light, in Gamal's eye?

'Close the gates,' he told the captain at the small lodge next door.

He went inside, as he would do each day, to watch them sitting around Farouk's old room in their armchairs listening, listening, listening to the voice of Menzies which came from the soft part of his neck.

'I would like to make it clear . . .' Mr. Menzies would begin; and that was always a lawyer's beginning, or an Englishman's.

But what was clear? Ah, Mr. Dulles's plan was clear. Hakim hardly heard it, but the absent Mr. Dulles assured Egypt that she could go on owning the Canal Company, although the operation of the canal itself would be in the hands of an international committee. Wasn't that very simple? Very clear?

Gamal smoked and did not laugh out loud. Did they think he was such a cringing idiot to want a pretence like that as a means of owning the canal, which he would not control, nor in fact own, nor in fact even share?

Menzies was a large, red, full-faced man, and Hakim followed him out. Menzies was heard to say to reporters outside: 'Don't I look happy? Don't you see that I'm using the President's car? That's a good sign, isn't it?'

It would be, if he was shot mistakenly for Gamal.

In the evening Hakim came back again to hear what Gamal would say to these extraordinary men who did not even understand what they were trying to do.

'What is your problem?' Gamal told them, shrugging a little and watching Hakim briefly as he leaned against the window, with the evening breeze from the river (smelling of mud) pushing down the back of his tunic, searching for his bones. This island of Zamalek was too unhealthy, too damp, and Hakim moved away from the window.

'What is your problem?' Gamal was saying. 'Freedom of navigation? I'm ready to discuss that. Tolls? I'm ready to discuss that. The British press charges I'm trying to build an empire. We can discuss that too if you want. But I tell you now, gentlemen, that I will not discuss Egyptian sovereignty. I refuse to do that . . .'

The visitors were polite and silent. Did silence signify embarrassment of intentions? Why should he mention such a thing to them?

'All right,' Gamal said, with a moment's exasperation, 'perhaps you would like to discuss British fears that I'm going to cut their lifeline of empire. But if I did that it would mean war with Britain. Do you think I'm mad enough to do that? And if I was so stupid, how could the international board that you propose prevent me from doing it in any case? Eh?'

The bushman looked worried and red faced.

'I can't go beyond my mandate,' Mr. Menzies replied solemnly—a very heavy warning from afar. 'I can only present and explain our committee's proposal. But I do assure the President that Egypt will not lose sovereignty by allowing an international body to control the canal.'

It was all talk.

If they wished, Gamal would guarantee their right to use the canal, even the unmentionable Israelis could use it if they wanted to, but the tolls must be paid to Egypt, and Egypt must have control of what was rightfully hers. Remember what it was for, gentlemen? Hakim could say it, but Gamal could not. Did anyone remember the Aswan Dam now?

'Let us negotiate the terms, not the principle,' Gamal said. 'The principle is not at stake. The canal now belongs to Egypt and nothing can change that. Believe me!'

But Mr. Menzies, wriggling like a lawyer again, said he had no power to negotiate on those terms, even if they recognized the principle, which they did not and could not.

Why was he here then? if it was not an impolite question.

He was here, the bushman said, to present and to explain and to warn. Nothing more. He had presented, and he had explained, and he had warned. That's all he could do.

'But they won't even negotiate,' Gamal complained tiredly when they drove away together in Hakim's Chevrolet. 'They only want it their way. Or they want to frighten me with the hint of force. But the only thing they know how to do is to try tricking us. They give us the Canal Company on paper, while they keep the canal itself. That's crude, isn't it? Why can't they see that I'm not a fool? Why can't they see that I don't even want to take anything away from them? Why can't they see it is Egyptian? And why can't they see that the Arabs are not to be deceived? Why don't they believe me when I tell them these things? Why do they obstruct us when they can't win? Why? Why? Why don't they listen to me, and why don't they understand?'

Gamal had almost lost his temper in exasperation, but what could a man do when he was dealing with deaf pretences, mute promises; talking to the sad faces of these solemn men.

'I listen and shrug,' he said bitterly. 'That's all I can do, *ya habibi*, because they shrug without even listening.'

Hakim said nothing. It was all right for Gamal to look into the eyes of his Arab brothers and say: *Believe me! Believe me, O brothers!* But what could a bushman do with a passion? To be burning with the Arab future was almost a terrible religion with Gamal. How could Australian horsemen know anything of the deep inlay of the Arab past and the Arab hopes; of the religion or the dream? How could he know? It was impossible, and Gamal ought to realize it and tell them to go, and never mind being exasperated by them.

But when he stood very near Mr. Menzies, in what used to be royal gardens, Hakim wondered what this man's country was like.

These pink, discoloured-looking people all appeared as if they ate too much raw meat and rode racehorses. The Australian soldiers in Egypt during the war had been the worst of all, little more than uncaged beasts who had ambled recklessly at large—playful, destructive and stupid. Was this their hero, this red man drinking official *limoon* (no whisky) and sweating in Farouk's old garden while Gamal swished away old Egyptian flies and tried to explain in English that Egypt was a very old country, and that ancient history was still an insoluble base for a nation to rest upon?

Egypt now was beginning to fulfil the destiny of her old glories, simply by being independent and by exercising a will of her own.

Whereas the faraway Menzies country was probably a country that reminded one of a provincial racecourse. Would the Australian bushmen weep if their Menzies was murdered in the streets of Cairo, as the Egyptian fellaheen would weep if Gamal was suddenly struck down by someone ill-begotten enough to want him dead and safely removed?

'We'll see,' Hakim said to himself in English. He saw Mr. Menzies make a big joke with the American, Mr. Loy Henderson, and Gamal smiled.

'You may yet die a hero's death,' Hakim announced good-naturedly to Menzies, but only the old banyan trees could hear it.

It was Fahid's day, today, to take a further barograph test for his 'A' licence, because the Air Force had disputed his first one. What a blow! What a stupid, vindictive thing to do to him after he had passed. But what a marvellous chance. Couldn't he, today, justify Zareef's misplaced confidence in him, even though Zareef's trust in him was really Zareef's secret blow at Captain Selim?

Captain Selim, the chief instructor, was afraid to allow Fahid to take up a plane on a further test; so Zareef took the responsibility for it instead, and thus, morally, Zareef had Selim on the run. Ever since the day Captain Selim had been afraid of their take-off in an overloaded Auster, Zareef had found his mark, and now he was being reckless with this war of responsibility.

'I'll take the entire responsibility for the test,' Zareef said impatiently to Selim.

'All right, Capten,' Selim answered, signing the clearance. 'But if he smashes the plane it will be the worse for you, not for him. Why do you trust him? He's such a *magnoon*.'

Fahid was a fool and everybody knew it, even Zareef.

Nevertheless, vocation itself was a factor, and Zareef took Fahid up in the Auster and went over and over the simplest rules for keeping the S-turns wide, and maintaining height in a turn, and for avoiding under-shooting and over-shooting in landing, because there would be no second chance with a barograph on board during a test.

The cross-country too would be a miracle of luck. But Zareef now gambled on the impossible, and he had taken Fahid with him in the Gemini every time he had flown to Alexandria on the Army A.A. co-operation flights, and he had allowed the boy to work out the course and find the landmarks, the few there were.

On these flights Zareef had recognized Fahid's suppressed fear of extreme height, which began at three thousand feet for most people who

454

were afraid of flying. This was very important. Usually a man who was afraid of heights could not adapt himself to the stillness of the panorama below, he became afraid of its slow passage, much preferring the closeness to earth and the feeling of passing contact it gave you, even though it was far more dangerous. The mad boy Fahid had this natural fear of higher perspectives, so Zareef had arranged for him to go up early mornings in the weather plane from Almaza, which had been his own training in heights up to twenty thousand feet, and Zareef still remembered nostalgically those unquenchable discoveries of space when he had been a student at Almaza.

Zareef then had always arrived in pre-dawn darkness to be sure that he could ask the weather pilot if he could go up. It depended on the pilot flying a two-seater, and not an old Gladiator or a Hart. In those dim, fine intimate rose dawns when the plane had climbed to its maximum, he had learned how to forget the old view of the earth and feel the freedom of genuine detachment from it. Usually the weather Harvard had climbed at its full angle of climb, flown off the top at eight thousand and twelve thousand and twenty thousand feet while the pilot took barometric readings and calculated drift and recorded temperatures and humidity. Then he had come down immediately without wasting time, so that the pilot could be home in time to eat breakfast with his wife. The pilot's wife would know when he was down to earth again because she lived in Heliopolis, and every morning she could hear the sudden straining roar of the Harvard's engine when the propeller pitch was fined down for landing.

'It's all habit,' Zareef told Fahid. 'A man learns to do something only by doing it, and by nothing else.'

'That's a stupid way,' Fahid said calmly. 'That means any fool could learn to fly.'

'Yes, if he does it often enough. But the clever ones learn quicker and do it better, and the fools make bad pilots.'

'Don't believe it, Captain. It's the stupid ones who learn easily. The clever find it difficult. There must be some reason why I find it difficult,' the boy said and laughed his shame away cynically.

'He'll probably kill himself sooner or later if he goes on flying,' Zareef thought, avoiding Fahid's thin, resentful, parrying thrusts of body and brain and eyes. He was certain to end up doing something violent and self-destructive.

A security officer was permanently at the airport now, and he was usually at work everywhere, developing the casual relationships of the hand-slap and the heart embrace, which Fahid despised.

'What do you think he wants? Why did they send him?' Barmeel asked

Fahid, watching this green-fringed lieutenant slapping handshakes on the engineers and the C.A.A. men who were fitting the barograph into the Auster for the test.

'He wants to see if there are any bombs in the plane,' Fahid said.

Were they still looking for echoes of Sam Hassoon?

The students were gathered in the leather lounge waiting for morning coca-colas and for the signal to start flying. Zareef was testing the other Austers and Captain Selim was late. Selim was not going to be here the day that Fahid was sent on a second test. He had more sense. It would have to be Zareef's entire responsibility.

'Do they think you're going to bomb Abdin?' Barmeel said facetiously.

'I might,' Fahid responded.

'That's what they thought Hassoon was going to do,' Barmeel tittered. 'Why do they still worry about it?'

'Merde!' Fahid said. 'That's how stupid you all are.'

Fahid knew he was the only one here, or anywhere else for that matter, apart from his father, who probably knew what Sam Hassoon had been doing and how guilty he was. Dropping bombs on Abdin? Was that what these idiots suspected? If they only knew . . .

'Perhaps they're not stupid,' he said. 'Perhaps I will drop a bomb on Abdin myself, some day.'

'Shhh!' Barmeel said urgently.

Everybody had heard it, and Fahid turned on the others.

'What are you afraid of?' he shouted at his student companions, who were simply objects large or small to him, ignorant or dull, or frightened or insensitive, or dark or fair. They were idiotic whenever they talked politics, anyway, and ever since Gamal Abd el Nasser had nationalized the Suez Canal they were showing even more pride in themselves than was decent. But Fahid's savage attacks on them had become so virulent lately that they tried to avoid him altogether. They had even ceased to ridicule him to his face because he was becoming too dangerous and reckless in his replies. They were now afraid of him.

'What use are you?' he said to them now. 'Are you going to protect Gamal Abd el Nasser? How? By your silly jokes? You're all soft sons of silly fathead fathers. You haven't even killed the Jews in Palestine. A Jew would look at any one of you, and you'd run away. Where would you get your courage from? Are you the ones that Gamal Abd el Nasser loves? I suppose you are. Are you the new Egypt? Oh, my God! Do you think anyone could be afraid of you? What will happen to you when Mustafa the night watchman and his asses turn and bite you, or Hefney the prop-swinger takes a gun and shoots at you? Where will your Gamal Abd el Nasser and your creased pants be then? Look at the old wretch selling *ful* in the middle of his donkey shit outside the gate. Was it for you or for him that Gamal Abd el Nasser had a revolution? Why, for you, of course, my darlings.'

'Magnoon!' they muttered and went outside.

Fahid mocked them all as they left. Barmeel tried to calm him.

'One of them will make trouble for you,' he warned Fahid nervously. 'They don't like it when you say that.'

'Let them,' Fahid said. 'What do you care?'

Barmeel was round, and he wanted peace: peace everywhere, even with Fahid. He knew that rebuffs meant war, and he did not want war, even with Fahid.

'Why do you talk like that?' he said appealingly to Fahid.

'Oh, they think it's all theirs.'

'What's theirs?'

'Why, everything. The English and the foreigners are running away, and the lieutenants of our fine Egyptian Army are taking over all the villas in Meadi. No corruption, oh no! Why it's only a brother or a sister who gets the house, who buys the business, who steals the money. That's a marvellous revolution. Why should I bother with it? Even this coca-cola community under the Haboob, where we learn to fly to be nothing—this is supposed to be a new revolution? What a joke. I wonder what you will be, Barmeel? Let's have a coca-cola, or send Ali for a coffee. What a life.'

Barmeel supposed he was too excited because of the test.

Captain Zareef had already landed a Besterman in a perfect landing on its flight check, and he came over to give Fahid his last instructions for the barometric test. The instrument was sealed and ready, and the security lieutenant had made sure it was not a bomb.

'Now, when you take off,' Zareef told him, his square hand capping Fahid's thin shoulder briefly, 'don't start over-correcting. Get to your climbing speed and stick to it until you are up to three thousand feet. Then you level off. Just sit back and go up. And when you start your turns, make them *wide*. You like to make them too tight and you lose height because you slip into the turn. Keep them wide and gentle. Don't hurry. Just don't hurry, *ya wallad*. Eh? And when you come in, make your approach gentle. You can always use your engine to make up if you're undershooting.'

'I think I'll just take off and never come back,' Fahid said to Zareef.

'Just don't hurry,' Zareef said, knowing he would never understand the boy.

Fahid knew it and wondered who would understand him, some day.

He strapped, buckled, started, taxied, turned, took off, climbed and remembered the things he hated most. The world of soft-skinned young men in white silk shirts. How they pounced around the streets, now that Gamal Abd el Nasser had made them men without the struggle to be men. He had made heroes out of fools, he had salvaged the conceit of a nation of mother's sons. Spoiled boys! Was that the purpose of their liberation? But it was not quite true. He remembered his cousin, Ramzey, who had been in the siege of the Feluga fortress. Ramzey had admitted fear and confusion, but he had not surrendered. But Ramzey was a hateless family-man who loved his village wife and his baby sons, who would die some day as an officer because it was still honourable to die simply. He was a simple man, although he too ate more than was good for him, and he believed in Gamal Abd el Nasser.

'I hate aeroplanes,' Fahid said aloud.

For a moment he had forgotten it, and he had done well. Now it bumped in the hot air and the engine roared unevenly in compensation, and he began to correct.

'If I fail this test,' he decided, looking at the altimeter which registered 2,800 feet, 'I'll kill Gamal Abd el Nasser myself.'

He wondered why he had come to hate Nasser so much.

'It's a trick,' he shouted aloud. 'It's all a deception.'

He knew the Army and hated its officers. Was that why he hated Gamal Abd el Nasser? Or was it for something he had failed in himself? He felt the burden of some future in him, but what could it be? What could it possibly be, he wanted to cry out. Nothing, absolutely nothing! He could only despise everything—the corrupt old pretences which Gamal Abd el Nasser had replaced by another, younger, and unformed pretence, this new pretence which he had encouraged in the boastful nature of every white-shirted adolescent in the streets and the countryside. Was that it?

'It must be more,' he could cry unhappily up here.

But it was hard to identify, up here, what more there could be; and what was worse than anything else was this blank, this lacuna, this chasm between all these pretences and the daily life one lived down there. Egypt would go on rotting in shame, and Gamal Abd el Nasser had done nothing more than make the shame a national selfconsciousness, uplifting only those young men down there who were too ignorant to know that something had failed, and that everything was wrong. Marvellous men believed in Nasser. But they were wasting their marvels on a man with one face, and no future.

'Merde!' he said, because he had gone too high.

He levelled off and throttled back and felt cool, almost cold. Here it was still, and the vibration suddenly alarmed him because the engine was quieter, and his reactions had time to work. His ears were quite dense.

'Now I'll give Zareef his victory over the Haboob,' he said.

He began the 'S' turns, and knew he would never grasp the balance between stick and rudder which made a turn exact and pure. The plane swung, it slipped, he tried to push it around with the rudder, it slipped

458

further, he corrected; but at least he was in some sort of a turn and he held the height. The height was all that mattered to the barograph and he did his first figure-of-eight.

Suddenly he laughed.

What possible reality was there in a man up here at three thousand feet above the earth doing figures-of-eight in an aeroplane? What did it mean?

'I'll be nice to *Barmeel*,' he said, and laughed again.

He completed his second figure eight and corrected his height because he had lost fifty feet, but that wasn't so bad. It was now his last turn and he concentrated on it sternly for the justification of Zareef's instruction, for Zareef's proud war with the Haboob.

'Habobb, haboob, habibi . . .' he sang through the last one.

He had completed it, and he cut the engine and adjusted the tail-trimmer and began a fast glide, correcting and over-correcting and looking down for the airfield. Where was it?

He was over the river and he made a steep gliding turn.

He did not like gliding or climbing turns because they had so little internal control in them, so little real direction. He came down in a straight glide, and he could see the blots of peasants in the fields, the white birds, the gamoosses, the wet glistening reflection of water under the soil, and he felt the rising bumps of heat which drew stresses and vacuums around the plane's wings and waltzed them up and pushed them down.

His approach was miraculously right, it must be the luck of Zareef. He saw a peasant's face upturned and felt like leaning over and waving to him in sheer camaraderie. He was standing there up to his knees in mud, his face grinning and his hands thick with roots or grasses, his gown wrapped around his waist. He grew there. That peasant had concentrated all the reality in his feet, not in his head or his hands. That was the earth coming up to him, and he knew now where reality was. It was right there. It was there if he didn't undershoot and hit the railway line and end up in the green muddy swamp near the road.

'I hate this too,' he said.

He hated the challenge of landing, but he resisted the temptation to level out too soon, and he held the nose down until it was six inches off, he swore. Then he eased back the stick and decided to hold it in the middle and let the plane land itself. That way he wouldn't bump. He waited. He waited. He waited. He drifted. He explored the marvels of reality. Then he landed perfectly, having allowed the plane to do it for him because it was far more able to than he was.

'All they have to do now is fail me on the barograph,' he said, down to earth again.

He waited for another Auster to land, and he turned around and opened

459

the engine and taxied much too fast across the dirt and dust of the field. If they failed him, he recalled, he would kill Gamal Abd el Nasser. Would he do it—down here in the dust where the world was fixed and all was pretence?

'I might,' he decided happily. 'I still might do it.'

CHAPTER SIXTY-ONE

JOLLEY had been gone long enough for Helen Mamoon to bring the office boab, Ismail, in with her every morning to bundle up stacks of the important files and maps in brown paper and take them away to the bank, where she had hired a deposit box. The box was already far too small for the amount of documentation which thirty years of oil-prospecting had accumulated, and she was storing the leftovers in a trunk which she would lock and leave in the hired garage where Jolley had kept his car. Nobody would bother to look there, and its rent had been paid a year in advance.

She ate a small bowl of yaourt and read the French newspapers. She could no longer read the Arabic papers because the boasting depressed her.

The *Bourse* this morning said that the Orient Line boats from Australia had been diverted from the Suez Canal and were now going to England around the Cape. On the tin trunk which Ismail was packing with letters and maps she could look over her morning *Bourse* and read a name in white paint:

'Lieutenant-Col. George F. Ainsworth. GHQ. ME.'

George Ainsworth had left his tin trunk behind him when he had packed up and gone to Burma in 1944. He had never come back and never written to her. That pale, masculine-looking Englishman had wilted at the thought of being possessed by the demanding eyes of a Circassian *mirligo*. She had wasted so much time on him that she could not quite laugh it off. But she did laugh to think of this last remnant of his, ending up as a hiding place for dusty papers and dead correspondence of an English oil company in Egypt, beginning: 'Yours of Feb. 3rd to hand . . .'

'Who's going to lift all this trunk, *ya sitt*?' Ismail asked her.

'Not you, Ismail,' Helen said. 'Don't worry.'

Ismail was old and diseased and dangerous. Among the office boabeen he was probably the least kind, although the most reliable: the spokesmen for all the others in this building and in the neighbouring offices. The boabeen sat on the benches under the lift in the morning, and they slept under the stairs in the hot afternoons. She imagined that they were always deciding what they would do when the mob broke loose again. Someone would pay for a moment's rudeness.

Only last week the boab of the block of flats where one of Jolley's friends lived had been insulted. Teddy Andrews, who was a car agent, had been struggling with another car parked right against his own, outside his flat, and when the boab had not come outside to give him a hand, he had gone inside and shouted rudely at the boab: 'What are you being paid for? Why don't you come out here and get this car out of my way. Come on.'

The boab had been insulted by his manner and had refused. He had thereafter refused to allow Teddy Andrews to use the lift to reach his eleventh-floor apartment.

Andrews had been forced to call on Helen to settle it, somehow. 'Any way you can,' he begged desperately. 'I can't go on walking up those stairs.'

Helen had tried to placate the boab, but he said to her that if the *hawaga* (the plain mister!) ever talked like that to him again, he would get his friends together one dark night and beat him up.

'He is sorry,' Helen had apologized. 'He would like to offer you this.' The envelope had contained two pounds. The boab had refused it and he had said, 'Let the *hawaga* apologize personally, with his own tongue. Then I'll take his money and forgive him.'

Teddy Andrews had stormed and refused, all in the privacy of his office. He had cursed the country, the people, and Nasser for doing this. To apologize to a boab was simply going beyond the blood. He would leave Egypt before he would do it.

'You can't talk rudely to these people any more,' Helen had warned him—not without reprimand. These Englishmen never knew how to talk to servants, anyway. They had neither dignity nor character enough to convince any boab of their supposed superiority; very few Englishmen by nature were that convincing. Now they were paying the price for years of undignified, imposed lordliness, the victims of which were now anxious to turn around and eat them. So they did. Teddy Andrews went on walking up his eleven flights of stairs, and the boab had said one morning to his friends in Arabic, so that he would be heard, 'Gamal Abd el Nasser is also making all these *affrang* walk a long way around the canal, you notice?' The others had laughed as Andrews fumbled for his car keys; and finally there was no alternative but to arrange his apology or be laughed at rudely every day.

Helen had tried to arrange it as a private affair, but the boab had made sure that all his friends were near enough to hear this Englishman apologize to him for being rude.

In gratitude, Andrews had sent Helen a large box of chocolates for her help, but they were bad for the liver, and Andrews had also decided to leave Egypt, so he had also sent her a bundle of his own files to be stored with Jolley's.

'Are they all such ninnies?' she was beginning to ask herself, preparing for a few moments' wider exploration of Englishmen and their sudden failings. But the outer office door was suddenly opened. Strange that she had not heard the lift. The other boab below should have rung her bell if someone was coming. The inner door was opened then, and three men entered the office.

'Sitt Mamoon!'

One of them was the sharp-eared tax man, and the other two were police captains in uniform asking for Jolley. Where was he? Why had he gone? Why was she packing up her office? Where were the company's books?

The whole thing was upon her before she could gather her wits.

'The company's books are in the bank,' she said hastily. They would have to wait if they wanted to see them. She tried to think quickly of other evasive answers about the books, but they showed no particular interest in the office accounts. They were obviously more interested in Jolley himself and in her; and she began to feel afraid of them.

'Why did he go away?' they kept asking, while Ismail the boab listened.

She had tried to send Ismail away, but they told him to stay and they asked him how many other trunks of papers he had packed, and were there many maps?'

'There are nothing but maps,' Helen told them indignantly. 'We have maps of every square inch of Egypt. We must have them.'

'Where are all the other maps, then?' an officer with his cap still on his head asked. The other one had removed his cap, so she answered this one as a rebuke to his rude companion.

'They are mostly in that trunk,' she said. 'Take them all if you want them.'

But she realized suddenly just what that trunk could mean.

In the trunk was a detailed plan and survey for every oilfield or potential oil-bearing area in Egypt, with roads and all communications marked, with ports and pipelines and landing fields and plotted capacities, with wells and pumping-houses and storage tanks. There was nothing secret about it to an oil company, all the foreign oil companies in Egypt would have such maps, but there could be something secret about it to secretive minds looking for suspects—for those enemy aeroplanes looking for targets.

'Where were you sending this trunk?' the polite one asked.

She knew how dangerous a lie would be now, and she told the truth.

463

'To Mr. Jolley's private garage where he keeps his car. It's already full of his boxes, awaiting his return.'

They asked for the keys.

She gave them up and felt her whole body trembling with both anger and fear, and she cautioned herself not to fight back, not to lose her temper, not to defend herself before it was necessary.

'Is that all?' they asked. 'No more papers?'

'Only in the bank,' she said as calmly as she could.

The impolite officer lifted up the empty yaourt jar from her desk, sniffed it, and then put it down and wiped his fingers on his handkerchief. He caught her sharp feminine eyes and removed his cap reluctantly, and told her that she must report at room 47 at the Ministry of Interior that afternoon with her own passport and her sister's, and also to bring with her whatever documents she had for her nephew, Sam Hassoon.

'He's a man older than you are,' she told the officer. 'I don't keep his papers. Anyway, he hasn't got any. You probably know that as well as I do.'

The officer shrugged and said: 'Bring what you have. Everything for all of you, including your sister who is visiting you.'

'She has a British passport, not an Egyptian one,' Helen said.

'Gibbi el kul!' Bring it all! The officer's throat swallowed the *kul* with a tightening of his neck muscles which suggested that he too was containing his temper and did not want to be argued with.

It was unfortunate that Quartermain had booked four passages on the Orient Liner which had been due at Port Said early in October, because owing to the tense situation in the canal area it was now being diverted around the Cape. It would not call on Egypt, and they had thus lost their escape passage home.

'I had thought Hanna would go with you and the children,' Quartermain said, when he told his wife what had happened, 'while Helen and I waited here and got out some other way. But the children ought to go in any case.'

'We should all go together,' Nona insisted stubbornly, 'otherwise I know Helen won't leave. We'll all go as soon as she gets her exit permits.'

'But we may not be able to wait that long,' Quartermain argued. 'Planes and ships are booked out for months ahead. I was lucky to get those berths.'

'Can't we get to Khartoum or Libya and go on from there?'

'We can get anywhere,' Quartermain said dryly, 'if we wait here long enough to find a fortune.'

'Helen will lend us some money. Then we'll all go together.'

Nona was still fighting for the right to rescue her sisters, but Helen

464

listened and realized that Nona was not giving her husband the chance to help without her insistence.

'It's not necessary to leave Egypt yet, anyway,' Helen said. 'After all, they're still talking to Menzies.'

'He thinks we should leave,' Nona argued. 'And I do too. But I won't go unless I know at least that you and Hanna have exit permits and can follow. I won't go . . .'

It was acrimonious and unpleasant. Hanna was upset also. 'Family decisions,' she said privately to Helen, 'ought to be reached without argument. It's terrible to see them arguing about it.'

But insistence, rights, and a sense of protection were bad company for family reason, and Nona flung off her demands as if she were standing on some high cliff with a wasteful and barren shore below. That barren, dry shore shrugged. He was ill with a suspected kidney infection, and he lay in bed looking grey and trunk-like, and partially disinterested. When Nona leashed back at him with her insistence on required family rights, he picked up a newspaper and began to read it and she left the room almost in tears.

Helen felt sorry for Quartermain and she allowed herself one second for the thought that Nona might be too harsh in her insistence, and too determined in her pronouncements. Nona was not easy to compromise with.

But Helen had to talk to Quartermain alone, and she sat on the end of the bed and rubbed one of his long toes sticking up under the cover of the sheet.

'She's worried about Hanna and me,' Helen explained.

'So am I,' Quartermain said sourly, 'but she makes it impossible to think this out calmly, so that everybody can get away if there is trouble.'

'I'll talk to her,' Helen promised, and said consolingly: 'Don't worry. And please don't you get sick, *ya hawaga*, because we're not going to be much good without you.'

'Let her do it,' Quartermain said in a huff, in a sad acceptance of his defeat, which had drawn in his face to the lightest shade of grey, like his hair, and made his soft eyes droop from their usual suspicious outlook into a bitter enclosure against everybody.

Something, she decided, was bothering this man quite profoundly. Whether it was simply this inexplicable running sore with Nona, or whether it was something to do with his complex politics, she could not guess. But she could not afford to be compassionate about him now. She needed his help.

'The police came to see me this morning,' she began, 'and they want to question me again this afternoon.'

465

Her discipline and her determination kept a rein on her indignation and her fears for a little while, but by the time she had finished telling him what had happened she had lost her nerve and her temper.

'Why do they pick on me? Since Swinburne and that other Englishman were arrested as spies, every British firm in Cairo is under suspicion. And everybody working for them could all be spies. It's so ridiculous and unfair. Most British concerns in Egypt are technical. They all have to collect or use technical information in Egypt, which Nasser can easily say is spying. Particularly Jolley.'

'Do you think it's Jolley, or is it Sam they're worrying you about?'

She knew what none of them knew about Sam, but she could not possibly know if the Egyptians were going to question her about Sam. She could only pray, *in sha'allah*, that they would not.

'Did Sam and Jolley ever meet?' Quartermain asked her.

'No, no. That's not what Sam did,' she said, impatient with his question. 'It was nothing to do with Jolley.'

'How do you know what Sam did?' he asked her. 'Do you know?'

'Of course I do, but if you want to know . . .'

'I don't. Don't tell me,' Quartermain said sharply. 'What I don't know I can't tell someone else. Don't tell anyone, ever. Don't talk about it even to yourself.'

'I don't intend to tell anyone,' she said, but it was beginning to be a strain, keeping so much to herself. She had not yet told Nona or Hanna about the police calling on her, or of their demands for passports. She couldn't risk their upsetting concern for her. Perhaps they would even panic, and then she would panic herself.

But she could trust Quartermain's judgment more than anyone else's, because he was so often right and never panicked, in fact he never seemed to be surprised by anything that happened. Thinking about him like that, she could even have admired his outlook if only he did not always dry it up with his own certainties, and sour it continuously with his expectancy of the worst—in the world's wrongs. The world *was* wrong. But sometimes it managed to be right also, although at the moment it was all wrong, all unfair, all frightening.

'What should I say to the police?' she asked him.

'If they ask you about Sam, tell them you don't know anything. Otherwise, tell the truth as near as you can.'

'I always do.'

'Don't let them frighten you. And if they do frighten you, try to keep quiet. Say nothing if you're frightened, not a word.'

'Oh, I'm used to the Security police,' she said contemptuously. 'They are usually polite at least.'

'Don't let them be too polite,' Quartermain warned her. 'When police-

466

men are polite—when they are decent and honourable and friendly, they are much more dangerous to you than when they try to beat you up. And never volunteer anything. Answer, but answer as briefly as you can. Don't say anything more than you have to.'

She knew all that too, but he warned her not to hand over her passport or Hanna's. She could certainly not take Nona's with her. Leave them all behind, locked up in her flat.

'But they said I must bring them.'

'Let the brutes come and get them. Tell them so,' he said viciously. 'Don't hand over your passport for any reason. And if they ask about Nona, tell them to come to me.'

Nona called Helen to come to lunch, and she got up and kissed Quartermain on the grey face. 'You mustn't worry about Hanna and me,' she said gently to him. 'You will have to go without us, but we'll be all right.'

'If you could get her an exit permit, Hanna can leave with Nona and the boys,' Quartermain said. 'I'll try to get them on a plane. You and I could follow. I have to stay here anyway, to see what happens.'

'Do you think the English will really try to take the canal back, by force?'

'If Menzies fails to get it back, if Nasser doesn't budge, if—if—if. *If* is the only real position on which the world survives at the moment.'

'The British would attack Egypt? I mean bombs and armies?'

Quartermain shrugged. 'I'll tell you the answer to that after this debate in the House of Commons about it. Real intentions sometimes show up through all that blah.'

'But the Egyptians would hate them for ever if they attack,' she said. 'Don't they realize that?'

She did not believe it possible. She admired Eden. Everybody did who remembered what he had done during the Abyssinian war, although she had forgotten what it was.

Had he resigned over the sanctions against Italy? Had he resigned be-because of Chamberlain and Hitler? Anyway, he was not a violent or a stupid man. Only a butcher or a fool would think of attacking Egypt now, even over the canal, even over Nasser.

'I'll try again for our exit permits,' she told Quartermain, hearing Nona coming down the passage. 'If I can only get Hanna's . . .'

Nona walked in carrying a tray with a plate of boiled and fatless chicken for him.

'Dr. Buelli will be here at five o'clock,' she said. 'He says you'll have to be X-rayed tomorrow, and he says you ought to rest.'

Quartermain's world of document and significance, of argument and typewritten statement, was scattered over his bed.

He had almost finished his dispatch on Mr. Menzies' mission, and

467

perhaps Helen would take it to the Cable and Wireless office, on her way to the Ministry.

Helen had already tried to find her friend Maître el Khony, but he was on holiday in Alexandria with his wife, presumably trying to prove to her that love was still possible, even when she did not *have* to love him. Even her cousin Makram was away in his province, which meant that she could not find any inside support for her contest in Room 47, which was at the very top of the crowded and hectic ministry building, near enough to the roof and the heat to compress perspiration from every pore of her body.

The hubbub of all those foreigners begging for papers had given her a headache. She was soaked in it by the time the Security police began to question her, so that at the beginning she was too physically uncomfortable to be upset by their silly questions.

The first questioner in Room 47 began by asking her very inexpertly about her past, pushing a pencil through his thinning hair and scratching his dry scalp with it so that she longed to tell him of el Khony's remedy with camel dung. Then he went away and another man appeared and sat at another desk and asked her the same questions, casually leaning over the back of his chair. They first asked where her passport and papers were, and she replied that she had not brought them because she was afraid they might try to keep them.

Both had asked it, both laughed at her honest reply; but they did not pursue it.

Finally a third man, an older man, arrived with a large pink file in his hand, and she recognized it by the traffic of the file on the other desks, in other days. It was her own dossier with the Ministry of Interior. She thought she also recognized the man, but she could not quite place him.

He was grey-haired, and he looked as if he had been an army officer. He opened the inner door of the office to allow some air into the room, then he filled in a small white card, looked at her once, wrote something on the card, and filed it in a long drawer on his desk with a thousand other white cards. Life and death seemed to have been written on that sterile little card and put away. Then he began to look at her pink file, taking a deep breath every now and then as if he had eaten too much lunch.

'Where is your nephew, Sam Hassoon, now?' he suddenly asked, quietly but clearly.

She was startled, having settled into the stillness of waiting and watching, thinking she had much more time to wait before he spoke.

'He lives in a *pension* at Kubbeh,' she said.

'Yes, yes. But where is he at this moment?' The officer looked at the clock and then looked at Helen, and she felt herself blushing as if she were hiding something.

'I don't know. How could I know?' she said.

'Perhaps he is asleep,' the officer said, turning the documents in her file again and blowing the dust from the edges occasionally.

'I don't know,' she insisted. 'How should I know?'

'Why did you want a *laissez-passer* for him?' he asked.

'So that he could leave Egypt,' she replied.

Her honesty did not seem to disturb him, but he began to look at her more often. 'Why does he want to leave Egypt now? Is he afraid of something?'

'He can't find work,' she said. 'And the police interfere when he does.'

Her temper was beginning to flicker already, and she decided now that she would battle this man to the ends of the earth for Sam's right to have his *laissez-passer*, his right to leave Egypt if he wanted to, and his right to be what he was—whatever he was. Was one man, casually turning over old pages in a dead file, going to define their fate and determine their future? She would never give in to him, no matter what he did.

He looked up and smiled at her. 'Would you like a coffee?' he asked.

'No, thank you,' she said stiffly.

'Please! I don't want to hurry this. Please, for my sake.'

She shook her head. 'I do not drink coffee,' she said firmly.

'But you will insult me,' he insisted, beginning the war for good manners.

She was about to say she was ill and could not drink coffee, but she would not admit a weakness to this man, she would not beg even that much consideration, despite his smile and his sudden compassion and the rules of courtesy.

'I'm sorry,' she said. 'I would simply like you to ask me what you have to. Then tell me when I can go.'

'But you can go now, if you wish,' he said.

'You have finished?'

'Well . . . no. If you go now, you'll only have to come back tomorrow.'

'Then let us go on,' she said.

So far they had spoken in Arabic, both overflowing from the colloquial into rival phrases of a more literate form to prove their superiority over the other in the tongue of their fathers.

'Where is your passport?' he asked then, in English.

'I am sorry,' she replied in Arabic. 'I regret, but I did not bring it.'

'Why?' he said in English.

'Because,' she answered in Arabic, 'because, I regret, but I will not part with it, unless you come and take it from me.'

He shrugged. 'It's not important,' he said.

She was wondering now what was important.

469

'Where is Mr. Jolley now?' he went on in English.

'In London,' she said, also in English, giving up the fight for the right to use her own language. It didn't matter here.

'Did he have his operation?'

'What operation?'

He handed her a small white letter. It was a letter from Jolley's English doctor, addressed to whom it may concern, informing them that Mr. Jolley must return to London immediately for a hernia operation, which could be serious if delayed. She had not been told about this letter, and presumably it was only one of Jolley's many dexterous proofs that his exit from Egypt was temporary, and for any reason but the real one.

'Oh, that!' she said inventively. 'That was not as serious as they thought.'

'Did he have the operation?' the officer repeated.

'I don't know.'

'Doesn't he write to you?'

'Of course he does. But not about such personal things.'

'Forgive me,' the officer said and smiled at her again.

'I would like the door closed, if you will allow it,' she said to him. 'I don't like sitting in a draught.'

'Of course.'

He got up and shut it and sat down again, and she realized that she was alone with him in the room, that the other one had gone and that the dull thunder of the pandemonium of the crowded corridors below was shut out. Every floor of the Ministry below was stuffed with arguing, frightened people trying to get papers to leave or to stay: Greeks, Italians, French, British, even Arabs from other Middle East countries. Below, it was a furnace of hot shouting. Up here it was also hot, but silent and heavy and menacingly disjointed.

He went on with his file-searching again. 'Was Sam Hassoon a good soldier?' he asked, closing the file at last and offering her a cigarette, which she refused. He asked permission and began to smoke thoughtfully, leaning back and looking just above her head at some soldierly distance in the field.

'I believe so,' she said.

'Why didn't the British give him a passport when they discharged him from their Army? That was a law the British had, you know.'

'I know that very well. But they said he was technically under civilian contract to Naafi. That didn't count as service in the Army.'

'Even though he fought with a famous desert unit?'

'Yes.'

'Wasn't he angry?'

'Of course.'

470

'He has still many British friends, hasn't he?'

'Yes. Captain Scott is a friend of his . . .'

She emphasized Scott's name as she might have emphasized Gamal Abd el Nasser's in the same circumstances. Scott, in that second, was their man. Let them swallow that friendship, along with their miserable suspicions.

'Oh, yes. Our English friend, Captain Scott,' he said, with a slight smile.

She sensed then that this man probably admired Scott. They all did. They all respected him, yet they too showed a sort of anti-English reluctance about him. Or was it simply a puzzle? Why should anyone mention Scott's name to them?

She thought he had finished with Sam, but he leaned on his elbows and asked how old was Sam now. Was he happy? Did he see his old friends from the airfield where he had worked? And how did he manage to live if he didn't find work? Was he having difficulty about money? And why hadn't his British friends helped him with the Embassy? Did the British Embassy mistrust Hassoon, perhaps? What did Sam himself think? Why couldn't even his friend the British Member of Parliament, Colonel Peacock, help him get a British passport? What a terrible thing when a man's friends were so powerless.

'His powerful friends couldn't help him get an Egyptian passport, either,' she retaliated. 'And he was born and brought up here, and speaks Arabic as well as you and I do,' she said to him in English.

He laughed gently. 'I wonder where Hassoon would be without you?' the officer said, bowing a little to emphasize the point, to make it an admiration.

'He has never had a father to help him,' she replied, but she regretted her sense of retaliation which had made her go too far. She should have left his dead father out of it.

'But Hassoon wept very unhappily when his father died in prison,' the officer said. 'We were very sorry for him.'

He became reflective then, and he looked up once when someone knocked. A young man entered and whispered something to him. The officer shook his head and the visitor went away.

'Ah, well,' he said, rubbing his forehead tiredly, or apparently so. 'Do you think Hassoon will ever get a British passport?'

'I don't know. I don't think so.'

'Why don't you go to the British and ask them for him?'

'Why should I go? Why should the British listen to me?'

'Because you are a friend of the British, and because you are so persuasive. It seems to me that they tricked him out of a British passport. That's a shame.' He raised his hands. 'They know very well that he is not

471

eligible for an Egyptian passport. So the least they could do is to let him have one. Why don't you try?'

She began to worry now, wondering if they did know what Sam had done. Otherwise why should they suggest such an extraordinary thing? Why was he making such a point about a British passport?

'After all,' he said, 'they do owe it to him.'

'Why?' she said, quivering with fear. 'He's not English.'

'Ah!' the policeman said mysteriously, smiling a little. 'That's true.'

He consulted his documents and she recovered, and then he asked her why her brother-in-law, Mr. Quartermain, had come to Egypt. What was his interest in Egypt now?

'To see my sister and me,' she replied.

'Do you know that he writes communist books?'

'That is nothing to do with me.'

'But don't you at least agree with him, sometimes? His thoughts?'

'He is a good husband and father.'

'He was in the same British Army unit as your nephew, Hassoon. And he is friends too with Mrs. Pickering and Colonel Peacock. Not so?'

'Also with Captain Scott,' she reminded him sharply, beginning to lose patience.

'We know,' he agreed, 'that he is a friend of Captain Scott. Does your sister Nona agree with her husband's ideas? Just a little, of course?'

'I don't know. Aren't you asking silly questions now? How can I answer a thing like that?'

'But surely . . .'

'I don't *know*,' she repeated angrily.

'Will you bring her to see me?'

'My sister Nona?' She was amazed.

'Yes. She wouldn't mind . . .'

'But *I* would mind,' she said suddenly leaping to her feet and demanding that heaven witness it. 'Why should I bring my sister to see a security policeman?'

'But . . .'

'Why should she have to explain herself to you?'

'I assure you . . .'

'But what is everything in the world coming to when we are all in fear and trembling of people like you, sitting up here and interfering in people's lives. What is it? You have no right . . .'

He tried to calm her, but he could not stop her now.

'I don't care what you say to me,' she cried. 'You have no right. Suddenly every human being in the world is surrounded by men like you asking such questions, terrible questions. I won't answer them any more. I

472

don't care what you do. You have no right. Aren't you ashamed for what you do? Think of your children. Think . . .'

'Please,' he cried. 'You are wrong.'

'*You* are wrong,' she accused. 'You are all wrong, and you are stupid as well. Do you think your nice face and your nice manners forgive you? You are a hypocrite. I would feel ashamed of myself if I answered another question. If you want me you will have to come to my house and take me away by force. Anything you take from me you will have to drag out of me. Do what you like . . .'

The rancid volume of her Arabic swept away his professional efforts to be patient and cunning, his good manners and his smile. He was hurt that she could abuse his kindness so. He was indignant that she should be so bad-mannered. But she was leaving . . .

'Ya sitt!' he called.

But she had closed the door on him.

She waited a moment, digging down into her handbag for a handkerchief, shaking and shivering with the ferocity which she was afraid would become violent. She had almost hit him. She was about to be tearful, but she would not weep. He would not see her weeping. She expected him to follow her, to seize her arm, to call the soldiers who stood near the lift.

Below, the noise of the crowded corridors made the place already her prison.

'I don't care,' she said in English. 'I won't accept. I hate Nasser. I hate them all.'

She walked slowly down the circular staircase, weeping and denouncing policemen. For the first time in her life she understood them. In future she would never show anything but hatred and contempt for them. They were even more hateful to society than the criminals they put in gaol. In the entire history of man's evolution from a primitive beast, she decided, the two most degrading products in the whole astonishing process were policemen and those bestial scientists who made germs and atom bombs.

'Why do you accept?' she wanted to cry out in anguish at the men and women she passed who were hurrying up and down the staircase carrying their lives in their hands: pieces of paper, exit visas, *permits de séjour*, and stamps which blacked in identity and name, dates, places of birth, quality, character and permitted existence.

Didn't they realize that in here they were already dead and buried?

'I'll never come back,' she told herself. 'They'll have to come and arrest me. They'll have to drag me out. But I won't come back here again—like a sheep to be slaughtered.'

473

ON Wednesday Sam had brought home a ragged twelve-year-old house-boy. 'To help me dig,' Sam said. But it seemed to be another one of Sam's follies.

Indignation was always stronger in Sam than economy. When little Abdullah had told him the story of his treatment in the household of George Souki, the wealthy Lebanese who had recently employed Sam as a wireless mechanic, Sam had immediately offered Abdullah work, and now paid him five piastres a day which was more than Souki had ever paid him and more than Sam could afford. But it was still considerably less than Abdullah needed to keep his half-blind mother and younger brothers on, even though they lived in a hovel on a roof in Shubra without bed, blankets, utensils, or even a primus.

'You cannot,' Nona had often told Helen, who was watching them work in the garden, and who forgave Sam this time, 'you cannot explain to anyone in Europe what real poverty is. Even when they talk of the worst poverty they know. Even though they've been to India or China or Egypt, Europeans haven't any real feeling of what it is like. They've never suffered it themselves by millions; that's why they'll never understand. They've never watched one of their own kind, their own children, killing himself with work for a penny a day and trying to keep his family on a ha'penny and being beaten and trampled on while he slowly dies of disease in the same horrible process. They don't even know what disease really is, or real starvation or infant mortality. They don't experience it. They have such academic theories about it, and something they call free-will or the L.C.C. or something for the débutantes, but even when they come to Egypt and look at the beggars, they still don't touch the lives of all these poor wretches who have to abject themselves entirely, terribly, simply to gain an hour of life, even a minute of it.'

Abdullah the servant boy had been stealing from Souki—a little sugar, a little tea, a few half-piastres, or a packet of envelopes which he could sell on the streets for a few piastres. With the proceeds he had fed his family on beans, but he had thus violated the trust and favour Souki had done

474

him by employing him as a house slave (Sam swore it was no more) for a few piastres a week, for twelve hours' work every day.

Since the British had left Egypt there was no work for tens of thousands of these hangers-on in the city. They had always served the English and the French and the other foreigners with their morning tea: swept their flats, ironed their clothes, run their errands: insuring all foreign life in Egypt against the effort of ever raising an arm or the trouble of filling a pot with water. But the British had gone. Souki the rich Lebanese had therefore been a godsend for Abdullah, who should not have abused this trust in him; and when Souki had caught him in his deficiencies, he had threatened to bring in the police if Abdullah did not pay back all of the twenty piastres he had stolen, within a week. Four shillings! Abdullah was put out on the street, where Sam had found him begging. Where could Abdullah get twenty piastres? Twenty piastres to Abdullah was a month's hard, full work, fifteen hours a day.

Sam had brought him home yesterday; Scott had given him the twenty piastres and Sam had given him a job in the garden for a few weeks, swearing he would break Souki in two if he ever saw him again.

Helen watched them both at work without knowing why she had come here to see Sam.

It was Thursday evening, a dusty yellow twilight, and she could afford the time. She would not go to the office tomorrow. Tomorrow, Friday, Ismail would be praying half the time anyway, and she still could not face the emptiness and the fear of that near-empty office. The police had taken away the tin trunk, and they had emptied the garage. They had not yet bothered her again, but she dammed back torrents of anticipation, knowing that they could come and collect her any time they liked now, the way they had once collected Sam.

She sat in the dusty garden deck-chair watching Sam and Abdullah planting bougainvillaeas. She felt, quite sadly, that she would like to gather up this twilight into her life. She was depressed, watching the thin blue curl of smoke from Sam's garden-fire lifting, wafting away, dispersing and renewing itself so transparently, so slowly that she almost went to sleep under its influence.

'How lovely this country is,' she felt, and repeated it tenderly to herself. 'It's so calm now, in the autumn.'

'Am I disturbing you?' Scott asked her.

She opened her eyes. 'Not at all,' she said calmly. 'I wasn't asleep. I must have been talking to myself.'

Scott guessed instantly that she was low-spirited, or very tired. She barely looked at him. He sat down on Sam's weed-box and made a joke about avoiding Sam's enthusiasm for digging. She did not smile.

'It's so fascinating,' he said, 'to watch Sam's sudden passion for it. It's so unlike him.'

'Do you think so?' she said, uninterested.

But then she could not put off her indignation any longer. Look at Sam. Look at what he had to do, simply because he couldn't get work now.

'Why does Nasser make it so hard for anyone who isn't a Moslem?' she asked him accusingly. 'Why does he imagine that all Christians and Jews are spies?'

He did not expect that, but he understood it. 'Do you think it's that bad?' he asked.

'Have you been to the Ministry of Interior lately?'

'No.'

'Why don't you go there, if only to see what it's like? All those miserable human beings begging for a scrap of paper. Why should men have such a right to say how others can live, or even if they can live at all?'

'It's getting to be hard on all the Europeans,' he agreed. 'But the Europeans here were once hard on the Arabs.'

'It's not only the Europeans,' she declared. 'Look at him.' She pointed to Abdullah who was in the freshly watered mud beside Sam. 'That's the place where he was born and where he will die: in the mud. Has Nasser done anything for him? He's the real Egyptian, isn't he? The fellah? Who *has* Nasser helped if he hasn't helped him?'

'Nasser hasn't had much time yet,' Scott suggested. 'When you remember what this country was like.'

'Do you really think that?'

'Four years isn't so long, when you think of the accumulated poverty of several thousand years.'

'It's long enough for Nasser to have given his officers all the advantages —his own class. Why is he against everybody else?'

'He's against Europeans ruling Egypt,' he argued. 'And that seems fair to me.'

'Oh, nobody blames him for getting rid of the Europeans. But even so —where are they to go? Egypt has also been their home.'

But that was not the point she wanted to make. She did not want to defend Europeans. She too thought their demise was a fair revenge. But she had lost the thread of her real complaint against Nasser. What was it? Was it even Nasser she was complaining of? All she was sure of was indignation. It was indignation which made her want to shout at the Europeans and Egyptians herding themselves obediently into the Ministry of Interior: *Why do you accept?*

'Why *does* everybody accept?' she asked.

'Accept what? You mean Nasser? Not everybody does.'

'No. That!' she said, and pointed to Sam and Abdullah.

476

She knew that was not quite right either. Sam had found a very long worm and they were playing with it like children. Abdullah touched its nose and it shrank to half its length, and they admired its healthy muscular wriggling before mercilessly cutting it into pieces and throwing it to an appreciative minah which was cheekily watching their gardening from a few yards' distance.

'Gobble, gobble, gobble.'

The worm had lost his life and the minah was a glutton and Sam and Abdullah laughed like schoolboys.

'You've lived here so long,' she said to Scott. 'Can you imagine those immaculate young officers ever fighting for anything worthwhile? Can you imagine the common soldiers or the fellaheen ever believing in *them*? I can't. I simply can't.'

'Perhaps you're forgetting how bad it was under Farouk.'

'I'm a woman,' she said, not stiffening but relaxing a little as if to be relieved finally of her burden of restraint. Why shouldn't she relax with this strange man? 'No woman in Egypt felt safe in those last months of Farouk's reign. A woman can always tell when things are at an end. The behaviour of men becomes so unpleasant and corrupt that they lose control of themselves, and they don't care what they do any more, even the decent ones.'

'The decent ones threw Farouk out,' he reminded her.

'So they did, but was that enough? Look at those two,' she insisted again.

Scott felt as if he were looking out of the train window again, watching the miseries of Egypt fly past behind the glass panel, scene after scene which were never to be touched, never experienced, never understood. The few people in Egypt's comfortable train were all protected so carefully against the contamination of their own conscience. He knew what she meant, but he thought her estimate unfair.

'Whatever Nasser's faults, Egypt is now Egypt,' he argued. 'That's a beginning, at least.'

'It was also Egypt under the British, and it was ruled well.'

Scott was surprised to hear her say that: this proud woman. Why should she, an Egyptian, feel so drastically favourable to the British? How could she possibly deny her own emergence?

'But even the British felt ashamed of what they did to this country,' he told her. 'I don't see how you can say that we ruled it well. We did not. We ruined it.'

'The British built everything Egypt has,' she argued. 'The roads, railways, the cities. Your own father must have engineered miles of · irrigation canals . . .'

'For growing cheaper cotton,' he interrupted. 'Even my father knew that.'

477

'But Egypt became rich on cotton.'

'And poor too,' he pointed out. 'When Britain came to Egypt, over eighty years ago, the fellaheen were much better fed and better off than when we left. We built the roads and the canals and the cities, simply to grow more and cheaper cotton, and provide the barest subsistence. We never built a mile of road or laid a foot of rail or irrigated even a village if it didn't help our own requirements. We actually ruined the agriculture, the old base, in order to get the cotton.'

'Even so,' she said, and she was watching the lovely night closing in on them now, growing darker and darker so quickly, 'even so, Egypt was better off. We were all Egyptians then. All of us, not just the Moslems.'

He knew her problem, he understood, he knew it was true; but he had no argument to it. To be an Egyptian one had to be a Moslem. To be (as she was) part Copt and part Circassian was not enough for the dream that Gamal Abd el Nasser dreamt. But who were the Egyptians? Across the streets of Cairo were banners which said: *Egyptians! Get up off your knees*. But the Egyptian people, the fellaheen and the mechanics, could not read it. So how could they do it? That was her real argument. That was what he saw himself. Was that Gamal's ultimate dream? Or was it of something else he dreamt, which simply moved his people into some sort of unity, into some sort of nationhood, some sort of belief in his own concepts. How did Abdullah or Helen Mamoon or Sam serve in the dream of Gamal Abd el Nasser?

'That's the tragedy of it,' he said, drawing deeply on his own experience now, and knowing it to be hers as well. 'The individual person is always lost.'

'I wouldn't even mind that,' she said, unshaken by that threat, 'if the misery vanished, if the poor benefited and the rich suffered. But I don't believe it to be so. It isn't so. You know he hasn't done that at all . . .'

But when Gamal Abd el Nasser had finally taught the fellaheen to read, when the mechanics became articulate—what then? Is that when they got up off their knees? Was that the dream?

'He has begun it,' he said doggedly, as if to convince himself also. 'It will take time.'

She shook her head. 'I don't believe it,' she said harshly.

The buttermilk eventide had gone completely now, the night was set and it would soon be cold, and without knowing why she did so Helen told him what had happened to her in room 47 of the Ministry of Interior.

'That's so stupid,' he said angrily, feeling sorry for her and yet sensing that it was unnecessary because she was too proud and too indignant to want pity. Not pity. Beware of pity. He knew her well enough to know that. 'They could have left you alone,' he told her.

478

'Do you think they are still interested in Sam?' she asked.

'I suppose they are. These things are never dead.'

'Then I'll never tell them anything. I'll *never* give in. I don't care what they do. And I won't even stop until Sam has got his *laissez-passer* and can leave Egypt. They can't go on blaming everything on to us.'

Defiant, yes! But he knew there were quiet tears in it also.

'Perhaps we'd better go in,' he told her, 'before they hose us down.'

Sam and Abdullah were beginning to hose the garden so that the night would hold the moisture and keep it warm in the earth. It smelled delicious, but it was time to go inside where Madame Salz and Becky and Alicia, Sam's sister, were in the dining-room expecting them.

The Wing Commander had obviously given Zareef back the Gemini to fly over Cairo for anti-aircraft practice, and Sam remarked to Scott joyfully: 'There's Ali!' He came in with his singlet soaking wet and his arms coated with mud, and Becky began to mother him with a towel.

'Do you think it's Ali?' Scott asked, hearing the Gemini high above.

Sam insisted happily that it must be. If it had been Captain Selim the Gemini would have been moaning with the wave-like sounds of badly synchronized engines. But that was one of Sam's prejudices against Captain Selim who was a good pilot, whatever his other mysterious failings were.

'What are you doing with five women?' Sam asked him.

Scott blushed. He had been listening to them gossiping in French about Leo and Phillip Lieberman. All agreed, pityingly, that Leo had little time left to live. Scott would have left them to their gossip, but it would have been too impolite and obvious.

'I was waiting for you,' he said to Sam.

It occurred to him then, looking at Sam, that Sam was a good influence on all these women. They were all in some way dependent on him. 'Dependent' was not quite the word, they were all concerned with protecting him or mothering him or possessing him. Sam was not aware of it himself, nor of the responsibilities involved—except for the new eyes of his wife when she told him to go and get washed.

Scott got up to leave, shaking hands with each of them and watching Helen Mamoon wipe away, with her cool dark-eyed certainty, the second's intimacy they had exchanged, however formally, in their handshake.

'Now they'll talk about you,' Sam told Scott cheerfully in the passage. He was a happy man, doing what Becky had told him to do. 'You can be sure.'

So they would talk about him. But there was nothing extraordinary in that.

They would probably pass from Leo and Phillip Lieberman to Françoise and himself, unless Sam told them that they must not gossip about his friend. Sam probably did not approve of his relationship with Françoise, because it was scandalous. He would rather approve of Lucy Pickering, because that was straightforward and understandable, and they were both English.

He listened to Zareef buzzing overhead like a distant bee in the night, and he felt glad that at least his friends were safe—if you could call anything safe in the flimsy world they all lived in.

CHAPTER SIXTY-THREE

THE Menzies mission had come to a dead-end. There was no agreement with President Nasser, no sign of a compromise on either side, but in order to avoid a final breakdown in this last hope of a peaceful solution the delegates had decided to wait over the week-end in Cairo, to break for a few days, and then try just once more.

Friday was a religious holiday anyway. Gamal would go swimming, and Hakim would never afterwards forgive the Egyptian Navy (privately, secretly in his heart) for providing, in uniform, one of the men who tried to murder Gamal Abd el Nasser that day.

In the hot aeroplane on the way to it, unknowing, Scott already felt bothered by the tension. He knew that Hakim liked to make excursions of fateful days, but what was this one all about?

Hakim was sitting back comfortably and recollecting that he had almost missed the most important moment of the revolution. He took off his cap and his shoes and put his two hands behind his head, and as they both vibrated with the skin of the aeroplane, he told Scott how he, with Anwar el Sadat, had been almost left out of the very event they had waited for all their lives.

'Believe me,' Hakim said thoughtfully, 'it was a narrow business.'

The plane was almost over Tanta, which was probably what had stimulated Hakim to recollect it. They both leaned over to look out at the green, living map of the Delta far below—tracks, roads, and glistening canals twisting through clumps of villages and towns to signify 'Tanta' which the Air Force officer had shouted at them from the head of the plane.

'You know, I was at Tanta on the day of our uprising against Farouk,' Hakim was saying. 'That's how I nearly missed it, because I was there making sure that the provinces would not stand in our way when it did come. So . . .' he took a dramatic breath of memory, '. . . when Gamal sent me a telegram to return quickly I hurried back on the train. But there was no one at the station to meet me and it was almost dark, and that's when I was silly. I was worried. I didn't go straight home, because I was also responsible for seeing that the Moslem Brothers did not interfere. I went straight to see Mohamed Farid to tell him to warn the Moslem Brothers to keep away from the army, once the uprising started, which I still expected for the next day. But while I was at Mohamed's place, Gamal came around to my house in his baby Austin to pick me up, because the uprising was planned for midnight that night. Gamal himself was going around personally telling everybody who should know. And the only two he couldn't find were me and Anwar Sadat, who was at the pictures with his children. He was even sillier than I was . . .'

'Didn't he know that the uprising was due anyway?' Scott asked.

'Of course he did,' Hakim said, 'but waiting is excruciating. Is that right? Yes? You have to do something. He didn't expect it until next day, either.'

'So he missed it also?'

'Wait,' Hakim said, shivering a little now because the plane was climbing. 'When I did get home that night, I found a note from Gamal telling me to be at Abdul Hakim Amer's house at 11 o'clock. *It happens tonight*, Gamal had written in our code, and you should have seen me. *Tonight!* I stood there and hit my forehead and called myself names, and then I ran downstairs and found a taxi and got to Abdul Hakim Amer's house.' Hakim laughed boyishly. 'I broke all records that night in that old taxi. I'd picked the oldest taxi in Cairo, and when I got to Abdul Hakim Amer's house there was no one there, except Anwar Sadat who was also left out, like me, and there we were, standing out on the street like two village girls.'

Hakim smiled, lost in it for a moment. 'Heh, heh!' he said, formally. It was such a good joke on himself.

'But surely you were there eventually,' Scott said. 'I remember you telling me how you went to the British Embassy . . .'

'Later, *habibi*. That was much later. I was there all right. Of course I was. Anwar Sadat and I cursed each other for fools and then got into his car and headed towards G.H.Q. What we didn't know was that the hour had been put forward by Gamal because Saad Tewfick, one of our Intelligence officers, swore to Gamal secretly that the King and the Government knew all about the uprising due the next day. They intended arresting each of us separately at home. So Gamal pushed the hour ahead, one day, so that the revolution would get rid of them before they could get rid of us.' Hakim sighed. 'Ah, what a day . . .'

Scott was also remembering the day. He had not been in Cairo on 23 July 1950. He had been in Port Said burning terredo eggs out of the bottom planking of a Folkboat he shared with Amin Fakhry, who had been helping him. Amin's brother (who was a doctor) had suddenly arrived on the Port Fuad side, where they were working almost under the Suez Canal workshops, and after a whispered conference Amin had hurried away with his brother, leaving everything in a second, without a word of explanation. Knowing that Amin could be impulsive, Scott had gone on murdering the terredo, using the old Roman method of burning straw under the planks to make sure there were no worms left alive, even though they were supposed to die a natural death after twenty-four hours' dry exposure; but Red Sea terredo apparently preserved their own moisture indefinitely, and even after a week on the hard they were sometimes still alive.

The revolution had not taken place in Cairo until midnight that night, but he remembered ever afterwards that he had been calmly painting the boat that day, the day Egypt had suddenly turned over in its sleep.

'The trouble is that I did miss the best part of it,' Hakim admitted sadly now. 'I'll never forgive myself, and my children will always regret it. By the time Anwar Sadat and I reached the Headquarters that night, Abdul Hakim Amer had captured the place with his pistol, just walked in through the G.H.Q. guards who had come over to our side. That was what *I* should have been there to do, but that stage of it was all over when I got there. Even the sentries, our own, wouldn't let us into the building. Imagine that.'

'Didn't they know you?' Scott asked.

'Yes, but I didn't know the password. Gamal had only been in control of the place for five minutes. Anwar and I were standing there by the military hospital fuming and arguing with an officer I know as well as I know you. But he wouldn't let us in. Password, *ya effendim*, he kept saying. We could hear the machine-guns inside the barracks going off. Then we caught a glimpse of Abdul Hakim Amer down the road through the gate and shouted at him as hard as we could *Abdu!*'

Hakim shouted above the aeroplane engines now as he had shouted then.

'That's how we got in. But we had already captured G.H.Q. and all the generals. We had everything, although we didn't really know then if we could keep it.'

'Is that why you went to the British that night?' Scott asked. 'Did you expect them to interfere?'

He remembered that episode from one of Hakim's previous stories— how he had walked into the British Embassy with Wing Commander Aly Sabry (now Gamal's secretary and right-hand man) and told the British not to interfere.

'We thought they might interfere, and that's what the British don't forgive me for,' Hakim said. 'When Aly Sabry and I were talking with Sir Walter Stuart and General Goooborn . . .'

483

'Golbourne,' Scott corrected.

'Gold-bourne. All right. Isn't that an Israelite name? Anyway, they were so angry that they couldn't finish a sentence. I had to help them both. They were both saying: *But when? But where? But what is the reason? But who is responsible for this situation? Oh, but we must be given some sort of information . . .*'

Hakim was laughing at his own English memory.

'Didn't the Embassy know that you had all your armour in front of the British camp on the Suez road?' Scott asked, knowing about that episode from Amin Fakhry, who had been in command of those tanks.

'The British didn't know anything. The British Embassy had to get their own General Festing out of bed in the Suez camp to tell him. Nobody knew. Not even Neguib knew. Farouk's Minister of Interior actually rang up General Neguib and got him out of bed and complained that his boys (Neguib's boys!) were making trouble. *Neguib's boys.* Neguib himself arrived an hour later at G.H.Q. looking bewildered. Then he started congratulating everybody all round and looking pleased, so we made him Commander-in-Chief.'

The plane had long ago reached its maximum height and now they both felt very cold. Scott rolled his shirt-sleeves down, and Hakim put on his shoes and called to his subaltern-adjutant behind him for a towel which was in his grip, packed by his wife for their swimming excursion. He told the adjutant to pour out some of the hot coffee his wife had put in the thermos and they sipped the coffee while the plane began to circle around what Scott supposed was some radar recognition point.

'When the British talk of Mohamed Neguib,' Hakim said, the striped towel around his thin cold shoulders, 'I understand them. Naturally, if they could get rid of Gamal, he would be their man, with his pipe and all his old-man's I-know-how-to-do-it. But Mohamed Neguib knew nothing. He would have patted Farouk on the back if we had allowed him to. What did he know of the revolution? Not a thing, except that we made him Commander-in-Chief, then President, then we took it away from him, and then gave it back again, and then we locked him up. That's all he ever knew, and that's all he'll ever know, whatever the British think . . .'

'Why do you worry about him then?' Scott asked pointedly.

'Because some stupid Egyptians also talk of Neguib, even now. When they think about him and plot to restore him, I don't understand it. That's when I lose my temper. How can they admire a senseless man like that? When he came that night, straight from his bed to the revolution, he was patting Gamal on the back and saying to all of us: *That's right, my boys, mabrouk, mabrouk.* My boys! I told him we were Egyptian officers and revolutionaries and not his boys at all. He patted me on the back. A silly man, don't you agree, *habibi?*'

484

Scott shrugged. 'At least he was for you and it helped.'

'He's not for us now,' Hakim said flatly. 'Somebody would like to kill Gamal and put Neguib back. Do you agree with that idea?'

'I never thought much of him for wanting the old politicians back,' Scott admitted carefully. 'What would have been the use of that?'

They had been circling a long time, and one of the aircrew opened the door of his compartment and said, 'On that side.'

They all looked out.

'There's Gamal,' Hakim said, and pointed out of the window.

Scott went to the seat behind and saw what looked like a smaller plane, pretty and white and silver and green, flying half a mile off and escorted above and below by Russian-made Migs. They approached close enough then to see Gamal's face in one of the small windows; he was smiling and waving to them. His children showed themselves in another window, also waving, and the pilot was grinning. The Mig pilots kept farther away, but they were faces and people, so clear in this family-like gathering at six thousand feet.

Then their own plane tilted its wing in a signal and swung away in a great curve and began to descend. Gamal Abd el Nasser's plane also turned away and was soon out of sight with its open-mouthed little escorts weaving back-and-forth behind it and above it.

'Everything is all right so far,' Hakim said as their own plane continued to descend. He was no longer in a reminiscing mood, however, and he waited impatiently for the hot bumps to end. It was only later when they eventually landed at the swamp-ridden airport at Alexandria that Scott realized he and Hakim were in Gamal's private plane: the Ilyushin the Russians had given him for his private use, and he guessed too that they were probably some sort of decoys for Gamal's safety.

'Masr!' Hakim said almost affectionately as the plane taxied in, indicating the unidentifiable Russianness about the decor of the plane which was simple but not quite coldly precise. 'When our Egyptian fellaheen build their own aeroplanes, it will be the same. But the same,' he said. 'When the Russians made their atomic bomb they must have made it the way the peasants would make it—the same.'

'It goes off just as well,' Scott replied.

'That's the miracle,' Hakim laughed and told a soldier to pick up his grip. 'Bring it to the car,' he said.

Waiting for them was the presidential black Chrysler, and now it was very obvious that they were decoys. They stepped into it quickly from the plane, the Adjutant got into the front seat, and Scott felt presidential and lost as the limousine sped across the tarmac of the airfield and out of the gates braced with salutes. It went on, around the edges of Ibrahimia, never approaching Alexandria itself, but entering a barbed-wire enclosure

485

near a coast-guard station which commanded a wide beach, a few white beach huts, and a small coast-guard signal station. There was nothing overlooking the beach except a solid cement water-tower, and here they would swim with Gamal.

Gamal was not here yet, but all was ready for him.

The gap in the barbed-wire was guarded by soldiers in fatigues. It was a quick and safe spot. The coast-guard station itself was not guarded, because it was in the perimeter. The water-tower was outside the barbed-wire, and it was simply a solid lump of cement which had once been painted cream.

Far behind the beach there were stable-like buildings, perhaps belonging to the sporting club which was somewhere behind, where the skeet-shooting and pigeon-shooting competitions were usually held. They could hear occasional shots now, but they were far away.

There were a few other people on the beach just outside the perimeter, the coast-guard and a woman in a black dress with two children. But they were not near enough to be important. There was another group a hundred yards away in the perimeter—three or four young officers who sat around in the sand, talking or occasionally running into the sea. But Hakim and Scott and the adjutant kept to themselves. They were almost hidden in a sudden rise of sand, and a breeze blew along the seashore which continued on to Stanley Bay and Bulkely, to the rest of the famous Alexandria resorts.

'This is where Gamal likes to come when he doesn't want to see any-one,' Hakim told him.

'Where is he?' Scott asked.

'His plane is very slow.' Hakim was being reticent now.

He had the picnic basket brought from the car and suggested a swim before lunch. They could undress in the white hut. It was Hakim who went first and returned, half-white in swimming-trunks, his thin arms and neck brown from his summer exposure. Scott used the same hut and felt the strange secrets of Hakim's clothes which made him feel like an intruder on another man's privacy, and he wondered what he was doing here, swimming on the beach of one of Hakim's mysteries. The morning was already blurred with it. He was not sure why Hakim had wanted him to come here in the first place, excepting that he had placed a great deal of importance on his meeting with Gamal. It might clarify so many decisions for him; he said so to Hakim, and he hoped so.

Why didn't Gamal come?

Scott dipped and swam and sat in the mid-morning sun, hiding his scarred diaphragm with a towel so that Hakim's memory would not be too disturbed by old wounds, and watching Hakim swimming with boastful, boyish skill. There was nothing cynical about Hakim's swimming. He meant it, and he came out puffing and waving his arms. He dried himself and lay down near Scott and it seemed to be the time now to talk business. Hakim asked him what he expected to get from Gamal.

'I don't expect anything,' Scott answered. 'I simply want to say good-bye to him.'

'You still think you will leave us? You are so sure?'

'I told you that this time I do mean it.'

'I don't think so,' Hakim told him confidently. 'Not today.'

Scott shrugged. How could you argue with such a man?

'Anyway, Gamal won't let you go,' Hakim said. 'He will ask you to stay. I'm sure you will stay with us. Of course you will, you'll see.'

Scott wanted to say: *Gamal can't do that*. But he felt that he had already put his whole life, momentarily, into this meeting with Gamal. And being face to face with him might also undo this other creeping involvement which Peter Dukes and Lucy Pickering had frightened him with. He did not believe Peter, however obvious everything seemed. Yet he was still afraid of something, and now Hakim made him feel mysteriously poised.

'Well?' Hakim said, after his long silence.

'Gamal knows that I've finished everything I can do in Egypt. He'll understand why I want to go. Why should he want to keep me here?'

'Let me tell you a big surprise,' Hakim said. 'You are no longer in the Frontier Department. We have already transferred you.'

Scott smiled cynically. 'Where to? Back to Survey?'

'Only technically—to Army Survey; although you are still under me. We want you to do something quite new. Very urgent. Something we ought to organize in Siwa in a hurry, before it is too late.'

'Siwa?' Scott rolled despondently onto his stomach with a perfect and unwanted picture of that south-western oasis in his mind. 'What are you doing down there? American oil surveys?'

'That's where your famous Tracks and Survey had its base in the war, isn't it so?'

'Yes, for a while.'

'That's where you set off into Libya and Cyrenaica behind Rommel's lines, not so? Didn't you know all those deserts and tracks that came in the back way to Egypt, and the front way as well? Weren't you the expert?'

'We were all experts then.'

'Didn't you go right across those deserts, unseen, with your small force? Anywhere you liked. Wasn't that your special task, *habibi*?'

'At the beginning, anyway. Later on we were swallowed up in another unit.'

487

'Well, that's what we want you to do. The same, the very same.'

'What do you mean, the same?' Scott sat up. 'A military unit? What for?'

'Now that is the question, and I'll show you.'

Hakim drew a map in the sand, showing the coast of Egypt and Libya, the deserts of Libya and Cyrenaica.

'What did you discover your friend General Church was doing all round here?' Hakim said to him, and drew lines along the coastal areas between Libya and Egypt. 'You don't know, do you? You couldn't find out, could you?'

'Not really,' Scott admitted.

'Well, let me tell you something we do know. Look. Isn't it so: if the British attack us, they will want to take an area they can safely hold, not so? That means the western desert. It always does. Which do they know best? The western desert. Which is nearer both to Cairo and Alexandria? The western desert. Which is hardest for us to defend? The western desert. Which is nearest Libya where the British have troops? The western desert . . .'

'You expect them to come from Libya?'

'From anywhere on this side.'

'And you plan a force that can go into Libya itself?'

'Of course. If necessary, that is.'

'But you have a whole Frontier Corps along the wire.'

'*They* can't go into Libya undetected, now can they? That would be illegal.'

Scott could see the point, but something else seemed to lie behind Hakim's idea and he did not like it.

'Why use me?' he asked Hakim. 'That's a purely military task. You've got plenty of soldiers who can do it.'

'But you needn't be a soldier yourself,' Hakim argued. 'Amin Fakhry, our old friend at Ghurdakha, will be responsible for it. You know what Amin is like. He's too impulsive. So you will advise him. You will be very calm and sure of what you are doing. It will save us so much time that way. You've already done it, you *are* an expert on long-range units, and we need it very quickly. If you don't want to be a soldier, *habibi*, you are not. Amin is the soldier. Let him do what you suggest. You can have everything—the best equipment and men we can spare.'

Scott tried to speak again.

'Wait. Don't refuse yet,' Hakim said sharply, wiping out his sand map. 'It has already been arranged. Ah . . . I almost forgot. More pay for you too. Amin Fakhry is already in Cairo. You might see him here today. He may come. I only saw him last night myself. I thought I would keep this as a nice surprise for you. Eh? You can even talk to Gamal about it. It's simple enough, isn't it? Don't you think?'

488

'Very simple,' Scott agreed testily, 'except that I have no desire to go back to that sort of work.'

'Not even for your old friends?' Hakim was saying.

'It's not that . . .'

'Why do you worry about being a soldier? That's not so important.'

Hakim was really saying: 'Don't you owe us something, even more than you owe the English, who would not even give you a job after the war and who always remind you of your disgrace? Hasn't Gamal always helped you? Hasn't Egypt accepted you? How can you get out of your responsibility now?'

'I am not a soldier,' Scott insisted. 'I'm out of date. Amin Fakhry can do it without me. Don't you realize that I've lost touch . . .'

Hakim clicked his tongue annoyingly.

'Does Gamal know?' Scott asked him. 'Did he suggest it?'

'You needn't worry. Gamal will agree very happily.'

'But Amin could do it without me,' Scott tried again. 'He's a professional. He doesn't need me.'

'Perhaps,' Hakim agreed in his specially tolerant voice. 'But we are calling on all the friends we can find now. All the soldiers too. It would be wrong not to ask you. You know that. Mr. Menzies will go back on Monday night, and yes—it will be over. We will never agree with him. What will they do then? They are already planning to attack us from Cyprus. It will come. And we will be ready, *insha'allah*.'

Hakim filtered hot sand through his thin distilling fingers.

But Scott was hammering at himself with the only defence he knew.

'I am not a soldier. I am never that again. I am not going to be. I must not give in . . .'

'Here we are,' Hakim said, sitting up. 'Here's your friend.'

The figure was familiar—a very large man in a white shirt and grey trousers, followed by two soldiers. It was a long time since he had seen Gamal face to face. Scott was brushing his hands free of sand, ready to greet him, when the expected and the unexpected happened.

He saw suddenly that it was not Gamal. It was his friend Amin Fakhry who was about the same build. Amin also had a moustache, and he was also dark, also large, also smiling. It could have been Gamal at that distance, except that Amin was more volatile and liquid if you knew him well, otherwise it was Gamal Abd el Nasser himself.

Someone else must have thought so too.

There were five or six shots from an automatic rifle, so close together that they were almost one sound. Where did they come from and where did they go to? Everybody stopped still for a second. Scott would remember all his life that second's frozen tableau before the obvious occurred to them. Then Hakim shouted at Amin Fakhry to get down.

'From the other side,' Amin was already shouting at someone.

Amin did not get down at all. He pointed to the white coast-guard station, and one of the soldiers with him began to fire from the small automatic he carried. Every other shot seemed to be a tracer, so that they could all see it hitting and chipping the walls.

'Look out for the woman on the beach,' the adjutant was shouting behind them.

It was sudden anarchy.

There were a few bursts of confused fire near them. One of the soldiers with Amin Fakhry had been hit, but Amin was now running towards the coast-guard station and there was a stunned sound of a great deal of firing at it from behind. They could see the shots ricocheting off its corrugated-iron roof.

'Stop it, stop it!' Hakim was shouting.

Scott had been lying flat on his stomach, the only poor target among them. But the others seemed to know what was happening, and what they were doing about it. Hakim began to run towards the coast-guard station also, and Scott followed him, feeling the hot sand burning his bare feet.

He could hear the woman on the beach below, screaming.

'What is it?' he asked Hakim, catching him.

'Ali! Ali!' Hakim was shouting, ignoring Scott.

That was for somebody else. By the time they had run out of the hollow, and then over the sand the two hundred yards or more to the station, the woman on the sea's edge had picked up the children and was running away in terror. But it was not on the coast-guard station that Amin Fakhry was now organizing the firing. He had gone outside the perimeter with the soldiers who were firing on the water-tower. An iron ladder went up the high legs of it, and Amin was already beginning to climb up.

'What are you doing there?' Hakim shouted at him. 'Amin!'

'He's up here,' Amin shouted back.

There were ten to twenty soldiers around the tower with hand-guns, two officers with pistols, as well as Amin Fakhry and Hakim's adjutant and the neighbouring officers who had been swimming. They had pistols in their hands, which seemed quite threatening to their own half-naked bodies.

'He must be in it,' Hakim said when he arrived.

'But he can't be. It's sealed over.'

The cement tank looked completely enclosed, sides, top and bottom.

'There must be a hole in it somewhere,' Hakim shouted to Amin. 'Go up, but don't fire into the tank. Get him out. Be careful.'

490

Amin was already at the lip of the tank, and by lying flat on the sloping conical roof he pulled himself up by spikes to the top of the cone. They had all moved back so that they could see him, and when they saw his hands grip the rim of the cone, only then did they realize that the tank was open at the very apex.

'It's open on top,' Amin called down in his excitable voice.

'Go up to him with some grenades,' Hakim ordered one of the soldiers who stood beside him in American fatigues, peaked cap and all, holding his automatic up high. 'Donkey!' Hakim bellowed. 'Don't point that weapon at the officer on the tank.'

Amin Fakhry was shouting something down into the tank, and the booming and muffled prison of the sound made it clear to them that the tank was empty of water. When the soldier had reached Amin with a grenade, Amin shook his head and turned around and shouted down at them:

'He's coming out. Be careful. Let him come.'

'Is there only one?' Hakim asked.

'I think so. Let him come, anyway. Don't fire.'

'Come down then,' Hakim told him, and he told the soldiers to wait until Amin was down, but then to keep their weapons pointed well up on the tank, but by no means to fire unless ordered to.

'Did you know he was there?' Scott asked Hakim. 'Who is it?'

'How could I know?' Hakim said heatedly. 'I didn't know the tank was empty, or that there was a hole in the top. They knew, I didn't. I'm a fool. I thought he was in the coast-guard station.'

'That was meant for Gamal,' Scott said. 'Why didn't you tell me?'

'Who else!' Hakim said, already savagely anticipating the head and shoulders of the assassin. 'Ah, my God! They really did it. Come down,' he called to Amin. 'And think!' he said. 'Gamal himself might have been here with his own family.'

Amin Fakhry was still up on the tank. He had put his arm down the hole and he helped a man up, pulling his arms and then helping him get his shoulders through. It was barely large enough for him to come out, and when he did so he was dressed all in white. His shoes and the bottoms of his trousers were filthy and wet up to the knees from what must have been residue slime in the tank. He was covered and stained with it on his back and side, and down his arms, as if he had fallen into it.

'Come down, you motherless beast!' Hakim cried, as if the assassin had the choice and would prefer to remain there. He slipped on the lip of the tank and almost fell fifty feet to the ground. All sighed with thankfulness when his hands held their grip.

Amin had to come down the ladder ahead of him because there was no room to pass. When he stepped off the last rung of the ladder, he saw his friend Scott but he did not shake hands because his own were dirty. He offered his wrist and looked at his own soiled trousers and shirt.

'Il est fou, cet idiot,' he said incredibly to Scott and whirled a finger near his head.

'What was he firing?' Scott asked Amin. 'I didn't even see the shots hit anything.'

There was no time to answer. The assassin had reached the bottom rung of the ladder and there were a dozen men to surround him. The soldiers pushed him and insulted him noisily and dangerously until Hakim told them all to stand back. The white shirt and trousers proved to be naval uniform, including the cap which the man had carefully carried with him, and which had probably caused his near-fall. Hakim looked amazed.

'Who are you?' Hakim asked him.

The man put on his cap and saluted, the worst thing he could have done.

Hakim was so incensed by such a claim to honour that he knocked the man's naval cap off and then leaned forward and ripped off the two rows of ribbons he wore pinned on his chest.

'You are not an officer. You are nothing,' Hakim shouted at him. 'You will not even leave here alive. When we have finished with you it will be terrible. You dare not even stand there like that.' Hakim, half-naked, was rigid with hate, and yet it was a cold ferocity. 'Get down on your knees.'

'Don't kill me,' the officer was saying through his terror-stricken throat and wide eyes. 'I beg you to treat me justly. I have done no harm. I have killed no one. I beg you to treat me properly. I beg you to consider my rank. I beg you to give me fair treatment, in the name of God.'

'Why didn't you shoot yourself in there?' Hakim said contemptuously. 'Eh? Murderer. Who are you?'

'I haven't killed anyone, I swear it. I beg you to treat me with honour,' the man babbled, but he was standing erect and waiting for his own courage to prove itself with their acknowledgment of his honour.

'Give him a pistol and let him kill himself,' Hakim told one of the officers in swimming-trunks who offered his pistol to the naval officer, butt forward.

'I will not touch it,' he cried, while the soldiers pushed him towards it. 'Don't force me to do that. I will not kill myself. I throw myself on your mercy, your sense of honour. In the name of God.'

Two brown tears were running down his face.

He was not more than twenty-five or twenty-six and a little too fat and short, so that his white naval clothes, stiff and starched, made him appear to be the same white thickness from top to toe.

Hakim snatched the refused pistol from the officer near him and it looked for a moment as if he would use it, as he had once used it on Scott.

His left hand automatically came forward to brace his thin right wrist, to prepare for the recoil.

But the intervention of a madman saved the naval officer's life.

'There is another one, *ya effendim.*'

Fascinated with this one, they had forgotten the possibility that another man might be in the tank.

Up in the hole, at the apex of the water-tank, another man was laughing and shouting crazily and he began to fire an automatic rifle with the speed and skill of a marksman shooting sitting ducks on a lake.

'Enough, Ramzey! They'll kill you,' the naval officer shouted out frantically. 'Stop it. In the name of God, stop it, *ya wallad.*'

Three or four shots had shaken them into a panic, and Amin Fakhry, being the likely target, was running in a comical zigzag across the open tufts of sand with a marksman chasing him with little explosions of sand all about him, until the firing suddenly stopped and the man in the tank fell down inside it, so heavily that they heard the booming crash within it, and a dead dull thud without.

'You wait down here like fools while that madman is there inside,' Hakim cried at the soldiers. 'Get him out.'

The soldiers leapt onto the ladder and went up to the tank one after the other, while Amin came running back and Hakim shouted at them to hurry. One soldier at the top slipped off the cone-shaped roof and slid down and crashed to the ground near them, so that they forgot everything for a moment to recover him, conscious, but with a broken back or broken legs, in terrible pain.

'We should have brought a doctor,' Amin Fakhry said. 'Get the jeep,' he called to a soldier. 'Go quickly and bring an ambulance.'

They left the soldier moaning where he was, under the tank, afraid of moving him, and they watched the progress of the others who were lowering themselves into the tank.

'Bring him out carefully,' Hakim shouted.

But even as he called out they heard a thumping and crashing inside the tank as if some desperate fight were taking place inside it, and the shouts of the combatants were booming out of the hole above them as the soldier on the lip of the hole shouted down instructions to his companions, struggling within.

'He's still alive in there,' Amin said indignantly to Scott. 'Did you see the way that fool chased me with those shots? My God ... I'm lucky. Look.'

Amin had two burns across his bare right arm, and a scratch on the back of his neck which was bleeding. Scott took Amin's handkerchief and dabbed at the wound, but Amin shrugged it off, and by now the tank was silent.

'He's coming out,' the soldier called down. 'Look out.'

This was a confusing and complicated operation, handing down a half-conscious lunatic covered in slime who jabbered nonsense and flung his limbs about wildly. But his body was too limp to offer effective resistance, so that when they got him to the top of the iron ladder two of the soldiers half-carried and half-dropped him down the ladder until he was finally a mess on the ground.

'It's young Bindari,' Hakim said bitterly as if he had expected it but was also surprised. 'Look at him!'

'But he's quite *magnoon*,' Scott said, amazed.

Young Bindari was horribly vacant-eyed, and he was folded up helplessly on the ground.

'What's the matter with him?' Amin demanded of the naval officer.

That frightened assassin simply shook his head unhappily and wiped his hot face, unable to talk.

'He's insane,' Hakim said. 'Look at him.'

Bindari's skin was pale and opaque, his tongue was just protruding between his teeth, and his eyes were staring up at all of them in the fury of a drugged man; and though he was a limp mess on the ground, he suddenly heaved himself up like an animal and cried out:

'It's the dogs that would eat me. You! Let's get out. Go. Go!'

He had leapt at Hakim like a beast, but Scott who was nearest swept his arms around Bindari and there was a violent struggle of sanity and insanity for a moment which made it impossible for the others to help. Bindari's legs and arms and teeth, and his whole body, flayed at Scott to get free. He was growling and drooling, and Scott simply held his grip and tolerated the blows. But then something happened to Scott also. What was in his arms? What was here but the very end of this dangerous world he had been living with? It was struggling in his arms, it was biting him and trying to kill him, and Scott's nerves could stand it no more and he imprisoned Bindari's whole body in an embrace which was going to crush him to death. Bindari became berserk. But the blood was in Scott's head, in his whole body, and he got his head under Bindari's chin and forced it back in the worst of all fouls, and the most deadly because it would snap his neck, and he crushed this evil thing in his hands until it was limp. They tried hastily to pull him away from Bindari, but he shouted out: 'Leave it! Get away.'

'You'll kill him,' Hakim was shouting.

'Go away,' Scott shouted back. 'Don't touch me.'

But the body was limp and the resistance was too ineffectual; and Hakim's startled expression and Amin's excited shouting of his name: 'Scott! Scott!' was a release from it. He allowed them to take Bindari's helpless body out of his crushing embrace and to lay him on the ground.

'Is he dead?' Scott asked, white and sick now.

494

'No,' Amin said. 'But he would have been, old sweetheart! You don't know your own strength.'

Hakim was still looking at him with a puzzled and amused interest, but Scott turned away impatiently.

On the ground young Bindari was crying and moaning, his face in the earth, insane and incoherent until Amin took a soldier's jacket and put it over his head. Then he became quieter, simply moaning and whimpering like a demented child.

'One ought to shoot a beast like that,' Hakim said in revulsion, but he was calm now and efficient. 'Why is he like that?' he asked the other one.

'But he's been drugging himself all day,' the naval officer told them through fresh tears. 'And he took too much. He was taking it all day, but I didn't . . .'

'Animal,' Hakim said hatefully.

Scott, in his own physical shame, felt the punishment of that word. He looked quickly at Hakim to see if there was a double-edged hint in it, but Hakim was already telling the soldiers to search the area in case there was another one hiding somewhere. And this time, to search it better than they had before.

It was over, Hakim said, when they had cleaned up the mess. 'So let's go up and have a look at this place.'

They had sent the wounded soldiers away in an ambulance, and they had strapped Bindari tightly to a stretcher and locked him—with his naval companion—in another ambulance which waited there in the sun for Hakim's decision. Inside it, Bindari was still insane, still moaning and crying out with a wild man's idiocy, shouting about dogs, begging someone not to walk in the canals, and arguing with someone else who might have been his father—laughing and mocking him. They could hear the babble coming from the ambulance.

'Pity that poor wretch with him in there,' Amin Fakhry said to Hakim, sorry for the other one who was hot and frightened but sane at least. 'Do you have to lock him in there with a madman?'

'Let him feel lucky to be alive,' Hakim said sharply.

They climbed the ladder and lowered themselves into the tank. Amin had found a large battery-light inside, which he switched on, and they could see that the assassins had been prepared to hide here for days. There were crates of tinned fruit and tinned food (anchovies and pickled mushrooms), some of them opened and eaten. There was a row of wooden crates, long enough to form a rough bench above the level of the few inches of slimy water. The stench was dead and horrible, still thick with the smell of his fired cartridges. There was a small kitchen step-ladder

495

which Bindari had obviously been standing on so that he could fire from the hole.

'If that idiot hadn't drugged himself into stupidity while he was waiting in here, and if that frightened wretch with him hadn't lost his head,' Hakim said, 'you would be dead, Amin. Even if he had fired one shot, accurately, and then quietly climbed down his ladder—who could have found him up here? We didn't know about this hole in the top. We could never have known that the shot had come from in here. What a fool he was,' Hakim said dispassionately.

They inspected the rifle in the light. It was a new American automatic with a cheek rest on the stock and a peep sight, a marksman's weapon.

'Fool,' Hakim said professionally.

He stood on the little kitchen ladder with the gun, his head out of the hole, and he fired one post-mortem shot across the dunes to prove the efficacy of the idea, but the clumsiness of its execution.

Satisfied, they climbed out of the tank and went down to the sea to wash off the slime. It was filthy stuff. Amin Fakhry was trying to clean it off his clothes, and one of the soldiers was helping him with petrol from the jeep. While Hakim was dressing, Scott asked Amin if he had known that he was acting as a decoy for Gamal.

'Of course, my dear. Hakim sent a plane for me last night. You know how he is. With his silent secrets . . .' Amin hooded his aristocratic eyes in a mockery of Hakim's lower mind.

'Does Hakim know who else is behind it?'

Amin shrugged. 'He must have a good idea,' he said and dabbed at his trousers, his neat professionalism revolted by the mess he was in. 'But why did he bring you here?' he asked Scott.

Scott had wondered himself about that, but a glance—a casual accidental glance—at the scars on his own stomach, the dark holes Hakim had once fired into him years ago, revealed it all clearly enough. Was Hakim so guilty about that, even now? Did he delight in showing up an English assassin at work? To hold up the mirror to Scott and thus equalize the guilt?

'Hakim likes to be mysterious,' he agreed with Amin carefully. He was still recovering his sanity. He was wondering, too, if this incident had returned Amin Fakhry back into the old fellowship and if Amin's real differences with Hakim had been forgotten. It seemed possible.

'Did Hakim tell you about our plan for a long-range column at Siwa?' Amin asked him.

'He was telling me just before you came.'

'Well?' Amin said, smiling with enthusiasm, sparkling with the confidence of having achieved something worthy of him at last. 'We can do it

496

better than anybody else, my old sport. Not so?' Amin forgot about his trousers.

'That's true,' Scott said noncommittally.

What else could he say to Amin? He still felt sick, and he was more determined than ever not to do it, even now. He could not argue with them yet—with Amin or Hakim. But he would *not* become a soldier for them, no matter what the moral pressure and no matter how much Hakim suspected him of English hypocrisy, simply because the possible enemy in view would be his own countrymen.

Amin stopped the soldier dabbing at him and began to enlarge enthusiastically upon the possibilities before them, and he was saying as Hakim emerged fully dressed from the hut: 'Let's try to settle some of it with Hakim now.'

But Hakim had forgotten, for the moment, the value of his new long-range raiding force, and he was telling the soldiers guarding the ambulance to get inside it and at the cost of their lives to let neither escape.

'Nobody will escape this time,' Hakim said to them. 'If there's a man in this whole country with even a breath of suspicion on him, he's going to pay a big price for his stupidity. Why have we been so gentle with these dangerous monsters all this time? These weak fools! They were never gentle with us.'

'But who is behind it?' Scott asked Hakim in a dead voice.

'Too many lunatics,' Hakim said grimly. 'And this time I'll lock them all up and keep them locked up. They can rot in darkness until I know who is in it and who is not. How could I forgive myself if I let one small-minded murderer escape, simply because I was afraid to suspect him of the worst? After this,' Hakim said, 'everybody must prove himself, otherwise he must be counted as an enemy. It's the only way. Believe me, it's the only way.'

It was obviously impossible for them to talk of anything else except Hakim's sad realization that he had been dangerously lenient. Amin reminded them that they had not yet eaten lunch, but Hakim rejected such frivolity and sent Scott back to the airport in the Chrysler ('Poor *habibi*,' he said. 'You don't look well!') to return to Cairo alone in Gamal's plane, while he and Amin drove away in the ambulance to finish the investigation of their inept captives, who would never again see the light of an Egyptian day—that seemed sure.

CHAPTER SIXTY-FOUR

NONA had heard innocently from one of her friends that Quartermain, her husband, had been seen taking coffee with a young woman in Loques', and though Nona shrugged it off and said nothing about it, he eventually discovered what she was being so contemptuous of him about.

Another woman?

She did not really believe it was serious; but why hadn't he told her about it?

'You'll just have to trust me,' he told her weakly now. 'Don't ever ask me who it was.'

'I don't intend to ask you who it was,' she said coldly. 'I don't even want to know. It's your business.'

He did not want to tell her yet about Sophie Mourad, the auburn-haired communist. He admitted to himself that he had sat there with her, fascinated by her youth, gulping healthily of it and romancing a little on the future of this Egyptian girl if she kept her course straight and became a proud, emancipated, Egyptian woman. What a lovely, remarkable woman she would be.

'Wouldn't you take the money?' she had begged him once more. 'How will we ever reach our people if we can't show them what their lives mean? It is important, and you would be doing a good thing.'

A good thing, she said.

He listened. He knew its importance. He understood the future she planned for her people with that photo-engraving camera and those bright young cheeks, those dark eyes and unflown banners of innocence. She needed no banners. But how had she discovered this war of the worlds, this dialectic of the unborn future?

'I'm not leaving Egypt yet,' he had told her. 'So it's pointless promising you anything.'

What other excuse could he offer her? Yet he hung on grimly to the rules he had made: absolutely no involvement in anything that would damage his family. That rule was particularly needed in Egypt now. He would not take risks, even for her bright future. But someone had been very clever to send this untouched young woman, who saw it in such natural colours. Where was the terror or the conspiracy of the fear of being a communist, when you looked at her? It seemed to be too naïve. Yet—try to show a lack of courage or try to deny concern, or display if you could any fear of the consequences. Do anything ignoble before those eyes? Impossible.

'No,' he said. 'I can't do it yet.'

'Will you tell us when you *can* do it?'

He shook his head reluctantly. He was not a well man. He could get worse too, under the thousand strains this life put on him. But now he was only under the strain of his conscience, and despite her great hopes for their future (with his help), Sophie Mourad had failed to persuade him. No matter what guilty pleasure he had enjoyed simply sitting there with her, he would not tell Nona that he was being asked to do a risky, conspiratorial thing. The less Nona knew, the better and safer for the family. He bore up very bravely with his wife, and with her headlong refusal to ask or even to quarrel about an unknown woman, and Nona drove him coldly into emotionless corners. Perhaps she trusted him implicitly, but even so she would not allow her faith in him or the jealousy to come out in the open, whatever happened.

But Nona felt relieved by better hopes. Helen had received a letter from Jolley in London offering her a job in the Head Office of the English Oil Exploration Company, should she find it necessary to leave Egypt during the present crisis.

'It's decent, anyway,' Quartermain admitted.

'At least you can come with us now, without worrying,' Nona said.

Hanna thus saw the end of their old life drawing near, but she was pleased for Helen and for herself—because she would go with the children. Where was life now if it wasn't with Nona's children?

But Helen herself wondered if she could work in a London office after a lifetime in Egypt.

'I don't think I could ever slave like those English girls—nine to five and hurry home in those crowded buses and tubes. What a strange life they live. What do they get out of it?'

'Husbands,' Nona said pityingly. 'What else can they hope for?'

Neither Nona nor Hanna yet knew that there was no hope of an exit visa. But Helen knew it, and she was looking for excuses to satisfy Nona, to avoid causing trouble between husband and wife.

Quartermain was back in bed after getting up too soon to attend Mr.

Menzies' last press conference. Did he have T.B. of the kidneys? Dr. Buelli had sent him to be X-rayed. The bill, which Nona had insisted on paying on the spot (not to Buelli who would never charge but to the X-ray clinic), was forty pounds.

'It's shocking,' she complained, knowing that it would make a big hole in Quartermain's close money calculations for their escape. 'In that way at least the English are impressive. In their hospitals you do see how civilized they can be.'

They were sitting on Quartermain's bed. Nona went on praising (in French) British hospitals for their intelligent realization that sickness should be free. Benjamin had been a difficult boy to get born. She had been confined in a private Chelsea nursing home, which had cost a large sum of money and had been filthy and badly run, and probably specialized more in high-class abortions than legal births. But when Hilal was due she had put aside her unpleasant memory of Egyptian public hospitals and had gone to St. Thomas's, to the public ward. There, the glimpse of the humane English had made her a social-service-minded Anglophile: that they should treat patients like human beings, that the red tape was negligible, the doctors helpful, the sensibilities of the highest . . .

'The hospitals may be all right,' Quartermain agreed dryly, 'but aren't private English doctors the richest benefactors to humanity the world has ever experienced?'

'You're so prejudiced,' Nona said.

'Not at all,' he insisted. 'I don't mind them making all the money they like, providing they call themselves medical businessmen and never throw in all this stuff about serving humanity.'

'They deserve to be rich,' she argued, 'and they do serve humanity. I would have been a doctor myself if women could have been doctors in Egypt.'

They had been gossiping after lunch, and now they left him to his siesta. He did not have tuberculosis of the kidneys. He simply had the solidified stomach (he told Buelli) one got from living with a wife who always applied her strongest emotions to the world's most deserving situations—such as Benjamin's naughtiness in refusing to wear shoes around the house.

That had meant two days of intense warfare, which mother and boy could happily withstand. But the father was in bed, and now he hid his head under the pillow while Nona mustanged her children into the bedroom for their afternoon nap. Benjamin wept, Hilal was scolded for sucking dirty fingers, and voices rose and fell happily as if the world must go to its doom as punishment for two dirty fingers and a pair of cotton socks. So it ought.

'Some day,' he told himself, 'something large is going to shock her.

Something important enough to penetrate even her wall of extraordinary values. Then let's see what happens.'

It was not meant to be a revengeful prediction. It was really a hope, which he often repeated to himself, to make the wait bearable. Some day the forceful values of Nona's everyday issues (such as who would go into the bathroom first) would be supplanted by others which might rise to the heights of: *it doesn't really matter.*

'It's a dream,' he groaned helplessly.

But he supposed he was only feeling sorry for himself.

The house was quiet; the house had been organized into cool autumn sleep. Hanna and Helen had gone to their own flat to meet their Coptic cousins from the provinces, and Nona came and lay down beside him in her cotton dressing-gown. But he was too tired now to correct the profound error of her whole approach to life itself.

Why pound at life when it was sometimes possible to caress it?

'Are you in pain?' she asked him, when he sighed.

'No. I'm arguing with myself,' he said.

'Even with yourself,' she said triumphantly. 'At least that way you can always win.'

In the middle of the siesta hour the telephone rang and Nona wondered sleepily who could be so inconsiderate. She answered it in the living-room and Quartermain heard her voice panic. He could hear her excited Arabic, and he had a presentiment that some new threat to his stomach was coming down the passage.

'The police have taken Helen away,' she said, shocked, her face taut and frightened. 'Everybody else was sleeping, and Helen was dressed, and they just took her off.'

'What for? Did they say?'

'No.' Nona sat down and got up again, starting to dress quickly.

'Did they say where they had taken her?' he asked, as upset as she was.

'No.' Nona was already pulling on her stockings. 'I'm going over to Hanna. Hanna said the police had already questioned Helen before. I didn't know that. Why didn't she tell me?'

'Helen told me,' Quartermain said. 'She didn't tell you because you panic too much.'

'What was the use of that?' Nona cried indignantly. 'Look what's happened now.'

'Shhh,' he said. 'Calm down. Has she actually gone with the police?'

'She tried to delay them, but they insisted. She had to go.'

'Then tell Hanna to come here.'

501

Nona had already become urgent in her panic, hurrying about the room. She was half-dressed and pinning up her hair.

'All our cousins are still there, having tea with Hanna.'

'Let them come here then. I can't get up and I want to talk to Hanna,' he told her. 'You're not going to do any good rushing over there. Helen's gone.'

Nona's stringy nerves began to snap painfully.

'What do they want?' she said, tearfully sitting down near him. 'Do you think they've arrested her? Oh, that stupid idiot, Sam. It's all his fault. Why did he have to get into trouble with the Egyptians? It was all because of his father. But it always comes down on Helen. Everything that somebody in this family does eventually falls on her like this. Nobody cares.'

'Everybody cares,' he corrected sharply, trying to stop her wasteful search for blame before his stomach dropped in a tight ball of iron down to his groin.

'But who helps her?' she demanded. 'Nobody! What can anyone do now?'

'Calm down,' he told her again. 'Nobody can help her if you go on like that.'

Her natural reply would have been, 'Oh, you're as bad as all the others.' It was coming . . . But Nona's terror for Helen was the one feeling she could not cope with in life—this sudden feeling of helplessness and of something beyond her control. What could she do?

'I'll get up,' he told her, knowing that she might suddenly collapse in overwhelming defeat if he did not do something. 'I'll see if I can talk to somebody.'

'But who can you see?'

'I'll find somebody,' he said. 'They're not going to hurt her. They probably won't keep her long.'

'How do you know?' she said. 'Look at all the Egyptians they've arrested for spying. And who knows whether or not that man Jolley was a British spy? That's what she gets for looking after the English. What for? Who cares?'

He knew he now had the advantage, but he could not take it. He felt too much admiration for her complete loyalty to those she owed most to. 'Let her alone,' he told himself. 'Don't argue against it. If you ever deserve that kind of passion for anything, yourself, you can count yourself lucky.'

'I get depressed in bed,' he told her when she said he should not get up.

She did beg his pardon then for being so short-tongued, but she didn't say anything more. She relaxed unhappily for a moment, trying to forgive him, before she went off to telephone Hanna to come and talk to her husband.

Sam had also been taken away by the police. One of his old friends, he had said, from the villa.

502

'What for?' he had asked indignantly.

No explanations and no questions answered (they said) so that when Scott returned from lunching with Leo Lieberman in Cairo, the household was upset. Even the *pensionnaires* who had never seen such a thing happen, although they always feared it might happen to them, were waiting for him. But only Becky was calm enough to explain what had happened while Scott had been absent. The police had knocked on the door at two o'clock in the afternoon and asked for Sam. Sam had known one of the policemen who was in 'civil' and he had gone off in his friendly way with them.

'He told me it wasn't serious,' Becky said in French. 'He swore it wasn't.'

Madame Salz was dazed, and Sam's sister Alicia had arrived in tears, beating her forehead. Together they were making a noisy, worrying situation of it in the darkened dining-room. What could Capten Scott do?

'Ne vous inquiétez pas,' he assured them. No, no; above all they must not disquieten themselves.

What else could he say? They all needed reassuring, except Becky. She was upset, but she had accepted Sam's word for it, trusting not so much the honour of the Egyptian police to return him, but to Sam's own assurance which she accepted without doubt.

'Good girl, Becky,' Scott said in relief.

He put his large hand affectionately on the back of her fine reddish hair. She blushed up her neck, and he realized that he had touched her without thinking because he was anxious to show his appreciation for all the help he could get.

'I can't do anything tonight,' he told them.

He couldn't explain that Hakim was not yet back from Alexandria and he would have to see Hakim. Who else was at work? Was this Hakim's temper getting the better of him? If so, Sam and Helen Mamoon (they had learned on the phone that she had also been arrested) might not be seen again for a very long time.

When Quartermain came to see him the next day, he knew what would be expected of him.

'Last Friday must have been black Friday,' Scott told him, telling him also what had happened in Alexandria. 'It was so bad,' he said, 'that I suppose Hakim simply gave orders to round up everybody. At least everybody already under suspicion. It's the only possible explanation. But I can't see why he did that to your sister-in-law as well, even if she was trying to get Sam a passport. What for?'

Helen had not come home overnight, and the police had refused to tell the family anything more. Quartermain still looked very sick, and he apologized for coming.

'As you know, I never do ask favours,' Quartermain told him tiredly, 'but if you've got any better ideas . . .' Quartermain shrugged helplessly for his own failure to think of anything.

Scott looked at him and said, 'You ought to get out of this country.'

Quartermain was like an old man. He looked as if he had been sucked dry by the heat; or perhaps he was tired out by the wear and tear of the harsh mockery—that thick armour he had put over his heart so that he could always defend his concern for the world without being laughed at for it—by anyone excepting himself. It was extraordinary how this country told on some people instantly.

On the other hand Quartermain found himself looking at a healthy man and resenting it. Considering what Scott had told him of his experience in Alexandria, he marvelled at Scott's resiliency, his apparent acceptance of all the world as it was and ever would be. In fact that healthy face and body seemed to be a denial of the world's responsibility. How could a worried man or a conscience-stricken man be so healthy? What had Scott cut out of his mind to have such a healthy look about him?

'The trouble is,' Scott complained, 'Hakim is moving in the most mysterious way possible. He always does. But it gets worse. I don't know why he'd arrest Helen. I think it's his bad temper now. I've never seen him like that before.'

Quartermain walked around stiffly and restlessly as if he still had a painful stomach-ache or a fever or a heart full of broken hopes.

'Oh, I can see the point to it,' Quartermain said dryly. 'Your friend Hakim simply wants to dig us all up, that's all. He can't help doing it.'

'What do you mean?'

'Who can blame him?' Quartermain asked of the world. 'I told you. The east is going to turn us all over, sod by sod, rose by rose, lie by lie. So Hakim isn't likely to let up on the process just to spare a few daisies by the roadside like Helen, is he?'

'That's truer than you think,' Scott told him, realizing that Quartermain had understood Hakim perfectly. Hakim would uproot them all, sooner or later. That was exactly it.

Quartermain was trying to laugh casually at the irony of it, but he could only reach a sad excuse for his cynicism. 'I've been trying to decide all day what I could do, to force them to let Helen go. I can think of all the stupid things, and the very brave ones, and even the dangerous ones, but they're all so ridiculous and useless. Sometimes I think that it's only a matter of shaming them. Do you think I could shame them into letting Helen go? Can I prove them uncivilized, something very frightening like that? You ought to know,' he said cynically to Scott. 'You're an expert at doing it yourself. What does one man do?—that's what you always ask. The trouble is I know the answer already. One man does nothing. The world gobbles up one stubborn woman like Helen or one stubborn man like you; simply eats you up. What can *I* do? Or what can *you* do? Nothing. Unless . . .'

'Yes?'

Quartermain was playing with the ridiculous again. 'Unless I deliberately sent out the story about someone trying to assassinate Nasser. Then I might make a *scandale*. I'm the only outsider who knows about it, aren't I?'

'For God's sake, no!' Scott begged. 'I wouldn't have told you if I'd known you'd say anything about it. That wouldn't help. Don't ever say anything about it. And anyway—it was Amin Fakhry they fired at, not Gamal Abd el Nasser . . .'

'I know that. So what will help?'

'I don't know,' Scott admitted, upset and depressed by this sad view of Quartermain asking the questions now. 'I'll do what I can,' he said. 'But not if it's going beyond any sort of involvement that I could defend. Somebody did want to kill Gamal, and I can't argue with that.'

CHAPTER SIXTY-FIVE

WHEN Hakim came back he was very enthusiastic about the new desert department he had invented, and he told Scott that Amin Fakhry was already sitting in his own headquarters in Abassia, in an old Nissen hut which had once been used by the British as the quarantine quarters for anyone suspected of fever or contagion, particularly yellow fever. Since then, Egyptian Army units had kept out of it for fear of some latent contagion from it. Surely the risk remained.

'You're not superstitious, are you?' Hakim said.

But now it was indignation which Scott unburdened without caution. Why was Sam back in prison? That was unfair. Why did Hakim round up people like Helen Mamoon, as if they were assassins? He protested. He almost accused Hakim of being cruel to a woman, but he knew through his colder nerves that he would make it worse if he went too far.

'Perhaps you don't realize,' he said to Hakim in Arabic, 'that every time you swoop down on these people, the way you do, by God, it wrecks their lives. What have they done? They don't want to kill Gamal. You know that. Why do you bother with such unimportant people? Do you do it because Sam is a foreigner? All right, but she is not a foreigner, anyway. She is an Egyptian . . .'

'But I didn't tell anyone to arrest Hassoon particularly,' Hakim replied, delighted with Scott's protests and his unhappy appeal, teasing him deeper into it as if to discover how far it would go.

'Who did then?' Scott asked, regaining some caution.

'It's simply the way these things are done,' Hakim said. 'I sent a message from Alexandria and told them to take in everyone under suspicion, no matter who it was. I was angry, *habibi*. I am still angry,' he said. 'We arrested fifty people, many of them Egyptians. Was Hassoon among them? I'm sorry, *habibi*. Was his aunt too? *Misqueena!* I'm sure she didn't want to kill anybody. But they can prove their innocence. I'm sure they can.'

'Then can't you let them out?'

506

'But we don't know enough,' Hakim replied in good-natured exasperation. 'We still need them.'

'They're not going to run away, and they're not going to hurt anyone,'
Scott insisted impatiently, wondering as he calmed down why Hakim put
up with his arguments at all. Why didn't Hakim throw him out and end
their strange and distended relationship, which seemed to have no more
point to it? How much longer would this contest between the Caliph and
the beggar go on? How beggarly must he become?

'I ought to warn you,' Hakim interrupted elaborately, 'that they both
want to leave Egypt.'

'What else can they do?' Scott said in a new fit of impatience. 'It's all
very well for you to make strict rules about who you can trust, Hakim,
and who you can't. But you make it impossible for some people to go
along with you. Why don't you let them feel like Egyptians? You make
their lives too difficult. Not only the foreigners, but even Copts and Christians like Helen Mamoon . . .'

'She is a very determined woman,' Hakim said admiringly in English,
as if they were sharing a delicate secret about her. 'Don't you think she is?'

'She has to be,' Scott answered. 'You're making things so hard for her.'

'That's true,' Hakim said seriously. 'But not all of them are innocent,
habibi. Not all foreigners are our friends, even those born and bred and
made wealthy here.'

'That doesn't apply to either Hassoon or Helen Mamoon.'

'In that case they are safe,' Hakim said, teasing again. 'They are much
safer where they are, for the time being. Patience, my dear.'

Scott felt warned then, and knew he had been a fool for losing his
temper. He needed a little time to restrain himself, so he picked up the
American rifle which Hakim had brought back with him from Alexandria.
It was leaning on the small table near Hakim's desk, cleaned and tagged.

'This morning,' Hakim said, taking it from him carefully and putting
it on the table as if he were afraid it might go off, 'this morning they called
Mr. Menzies home. Do you think that means war, now that *someone* has
failed to kill Gamal? In any case, Mr. Menzies is lucky to be going home.
What do you think I would have done if someone had shot Gamal? I
went to the airport this morning to see Mr. Menzies off, and I happened
to have this rifle in the car with me, and I thought then: "How easy it is,
really, to kill somebody, if you keep your head." I could have picked up
the rifle from where I was sitting in the car and finished Menzies off with
one good shot. And who would have been the wiser? Who would have
suspected *me*? When he turned to wave at the press photographers I said
to myself: "Good-bye, Mr. Menzies. Only I know how lucky you are." I
had decided he was hardly worth it, although I was tempted to frighten
him a little, the way we were frightened on Friday.'

'What good would that have done?' Scott asked, amazed, although he knew Hakim was exaggerating.

'What good would killing Gamal have done? Ask your own countrymen that, my friend. Ask them.'

'That's nothing to do with me or my friends,' Scott pointed out.

'How do you know it isn't? That is my point about shooting Mr. Menzies. How can you possibly know who would like to kill a man? Who would have suspected me? Oh, well, perhaps you are right in this case.' Hakim sighed. 'Why should I quarrel with you?'

Scott waited.

'But you must admit that too many people are interested in getting rid of Gamal, particularly the British. Do you blame us for arresting all suspicious persons, even your friend Hassoon?'

There was no argument to it, there could be no argument; but as Scott was leaving, Hakim held him back and gave him a bundle of photographs of young Bindari who had been put in a criminal asylum, he said, still raving mad. Hakim added as an afterthought:

'Did I ever tell you who first told us that Hassoon was working for the British? I did tell you . . .'

'You only told me it was an Englishman.'

'But I didn't tell you *who* told us?'

'You like to reveal things of that sort by painful fractions,' Scott said dryly with his stubborn resentment implying trickery in Hakim's behaviour now. 'And you usually think it's such a good joke.'

'Well, it is. It was that old man, Peter Dukes,' Hakim said.

Scott felt like striking his own heart. 'But he's a British agent himself. Why should he tell you that Sam was working for the British . . .?'

Hakim pulled a wry face. 'Why would Peter Dukes tell us many things?'

'But you can't believe him.'

'Oh, but I'm glad we did. But we also take your word,' Hakim pointed out, 'and you are a much older friend. Aren't you going to be a great help to us? You will now be able to show the English that there are other kinds of Englishmen. You will help Amin and we will be grateful. You have decided, not so?'

Scott had decided once and for all that he would refuse. He was determined to hold out. But even the look on Hakim's face now was a warning to him of the consequences, if he did.

He knew then that he was Hakim's hostage—not only for Sam and Helen Mamoon, but for the whole perfidious British race as well. Was he any different from the others? Could one Englishman prove he had other values besides being English? It was in Hakim's eyes, and though Scott's heart was not deep enough to bother with his honour any more, he knew

508

that he represented the only safety for Sam and Helen Mamoon. Hakim could not have made that clearer if he had written it down, to be signed and sealed: his loyal services against the lives of his friends.

'All right,' Scott said, pushing away those stark photographs of the mad young Bindari whose eyes and face were now beyond saving. He knew that Hakim was reminding him of his own folly rather than Bindari's. 'I'll help Amin with his desert force, if you insist.'

'Good. That's so good. I knew it, because we do need you. I tell you, my dear, you have the experience, and we are in a hurry. And you mustn't worry about your friends. They are quite safe where they are, they can remain safe with us. Don't worry about them.'

Scott nodded. He understood. The price Hakim had put on him was going to remain high. Let him act perfidiously for just one moment, and his friends would probably pay the penalty for his English betrayal.

'Where is Amin?' he asked.

'Right across the barracks. I'll send Ahmed with you. Just call him in.'

'What do you think will happen, now that Menzies has gone back?' he asked Hakim, knowing that it was important now.

'You know the English better than I do. What do *you* suppose they can do? Bomb us? Or will they send warships to teach us a lesson?'

'They might,' Scott said savagely, giving Hakim a little of his own medicine.

'Do you think they could be so stupid?'

'Of course they could be. Who could be stupider than the English?' Scott said sarcastically.

But Hakim laughed generously. 'I don't know, *habibi*. I honestly don't know.'

They were making cynical jokes against each other, but even Hakim (in that secret heart) could not seriously believe that the English proposed to use force.

CHAPTER SIXTY-SIX

SCOTT did not really worry about the British using force. He refused to be tricked by this talk of a crisis. It would pass. It always did.

He was worrying instead about the combined trickery of Peter Dukes and Hakim, and he was trying to suppress a desire to make Peter Dukes pay some terrible penalty for his betrayal of Sam. If he had caused Sam's trouble, then something quite nefarious and evil was behind it, and he would settle with Peter Dukes somehow.

Peter's office, however, was locked and apparently abandoned. For a moment he was glad that he had thus escaped the necessity for finding out, at last, the root of this evil business. But he could not escape it so easily, and he knew he must try the Turf Club where Peter Dukes lived.

The original Turf Club, almost next door to Peter's office, had been burned down during the Cairo riots. The new one was on the top floor of an office building which the mob could not easily reach if they ever wanted to set fire to it again or throw the club members out of the windows.

He asked one of the club stewards for Peter Dukes, standing at the little fort of cubby holes thinking how sadly unprepossessing this small island of lost British privilege was. An old steward told him that Mr. Dukes was in the hospital, but Major Runciman might help him.

Scott tried to withdraw, but Major Runciman was called. He had heard and seen Scott, and he was already approaching from behind a writing-table where he had been working over stacks of letters and files. Runciman was not the club secretary balancing the books, but a battered Englishman doing his agency business in the safety and surroundings of his friends. Runciman had been caught at his office in Adly Pasha street during the riots and his office and his clothes had been set on fire. He was still scarred unpleasantly from the neck to the top of his head, which was half-bald on one side as a result.

'Isn't it Scott?' Runciman said. 'I heard you asking for Peter. Do come in, will you, and I'll put you onto him.'

Runciman was enticing him into the writing-room.

'Let me get you a drink. Albert . . .'

'No, no,' Scott said stiffly. 'I'm in rather a hurry.'

'That's all right. I'll have to ring the hospital for you. Peter's been laid up. Come in, old fellow. Just for a moment.'

Runciman had been a Cairo lawyer before the war, and an Adjutant-General's lawyer during the war. He had probably made a fortune in Cairo in the thirties with his prosperous legal business, specializing in Government contracts, but nobody knew what had happened to his money. Some said his wife had squandered it in England, living in expensive country houses and never coming to Cairo to see where the money came from. After the war, Runciman's legal business had been ruined by the Egyptianizing of all local business and the closure of the Tribunaux Mixtes. He had not been able to retire gracefully on his savings, so he had taken on instead the rather crass (for him) work of selling a popular make of British motor-car. He had probably made another fortune, which he could not get out of Egypt now and which he kept secret from his daughters who never came to see him.

'I don't think I've seen you since the war,' Runciman said.

'That's true,' Scott said civilly. 'It must have been in 1943.'

Runciman, more than most people, probably knew all the details of Scott's court-martial, because of his war service with the Adjutant-General's department. Formerly, Scott's sense of enmity (which had been simple and one-faced) would have identified Runciman as one of the people on the side of his downfall, and he would have withdrawn from this situation without bothering to be more than polite.

'It's so astonishing to see you still here,' Runciman said, trying to warm up to Scott.

'I might say the same about you,' Scott answered. 'Most people have left.'

But Scott was upset to see him. Even his scarred face was pitiful. Six years ago this man might have greeted him, but barely so. Ten or twelve years ago Runciman would not even have been polite. Now he called over the others in the club, those who were in the writing-room and some from the bar. Three or four other Englishmen, all recognizable to Scott as old Cairo inhabitants, were suddenly at hand being friendly; reservedly so, but friendly.

What for, he wondered.

'We should see you more often, now that you've left Ghurdakha,' one of them said. He was a Cable and Wireless man named Fortescue Privett.

A drink was put in his hand. He looked at their puzzled faces. He wanted to go away, but he could not be so impolite now. Why? They didn't seem to know themselves why they were asking him if he was staying in Cairo permanently, and why he was answering them with such polite answers. 'Yes, I think so.' Had he seen Peacock when he came through? *Yes, Peacock had come to see him.*

But what did they all want?

They looked hungrily into his eyes for something.

It seemed to be something he was holding back and would not give, but what was it? Perhaps they were not asking him for anything. Perhaps they were not being more than delicately friendly. Yet he felt it, and he felt too the tight unit they had made with him, standing by the window looking out on the dry limbs of a dusty palm tree or a sad rooftop. They were united for a moment so that the old sense of a lost continuity came back, the old Cairo, the refreshed memory of what it had been for them because he was of it. He had walked in on them, a lucky and unexpected remnant from a lost world, and they clung to him for the smell and the recollection of it, nothing more, and it didn't matter that he had never been a part of their world at all.

'I rang Peter,' Runciman said, coming back from the phone. 'He's in Dr. Mourad's private hospital in Gizeh. You can go there now if you like.'

'Is he very ill?'

'Not at all. He had his appendix out,' Runciman said, and only then could Scott escape them before they tried to capture him permanently. He would not have been any use to them after a few hours anyway, because the monotony, habit, and perhaps the rancour of bad memories would return and spoil their discovery of a remnant like him, thrown up from the good old days.

He left them quickly and he tried to shake off their after-effects, but the meeting had made him feel how children and middle-aged adults feel when they sense their own mortality, and he was thinking it out in the taxi on the way to the hospital. He decided that he was now at that age in life when the half-way turn-over takes place. Youth is gone because the past is gone, and the remainder of what time is left cannot be so easily lavished on new attempts at beginning a life. He was not even thinking about Sam but of himself when he arrived at the hospital to see Peter Dukes.

He meant to be revengeful with Peter, but the yellow stain of the man lying sunless in white sheets in the private hospital bed made him ask instead how Peter was, and whether it was all over. What was the use of trying to punish this man?

'Oh, it's nothing,' Peter said casually, sitting up. 'I wondered when I'd see you. I didn't think you'd bother to come here, though.' Peter was happy and glad to see him.

'I had a particular reason,' Scott admitted, 'but I don't want to bother you if you're sick.'

'Why must there always be a reason?' Peter said cheerfully. 'I'm glad you came, anyway. I get lonely, and it's a rotten feeling at my age.'

But Peter looked happy, not lonely, in this smart aseptic cement villa which was the most expensive private hospital in Cairo. Dr. Mahmoud Mourad, who ran it, was Cairo's best and most expensive surgeon. Peter said he was still in love with his life, just enough anyway to put it into the best hands, instead of going to those English, French, German, Austrian hacks who were all supposed to be better than any Egyptian doctor—if you felt that way about Egyptians. That was good for anything except surgery, he said.

'He's great,' Peter was saying enthusiastically of Mourad. 'I didn't know a thing about it. Didn't even have anaesthetic. One of those spinal jabs. I heard the whole thing being done. I could even smell the cigar smoke on Mourad's clothes. None of that sick smell. I wonder why the devil I waited this long to have the damn thing out. But I've been so wary of doctors. They're so bloody sure of themselves, and usually they're so colossally wrong.'

'They say he's very good,' Scott agreed, trying to come stubbornly to the point. He asked Peter then if it were true. Had he told the Egyptians about Sam?

'Are you still going on about that?' Peter said with his vulgar good temper. 'Of course I told them about Hassoon. I had to.'

'What exactly did you tell Hakim?'

'Nothing much. I've forgotten. I suppose I told him that Hassoon was in touch with Bateman.'

'With Bateman?'

'I think that's what I told him. I'm surprised Hakim didn't tell you himself. I've forgotten, exactly . . .'

Scott felt all explanations slipping away from him. There were never reasons or explanations with these men. The point was always to extinguish the reasons and the explanations before ordinary men got hold of them. 'How do you know that Sam was working for Bateman?'

'Didn't you know?' Peter said.

'I knew he had seen Bateman, but I don't believe he did anything for him. What could he possibly have done?'

'Have it your own way. Oh, don't be so bloody stubborn, man. You knew Sam Hassoon wanted a passport. The British wouldn't give him one. Lucy Pickering sent him to Bateman for help. What did that little puppy-dog do? He put your friend Sam to work. He promised Sam a passport in exchange for a few favours.'

'How could Bateman have got him a passport,' Scott argued, 'when even Tim Peacock couldn't?'

'Hah!' Peter said triumphantly. 'You tell Hassoon that. These poor

s

bastards without passports and papers will believe anything. They listen to any fool's promises. I wonder what's going to happen to all of them,' Peter said with a moment's dry regret. 'I often get a bit depressed when I think of some of those poor devils.' He shrugged. 'Actually, if they'd been clever they could have had papers, particularly the Jews. Now it's too late to be clever, because it's too dangerous.'

'But why did you tell the Egyptians? You must have been mad.'

'I told you once before, Scott. I even warned you. At least I tried to warn you. I had to stop Bateman's capers.' Peter was folding a letter to fit into an envelope which he licked carefully and then sealed. 'First time I've managed to write letters home to England in years,' he said pulling a face because the glue tasted so horrible. 'I found a long-lost sister living in Bristol, married to a Welshman.'

Scott had long ago run out of indignation with Peter, and now he was little more than curious: an indignant curiosity. How could he ever understand a man like Peter Dukes? It was impossible to understand him.

'You might have put a stop to Bateman,' Scott said to him, 'but Sam got the worst of it. Bateman managed to get away.'

He had read it that morning in one of the more scandalous Arabic newspapers that an Englishman, unnamed and wanted for questioning concerning a conspiracy, had removed himself hastily to Libya. They could not give his name, they said, but he was well known to the authorities as a British agent. They had also hinted at a plot to assassinate Gamal Abd el Nasser.

Apart from this, no one seemed to know anything yet about the attempt in Alexandria. For one reason or another Hakim was keeping it a secret. It could wait.

'Bateman had left before that little incident in Alexandria,' Peter told him.

'How do you know?'

'Don't always ask that same silly question. It's not difficult to know things, after they've happened. Moreover, it was Hakim who let him go deliberately.'

'You mean Hakim didn't know about Bateman?'

'Of course he did. He knew. But he knew if he stopped Bateman leaving, he would reveal just how much he knew. He didn't want to do that. He wanted it all to happen so that he could catch all the Egyptians involved. He didn't want to spoil it all by stopping that silly young bastard getting away.'

Scott did not question the trickery of it, only the results. 'Bateman gets away,' he complained, 'and Sam has to stay.'

'That's Sam's bad luck,' Peter admitted. 'But it's also his own fault.

514

Do you think he had anything to do with that shooting in Alexandria last week?'

'How did you know about it?' Scott asked again.

'I told you about it, didn't I? You were too stubborn to listen.'

'I know what you told me. But how did you know it had actually happened?'

Peter put his hands together piously. 'You poor naïve chap. Poor old chap,' he said. 'When I start to write my memoirs I'll tell you all my secrets. Anyway, *did* Hassoon have anything to do with it, or didn't he? Tell me honestly?'

'Definitely not.'

'Did Lucy Pickering or Church?'

Peter was joking, but Scott had made up his mind about Lucy, and Church also, and having faced that already he did not want to face it again—with Peter Dukes as the inquisitor. He had asked himself in the plane, in the loneliness of that empty plane coming home, if he honestly thought Lucy and Church were capable of involving themselves in what he had just seen. All the coincidences pointed to their involvement—the *pension*, Lucy's visit to the Bindaris' estate, her association with Bateman, and so many other obvious factors, but he had made up his mind not on the coincidences and the evidence, but on what he understood of them, and he knew they were not murderers. How else could you judge people?

'No they would not do a thing like that,' he told Peter now 'Church may go around looking for good landing-places, and Lucy may make teasing remarks about Nasser, and even do foolish things, but she would not plan a murder, nor would Church.'

'Then who would do it?'

'I suppose Bateman could, or perhaps even you could,' Scott said coldly.

Peter thought it a great joke. 'You may be right . . .'

'Anyway, Sam didn't. And that's the important thing.'

Peter shrugged. 'Nevertheless, he was involved with Bateman. And those fellows used Hassoon, I didn't. Why get angry with me?'

Peter was right. He was angry with the wrong man.

'You should never have told the Egyptians,' Scott insisted. 'That was cruel.'

Peter kept his good temper. 'Never mind. They won't do much to him. I doubt if they even know what he was doing for Bateman anyway.'

'Do you know?'

'Not the slightest idea,' Peter answered. 'But I hope it wasn't anything to do with Alexandria. If it was, Hakim will have him shot. For sure.'

Scott got up and was leaving in disgust, saying, 'I can't even see the point to it. I simply don't see why you did that to Sam.'

'Don't go,' Peter begged. 'Stay awhile. Let's talk about something else. You're the only visitor I've had. Look . . . it'll all come out in the wash.'

'Sam won't come out in the wash,' Scott said, not meaning to be clever.

'You never know what can happen. Anyway, the danger is not Sam, but something else, because some fool in London can still listen to idiots like Bateman. Yet, even if they do, sooner or later they'll have to realize that Nasser is the best bet we have in this part of the world. They have to realize it. So why don't you help me make them realize it before something else happens?'

Scott said he was not interested in the machiavelian aspects of Peter's world. Yet it remained Peter's final justification.

'After all,' Peter said, raising his voice so that Scott could hear even as he closed the door, 'at least we got rid of that dangerous little bastard, Bateman. It was worth it. Bateman will never come back here.'

The price was Sam, the end was Bateman. Peter had won a trick.

But Peter was a sick man. Wasn't Peter yellow and sunless?

Scott felt like a listless man, however, walking under the dried-up flame trees of Gizeh in the autumn smoke while Peter was singing happy songs in his hospital bed. Perhaps the sick man wasn't so sick, and perhaps the healthy man wasn't feeling too good.

CHAPTER SIXTY-SEVEN

FRANÇOISE was also in Cairo. She was at Leo Lieberman's flat waiting for him, and she had telephoned for him to come quickly.

He felt relieved, unbent with the thought that he would see her. But her neat black elegance was too well-groomed to shatter his heart today, and she was excited about something of her own. She was somebody else today. Not that she was unusually dressed. But in Cairo, and in Leo's decorated flat, she made the air too sharp with nylon and French perfume, because she put on her best clothes when she came to Cairo. When she was like this he wondered how he had ever had the courage to expect even a glance of intimacy from such a fashionable and sophisticated person whose life was entirely her own, far away from his.

What use was he to this pretty, metropolitan woman?

'I'm going,' she said excitedly. 'It's arranged. I have everything.'

Leo had used his money widely, and perhaps wisely. She had both an exit permit on her French passport, and a passage on a Greek boat leaving from Alexandria for Marseilles at the end of October, in less than a month.

'Did the Egyptians give you a re-entry permit?' he asked her.

'Why do you ask that?' she said. 'Do you want us to come back here?'

'I don't know that I can leave,' he told her. 'Not yet.'

'But you promised that you would leave with me, the moment I had arranged everything.'

'It's very difficult at the moment,' he repeated. 'I can't.'

'Why can't you leave? What's happened?'

He could easily tell her that Sam had been arrested again, and Helen Mamoon also; but that was not the whole of it. How could he explain his predicament to her, when it was inexplicable to anyone but himself and Hakim? It was not enough to say, simply, that Sam and Helen Mamoon's freedom might depend now on how he acted. It was not that simple, even to his own mind.

'But I've already arranged everything,' she said, sitting down near him. 'We have two cabins on the Greek boat. Leo arranged it so that Mireille and I can be together and André can be with you. I've told Monsieur Beauvoir that I'm leaving, and I can't change my mind now. I simply can't.'

'Then you must go alone, Françoise. I'm sorry, but I can't leave here yet.'

'Why not?' she demanded again.

'The Egyptians won't let me,' he said to simplify it completely.

'I won't go without you,' she told him. 'What will happen to me if I just leave like that? I might never see you again. I won't ever go alone.'

'I didn't realize that you were going to arrange it so quickly,' he complained. 'If I had known . . .'

'But what did you expect? You said that you would come. You had decided it yourself. You said so.'

'Other things have happened, Françoise. I simply can't leave just yet. But I'll follow. You ought to leave as soon as you can, and I'll come by plane.'

She was angry now. 'I don't believe you.'

He became angry himself. 'Do you think I want to stay here any longer than is necessary now? It's such a mess. I can't get out of it quickly enough. But I can't leave—just like that.'

'That's what you say. But I know you don't really want to leave here at all. You never did.'

'That's silly,' he told her. 'Don't say it. Please don't say that.'

'Je t'en supplie,' she said. 'Please come . . .'

She had even *tu*'d him deliberately to give some promise to it, but he decided that she was not being honest. He swore to himself that she was not so simple as all that. If Françoise had been at her simplest—worried about her children and bitter about the cynicism of her husband and the Egyptians, if she had talked of the disappointments of her life and asked him to set about repairing them for her—one wholehearted gesture (he swore) would make him abandon the troubles he had accepted on other people's behalf. But (he looked at her—he knew) Françoise was not promising anything of herself. The French language was simply not the language of a promise to be believed, and there was no real enticement in the supplication of *tu*.

'Tu a promis!' she said. 'Et maintenant tu veux m'abandonner.'

Don't, he wanted to say to her, don't say that now.

'I don't want to abandon anything,' he said. 'That is why I have to stay. I've got to stay.'

'Et moi?' she said bitterly. 'Aren't I that important also?'

He could not bring himself to explain it because it would become foolish the moment he said a word to Françoise. What was Sam or Helen Mamoon to her?

'I will not go,' she told him. 'And it will be your fault.'

He shook his head as if he did not want to hear it. 'I'll follow soon,' he promised weakly. 'I can promise that.'

But even as he said it he knew that he was promising something that seemed hopeless already. He did not really want the responsibility any more for what they were promising each other. He did not want the responsibility for deciding her upheaval, her divorce, her prospect for another life, because he knew there was no real truth in it. He felt it, standing here with her arms through his: he had promised himself to something that was dead already, because he had long ago betrayed it himself with Lucy Pickering; and Françoise had never given it substance, not even on the shadow of a promise. What hope was there for either of them now?

'But there's another problem,' he began to say.

'What other problem?'

'It's not important,' he said, because it was not possible to tell her about Lucy Pickering. It would never be possible, and he could hate her for making it so impossible.

'Voilà Leo,' she said.

They heard the lift door outside.

'I suppose you'll have to tell Leo I can't go,' he said to her quickly.

'Of course. Don't you want to talk to him about it?'

'No, I don't. It can't make any difference, Françoise.'

'I must tell him,' she insisted.

'All right, but it is really something between you and me, as far as I'm concerned. I don't want to talk about it with Leo, so please wait till I've gone.'

'Comme tu veux,' she said carelessly.

The tu-ing embarrassed him now, and he could not even look at her. They heard Leo struggling to the door, dragging his feet along the parquet passage outside the flat.

'I wish he would get a chair with wheels,' she said unhappily, 'but he doesn't want to. It's terrible to see his face when he walks. It's terrible.'

Leo opened the door, and even by their manner and their eyes it was obvious that they had been quarrelling, but Leo had a good grip on his pipe and he greeted them with a smile over his teeth and under his painful eyes. Françoise was right. It was almost unbearable to watch him reach the couch and fall into it. But, watching him, Scott realized that Leo now stayed alive by his rejection of pain, or rather by his rapprochement with it. What else gave him the power to stay alive?

'I was at the museum,' he told them. 'It's so hot.' He was sweating with his effort.

'On such a hot day?' Françoise said, calling the servant to make coffee

519

for them. She knew Leo needed it, even though it was not good for him.

'I was with the under-director. Do you know what I'm going to do?' he said, breathing heavily and looking slyly at Scott. 'I'm going to have some of the Tutankhamen jewels copied in gold, exactly, and then there will be two copies—like the British crown jewels.'

'But that would cost a fortune,' Françoise said. 'It's all gold.'

'Think of the work rather than the gold,' Leo said in his garish French. 'It will be lovely—beautiful.'

'What are you going to do with the copies?' Scott asked him politely. 'I mean—what's the point of copying them?'

'Wouldn't every museum in the world like to see them?' Leo told him. 'The Egyptians will never let the originals leave Egypt, but they will surely allow the copies.'

'In real gold?'

Leo knocked out his pipe. 'The gold is unimportant,' he said again. 'It's the beauty of it. How beautiful the amulets are, the head pieces.'

Scott marvelled that Leo trusted him with the idea. It would be brilliant if it worked. It was one way to get a fair share of his fortune out of Egypt. Leo could easily arrange for some museum to ask for the copies, and after that he would hope for the best, if not for the jewels themselves then for the market value of the gold. Was that what Leo wanted?

'Did they agree?' Scott asked.

'So far, yes. My goldsmith will work in the museum itself. But it will take time. The copy must be exact. Some of it is certainly the most beautiful of all the pharaonic designs. Particularly the necklaces. The rings are too big. I will keep some for Françoise too.'

Françoise was being irritatingly busy in the kitchen with the servant, and Scott asked him if there was any news of his brother Phillip.

Leo nodded his head, wiping away the perspiration with a damp handkerchief. 'The British told me that the Egyptians made no charges, so they are going to release him next week and expel him from Egypt. You know that there is quite a lot of money traffic to the Lebanon with Egyptian thousand-pound notes. I think they were trying to trace some which Phillip had, but they'll never find them, I'm afraid. I heard the other day of a man who took out a one-thousand-pound note glued under the denture of his teeth.' Leo shrugged. 'How can you trace that sort of money? They can't blame Phillip if some of the notes he had are missing. He traded them.'

When Françoise came in with the coffee, Leo said, 'Let Ahmed do that.'

'In France there will be no Ahmed,' Françoise told him, embracing this interest in herself so that they could not transfer it elsewhere; but she was still concerned for Leo and pulled a coffee table near him so that he would not have to reach forward.

'So, she will leave us,' Leo said with a flattering sigh.

'But I'll come back when I have fixed everything,' she said. '*Je t'promets*, Leo. I don't care what happens, I will come back.'

Leo looked quickly at Scott and smiled a little.

Françoise did not notice it, because she was now defending herself with the cool straight-legged guardianship of femininity with which French-women made their sex aggressively sure of itself. She did it very well. Her knees were joined together when she sat down. She was confident and chic. Her angry little shrugs were very expressive; and though it attracted both men, it also forced them into a selfconscious silence until Scott said he must go.

He said good-bye to Leo, and Françoise came out to the lift with him where he kissed her lightly, aware now that she was being very sure of herself against him.

'I'll come to Port Said in a week to see you before you go,' he said. 'And I'll take you to Alexandria to the boat.'

'Comme vous voulez,' she said without rancour.

He wondered what had changed her mind, her mood. He would never know. Yet she seemed sure of him; and he did not feel so badly. She seemed to imply now that she need not worry after all. After all, *l'anglais* was a man of honour, and she could depend on that to face the future with.

CHAPTER SIXTY-EIGHT

EVERYBODY interested enough, and Peacock also, could see what was happening. London was full of French officers in civilian clothes. And everybody who cared knew that the special debate in the House on September twelfth and thirteenth would settle what the Government would now do about the canal, and about Nasser as well.

Peacock said to his wife, Eileen, that the extraordinary always showed the House at its best, and he made sure that she had a ticket to the gallery. Something impressive was sure to come out of it, because tension in the House was always infectious, even to Eileen who was inclined to be phlegmatic about politics.

Eileen rarely went to the Commons, even when he spoke sometimes in the very loose debates on the Government's agricultural policies which drove the farmers themselves to threaten suicide. She always teased him afterwards for anything he said, convinced that he knew nothing about farming—that is, politically. Whereas he felt that, even though he was only a tax-loss farmer, he had been born with a west-country head on his shoulders and a sound grasp of the two aspects of political farming which mattered most.

The 'muck and mystery' school influenced most British farmers, because no matter how much fertilizer was added to the soil, no matter how it was jagged-up with fancy chemicals, the fact remained that there was no artificial way invented yet to replace the vital natural humus which kept the soil fertile. Only livestock and grass could do it, and farmers understood this only too well. One could begin any debate at this point, and sooner or later someone (probably a farmer-member on the Government's own benches) would accuse the Government of ruining the English heritage of good natural soil by its emphasis on chemicals.

Apart from this grass roots bitterness, one needed to know something about marketing to understand the British farmers' other odd mentality. All farmers (no matter what they grew) felt that the Government ought to guarantee them sure markets and stable prices for their products. Very natural. But then the Government ought to step right out of the way, while the farmers got on with the job producing as much as they could to supply the market and make a profit. But administrators and boards were always interfering, and that was usually when the arguments became acrimonious, particularly in committee sessions.

Whenever Eileen listened to his own appeals for non-interference in farmers' affairs, she protested that all British farmers were hypocrites.

'They expect the Government to pay them lavishly for everything they do, yet they always complain when the Government tries to see how the money is being spent,' she had said, after one of his contributions to an adjournment debate in which he had castigated his own party's policy on grazing, which was starving the farmer off his own land.

But he knew what she meant, and there was something comic about it.

He always found himself, on the one hand, defending the farmers' absolute right to a guaranteed fair price for potatoes, set by the potato board; but then he would have to ridicule the inefficiency of the same board when it bought potatoes for a high price from the farmers and sold them back to the same farmers at a lower price to be used as fodder. You patted one side of the cheek and slapped the other. He supposed it probably was ridiculous to the uninitiated. And though Eileen was really a country girl by nature, she firmly refused to be initiated.

When she did come to the House, therefore, he usually had to defend himself against her jokes.

'It's such a lot of sham,' she said with a look of good-humoured distaste for it.

It was probably her schoolgirl's contempt for 'side' which made her laugh at the professional politicians in the House. She was also a soldier's strongminded daughter, and perhaps that also affected her. She certainly did not play the politician's wife in London. In the country she was friendly with the people who mattered to him, but not by politics. It was rather by chasing hair-streak butterflies in some dell with the children or breeding the moor ponies she liked so much, or simply caring for some rotten old oak by Westward Ho! or hunting because she liked to hunt. That was enough for the sort of west-country people who had liked him well enough to go on supporting his candidacy through three parliaments. Of course he had never let them down, and he was also wealthy enough to keep their profound respect.

But when Eileen came to the House he began to feel it through her eyes.

Once, on a surprise visit to the strangers' gallery, she had begun to write him a note to be sent down by the attendant, but before she had put her little silver pencil to her notepad, one of the gallery attendants had rushed up and said to her: 'You can't write in here, madam.'

Make a note in the House?

523

When she had defied the usher messenger, he had shaken his head firmly and she had been asked to leave the House. She had not reminded them of who she was, and she had laughed at her husband all during dinner. She said that in the first place to get into that precious place, as an ordinary member of the public, she had passed through ten suspicious policemen, she had been forced to give her name and address, and she had been treated altogether like a criminal going to church; and finally that ridiculous man had told her she could not write. How could she take any of it seriously?

'And anyway, there were only eleven of you down there,' she said. 'I counted you. And I couldn't understand a word anyone said. And even before you started, when the Speaker's procession came through the Hall, I went up to see it again, but it was all so pecksniffian that I couldn't bear it. You all looked so black and dingy, like mousy old-fashioned clerks. The man who held up the Speaker's tail was all worn out across the shoulders like a hen moulting. You are all pickled-Dickens.'

She laughed, but sometimes she was right.

But he did wish that she would take him more seriously, although nobody else did. The whole House usually became inscrutably Chinese and good-naturedly bland whenever he spoke.

Even so, nobody hated him on either side of the House, and he hated nobody (except Monty Mathieson who had now become a terrible black mark of a man). Usually too they would all laugh when he had only begun to make a funny remark. He seemed to invoke everyone's sense of humour, which then stirred his own. It was a funny circle, and he did not always like it.

On the other hand Eileen's sense of humour almost made love to him, so he never minded that. She was always most affectionate to him when she had the devil trailing around her tongue, and the mischievous eyes of a schoolgirl which seemed to want to wrap him up like a baby and tease him. He loved her most when she was like that, although it usually cost him a great deal of his dignity.

Of course he had admired other women, and he always liked to be with pretty women and to look at them; but he had never been able to go very far with them because of these strange influences which Eileen had on him (with the fun she made of him, and the eyes that told him a great deal sometimes). These were always the bridge he could not cross to reach another woman, no matter how enticing or beautiful she might be. He was loved by his wife (even though she was not going to respect him as a politician) and he would always have that.

But today he wanted her to see what he could do in the House, to prove the seriousness of it. When she was up there, when he could see her

524

handsome fresh face and her almost perfect English style, when he could look up and see her teasing him, he felt uncomfortable.

What would she make of this session which would decide what the Government would do finally about the Suez Canal? It would give the Government an idea of the temper of the House, the temper which would decide for them what decisions they could safely pursue, whether it would be action or inaction.

The House was packed; so many pink shrimpish faces.

He could feel the tension, because no one on the front benches had their feet up on the table, and there were no question papers floating around.

After prayers, after the Speaker had announced the writ for Chester-le-Street, after Mr. Gaitskell had asked if there were any statements of business and Mr. Butler had replied 'Yes, Sir,' and after the motion for the adjournment was made, after the Question was proposed, after the adjournment itself, Sir Anthony Eden rose and put his knuckles on the box.

Peacock looked up at Eileen then. She was not looking. She was taking off her ear-rings, and he never did remember much of the debate that followed, excepting that they went on arguing all day about the morality of force or not force.

So she was not impressed! He was so resentful; and because nothing was going to impress her now (she had made up her mind) he fell into a rare feeling of huff and he decided absolutely that he would resign his seat at the end of this parliament, ask for the Chiltern Hundreds and see how she would like that. She would regret it then.

He lived out many a subsequent scene, and the debate proceeded without him, until Sydney Silverman kept interrupting the Prime Minister (who was outlining as best he could his attitude to Colonel Nasser) so much and so annoyingly that Peacock stirred himself and shouted: 'Be quiet, Sydney!'

He ought to be contributing something more to the debate himself. After all, he had seen Nasser. After all, he was trying to specialize in Middle Eastern affairs. But twelve years' sitting in the House had developed a philosophy of hearing, by which one scooped off the cream of what was said. Or rather the cream slopped down onto the brain from somewhere when the key-words were said. Today they were heavy and thick: *military measures justified* and *military measures limited in scope* or *charges of sabre rattling at Egypt are ridiculous.*

What a silly phrase anyway, *sabre rattling.*

He listened patiently and decided to let them get on with it. 'If they are going to go into Egypt I wish they'd do it and stop all this silly talk in the House. What's the point to it? It won't make much difference if they've already decided to go in.'

525

He wriggled impatiently on the bench because Eileen already had him feeling as if he really were in church.

'Damn,' he said and looked up, but she would not catch his resentful eye.

He leaned his head back and looked at the Speaker and suddenly caught him at it. The Speaker had put his right hand slyly under his robes, into his waistcoat pocket; there he had extracted from an inside pocket a jujube, which he raised slowly and with great dignity to his mouth. He popped it in under the excuse of scratching his nose, just as a Government member was saying that the use of force against Egypt was justifiable, not only by international law but by international morality as well.

'Hah!' Peacock mumbled. 'Eileen saw that, I'll guarantee.'

He felt more and more like a sinner in church. She had infected him so much that he began to wriggle again on the bench and feel the dinginess of the chamber. Why did they have to have green benches? Why not red? And this grimy Victorian gothic was hideous.

'Look at old Gwillam,' his neighbour behind him said into his ear.

That was a standing joke. The Honourable Member for East Llanelly, William Jones, sitting opposite, always forgot his handkerchief. Sooner or later he would quietly wipe his nose on his sleeve or he would leave the chamber and go to the nearest toilet and tear off some of the paper towels over the wash-basins and come back sanitary.

'Do you think he'll walk out?' his rear neighbour asked.

'No,' Peacock whispered. 'He'll use his shirt-cuff.'

Gwillam rolled back his coat sleeve a little and discreetly wiped his nose on his shirt-cuff. He was an old, chapelish, ill-mannered man; but Peacock disliked his own laughter at the man's expense. Although Eileen was proved right. They were all so pickled-Dickensian.

Behind him, Paul Douglas kept on prattling, because Paul had to whisper to someone sooner or later. Like a schoolboy in class, he couldn't keep quiet for more than five minutes during any debate.

Peacock ignored him and took out an envelope from his pocket and began to work out how much it would cost to feed and train a decent hunter into cross-country steeplechase condition: given a good horse to start with. Say two hundred guineas for a long-nosed brute with solid knees and a deep chest. Then, on the basis of hunter costs doubled, and of what he knew from experience, another two hundred a year for a couple of years—and who knew? Eileen might win Aintree with it. That was almost a human failing with her. She liked stamina and long wind, and the sort of doggedness that broke its neck or went on for twenty-eight jumps and won it. That was her hockey training. But it was such an odd, amateur, farmer's sort of race, which anyone could win with anything that could stay the course, even if it was sired in the knacker yards.

'It looks as if we're going to go in,' Douglas said through bad teeth into his ear.

Douglas was a fool. 'In where?' Peacock asked.

'Listen to what he's saying about Nasser,' Douglas said. 'Never mind taking notes for what you're going to say.'

He put away the envelope and felt angry with Eileen. He would not look up.

He sat forward, screwed up his face, and tried to listen.

Off came the phrases, scoop went the mind. The cream of their indignation came down in dollops. He wished they would behave, though, for Eileen's sake.

'If they'd only shout at each other,' he said to justify some of his claim for real contest, which she refused to treat seriously.

He thought about the dinner he had had at Hatis, eating kebab with Helen Mamoon. Oh, damn Eileen!

'Did you hear that?' Douglas's voice almost slapped him on the back.

Of course he had heard it. He knew everything that was being said without hearing it. Force, or not force, that was the obvious question. Government was reserving several kinds of right to use force. Gaitskell warned them rather doubtfully not to. So the rest didn't matter, unless of course they invoked the UN charter. No doubt they had all made up their minds, anyway. The Opposition weren't putting up any real resistance. It would serve Nasser right, because nobody could take this sort of behaviour, not really. Nobody in the House was for him, on either side. It was too silly to let a strong oil-haired chap like that run the sort of race he wanted, elbowing out everybody else. Everybody was right. They were only disagreeing over details as usual. Ah, well . . . He looked up stoically then.

Eileen had gone.

He already felt lost and wasted in here without her; in a second. But he would wait awhile to prove his independence.

After Gaitskell it would have to be Clement Davies.

Eden looked ill. When his hair looked so dull he was almost certainly having stomach trouble. When he spoke in that curious lisping way, he was tired. Gaitskell looked like something of sap carved out of a red pine tree, and when Clement Davies spoke there was a sound of breakable crystal balls popping; slowly, clearly, but popping.

Force or not force, that was the question.

Old Raikes was getting up saying: 'Nobody wants force, nobody wants war for the sake of war.' And Sydney Silverman was erupting again with the United Nations Charter. Henderson, Shinwell, Patrick Wall, Awberry,

Paget, Blenkinsop, Hinchinbrooke, Burden, Brooman-White, Monty Mathieson (horrible chap), Orr-Ewing (Charlie), Bell, Beamish, Winterbotham, Crossman, Strachey, Zilliacus, Beswick, Hunter, Davies, Mellish, Boothby, Pitman, Partridge, Hutchinson, Hughes, Stross, Wedgwood-Benn, Robens, Edelman, Ellis Smith, Simon, Hunt, Rankin and Younger went on ringing over phrases like old men ringing church bells until the Motion lapsed without the Question put, and he had not even been out for dinner.

But he had stuck it out for seven and a half hours to prove to Eileen that these things really counted. He even stayed the extra half-hour while George Wigg complained about the army reservists being called up for the emergency.

Anthony Head kept saying, 'I am coming to that. But I *really* am coming to it.'

Everybody laughed.

The Speaker slipped another jujube into his mouth and the boom of half past ten closed the time limit, and he left the Chamber stretching his legs to unwind his tangled shirt, wondering why Eileen affected him like that in the House. He never enjoyed it when she was there, so why did he ever persuade her to come?

CHAPTER SIXTY-NINE

AMIN FAKHRY was being very energetic, hurrying Hakim's new compact unit into order before the enemy was at the gate. What sort of men should they get? That was what worried him. Whereas Scott was saying to himself every day: *How soon can I finish with it?* But he would do it properly, and they worked hard, inspecting, arguing, and laying down first of all (Scott insisted) the basic idea of it, before they began the practical side of training and assembling.

Amin was impatient, however, to get the men. He considered and speculated and formulated a type every day.

'Les types,' Amin said with his St. Cyr nervous system, 'avec toute l'individualité pour agir. Discipline, oui; mais l'individualité surtout.'

Scott pictured his own individualist, Ishaak his driver, who had been too individualistic for the kool-cola company and too individualistic for Scott to trust with any task on his own. And the orderly Egyptian soldier —brown-skinned and obedient and courageous and thick-booted—a peasant who hated fighting (didn't all good soldiers?). The Egyptian soldier was not yet the man his officers would like him to be. Why? Because he did not yet trust his officers. Amin knew that, and worried.

'We want good mechanics,' Scott argued patiently in their Nissen hut with the sounds of barrack-square athletics going on all round them outside: *Hup-wuntwothree-hup.*

'Tu parles!' Amin said with his fine, nervous hands protesting. 'What can mechanics do in the desert except drive the trucks?'

'Mechanics are always good improvisers,' Scott pointed out. 'They always know how to make the best of what they've got, and that's what you need.'

Amin's smile was superior and tigerish and handsome and soldierly.

'Ça, mon vieux, ça c'est la pratique anglaise,' he said.

They argued in French. They would decide first on the equipment, because the men would have to be found one by one.

'And don't worry,' Scott said. 'It ought to be a small unit, so you can

529

easily find the men. Almost any man can be good at it. Pickering proved that to us. So first you've got to get the stuff for the men to work with.'

They passed documents in Arabic across the dusty table they shared—lists of available equipment for reissue and plans of Egyptian Army unit reconstruction which were just beginning to come into effect. But Arabic was unreadable in military jargon. It was simply not a military language, and because he was not an Arabic scholar Scott put aside as much of the paper-work as he could and said that the first thing they had to find (now that they had an idea of what they would start with and before they finalized anything about men or equipment) were spares. They should settle only on that equipment which had plenty of spares available. Weapons were Amin's responsibility and that was something else. Therefore spares were the best place to begin the first practical existence of the unit in creation.

Even the inspection of trucks and tyres and jerrycans was a nuisance to Amin. But he was a good companion and Scott did not have to worry about what he said, nor did he have to play games with the balance of mental power, as he did with Hakim. Amin's old contempt for Hakim had once been personal as well as military. To see them friends again was almost satisfying to Scott, except that it revealed how clever Hakim was in using these olympian arrangements of compromise.

For what reason?

The old enemy was at the gate. Not the Israelis, but the British.

'Even so,' Amin said to him one morning over a newspaper report of another incident on the Israeli border, 'we ought to go and look at Gaza.'

'Gaza? What for?' Scott demanded. 'We're supposed to be working west, not east.'

'Nevertheless,' Amin argued, 'we ought to see what's happening where it is happening. Come on, we'll ask Hakim. Perhaps we can pick up some good men there. I want to see Loutfi, who is there. He would be a very good desert navigator.'

Amin asked, and the request was granted. And Scott—in terror of his peace of mind and of his unsoldierly heart—found himself in the very neck of this little war he had tried never to think about—this dangerous eruption on the edge of the sea—the Gaza strip between Israel and Egypt.

The sand trenches and barbed-wire on the border of the strip made long lines like birthday messages on a yellow cake. Across the dented, shaven desert (which looked as hard as cement), somewhere over there lay the Israeli patrols who were waiting for a stray leg to appear on their side of the wire so that they could open fire with the 20-millimetre guns they kept ready for the first long-range shot in defence of their . . .

'Their what?'

It was only here that no one could say what it was. Nobody discussed. Nobody investigated. There was a canal crisis which went on every day now in the Security Council in New York where the rivals for it formed up legally on one side or the other and proposed and counter-proposed. But no one here followed it closely. They all knew out here on the troubled frontiers that when war came it would not be the result of some legal decision on the streets of New York, nor the exhaustion of some international moral limit which, stage by stage, by its historical logic, would come to the moment when one side said: *I declare war on you.* Nobody here watched the comings and goings in Paris, London and New York. They knew that it would start by some intangible decision at some indefinable moment.

There were, out here, other reasons for war, not legal ones. Here they were military reasons, and they waited upon their military orders to begin it or to expect it from the other side. And meanwhile the newspapers did not decide their feelings for them. The searchlights and the routine precautions did, the waiting did, the inevitable did.

Meanwhile, also, the desert went on wearing out its daily ration of daylight; every dawn the sun lay long yellow shadows over low pillboxes, towers and sandbags: the same for the enemy on one side, the same for the enemy on the other.

It was only when he heard the regular shooting every night (their mutual nervous warning to keep everybody on their toes) that Scott felt the unpleasantness of it. The searchlights would go on, the big blue glare would cut the night to ribbons, and the garish silliness of it would send him down below to his bunk. When he heard the shooting which soon followed the beam of light, he knew that he was already too old for it. He was too saddened, too ruined. He simply confirmed, again, that he had never really been a good soldier. He had been good in the desert—never failing, but he knew that he had always avoided the deadliest part of it which made war possible at all: this formless and dangerous emotion being exercised here. He had never felt this kind of ferocity.

'It *is* a waste,' Amin said sadly, as if he had recognized Scott's sorry mood. 'But why do you worry about it, my dear?'

They listened to the reckless pot-shotting above them.

'I was thinking that I've done it all before.' That was only half the thought, but it would do.

Amin shrugged. He was not much younger than Scott, but Amin *did* despise the Israelis. He had to. The night shots, which flew in rainbows of tracers across the borders, were simply the daily exchange of their new hate and counter-hate.

Why?

531

A week ago on the northern borders, the Jordanians had ambushed an Israeli patrol and killed six Jews. The Israelis had retaliated by killing twelve Arabs. The Jordanians had then killed three more Israelis. The Israelis had finally brought up planes and artillery and had killed heaven knows how many more Arabs in a village across the barbed-wire frontier. And tonight, on this Egyptian border, both sides were firing recklessly under the searchlights, hoping to kill anyone at random.

'Some day soon it will come,' Amin said under their petrol lamp in the seaside bunker they occupied, 'because we can't live with that thing over there.'

'Is it so important to you?' Scott asked.

'No, it's not so important now. But the Arabs will eventually be one people, if they ever get over their contempt for each other. Then we will not be bothered. We will simply not be bothered by little Americas, and the horrible scars of Europe. They are too late to force more foreigners on us. You know, they are not even Jews. The ancient Jewish tribes died out of Palestine two thousand years ago, and even then they were a minority in Palestine. These people today are the scattered dregs from the slums of the world, forced upon us by the very people who hate them, and who want to get rid of them. Why should we have to save the European conscience by submitting to these European Jewish ambitions? Let the Europeans give them land. They murdered the Jews, we didn't. In fact, it's the Jews now who are anxious to murder and to steal from us.'

They heard a night patrol of jets go over, and Amin was out of bed again standing out in the desert night watching them excitedly. But these noisy little Russian planes had disappeared in a red trail of hot gases long before Amin had stumbled in his bare feet over the loose stones which active front-line soldiers made a point of honour not to clear away, because that would have been barrack-square mentality—something they must not have here.

'It's not very serious yet, and I don't like it here,' Amin said in his civilized French, his soldierly response. 'It's not an honest war. But I can't help wanting to stay here and fight it, can I?'

Scott wondered only how he could get through another day and another night of it. He was already thinking of the relief and the safety of wastes where men had barely set foot.

Perhaps the world's frozen white continents would be the only escape for him, once and for all; if it was not too late. And once he got himself clear of this commitment to Hakim, and once his friends were safe and free, and once he had fulfilled his promises to Françoise, he would take that offer up again. There was more hope for a man at the frozen poles of inaccessibility than there was here.

CHAPTER SEVENTY

THERE was a long lull in the canal crisis, but then suddenly so many
things happened. On a mid-October day, Zareef had been rearrested.
This was also the day when Budapest students were demonstrating
angrily against communism in support of Imre Nagy, who said he was a
loyal communist.

On this day, Fahid's second barograph flying test was accepted as a
pass and he was given back his 'A' licence. He went to Zareef with it in
his hand and said:

'Now you can go to the Haboob, Capten, and laugh it off. If you can
teach me to pass a test twice, you can teach a donkey to fly. Not so,
ya Capten?'

A few hours later Fahid was not quite sure whether anything could be
laughed off any more, because they had sent a small car to take Zareef
away.

'Why don't you refuse to fly?' he snarled at his fellow students when
they mumbled excitedly in their afternoon boredom that Zareef had been
arrested again. 'Why don't you go and throw the Haboob and the director
into the swamp?'

'Throw the donkey out,' someone said.

In the lounge, on the gritty leather chairs, they were reaching conclu-
sions about Zareef which were not likely to hurt anyone, even Zareef,
although they hurt Fahid. He rolled up a magazine and threw it among
them and walked over to the director's office.

'Ya Rais,' he said most respectfully with his brazen eyes looking at the
Wing Commander's compromising face, the face of a man who was weary
of temperament in others, 'I don't see how you can let Captain Zareef be
taken away like that.'

'What's that?' the Wing Commander said, astonished.

'Ali Zareef is not a Jew. He's done nothing more dangerous than teach
stupid people like me how to fly. Why do you let the police come and take
him away? Why don't you stick up for him? Why don't you ring up the

security and demand that they let him go? You know he has done nothing at all.'

'Are you ill?' the Wing Commander said dramatically. 'Have you taken leave of your senses, boy?'

'Nobody has any sense here. If you and Captain Selim behaved like men, they wouldn't keep taking Zareef away. Everybody knows they take him because he was flying Hassoon. They think Hassoon is a spy. But nobody tells them that Zareef isn't. Why don't you? Eh, *ya Rais*?' Fahid's appeal for Zareef's sake had the character of a man kicking a dog.

'You are suspended,' the Wing Commander shouted in a fury.

'I know . . .'

'Go! Get out! I will telephone your father.'

'He will agree with you. You will all agree . . .'

'Get out.'

'Why is there no law against cowardice?' Fahid said contemptuously, but the Wing Commander, in terror of the consequences, chose not to hear it.

Fahid walked out and around the dried-up flower-beds like a man with a mission. He saw the students gathering under the control-tower to begin their morning instruction under Captain Selim and a young Air Force officer whom the Wing Commander had insisted on borrowing. That was easier than demanding Zareef. There they were—crowding around the pale young Air Force man in admiration.

'I ought to burn the place down,' Fahid cried. 'Oh, my God! There aren't any fools bigger than I am. What am I doing out here flying these stinking things, up and down, up and down? What's it got to do with anything? What will I become? Am I supposed to become one of those small blue gods who walk up the corridors and fly away and then fly back again and go home and think about oil pressures? What for? To do that for twenty years, to sit up there in the sky, nowhere at all, on a leather seat for twenty years twisting things and turning knobs this way and that. What for? Is that why I am alive?'

The students saw him coming and knew they would be embarrassed. Barmeel spoiled their firm front of dignified silence.

'What did he say?' Barmeel asked querulously. 'We heard him shouting at you.'

'He said you were all monkeys,' Fahid said. 'He said you were all cowards. He said that if you were good new Egyptians you'd burn the place down in protest. He made me chief instructor, and you're all suspended as a protest.'

He was behaving like a madman.

He felt quite sane. 'Protest!' he repeated. That was a word. *A'tag*, it said in Arabic. It meant what it always meant: I complain, I am against or

534

I protest. But they couldn't even protest. And what was a protest anyway? Nothing.

If only he could say to them: 'Listen, you idiots, let's go and pull the director's nose and then pull all the security policemen's noses and then tear up a few pictures of Gamal Abd el Nasser, just for the revelation of it. Let's go. Let's *do* it.'

But there was nothing to do. Every frightened face which looked at him was dreaming of the corridors of aeroplanes and a pair of wings on their pockets. Did they have no wings on their hearts?

'Ah, my God,' he decided drastically, 'if I'd been born a peasant I'd feel like a man. At least I'd dig up the mud, and kill my wife if she misbehaved, and feel like a brother when we all starved to death. And even though I ran away in terror from everything that frightened me, in my heart I'd know what I was, and what everyone else was. That would mean something.'

But would a peasant slaving in the mud and dying of bilharzia say: *I protest!* A fellah couldn't even say that, because he knew it was hopeless to say it. Protest to whom? Only the privileged ever protested. It was the whine of a spoiled boy. The thing to do was to chuck them all out. Everybody.

'Did the Director suspend you?' Barmeel was asking him.

The others had deserted him to watch the first flight with the new instructor. Who would the lucky pupil be? Naturally it was the prize Lebanese student who had flown solo in four hours twenty minutes, a world record.

'Of course he suspended me. I told him you were my best friend, Barmeel, and I said you agreed with everything I said.'

'You didn't.'

'Of course I did. He suspended you too. So let's go.'

Barmeel recognized a joke, however, and though he laughed, he felt sorry for Fahid.

'What are you going to do, Fahid?' he asked.

'I'm going to the police myself,' he said. 'I'll pull their filthy noses.'

Fahid never saw anyone close enough, or important enough, to pull noses.

As far as he got he was asked (with astonished shoulders and indignant eyes): *What was it to do with him? Who was he? And who was this Zareef?* He was told to go home and mind his own business, and they telephoned his father who laughed at them.

'Let's see how honourable our English friends are,' Fahid told himself, and he began to look for Scott.

But long before he traced Scott to his office in the barracks, Fahid was

535

saying instead: 'Let's see if he is such a friend of our revolutionary heroes? Or let us see if he's a big joke.'

Scott had not heard until then that Zareef had also been arrested.

It had not occurred to him. Who would tell him? In fact he had only learned the day before that Lucy Pickering had discreetly disappeared again. Had she left Egypt? He did not know. His conscience had kept him away, but he had telephoned her in Alexandria to discover that she was not there. But when he tried her Cairo hotel again he found a note from her saying that she had gone to stay with a friend at the Embassy for a few days and that she would call him when she returned. Was she hiding out, just in case?

'Isn't there anybody at the aerodrome who can vouch for Zareef?' Scott said to Fahid, who grinned with bitter delight for the evasion.

'They have never heard of Captain Zareef,' he said to Scott. 'He has never existed.'

'But Captain Selim should help.'

Fahid had looked at him as if he were also trying to wriggle out of it —no different from all the others. Then he turned away with a cynical little bow and said, 'Goodbye, Capten. *Salaam Alekum.*'

'Wait.'

But Fahid had gone with a sick little laugh.

Go to Hakim and beg for one more friend, one more favour? Another hostage for the world?

Scott tried to walk across the barrack grounds, over the dusty roads and through the little streets of cement huts and lorry parks to Hakim's office. But he could not do it. He could not pick up a phone and say to Hakim: 'Listen, Hakim, don't do it. Not all of them. Not Zareef. All Zareef ever did was to fly us down the wadis.'

Zareef was an Egyptian and a Moslem. He was in prison for knowing Sam. Or did Hakim think he might drop a bomb on Gamal Abd el Nasser from an aeroplane? It was possible; anything was possible, he admitted. But surely not Zareef. Surely that was absurd to everyone but Hakim.

He could not even ask help of Amin Fakhry who had gone out to inspect some of the men the Frontier Corps were offering him, and Scott left the quarantine hut and walked home, feeling as if there were no more answers to any questions of any calibre. He had no more solutions, not even to the requirements of a friendship.

But he must talk to somebody. He could not go on being stoically numb about it, so he went to see Quartermain who was in bed again, eating crackers in chicken broth.

Quartermain listened sadly to Scott hunting desperately for some kind

536

of a reason or the gleam of a solution. Sam, Helen Mamoon, and now Zareef . . .

'You can't help it,' Quartermain consoled. 'What do you think one man is supposed to do—alone? What can he ever do alone?'

'I don't know. When I live in the desert, none of this touches me. The moment I come back here I am trying to solve the unsolvable. I can't go to Hakim ever again, not even for Zareef.'

'They'll let him out. Surely they'll realize that much.'

'He should never have been taken in,' Scott said bitterly. 'The trouble is, though, that I know Hakim is right. After what I saw in Alexandria, I know he has to do it.'

'Do what? Arrest Zareef?'

'I don't know about Zareef or Sam or Helen. But I do know that he's right to mistrust anyone who is not like him. If I were in his place I'd do the same. Do you know how much intrigue goes on? I simply can't blame him. That's why I'm helpless this time.'

Quartermain rustled among the papers on his bed and handed Scott a sheet of paper which was typewritten without capitals or punctuation or paragraphs.

'Read that!' he said to Scott.

'What is it?'

'The Egyptians released the story today. It's that incident in Alexandria, but all they say is that someone fired shots at an Army officer, although it was part of a plot to assassinate Gamal Abd el Nasser. They admit that two of the assassins were caught.'

Scott did not read it. 'Do they blame anybody?'

'They obviously hint that it's the British who would like to get rid of Nasser, but the British say that themselves.'

'True enough,' Scott said.

Quartermain lay back a little. 'And my friend Jack de Brazio swears that they brought one of the assassins to Cairo in chains. They say he'd gone completely berserk.'

'That's young Bindari again.'

'I thought so too. And something else occurred to me later. Wasn't Bindari a friend of Lucy Pickering's? Isn't that where Peacock went—to their estate?'

'Yes, but don't look for reasons there.'

'Why not?'

'I don't know, but even Hakim doesn't look that way.'

'Then he's a bloody fool and so are you.'

'I went to Alexandria to satisfy myself about that.'

'And you're satisfied?'

'Yes.'

537

'They proved their innocence?' Quartermain said cynically.

'No. You can be cynical, but I know that neither Lucy nor Church are capable of it.'

'You poor sap,' Quartermain groaned. 'They're capable of anything. Look what they did to you. Between them they more or less assassinated you, didn't they?'

'That's hardly the point. I know everything can point to their part in it. The *pension* where they live and knowing Bindari and plenty of other reasons, but if I can't believe in what I know of them as human beings, what can I believe in?'

'I couldn't say, but . . .'

'You have your beliefs, and strange as it may seem, Quarts, I have mine,' Scott said. 'You used to talk about class, Pickering used to talk about the man. I don't care much for either, not any more, but I'll stick to my own knowledge of people, if you don't mind. I'll go on judging them as I see them, and I'm not going to give that away to anyone yet, not even to Hakim's suspicions or to your crazy theories.'

'That's okay. But don't be surprised if you suffer a terrible let-down sometimes,' Quartermain insisted.

'I'll have to take a chance on that.'

Quartermain shrugged. 'I suppose you're almost right. But you're too naïve about it. I can admire you for never abandoning your friends. And if I ever get into terrible trouble I know who I'd depend on most. But even so, Scotty, granting that you're going to defend a man despite everything, you ought to remember sometimes that some men, like Church for instance, have bigger things in *their* minds than your faith and trust in their innocent faces.'

'Don't worry,' Scott said. 'I'm not that stupid. I know Church is busy being a soldier, and surveying the land. So is Lucy, probably. But that's comparatively harmless. So long as they're not mixed up in trying to get rid of Nasser.'

'All the same thing,' Quartermain said sadly.

'If I thought that, I'd abandon Sam and the others too. I'll never believe that.'

'All right, all right!' Quartermain said. 'I can't argue with you. My stomach won't allow it. You know Lucy Pickering and Church better than I do, but *I* know they'd do anything . . .'

They heard the door of the flat opening, and Benjamin and Hilal were running along the passage. The grappling rush of the two boys crushed all the paper-work on the bed, and the father was hammered. Small fingers probed his heart to see if he trusted them beyond all possible doubt.

'Shhh!' he said, when it became too much. 'Calm down, the both of you.'

Hilal was speechless with the only spoken words he knew properly: 'Put it there.' That meant put anything anywhere at any time. 'Oh, be quiet!' Benjamino insisted, gay eyes, gay face watching Scott to see if he was going to bend or resist him. 'I want to ask him something.'

Benjamino asked Scott to make a paper dart, if he knew how to.

'I haven't any paper,' Scott told him.

'Use that,' Quartermain told him.

It was Quartermain's dispatch still in Scott's hand. Scott put it down, unwilling to tear up a man's work so easily. He found an unused piece of paper and began to make a dart most carefully, saying in embarrassment, 'Let's see now . . .'

Long before he had finished it, Quartermain had completed one which he threw across the room. The boys went after it as Helen Mamoon stood at the door watching them.

'I didn't know you were here,' Helen said to Scott. 'I'm sorry.'

Scott felt surprised for a moment, and then he realized that it was Helen Mamoon all right and that she was free and that he felt one of those moments of complete relief in life which comes only rarely for a man so riddled with self-defences. It was greater than relief; he was willing to consider it a form of salvation, even though he felt broken—not on her behalf but by some large exhaustion of himself.

'I didn't know they'd let you go!' he said. 'I knew they would, sooner or later. But I didn't realize . . .'

He was looking at her as if he had not seen her for a long time, and she could not help smiling at his astonished face.

'Yes. This afternoon,' she said.

'Now we can all survive,' Quartermain said to her when she kissed him. 'We were all about to do something drastic. I think I would have shot Nasser myself . . .'

Scott was still watching her. 'Have they let Sam out as well?' he asked.

'There's no sign of him yet,' she said.

He had to apologize then, even for his presence, even for his sudden existence. 'But I can't tell you how pleased I am!' he said.

'What are you doing?' she asked him, looking at the paper in his hand.

'I was just about to go,' he told her.

'No, you weren't. Don't go yet. I wanted to see you, anyway.' Her eyes now were where they should be—on his face or on his nose or his eyes. 'I have to thank you, I know, for using your influence. I suppose that's the only reason they did let me go.'

'Don't think about it,' he told her. 'It was all a mistake on their part, anyway. I couldn't understand why they did it.'

'I don't think it was a mistake. They'll probably do it again.'

But Scott was blushing. He was guilty without knowing why. Simply to

539

see her made him feel his guilt. What guilt? Why should he feel that way?

She saw his embarrassment and felt sorry for him and decided to ignore him so that he could get over it. She kissed Quartermain again and said: 'How is the *hawaga* feeling?'

'Like that!' Quartermain said, taking Scott's dart and throwing it with lucky accuracy at his own reflection in the dressing-table mirror.

The dart slid off the mirror and zoomed out of the window. The boys were ready to jump up on the window ledge to see where it went, but the father leapt out of the bed and plucked them from the heights before they could take the plunge.

'I told you never to go up on the window ledge,' he said to them angrily, and threatened them with a hard, thin, worried hand.

Scott was glad of the relief, watching a world he did not know. He admired Quartermain as a father, but did all people soak up their children like this? He watched Quartermain soaking up his sons. He looked at the boys enviously. They were too young to know much else but love. Love must be the one thing in their lives which children did not have to worry about—given innocence and safeguards against cruelty, and given their ability to forget all hate and to live on each second as it came. Given these simple emotions, love was childishly easy.

'Come here, boys,' Scott said to them, 'and I'll make you a snapper.'

'I know how to make one myself,' Benjamin told him.

'You do?' Scott said, taken aback, disappointed, accepting it as truth or rejection or disinterest—all the things it was not. He felt Benjamin's eyes on him and he knew he had been reduced or bent or whatever it was that children did to survive the inchoate world of adults.

'Let's see you make it,' Quartermain challenged his son.

But Scott did not want the boy's bluff called. He started to make a snapper out of a sheet of paper, aware that father and sons and Helen Mamoon were watching him, as he put his glasses on, to see if he could manage a simple relationship with two small boys.

He worked carefully. It required a great deal of attention. He fumbled. Then he failed.

'I've forgotten how to fold it,' he said helplessly.

There was plenty of help ready. Quartermain and Helen Mamoon were telling him to fold it that way and this way. They argued. They had their heads together over Scott's square fingers. They were all bound to succeed.

Then Nona Quartermain arrived and asked, 'What are you all up to?'

She greeted Scott and picked up a wad of paper from the floor.

'Outside, boys,' she told her sons. 'It's time for your supper.'

The rule of law had reached this recklessly primitive community. Nona brought traffic lights, roads and policemen. She sent the children to the bathroom to wash their hands for supper.

'I must go,' Scott said, carried away by civilization.

'Won't you stay to dinner?' Nona asked him, open-eyed and friendly. 'I think Helen wants to talk to you.'

'I'm expected at Madame Salz's,' he told her.

He was not expected, but he was in retreat before any force, even Nona's feminine force, which ruled everything here with such absolute authority. So much so that Nona did not argue. She and Helen left him alone with Quartermain, and when he had said his happier farewells, Quartermain looked at him thoughtfully for a moment, as if he was going to ask Scott for a new favour. It seemed to come over his troubled face—that reluctant, dry look of Quartermain's.

'Do you think you'll be leaving soon?' he asked Scott.

'I can't tell. It's still not easy for me, at the moment. But I'm still due in London for that antarctic interview. I'll get there. What about you?'

'I shall get up and leave the moment I can keep one meal safely in my stomach,' Quartermain said. 'That is—if I can leave Helen in your care.'

'But I may not be here,' Scott said.

That was disappointing. 'Helen is obviously afraid—and so am I—that they will arrest her again,' Quartermain said. 'What do you think?'

He wanted Scott's denial, but Scott threw up his hands helplessly. 'No one can guarantee they won't do it again,' he admitted. 'Not the way Hakim is feeling. I'm amazed Hakim let her out. And if I'm not here, in Egypt, I won't be able to do much for her, will I?'

'That's what I'm worried about,' Quartermain said. 'If Helen and Hanna could get their exit permits, they could leave with us.'

Another little grain of influence? An exit permit?

How could he tell Quartermain that he, Scott, and Helen and Sam and Zareef were all hostages to Hakim now for the behaviour of the world, for this new and universal rule of life which demanded that you prove your loyalty by subtler means than birth, death, and duty?

'I can't really promise anything,' he said, and left Quartermain sitting up in bed, nodding and understanding, but in a dilemma of his own.

On his way out Helen Mamoon drew him onto the balcony verandah where she began to be graceful to him in English.

'They didn't harm you in any way, did they?' he interrupted.

'No. Egyptians aren't brutes yet. But if they go on like this they *will* be, Captain Scott. Why don't you tell Nasser that, if you see him?'

'I don't see Nasser; but I'll tell him if I do.'

'If he wants to make bitter enemies,' she added unhappily, 'he's doing a very good job of it. With me, anyway.'

They had argued this before, but they had something different to consider this time. Before, she had only been indignant. But look at her now. She was frightened and angry. What exactly had they done to her?

She said they had kept her in one room with an iron bed and a washbasin and allowed her out only to go to the lavatory. They had questioned her mainly about Sam, but they had also started to question her about her family. Then suddenly she had been let out into a garden. They had been quite polite. They had not called her names. But anyone who sat for days in that strange bare house hearing other women (she never saw them) weeping—and weeping yourself when you had to—soon forgot that there was another world outside, and it was frightening that human beings could suddenly trap you like a fly. There was no one besides yourself, and no way for the world to reach you. Everything else ceased to exist . . .

'They submerge you!' she said. 'I felt it, even after a few hours in there.'

'I know.'

He did know. They had all forgotten that he did know, this fear which remained with you for the rest of your life, this 'submergence', as she had rightly called it. Hadn't that been the price he had paid, also, in Abu Suwair? It still governed his life—that submergence.

'Quarts said you are anxious to leave Egypt,' he said to her.

'What else can I do?' she asked him helplessly. 'Oh, let Nasser have it his way. All I want to do now is to leave this wretched country.' She was pacing up and down on the balcony holding her elbows, containing herself. 'Let him say I'm not Egyptian. I don't care any more. I once regretted that I wasn't a Moslem. Now I wouldn't be anything but what I am. I don't even want to think the way they do. All right,' she said, accusing him and everyone else behind him, 'I'm not Egyptian. Yes, I am! But I'm not a Moslem. I'd learn to hate them. If they want to say I'm not Egyptian, then let them say it. But they must let me go. If they don't want me, I don't want them. I give them their Moslem Egypt, if they'll only let me go somewhere else.'

She was distraught by now, and he tried not to see her tears.

'I'm sorry,' she said. 'It's not your fault.'

'It's a pity that nationalism gets so much out of hand,' he agreed unhappily. He meant to be helpful, but he could not help antagonizing her by saying what he felt. 'But I think if I were an Egyptian I would probably feel like them. They can't help it either.'

'Oh, so would I, if they would let me feel that way. But they don't.'

That was the real exclusion—the exclusion of all others. That seemed to be the only way a national existence could emerge.

'But now I don't care. All religions are a curse, anyway; and if they would just let me go I would gladly go. I'm determined to go.'

One grain more of influence? An exit permit?

He could say nothing at all, and she was considerate enough or proud enough not to ask. She walked to the balcony door to let him go. She showed him out. She shook his hand, still holding her nerves in their safe prison. While they were standing at the lift door Benjamin erupted underneath them with wet hands to press the lift button.

'You'll get an electric shock if you do that with wet hands,' Scott warned him quickly.

Benjamin looked interested, but he was not going to be frightened by the electric shocks in life. 'I do it all the time,' he said.

But Nona had followed him. 'Come inside,' she told him.

Nona's voice was probably too strong, too determined, but Scott felt a sudden admiration for Nona. Someone had to make sure that diversions never got in the way of things that ought to be done.

At least Nona's world was a sure world, and her children ought to be thankful for it.

CHAPTER SEVENTY-ONE

SCOTT had almost given up thinking about Sam, but Helen's release had given him some hope for Zareef. He did not like being cunning, but he suggested to Amin Fakhry that they ought to have a small plane working for them, if they were to operate from Siwa.

The lack of a plane had always been the bugbear of Pickering's life, in the British Army's Tracks and Survey unit. Pickering had even tried to get a plane from the R.A.F. (Scott told Amin) but the way the Air Force had wanted to run things, their sort of small plane would have been useless for the irregular sort of flying they wanted it for. The answer had always been to have your own small plane, and to keep your own pilot in the unit —a man as irregular as everybody else and as good.

'You want a pilot who can land absolutely anywhere, like Zareef did with me,' Scott told him.

Amin Fakhry knew Zareef. Amin had also flown the wadis in the Gemini, and anything that seemed as logical as Zareef's inclusion would be hard to deny. Amin agreed. He would take it up with Hakim. Hakim (Scott hoped) would tell him that Zareef was in gaol. Then Amin would lose his temper and get him out.

A late October khamsin had rasped Cairo's nerves until every Englishman left in Egypt longed for a good downpour of British rain. In a few days now they would have it—almost literally so.

It was an auspicious day for Scott.

For breakfast every morning he ate one poached egg on two pieces of toast. He cut the egg in half, and then slid one half of the egg onto one piece of toast. Then he turned everything around to fit the slope of the plate so that the yolk soaked back into the bread and did not make a mess. It was good engineering.

'After all these years, you still eat that English breakfast,' Madame Salz complained. 'Have some pickled herring. Just a little . . .'

Becky and Madame Salz ate anchovies and olives and white cheese for breakfast. Scott usually refused, but today it was an important day so he reached over and took a black olive.

'Just one,' he said, when Madame Salz instantly tried to give him half a dozen more, and some salted cheese as well.

'Don't corrupt me,' he said to Madame Salz and explained to them that today he would deliver to the Survey Office in Dokki the last tracing of an unimportant feature on the el Tih plateau which covered the central formation of the Sinai. In five years he had drawn over five thousand such maps, and he had delivered them himself month by month to the Survey Office. There he had checked the finished maps, which were over two years behind him on the drawing-board and four years behind in the map issue.

'Don't your surveys ever finish?' Becky asked him when he had told them why it was an important day for him.

He was really trying to be cheerful for them. Every morning, since Sam's arrest, he had tried to divert them somehow from thinking of Sam, and he had unconsciously tapped into himself to do so. He had told them a great deal about his boyhood, his early youth at university in England, his father and his mother. Now it was his work, and it didn't matter if they understood about maps or not. Becky did understand somehow. She showed it in her pale, freckled eyes which admired him and respected him so much.

'A survey only finishes when you want it to, Becky,' he joked. 'Usually it's finished when you've decided it's time to do something else.'

Had he decided to do something else?

'No, no,' he said, realizing her fears. Becky was worrying about his other plans. Would he leave Egypt before Sam was free? 'Don't worry,' he said to her, although she had said nothing to him about it. 'I won't go until Sam's all right again.'

Becky knew about his hopes of going to the antarctic, because Sam must have told her. She also knew—in her natural and youthful heart—that he had other emotional reasons for leaving Egypt. She was well aware that only his feeling for Sam and his other friends kept him here now.

'Don't worry,' he repeated often for them. 'It will be all right soon.'

They believed him. Sam was still silently hidden away somewhere by the Egyptians, but it was all right while Scott went on assuring them every day, even though he had closed up his own hopes.

He took his blue bundles of notes and his scrolls of tracing-paper to the Survey Office and left them in the map room and went away without taking coffee with the short-sighted Colonel, a new man whom the army had appointed to speed up the map issue. He was avoiding all questions, all talk, today.

'What news of Françoise?' he asked Leo on the telephone, because Leo had come back from Port Said the night before.

'She is getting ready to leave now,' Leo told him. 'She is expecting you in Port Said soon. It's only ten days now.'

'I know, but I can't go yet,' he told Leo. He had written Françoise, he had been gentle and loyal in his letter, but he had not faced the real issue of whether he would go with her or not. 'Did you manage to get her a return visa for Egypt?' he asked Leo.

'No. I think it's impossible now. But she will go even without that. I only hope it isn't too late to leave. Did you see the news this morning?'

'No. What's happened?'

Scott had given up buying the newspapers regularly. He had decided that he could wait for events to happen, hoping that way to escape the confusion the newspapers caused.

'The Americans say that Israel is mobilizing,' Leo told him, 'and everybody is talking war. Mr. Selwyn Lloyd and Eden are back in London from Paris, and the Russians say they were there to prepare an attack on Egypt.'

Scott shrugged figuratively. The newspapers played with war like dangerous children. He could not blame Leo for taking it all seriously, but he was not going to have the mania thrust on him any more.

There was even more sense in Amin's preparation, since they were genuinely for war, and there were no lies and there was no hypocrisy in Amin Fakhry's plans for the defence of his country.

'We ought to go and look at Siwa soon,' Amin told him when he walked into the quarantine hut.

'Whenever you like,' Scott answered. 'Everything is ready to shift you down there.'

'In fact, Ali Zareef can fly us down on Saturday,' Amin suggested, pleased with his surprise.

'Ali? Did you settle it with Hakim?'

'Of course! Hakim thought it was a magnificent idea. Marvellous. He will even get us a small plane. Zareef will fly it. What do you think of that, *mon sport?*'

'That's about everything we need to start with,' Scott said, smiling happily. How could he show his gratitude to Amin? He did not try to. Amin was being deliberately busy, to spare them any embarrassment about it, any talk of it.

They understood each other very well, and Scott called in the new supply corporal to see if he had managed to find any of the sun-compasses which the British must have left behind in Egypt, somewhere. Nobody could navigate a desert efficiently by car or truck without one, and he would have to uncover at least twenty, otherwise they would have to be

546

specially made, an expensive and difficult business to be avoided if possible.

He felt now that he had only one way of convincing Hakim to let Sam out, and that would be to say to him: 'Let *me* be responsible for him. It's only Sam now, and Sam will always be here if you want him, I can promise that.'

He had to try. His word for Sam was all he had left.

But he felt now like a soldier reporting to a Headquarters, when he went into Hakim's little compound, and he hated the feeling.

Hakim listened and then ignored it and pointed to the newspaper on his desk. 'You know, *habibi*, they are definitely going to attack us.'

'Who is?' Scott said, bringing his mind slowly into Hakim's focus.

'The same animals. Who else? They couldn't kill Gamal, so now they are actually ready to use real force. I'm convinced of it, even if Gamal isn't.'

'I thought you might have meant Israel,' Scott said.

'But I do!' Hakim said contemptuously. 'Only it's not the Israelis we have to worry about now. They'll never attack us unless the British and French do it with them, and that's what they are getting ready to do. You see how many French troops have arrived in Cyprus now? Parachutists! *Les paras*. They do want to frighten us. Well, are you ready for them, dear friend?'

'Almost,' Scott said with difficulty.

Hakim looked at him and guessed his sickness.

'I don't understand you,' Hakim said. 'Why do you worry about Hassoon so much? He is perfectly safe. No one will hurt him. He eats well, and he sleeps well and he lives in a nice house with a garden. Why don't you let him stay where he is for a little while? It won't hurt him.'

'It hurts his family.'

Hakim rubbed his fingers on his face as if he were fed up with people begging him for lives, for families, for a second's respite from this struggle to hold a nation together against the petty but dangerous inroads which some men made on it.

'Does it?' he said. 'Is his family so important to you also? Do you give them protection also?'

'I simply want to end this unhappy business of Sam, Hakim. I'll be responsible for him. He won't do anything, I can swear it. I'm not asking for more than his release.'

Hakim looked at him and shrugged.

'You're very persistent. You are a good friend to have, *habibi*,' he said, and it was impossible to tell how slyly or how truthfully he meant it. 'But you give your devotion to strange causes.'

547

Scott waited, feeling Hakim venturing out a little, afraid now to stop it with a word, even an appeal.

'But I told them to release Miss Helen Mamoon and the pilot. I did that for you. Isn't that enough?'

'I know, Hakim. I appreciate it. They are grateful too. You don't know how grateful they are, and you've done the right thing, believe me. They are absolutely harmless people. But I know that Sam too is not a dangerous man. You don't need to keep him locked up, I assure you.'

Hakim sighed elaborately. 'Do you think I want to keep these people in prison? It's terrible, I know. But you saw what happened. I swore I would never take a chance again—not with one single man whom I could not trust, and I don't trust Hassoon. How can I?'

'Let us say you trust me then. I'll take the responsibility.'

Hakim looked at him then and threw it all away dramatically. 'All right, my friend. I trust you. He can go. But I'm a fool. I break my own word. And I hope that heaven will forgive me, but how' (he raised his eyes a little) 'can I resist a man who begs me so insistently to save a friend? I am not a sly man. I'm not cruel. I'm a religious man. But I'm a fool too. But he can go. It's done, *habibi*, and you can be with your friends.'

Scott felt that magnified relief a second time, and though he thanked Hakim as profusely as he could, he dared not quite believe that Hakim had done it, and he did not believe it until Sam arrived that same evening, in the very palest of evenings, in a taxi, calling out to Becky and Madame Salz and borrowing a pound to pay the taxi fare and looking no different, no more worn, no more unnerved than before.

Scott envied him his large and unsullied heart, and he asked himself, inspecting his own wounds, if Hakim had thus shown, this once, a sense of largeness and sympathy and understanding and trust—a belief in another person's feelings besides his own. It was possible, he wanted to believe it of Hakim, but in his self-defensive mind he was too frightened of what came next to give anyone that much faith, particularly Hakim.

He had read the papers also, and he too believed that this Suez dispute could only end in a war now. And what would happen to all of them then?

548

CHAPTER SEVENTY-TWO

THE fox-hunting season in the West Country did not open until October 31, a day early anyway, but Eileen's plan to beat the hunt servants over the fences had been in preparation all summer.

This October had been a darling month. The Pony Clubs were out. Some of the local crops were late, but even over the uncropped ground and in the bottoms, a good rider could find the compromise between the hedges and the hidden paths through the soggy bottoms which might provide a good opening, when the moment came.

'For heaven's sake, why don't you let that fellow lead the pack and be done with it?' Peacock tried persuasively when Eileen was looking at him *like that*.

'I simply don't like the man,' she said.

It was her pigheadedness, her fun, and it was also the iron will in Eileen's heart.

'But why exaggerate?' he appealed.

He was afraid that she would take a reckless and independent course through the fields and hit a ditch, or worse—tangle on a wire which any overgrown hedge might conceal.

'He's such a bad-tempered man,' she told Peacock. 'Nobody enjoys it when the huntsman is so arrogant. The pack try to split up, the riders are rude to each other, and even the horses feel it; and I suppose the wretched fox as well. He's a rotten huntsman and that's all there is to it, darling, and I refuse to follow him over anything, like all those dried-up women who reek of gin and shout nonsense at each other all day. It's horrible. He's their type, but he's definitely not mine. I won't follow him, and anyway—hunting is still the art of going first, and I'm going to go first.'

Eileen loved the older version of the sport.

The morning sounds were muffled and autumnal. A grader or a binder was rattling behind a tractor near the pigeon copse, and the compressor in the milk-shed hummed and vibrated waves of work into the air. There was a community somewhere of dogs, chickens, and hungry pigs whose

549

pedigree Eileen refused to allow the farmer to register because the charge was ten shillings a litter. Eileen simply wouldn't give in to such official banditry.

'Please be careful,' he begged her.

She was waiting for their nagsman to groom off the few stray hairs of the beast she had schooled for months simply to take down the bad manners of a ripe-faced huntsman. Was it worth it?

'But I'm only doing what anyone should do. Why don't you come along, darling? You might be a great help. You might encourage the pack.'

'I might be very funny too.'

'Honestly . . .'

'You always laugh indecently when I appear in that get-up,' he complained. 'I don't mind being knocked about on a polo field, but even the way that grey's belly rolls and rumbles seems clumsy to me.'

'He's very good!' she said, caressing her grey hunter which had been as woolly as a bear and pot-bellied when she had bought him in Ireland in May, and now (Peacock had to admit) he was square on his legs, his head was well up, and his coat was as smooth as grey butter.

'Boysie,' he said to the old nagsman who had been a hunt servant himself and who, like Eileen, deplored this transformation of local hunting from a hearty west-country farmer's sport into the harsh-voiced battle of quick-moneyed women with flashy cars that were too expensive, and drinking that was too near the gin mill. 'Boysie,' he said to this cunning old man. 'Get on Janie's pony and go as far as the railway lines with her.'

'Oh, don't be so daft,' Eileen told him.

'One day one of those hooves will slide along a line,' Peacock said to his wife, 'and you'll knock your head on the rails. You walk across . . .'

She was gone.

She would practise crossing the railway lines by cantering beside them and crossing them obliquely without losing stride. That was dangerous. She should turn direct across them and break step and walk the horse over, but she was intent on arranging all possible advantages.

'It's that cunning old devil who's put her up to it,' he said, looking at the spindly-legged Cornishman who never looked directly at anything. His eyes seemed to observe in two different directions at the same time, and the grey nubble of his beard looked like badly-cut grass, neither shaven nor unshaven but a little of both, with queer yellow patches around the mouth.

'Cunning old devil,' Peacock said resentfully. 'He's got it in for that fellow Stevens, and he's using Eileen to pay him back. He's putting Eileen up to it, and she's falling for it.'

He turned away in disgust.

He should have been at the House today because there were four questions down for Heathcote Amory on a silly statement he had made that only a fraction of one per cent of the harvests had not yet been gathered. That was like holding a red rag to a bull to any farmer, because the wet summer had ruined half the corn crops, the blight had annihilated the potatoes, and the beet had been late. He ought to be there to back Harvey who had tabled the question.

'Alice,' he said to one of the girls cleaning the breakfast table. 'Where are all the papers? Where did you put them?'

'In the geranium room, sir,' she said.

The geranium room was his own invention, or rather the title was. Eileen had built a three-sided glass-house at one end of the breakfast-room. She had packed it with geraniums, so that when they ate breakfast every morning they could taste and smell geraniums, and when he sat in the glass-house in a cane chair in the cold morning sun reading *The Times*, he was suffused with geraniums.

'They do stink,' he said over the news.

The middle page of *The Times* this morning had a picture of the insurgents in Budapest pulling down a 24-foot-high statue of Stalin after cutting it through the legs with a blow-torch.

'And another redskin bit the dust,' he said sadly.

He did not like to see such things happening. Effigies ought to be effigies, and once something was up it ought not to be knocked down. Admittedly Hungary was in the middle of a revolution. Nagy had ordered all Russian troops to leave Budapest, and he had a clear picture of those Russian troops, communists, opposing them. Not that the Russians were beasts or the communists lunatics. It was simply that the Russians were heavy-footed, and that nobody wanted or liked the communists (how could they?). That left the decent fellows to solve it somehow, as they probably would—given the chance.

On the other side of the page, Eisenhower had warned Ben Gurion that any 'forcible action' against Israel's Arab neighbours would endanger peace. The Americans were worried because the whole of Israel had been mobilizing for weeks. What for?

'All very well for Eisenhower to talk that way with a couple of fleets in the Mediterranean and stacks of atom bombs. But what does he expect the Jews to do? Even so, they're a confounded nuisance,' he decided.

He held his breath for a moment to forget this heavy odour. How did Eileen stand it?

'I ought to go back,' he decided, letting his breath out, thinking of the House this morning.

But he did not like to leave Eileen until this silly plan of hers was over, tomorrow. If she succeeded, if she took the field in front, if the whole vanguard followed her instead of following the huntsman, and if the hounds also took out after her (and therefore half the hunt equipage as well) there would be a horrible scene with that ugly huntsman Stevens who would become rude, because the normal barriers of class or what-have-you disappeared when Englishmen went hallooing.

Perhaps Eileen could manage all that. But if she became too determined to cut the huntsman out of the field tomorrow she might try to do something silly, in the hockey sense; and he had a frightening picture of Eileen with a broken back on the railway line, or strung up painfully on some fence, terribly injured internally which would be worse than outright death.

'That idiot!' he said to all.

With that kind of frightening picture in mind he could survive *The Times* and the eventful atmosphere which was pulling at him to rush back to the House because a major event of some kind was sweating itself out of the crisis in Hungary or the Middle East or somewhere. Hungary? Israel? All those French officers in London? Would the French start something?

'Did she get over the rails safely?' he shouted to old Boysie through the window over the flint wall where stark veins of old plum trees crawled in knots, upwards.

'Aye! That she did, zur. But there's the Antrim's bull they've put in the old bottom, and she be gone now to zay it's unlikely company in the field in the morning for the hunt, and to lock him up for a day or two until all season be done.'

'That's all she needs,' Peacock moaned to himself, sitting down. 'A wild bull in her way. D'you think that would stop her? Oh, no! Not Eileen.'

'I knew something would happen. I felt it,' he told Eileen on the morn itself and leapt out of bed. 'What time is it? I'll miss the 8.14. Damn and blast it. There's going to be a war now, for sure. Why didn't you get me up earlier? This means I can't be in the House until half-way through the afternoon, and there'll surely be an adjournment debate after Questions on it. I'll miss the whole thing . . .'

It was a fine, patchwork day for the opening. Thank God the ground wouldn't be too wet. Eileen was already dressed in her very long split riding-skirts, which she insisted on wearing although he forbade her to ride side-saddle. That was where he drew the line. She was bathed before him. She had written a letter to Janie and Pam who were back at school, and they were calling him down to breakfast—Eileen's mother and her friend who had come over to see her give Stevens a jolt. With what? Oh, damn! It was already a morning of jolts.

'What's happened?' Eileen asked him.

552

The Israelis had, this morning or last night, invaded Egypt. 'The silly bloody idiots,' he said. 'What did they want to do that for?' 'But everybody expected it,' Eileen said. 'Even you.'

'They must be on the canal already. On the canal! They're charging down Allenby's old road as fast as they can go, with absolutely nobody to stop them.'

'I suppose it will all be a horrible mess,' Eileen said, going downstairs.

Eileen knew her wars well. Her father was a late flower of Allenby's, of that same hot road to Palestine which skipped the last war and lay farther off, in the mirligo of Turks and puttees, and the brown khaki barrack years under Mount Carmel when the English grew gardens under old skies and stayed for ever, simply because not-being-there was inconceivable. Like Eileen the English soldier was as native there as a palm tree, and the longing of an English street boy for the future sounds of eastern afternoons was (they said) his heritage. But Eileen, walking down this English staircase, remembered the gayest sounds in all her life, which were the sentry challenges (she loved that military bark coming across the walls and empty courtyards at night), and the spitted-and-polished and flushed subalterns who dressed so well and danced every night on flowered, dry, creaking verandahs, the very thing Eileen had tried to simulate in the geranium room. Heat? No! Sun? Impossible in England. She had wanted a warm, cloying place to sit in, where the tiled barrenness of the floor suggested the uplands of a dry outpost. Even the cane chair was hers, was theirs, was Palestine's. Not Israel's. These sudden interlopers from Warsaw and Hamburg had pushed their way in with brown-paper bundles and shekels and wizened eyes. It was a sad loss for Palestine. And Israel was already on the canal.

At Totnes, in the train, Peacock understood it. It was 11.20 and the hunt would be moving off down the old flint road, which became a ford.

There would be a war of some kind in the Middle East. Of course nobody was supposed to have planned it, but at least a dozen people in the House knew that after Eden and Selwyn Lloyd had been in Paris, Ben Gurion had flown from Israel to Paris on October 22 and had landed secretly at the military airfield of Villacoublay and talked there with Guy Mollet. It was really an American intelligence guess. The French had supposedly told no one. The Americans had tracked everything on radar. They knew about the Jewish Prime Minister's white hair, and perhaps Guy Mollet's black hat arriving from Paris. The Americans had known everything.

'They do stick their noses in,' he said bitterly.

By now Eileen would be taking the first fence somewhere over the stony furrows, the ground he disliked most. If her grey became nervous

in the crowd—which the beast would be experiencing for the first time—
and if Eileen got too determined, and if Stevens that lout began to be
vicious and provoking with the pack, Eileen would probably cut loose and
go all out on her own, once the halloo was on. She had certainly inspected
every inch of possible ground all summer (the soldier's daughter, admirer
of Scott's famous reconnaissances) but there was always a hazard you
could not anticipate. Even a soft patch would bring down that big brute
of hers which might fall heavily on her.

'I refuse to worry about it!' He swore, and looked at the old lady opposite who simply misunderstood him.

'Yes, isn't it!' she said, looking at the wretched weather hitting the train
window.

What would happen today in the House?

'Everybody will get reckless,' he decided.

He had once been reckless himself, when he had shouted at Strachey
across the floor, during the dark days of the Malaya campaign against the
communists, when Labour was the Government:

'Soldiers (if that's what you want to call yourself) should not carry
shotguns into battle.'

When Strachey had been Minister of Defence, he had gone into the
bandit areas of Malaya (it was reported) carrying a shotgun. For Peacock
that had been a terrible thing to do, if it were true. Didn't he know, sym-
bolically, what a shotgun did to a man when it hit him?

What were they doing now, he wondered.

The flurry of come-and-go down the gangways, of papers in hand, the
bob of men snuffing themselves ceremoniously to the hidden altar which
traditionally bound the Speaker to that hidden holy virgin behind his
chair, some said in parliamentary deadlock.

But the finest remnant in the House was not that silly business about
the Speaker's chair, nor was it the document of regicide in the Lords'
library, or the Gothic habits in the Chamber; no, the best thing in the
House was the forgotten table in the cloak-room near the crypt where
members kept their cricket-boots, skis, and Homburg hats. Under that
old table, on the flat surface of its lower supports, were the restless scars
where Cromwell's commoners had dug in their spurs so that they could
unstrap them from their high hip-boots.

He could never see that table without seeing the act. The whole place
must have stank of the stable in those days, such as it was. He saw their
faces, and felt their tremor of sudden authority. They had meant it. It
wasn't so much that they had murdered a king (a bestial thing to do), but
that they wore hip-high boots and draconian jerkins and moved like men
who need not be explained to Eileen, because she would admire that side
of them—those men—most.

'Scotty!' he thought. 'He's in the thick of it out there.'

It was after 12 o'clock, the train was running late, and he was already feeling hungry.

'Why didn't Scotty get out when he had the chance? Now what happens? What the devil is he going to do. Particularly if we go in?'

Rain almost perforated the train window. 'Rain! Oh, damn!' he said.

If the grey's hooves got thoroughly clogged with mud he would start acting heavy-footed. That was when you started to nick the tops of fences and stone walls, and down you came in a horrible mess.

'Curse the field-master. Curse the idiots who take it seriously!'

But he was losing his anger, because he knew that by now Eileen had either scored her victory over Stevens the ill-mannered clout (yes, clout!), or she had failed because the hounds had kept clear of her, and the loyalists had followed the hunt-master. Or the fox had taken a bad course which favoured the small horses or even the ponies, and left Eileen miles behind. Or perhaps she was down somewhere on her back, mangled and wet, and behaving bravely only for the useless honour of being a good loser with a broken neck.

What, in the name of heaven, was the use of that?

CHAPTER SEVENTY-THREE

AT midnight, Quartermain heard someone hammering and ringing at the front door of the flat. Nona awakened, and she also heard it. 'Don't go,' she said. 'It may be the police.'

Quartermain knew what he ought to be afraid of, because he had again talked with Sophie Mourad, the communist, only the day before. But he said irritably, 'Why the police? Why do you always look for panic?'

The hammering and ringing went on, and he hung a raincoat on his limbs and went to the door, saying: 'Who is it?' before opening it.

The reply came in Arabic, so he gave a little shrug of fate—thinking how foolish and how careless he had been to see Sophie Mourad again and so openly. Then he opened up.

'Mister Quartermain . . .'

An Egyptian in a khaki jacket stood in the unlit hall. A soldier, perhaps. But he was in fact a messenger, one whom Quartermain recognized.

'I told you!' Quartermain said angrily to him. 'I don't want that stuff.'

The messenger came from the Middle East News Agency, an organization which President Nasser had recently set up to replace the old Arab News Agency which had been paid for by the British Embassy.

'Kwayis!' the messenger said appealingly, and added in English, very carefully. 'It's good, *ya hawaga!*'

The Middle East News Agency was indeed very good. Every day last month this messenger had arrived at Quartermain's door at 10 o'clock in the morning with a thick envelope of duplicated information—translations of news and comments in that morning's daily Arab papers. They had become Quartermain's best source of information on Egyptian politics and opinions, which was otherwise unobtainable because Nona and Helen would do no more than glance at the Arabic papers.

After a month of it, however, the Agency had sent Quartermain a bill for fifty pounds and a further account for the next six months to come, totalling in all three hundred and fifty pounds. He had hurriedly returned the bill with an indignant letter refusing more copies of the service, and insisting that he had never asked for it in the first place, and, having considered it a free service, he certainly would not pay the fifty pounds demanded for the past month.

'You must take it,' the messenger was saying now in Arabic. 'Please. I beg you.'

Nona appeared, wrapping her gown about her and asking in Arabic what it was. She too protested in a surge of awakened Arabic to the messenger.

'You come here at this hour with your silly envelopes. Who told you to do such a thing? The *hawaga* already told you he didn't want it. At this hour? Why do you wake people up in the middle of the night? Go away.'

'Ah, forgive me! I swear, *ya sitt*, I wouldn't do it. On the grave of my mother, *ya sitt*, I wouldn't; but I was told that everybody must take one. It is very important. Why doesn't he just take it? It won't hurt him.'

Nona began to argue, but Quartermain took the envelope and told the boy to go, although Nona held him back to give him two piastres, since it wasn't his fault.

'I'll go around and see them in the morning,' Quartermain said. When the door had closed and the boy had gone he opened the envelope and read the duplicated announcement that Israeli forces had entered Egypt, and were operating around the el Kuntilla area of the Sinai, although no real clash between Egyptian and Israel forces had yet been reported, up to 11 o'clock that night.

'No wonder they insisted on my taking it,' he said. 'It's a war.'

'What does it mean?' Nona asked, reading it over his shoulder. 'That the Israelis have actually invaded Egypt? Have they started a real invasion?'

'It looks like it,' he told her, but then he shrugged. 'I don't know. The Israelis are always up to something like this. It might be a bluff. They're so machiavellian that it could be a trick.'

Nevertheless, he decided, it was not a trick this time.

He knew that Jack de Brazio would also be awakened by the same knock, and he telephoned the hotel. Jack was not there. Ella said he was out trying to get an interview on tape with some sort of official military spokesman. Earlier that night, she said, the Egyptian Army had announced that an Egyptian plane, flying from Damascus to Cairo, had been shot down by the Israelis.

'The Israelis obviously tried to murder General Abdul Hakim Amer,' she said. 'He was in the plane that left just after it.'

Could there be any bluff about that?

Only that afternoon he had been arguing with Jack de Brazio about President Eisenhower's warning to Ben Gurion. The President had sent two messages to Ben Gurion of Israel expressing (they said) grave concern, urging Israel (they said) to take no forcible action which might endanger peace. The President had been informed that Israel was fully mobilized, and the President had not heard of such large-scale mobilization in Arab countries neighbouring Israel.

'What's he worried about?' Quartermain had said.

They had gone to the ticker-room at the American information office and the President's press secretary, Jim Hagerty, had (he might as well have) hammered out personally word for word on the tape his reply to the reporters who had asked if Ben Gurion had ignored President Eisenhower's warning.

'That assumption,' Jim Hagerty had said, 'is one I am not taking.'

However, the tape went on, Mr. Eban, the Israeli Ambassador to Washington, had assured Mr. Dulles that Israel would not start a war.

'Somebody's going to begin it,' Jack had said.

But Israel was not their argument. They had been arguing about Eisenhower's sudden policy of restraint. What was Eisenhower afraid of?

'Oil,' Quartermain said.

'Oh, balls,' Jack had said. 'Eisenhower knows that if it blows up here it will blow up everywhere. He's trying to stop a war.'

'Why should he care about that,' Quartermain had argued, 'except for what you'll lose out of it? Do you know where most American oil profits are made? Do you think they come from Texas? It's all made here, where the labour costs are so fantastically low. Standard Oil make their zillions here. They barely break even on Texas oil. That's all Eisenhower sees going up in smoke.'

'Why can't you give a man the benefit of the doubt, just once?' Jack had said. 'Even Eisenhower.'

But the trouble with being right was that you could not allow a man the benefit of your doubt—however ungenerous the attitude seemed. The ungenerous Quartermain had dried his moustache. He had said that perhaps he felt sorry for Eisenhower. It was very hard for a sick man to get out of the dangerous situation his Israeli friends had put him in.

And now the worst had actually happened, despite the Israeli Ambassador's promise to the President.

In the morning, in the newspapers, it seemed worse. Nona's unnerving desire to become angry was not going to make the situation any easier, even though it was Quartermain himself who suggested that Benjamino ought to stay home from school.

'Don't let them out of your sight,' he warned her. 'And stay at home.'

'Have the Israelis got bombing planes?' she asked, looking (he was certain of it) for something to panic about.

558

'No. No. I don't know. Of course they must have bombers. But I can't see them reaching Cairo. What are you panicking about?'

'What I'm supposed to panic about,' she announced. 'My children.'

'You ought to have thought of that before,' he retaliated bitterly. 'I wanted you and the children to leave weeks ago. They're still here, and so are you. Are you satisfied?'

He was shouting.

Benjamino was calling out that the school bus was waiting: he could hear the tooter blowing, the children shouting for him.

'Go downstairs and tell the surveillante you are not coming,' Nona told him. 'Hurry . . .'

'Why?' Benjamin asked. 'I'm ready . . .'

Nona opened the front door and sent him below with a threat of a hiding.

'That'll help,' Quartermain groaned, closing his eyes and ears against it. He had been ringing B.O.A.C. and T.W.A. to see if he could find a place for them on any aeroplane leaving Cairo, but Cairo airport had been closed to all traffic coming and going since early morning. The last plane had gone, and it was reported that Lady Trevelyan, the wife of the British Ambassador, by astonishing good luck had just managed to get on it.

'I'd better go and find out what's happening now,' he told Nona. 'But for heaven's sake—whatever happens while I'm out—keep your head and don't get into a state about it.'

'I'm not in a state,' she replied. 'And if I am you put me into it.'

'All right, all right,' Quartermain said helplessly, sucking in his painful stomach and leaving the house in a huff to find Jack de Brazio, who would know everything that was happening.

CHAPTER SEVENTY-FOUR

HALF-WAY down the parade ground at the Abassia barracks a hundred Molotov trucks were queueing up to go somewhere, and Amin Fakhry was taking Scott in their jeep to inspect them, and to see the rich treasure of Russian spares which had recently arrived: crankshafts and half-shafts, dynamos and water-pumps, distributors, carburettors, bearings, springs, wheels and even light-bulbs, all neatly piled in an old hangar which had become the storehouse for all this newly-acquired Russian material. The hangar was dark and cold and empty, save for these piles on the floor, on the rows of shelves, on the trestle tables. Mechanics were working on some of the new trucks at the open end of the hangar and the thundering roar of the engines inside was unbearable.

'See!' Amin said impatiently when they were out of it. 'All the spares we would ever need. You don't like the trucks, but look at this hoard.'

Amin was bad-tempered because he was being bitterly frustrated. He had hurried urgently to Hakim when the news of the Israeli attack had reached him, but Hakim had simply told him to get on with what he was doing.

'It's going to be a waste of time now,' Amin had complained.

'Get on with it,' Hakim had said impatiently. 'You'll have an aeroplane tomorrow. You can go down to Siwa and begin organizing your base.' And when Amin had asked what was the use of going that way—west to Siwa, when the war was east in the Sinai, Hakim had said: 'How do you know the British won't come in that way now?'

Amin Fakhry could not be appeased, however. What was the use of Siwa with an Israeli attack on? Yet what else could he do? Hakim had been too busy to argue further, but he had told Amin that the battle for the Sinai had not yet started anyway. The Israelis had dropped a parachute battalion somewhere between the sea and el Kuntilla. All night large planes coming from some mysterious base had dropped them supplies. The Israelis had also moved in from Negev to somewhere south-west, obviously to join up with the parachutists, and they had broken out of

Eliat, the Israeli port on the Gulf of Aqaba and were probing forward in-
and, well into the Sinai. It was a complete frontal attack along the whole
border, but there had been no battle yet, and there might never be . . .

Amin and Scott had already argued about it over the maps in the
quarantine hut.

'I can understand why Gamal wanted to keep the Jews out of every
little piece of the Sinai,' Amin had complained. 'But why didn't he tell
the Germans to build the forts farther back, on the line of the plateau?
Why did he build the defences right on the borders? Even on the Gaza
strip? What's the use of that? He depends too much on our new Russian
jets and the Air Force to keep the Israelis out of the desert. But something
always goes wrong with the Air Force. The weather's bad or the landing-
fields are too far away. It's always dangerous.'

'Nevertheless, a dozen planes with a free hand can wipe out everything
visible on the desert,' Scott argued. 'It was always true. The Israelis will
be very exposed to air attack.'

'What are *we* doing with our ideas, then?' Amin had said, drama getting
the better of his judgment, his old critical impatience getting the better
of his restraint. 'We're supposed to be organizing a unit to operate long
distances over open desert. What will planes do to us?'

'If it's a small unit it's safe,' Scott had pointed out, knowing that Amin
was well aware of the difference. 'Armoured cars, tanks, infantry in trucks
are all hopeless. An army in the desert is hopelessly exposed to air attack.
Gamal was right. You can hold the forts on the coast and let the air force
do the rest . . . providing you have an air force, and this time you
have.'

Everyone knew that Nasser had concentrated on buying jets from Russia for that purpose, not for their air value but for their land value. But
Amin Fakhry would never give up the soldier's fear of an unreliable rival
like the Air Force doing the soldier's job for him.

'Let's get back to the hut and look at the maps again,' he said now, when
it was no longer possible to pretend interest in these unwanted trucks.

At the hut they spread out the poorly scaled maps which Scott said
were years out of date. Amin sent the orderly for any others he could get
from the Ordnance officer near by.

'It's so open,' Amin moaned, looking at the vast areas of the Sinai—
most of it undefendable.

'The Israelis will have to stick to the roads, none the less,' Scott argued.
'They can't cross the high Tih or the mountains any other way. Although
there are other ways . . .'

The 'other ways' depended on what Scott himself knew of every wadi
in the plateau. The Sinai for him was not a relief map of dotted wadi lines
ploughing up towards the north-western plains; it was more intimately

561

full of so many back doors which could show him a way behind any route
the Israelis could take.

'But nobody knows all this stuff as well as you do,' Amin said. 'Nobody
there, anyway.'

'But there must be a more detailed map issue,' Scott said. 'They have
printed small charts already, I've seen them.'

'And the Jews will have very good aerial surveys,' Amin went on bitterly. 'Better than ours, probably.'

'That won't tell them what the going is like,' Scott said, 'and that's all
that counts if you want to move over open country.'

Amin was sick with worry, with pessimism. He was not worried about
the outcome (he was amazed that the Jews were foolish enough to try
breaking through the Sinai), he was hotly impatient, as he had been before,
with the lack of military foresight, and the slow military reaction to a
purely military situation.

'They're not doing anything,' he complained.

'How do you know . . .'

'But look at us!' Amin suddenly exploded. 'We're just sitting here talking about it.'

Scott sat down cautiously, a deflating and almost disinterested thing to
do in the face of Amin's nervous excitement.

The phone rang and Amin leapt on it.

'*Iowa, ya sidi* . . . yes . . . yes . . .' Amin looked disgusted and hung up.
'It's that idiot Ahmed asking me if he can borrow our jeep. Let him have
it. What's the point to it now?'

Tomorrow their first four officers and fourteen men were due for inspection, men picked by Amin on their acquaintance or their record or their
specialized qualifications: wireless, explosives, navigation, repair mechanics, intelligence.

'I shall kill Hakim if he doesn't let us go. I'll insist. Come on!' Amin
told him excitedly. 'If we both go to him it will be impossible for him to
refuse. Don't you know that whole peninsula? Even if we're sitting in
some base headquarters on the coast, it's better than here. You know all
the country. You made the maps. Think of your experience. What are
they waiting for? You can convince Hakim better than I can. He's still
afraid of me, because I know more about soldiering than he does.'

Scott saw all the opportunities which Amin saw. So many frustrated
hopes and intentions. Amin would be a good soldier, the right person to
be there. So easy to go with Amin, to say: *Yes, it's the best way. I should go
so let's go.*

'No use me going,' he told Amin calmly. 'You can persuade Hakim
without me.'

'But I want you to come.'

562

Scott shook his head and sat there under sentence. Why not? Why houldn't he go? Didn't he know all the terrain being fought over? Wasn't nat a consideration too valuable to be passed over, either by his own nysterious diffidence or Hakim's stubborn silliness? And his experience— robably greater than any soldier in the entire Egyptian Army.

'It's your chance,' he told Amin. 'Hakim will let you go.'

Amin looked surprised and disappointed. 'What chance? Why do you nink the Jews attacked? To give me a chance?' he said, as he left in a emper.

Scott had not meant it that way. He had simply said it to avoid the nisery of going where Amin might lead him. He felt as bitter as Amin bout the Israeli attack. They ought to be crushed for it. If he were Amin e would want to be in the heart of it. But he had many proofs and justi- cations for not being there.

Above all, he could not give himself up to being a soldier, no matter what the cause, or how great the need. Of that he was certain.

'I simply can't do it,' he said miserably. 'I can't.'

But there was no one present to listen.

CHAPTER SEVENTY-FIVE

THE Tripartite Declaration made by Britain and America and France in 1952 had been an absolute guarantee of stability in the Middle East. The three powers had agreed to come to the aid of any country in the area which was attacked by any other. This, they felt, would protect the *status quo* at least.

'Technically,' Mr. Emanuel Shinwell, the Labour M.P. for Easington, was saying in the House debate on the situation, 'technically she (Israel) might be at fault in the terms of the Tripartite agreement and in the provisions of the U.N. Charter, but has there ever been any country so provoked, bullied, accused, and castigated . . .'

Who could therefore blame Israel, they argued, and why therefore stop Israel's aggression, which was not aggression at all?

But Israel was soon forgotten in the debate when Sir Anthony Eden rose to tell the House that Britain and France had just sent an ultimatum to Egypt and to Israel instructing both countries to withdraw all their forces ten miles from the Suez Canal within twelve hours. Otherwise Britain and France would intervene.

'About time,' Peacock shouted at the top of his voice with the others even before he had quite settled in his bench, still feeling damp and saturated in smoke from his long train journey.

In reply to the Premier, Mr. Gaitskell called the situation grave, and asked the Prime Minister by what authority Britain and France were justified in armed intervention; to which the Prime Minister answered firmly that it was very justified. 'The spirit of the Tripartite Declaration —and more than the spirit—is operating in our minds.'

Only a few men wriggled uncomfortably in the packed House and wondered who had attacked whom. Everybody was tense and ready to be upset, to be angry, to be quarrelsome.

'Oh, do shut up!' Peacock shouted again when Shinwell kept dragging in Israel, and Israel wasn't the point.

What exactly was the point?

How was it, for instance, that over five hundred men could sit in the House and not draw a little map on their question papers to see what was being asked by the Anglo-French ultimatum? If Egypt, who had not attacked anyone, agreed to it she would be handing over to Israel the entire Sinai peninsula as well as the Suez Canal, she must abandon all her armies fighting the Israelis in Egypt, she must move her own frontier back over 100 miles inside Egypt. Whereas Israel (presumably the aggressor under the Tripartite Declaration) in accepting it would be moving her frontier 100 miles inside Egypt, she would have without a struggle what she had often claimed was religiously and physically hers—the entire Sinai peninsula.

Peacock did not feel happy about it because he did not like Israel, but 'Hear! Hear!' he said, because that was the atmosphere on his side of the House.

It was grave.

This was the sort of thing he had tried to impress Eileen with, but impressing Eileen seemed hardly important now. Gaitskell, still prattling on, asked for a delay before any military action was taken under the ultimatum. Eden was saying painfully, patiently, that he could not guarantee it, he could not delay anything. Fighting between Israel and Egypt was going on now in the vicinity of the canal, in which Britain had large quantities of shipping.

'That is why,' Eden said, his voice obviously weak, his knuckle-rapping on the dispatch-box tenuously fragile, 'that is why I can't give the undertaking that we would not take action.'

It was not a pleasant chamber, and Peacock pitied the Prime Minister who looked sick. He felt the debate becoming more and more unpleasant, not for what was said but for who was saying it. Even to look at all the faces opposite made him wonder if he would ever trust one of them again. He didn't dislike them (excepting Monty Mathieson), but today they seemed particularly untrustworthy and alien and yet frightened. They were scared for themselves, he felt sure.

'I don't think I should feel that way about them,' he said, listening to Denis Healy talking perfectly with his party's intellectual passion.

'I think it would be both a crime and a tragedy,' Healy was saying, 'if, at the moment when freedom and national independence are being suppressed by Russian tanks in Hungary, this Government did anything without international support . . .'

Trust Healy to throw in the Russians. Paul Douglas always said that Healy was always throwing up the Russians, rather than throwing them in.

'Never mind that!' Peacock cried with the others on his side. 'Stick to the point.'

There were altercations.

'Sit down!' Peacock shouted angrily.

But he wished they would all keep quiet. It was difficult to grasp this to think clearly while the other side was moralizing. Healy particularl annoyed him. He thought of Healy as an Irish Catholic intellectua socialist, and the Irish Catholic part, at least, seemed to be bad luck fo Healy.

'It must be the Monmouth or the Puritan in me,' he said self-critically 'I oughtn't to think like that about Healy.'

If the Ashleys of Dorset had acquired their lands at the Reformatior and all those other Puritan Peacock families of Somerset had gone to th Duke of Monmouth's cause, it was hardly the reason to criticize Healy

Nevertheless he wished they would all shut up. He realized, sadly, tha middle age was beginning to make him think; and what he thought abou these days was not the Puritan Ashleys so much as the Hastings and th Peacock side of his father's family who, at Monmouth's time, had bee original enough to have red hair. One Hastings had 'kept all manner o sport hounds that run buck, fox, hare, otter and badge', and hawks tha were vicious; and every yeoman's daughter had done very well by hin they knew all about his amorous approaches; but he had been decent t their men who had always been welcome in his house.

'That's the sort of thing Healy can never have, an Oxford educatio notwithstanding.'

The debate was winding up. They had attacked Selwyn Lloyd, an Lloyd was defending himself. Peacock's mind, listening for a while, rea into it already the mustification which *Hansard* would convey of Lloyd' speech in the morning.

'We have never claimed,' Selwyn Lloyd was saying, 'that we hav acted in agreement with the Government of the United States. (Oppositio cries of "Oh!") We have certainly been in close touch with that Govern ment (Ministerial cheers, and Opposition counter-cheers and cries o "Oh!" throughout the controversy). We have never said we have acte with their approval and authority. (Renewed Opposition cries of "Oh! and dissent.) And we believe the decision we and the French Governmen have had to take in our own rights (Loud Ministerial cheers, and Opposi tion laughter and cries of "Oh!") is a decision in the interest of peace i that area. (Renewed Ministerial cheers and Opposition dissent and crie of "Oh! Oh! Oh!")'

That was the end of the day.

Tomorrow there would certainly be a war. Would there be Oppositio cries of 'Oh!'? He only had to remember Nasser's face to know tha Nasser would never agree to any ultimatum.

The Speaker mumbled the adjournment. It was almost midnight, an Peacock wondered what was the matter with him. Why did he feel thi way, almost numbed and impatient? He must be catching a chill. He did not go down for the usual drink with Sandy Buchan who would soon come down to do some shooting, but went straight to his London flat thinking that it must be himself. Yes! He hadn't caught the gravity of the House with that usual feeling of excitement and pleasure. The House had not been satisfying. But it must be the chill, and that voice of Healy's.

'I suppose if I ring Eileen now at this ungodly hour,' he decided when he opened the white front door of the warm but damp flat overlooking the river, 'she'll wonder what's up, and rag me unmercifully.'

He knew that if anything had happened to her they would have sent a telegram to the House. All he had to worry about now was whether she had tangled unpleasantly with the huntsman, whether she had actually pulled it off and beaten him.

'Even if she did?' he said with a shrug, pouring himself a medicinal cognac from the small cupboard he kept locked in the living-room. It was a lovely white flat, bright and thick underfoot, but he missed Eileen.

'Damn climate!' he said, hating his depression.

He thought of Cairo and of what history was suddenly doing to it: not the Israeli advance, but the end of all that had been best in it, and the end of the life he had enjoyed most (he had to admit). To be back in the warm afternoons on any pitch, even a cricket pitch, when Cairo was softening down for the evening, or walking the hot streets in desert boots and a crisp clean uniform, brushing off the beggar-boys who were such filthy, cheerful little vandals.

'I wonder what Scott's doing?' he asked himself. 'I don't suppose they'll lock him up.'

Then he pitied Sam Hassoon, who was, after all, Jewish, and the Jews must be having a difficult time just now in Cairo. Probably being thrown out of windows. He should have done more for Sam, but it was too late now. And what about Lucy Pickering and Church, and probably Quartermain also? They must all be caught.

He wondered what all the other Members were thinking about as they got into bed tonight. Probably tomorrow's debate.

'It must be me,' he decided accusingly, certain it was his chill, resenting introspection, and being suspicious of it. When he thought about Healy again, he said: 'I really am very badly educated . . .'

'CAPTAIN ALI ZAREEF was thrown out of the school,' Hefney the prop-swinger told Sam when they met casually on a Shubra tram-stop. 'They suspended him.' Hefney brushed his hands together. 'Finish Captain Ali.'

Sam forgot for a moment that he was a Jew. This was the morning of Israel's attack on Egypt, and Hefney, who was a simple Moslem, might feel bitter and violent about it.

'But why did they suspend him again? He did nothing at all.'

'Poor Captain Ali has been in trouble all the time since they sent you away,' Hefney told him in Arabic. 'They think he wanted to blow some-one up.'

Sam knew what Zareef had suffered, and he had felt unhappy about it. But he also knew what Hefney apparently did not know yet: that Ali Zareef would now work for the Frontier Department, for Amin Fakhry and Scott himself.

'Why aren't you working today?' Sam asked Hefney. 'Have they closed the school?'

'It's Monday,' Hefney said.

Sam had forgotten it was Monday. There was never any flying at Gedida on Monday morning. It was a tradition left over by the British who had realized that flying on Monday morning could be dangerous after a too-cheerful Sunday night. Hefney, too, was something the British had left behind.

'I'm going to see the doctor about my bad foot,' he told Sam.

Hefney was a grey and ageing Cairo peasant who had spent thirty years swinging aeroplane propellers. He had started as a boy after the First World War working for the English instructors at Almaza. In 1925 he had been employed at a piastre a day pulling the chocks away from the wheels. He still did so. An important but unrealized sound at Gedida was Hefney dragging four chocks across the gritty tarmac behind his sloppy feet on a hot day. He had swung propellers of so many generations of English light planes. The very first had been an old Avro 504K, and then

568

when the British Royal Air Force were still mixed up in it) Harts, Hornets, Gypsies, Tigers, Austers, and then a few later models which started by battery. The battery had to be plugged in and dragged away. He had known all the generations of Egyptian pilots who had passed through all the crises of flying, of politics, of school politics, of Egyptian politics. He had outlasted them all. He knew all those who were good and bad pilots, and those who were good or bad men according to his values, which were quite liberal.

But he did not think about aeroplanes any more, only about getting a warm coat for winter from someone, and finding work (some students were rich) for his youngest sons of twelve and fourteen, and working husbands for his fifteen-year-old daughters who were always a problem. He had ten children. He had learned so many tricks about aeroplanes, and he knew so much about flying them (although he never went up at all) that no one took any notice of him. When he gently tapped the carburettors of a Hornet moth with a little pebble to break an air-lock he was doing something he did not even know he was doing, or how he had learned to do it. He had once been a peasant boy, and now he was an old man who earned 10 piastres a day and could not afford a pair of shoes, although he wore those cast-offs which thoughtful instructors or engineers or pupils gave him. He was clean-shaven and secretly took sides in disputes, often both sides—dependent on whom he was talking to. But he had his favourites, and though he knew that Captain Ali Zareef was not always lily-white in his dispute with Captain Selim, and though he knew that Captain Selim was not a cruel man, even if he was a weak one, it was Captain Ali Zareef who had been the most obviously dedicated pilot of them all.

Hefney's tram had come and gone, and Sam stood there alone for a moment, his conscience worrying him unnecessarily because he knew that Scott had already extracted Ali Zareef from trouble, and had found him another job as pilot—perhaps even better than the school. But it was a shock to hear about his actual dismissal from Hefney, because the old atmosphere of the aerodrome itself had reached him again, and he knew that he ought to go and see Ali Zareef and make sure that he was all right.

'Why did the Israelis attack?' Sam asked Scott impatiently at dinner. 'The Suez Canal is nothing to do with them.'

They were eating the very dish Madame Salz had decided by observation was Scott's favourite: fatta, a chicken broth poured over rice and native bread with square lumps of veal sprinkled on top. Fatta was generically dunking, Egyptian dunking. The peasant would make fatta with lentils and soak his flat bread in it. Madame Salz made her fatta the way a pasha should make it, but she swore they were too mean to do so

569

well, and she knew that Scott would eat it with relish, two helpings a
least.

It soothed Madame Salz from a frightening day.

It ought to soothe Captain Scott, who had been very low and silent an
even miserable lately; if his solemn, thoughtful face was any indicatior
of what was going on within. *Ce pauvre homme!*

'It's that Lieberman girl in Port Said,' she had told Becky.

'Perhaps it's the Englishwoman,' Becky had said.

'No. No. The Lieberman girl won't divorce her husband and marry
him. She wants to get her cousin's money first. I know.'

Scott ate the fatta with relish none the less, and Sam also.

'I don't know why they attacked,' Scott said reluctantly to Sam. 'They
can't possibly win.'

Every other person present was a Jew, and Sam had asked the questio
for the others. What did any of them know about Israel? A moment's pride
a second's deep racial and religious satisfaction. But Sam could no
answer the question for himself, or for them, because he was a Jew who
was not necessarily an Israeli.

'Perhaps they don't want to win,' Madame Salz's oldest boarder said
'Perhaps they know it's hopeless.'

Madame Salz had only two boarders at the moment. This one was ar
old Russian named David Kosnoff who had wanted to marry her fo
many years, but she had kept her head. David Kosnoff had even brough
in a marriage-broker to persuade her, two or three years ago, even thougl
he was living in the same house. Someone had to present his good point
and his assets clearly and favourably. Madame Salz had listened breath
lessly, flattered but not quite convinced. She did not know why she had
rejected an offer which would have left her well off when he died. Bu
she had felt that she was happy enough as she was, at the time, with he
good friends and her daughters and their husbands-to-be, who sh
imagined would be fine, well-off, family-loving men. Sam was not quit
her old idea of a successful husband, but she was happier now with San
than she could be with her other daughter's husband, who was a Germar
Palestinian, a thief and a cheat and a betrayer. Sam was honest and simpl
and in love with Becky; and his friend Scott was a guarantee of his honoui
and of his safety in Egypt, despite the trouble he had been in, which sh
did not understand anyway.

'Jews have to defend themselves,' the old man, David Kosnoff, said
'That's why they attacked. But they should only punish, and then with
draw.'

'And what do you think the Egyptians should do?' Sam asked him i
French. 'Punish the Jews and withdraw also? Why did Israel start it a
all? Don't they ever think of anyone but themselves? It's silly.'

This was an argument before the Anglo-French ultimatum, which came pon them that evening on the radio. And then it was not only Sam look-g for comfort and explanation from Scott, but Scott sunk into dejection, linging to Sam's innocent indignation as the antidote to stupidity and iolence.

'Don't worry,' Sam found himself saying, consoling, encouraging. Somebody will stop it, Capten.'

Scott shook his head. 'Nobody will stop it. Nobody cares that much.' He had never felt so wretched and ashamed in his life.

Lucy Pickering suddenly appeared (from the Embassy? from Alexan-ria?) when Gamal Abd el Nasser was rejecting the Anglo-French ultima-um on the radio. Nasser said it was an attack on the rights and dignity of Cgypt, and a flagrant violation of the United Nations Charter.

'I was terrified that you might not still be in Cairo,' she told him, greatly elieved.

He had found her knocking at his door at half past seven in the morn-ng, with Madame Salz's worried face behind her. He did not like having er in his room, but he brought her in and turned off the radio. Was it a ristine or private place always? Or was it simply a well-guarded self-onsciousness, a room which had always closed him in safely on himself?

'I tried to get a train from Alexandria last night,' she said, still breathing urgency, 'but I had to hire a car, and it was a beastly journey at night and o expensive. I gave him every penny I had, and I must look frightful.'

'I thought you'd have gone away by now,' he told her. 'You'll never get ut of Egypt now, unless you have a diplomatic passport.'

'I don't care about getting out. Could I have some coffee? Is that your reakfast? I came straight here to see you, and if I could use your bath-oom. Although that ought to wait. I simply have to talk to you.'

'Did they bomb Alexandria last night?' he asked, feeling flight and urgency in her face. Her hair was unbrushed, and her calm blue eyes were estless.

'No. They didn't bomb Alexandria,' she said in surprise. 'But why do ou ask?'

'I thought that was why you had come down here,' he told her.

'Please get me a cup of coffee,' she asked him, 'and lend me a towel.'

He gave her all the means of restoring herself, so that she was clean and rushed again, and she sipped her coffee deliciously, sitting on a tin trunk vhich he had covered with an old Bedouin mat.

'It's lovely,' she said between sips. 'I did need that.'

'What about your breakfast?' he asked her.

'Later,' she said. 'Do you think they will intern us?' she asked then. That is—Church and me. What do you think?'

571

'What can you expect?' he said.

'It's worse than that,' she went on. 'Is there any way you can persuade the Egyptians to allow Professor Maudie to be shifted to a hospital in Cairo?'

'Now?'

'Yes. It's going to be terrible in Alexandria, being a port. Jack Church won't leave her, and he's afraid that they'll bomb the harbour. She'd be much safer in Cairo. He asked the hospital yesterday if she could be moved, and they say *Yes* if the Frontier Department agrees. That's you, isn't it?'

'Doesn't Church know that the British and French have declared war on Egypt?'

'Of course he does. That's what he's worried about. But that's hardly Maudie's fault, and she should not suffer because of it. Can't you ask somebody to telephone or write a note? Something, to bring her down to Cairo.'

'Why does Church think they're going to bomb Alexandria?' he asked. 'Does he know?'

'He might know,' she said with an impatient shrug. 'What difference does it make? He simply wants to get Maudie out of the way.'

'I can't help that,' he said, walking up and down restlessly, indignant and angry already by her fantastic sort of innocence, or was it ignorance? 'I can't help you,' he said. How on earth, he asked her, could he approach the Egyptians now—himself an Englishman, to ask help for another Englishman, when a British army was about to launch an attack on Egypt?

'They're obviously going to invade Egypt, yet you expect them to help you.'

'I don't see it like that,' she argued impatiently. 'Don't be silly. It has nothing to do with what the British are doing. This is simply getting Professor Maudie to a safe place. She is still terribly ill, and it may kill her.'

'It may kill a lot of others also,' Scott said.

He couldn't understand her. Was she so inherently insensitive, so English, so armoured against reproach or fault that she could not see what she was asking of him? For a moment his anger and bitterness came back.

'No, no!' he warned himself. 'Don't get involved in arguments like that with Lucy. She'll never see the point, if there is a point, and you'll be in the wrong.'

'Anyway,' he told her wryly, 'I've had my last favour from the Egyptians after this morning. I don't think they'll ever listen to me again, not now.'

She put down her coffee cup and sighed. She was not surprised, but she was watching him carefully and suspiciously. What was he really thinking

572

Her look was investigating him and he was sitting on the edge of his desk feeling like a strange man in his own room, in his own feelings.

'What will you do now?' she asked.

'I don't know. I suppose they'll intern us all.'

'Not you, surely?'

'Why should they make an exception of me? I ought to be locked up with the rest of you.'

'But you're on their side,' she argued. 'Aren't you angry? Don't you want to fight the British or the French or the Israelis, or whoever you blame?'

'What for?' he asked. 'It's too late.'

'Why do you say that?' she demanded.

He did not answer. Every emotion about it had already been washed away from him. He was no longer indignant or angry. He had longed hungrily to feel both, but he had (just now in the dead of night) reached a bearable state of resignation and understanding—the realization that all of this was inevitable anyway.

'It had to happen,' he said helplessly. 'What can I do to change it?'

He knew that not a man or a nation could stop this hearty British destruction of a country so inferior to itself. If the British wanted it so, then how could it be stopped? If the British had failed to murder Nasser, failed to restore the old days by an assassin's bullet, then they would certainly not fail this time.

'Don't be so weak-minded,' Lucy was saying, jumping down from her perch and putting down her cup. 'You ought to be losing your temper and goading your Egyptian friends into putting up a terrible fight. That's what I thought you would be doing. How can you sit there and wait to be locked up like the rest of us? Don't they expect more of you than that?'

'They expect me to behave like any Englishman.'

'They *don't*!' she insisted heatedly. 'They imagine that you have a sense of honour at least. They expect you to do anything on their behalf, and to say that you'll fight the horrible, beastly British.'

'Don't try to stir me,' he warned her, 'because I know very well that you don't believe a word of it yourself. I know from experience about you. Are you shocked by anything the British are doing?'

'Of course I'm not. I'm even sorry they waited so long to do it! Oh, it's too late to argue that with you now. I don't believe in the same things you do here. But I told you once before—I'm willing to believe in *you*.' She stood facing him, a puzzled look on her face, as if she were waiting for him to explain himself, or to understand her. 'I know what *you* should do now. And sitting there, being miserable with yourself and shrugging helplessly, isn't what you ought to do.'

'We will never agree about that,' he said, 'so we ought not to quarrel Let it go.'

She broke away from him then as if it were all clear. 'Why is it,' she cried at him, 'that you always refuse to see what I am offering you?'

'I don't want you to offer me anything,' he said defensively.

'I simply don't understand you! Never. Excepting that you make me think what a stupid and weak object a man is. Women go around looking for a man who can live up to himself, but my God, how rarely do they find one?'

She was walking around his room now, looking contemptuously at everything, at every part of him. It was *him*.

'You're such a man, aren't you? Look at this room. Look at you. But do you know what it's like to be a woman? Do you have any idea of the waste we suffer because the world is designed against us, and because men like you are so stupidly inadequate?' She faced the pictures on his mantel shelf. 'Pictures. You are all so sentimental and pompous and frightened—mainly of yourselves. Women are such *fools*. Even when a woman knows she is superior to any man, she is still willing to go on looking for one who might get himself up out of the mud. I'll never understand what happened to the matriarchy.' She turned on him. 'Yes, I do understand. Women simply knew they were stronger and cleverer and better than men, so they simply gave up and let the men assume the pretence. That was the mistake. The pretence of it. Look at you! You're a monster. You're so big, aren't you? But you're all pretence. You have nothing. None of you have.'

He sat down and watched her drawing this fire from some cold reserve. She was tired, and she was goading herself deliberately with it and pulling it out in thin harsh shreds of herself. But why did she do it now?

'I've tried twice to make something of a man,' she was saying more wearily now. 'But I failed. Oh, how I failed. Because there was never anything to make. Pickering' (there was his picture, among his friends) 'was a silly eccentric. Oh, he was! And all I could do was try to pour something into that oddity, hoping it would mould itself into something forceful and worthwhile. But he was too crazy to do anything but play. He played! Oh, you did!' she said at Pickering's youthful, faded picture among his soldiers. 'He played at himself, played at being different, played at being soldiers, played at being a father and husband and man. It was the best he could do, and it still made him superior to most men. Then you . . .'

He blushed now, as if she were insulting him in a room full of people.

'What I thought I'd found in you was the purpose at last. But like all things in a man it becomes its opposite when it's pressed to the point. You were a coward. You ran away from yourself. And I came here, all the way, thinking after all these years that I had been wrong to leave you. But

574

I wasn't wrong at all. You deserved it. Now you are doing it all over again, and I can't stand to see it . . .'

'Shush!' he said to her, standing up and laughing at her because she was no longer serious. She could not be serious. 'I can't be all that bad,' he said.

'But you are!'

'Never mind,' he told her gently, putting his hand on her shoulder and on her hair. 'It's too late to change now, Lucy.'

'It's not even that,' she said, giving in, leaning against him. 'I do have to blame someone, don't I? And I can always blame you. I have to. Even when you're not there.'

'I don't mind.'

'Yes, you do. But I miss you. I wanted just to come and see you, but I couldn't. I always say to myself—next time I shan't open my mouth and say terrible things to you, but I do. I don't want to be so mean, but you're so weak.'

She was still leaning on him tiredly. 'You're not being mean,' he assured her. 'It must be the times we live in, I suppose. I seem to be angry myself all the time, and I can't stop it.'

'Perhaps we've both changed too much,' she told him. 'It's not you really, I know that. It's *realization*! Don't you understand? I mean, for us. When we were younger, love was mainly a simple sort of desire, a pretence even, and so terribly clumsy and frustrating. But love now would be such a complete freedom, if you could only see it and take it.' She leaned away from him and inspected him very simply. How brown she was, so pale-eyed and so smooth-faced and so briefly, briefly hopeful. Don't you ever understand what I'm offering you?'

'I understand you, Lucy,' he told her quickly. 'But we are only making it more difficult for ourselves.'

'Can't you trust me?' she begged.

He did not know, he would never know; so he could not answer her truthfully. He could only avoid her. 'It's too late for us . . .'

She nodded and moved away from him. 'I know I always know it is,' she said calmly. 'And it must be my fault. I should have been more careful, I suppose.' She was once again the obliging woman she said all women do become—effacing quickly whatever strength she was trying to share or give away. 'It's always been my own fault.'

'It's nobody's fault,' he said virtuously. But he disliked his own apologies. 'It's simply that time passes, and other people become important too.'

'Are you really in love with that girl in Port Said?' she asked.

He would not say. 'I'll marry her as soon as we can get away,' he replied. If we can ever get away now.'

'Have you a right to do that to her?'

'I have no right *not* to do it,' he told her. 'She expects . . .'

'She'll know.'

'She'll know what?'

'That you don't love her.'

'She'll never know any such thing. And perhaps she doesn't want love any more, not the way you think of it.'

'But *you* will,' she said warmly. 'You'll want it.'

Perhaps he had never loved Lucy Pickering as he could love her now, when she spoke simply and abandoned her own hopes and her own ambitions, warning him for his own sake. But it was only partly Lucy, partly her eyes, partly her face, partly her manner and her hopes. The other one lurked about, and swore to terrorize him if he ever believed in the gentility of the soft Englishwoman he saw now. His stubborn fears and his suspicious emotions would always doubt her. And what he saw in that second in her heart, was gone the next, and the issue was over.

'And you really can't help Jack Church?'

He had forgotten the war completely, but she had easily remembered it.

'Honestly I can't, much as I'd like to,' he said.

'Then I must go back to Alexandria before they catch me here,' she told him. 'I suppose I'll have to wait for the Egyptians to find me somewhere. Do you think they will put us under house arrest? I suppose I can survive it. But I hate to think of how Jack Church will feel if he can't see his Professor, and if he's down there all alone and miserable. He'll feel awful. Do you think they'll be cruel?'

'That depends on how cruel we are to them,' he suggested harshly despite himself.

'But they brought it on themselves,' she said.

He kept his temper and took her to the corner where she could find a taxi. She borrowed a pound from him, and she turned around calmly as she was getting into the taxi and said to him, 'I feel much better now. I knew I'd feel better if I came to see you.'

It seemed more like a form of dismissal, however. Had he served his purpose for her? He suddenly felt all his mistrust of Lucy return, only to disappear again because she had disappeared. Then he felt very lonely walking along the dusty streets towards Abassia, where even the Egyptian seemed to have forgotten him.

CHAPTER SEVENTY-SEVEN

QUARTERMAIN took his last walk around the city, which was now at war.

There was nothing warlike to see, except the lorry-loads of brown-eyed solemn soldiers and covered anti-aircraft guns in convoys passing through the streets. But there was a nervous, hidden expectancy in the traffic, in the movement of each person. There was a feeling of disaster that could not quite be seen.

He had walked up as far as the British Embassy to see if there was any chance of the Embassy getting the family out of Egypt. But at the gate he had faced the reality of his stomach, which would not allow him to go on in and ask for help. On the other side of the fence, where the Chancery garden was, he could see clerks and secretaries piling up secret papers or old bills on a bonfire, to make sure that everybody understood that they were doing what diplomats are supposed to do when war breaks out—burn the evidence.

'Silly bastards,' he said, turning away.

Only profanity occurred to him. What was the use of being right now?

'Did you arrange anything?' Nona asked him when he came back, hurrying home because he did not like to leave them for too long.

'No. They couldn't do anything,' he lied.

He could look at his sons, kept at home from school, and he could ask himself why he dared to take a risk with them rather than walk in the gate of the British Embassy and beg them for help. 'I have to risk them for something,' he told himself, 'and I suppose they'd forgive me for it.'

Helen and Hanna were also waiting in the flat. They thought they ought to move in to stay, but Quartermain had said it was not such a good idea.

'We should all be together,' Nona insisted.

'What's the use of that?' he said. 'Hanna and Helen are Egyptians. They're not going to be interned. But probably we will be.'

'He's right,' Helen said. 'Only, let Hanna stay to help you with the children.'

'And leave you alone outside?'

U   577

'Oh, heavens,' Helen said. 'I'll be all right. They're not going to kill me.'

'They may arrest you again. They're sure to be thinking of it.'

'Do you think it would stop them arresting me if I come here?' Helen argued.

'And if the British start bombing?' Nona persisted.

But Nona was already defeated by a situation she could not control. She hoped (she said) that the Russians would drop a bomb on the English and teach them what it was like to be treated the way they treated others —like insects.

'The British won't bomb civilians,' Helen argued.

Nona laughed ironically, because the news from that point of view was not encouraging. They had heard it that morning on the B.B.C. from London.

'All civilians in Egypt,' the B.B.C. had announced, 'are warned for their safety to keep away from all Egyptian airfields from now onwards until the Egyptian Government accepts the request of the United Kingdom and French Governments, delivered on October 30.'

'Please don't go out,' Nona begged her husband.

'Why not?'

'They're going to bomb us. They admit it. The people in the streets will be angry.'

Though he was a British subject, Quartermain could still walk to the telegraph office. He could still send his dispatches to the Northern Allied Agency, who were sending him a cable every hour asking him for specific details, employing him for the duration of the war, encouraging him, urging him. 'Oh, damn them!' Nona said. But it was partly salvation. At least they were Americans, and the Americans at the moment were being sympathetic to the Egyptians.

'It'll be all right,' he told her. 'And, anyway, let us wait until the trouble starts before we worry about it.'

'They'll tear you to pieces on the streets,' she said. 'Think how they must feel. If the mob turns loose again . . .'

'Nasser can't have mobs getting out of hand,' he said. 'It's all very calm.'

'It won't be calm for long,' she insisted, 'when the British start bombing. You wait and see.' But she already knew that she was fighting for their safety against impossible odds.

Scott had already sent a telegram to Françoise telling her to come to Cairo, but now he telephoned her in Port Said, surprised that it was still possible. Had the British or the Israelis bombed the city yet? The ultimatum time was already up, and something was sure to happen.

'No, no,' she said, '*mais il y a des rumeurs, toujours des mauvaises rumeurs*. The office is closed,' she said, 'and M. Beauvoir says that the French will be here soon.'

'Françoise!' he shouted into the instrument in Madame Salz's front hall where the phone stood on the mantelshelf under a mirror with a golden border, facing which it was difficult to avoid your own eyes, your own doubts and deceptions, when you spoke. And when you shouted you were shouting at yourself.

'Françoise,' he shouted with all the conviction he could muster out of his concern. 'Get the children and come to Cairo. It doesn't matter what happens. Come down here tonight if you can—even if you have to hire a car.'

'They've stopped permits for the canal road,' she wavered back at him 'I can't leave here until the train on Monday morning. *C'est affreux ici— il y a toujours des rumeurs.* I'll come on Monday by train. There is no other way now.'

'I'll meet you,' he shouted. 'But try to come before.'

'That's all, that's all,' an Arabic operator's voice interrupted. 'Terminé,' she said in the gritty French of the telephone. 'Toutes communications avec Port Said sont terminées.'

He put the telephone down and wandered out restlessly into the Kubbeh Garden streets, walking about in the night without knowing what he should do.

The suburbs were strange, lonely places. How did life just go on? How did these people live out their lives so helplessly? He tried to think himself into someone else's safe, unbothered existence in these streets, but he knew nothing about the people in these old dry houses behind dark gardens. Bats zoomed recklessly around an old French villa, where boabs sat on kitchen chairs at the iron gates talking quietly. They stopped talking when he passed them. That was unusual. Why should they notice him in the darkness?

'What do people do?' he was asking himself.

It was a hopeless question.

When a man set out walking in the night to solve the problems his conscience had forced on him, he usually found that he had nothing coherent to say to himself.

'People do nothing,' was his answer.

They would wait for the war to reach them, just as he would wait. War was very tempting to soldiers. But who fired the first shot, and who gave the first order, and who conceived the beginning and the end, while these people and himself waited in his dead suburb to face ten thousand other decisions about their lives made by other men? Even soldiers knew nothing, but simply reacted at what was done to them.

'At least soldiers have to act or react,' he told himself, still under the sting of Lucy's attack. 'That's something.'

But he was already suspicious, and perhaps he was admitting, finally, that he was and always would be a soldier at heart, because he had only managed to find in soldiering what he wanted to find in life itself. He could not deny it. Soldiers served, soldiers were coherent and directed at specific tasks, soldiers worked in a disciplined collective, they tried not to surrender to pain or threats of destruction; they covered great distances and captured the fleeting social force of unselfish objectives; and above all they endured when they had to, even when they were afraid, because there was a greater influence working on them than the primitive private fears of their own frightened minds.

Yet they did it all for what they could not understand or control, or even initiate. Soldiers were also helpless. They were as much on the wind as the blind bats and the talkative boabs gossiping in the night.

'I'm not going to get involved in that, whatever Lucy says,' he warned himself again and went homewards.

But what must he do tomorrow morning, for instance, when tomorrow morning came?

'Get on with it,' he advised himself. 'Go on with what you're doing.'

He could do nothing else except go on like everyone else. He would simply go to work like everyone else, and he would do what he was supposed to do. He would wait—like everyone else—for one of these ten million decisions made by other men finally to reach him, to do with him what it liked.

But it would not make of him a soldier. Nothing would.

Amin Fakhry had gone, anyway. In the morning he was simply not there. He had left a note saying that he had persuaded Hakim to let him go. Where was he now? Hakim had sent him to where the B.B.C. this morning had said the Israelis were fighting—down the last road from Nekhly to Suez. The B.B.C. said the Israelis were almost on the canal already, but who could believe the B.B.C. when you were sitting in Abassia barracks, with no particular urgency pressing the soldiers marching around the parade ground in fatigues.

He had tried to see Hakim, but Hakim had also gone, and Scott was left with his own decisions—to accept delivery of fifty 12-volt batteries and a diesel generator to be sent on to Siwa, to send away fourteen men who came to be inspected in immaculate uniforms. Would they enjoy being inspected by an Englishman to prove themselves worthy of being Egyptian?

'Tell them to report to General Hakim,' he told Mahmoud the sergeant who had come into this with Amin, and whose impersonal and non-commissioned authority was already beginning to gall.

'They came from General Hakim,' Mahmoud said condescendingly.

'Send them back,' Scott told Mahmoud as carelessly as he could.

He had telephoned Hakim through the hoarse-voiced efficiency of the Abassia military exchange and he had learned then that Hakim had gone. Hakim was elsewhere.

Were they being cool? Could he show his face again?

But Ali Zareef arrived, as friendly as he had always been.

'Ahlan! Ahlan!' they said to each other.

Zareef had a few heavy sighs from his navigator's heart for the terrible situation, but otherwise it was not so bad. Their new plane had arrived at Gedida from Heliopolis and was waiting for someone to come and take delivery of it.

'You must come!' Zareef said. 'It's a German Fieseler. It's rather small. It might be a little too slow, but it will land anywhere.'

He ordered coffee for Zareef over Zareef's heart-holding protests.

'You can't come in here and refuse,' Scott told him.

Zareef refused politely, in order to accept. He was being particularly nice, as if he knew what the other man was suffering in unhappy divisions. To be a soldier, and to be an Oriental? What use were English manners, which were superficial, compared with this game that he and Zareef now played of protest and counter-protest over the arrival of a cup of coffee? They were really offering each other what English good manners could never offer—the search for the sensitive man under the protests. It forced the most insensitive into a delicacy of feeling; and over Zareef's *habibis* and his own *min-fadlucks*, over the form and the monotonous repetitions, he knew that Zareef was being gentle with him, encouraging him to come, to feel like a friend, to be welcome as he had been, to be what he always had been—never to imagine that his friends were going to turn on him because of what had happened.

'Please come out this afternoon,' Zareef insisted again. 'You must see your new plane.'

'All right,' Scott said.

'Welcome! Welcome!' Zareef said in advance, leaving hurriedly.

He told Sam at lunch-time that he was going out to see Zareef at Gedida airport, and Sam said that he would like to go too.

'If it's no trouble,' Sam added.

Sam, for one, was not going to think, above all else, that he was a Jew and would not be welcome on an Egyptian airfield. He was thinking about Ali Zareef, whom he had not seen since leaving Gedida. The reminder from Hefney had made him worry now about his responsibilities.

Even so, was it possible for a Jew not to think of himself at all times as a Jew, particularly now? There lay the problem of the race, and Sam seemed to have solved it by being himself—a careless man sometimes, a responsible one at others, but with other criteria and other values besides the clannish huddle of defence which drove a strange people into the corner when quite often they could be themselves among others and suffer no damage. Sam forgot, or Sam did not insist, or Sam simply wanted to see Ali Zareef—nothing else occurred to him. Wasn't friendship as valid as all that fanatical racial sorrow and its harsh self-consciousness?

'It's no trouble,' Scott told him. 'You can come in the jeep with me.'

Scott did remember what Sam was. But what was the difference now between himself and Sam? Weren't they both the outcast samples of the enemy snarling at the gates? And anyway, Gedida was not a military airfield. Sam could come in Amin's jeep, and no one would know the difference.

'I'll pick you up at about 4.30,' he told Sam.

'At the workshop.'

Only a few days before, Sam had taken a job working for Leo Lieberman, learning watch-repairing. But he knew that Leo wouldn't mind his leaving early this once to see a friend. Sam had repaired enough instruments during the war, and afterwards working at Gedida, to pick up the rudiments of watch-making faster than Leo's Austrian expert could teach him, assuming Sam (being an Egyptian Jew and not a European Jew) to be a big fool. Sam had said, 'I know all that,' when the importance of the jewelled bearing was explained to him. Sam's large fingers were delicate enough to solder the tiniest whiskers of a transistor circuit, and it was all the same principle, anyway—bringing everything to bear together at the same time: eyes, tool, intention, screw and whatever else you wanted on it.

'You'll never learn,' the Austrian had said to him, but Sam had decided that he could learn well enough without any more instruction.

In the meantime he had left the garden to little Abdulla, but today, after lunch, he supervised the shifting of Madame Salz's personal collection of pot-plants—chrysanthemums and geraniums—from the wall of the house to the base of a tree, where he had made a circular path.

'What about the tortoise?' little Abdulla asked. 'That's where he sleeps almost every day. He will eat the leaves . . .'

'He can sleep somewhere else,' Sam said. 'He's got a whole garden.'

'But, *ya hawaga*,' Abdulla insisted. 'He already loses his way, since you changed the paths. I swear he's lost. He looks at me sometimes, and he says: *Breaking up of my home! Terrible tidings all round me! What can I do?*'

'He's too cheeky,' Sam complained. 'Some day a dog or a kite will get him. He ought to find a new hole.'

He and Abdulla had watched a kite diving on Felu the day before. It

582

had been an exciting contest in anticipation. Felu had pulled in her (or his) head at the exact moment that the diving kite had reached out for it with beak and talons. It seemed inevitable that some day, sooner or later, Felu would be a little slow, and her long and happy life in this old garden would come to an end.

'She's a silly beast,' Sam said, refusing to allow a tortoise to put something over on him.

It was a familiar journey to Gedida airport, particularly if one began to wonder if the city would be bombed and destroyed.

Dodge the trams in Bulac, the native quarter, and watch an ass ridden at full speed on the footpath, miraculously hitting nobody. The jeep stopped in the heavy traffic. An old man sold holed bread on a stick, and another one stood silently behind a marvellous hexagon—a glass pyramid with sweetmeats in it. They were all so familiar and unnoticed on other days. The man who sold bowls of milk curds swept flies away from his netted safe, and another one stoked a little oven with roasted pistacchio nuts—it also had a little chimney with blue smoke coming out of it. They all cried and sang what they had sung every day of their lives, and would go on singing until they were interrupted by catastrophe or death. At each end of Shubra bridge there were four new soldiers on guard, but at each end there were also the sweet-carrot sellers flanked by the ragged street children begging for a morsel.

Scott felt that he knew everything about them, and yet nothing. They were polite and charming people, all these street people, *desiring* to oblige and help. They helped each other, they tormented each other, they lived with each other. All business seemed so casual and intimate and argumentative between them; so deep; but all discussion was direct and equal.

'I hate this street,' Sam said, disliking the crowded noisy delay. 'Why don't they clean it up?'

But Scott was afraid for them. He could look at them and wonder if anyone, even Gamal Abd el Nasser, had touched their lives. He could already feel the terror of one bomb among them, one death, one reckless bullet. What for? They were blameless, yet they would be punished. It seemed ironical, though, that by its contempt for all things Egyptian, British rule had finally made the Egyptians aware of being Egyptian. They were all aware now, all of them, even the beggars. If Gamal was driving through this street today, he was surely saying, 'These are us—the Egyptians; all these ragged donkey drivers; and all these homeless, dirty, happy, miserable children, these filthy garbage collectors and sugar-cane vendors, these barefooted workers and very poor plumbers.' Scott remembered the day he had seen a barefooted plumber with his canvas bag on his back limping cruelly all the way (ten miles) into Cairo from some village near

583

Gedida, a swollen and infected foot dragging dirt and blood behind him, so resigned that he had not attempted to ask anyone for a lift, and no one had thought of stopping for him, including himself in the comfort of the white airport bus.

Were these the people who were going to stand up to the British and the French and the Israelis? Could they stand up to a civilization in which the brutality was better organized? Scott felt helpless then, because he knew they were helpless.

'The British say they're going to bomb the airfields,' Sam said, from the back of the jeep where he was hunched up in a tweed jacket. He had put on his best clothes to pay his visit to Zareef. 'I hear it on the radio.'

'I know,' Scott said. 'But they'll probably be after Almaza, and the other military airfields.'

'At night?' Sam suggested.

'Who knows?' Scott said. 'It's strange how everybody is waiting for something to happen, as if that's all we can do—just wait.'

'What else?' Sam said.

It was a still day, and when they swung into the gates at Gedida airport, it all came back to normal. Particularly for Sam. It was all the same—there were the yellow Shell wagons of petrol, the met. cage and the brown copper rain-trap on the little lawn, the train and the sugar-factory smoke drifting behind, the dry brown-green stubble of the small airfield. The wind-sock sagged, and the low hangars looked like small lumps of dirty sugar. There were small aeroplanes on the tarmac, and mechanics were working on them. But they discovered that all school flying had been cancelled at Gedida as of this morning, owing to the situation.

'Ahlan! Ahlan!' Zareef said. And when he saw Sam he seemed not quite sure, for one second, but then he greeted him anyway, as if he had not seen his old friend for a long time. 'Ahlan, ya sidi.'

'Ya Ali!' Sam said, embracing him.

There was nothing much to be done. It was no more than a courtesy visit and Scott looked at the Fieseler and saw its faults.

'It's not big enough for two wounded men to lie down in,' he told Zareef.

'Unless their feet go down into the fuselage,' Zareef suggested.

'Could you still fly it with the weight back there?'

'If they don't have thick boots on.'

How still it was when they laughed. It was almost evening.

'Why did they paint it yellow?' Scott asked.

'That's the easiest colour to see if you force land.'

'I know that, but it's no use for us, Ali. We don't want to be seen.'

'They probably didn't realize what we wanted it for.'

They looked at it for a long time. Scott had no great interest in aeroplanes, except that Ali Zareef was a good pilot. But they stood under the wing and discussed it. They could not try it out because all planes were grounded and the airfield seemed depressed with some sort of expectancy. Mechanics were tightening something on the tail of a Tiger Moth, which was set up on a trestle on the tarmac. Bambo the mechanic was bleeding from a slip he had made with a spanner, and he flicked the blood off his hand on to the gritty tarmac.

Sam, tactfully leaving Scott and Zareef to their business, had gone to see his friends the firemen in their open-doored brick house. They wore black jerseys and berets and high leather boots and big black moustaches. An old man was weeding the meteorological department's lawn, and another was picking pansies and marigolds from the borders to put them in a jam-jar in the control tower, which was his way of reminding the control officer that a monthly two-piastre tip was due. Tomorrow it would be the director's office, and then Captain Selim's unused room, and then patience for another month until he could earn another six piastres. His flowers would never be noticed in the control tower, not today, anyway. Even the phones were silent today.

'Ahlan!' Said the driver of the fire-engine said to Sam. 'Health and happiness, *ya sidi*!'

'To thee!' Sam said. 'How are you, Said?'

'All well?' Said asked in return.

'*Merci*, and thee?' Sam asked.

'El humdulillah.'

'God be praised! Fifteen years waiting for a fire,' Sam joked.

Sam put up with the politenesses. He spoke seriously to Said's small son, Mish-mish: little apricot, little black-faced apricot. And then he ordered coca-cola for everybody in sight. When the new sofragi brought them, but short-changed him, Sam (after a lifetime of being cheated) began to argue with the sofragi indignantly as if he had just discovered cheating for the first time in his life.

'Ah, good Lord!' he said. 'He brings me back one small piastre, and I'm supposed to leave him with twenty. What does he think I am?'

The sofragi ran off to correct it and the firemen laughed at Sam's indignation. It was all part of the quicksilver of life, it was fierce and relative. But Sam had never been interested in relativity. For him it was genuine outraged innocence.

'In God's name I made a genuine mistake,' the sofragi begged, returning and handing over the twenty honest piastres.

'Hah!' Sam bellowed in contemptuous disbelief, taking the twenty piastres and then returning five in an overwhelming tip to show the power of his contempt.

They laughed at Sam, it was a relief. They knew him. Especially today,

U* 585

which was tense and depressing with this expectancy of the war, which had not yet touched them but which was now being fought out in their nerves all the time.

The students had arrived in the morning, but only half of them had come back after lunch. These few were walking over the airfield in groups, or sitting in the leather lounge drinking coffee at Barmeel's expense, talking about the only thing they could talk about.

The boy, Fahid, had also come back with them because he knew that Captain Ali Zareef would be showing off the Fieseler. The afternoon might therefore be worth something.

'Gossiping!' Fahid said cynically to Sam and the firemen who were squatting against the wall. 'Like women.'

Sam had never deigned to notice students, except to greet them when they greeted him. He had never fallen in with their banter, he had maintained a disinterested dignity with them. This one, though, was always difficult. Fahid, the son of old Rahman the lawyer, could be friendly and cruel and very dangerous, so Sam tried to ignore him.

'Did you come to see your old friends?' Fahid said deliberately to him.

Sam did not answer.

'They're all at home with their mothers,' Fahid went on. 'They are out there, talking their heads off. Look at them—talking, talking, talking.'

He swept a cynical arm at the students walking over the stubble.

The phone in the control-tower rang and everybody heard it.

They heard the control officer answering it. Then he put his head out of the window and shouted out excitedly to Zareef:

'Ali! There's a yellow alert. Get the planes in.'

Where were Captain Selim and the director, they wanted to know, as they ran to help.

'They're drinking coffee at Almaza,' Fahid said as he began to hurry towards the Fieseler and the other three planes on the field, 'helping the Air Force win the war.'

'Oh, be quiet!' Ali Zareef said to Fahid in anger.

There was sudden haste, but no real belief in anything frightening. A yellow alert was only half-way to being a real one, and they had already had two that morning, which had been false. The telephone in the control-tower rang again, and this time it was Captain Selim calling from Almaza making sure that the planes were in the hangars.

'Why don't you spread them out, around the airfield?' Scott said to Zareef.

'What for?'

'If you put them all in the hangars they'll all be hit.'

They knew that. But who believed, even now, in the yellow alert—this

586

half-way threat which did not quite come, and would probably never come.

Yet it did come.

Hefney the prop-swinger was gathering up the green leather cushions he had washed (almost a dozen—two from each plane) and he and Zareef were carrying them in, piled up to the nose, when they heard anti-aircraft fire clapping at the evening sky in little knots over the desert somewhere. Almost instantaneously the soggy thunder of explosive sucked up the whole body of the little airfield. The power of its upheaval and the thunderous hot air crushed out whatever came within it.

So much came within it.

Zareef came within it, Hefney the prop-swinger came within it, three of the students on the field came within it, the old man weeding the meteorological lawn did, and Bambo the mechanic with the bleeding finger, and some unseen peasants somewhere in the fields beyond, working by the canals, where the last four bombs had gone wild and had sown small volcanoes across the barseem and the maize, the lettuces and the watercress.

Not a man was left standing.

The Shell petrol-wagon was blown to pieces, the hangars and two planes were set on fire, the fire-station was knocked down by the blast and every window in the control-tower was smashed, cutting up every man in it. The lawn was burned to extinction, the flowers ripped out and chucked by the roots against the wall of the director's office, and the door of the accountant's office was lifted off its hinges and thrown over the mud wall into the neighbouring fields.

And Ali Zareef?

He had, in the mental division of a second, seen the string of bombs plucking up the earth on their way to him. The instinct of those like Sam and Scott, who had seen bombs before, was deep enough and quick enough to plunge them flat on the earth at the first sound, the first hot lick; but Ali Zareef and Hefney the prop-swinger had never seen a bomb in their lives, and they were standing close together watching it. They stood there quite still, stupefied, their arms full of green cushions, until they were severed from the earth in a million hot places, a disappearance so complete that it was more horrible than the mess of mangled friends which was left lying there in the dust behind them.

CHAPTER SEVENTY-EIGHT

THERE was terror, but no panic. There were not enough people to cause panic. They lay down as the anti-aircraft cracked lightly at the darkening sky, but they did not even see the planes, which were too high. One more string of bombs cut off the far end of the airfield and went on recklessly across the country into a canal, blowing a thin column of black water into the air, and that was all.

That was all, and nothing could be done about it.

The hangars were already burning, but the fire-engine was crushed under its brick shed, and some of the firemen were trapped in it. Said, the driver, was under it. Two students were wounded in the field, and Bambo the mechanic was lying outside the field, dead on the roadside, his crushed finger still bleeding gently.

'The planes. Get the planes out.'

Why the planes? Why bother with the planes now? But they all ran around the craters and the smoke and fire to one side of the wrecked hangars to start pulling at a Tiger Moth and a Besterman which were still standing among the burning tangled mess.

They might roast alive, but they must get the planes out.

It was a wasteful desperation, a sad defiance in which Sam was the most reckless and the most furious. But the Tiger Moth was all they could reach before the volatile silver paint and the oil-drums in the hangar caught fire and blew up in green flames, shooting out of the holes in the curved roof and the gaping sides, which were a twisted mess.

They watched it burning then and collected themselves in a little group.

'I didn't even see them,' Barmeel was crying to the others, the tears pouring down his cheeks. He had been walking on the field. Would it have made a difference if he could have seen the bombs which had scooped away his two companions so casually?

Fahid Rahman was walking into the nightmare saying helplessly (slapping his hands together with each movement), 'La howlillah! La howlillah!' Each slap of the hand was the Arabic moan, the stunned recognition of a terror which had finally reached him.

It reached them all.

Scott too was pushing frantically on an aeroplane to save it, but he gave up.

'But why did they do it?' Sam was shouting as they retreated from the fire, scorched and torn. 'There was nothing here. Nothing at all. I told them. But I told them.'

That seemed to be irrelevant now.

In the flames, in the searing hot smell of burning oil, dirt and metal, night had fallen gently on chaos.

'Hurry up! What are you waiting for, you fools?'

Glass and great recognizable lumps of aeroplanes and debris were crushed underfoot. Men began to run to and fro now, and the unity of their original shock was lost.

Scott moved irresolutely with the rest of them, as if he had no more right now than simply to join in. But Sam called for his help. With two firemen, Sam was tearing away the crumbled walls which had crashed in on the fire-engine. Said and another firemen were in it somewhere, and they could hear one of them groaning agonizingly:

'What happened?' he was asking like a child. 'What was it? Did the petrol-wagon blow up? What was it?'

Nobody answered him as they worked in the thickening darkness, and Scott lost himself coldly in this flickering torchlight from the hangars. When they had cleared the bricks and reached the inside of the fire-station they could just see Said lying crushed by the shoulder under bricks and steel boxes.

'Lift it up, for God's sake!' Said cried out.

Sam bent down with Scott to lift up a long and solid steel bench filled with tools and vices and heavy equipment, which was blocking the way of the others, who were pulling down the lumps of bricks and hurling them away behind.

'All right, Said. It's me, it's me,' Sam repeated, as if that would comfort him for sure.

Sam had seen worse than this when he had served in the desert with the British Army in the war, but he seemed to panic the nearer the diggers came to Said's dark face, and he became frantic under the tremendous iron burden on his back—that heavy bench—when the others did not hurry to clear the stuff away.

'Crawl through!' he shouted at the firemen working under the bench which he and Scott were still holding on their backs. 'What are you waiting for . . .'

'The other end will collapse,' they shouted back.

589

'Never mind that!' Sam cried angrily. 'Crawl through.'

It was too dark and flickering, and they had to be careful of what was farther along. The whole wall might collapse, and Said moaned in pain.

'Can you hold it up alone if I let go?' Scott said to Sam. 'I can get into the fire-engine and turn the lights on . . .'

'Yes, yes,' Sam said impatiently. 'Go on.'

Scott lowered the iron bench so that it shifted from his shoulders (its entire weight) onto Sam's, and he crawled over the rubble and put his body through one side of the open cockpit of the fire-engine and groped for what would be a light switch, turning on everything until one head-light showed its dirty aura through the dust and the rubble. It showed up a man's feet without boots on, and a small hand.

Said was easier to free now, because the firemen did not have to worry about something unseen collapsing on them. They took him away, un-conscious. Then, by crawling under the fire-engine and making a hole in the rubble in front, and coming up through the little tunnel he had made, Scott reached these other two figures, and he cleared the rubble of bricks away from one of them—a very broken thing which had once been whole and alive. Scott did not have to think about death there, and he went after the other one; and only under his own shadow, through the frenzy and denial of his imagination which had ceased to be reasonable, did he realize, when he came to it, that this one was a child.

'*What can a child be doing here?*' he asked, unbelieving and sickened.

He tore away the bricks and found the small dark head crushed and twisted, the body in its cheap grey *tablier* a lump of irreconcilable parts—so irrelevantly lifeless that it was hardly possible to believe it had ever been alive.

'It's a child!' he shouted back at Sam.

Sam groaned aloud from under the bench and ground his teeth.

'It must be Said's son. It must be Mish-mish!'

Scott remembered Said, the fire-engine driver, often bringing his son to the airport on Fridays, the Moslem school holiday; as Ali Zareef had done sometimes. As they all did. Today was not Friday but there was no school today because of the situation, and the children had been sent home.

But why had this stupid man brought his child here, to this airfield, when he had been warned over the radio by British Headquarters, the British chiefs of staff themselves—perhaps even by the British Prime Minister, that Egyptians must stay away from airfields today?

'*But why bomb our Gedida?*' Said had thought. '*There's nothing there.*'

That was the innocence of Africa in him, and he had suffered the penalty of his innocence, or rather, his son, Mish-mish, had.

Scott could not touch the boy.

'Come and help me,' he shouted to the firemen. 'Crawl under the engine.'

He had never seen a dead child in his life before. There was death of all kinds, but none like this. What could a man of his nature do? Weep? Could he bring all his life to bear on this moment and realize that everything else was irrelevant; that the truth of life lay dead before him, and that he had partaken in its destruction?

He simply could not touch the child with his English hands.

'What have they done!' the fireman cried when he reached Scott. 'Aieee! What did God do today? What in God's name is the meaning of it? In God's name. Misqueen! Misqueen!'

'Be careful,' Scott found himself shouting at them, although it was too late to be careful now. It was too late for anything now.

Darkness had not helped, and when the jeep came back after taking two of the lightly wounded students into Kasr-el-aini, they could do nothing more except watch listlessly while the hangars burned themselves out, and watch nervously for another raid, which did not come. It was not necessary.

'Come on now, Sam,' Scott called. 'We can't do anything more. We'd better go home.'

Sam had worked recklessly with the firemen—black, burned and torn— saving what they could from the edges of the fire, the boxes of tools, the spare wheels, log-books, clothes, rolls of cable, anything at all that could be rescued from the wreck of the hangars.

But it was now ten o'clock at night and there was no point to lingering here, except to satisfy this strange desire to see a tragedy out to the end.

Scott offered a lift to anyone who wanted it, but no one bothered. They would wait for their own white bus to come back. In a moment, standing near Fahid, he said sympathetically to the boy:

'What about you, Fahid? You must have had enough.'

Scott did not remember seeing him at all before now, but he was standing there with a sick, white, perhaps frightened look on his face, and Scott felt sorry for him.

'There's room in the jeep,' Scott told him. 'You ought to go home.'

Fahid looked over at him then and simply said, 'Yabn 'ishsharmuta!'

'But what's that . . .'

If he had heard right it was possibly the most insulting thing a man could say to another in Arabic, and Fahid repeated it calmly.

'Don't say that,' Scott said, blushing in anger despite himself.

Fahid cried out in sudden temper then, and raised his arm and hit Scott across the face as hard as he could.

'Wait!' Scott said, stung and hurt. 'It's no good doing that . . .'

591

'Why not!' Fahid shouted at him. 'Why not, eh? Should I kiss you like a brother . . .'

Fahid's sick face was unpleasant to see and his mouth was slightly opened, which made him look like an animal that was frightened into a defensive terror, preparing to attack.

'No, no!' Scott cried desperately, but the boy was hitting him again until Scott held his thin arm in a tight grip and held him off. Fahid struck out with his other hand, and then suddenly he wrenched himself free and said, 'Where is the pilot now? Where is Captain Ali now?' He was in tears, and he pulled away abruptly so that Scott felt a frightening division of himself for the first time in his life: a man tearing away from him like that.

But Scott was also upset and angry now, and he got into the jeep with Sam and told the Frontier Corps driver to take them home.

'They could have spared this miserable little place,' he said bitterly to Sam, trying to overcome the shame of Fahid's blow which still sickened him.

But Sam said nothing.

They were out on the dirt road in the night running along the railway line, and by looking back they could see the low fire of the hangar burning blue and green in the night.

'Who will tell Ali Zareef's family?' Sam said then, as the pain began to return, as their removal made the realization terrible.

'I don't know, but I don't think we can do it,' Scott warned him. 'Not me, nor you, Sam.'

'But somebody must do it,' Sam said.

'Perhaps they've telephoned already,' Scott suggested, knowing that Sam was weeping quietly to himself—something that was not difficult for Sam normally, but perhaps this time it was real pain.

'Ah, but it's my fault!' Sam burst out as they choked through the dust of the dark village. 'It's all my fault. The English bombed Gedida because I told them about it,' he said. 'I told them. It was me who told Bateman what was there. I told Bateman what was there. There was nothing there! But he kept pestering me to know. How did I know what he meant it for? I will *kill* him when I see him. I swear it.'

'What did you tell Bateman?' Scott asked sharply, not yet understanding it.

'Everything. Even about the fire-engines. He wanted to know everything. Poor Ali Zareef. *Think* of that Englishman! Think of what he asked me to do, and what I did! Think of what he's done . . .'

'But Gedida isn't even a military airfield,' Scott said. 'Bateman knew that.'

'But I told him too much,' Sam bellowed. 'He insisted. How else was I ever to get a passport? They make us into beasts. I begged the English for a passport, and look how they cheated me. What do they all think we are made of? I wouldn't have told Bateman anything. It's not my fault at all. I swear I didn't want to do it.'

'Then be quiet, Sam. Don't talk about it now.'

'Ah, but look what I've done to poor Ali Zareef.'

Sam was sobbing with his guilty heart for his unbelievable crime, and Scott finally knew what he had never wanted to know—what the Egyptians must also never know, because they would justifiably shoot Sam now for that small betrayal.

All the way home, Sam ground his teeth and smashed his great fist down on his knees in despair, but he could not wipe it out. The anguish of it had only just begun—and he was already threatening himself so seriously that Scott stopped the jeep and got into the back seat with him to make sure he did not throw himself out in one of his elaborate moments of grief and guilt. He sat there swaying and moaning and saying:

'If I could kill that man! Why have I done such a thing to Ali Zareef? But everything makes us do it. Why are we hated so much? I can't forgive myself, though. No. No. I can't, before God. How can I? And who will tell Ali's family and his children . . .'

Scott knew he could not console him out of it, and he did not try to.

CHAPTER SEVENTY-NINE

THERE had been astonishing scenes in Parliament—an uproar; and the Speaker had been forced to suspend the sitting for half an hour because Opposition members had refused to keep quiet on a profoundly technical argument on the Government's Suez behaviour. The Speaker had tried to define the motion as a general one, but the Opposition had been shouting out 'No! No!' so often and so recklessly that the Speaker had said angrily:

'If the House will not listen to me, I shall suspend the sitting.'

The front benches were trying to make themselves heard, trying to quieten the bedlam of shifting back-bench anger behind them: Gaitskell was standing up, and the Prime Minister looked nervous and upset by it. But the shouting went on, heedless.

Peacock too found himself shouting with the rest of his colleagues: 'Shut up!', 'Behave!', 'Sit down!'

So the Speaker had suspended the sitting for half an hour. He got up irritably and walked out, while everybody was still feeling stunned that he had actually done it.

Peacock laughed out loud. 'By God, he did it,' he said admiringly but unthinkingly to his neighbour on the bench, who was an old family doctor from somewhere in the Midlands, or was it Cumberland and the border country?

'Resign!' the Opposition were shouting at the Prime Minister as he left; and Peacock again joined his friends to shout across at them angrily: 'Shut up!', 'Get out!'

'Just in time for a spot of tea,' the Doctor said, brushing off his waistcoat as he waited patiently in the midst of these schoolboy cries—this well-known parliamentary uproar.

What had started it, anyway?

Questioning Mr. Anthony Head, the Minister of Defence, on the statement he had read to the House about Egyptian airfields being bombed, Mr. Gaitskell had wanted to know if Britain had actually declared war on

Egypt. If Egypt had already been bombed, then the Opposition were primarily worried about the protection which might, or might not, be afforded captured British troops in Egypt under international law, if no declaration of war had been made. What was the legal position? Would the Egyptians have the right to shoot them out of hand, for instance? This ought to be cleared up.

'Blasted, idiotic hypocrites!' Peacock said furiously as he formed in the bustling, noisy queue to get down the gangways and out. 'What did they have to go on making a fuss about?'

'What's that?' the Doctor, behind him, asked.

'It's getting too silly,' Peacock shouted at the Doctor.

The Doctor never did say much, had never made a speech in ten years in the House, and he smoked scented pipe tobacco in the smoke room as if taking that silly name to be literal. He had once tried to persuade Peacock to attend his youngest daughter's wedding in the House chapel seven or eight months ago, or to attend at least the reception tea on the terrace afterwards. Strawberries and cream were coming back all right. But Peacock had escaped the embarrassing gentility of it with some hurried excuses, and now he was always embarrassed instead by the fellow's presence, and hurried ahead when the noisy blockage had been cleared from the floor. An usher messenger stopped him at the swing doors and gave him a message, which had come direct from the War Office.

'The War Office messenger is waiting, sir,' Hardy the usher told him.

'Just a minute, then,' Peacock replied and tore open the buff envelope and read a handwritten note which said: 'Dear Tim: Can you come over urgently to see me when you get a moment? Don't leave it too long. Yrs. George Astley.'

Peacock took out a pen and scribbled on the back of it: 'Dear Georgie, You'll have to come to me. I can't leave the House. Come to the Strangers' Bar and send in for me. Yours Tim.' He folded it and gave it to the usher and said: 'Find an envelope and stick this down, will you, Hardy, and give it to the Don R. or whoever brought it. And if anybody wants me, I'm down in the hairdresser's shop.'

'Yes, sir.'

Peacock saw another Member, Galsworthy, obviously approaching him through the other excited groups of M.P.s as if to waylay him, so he fled, feeling oddly that he was running away from everybody these days, without knowing why. He really needed the peace and quiet of the barber's shop to ease him off. Why did the House affect him that way lately? It must be Eileen's influence coming back, or that interminable irritation from the other side.

'Tim . . .' someone said.

'I must just go downstairs,' he cried, without caring who it was. 'I'll be back in ten minutes.'

He ran out and then down the cold stone steps and into the warm old-fashioned barber's saloon. It was quite up to date in some ways, mechanically, but he always imagined old Curzon down here weeping quietly to himself when something went wrong upstairs. It *was* Curzon, wasn't it, who had always been in tears? It was Curzon, wasn't it, who had once wept so profusely during a Cabinet meeting that another minister had been forced to say to him firmly: 'Come along, old chap. None of that!'

George Astley found him still in the barber's chair with his scalp being gently massaged, and Peacock said to him: 'Georgie! Since when, old chap, am I supposed to come to you? That was a bit of cheek, wasn't it?'

'Not really,' Astley answered, always (since school days) cheerfully impervious to cheek or the sense of it or the meaning of it. 'I simply thought it would be easier for you to get away. You must know how frantic we are.'

'What do you think it's like here?' Peacock said.

'Oh, bedlam as usual, I suppose,' George said. 'Hurry up, will you, because I haven't much time, and it's rather important.'

'That'll do, Wright,' Peacock told the barber. 'Just brush me up and let me go, will you? And don't put any powder down my neck. It gets all over my coat, and if my wife's in London she wonders where the devil I got it.'

'Yes, sir,' Wright said as they all laughed and smiled and bustled.

'How is Eileen?' George asked.

'Oh, unquenchable,' Peacock said rather sadly as they went upstairs. 'She's been in a lot of hot water with the local hunt; and I can't work out yet who won it. I think someone is going to sue her or expel her—or she's going to beat somebody up. I don't know yet quite what happened. Too confusing.'

'She'll win,' George said. 'Don't worry. Eileen's her old man's daughter.'

George was a robust, handsome Colonel, not particularly a soldier in his present attitude, although that was certainly what he was. He had grown, lately, into one of those fresh-faced upper-class Englishmen, just entering forty, who had never had a day's upset in their lives, and were therefore about to enter middle age with the temperament of a schoolboy: impervious in some ways, always secure, but absolutely without prejudice in anyone else's favour, excepting quite simply and not unpleasantly his own. He was a good chap to all, and Peacock had been his friend for twenty years, since they had been subalterns together.

The difference was that George had stayed in the Army and Peacock could look at him and suppose that Georgie was what he would have

596

become himself if he had stayed in the service and made a life of it. Yes, he was a professional, a simple and likeable chap, really, but with something missing. But there was no guile, and everything was pretty straightforward stuff to George.

'Do you remember Alan Dawnie?' George asked him.

'Very well. I suppose he's still trying to blow somebody off a hill.'

'No, no. He's been with us, and this was partly his idea.'

'What idea?'

'I came over here to persuade you to go and take a look at what's happening, Timmo. Somebody's got to see it, and you're about the only man we can trust in this whole bloody place.'

'Yes, but look at what?'

'Well, Cyprus, anyway. After that, anywhere you like. God knows . . .'

The bells had gone and the half-hour suspension was up by the time they sat down at the table under the mullioned window of the Strangers' Bar.

'What are they gassing about, anyway?' George asked over his whisky.

Peacock held a small glass of sherry in front of him without drinking it. He did not need a drink, he did not even feel like drinking.

'Motion of censure,' he said.

'Yes, but what are they saying?'

'Oh, the Opposition is biting its nails about the Geneva Convention,' Peacock told him, not hurrying now, not anxious to go back into the Chamber. 'They want us to swear on a Bible that we've actually, legally, declared war.'

'What do they think we've done?' George said. 'Called another conference?'

'No, no. They'll go on raving about legalities all day.'

'Good!' said George. 'That'll give me time to tell you what's really happening. That's why I came over. But you'd better be careful, because I'll get a terrible shock from somebody if it ever comes out that I got you into it. You know what happens if we're caught meddling in here. But this time somebody's got to meddle, otherwise we're going to be blamed for all the muck-up, and it looks as if there's going to be a proper muck-up. That's what I wanted to see you about.'

'Never mind about that yet,' Peacock said. 'Just tell me what's happening on the canal. We don't know a thing, as usual.'

'Nothing much is happening yet. That's the trouble. Mostly R.A.F. stuff. Every big airfield in Egypt is being bombed every fifteen minutes, day and night. By now nothing will be able to walk or crawl—not for days.'

Peacock shuddered appreciatively.

'We ought to be landing tomorrow morning or the next day. I don't

597

know. The French are breathing down our necks to get going, and we're doing nothing. We can't hold off much longer, though. That's what's causing this silly chaos.'

'Oh, hell,' Peacock said. 'Why did we have to get mixed up with the French?'

'Don't down the French yet,' George argued. 'They're savages, I know, but we might have gone in days ago, weeks even, if we had kept our part of the bargain. The French are frothing at the mouth, waiting to go. So are we. But you silly beggars are sitting in there talking your heads off while we wait to get on with it. It's going to be a genuine debacle if we delay it much longer, and that's why Alan Dawnie thought one of you ought to go to Cyprus and take a look at things so that whatever happens, somebody can get up in your Parliament and take some of the blame off us . . .'

'But the Minister will do that,' Peacock argued. 'He's not likely to walk out on you.'

'I know he won't. But, listen, Tim. Let's be an open book. No politician ever sticks up for anything but himself or his own mistakes. And, anyway, no Minister will ever be able to tell the half of it. Not now. It's too much of a bloody mess. Don't you realize that we've been working on this with the French for over four months now? No Minister can say that, can he? Ministers have to be innocent, don't they? I'm not blaming them, but what happens to the poor bloody man on the job? He gets the worst of it. Everybody's going to be down on him, unless someone can say it was all very different. And that's what we count on your doing, if you can get away—even to Cyprus, just for a few days.'

'But what's the point of my going to Cyprus? What the devil can I do there?'

'Nothing. But if anybody started putting the can onto us, Tim, you could at least say you've been there and seen otherwise for yourself.'

'My God! It would have to be done in very thick secrecy,' Peacock said then. 'They'd stop me . . .'

'Please yourself how you do it,' George said seriously, 'but if I were you I'd simply get up and go without saying anything to anyone. We'll get you there and back. Only it ought to be tonight. What will happen, in there, if you disappear for a couple of days?'

Peacock shrugged. 'Nothing much, except that someone will notice it. I suppose I could have 'flu, but I have to stay for this sitting, because I'll have to show up at division when the vote is put. I don't want the Whips to start looking for me, and I don't want to pair.'

'When will they vote?'

'Later on tonight.'

'That's all right, then. You can leave afterwards,' George went on

598

blandly. 'There's a transport going every night at about midnight with couriers and stuff. You can get on that.'

'I haven't agreed to go yet, old chap,' Peacock said. 'It's not quite that simple.'

'Why not?'

'I still don't see what I can do. I simply don't know enough about what's happening to take a chance like that. What for, George? They'll cut me up into little pieces if the House . . .'

'But that's it. You ought to understand how it's being done. That's the very point,' George said and walked over to the bar and got himself another whisky and walked back to Peacock who was staring out of the window at the river. 'While all you politicians have been doing the wrangling,' George said, with no little contempt, 'we've had to do all the work. We've been hard at it since Nasser snatched the canal in July, and the French were already fiddling around with the Israelis before that.'

'The Israelis?' Peacock looked around hastily.

'But they're nothing to do with us,' George said quickly, lowering his voice. 'They actually wanted to attack Jordan, but the Minister told them if they did that it would be the worse for them, so the French fixed it for the Israelis to go for Egypt. The French are handling the Jews, though. But we have to handle the French, and it's not so easy, because they're in such a bloody hurry.'

'You mean they're going to get there before us?'

'Not yet. It's not that. But they've been flying over here every week for months with some new scheme or other for blasting the poor bloody Gyppos off the map. But, anyway, we've had the joint plan ready and waiting for a month. The French want to get going on it, so you can see why they're going to be uncontrollable if there's any more delay . . .'

The Member who had tried to waylay Peacock earlier—Galsworthy— had entered the Bar, the only other person in it now besides themselves and the waiters. He seemed to be looking for someone, and in order to avoid him Peacock leaned forward earnestly and said to George:

'Well, go on. What's the rest of it?'

'All right, all right. You need to have seen some of those French schemes to believe them, that's all. But at least they've got the right basic idea, which is to hit very hard and quick.'

'Bloody French, all right,' Peacock said, 'if it works.'

'Who knows?' George said. 'Their first idea was simply to drop their *paras* right down the canal. Talk about Al Capone. You've never seen anything like that collection they've got in their parachutes; staff and all. We had to point out to them that Nasser had 400 planes and about the same number of tanks; and what would happen to their famous *paras* if support became difficult. It's axiomatic, old boy . . .'

'Very,' Peacock said suspiciously.

'We actually had to insist that they abandon that idea. So we got onto a general plan, and persuaded them to consider it an air, land and sea operation from the beginning, with some kind of combined staff.'

'More fool you,' Peacock said. 'Why did you bother them?'

'Because we had to persuade them to take it more seriously. They moaned a bit about all that weight being used, but they agreed finally and then they were sending over more plans, like daily rockets. We almost ran out of code names keeping up with them. We didn't know what was up at first, because only the P.M. and the Minister of Defence and the Palace saw the stuff, but we did know that we were going to supply three-fifths of the force with fifty thousand men, and the French were bringing in two-fifths with thirty thousand . . .'

'Are you telling me classified stuff?'

'Of course I am,' George said, with a down-to-earth whisper in this cool impersonal piety of the Strangers' Bar which, if heard, might have meant George's loss of liberty.

'Then I don't think I want to hear it,' Peacock told him firmly.

'Don't, for God's sake, be like those other bloody fools playing blind-man's buff in there,' George answered. 'Why do you think I came to you? We all agreed to tell you. We need your help. And, anyway, it's not going to be a secret very long, when the French start talking. So I'm just preparing you for our side of it. That's the point. The French are getting mad, and they're bound to spill it out all over the place, sooner or later, just to save their faces . . .'

'What am I supposed to do with it, Georgie, if it's classified information? I can't use it in the House.'

'Not directly, but there are always ways. And why should we be caught with everything down?'

'Who's going to run it, anyway? Us, or the French, or the Israelis?'

'We're running it. Keightly is, with Stockwell doing the land forces. Barjot, the Frenchman, is only there as Deputy and to think up new and crazier ideas. But we've got the entire French and British fleets stuck into it, about 200 ships and God knows how many carrier planes. They're all waiting at Famagusta and Limassol to get going. And all the combined air force is filling up the whole island. It's a fantastic sight. I haven't seen anything like it since Normandy.'

'Well?' Peacock said doubtfully. 'What happens now?'

'I wish I knew,' George said helplessly. 'Nobody seems to know. We're just waiting for the word to move, and it doesn't come. And it's going to be a muck-up, I tell you. I know it, and you ought to help.'

'What a bloody mess,' Peacock said.

'Isn't it?' George agreed.

600

Silence. Townsend the barman was discreet enough not to hover, but lonely enough to make a clatter of glasses on a tray, an almost shattering noise.

'What do you think, Tim?' George asked. 'D'you want to come?'

'I don't know. And, anyway, I ought to go back in and see what's happening. Can you wait?'

'How long?'

'Half an hour.'

'Half an hour?' said the soldier. 'Okay. Go ahead. You trot in and see how it's going. But do make up your mind pretty soon, for God's sake, although I don't see how you can hesitate.'

Peacock became wise. 'Don't be so impatient,' he said, knowing all about George's contempt for hesitation. But Georgie knew nothing about these sound-proof, world-proof walls. The outside world never came in here like that. In here this particular world was complete in itself, and other aspects of life (such as making-up-your-mind) usually changed character completely in here.

'Yes—trot along,' George said encouragingly.

Peacock saw the old smile of contempt on his old friend's face, the soldierly world at work. He *was* trotting along, and he couldn't deny it. But what a wretched phrase.

'Oh, George can't help it,' Peacock said as he went into the gangway and bobbed at the Speaker and found a corner in one of the back benches.

Yet the thought persisted.

Perhaps Georgie Astley was right. So much of this sounded silly now, even allowing for Eileen's influence on it. He tried to listen. He tried to scoop the old cream. Who was talking? He focused his eyes on Chuter Ede opposite. What was that fellow saying? Something about Captain Waterhouse, who had said (from Peacock's own bench) that if the Government had not taken this action in Egypt 'there would have been an absolute certainty of war'. The Opposition had laughed and asked what had they got, anyway, if it wasn't war. They were still worked up about the legal convention, and Chuter Ede was making a joke. He was saying that Captain Waterhouse had obviously imposed *his* will upon his own Front Bench. (Laughter!) Peacock groaned a little. Somebody else was now talking about the United Nations, where no doubt someone was at this moment standing up talking about the United Kingdom. Some little feller on the other side was saying that the Prime Minister ought to resign. Peacock, who had perfect eyes, suddenly felt too short-sighted even to see who it was. What little bastard was it? Then there was Bevan, saying that he had never known feeling in the House to run so high. Feeling was very high indeed, and Peacock felt it boring him, and he filled out Bevan's speech with *Hansard*'s ironical laughter. What did Bevan know about it? What did any of them know about it?

'Nothing!' he decided, and got up to go.

It was already very simple. Better be in the war itself than sitting here sunk by waves of talk about it—of loud Opposition cheers and Ministerial cries of 'Sit down!'

'Tim!'

He emerged from his daydream and looked at Galsworthy who had sought and finally collared him. They went out together, bobbing at the Speaker together, while Galsworthy explained what he wanted.

'There's going to be an end-of-season apéritif for the Yacht Club,' Galsworthy said (speaking, he said, on behalf of the entertainment committee of the House of Commons Yacht Club). 'Just to hold everybody together,' he said. 'Could you lend us your flat for the evening—on the eighteenth?'

'The eighteenth?'

'Yes, but it could be the nineteenth if that suits you better.'

'No, no. The eighteenth is fine. But hold on. Am I supposed to be there?'

'You're a club member,' Galsworthy joked. 'You're entitled to be.'

'Oh, all right,' Peacock said and got away. 'But I might not be there myself.'

He didn't really dislike Galsworthy, but somehow the man always made him feel entombed. There were always men like him who roamed these corridors, making a whole life of it. What for?

'We'll provide the drinks,' Galsworthy said after him.

Peacock nodded and found George talking cheerfully to Townsend the barman and eating a packet of nuts on the bar, ruining his appetite for dinner. 'If I did that, I'd get as fat as butter,' Peacock thought.

'All right, old chap,' he said to George, moving closely away with him. 'I'll come along. What time do you want me, and where?'

'Eleven o'clock at my old office,' George said, and picked up his raincoat and threw it, folded, over one shoulder. 'You could have a word with Dawnie too if you can get there earlier.'

'I'll try,' he said, and when George had gone he went into the common room to ring Eileen so that she would not worry.

But Eileen was still not at home. The maid said she was at her parents' house, so he decided to ring her from the flat later, when she had returned. Then he could find out what had finally happened over that stupid hunt.

'And I wonder what Eileen's old man is saying tonight,' he asked himself with sudden interest, thinking of Field-Marshal Warren, who had also fought his wars over the same ground.

He did not want to go back into the Chamber, so he read the evening papers until the division bell went. Standing Orders allowed him six

602

minutes to be in the Division Lobbies, but he filed past the gate among the first and gave his name with the Ayes, so that the Government won the vote against the motion of censure by 324 to 255. The Government's own amendment, congratulating itself, was carried by one less vote, by 323 to 255 (somebody had rushed out to have dinner); and the substitute motion (approving the Government's actions) was carried by 320 votes to 253 (which meant that six members had now gone to dinner, including Peacock).

When he went outside, however, he could not get through the streets beyond the main gates of the yard, because there were three or four hundred people demonstrating angrily and shouting slogans against the Premier and the Government.

He stopped to watch them. Mounted police were driving into them sideways with their horses, pushing the crowd back, and Peacock shivered at the thought of being bumped by one of those black brutes.

'Look out!' he heard someone shout.

A woman suddenly went down, and a youth tried to drag her free. Some of the bobbies on foot pounced on him, however, and cracked him with their knees in the stomach. Then they threw him clean over the low wall into the yard behind.

'Silly fool!' Peacock said sadly and walked back in, to leave by another exit.

In the House itself, the debate continued among those who were left. Mrs. Braddock complained of the incident which had just taken place outside the House, and she said that every one of the people on the Government side could be branded a murderer of every working-class (i.e. *British* working-class) boy.

Uproar.

The Speaker called for order.

'The word murderer,' he said to Mrs. Braddock, astounded, 'is forbidden in this House.'

(Ministerial cries of 'Withdraw!')

Mrs. Braddock said—moving her huge shoulders in a curious and impatient gesture—'All right. I withdraw the word murderer,' she said, 'and I'll say slayers instead.'

There were shouts of assent from the Opposition, and from the Government benches the parliamentary cries of 'Oh! Oh!'

CHAPTER EIGHTY

HAKIM looked like an energetic and happy man—his thin body seemed almost muscular, and his sharp and hidden and teasing face was different.

'I know why you've come to see me,' Hakim said to Scott.

In his more impatient and warlike confidence, he was walking up and down the barrack-room office crushing underfoot the screwed-up paper of memos or messages or Reuter dispatches which were strewn over the floor.

'But what do you worry about?' he said. 'We don't blame you. What have *you* done? Don't worry.'

'It's nothing like that, Hakim. I don't want . . .'

'You are safe. If you want to leave Egypt, the British Embassy are sending a road convoy to Alexandria tomorrow with eighty diplomatic staff to get on a Greek ship. You can go, my dear. And don't say you're not a diplomatic staff of the British Embassy. Ah, hah! We'll give you that as an honorarium. We'll force them to accept you. That should make you laugh . . .'

'I didn't come for that,' Scott said impatiently. 'I came to ask you to let me do what I can to help.'

'Eh? What?' Hakim said, as if he hadn't heard. He was snatching up a copy of *Le Monde* which the outside duty corporal had put on his desk. He threw up his hands. 'Where did this come from? We are all so civilized, by God. We still have the English and French newspapers from some-where, even up till today. And the English cable services still come direct. Sir Eden says he doesn't want to force us to do anything. Anyway, what can you do?'

'Anything useful. You know better than I do what's wanted. If my own experience is of any value to you, then use it, Hakim.'

Hakim suddenly became the previous, knowable, calculable Hakim: the sly yellow sky in his eyes, and the old game of hide-and-seek around his heart.

'You do want to help?'

'Yes, there must be something I can do. I don't care what it is.'

'Oh, but you must care,' Hakim insisted. 'Would you, for instance, broadcast to those British troops in Cyprus getting ready to invade us? My God, when I think of them . . . Would you tell them what a brutal crime they are about to commit?'

'If you think so.' Scott tried to judge Hakim's meaning, but he was unable to judge anything, even what he was doing.

'You would actually do it?' Hakim interrupted. 'But it would be terrible, if you did that. Wouldn't it? Of course it would.'

Scott was not feeling anything normally. He had not slept that night. He had listened to the R.A.F. pounding Almaza and Cairo West, and the Ismailia road somewhere, all night, all morning. He had been saving Sam from near insanity, and Becky from the fright Sam had brought home. She had never seen him like that—wailing helplessly.

Scott also felt that he had spent the night pulling off his own crown of thorns, something which had never fitted him anyhow, because he had always needed more than intellectual wounds to penetrate and punish him, to hurt him, to justify, or to satisfy his burnt-out conscience. But what was he here for?

'Why can't you see how I feel?' he wanted to say, as he watched Hakim. But who could know how he felt? What had happened to him? It was not even clear to himself, and yet he was sitting here trying to convince Hakim that he had some sort of responsibility for what had happened.

'I'll do anything you think useful,' he said doggedly; but he was disappointed and impatient, suspecting Hakim of an old game of teasing him.

'Good,' Hakim said simply, as if that were enough.

'But you ought to realize,' he warned Hakim, 'that British soldiers won't listen to me. If they read the English newspapers they already consider me a sort of traitor. That's not what I meant . . .'

Hakim was watching him, amused. 'Too degrading, *habibi*?'

'I'll do it if you insist,' Scott repeated deliberately, 'but it's so worthless that I don't see the point to it.'

Would Hakim go on punishing him like that?

'Ahhh . . .' Hakim exhaled, as if he were finally impatient with himself. 'No. I wouldn't ask you to do it. Why would I ask you to do a thing like that? Aren't you an honourable soldier? What do you think I am?' Hakim was serious. 'Go home, *habibi*. Go back to your own country . . .' Hakim sat down at his desk in a businesslike way. 'I shall arrange it all myself.'

Scott became angry then. 'Go home, you say! Go home where, Hakim? Where do you think my home has been? I've lived as long in Egypt as you have. I was nine when I came here. My mother and father died here. You can't tell me to go home like that.'

'I know, I know,' Hakim said. 'But I only want to spare you the

605

embarrassment, the horrible bad luck of fighting your own countrymen.'

'That doesn't matter now,' Scott said.

'Are you so sure? Can you say so?'

'I'm very sure,' Scott insisted. 'Why would I come to see you?'

'You think you will be a soldier for us?'

'Why not? That's the only thing I can be.'

Hakim shrugged. 'What can I tell you to do then, *habibi*? Do you know our situation? No, you don't. We hardly know it ourselves.' Hakim got up again. 'Early this morning,' he said crisply, 'all our new air force was wiped out by the British and French bombers—thousands of them were all over our airfields. We have only managed to get a few Ilyushins away to Luxor, out of range. What chance did our few fighters have against the entire air force of Britain and France? They're pouring bombs on us like rain. And I don't even mention the Jews.' Hakim kicked his way through the mess on the floor. 'But the Jews simply do the boasting while the British and French do the killing.'

'What about the Sinai?' Scott asked.

He had listened to the Israel radio in English and Arabic, and the Israelis had said that they now held all the Sinai. He did not believe it.

But even if it were true, Hakim was not going to be upset. He was still confident, still thriving on the validity of something right—perhaps the validity of war itself, because he became sourly and coldly dispassionate when he unfolded the catastrophe of the Sinai.

'The Jews,' he said, 'are already claiming that they have had a great victory in the Sinai. But they've hardly fired a shot. The French air force did it for them—bombing all our bases and smashing all our defences to nothing. You see how it is? The British destroy our air force. The French destroy our emplacements. Then the Israelis walk in. It was a very good plot—all of them knowing exactly what to do. The French were even bombing us all night, and they even sent a French warship to shell our Rafa fortress to nothing, before we'd even fired a shot. Then the Israelis walk in and claim a great victory. But they haven't got Gaza yet, and the French have been trying to smash it to pieces with ships and planes for two days.'

'What's the use of Gaza now, if it's so exposed?' Scott said, trying to think and act on it as a soldier might. But Hakim needed no argument.

'I know that,' he said. 'All our tanks, our columns of transport, our infantry—almost everything that could manœuvre and fight around it are simply smashed by the French air force whenever they try to move. Even when the Israelis landed parachutists on Mitla, half-way across the Sinai, they couldn't have done it without the French clearing the way and dropping them supplies from Cyprus, without the British destroying our air force. That's their plot. The Israelis even claim to have captured one of our destroyers, the *Ibrahim el awal*. But the Jews never fired a shot at it. Four French warships attacked it and fired on it and holed it and sailed it into Haifa harbour. It wasn't even a destroyer, it was a small dirty frigate and it wasn't even supposed to be at sea. But the Jews are claiming that victory too. Some day we will fight the Jews, oh, my God, yes—we will fight them! and then let us see if they can boast of the result. But let them wait until it's them and us—alone. Who are we fighting now, *habibi*? The entire British and French armies, their fleets and their air forces. Millions of pounds and thousands of guns and planes to invade us. More, they say, more concentrated anyway, than they landed in France against the Germans. Are we supposed to be supermen and fight three aggressors while they all laugh at us for running away? Of course we are running away. You know all about desert fighting, don't you? Would any British general keep his army in the Sinai with three nations attacking him on all sides? We can't get out of the Sinai quickly enough. It's a horrible death-trap for us now, with so much against us. All we can hope to save now are some of the men. Everything else is gone . . .'

'Then it's completely over. The whole Sinai?' Scott asked, astounded to hear it confirmed so calmly from Hakim himself. 'What about the gulf road?'

Hakim shrugged again. 'We had to let it go. We're not stupid. Why fight there when we can be defeated there? Wait until they have to fight us in the Delta, in the muddy fields and water canals. Then the war will begin.' Hakim drew a deep breath for that prospect. 'We will simply be cutting all their throats, one by one, in the middle of the night. And even if it comes down to that sort of a guerrilla war, as it probably will (and Gamal thinks it will), they will never win a victory, none of them. Even if we have to murder them, one by one, we will do it. I swear to you we will do it.'

Hakim was denouncing an enemy—three enemies—but he was looking at Scott as if to shoot every word, every thought, at an available target.

Scott felt it all. Hadn't he always been the target for Hakim's conscience? Yet there was no sign of Hakim's cat-and-mouse game this time. Perhaps Hakim was not taunting him after all. Perhaps he was pitying him.

'You are a strange fellow,' Hakim said to him suddenly as their eyes met calmly and equally. 'Why do you call yourself an Englishman?'

Scott wondered now where this was leading. Perhaps the old jokes could not quite leave Hakim. But whether Englishman or Scotsman, he did not feel like denying even small truths to Hakim. He knew he could never feel morally safe again if he did deny it.

'I'm not trying to deny what I am,' he told Hakim. 'And I can't be anything else but British. But don't hold that over me now. Let me go with Amin Fakhry, wherever he is.'

'Amin Fakhry is probably dead or captured,' Hakim announced. 'He had gone to find Mohamed Ahmed, to help him at the foot of Mitla, when the Jews dropped their parachutists. But the French have been bombing all around them, and we don't know what happened there afterwards.'

Scott knew that he could not feel any more tragedy. Was Amin dead too? He had run out of sorrow, it didn't matter. How could it hurt now?

'But Amin will turn up,' Hakim said, 'if he's alive. Don't worry yet. He went to the Survey office before he left and took all the finished proofs of your charts with him. Amin has probably done something silly. He was too impatient. But he'll walk back if he's still alive.'

The outside corporal had brought in coffee. Until now, Hakim had not hurried over this interview, but he was looking at his watch. He pushed Scott back into his seat when Scott rose to go, insisting that he finish his coffee.

'Wait, *habibi*. I'll be back in a little while,' he said. 'I have something to do first.'

Hakim went out quickly and closed the door behind him, and while Hakim was gone Scott tried to read what the world thought of the British and French attack. There were *Le Monde* and *The Times*—the last copies to reach Egypt. The British Government had not censured itself, anyway. It had won its vote of confidence from the House, and Sir Anthony Eden had called the bombings a police action, nothing more, and said that Britain had no wish to impose a solution on Egypt.

Was there no dissent?

He read the thin aesthetic columns of English. Mr. Nehru said it was naked aggression, but everybody knew that Mr. Nehru was no less an English gentleman than Sir Anthony, in which case words and honour in politics meant nothing. The Americans were angry and *The Times* said that Washington felt tricked, because it had all been done without them knowing about it; they should have at least been told. There would also be a vote tomorrow in the United Nations Assembly, where the Americans had called for an immediate cease-fire . . .

'Politics,' he said bitterly, and put the papers down angrily.

Who could trust any of it?

'Nobody will stop it,' he decided aloud. 'Nobody.'

He tried then to think of some specific task he could suggest to Hakim. He must be able to tell Hakim what he could do. He stood up and stared at the old and useless map which included the Sinai peninsula, trying to force the feeling of war into him. Why was he so reluctant still? Why couldn't he feel like a soldier, when his anger and his conscience demanded that he be one? He had made his decision; yet he could not stir up enthusiasm or hunger for the action.

'Go to the Sinai,' he told himself. 'You can help Amin get in behind their backs. That is probably what Amin will do, if he survives it. If only I could find Amin, I'd be all right.'

That seemed to be the obvious thing to do. Yet he knew where the real enemy was, and he would not be able to avoid it so easily: he would have to face the British and the French sooner or later, although so far the British and the French had done nothing more than bomb, and the only enemy armies inside Egypt were the Israelis in the Sinai.

'Well, *habibi*?'

Hakim had come back a little more impatient, obviously anxious now to end it. He behaved in fact as if he had been talking to someone about his English friend, Captain Scott. Hakim did not look at him, but stared at his cold coffee as he drank it.

'Uhhh!' he said and spat it out into the waste-basket. He wiped his mouth. 'We are waiting for the British land forces to attack today or to-morrow,' he said then. 'Would you wait until we see what happens? We will think about you. But it's difficult now.'

Hakim knew. He knew what his fellow revolutionaries all felt: that one trustworthy man could never make up for an untrustworthy nation. They must first see what these perfidious people were going to do before they allowed one man to act as the conscience for them all. Scott felt his own guilt then, as if he were actually trying to deceive Hakim in asking to help.

He got up to go.

'Ah, I'm sorry, *habibi*. Truly I am.'

Hakim put his arm on Scott's shoulder in a pitying gesture, an apology. There was no more of the old raillery, the torturous game Hakim had played with him for fifteen years. It had disappeared casually in Hakim's condescending grip.

'Never mind,' Hakim said to him gently. 'We are all the same. Yes, we are. Don't feel so badly about Sir Eden. Don't feel so badly that they've done this to us. We expected it, didn't we?'

'That's no consolation to me,' Scott said bitterly, knowing that he had failed. 'Or to you. I told you, Hakim, this is also my home. Who can see people murdered by bombs,' he cried out. 'Even children . . .'

Hakim clicked his tongue in Arabic sympathy. But even in Hakim's sympathy Scott felt how firmly he was now being eased aside.

'Listen, *habibi*,' Hakim said gently, consolingly, 'I have always been your friend. Haven't we been friends for a very long time now? Yet look how it started. When I stood outside the gate of your house fifteen years ago and fired bullets into your body, I believed I was doing the right thing. Yet as soon as I had done it (like Gamal that day) I knew I had done wrong.'

Scott tried to interrupt, but Hakim would not allow it.

'Wait . . .' Hakim said. 'I knew I was wrong—not because I had tried to kill you, but because I had not trusted you. Gamal was right. We must always trust our friends.'

'Then trust me now,' Scott urged.

Hakim went on thoughtfully as if he had not heard him. 'I don't think I was able to trust anyone in those days. It was too dangerous. I trusted only one person in the whole world then, and that was Gamal. I have learned otherwise since, but it is too late to be of any use now. Perhaps I still don't trust anyone; no one, that is, but Gamal. Even now . . .'

'But all that is over,' Scott said, astounded that Hakim should have mentioned, for the first time, the memory of those shots which had cursed their relationship for so many years. Or had those shots formed their relationship?

Scott felt that he was only now beginning to see what it meant. 'I always understood why you fired at me,' he told Hakim. 'I knew then that you would realize eventually that I had tried to help Gamal, and not betray him to the British. There's never been any need to worry about that, not for all these years anyway.'

'I know. I know,' Hakim said quickly, as if he did not want too much of a reminder. But he could not quite leave it alone himself. Perhaps he had suddenly been relieved of his guilt. But by what?

'You are a great nation,' Hakim was saying, holding Scott in a gentle grip as if afraid he would slip out of the door before he could make his last point, 'but your great and powerful nation is made up entirely of assassins. Did you know that? How else did you become great? You realize that they are much worse than I was? Why? Because, *habibi*, they murder without thinking, or without real cause. All your English brothers will pour bombs and burning petrol on us without knowing why they are doing it . . .'

'Duty,' Scott said. 'What else can they do?'

'Duty? Perhaps. But that sort of duty is only a stupid man's excuse for not thinking. They will all do it without thinking, except Sir Eden and Mr. Guy Mollet—both of whom I will gladly kill personally should I ever have the chance, and I will feel right and justified in doing so, because at least there will be reason and justification in what I am doing if I kill them. And a great deal of thought too. In fact, I should have shot that bushman Menzies that day and settled it all. But wouldn't your brothers have been shocked? Yet *he* knows why we are being murdered. So does Sir Eden, Sir Churchill and the generals.'

'Nobody will respect them after this.'

'But I respect them,' Hakim said, 'because they are murdering us for a reason. Do you see my point? I only despise the rest of the English because they do it for what they call their duty, unthinking and like sheep. Or because they imagine we are an inferior and stupid people and deserve

610

no less. Is there any crime so great as that? Should I be condemned, *habibi*, for once trying to kill you, believing that you had betrayed our revolution and our people to our enemies? My only sin was that I made a mistake, in your case. But it is someone else's sin, now, that they are trying to mass murder poor ignorant men with fire and bombs, while they would still condemn the lone assassin who does the work just as well, perhaps better, since only one man dies with one assassin's bullet. But how many will die today? How many men, women and children—with their fusillade of fire on us. You see, *habibi*? You *must* see that I was never a criminal. Only a revolutionary for my country. Who are the criminals? Not the bandits or the black-faced assassins they talk about. It's your English brothers. They wish to rule us. We will not be ruled,' Hakim raised his thin shoulders stoically. 'The few shots we fired at our politicians long ago in support of our side of the argument, the few men we killed to liberate ourselves, are little things, don't you think, when you compare them with what is happening to us now? Don't you agree?'

Scott could only agree, but he knew now that Hakim was also justifying himself. Had it taken Sir Anthony Eden to rid Hakim, finally, of the stigmata of his own conscience—the five shots he had once fired at Scott, the poor attempt at assassination which had failed? Was this English crime to be the overwhelming justification for Hakim's attempt to kill him?

'It's finished and done with long ago. Why talk about it?' was all he could say to Hakim, knowing now what it meant?

Hakim agreed willingly enough. 'That's right,' he said. 'Yes, you are right,' and he gave Scott a playful pat on the shoulder in farewell and released his arm at the same time, so that Scott felt how useless he was to Hakim now.

'But think about what I suggested,' Hakim told him. 'Really, my dear, you should go home. It will only upset you to stay in Egypt now.'

'I'll think about it,' Scott replied. 'But I know how I feel . . .'

'I understand that too, but you should go home,' Hakim insisted again.

In Hakim's last gentle tap on the shoulder there was a great deal of pity, and a final but fleeting dismissal.

611

IT was the second day of the war (before the security police finally came to take him away), and Quartermain did his best not to argue with Jack de Brazio, not to lose a friend in an emotional argument. It was not about Egypt, on which they could agree, but about Hungary—a subject which was so raw now that it was better left alone until the bad temper about it (even Jack's) died down.

But this time it was difficult to avoid, and they both knew they were on the verge of falling out bitterly over it.

They spent the day (like the day before it) on the roof of a block of flats on the edge of the Heliopolis desert, near the Almaza airport, watching the British jets pound Almaza airfield into ruins.

Further away, but visible with field-glasses, other British and French planes made happy toboggan runs with their jets over Camp Huckstep, one after the other. They could feel the crush of the explosions in the air, even here. To the south-west they could also see low-flying planes making runs on Embaba airfield, and on the Cairo radio station to the east, and also somewhere else to the south. What was that?

'There's nothing over there,' Jack said.

'Probably dumps,' Quartermain replied.

Jack had his Greek cameraman; and while the Greek took cinema shots of the Almaza bombings and the anti-aircraft fire with telescopic lenses, Jack spoke a commentary into his portable wire recorder. Jack had given up trying to reach the Sinai fighting, where the Egyptians did not want their debacle recorded, even by Jack. This was a poor substitute, watching bombings; but Ella had stayed in Cairo to report what else was happening there.

'Nothing's happening,' she reported, 'except that Nasser has admitted in a communiqué that all Egyptian forces are out of the Sinai, and that they're waiting in the Delta and the Canal area to confront the French and the British, should they also land.'

Today was Sunday, and it had been quieter on the roof than yesterday

when they had watched thirty British air attacks in one day, first by Canberras, then big Valiants flying high and thundering unmercifully, and
then French Thunderstreaks. Almaza had disappeared in an eruption of
dust, smoke and high explosives. The French planes, making rocket runs
on Huckstep, had set fire to long rows of tanks and transports which were
naïvely assembled there, because Nasser had not believed that the British
would attack.

'It's his own fault,' Quartermain said when Jack told him about it.
(The American air attaché had told Jack, and some high Egyptian had told
the attaché.) 'What did Nasser think the British were going to do? Beg
him to let them in?'

'Their air force is gone,' Jack said. 'It must be completely out of
existence by now.'

'And there goes their entire parachute transport as well.'

Quartermain pointed to a distant corner of Almaza field, where they
could see the disastrous ruins of a hundred American- and Russian-built
transport planes still burning. A French Thunderstreak was roaring over
even as they spoke, obviously taking photographs. They stood up to watch
this blue-and-black gnat shoot in at ground level and run across the airfield, almost touching it.

'Don't bother!' Jack shouted to his cameraman. 'Let it go.'

There was nothing to interfere with the plane, except a few tracers from
a hidden machine-gun near the water-tower. Not worth bothering about.

'It's all over,' Jack said, then he sat down on one of the washerwomen's benches. 'It's finished. Nobody can win a war these days without
an air force. In fact, it all goes to show you that a small nation like this
one can't win a war at all, unless another big nation moves in to help
them . . .'

'It's not over yet,' Quartermain suggested stoically.

'The rest doesn't matter,' Jack said. 'Bonney, the air liaison expert at the
Embassy, was telling me yesterday that those first British raids at night
were made from five miles up. These big bombers fly at practically the
speed of sound, and nothing can touch them up there unless you have a
most elaborate system of radar stations, central operational control, split-
second control of fighters on the ground and in the air, and ten million
other details the Egyptians aren't even capable of. You can guess what
will happen if they really start bombing this place indiscriminately.'

'It still ends up fighting on the ground,' Quartermain insisted, 'and that
hasn't even started yet.'

'But there's not going to be anything left on the ground to fight with.'

Their roof was bathed in Sunday sunlight. They sat under the dripping
lines where the native servants of the flats below had hung up the washing.
They had brought their lunch, and from time to time Jack had gone down

to the flat of one of the cameraman's Greek friends to ring up Ella to see what else was happening in town.

'Still no British or French landing,' Jack had reported after Sunday lunch.

'Why? Why? Why?'

Why hadn't the British followed up their bombings with a land invasion from the air or the sea?

Jack had brought up the message sheets from a wire service, which a messenger had left for him in the flat below, and they looked for the answer in these. Mr. Dulles, they reported, had called the British and French air-raids 'rash and violent attacks which cannot be considered as other than a grave error'. The American resolution to the General Assembly had asked for a cease-fire and the withdrawal of forces back to the armistice lines—carried by 62 votes to 2.

'Maybe that's why,' Jack said. 'Maybe they're frightened of the UN.'

'If Eden and Mollet have come this far,' Quartermain argued, 'they'll go all the way, whatever the U.N. says. They're . . .'

'Eden,' Jack read on, 'has said that Britain will go ahead with what she is doing. He refuses to stop bombing.'

'Look out!' Quartermain shouted from the wall. 'Here comes a new one.'

'Stefano!' Jack shouted to his cameraman who was perched on the highest point they could find on the roof, a high cement peak over a lift well. 'Start shooting. This one looks as if it's going to drop something.'

It was a smaller plane than the Canberras, and though it had R.A.F. markings they had not seen it before. As it dived low and comfortably over the field it released two banks of gaily painted rockets into an airport building they could not see. As the rockets left its wings, the plane itself seemed almost to stop in mid-air for a moment in recoil, but the jet of flame from each rocket streaked on down under the plane to earth. It was only a second before the explosions lifted an entire corrugated-iron hangar and flung it through the air like paper in the wind.

'God almighty, this is going to be too much,' Jack complained. 'They must be doing it now for practice. Why do they go on shooting this place up?'

Another plane of the same kind followed it in, and a similar burst blew more fragments of Almaza into the air. The plane's wavering, streaking wings went low over their heads, burning the air above them—so close that they could see the pilot's pleasant face, in its massive space-man's casquette.

'You're having a bloody good time, aren't you!' Quartermain shouted at him as he went over.

'You can't blame him,' Jack said.

614

'Can't I?' Quartermain replied. 'He won't look so pleased with himself if the Russians send a few planes and pilots down here as volunteers. Then he'll meet his equals, and what are we supposed to feel then? Pity? Patriotism? Anger . . .'

'The Russians' was not a good reminder between them.

Jack had been reading other Agency messages which said that the Russians had bombed Budapest or were bringing up tanks.

'The Russians are being as reckless there as the British and the French are here,' Jack said, unable to suppress his feelings of indignation any longer. 'If the Hungarians don't want the Russians, then that makes it a legitimate revolution, no matter what you say.'

They had been eating their favourite snack of ham sandwiches and beer under the clothes-line. Quartermain had already denounced the uprising in Hungary as one of the evil monstrosities thought up by Allen Dulles and the billion dollars which the American Congress had voted for encouraging revolts in Eastern Europe. Was that a legitimate revolution?

'When Hungarian university students, such as they are,' Quartermain said now, 'go running down the streets looking for what the world supposedly owes them, it's no revolution, Jack. Students, as Somerset Maugham says, are the scum of the earth. They always clamp onto the backs of their own society looking for special favours. I don't care what country they're in. They haven't the sense, the experience or the humanity to know how ignorant and dangerous and unworthy they are.'

'Prejudice,' Jack cried. 'You're out of this world. How can you be as blind as that . . .'

They could not solve it that way, and they broke away again to watch another bombing run on Gedida this time, far away over Ali Zareef's grave.

Were they newspapermen? Were they simply professional onlookers arguing dispassionately over an unavoidable tragedy in order to discover the truth?

Jack would worry about that, and he would come back to it and marshal his facts. Look at Imre Nagy, a communist, and Anna Kethly a socialist.

'Even the workers themselves are against the Russians, it's a fact,' he said.

'You'll never understand facts like that,' Quartermain retaliated sharply. 'You don't know anything about workers. You don't even know anything about class. The only American who ever knew anything about class was Jack London, and look how you killed him off.'

'Who killed him off?'

'What American reads *The Iron Heel* any more? Nobody. You read George Orwell, and anything he writes is just a vomit of Jack London.

You think that's what the other side is like? If you had any brains you'd see that *1984* is what the Americans will be like, not the Russians.'

'What's Orwell got to do with it? How did you get onto him? Why do you always find an old hat like him to kick around?'

'I've forgotten,' Quartermain admitted, trying to change the subject, knowing it was going to ruin them if they kept it up. 'I've forgotten the point . . .'

'You only make one point,' Jack said heatedly. He had lost his sense of humour now.

'And you never think . . .'

Their understanding was so different—that was what he meant. Their facts were different and their condemnations were diametrically opposed; so they could not argue calmly, and it was becoming increasingly difficult even to agree on disagreeing, and this time they were only saved by a telephone call from Ella. Somebody had called up to them for Jack.

'Come on home,' Ella told Jack on the phone. 'It's getting too dark now, and Nasser has been driving around the streets all afternoon in an open car, just to show Cairo he's not worried.'

'That's going to do him a lot of good after what we've seen out here,' Jack bellowed into the phone. 'Nasser is finished . . .'

They left the flats and drove through the cool blue city darkness into Cairo, but when they reached the station square which was simply a pool of night before them, a new raid was signalled. They were forced by police to leave the car, and while they hid in a doorway, in lieu of a shelter, they saw a snowstorm of leaflets coming gently to earth, while Egyptian Bofors made big red holes in the night sky over them.

Jack ran out into the roadway and picked up one of the leaflets, and he found a torch in the car so that they could read it, smothering the light in the doorway shelter. It was written in English and Arabic, in the name (it said) of 'the Allies'.

'Remember,' Jack read from the leaflet, 'that we have the might to obtain our objective, and we shall use it if necessary . . .'

'Let's get back in the car and go home,' Quartermain suggested.

'Shut up a bit,' Jack said and read on. 'Either accept the allies' proposals now, or accept the consequences of Nasser's policy, which will bring heavy retribution not only to the few who are guilty but also to you —the many who are innocent.'

'Very delicately proposed,' Quartermain said.

'What else can they say?' Jack argued, belligerent beyond reason now. 'That's what they mean, isn't it?'

'Let's go home. I'm hungry,' Quartermain said again.

'They're all going to make sure the innocent suffer for the guilty,' Jack said bitterly. 'That seems to be the point of this silly bloody war.'

'Has there ever been a war,' Quartermain asked wearily, 'when the innocent did not suffer for the guilty? What do you think wars are for?'

'I don't know any more,' Jack said in his angry mood. 'I've reached the point where I don't know . . .'

'Then all you've got to decide,' Quartermain told him, tempted dangerously out of his pacifism, 'is which side is right and which is wrong.'

'I'll leave that to you and your crazy ideas,' Jack snarled. 'But I do know this—you're just as cynical as they are.' He stuffed the British leaflet in a pocket as they got into the car. The raid was over. 'How can you be against this sort of thing here, yet all for what's happening in Budapest? Ah, Quarts, come on! Don't be so rigid. Be honest! It's all one and the same thing, it's brutal, and if you say otherwise you're being so bloody hypocritical that you ought to be ashamed of yourself.'

Jack had lost his sense of humour again, and Jack was also being personal, and Quartermain flushed under the attack and began to reply.

'If I'm hypocritical you're being stupid . . .' But he knew already that if he continued this angry sentence it would end in a personal exchange of insults which had nothing to do with who was right or wrong. A friendship was at stake for a word now, rather than for the need to be right.

'I'm being what?' Jack shouted belligerently.

'It can wait,' Quartermain told him. 'I just want to survive this ride home. If you must drive like this, for God's sake watch out. We'll be the first casualties.'

Quartermain kept quiet after that, and Jack drove through the blackout in a terrifying race down the dark streets of Bulac, where they almost hit a stationary tram. To avoid it they had to mount an island tram stop. The front wheels cracked hard onto the kerb, nearly throwing them out, and Jack had to lurch the car around onto the wrong side of the road, then bring it back again over the tram-lines. Another car without lights barely missed them, coming from the other direction.

At the end of this little adventure, Jack sighed in relief.

'It's a bloody cynical world,' he said sadly, and began to relax then because he too had seen all the dangers.

But Quartermain wondered now if his stomach could take much more of this punishment, and he hung on silently until they were outside his home. There they parted friends, agreeing very silently to disagree, which was better perhaps than throwing away their friendship.

But perhaps they knew it would never be quite the same again.

It had begun as a bad day, and it had to end as a bad day.

The dinner at home was a sad dinner of cold veal because Ali, the cook and servant, had disappeared, and it looked as if his feelings for the British had got the better of him.

Nona had gone down the back stairs to ask about him from the neighbour's cook, who swore that Ali had not taken away his clothes from his servant's room upstairs, and that probably he was worried about one of his sons who was a conscript soldier. Ali might have gone to the barracks to see if he could find out if there was news of him in the Sinai.

'He should have let me know,' Nona had complained.

'If he felt so worried about his son,' Helen pointed out, 'he wasn't going to think about you, darling.'

'Perhaps I'm worried about him too,' Nona said indignantly.

So she was, and Quartermain knew what she meant. He knew what her feudal arrangements with servants were like. Nona had one clear rule: she was sure that they were servants, and they must be sure that she was their mistress. She made it a simple relationship, which meant that she had to obey the rules as much as they did, and within the rules this permitted a leeway of generosity on both sides. There was a certain unequal equality about it and there could be no abuse. Not like the Cairo English, for instance, who (out of their own instinct for being lackeys themselves, she said) had always abused the relationship continuously and horribly to the cost of the servant. They were not really fitted to have servants.

'He'll be back,' Hanna said, because Hanna also knew another part of Ali well. 'Where would the poor wretch get a job now, with all these troubles?' Hanna said. 'It's difficult enough as it is, with the foreigners gone. And now there's a war. Where could he go? He'll stay with you as long as you pay him,' she said.

'Hanna's right,' Quartermain told her. 'He'll be back, so don't fuss.'

'I'm not fussing,' Nona said. 'If he's gone, he's gone. Whatever the reasons, I can't blame him if he did abandon us, that's all.'

They did expect him back. The front door and the back door of the flat had the same bell, and when it rang they thought it was Ali returning. Nona left the table and went to open it for Ali because no visitor was likely to be at large on these blackout nights, with this fear and expectancy in the streets. The British might bomb the city itself any minute. Hadn't they been flying overhead all evening dropping threatening pamphlets, while the guns burst the night open?

Yet it was the front door, and it was a visitor.

'Who was it?' they asked.

'Shhh!' she said coming back to the dining-table. 'I don't know. He's waiting in the outside room. He's an Egyptian. It's for you,' she told her husband.

618

Quartermain left his custard and went into the living-room. It was Rushdi the communist dye expert.

'Good night, Mr. Quartermain,' he said. 'I was afraid you might have already left.'

'Left?'

'Left Egypt,' Rushdi said.

'What makes you think that? Do you think I can leave?'

'I don't know,' Rushdi replied and asked if he might talk to him confidentially. Quartermain said 'Why not?' and took him into the salon he had been using as a work-room, while Rushdi apologized for his unannounced arrival.

'Never mind,' Quartermain said, taking Rushdi's coat. 'Sit down.'

'We have sad news,' Rushdi told him, putting his plump but firm body so deep into the chintz armchair that his feet jumped off the ground. 'The police have arrested many of our friends, including Sophie Mourad. Do you remember her?'

'Very well,' Quartermain said, and though he felt a surge of dismay, he also felt all that rush of pleasure he had experienced in the attraction to her youth—her chestnut hair, chestnut eyes and all that innocence and hope. He did not try to tell himself it was sentimental. 'When was this?'

'Only this morning.'

'For being a communist?'

'They don't say, but that must be the reason,' Rushdi said unhappily.

Quartermain nodded. 'That'll be the reason all right. But why do they do it now? Aren't you all for Nasser against the British?'

'We have made a statement. Our friends in gaol have made a statement supporting Gamal Abd el Nasser against the foreign attack. But that doesn't make any difference to the Security Police.'

Mr. Pickwick told him how much worse the police had become lately. They were, in fact, more vigorous about hunting communists than they were about anybody else, and all together over fifty people had been arrested in a month.

'Gamal Abd el Nasser is not behaving correctly,' Rushdi said simply.

'On the contrary,' Quartermain told Rushdi. 'It seems to me he's anticipating his future troubles. If he survives this British attack, he'll have to worry more about communism than about the British. Don't you realize that the British are making one communist an hour in the Middle East, since they started bombing Egypt?'

They argued about Nasser's incorrect behaviour, but Quartermain wanted to ask him about Sophie Mourad, who was so young and so unprepared for the trouble she was now in. Would Sophie talk about her friends, including himself?

619

'I came to ask you again if you would take the money for us when you leave,' Rushdi said. 'It's even more important now.'

'I can appreciate that,' Quartermain said. 'But do you think the Egyptians are going to let me leave? It's a wonder they haven't picked me up already,' he said.

'But surely they will expel you.'

'They might,' Quartermain agreed, 'but how could I help you then?'

'Take the money now,' Rushdi said.

'And if I am interned instead?'

Rushdi seemed puzzled. 'I don't know,' he said. 'We did think that you would all be sent back to England.'

'And if I am? Don't you think they'll strip me to see what I might be carrying?'

'I'm sorry,' Rushdi said, and added, in a slight but insistent whisper: 'But it's very important to us. No one else can leave Egypt at all now, not even Egyptians.'

'Nor can I.'

Rushdi was disappointed to see Quartermain so helpless.

'Even if I did get your money out, and paid for your engraving camera, how could you get the thing into Egypt?'

'Through the Sudan,' Rushdi said. 'We can arrange to get it in from there.'

'Is there absolutely no other way you can get the money to England?'

'We've tried, but we have lost too much. We think that you would be very clever, and would succeed, and would do what we want done in England. You understand, and we trust you very much.'

'Why?' he asked Rushdi, who looked quite startled by the question.

'Oh, but you know why. You are a friend of working people everywhere.'

'Too many friends of working people everywhere have turned out to be traitors to them.'

'But you are trying to be cynical.'

'I'm trying to be cunning. I don't see why you should trust me.'

'But we do. I know that _you_ would trust me.'

That was very true. Anybody would trust Rushdi at a glance. But Quartermain's old moustache (which he had lately thought of cutting off) was the camouflage for a mouth that registered pain as well as suspicion. Yet it was set against both sometimes. He smiled and said nothing. He looked at Mr. Pickwick's innocent face. How could a man be so completely benign when there must be some sort of a price on his head? Sooner or later he must be caught. Was he really so Pickwickian? A man could become very fascinated in speculating about Rushdi. So far, the world had always managed to find a new kind of face for a conspirator— once the old kind became ridiculous—whether it was sinister or innocent, terrifying or kindly. But whoever portrayed these days the men who devoted their lives, often dangerously, to rescuing their own people? These days it was Dr. Albert Schweitzer who was quite respectably heroic, although he had been rather late saying anything bad about the atomic bomb. But where would Schweitzer be here? An energetic life-giving service to the poor, a hospital, a devoted following, a philosophy for charitably serving the downtrodden; but never, never, never stirring them into a passion of revolt against their misery. Where then was Beethoven or Bolivar or Lenin with the idea that it could be done? Where, for that matter (when you looked at Rushdi), was Gamal Abd el Nasser? Was Rushdi the man who could take Egypt farther than Gamal Abd el Nasser had dreamed of, and glorify a peasant and workers' revolution into a dream for all the other miserables of Asia? Was Rushdi the man?

'You must be in trouble, now that the girl is arrested,' he said to Rushdi. 'She's so young.'

'Sophie will not be frightened,' he insisted. 'She understands.'

'Of course she'll be frightened,' Quartermain told him impatiently. 'How can she help being frightened? Have you ever been in prison yourself? Do you know what it does . . .'

'Not yet,' Rushdi said, lowering his eyes modestly. Quartermain felt then that he had made a stupid remark. Yet reality was reality. Could Rushdi imagine how isolated and terrified that young girl must be now?

'I don't think she will talk about you,' Rushdi consoled.

'I wasn't even thinking of that,' Quartermain said indignantly, but he was. He knew they must all be thinking it, even Rushdi.

'Then you will not do it?' Rushdi said, disappointed in his man.

'I *can't* do it,' Quartermain insisted. 'I can't leave Egypt. I'm an enemy subject, or I will be.'

'I understand. But if it *is* possible . . .'

'If it's ever possible I'll tell you,' Quartermain said.

'We know there are risks . . .'

'So do I,' Quartermain said, and pointed at the door. 'In that room are my children. In that other one are my wife and family, who are Egyptians. Did you know that my sister-in-law had been arrested once already, and that my nephew who is Jewish also . . .'

'Yes, I knew,' Rushdi said.

'Then you know why I must be careful. Don't you think they're watching me very closely—my whole family?'

'Of course . . . they watch us all.'

'Then don't expect too much,' Quartermain told Rushdi and stood up.

'I'm sorry,' Rushdi said, not hiding his disappointment, looking at Quartermain through his spectacles as if he had hoped for better things and must now sadly accept final defeat. He put on his coat and patted its

621

pocket, the innocent bulge of a thousand pounds in English money, and he thanked Quartermain for his hospitality.

But as they were leaving the room Nona entered it with a tray of coffee —the very minimum requirement of Egyptian politeness and good manners, no matter who the unknown visitor was.

Rushdi was instantly apologetic in Arabic to Nona for disturbing her, for being so rude. But Nona insisted so formally that he sat down with his overcoat off and sipped the coffee and spoke of nothing important—the blackout, and how he liked to walk, how he had learned in England how to walk. Then he begged to be excused. The right amount of time had passed, and they let him go.

'What did he want?' Nona asked when the door had closed. 'Who is he?'

'He's a man named Rushdi and he wanted me to take a thousand English pounds out of Egypt illegally to buy some printing equipment with,' he told her.

'He must be mad,' she said indignantly. 'You didn't agree, did you?'

'He doesn't want it for himself,' he corrected slyly. 'He wants it to start a revolution among the peasants.'

'That man?'

'That one.'

'Oh . . .' she said. She understood, but she hardly believed.

'I wouldn't tell Helen or anybody else,' he told her.

'Why should I want to tell Helen a thing like that?'

'You might want to. It's interesting. But for her sake she ought not to know anything about it. You ought to forget it too. I shouldn't have told you.'

'Oh, don't be silly,' she said.

Within an hour the Security police had come to take him away.

It was almost midnight and two special Security police officers and a soldier rang the door-bell. Helen and Hanna had just left, and Nona invited them in boldly to show them that they were hiding nothing. The officers came inside looking embarrassed, telling the soldier to wait outside

'You must come with us, *y'effendim*,' they told Quartermain regretfully.

'What for?'

'It's not for us to say,' they told him.

He tried to ring the Press Department. It was too late and there was no answer. Nona did not attack them, and Quartermain did not argue. They too felt guilty. The hand of doom was always the policeman's, and Quartermain demanded nothing, not even the respect and right which might be his as a newspaperman. He did not believe in that either.

622

'Are you going to let him come back?' Nona asked them.

'Perhaps. But he won't be harmed, *ya sitt*. It's all right.'

'Can he telephone me?'

'I don't know, *ya sitt*,' the young man said with a smile. 'I must simply do as I'm told. Forgive me. Don't worry, *ya sitt*. I swear he will be all right.'

'And what about me?' Nona asked.

'You must stay indoors. I must have both your passports.'

'And my children?' she said.

'They can go out with a nurse,' the officer told her. 'And your cook can buy at the market for you. There will be a soldier at your door.'

Nona did not lose her head, she did not lose her temper. She asked if her husband had to take a bag, and the Security Officer shook his head. What did he know? Nothing. Nona thought he ought to take something to eat, a piece of cold veal from the ice-box, but he said he would only forget it in his pocket.

'You'd better ring Hanna,' he told her. 'Tonight.'

She would have to stay alone in the flat. She could not, under any circumstances, spend the night alone. That was what the mysteries of black washerwomen and their Egyptian tales of night had done to her as a child.

'I'll be all right,' she said firmly. 'I'm not going to worry about that now. But don't let them make you say anything you shouldn't. And tell them you must telephone me. Please, darling. Insist.'

'I'll insist,' he assured her, and tried to be affectionate.

But in parting there was no room for anything except the reserve of fear which one felt for the other, the fear also that something had ended and something else begun.

'If I don't come back,' he told her, 'you'd better ring Jack de Brazio. Jack'll do what he can. He's an American, so he won't be locked up.'

'Why not your friend Captain Scott?'

'He has his own troubles.'

'You always say that.'

'This time, sweetheart,' he said to her, 'I'd sooner be in my own shoes than in Scotty's. He can't even help himself . . .'

'Do you think they're interning you? Is that all it is?'

'I suppose so,' he said quickly but doubtfully. 'If they start bombing Cairo,' he warned her, 'take all the money out of the bank and go down to Luxor. Get the children out of the way, whatever happens. Don't worry about me—I'll be all right.'

Was that really all it was—internment? Or had they heard of Rushdi, or had Sophie Mourad lost her youthful confidence and her naïveté as well?

623

He put on his coat and kissed Nona as gently as he could, determined in that last instant to shave off his moustache which had dragged him down to this sad view of the world. It was only when he was out on the street that he realized that he had not looked at the children. But they were on their own now, and they would have to do without him.

CHAPTER EIGHTY-TWO

FRANÇOISE, who was thirty-three years of age, had not suffered at all during the world war.

What she had experienced in Egypt at that time was the moral pressure upon her teenage of the British soldier looking for companionship and love. She had been terrified of them, of what they might do to her if they touched her, and she was therefore never in danger of casual involvement. Other than this she could not remember a sound of gunfire or a feeling of panic, or even a frightening sensation of war at all.

On this Sunday in Port Said, when the children were at home, the sound of it, at least, came to her. They heard the first bombing of the water-front out by the mole, with the sun still shining, and people still strolling in the streets taking little notice. She felt instantly that something terrible was going to happen to her, and that all her preparations for leaving tomorrow would be useless.

'Close the shutters. Quickly,' she called to André.

So far, in two days of war, there had been no panic. The Jewish army from Israel was on the other side of the canal somewhere, and Egyptian soldiers in retreat had filled the city. But no one was crying out *Down with the Jews*. It was impossible to telephone to Cairo because all lines were reserved for official use only. It was also difficult to get money out of the French banks. The train to Cairo had stopped running because Ismailia had been bombed. But Monsieur Beauvoir had told her of a comfortable truck, run by the Banque de Provençe, which would take her and the children to Cairo on his recommendation. She was ready to leave as planned the next day, on Monday morning, although she did not know, really, that she should go.

'In my opinion, you would be silly to go,' Monsieur Beauvoir had told her.

'But why should I stay here?' she had replied. 'It's terrible. All the rumours . . .'

It meant leaving her flat and everything she owned in it. It meant so much more—to take the children away, this time for ever. Everybody said that Cairo was now more dangerous than Port Said. Cairo would be bombed. Yet she knew that she would never feel safe until she saw again the English face which would secure her against all this terrible trouble.

'Les rumeurs . . .'

Her telephone had poured them out for days—that all French subjects in Cairo had been arrested, that all the Jews in Alexandria had been thrown out on the street, that the British had landed in Suez, that the French had kidnapped Nasser . . .

And Monsieur Beauvoir, whom she had telephoned in his villa in Port Fuad to get his help, had kept saying that she was foolish to go now. The French would arrive any minute. Perhaps that was the reason for all this noise and shooting. She could hear explosions.

'Et alors!' she said nervously, as each one shook the building a little.

'The Egyptians are sinking more ships in the canal,' André said. 'That's all.'

He knew more than she did these days, and the sight of those sunken ships deliberately blocking the canal had driven the sense of disaster very deep. It was bad enough that the office was closed, and it was sad that she must now consider all her life here over, for ever. But to see the canal itself being blocked seemed to make it a calamity for everyone—for the world.

'You, be quiet!' she said to her son, trying to quench his know-allness, because sooner or later it would upset her. There was nothing these days on which André did not answer back, knowing all about it; and though her mind was French with her children, she detested their childish French ways, the mocking certainty of little French answers.

'But it's true,' André said.

'Then it's true!' she shouted angrily. 'So be quiet.'

She had dressed them in their best clothes, in their white woollen socks and white shoes; André in his grey blazer, and Mireille in a white skirt and blue jumper.

'We'll go and see,' she told him.

'See what?' André said. 'There's nothing to see . . .'

His small hands said all, and to refrain from slapping him she allowed herself to feel how glad she would be tomorrow, just to see *l'anglais* waiting for her, and to have someone at last to take a firm hand with André. She knew that she was steadily losing her battle of authority with him.

No amount of military chaos would ever startle Peacock. He had an unflurried attitude about it because he had seen more than most during the war. Yet he did not like to see this tangle of nerves and disagreement under the mountains (they said) of Homer, and there on the wine-soaked sands, Aphrodite's birthplace. Cyprus was not a very reassuring place.

626

In one long day he had met a few old friends in the tents, in the strange little white villas they had built to house the Generals, on the verandahs, in the deckchairs of the messes, and up on the high rugged hill in the white barracks. There were Generals he had known even as schoolboys, all performing like professionals in a situation which seemed so confused with Anglo-French dust that he began to feel confused himself. Operation Hamilcar, Operation Musketeer, Operation Omelette. 'It's all *omelette à la Barjot*,' the English were saying.

George, at the last moment, had come to Cyprus with him. At dawn, wonderfully exhilarating, they went over to see the French base at Tymbou, which George said was the most fantastic thing he had ever seen in his life—this complete parachute base which had arrived in big Nord 250s, which were all over the field looking like horrible beetles. Then they had driven off to Akitori where General Brohon the Frenchman had set up his operational headquarters with the R.A.F. This airfield was also packed with planes, jet bombers and jet fighters and transports, both British and French. Around the perimeters, the tents of the French parachutists were clustered together like hordes of little green goats on the Greek earth.

'We said they could bring in five hundred, and they brought in three thousand troops in two days,' George said, always admiring. 'They want that bloody canal so badly that they don't seem to care about anything else. But we'll have to watch them closely. That's obvious now.'

'What are we supposed to get out of it if the French get the canal?' Peacock asked.

George looked disgusted. 'You ought to be able to tell me that.' He pointed to an operations tent in green and grey canvas and said, 'Don't, for God's sake, wander in there.'

'Why not?'

'Don't even ask why not. The General's been telling the French that if he ever saw an Israeli on Cyprus he'd throw him into the sea personally.'

'And you mean to say there's an Israeli liaison officer sitting in that tent?'

'We can't help it if the French don't keep the General informed. Don't go near it, that's all. The French would probably shoot you up, anyway. They're all so trigger-happy.'

Peacock wondered then if any of them knew what they were doing, or if he understood this kind of war.

All over the island the piled-up queues of jets and monstrous transport planes suggested a new kind of war to him. It was different from his day, and this perpetual thunder of transport planes coming and going (going where? to Israel? to the Sinai?) was the backbone of George's kind of war, and it was noisy and disorderly.

627

'It's changed too much,' he complained to George. 'The Army seems to have become a small part of the Air Force Is it all like this?'

'More or less,' George admitted. 'It's all airborne now.'

Even the uniforms were different. The French looked like wild bulls. They wore patchwork parachute uniforms, high boots, odd-coloured caps which were blue, red, green. They drove green jeeps around the airfield in dusty frenzy and smoked languid cigarettes like heroes with easy killing on their minds. He had only seen a few British parachutists so close, but they too looked the same, although they were not quite so self-conscious as the French, who looked so savage that Peacock wondered where they could have come from.

Before dawn, before he had seen all this, and almost simultaneously with his own arrival from London, the Minister had arrived in another Canberra and Peacock had kept half-hidden, in case the Minister saw him. He didn't want trouble yet, and though George had cleared him with the guards, he was careful about watching their conference. George had said that the French were arguing. The French wanted to go in now with parachutists, even now: do the whole canal with parachutists and never mind the risk and never mind waiting for the sea landings. What was holding up the English? Why did they insist on following up with sea landings which were not necessary?

The Minister was talking to them in the old green waiting-room of the Akitori airfield and Peacock sat alone outside it while George attended his General.

'You might have told me the Minister was coming,' Peacock had complained when they had heard about it on landing.

'I honestly didn't know,' George said. 'The General told me I'd be needed, that's all I knew.'

Occasionally, as Peacock looked out of the window at the brilliantly lit airfield, which was like a bright yellow circus-tent under the searchlights, he could sense the hesitation, somewhere. The reluctance or the fear, finally, to say: 'Let's go!'

He did not like the French, he had to admit, but with George's enthusiasm for the speed and imagination of their military mind, and looking at these frightening characters in their mysterious and ritualistic dress, he longed for something more old-fashioned.

'This side of Cyprus,' he wrote seriously and conscientiously in his small notebook (since he must begin to fulfil the purpose he had come for), 'is one large fantastic camp. Every square inch of military terrain is an awful mess of barbed-wire, equipment, jeeps, guns, and aeroplanes. The roads are packed with vehicles. If the Russians—(everybody here is talking about a Russian build-up in Syria; but a French reconnaissance, to calm British fears on the subject, revealed nothing new on Syrian airfields or in Syrian ports)—if the Russians decided to drop one bomb on these airfields there'd be nothing left of this invasion at all. Why don't the Egyptians try to bomb it? I don't suppose they've got a plane left. At night they go to work in full lights, under arc-lamps; and all day the planes are taking off as if it were a private Anglo-French exercise.

'Yet it's very hard to imagine, here, that any of it is going anywhere, because the invasion hasn't even started yet.'

He got up from the little table he had found in the airport building, and he looked in again. He could see the Minister pointing to a map. He could see the smallest General in the world talking, and he could hear the French elaborating the simplicity of their simple plans. They wanted the canal very badly. George was handing up memoranda.

What were they deciding? Were they worried about American opposition? Russian intervention? It must be political. The French were reckless and didn't seem to care who thought what; but the Minister must be taking it cautiously. Had Israel accepted the cease-fire? 'Almost certainly,' George had said. But what was the use of that without Egypt? Were they now giving Nasser another chance to accept? Was that the delay?

'Nasser'll never accept,' Peacock decided in his own private debate, remembering that face again, knowing it for a certainty.

'Sir!' the sentry with a carbine said to him as he started to walk outside to the airfield.

'Oh! Sorry,' Peacock said and showed the pass George Astley had given him.

'That's all right,' the boy said, handing it back.

'Are you allowed to talk?' Peacock asked him.

'Only if necessary, sir,' the guard said. 'Do you want something?'

'No. No. I was just wondering if I can walk about a bit, outside.'

'I wouldn't walk too far, sir. If one of our chaps doesn't challenge you, one of those Cypriot terrorists might.'

'You mean they're so near?'

'They even cut our wires to Nicosia. They got a Frenchman outside Timbuyu the other day. A civilian.'

'I'd forgotten about that,' he said, realizing that he was in sports jacket and trousers, the uniform he must wear for this war.

He supposed it was this dress which made him feel so lost and out of place here. It had all happened too quickly perhaps, and George had not been able to clarify much. He would never be able to clarify anything, really, because he wasn't the type. Anyway, George had also been surprised by the Minister's visit. As for himself—being more or less a secret guest of George Astley's and the General's seemed to mean keeping out of the way of everybody, or simply tailing behind George like a terrier, trying to be inconspicuous, which was not particularly easy.

629

'All right if I spread out here?' he asked the sentry.

He wanted to lie down on a comfortable-looking baggage trolley. He had not slept enough in the plane, and it was now almost four o'clock in the morning. After spending all day yesterday (was it only yesterday?) in the House, he was beginning to feel it.

'That's all right, sir,' the boy said, as if he had practised that phrase many times.

Peacock hardly heard it. He had put his hands under his head and he had gently fallen asleep.

Amin Fakhry had been shouting into the telephone to make Hakim understand what it was like in Port Said, to show him that it was suicide not to act more forcefully now.

'The British have been broadcasting in Arabic,' he told Hakim. 'They're telling the population to move back from the sea-front as far as Shareh Tewfik. They're actually *telling* us what to expect.'

'I know that,' Hakim said calmly. 'It's no good falling for that.'

'But it's logical,' Amin shouted. 'That's where they *would* land. The beach is good. There aren't any obstacles. It's absolutely certain, *habibi*. Don't you know what's been happening here?'

'Be quiet,' Hakim told him. 'Don't talk like that.'

'Listen, Hakim. The Jews are just across the canal. And all the Governorate here has done is to hand out guns to civilians who don't know how to use them. What's the use of that? Let me at least tell the anti-aircraft command to withdraw the Bofors from the sea-front and set them up farther back in the streets. That will give us some sort of concentrated fire on any landing-craft coming in.'

'Billahi Aleik!' Hakim appealed wearily. 'Will you mind your own business.'

'What's the use of saying that to me here,' Amin shouted back.

Why did Hakim refuse to understand? Obviously the hot lick of war had not reached him at all in Cairo, and he was sitting there simply waiting for something to happen before making his decision. He was thinking like a politician instead of like a soldier, and acting like one. It was the same old argument. It was always going to be the same argument. But now Amin was afraid that Gamal was thinking like that, and Hakim Amer and everyone else. Didn't they realize what was about to happen?

'Listen, Hakim!' he went on as he closed the shutters near him against the bright noise of the street far below. 'You don't know what it's like, I tell you. It isn't a frontier war this time, it's a whole strategic attack. The Jews have pushed up everything. When I arrived near Mitla the French had bombed every gun-hole we had, and we couldn't even get a jeep onto the road. It was hopeless. I didn't even try to join the mortar company

630

which was all that was left. And who thought of sending mortars alone to face parachutists? What was the use of that? Who thought of it? Why didn't they have some kind of support at least? They were being cut to pieces by the Jews with anti-tank guns firing flat at a few hundred metres. It was terrible. I didn't even look. I simply came back to warn you that it's no good. I was going to come back tonight, but when I saw what was happening here I decided I'd better stay here. It will be the same thing here. Let me get some of the guns organized and set up in the streets . . .'

'No! Do as you're told, Amin. You wait there for further orders.'

'There won't be time for further orders.'

'Will you stop that?'

'How can I stop it!' Amin cried desperately.

He seemed to be alone in this clean modern building which ostensibly housed a department of the Ministry of Agriculture, but Hakim had taken it over long ago for the Frontier Department's intelligence against spies and smugglers, for their counter-intelligence on ships and foreign activity in the city. Now it was empty because it was Sunday; intelligence was not working, and down below the ordinary sounds of a Port Said evening were beginning, the sea air was warm and damp, the city was friendly, the people strolled, the Christian church bells tolled.

'We can't defend the city,' Hakim told Amin patiently. 'It would be a death-trap for tanks and guns, for any organized resistance. It's got to be done by the Police chief, Rashid, and the Governor, and by the population itself.'

'But the Canal zone police aren't even equipped for it.'

'You don't understand . . .'

'*You* don't understand,' Amin insisted. 'The waterworks and the sweet-water canal and the bridges are all that matter here. If we could hold them we hold everything the city needs: the water and the road down the canal. And what about Gamil airfield?'

'Only a fool would try to hold on to everything like that. Don't talk about it! Don't interfere with Rashid and his police. He's handing out arms. It's Gamal's own orders. Let the people fight for themselves, any way they can. Do as you're told, Amin!'

They argued the impossible, and Hakim lost his temper.

'You should have stayed to reorganize units on the peninsula, as you were told to . . .' he said, but Amin interrupted heatedly again.

'What units? There were none left to reorganize. There was only chaos all over the peninsula. Why do you think I came back here? I told you what would happen if we ever lost air support. Somebody's to blame for that. No, I won't be quiet. Do what you like. I won't be quiet. If you were here you wouldn't be so calm.'

He could not blame Hakim, who had hung up on him.

But Amin walked out angrily, and he went down to the ground floor by the stairway, afraid to take the lift in case there was a bombardment which might trap him in it. He saluted the frontier guards who guarded the street door and he hurried down to the water-front to see again what could be done to anticipate the landing. But even as he reached it, the air bombardment began.

Port Said was a French city, and it had worn out like a French city—a peeling, tilting greyness hung on the buildings. On the verandah of a hotel overlooking the canal breakwaters and the sea it was Sunday tea-time. French, Greeks, Italians, Egyptians and also those English civilians who had come months ago to evacuate the canal peacefully and officially, were sitting on the verandah taking tea or coffee and cakes, looking out over the Mediterranean by the giant mole, beyond the canal mouth and de Lesseps himself—the statue erected by the French on the western side of the sea wall.

Into this calm Sunday air a British jet suddenly plunged over the town, skimming low over the sea-front and firing a bank of rockets at the two blockhouses at the end of the mole, where there were four anti-aircraft guns emplaced. They disappeared for a moment in the cone of fire and stone-dust and water, and they were out of action before they could reply.

The old kind of Sundays were now over, and the city was suddenly aware of itself, or of a new kind of Sunday afternoon.

Two more planes came in low from the sea whistling unmercifully in their jet vertigos. The first one flew right down the seashore, almost on the sand, and all the Bofors emplaced on the beach followed it with ineffectual fire, while right behind it the second jet let off rockets and machine-guns and bombs at the Bofors' crews, blowing most of them into the sea.

'Now perhaps he'll believe me!' Amin cried out in first thought, in first anger.

Considering the speed of what he had seen, it did not take Amin long to bring his logical military mind to work, and he thought instantly of warning the other Bofors' crews farther down the canal, to tell them to rush up here and do what they could. He turned back and ran along the street by the Tribunal Mixte, to where he had seen a gun a few blocks back.

Even as he ran, even as he found them, he shouted at them to shift the gun nearer the north beach with the truck and ammunition trailers. But the British jets came in from the sea, and they finished off the easy destruction of all the seashore defences, obviously in preparation for their ships which would land the troops on the beach there.

Amin ran back to the water-front and went into the hotel and told the lift-driver to take him to the top. He found a way out to the roof, and he stood there, under the rocketing noise, looking for any sign of an invasion fleet out to sea. There was nothing to be seen excepting this panorama of burning noises, of jets and rockets and bombs, and once more the second Bofors firing from the beach.

The second Bofors' crew had set up their little black gun near their dead companions, and logically they met the same fate. He watched them explode into the air with fine Nile sand and great holes of muddy water flung as high as the buildings.

There were no more anti-aircraft left on the seashore now.

But all over the roof-tops there were policemen and civilians firing hopelessly and wildly at the jets with machine-guns and machine-pistols and rifles.

'That won't do any good,' Amin shouted at a policeman near by, his wholly professional heart rejecting this wild anarchy of un-military resistance. 'Stop it!' he shouted at them.

The policemen took no notice and went on firing.

And now the third Bofors had arrived on the beach. It fired a dozen fast rounds, quick passes at impossible targets—two smaller and faster planes which zoomed crazily down the streets (almost flying at street level with one wing down), and the end was always inevitable. One little dip from the plane, one shallow arrival of boiling gases, and the dozen brown-and-khaki figures were blown up in tunnels of sand which drifted across the road and rained down on Amin, standing on the hotel roof.

It was over. The work was done.

He must find Rashid the Police Chief now. That was his only hope. He ran downstairs again, and as he left the hotel the waiters were already putting back the chairs which had been dragged away or knocked over near the windows; and a few blocks away, in Shareh Tewfik itself, there was no sign of disturbance. There was no concern about the bombing at all. What had been happening on the seashore? People had come out to watch it in a curious sort of safety. On the safe end of the mole they stood around for a little while talking, before going home. There were even children, and he could see the foreigners, the Italians and Greeks, talking together in little groups. All along the streets as he hurried, he passed the civilians whom Rashid had armed. They were usually standing by the black-coated policemen who guarded the banks, the post office, the water-works, the canal company's buildings, and all the various headquarters, of which there were too many.

Far too many in Amin's harsh estimation now.

'Never mind Rashid!' he told himself as he watched these little groups of amateur soldiers clinging together. 'It's the Governor who ought to organize a military defence. What's the use of thinking like Hakim? Somebody has to organize it properly.'

He called a taxi and told the driver to take him to the Governorate. 'Hurry,' he said, 'before that bombing starts again.'

The Cyprus delay was over. The Generals had finished arguing, and the Minister had decided what should be done. Barjot's plan would be accepted. Operation Telescope and Musketeer would be sanctioned. London had already set the time, then cancelled it, but after midnight on Sunday they had changed their political minds again, and Peacock lost another night's sleep watching the 16th Parachute Brigade queueing up to be in position for the Hastings aircraft to take off.

'Stick order,' the officers were shouting. 'Don't fiddle about.'

The floodlit Akitori airfield was a yellow rose in a desert of night, and every man tightened the pack on the back of the man in front of him, and then checked his own harness and smoked, sitting down finally to wait, as soldiers must always wait for orders, for weapons, for time, for delays, and this time for a carefully calculated moment long before dawn. It would be dark when they took off from Cyprus and just dawn when they dropped on Gamil airfield which was flung out to one side of Port Said between the sea and the muddy shores of Lake Manzalah.

'I don't think I'd like your job,' Peacock told the nearest officer, who was dressed like a rag-bag and who was trying to persuade a small transistor radio to work.

'American!' the officer said of the radio, not concerned with Peacock's delicate fears.

'What's it for?'

'I want to hear the B.B.C. broadcasts, so that I'll know what's going on,' he said. He told Peacock that carrying a private wireless set was definitely against regulations, sir, but he thought it was better to be well informed about the war than well regulated. Nobody in the middle of a war ever knew what was going on, wasn't that right, sir?

'Good idea,' Peacock shouted above the roar of the yellow dust set up by one of the Hastings, warming its engines. 'Wish I had one myself.'

It was coming to something when Lieutenants told him what they were doing against regulations. He must look the kindly sort, he decided unhappily. Was that how he looked? He felt so much older than these young men—officers and troops alike—that he had to accept the role, he supposed. After all, he was once removed from them, just once removed; far enough removed to realize that this was their war and not his.

'Anyway, why don't they let you carry it? What's the matter with it?' he asked when the engine roar quietened a little.

'Weight,' the Lieutenant said. 'Six more pounds, when you're dropping from five hundred feet, and the free fall is a little too fast. A few more pounds and it's all added to weight and volume, you see, sir. They say the

French are going to drop along the very narrow strip between Lake Manzalah and the canal itself. I don't think I'd buy that one,' the Lieutenant said. 'A hundred yards wide with water each side, and the air full of flying missiles. If their taxis make a mistake in drift they go into the drink, and believe me, sir, with all the stuff those Frenchmen carry, they're not likely to come up again.'

The boy himself made no impression, only what he said. Was this the new language of the new war? If so, how old-fashioned he felt.

'I'm off,' the boy said. 'Excuse me, Colonel.'

He had also been waiting. Now he was instantly busy, after this polite chat with this unknown Colonel. He went along checking his men, saying:

'Burroughs—don't get drunk with power on that hand-set. Use it for orders given you, not your own brilliant ideas.' ('Laughter,' Peacock noted mentally, and 'Yessirs!') 'And when Phillips looks as if he's hiding from trouble, leave him alone. Don't tease him. He's got to keep his head down so that the rest of you can get his signals. And listen to them, d'you understand?' ('Yessir!' 'Okay, sir!')

Peacock felt better, though, because he was no longer hiding. George had fixed it with a few strokes of the pen and two friends at the back of the Minister's party who knew Tim well and could be trusted to say nothing too soon. They had arranged for Peacock to be called up from reserve, given a temporary commission as a Lieutenant-Colonel and assigned to liaison duty with George and the General. He had already drawn a battledress, cap, pistol and etceteras, which Peacock now wore uncomfortably. He felt a little like a mirage of his younger self, a phantom, and perhaps even a fake. Was he still a soldier, and would he ever understand this sort of war?

In an hour or two he would find out on the beaches of Port Said.

When the planes came over again on Monday morning, Françoise was already up and dressed, ready for Monsieur Beauvoir who would come in his car to take her to the Banque de Provençe.

She had wondered why Beauvoir was being so helpful and so genuinely kind to her. She thought of her old feeling of ridicule—those four years of office routine with Beauvoir, the ridiculous little Frenchman. But all that life was gone now, and perhaps that was why she felt so changed towards him. They had both been uprooted. Poor Beauvoir. What would he do, now that the Egyptians had thrown them all out? He would hate to go back to France. He would never be able to live in France as he did here, on the Port Fuad side of the canal in a lovely villa with three servants. It seemed shameful, though, to remember her contempt for him. He even had to leave his car overnight on this side of the canal because the first ferry from Port Fuad might not be here in time. He would come over on a hired launch, get his car, and then pick them up and take them to the courtyard of the bank.

The baggage was all ready below, in the boabs' room under the staircase. Having tipped the boab more than enough, she felt that it was now simply a matter of going. Only to go! The flat was clean and organized to vacate. She had left it as perfect and as polished as she could, with old sheets over the chairs and carpets rolled up in mothballs. She had six more months on the lease with the Italian landlord, and perhaps she could come back to settle her affairs here when she had settled her other affairs *there* . . . if she could get *there*. But first she must not think of doing anything but reaching Cairo and *l'anglais* and Leo.

'You hear,' André told her as they ate very early breakfast in the clean kitchen for the last time. 'They're bombing again . . .'

It was true. It was not yet seven o'clock. The dawn was roseate outside the windows, and damp. From the sea-front they heard the noise of the explosions which shook the flat again. They were far too close.

'It's the airfield,' André told her. 'Something is happening.'

'Never mind that,' she said sharply. 'Finish your tomatoes . . .'

Mireille became frightened, and asked if Monsieur Beauvoir would come, and if the truck would wait for them. Like her mother she wanted *l'anglais*, and she wanted Monsieur Beauvoir to hurry up.

But Monsieur Beauvoir did not come. Seven o'clock, and he should have been here; but seven came and went. She looked out of her high window and saw the first formation of huge French planes flying low over the canal, right down the canal, curling over the Sherif basin and then throwing something out.

The sky was filled with explosion all around these monstrous-looking green planes, and the children were shouting in excitement above the noise.

'*Les paras*,' André shouted.

It was true. She saw the parachutes suddenly bursting in air like pale green, gold, white and yellow bubbles.

'Oh, my God,' she said. 'We'll be too late now. Where *is* he?'

What did she know of what was happening except that there was a truck waiting in the courtyard of the Banque de Provençe to take her away from all this? She was weeping. Where was Monsieur Beauvoir? Would he never come? André had run out on the other balcony and was shouting in his certain little voice from there:

'*Vers la mer. Les paras anglais* . . . Look at them, mama!'

'Come inside,' she screamed at him suddenly.

She slapped him hard and he began to cry, Mireille also.

The sky outside was so thick with the murder of gunfire that she heard

636

it coming even from the street below and from the gardens behind the Governorate. She closed the shutters and turned the lights on and telephoned Monsieur Beauvoir. 'J'écoute,' his wife had answered. Yes, but he had left. But Madame Beauvoir could hear the firing also, and she was very worried about him. Hadn't he arrived yet? What was happening?

'I don't know,' Françoise told her, never having liked Madame Beauvoir because she was always a *mauvaise langue*, and had always encouraged Roberto to find a wife among the French girls rather than the local girls, even after they had married. 'There are parachutes dropping. André says they are French,' she told Madame Beauvoir.

'Thank God for that,' Madame said. 'If it's only true.'

She did not ask Madame Beauvoir what she ought to do now. She said she would telephone back if Monsieur Beauvoir arrived, and she hung up.

'He'll come,' she said to Mireille, but she did not believe it now.

She waited. She stayed inside with the shutters closed, trying to keep André and Mireille calm, determined to wait. But she could not sit and wait any longer. She told the children to wait and to keep still, and she took the lift downstairs to the street, hoping Monsieur Beauvoir was there. But the street was now filled with frightened people in their pyjamas who were trying to see what was happening. The police and the amateurs of the Liberation Army were rushing about with guns, their eyes in the heavens. The roofs above were filled with firing rifles, and the gardens behind were thundering with cannon.

'Are my children safe here?' she asked a policeman wearing a tin helmet.

'Go inside and stay inside, *ya sitt*,' the policeman told her. 'Everybody is shooting. Everybody . . .'

She went back upstairs, certain that Monsieur Beauvoir would never come now, and certain that she dare not take the children into the streets.

Upstairs, Mireille was talking to Monsieur Beauvoir on the phone. He had gone back home. There was too much firing in the streets. Nobody would take him across the canal.

'Stay indoors! Don't move at all!' he told her in his excited office voice. 'I'll try to get across later. But don't go outside. Our *paras* have arrived. They are dropping on the waterworks now. I saw them with my own eyes. It will be all right, don't worry. The French and the English have come back. Now it will be all right. I told you . . .'

It would be all right, perhaps.

But Françoise knew now that she would never reach Cairo today, perhaps not at all.

Amin Fakhry had been awakened by the first explosions of anti-aircraft from the Gamil airfield. He had slept in the dispensary of the airport's passenger building, because his instinct had told him that he ought to be near the sea-front and the airfield if something happened.

The Governorate had sent him with a squad of Sudanese from the Frontier Camel Corps, and half the night he had kept them at work filling oil-drums with sand and rolling them over the airstrip so that British planes could not land. It was not such proud work for a Colonel, but at least he had soldiers, and he would not wait until Hakim made up his mind what to do with him. This would be the place.

But now the British were here already—the bombers first.

The anti-aircraft must have seen the attack coming because they were already firing when the British planes were making their first bomb runs. 'Out! Out!' he shouted to the Sudanese who were sleeping in the customs' rooms on the benches. 'Hurry.'

By then, bomb after bomb had put a blanket of flying earth over the airfield and even as they ran clear of the airport building and leapt into the perimeter ditch, there were rockets hitting the earth near the control tower. They crouched down in a little ditch which was the only shelter possible in this barren stretch of salty earth. Earth and bricks rained down on them. The customs' shed was on fire, and though the Bofors' batteries were firing at the string of British planes, which were now following each other across the field, it was not going to be the end this time, that was clear. Amin knew now what was happening. A flight of big four-engined planes came low behind the bombers from the sea, and Amin watched fascinated, knowing what they meant as they lost height gently and ran so low across the field that he could see their propellers turning slowly.

The first plane seemed to waver once.

Almost instantly he could see the men jumping out of the open sides, and then pink, green and yellow parachutes began to burst like hundreds of thistle seeds, one after the other, right across the field. They fell so quickly that surely the pendulous black figures on them would be smashed on landing. Only when he saw the first man hit the ground did he remember where he was.

Amin's professional logic was always ready to work, and he did not have to think about what to do. He told the Sudanese to concentrate all their rifle fire at the same single target, and told them which one it should be. Always the nearest. And though he knew the nearest man on the ground was over a thousand yards away, he knew how demoralizing that amount of rifle fire could be. That was all they could hope for.

'There, there, there!' he shouted, indicating the direction.

The rest of the airfield was thundering now with Bofors' fire, and the three-inch mortars of the airfield defence were firing from the weapon pits near the edge of the Manzalah lake, but Amin knew already that defence was not going to be of any use. It was too defenceless to hold out.

He had to think properly now.

'What is my object?'

He went over all the old lessons for section commanders, which was all he was here; and it was always the question and answer of the instruction book that came to him. 'My object is to destroy the enemy.' Very logical. But there were several more questions which led to the final one. 'What course is open to you?' And the easy field-exercise answer: 'Decide your plan and carry it out.'

But he knew that no plan of his would apply here. Withdrawal was the obvious answer. Already the airfield on the far side of the road, which led to Port Said, was in the parachutists' hands, and the only way out now would be by the marshes of Lake Manzalah behind the field across the road. He knew there were two frontier corps anti-smuggling launches at a little quayside at what was called the Tanitic mouth. He had once used them for duck-shooting. Better to go that way than try to go back to the city by the narrow strip near the cemetery, because the English were certain, if they had any sense, to cut the whole strip off.

'It's no good waiting here,' he told the four men nearest him, almost casually, because it must have been obvious to them also. 'The bombing is over.'

'Look . . .'

The faster planes were coming back, and this time they were choosing individual targets—the guns and the mortars in the pits. One after the other, the small English jets flew noisily over the field and fired rockets and heavy cannon at each of the defence positions. Amin could see curly black lines of rocket trails making hairpins in the sky.

'God! It's a terrible thing to be so helpless,' he cried out bitterly. 'It's unjust.'

To watch, to feel the whole field of his professional military education being demonstrated before him. It was not his French method, but the English method. But what was the difference? None. It was all the same. The only thing different was what they said to each other in order to get it done.

'Move out!' he told the Sudanese who were as fascinated as he was and were not showing any signs of panic at all.

'But where to, y'effendim?' They too were surprised. They thought he was ordering them to move forward.

'By the lake. Move out behind the sergeant,' he told them, 'and keep your backsides down, and don't turn your faces upwards.'

He knew why he was getting out. It was for the same reason that he had made Ghurdakha bearable. He could operate anywhere except where confinement or capture seemed certain. He would not survive that. He could see the future here. It was going to be a steady enclosure under

639

heavy fire, and he must escape it and have some feeling of manœuvre, of fighting an open war not a closed one. That was all that mattered. Even the streets of Port Said would be better than this flat, confined, exposed encirclement.

As they ran, low and carefully, one after the other, a new flight of large parachute planes was approaching, and quite clearly they were going to cover this side of the airfield now.

'Run. Never mind crouching now. Run,' he shouted to them.

Sweat saves blood, they were taught.

But Amin knew they would be lucky to escape this time.

Sergeant Roberto Rolland had not been trained long enough as a *para* in the Colonial Regiment to be cold-blooded about this very low jump out of the back door of the Nord, which had carried him over the Ferdan bridge. A little push from the signals Lieutenant behind (who understood) and he had gratefully fallen out a few seconds behind the white canister of medical supplies he had already kicked out ahead of him.

Smoke-bombs had almost blotted out the bridge, but he could see it from time to time. He had once lived in Port Said for five years, but he could not remember the details of the waterworks or of the double bridge over the road and the sweet-water canal, which he was now looking for as he came down, jerking and twisting towards the small strip of salt-fringed sand near the road.

He saw the white canister he had pushed out suddenly burst open in the air as one of the Egyptian shells from the bridge hit it. Looking down on those guns around the bridge and across the canal gave him the feeling of looking down on frying, bursting eggs—yellow and white bursts from each muzzle. But how extraordinary that there should be any firing at all. Was it possible that any Egyptian would stay and do that? It was not a contemptuous thought for Roberto, only a puzzled one. He had been confident in the impossibility of it, and now he was a little afraid for the first time.

'See a hole and drop into it,' they had repeated often enough in their knockabout banter, in their unique *para* bravado. What made a parachutist so different? Was it his close-cropped hair and his rations, his pay? Or was it his certainty that he had no other authority outside the force itself, a little French *para* world of its own?

Roberto was no philosopher. He was like his son—confident in his own judgment, in his own replies, in his own condition. But not so confident in others. He too wore a little of the *fiche-moi* at the heart's edge.

He saw a hole when he hit the ground, knees slightly up and knees together, and he leapt into it even as he tore the harness off, because he could see the burst of what he supposed were mortars cutting up the sand.

For the time being he only thought profanity, profanity, profanity.

A Lieutenant had leapt into his hole and asked him angrily what he was doing.

'Get out and look for the VHF radio,' he told Roberto.

'I've forgotten the colour of the canister,' Roberto said. That was bad.

'Yellow. Go on.'

As Roberto crawled out cautiously, he suddenly realized he was being too cautious for these close-cropped types, so he began to run around, crouching but looking for the radio canister until he heard the Lieutenant shout out to the Englishman who was with them:

'I've found it. On the edge of the lake.'

The three of them lay on the white-frilled strip of this salty, wavy side of the road, and the Lieutenant told him to hold the thing upright while he opened the face and turned the dials and shouted until he got the crackle of some voice from an aeroplane above.

'Do you get all that gunfire on the other side of the canal?' the Lieutenant asked the aeroplane urgently. 'It's doing the damage. There's a tank there and a machine-gun.'

Their jeep and a 106 gun with it, clumped airily under a nest of big parachutes, was swinging down over the canal to make a perfect but useless landing in the water, where it was blown to bits by Egyptian fire. There was another Egyptian tank near the bridge, and the Lieutenant told the Corsairs (the planes from the French aircraft carrier *Lafayette*) to go to work.

'Now get over to the waterworks where you belong,' the Lieutenant told Roberto sharply. 'You're here for Captain Fernand to use. Go on . . .'

Roberto left the beach and loped across the sand to the tower and the villa. It was Captain Fernand who would need him. That was the arrangement he had volunteered for. Why else would he volunteer? He did not puzzle himself too much about it, but he did not doubt that he would see his wife. But what for? To try to make up to her again? To try it? To satisfy the sudden eruption of curiosity about his children, whom Monsieur Beauvoir had described in a letter as *parfaitement gentille, fières, et vraiment français*? To appear, suddenly, and dramatically like that because he had been restricted in Cyprus and could not let them know he was there?

Perhaps he was not sure yet what he wanted, or even expected.

When he had left Port Said and Françoise in 1953, he had become a small functionary in the Army, just as he had once been a small functionary in the Canal Company. In Algiers he had been a clerk of works to the Army engineers who inspected all local work done for the Army under contract; and under Roberto were a dozen local Algerian labourers whom he administered in workshop Arabic, which was near enough to the Arabic he had learned in Egypt. In Port Said he had once been administrative clerk to the engineers in charge of all repair shops in the basin on the Port Fuad side, where the dredgers and launches and pontoons were serviced. In both places he had developed a distilled frame of mind about the work, only regretting that Algiers was not like Egypt, which had been more liberal and more comfortable, and the Canal Company had been freer than the Army. He did not even mind being a soldier. But though he had spent so much of his life outside France, he knew he was not a Colonial at heart. He had never learned to like the *colonistes* anywhere, particularly in Algiers. No matter what they said, they were not even strictly French. In fact, they no longer even called their mother country 'France' but simply referred to her now as *le metropole*.

'Roberto,' his Colonel had said to him one day, 'didn't you work in Port Said for the Suez Canal Company?'

'That's true,' he had replied.

'Then go and see the intelligence officer of the 3rd Parachute Regiment.'

Did he want to go back to Egypt? Would his knowledge of Arabic and the canal and Port Said be of any use? Of course!

Here he was, therefore, in this noisy and dangerous eruption.

'Don't walk about like that,' someone shouted at him now from the garden of the waterworks' villa he was approaching.

He had slowed down to a walk. He had crossed the road. The French *paras* were firing their machine-pistols into clumps of bushes around the lorry park of the waterworks, and he could see the red berets of the other company who were running into the garden of the director's villa firing at everything as they were taught to do—not at men, but at bushes and windows and mounds of nothing where men might be.

He ran into one of the little lanes of the water basins, and he fired a burst from his carbine at the lock gates, behind which, quite possibly, an agile Egyptian might be hiding.

'Give that shed a burst,' someone shouted to him.

But even as he swung around to fire at a lean-to on the water's edge, a parachute officer came out of it with his arms full of landmines, which he threw recklessly into the water, and Roberto recognized the medical officer—who would surely shout to him for assistance if he saw him, so Robert ran on into the villa garden where the Colonel had already established himself inside. Already, in this little pool of calm, his brother *paras* were walking about showing amazement that it was all so French.

'But the lot!' one said. 'Even the magazines. Look. Here's a *Paris Match* only two weeks old.'

Didn't that prove the validity of their presence? Who had built the canal? Who had invented it and engineered it and trained these Egyptians who were now running it? Who, therefore, had a right to return to it?

'Where were you?' Captain Fernand said to Roberto as he went up the stairs of the villa to take a look inside.

'I was helping with the radio.'

'Where is it now?'

'On the other side of the road, near the marsh.'

'Go and tell Lieutenant Moreuil to bring it here,' the Captain said.

Officers always spoke to Roberto as if they were annoyed with him, as if they wanted to penetrate his self-confidence. Was there something impervious in his manner which annoyed them, some unfinished defiance from childhood?

'Be useful. Carry your weight,' Captain Fernand snapped at him as he left.

He would have to go back across the little canal and the open ground. *Ça va*. He was not afraid. But he could hear the sappers shouting to their Major that the little bridge over the canal was cleared. The Egyptian mines had not gone off. There was still plenty of firing from the Egyptian mortars in the thickets behind, however, and snipers also; but he ran back hurriedly, diving into a hole only when the Corsairs made another run on some of the Egyptian positions. He didn't trust anybody, least of all those French navy pilots. He had only seen four Egyptian soldiers near the bridge, all dead, and he had fired at nobody.

'*Merde* on everybody,' he said calmly. 'Thou also,' he said at the planes whining overhead.

Roberto had thus learned enough about war already. *You* don't do much of the killing, something else does. Someone else in an aeroplane or a tank or behind a cannon or dropping mortars down a barrel. In fact, cannons fought the wars; only the men behind them were stupid enough to serve them and be killed.

In the afternoon it was quiet enough to send a jeep down the canal road to see how far it could go, and Captain Fernand called Roberto in from his guard duty on the villa steps to help the Colonel telephone to some local resident of Port Said with authority in the city.

'Telephone?' Roberto said, amazed. 'Is that still working?'

'Never mind that,' Captain Fernand replied impatiently. 'The Colonel wants your suggestions. He must find someone who can talk persuasively to the Egyptian authorities.'

'Why not the Canal Company administrator?'

'Idiot,' the Captain snarled. 'An Egyptian. Don't you know who is important here? A director of a bank . . .'

'The Bank Misr in that case,' Roberto said calmly. 'It's the most important Egyptian bank.'

Sitting in the villa they tried to telephone the Bank Misr, but there was no one there. As if convinced by their failure, they took no more notice of Roberto, but tried one telephone number after another, until they found someone who said he could contact General Moguy, the Egyptian Commander of the district. But it would take time.

They must wait, and Roberto was sent back to the stairs outside. His companion here was a *coloniste* with a dislike for *les metropolitains*, a suspiciously dark-skinned Frenchman whom Roberto suspected of not being quite-so. Was he fractionally Arab or Jew or Spanish?

'What are they doing in there?' he asked Roberto. 'Ringing up Paris? If we don't get moving on the Suez road, the Jews will be there before us from the other side.'

Roberto knew it wasn't the Jews they were worried about, but the British. Captain Fernand was not even bothering to hide it.

'If,' he had said to the Colonel, 'we can collect the surrender of the city from this Egyptian General, we won't have to worry about the English behind us. We can get on with it. Particularly if General Massu cannot move down the other side of the canal as he hoped.'

'Nevertheless,' the Colonel had said, 'the British will have to know. Otherwise they'll be bombing us as we go.'

Roberto witnessed thereafter one of the most complex little scenes in world history—the attempt of the new occupiers of the waterworks to collect the surrender of Port Said from an Egyptian General who had been telephoned across the city, and who arrived in the evening in a limousine. But preceding him by a few hours came a British brigadier, who stepped out of a helicopter in the villa garden in response to a radio message which went first to the British fleet on its way for the morrow's sea landings, and then to Cyprus where the Commander-in-Chief of the operation had given his consent for an attempt to negotiate a cease-fire with the Egyptians.

But the arrival of *les anglais* mucked it up.

The Egyptian General, Abdul Wahid Moguy, said that he had come to arrange a temporary armistice (nothing more) in order to attend his wounded, which included many women and children in the bombed city. The French said that they only wanted a cease-fire, an agreement quite simply not to go on shooting. The British (who had taken all the chairs out of the room so that the Egyptians could not sit down) had come to arrange a complete surrender, unconditionally.

Roberto had heard. They had all heard through the windows. But Roberto spoke and understood English, and when he heard the English and the Egyptians bitterly arguing, he knew that they must hate each other, and he laughed. But then one of the Englishmen warned General Moguy that if the city did not surrender, perhaps ten thousand innocent people would be killed at dawn tomorrow in the naval bombardment which would precede the landings.

'But that will be murder!' one of the Egyptians said in Arabic.

'Your fault and your responsibility,' one of the Englishmen replied in perfect Arabic.

General Moguy left the villa angrily, saying he had no intention of surrendering the city, but he would consult Cairo and he would telephone before midnight. Nobody saluted their departure. The parachute guards had laughed at the weight of their side-arms, at their stiff procession, at their comic Egyptian *esprit d'opéra*.

And Roberto watched them go off into the darkness and he began to wonder if he would see his wife or his children at all.

He was staring into a cabinet of expensive French porcelain. In the annoyingly white perfection of this old sugar-bowl and cup he had seen a little of the pyrrhic character of Françoise, the all-white perfection she demanded of the body, of the furniture, of the food, of the exploratory fingers, of the loving tongue.

'Rolland!' Captain Fernand bellowed. 'Are you there?'

'Yes, my Captain.'

'Find a torchlight,' Captain Fernand told him. 'You're coming with me.'

'Where to?' he asked boldly.

'You will show me the best way to reach Port Fuad. I want to see Colonel Fouchet who is somewhere near the Sporting Club of Port Fuad, with General Massu. Do you know where it is?'

'Certainly. But how do we cross the canal?'

'*I* don't know! That will be your problem when we come to it. We don't want any delay. We don't want to be sitting on Port Fuad when the British warships start their bombardment in the morning.'

What was Françoise now? And the children?

He had perfect confidence that they would be quite safe.

'*Merde* and profanity on the English,' this free-spoken parachute Captain said, as they set out in a jeep to go as far up the road as they dared, towards the city. 'They take their time and they take everything else. We could have been in Suez by now. What are they afraid of? That we'll take the lot, before they even get their arses off the ground. There'll be *merde* all over the city tomorrow, if they go plodding in . . . just plodding in . . .'

When the British naval bombardment began next morning, Françoise was asleep fully dressed and exhausted in the bed she had made up in the children's room. She had Mireille with her, and they awakened together when the far-away sound of explosions reached them. Mireille sat up, and at the same time they felt the air cracking with the first shells.

'It's the bombing again,' Mireille said, 'and it's still dark.'

645

Françoise turned the light on. It was six o'clock in the morning and she told her daughter to go back to sleep, not knowing for a moment what else to do. Perhaps they should go downstairs, if the bombardment got worse. But she felt safer in her own safe surroundings. Better to be here than in the little corridor under the stairs below, where the boabs and the servants slept. But not in the bedroom. It faced north.

'We'd better get up,' she told Mireille. 'We must dress and be ready.'

'What for?'

'I don't know. Just dress,' Françoise said.

André slept on, although the crash of the shells landing near the esplanade was having its effect.

Only yesterday afternoon she had telephoned to some of her friends asking them what they were going to do. Monsieur Beauvoir's telephone had been cut off, but there were other friends, and many more rumours. Her friend Giselle Corbo, who was married to an Italian, had told her that all the French had gone to the Eastern Hotel facing the canal, because there were rumours that the hotel was not going to be bombed, and anyway it was the best. The Italians were going to the Italian consulate, where the Consul had prepared a special shelter. The Greeks were going to the Cathedral, which was sure to be safe. Everybody had somewhere to go. But Françoise knew that though her children were French, and she had a French passport, the 'French' in the Eastern Hotel did not mean her. Nor was she Italian or Greek, or anything else. She was Jewish, and only the Jews and the Arabs had nowhere to go which might imply protection or safety from the bombardment.

But by late last night the rumours over the telephone had also said that there was a cease-fire, and that the war in Port Said at least was over. No more bombs would fall.

She had gone to sleep thankfully on that rumour, although another last rumour from Giselle Corbo had said that all those Europeans who had any sense were fleeing to Port Fuad across the canal, because the Arabs in the native quarter of Port Said had been issued with guns by the Russian consulate.

'*Tu peux t'imaginer!* You have seen them in the streets. When they get loose with their guns they will murder every foreigner in Port Said,' Giselle had said.

But Françoise's logic worked the other way. If the Arabs had guns, they would more likely try to loot the big villas in Port Fuad. And anyway, she couldn't walk the street safely now, to reach the other side. And now would she ever cross the canal? Monsieur Beauvoir had said that the ferry had stopped.

André was still asleep when the shutters of the bedroom were suddenly wrenched open, and a hot shattering explosion was forced into the room.

646

'Maman!'

She saw glass flying into the plaster walls, and without knowing what she was doing she had picked André up and was dragging him out through the bedroom door, where Mireille was standing half-dressed in her fright.

'Viens!' she cried at Mireille. 'But quickly, quickly.'

She pulled Mireille by the arm and slammed the door, and one after the other there were explosions shaking and shuddering outside. The building was rocked under an encirclement of shells, which were fortunately of small calibre, because at the last moment the British had decided in the name of humanity (they said) to shell the city with small warships instead of large ones.

'What shall we do?' Mireille was crying.

'Be quiet,' she told Mireille gently. 'Please, darling . . .'

'Oh . . . it's only to frighten the Egyptians,' André said contemptuously.

Françoise looked at her son for a moment and realized (no matter what the reason) that he was fearless. She felt the sudden lack—the whole lack of a man who might have instilled even more into her son than this blind confidence in himself. But that was clearly the shadow of Roberto gradually emerging in him, and it was not unpleasant now. At the moment it was strangely and profoundly comforting.

'Why don't we go downstairs?' Mireille cried.

'No. Not yet . . .'

Each shell now was wrecking some building near by, they could hear it. She felt the plaster falling from the walls as she told Mireille to finish dressing. She had left all of André's clothes and their shoes and socks in the other room, and when she rushed back to find them, she was suddenly aware of the chaos. Broken glass was strewn all over the floor, cupboards had been blown open, the two big chairs had been knocked over. Her poor furniture. She gathered up their clothes and their shoes, which were full of glass.

The lights were still on, but they began to waver as she ran out. The lights went out after a particularly heavy explosion which brought the windows of the living-room in on them.

'Don't cry, don't cry,' she begged them and grasped them both, holding what she could of their clothes and groping her way to the front door.

They did not cry, but they clung together as each explosion seemed more intense than the last, and when she was outside on the staircase they could see the red-and-white flash of each burst.

'Françoise. Is that you?'

'Yes, yes,' she answered, frightened of the familiar voice. 'Who is it?'

'It's Beauvoir. I came to help you . . .'

Monsieur Beauvoir was on his way up the dark stairs, and she thanked

647

heaven for this small man who had appeared like a god. Beauvoir took Mireille by the hand because he was too small to carry André, and they started to grope their way down the stairs, discussing as they went what they should do.

'We must get out of the area,' he told her.

'But the streets are dangerous.'

'The British are only shelling the first four streets. It's better to go nearer the canal. They will not hurt the canal. They need it.'

But they waited under the staircase while Françoise finished dressing the children. Their feet had been cut by broken glass. Other people from the apartments were running downstairs with children, and some were crying out that there were dead and wounded on the top floor. All the servants sleeping on the roof had been killed, the boab said, but Françoise tried not to hear, and she listened instead to Monsieur Beauvoir explaining in his small boy's excited voice how he had come.

Monsieur Beauvoir had done a very brave thing. Having left his Peugeot car on this side of the canal near the esplanade for their planned Monday morning departure, he feared that it might be wrecked by the bombardment. He had heard the British broadcasts from Cyprus, warning everyone in Port Said that the first four streets would be bombarded. No insurance company in the world would settle for a car destroyed in war. With this in mind, he had found a Canal Company employee (a Greek) who could work a launch, and they had crossed the canal at five o'clock this morning. He had shifted his car near the yard of the Canal Company's building, because now that the French were coming back they would certainly not bomb the Canal building, unless the Egyptians fought for it, which was possible, unfortunately.

'We can't wait any longer,' Monsieur Beauvoir told them, and the shelling had shifted its emphasis to some other part of the town. 'It will soon be too light to cross the canal safely.'

'But the children?'

'They are not safe here,' Beauvoir insisted anxiously. 'We must go.'

When they went outside they saw the bodies of policemen, soldiers, civilians and children strewn along the street in the rubble of masonry from the houses opposite.

'Oh, my God! That the children should see this,' Françoise sobbed, although the darkness of near dawn was sufficient cover to hide the worst of it.

They had a long way to go, but one rumour became true. Once they were a few blocks south from Shareh Fayid there was no sign of damage, although the street lights were out here too. Behind them, however, they could still hear each shell doing its damage. To the west the Governorate and the native quarter were already on fire, and the whole sky was black with smoke which turned purple in the first light of dawn which filtered painfully over the horizon from the Sinai. It was almost light when they reached the commercial basin where Monsieur Beauvoir had left the launch.

'I knew it would be safe here,' Monsieur Beauvoir said, thinking of his car under the shadow of the green domes of the Canal Company's building.

André saw Egyptian soldiers with guns leaning out of the windows at the top of the building and he said: 'They have guns, Monsieur Beauvoir. I told you.'

Beauvoir looked up and cursed these Egyptian soldiers because they would ruin everything if they decided to put up a fight for the building. Everything would be destroyed, including his car.

'Idiots,' he said as he beckoned impatiently to the Greek who was starting the engine of the old black launch. 'It's that stupid Security policeman, Rashid. The Security police are stopping everybody from surrendering. It's a shame.'

The launch came alongside the slimy steps of the basin and Françoise fell heavily as she was about to step into it. She hit the side, and then rolled over into the launch, covering herself with oil and green mud.

'Are you all right?' the Greek asked as he picked her up.

'Oh, yes, yes,' she said, barely able to speak.

But she knew she had hurt herself seriously, even as she felt her body take the fall. She could not groan nor cry out now because the worst was still before them, and as they set out across the canal they could hear planes coming over in the first light and machine-gunning both sides of the canal.

'Go further up,' Beauvoir told the Greek. 'The Egyptians are firing at the planes from the old barracks.'

Monsieur Beauvoir's own fear, which was obvious, seemed to make him even more courageous. But Françoise felt her whole body stiffen in pain, as if her back and all her ribs were broken. Every breath was a torture, but she heard André and Beauvoir prattling together as equals and she knew that her son was more at home with him than he was with her.

But she hardly remembered or saw the end of it.

She could not hide her pain much longer, and as they passed through the dock islands and reached the old chantier landing on the Port Fuad side, they were sprayed with water from bombs which suddenly strung out across the canal and the landing. On the landing itself there were cars and jeeps and guns, and bodies of Egyptian officers flung out of their smashed cars, or in the water. It was only the revulsion and shock of what she was seeing which made her breathing and her grip on Mireille seem possible.

'Don't look! Don't look!' she cried at them.

Y*   649

'It's all right now, it's safe,' Beauvoir was saying to her.

But safety only served to drag out a longing to wail, to give way to pain, a desire to succumb, to give up, to go to the wall, which was always inevitably the fate awaiting her and her people and her children. To cry out . . .

André went on with his silly French chatter.

But Françoise could not move another step, and when she saw another dozen bodies of Egyptian soldiers lying on the roadside—those familiar yet unnoticed figures of her entire lifetime—she sat down on the kerb near them and began to cry.

Nobody knew what was happening, and the rumours along the vibrating grey walls of the invasion ships at sea were as thick as they had been on shore. Weren't rumours the tentacles of war? They said that the French were in Suez already, and that Cairo had surrendered unconditionally; the Americans had sent submarines to intercept the fleet (true, American submarines had been seen); American planes had mucked-up the fleet's radar so that Egyptian planes could come in safely and bomb the ships (American planes had been buzzing the fleet); and the Russians had been seen landing in force all along the Libyan coast.

Peacock himself had heard the B.B.C. broadcast announcing a cease-fire in Port Said, but even as the yawning mouths of the transports were opened up to let the LCT's off, the soldiers heard otherwise. And when Peacock, on the aircraft carrier *Theseus*, stood on the chipped deck watching the noble sight of the seaborne landings, he could hear the early-morning battle of Port Said still being fought.

'Well,' a naval officer said to him, 'if there ever was a cease-fire, the barrage this morning put finish to it.'

'I can't believe we could be that slipshod,' Peacock said.

He had transferred with George Astley and the General to H.M.S. *Theseus* last night, and the General had told him, officially, that he would share the job of liaison with Astley—to make sure that field contact with the French was kept very close at all times; they must keep a particular eye on the French *paras*.

'Otherwise,' the General said grimly, 'they're going to run ahead on their own initiative when we're not looking.'

'I'm glad we didn't get involved in that Gamil airfield business,' George said as they lined up on the deck waiting their turn to take off. They had originally planned to land on Gamil after it was taken, but that was no longer the plan. 'They are still fighting for the barracks, and Jackie Goldbourne says he can't move a man along the eastern end of the field yet.'

They would land instead with the Marine Commandos in one of the helicopters from the *Theseus*. While they argued on the wet iron deck under the eaves of the radar platform they watched the fantastic noisy sight of these whirlybirds coming and going. The *Theseus* had nothing but helicopters aboard. She was packed with them. They watched the helicopters clatter off in pairs to form a long procession, taking ten men at a time.

'Number five group.'

It was time for them to step into the chipped and battered-looking behemoth which flap-flap-flapped in a clumsy way as it took off and barely skimmed the sea.

George held his ears. Peacock stared at his shoes. They were his own, not issue. They were black and they should have been brown.

The helicopter flapped them down like a sitting duck near the police headquarters, almost opposite the Canal Company's building. The door slid open, and George and Peacock leapt out and ran for the cover of the nearest building, ducking under the whirling high blades.

It was horribly deserted.

They waited for their small headquarters escort to follow them, three men with carbines and Sten-guns, and five others who were to join up with their own unit near the customs house.

'Off you go,' George shouted to the five men casually.

The helicopter took off with a twisting lift, and when it had gone there was a merciful silence, or so it seemed until they heard the rattle and clatter of firing all around them.

'Good God! Listen to it.'

'Nobody's taken the town yet,' Peacock said in agreement.

He had known it. In fact, they had been dropped off here to make a rendezvous with Egyptian officers at the Canal Company's office, arranged for 11 o'clock. The French had sworn that the Egyptian Governor of Port Said would be here at that hour to surrender the city. General Stockwell and the French commander, General Beaufre, were also expected. But from the police post above them they were suddenly sprayed with heavy machine-gun fire, and they took to their heels as they saw the navy launch in the canal, with the allied Generals in it, swinging around under fire from the Egyptians in the canal building.

'So much for the rendezvous,' George shouted as they ran.

The naval launch swerved off under fire, and landed the Generals a little higher up the canal near the customs house.

'Now what?' Peacock said. 'The usual muck-up?'

'We ought to head for the Italian consulate. There's no rendezvous here, that's certain. Look at that.'

The entire roof of the company building was alive with rifle and machine-gun fire, the tracers were shooting up the canal, almost bouncing off the muddy water.

651

'Where the bloody hell *is* the Italian consulate?' George said in a panic then. 'I forgot to ask.'

'Near the cathedral, sir,' one of the young Marine escort said efficiently.

'Do you know how to get there, Tim?'

'Good grief, no,' Peacock said. 'I don't know the place that well.'

They settled it on a map which George had taken out of his battledress pocket. They were both armed with carbines and loaded with pouches, and they decided on a course four blocks north and then seven blocks west. As they looked straight down the street they were in, they saw two tanks firing into buildings at the very end.

'Centurions, sir,' the Marine corporal shouted. 'They've landed.'

'They've got them too, Corporal,' George said. 'Let's turn off here.'

They made their way to the west, and Peacock tried to digest what George had already digested so easily in this confusion of order and counter-order, of plan and fantastic counter-plan, of speculation, half-truths, rivalries and muck-ups.

The one real thing about it seemed to be that he was walking the streets of Port Said. It was true. He felt, for one moment only, the morning's glory—the black violence all around them under the smoke and the dust. He felt momentarily liberated, and for the first time in weeks he managed to lift off a little of the gloom which had plagued his thoughts lately, and he felt like a man who was doing what he must do.

But what could they do?

Already they knew that the city had not surrendered, far from it.

'Look at this bloody place,' George complained as they hunched cautiously under the shelter of the buildings while the clearing group of their section went out ahead.

'It'll take weeks to clear the town at this rate.'

'What's the point in going to the Italian consulate?' Peacock asked then. 'What are we waiting around like this for?'

'The Consul is the one arranging the surrender. That's where the others must have gone,' George said.

They were turned back twice by rifle or machine-gun fire and grenades, which their two marines replied to, but George stopped them.

'Keep it for something serious,' he told them. 'Never mind back-chatting with those madmen on the roofs. The carrier planes will be over later to deal with them. Just keep your eye on those close enough to do us damage.'

Peacock knew already that he did not feel worried by this roof-top fire after so many years of not being fired at, but after his brief feeling of youthful emergence he was already beginning to feel the sadness drag him down again. He could not explain it. They passed a sudden little pile of

652

sandbags and rubble, terribly messed up with the broken bodies of Egyptian policemen.

'What a bloody mess,' George was saying with his perfect understanding of chaos. 'The French have finally tripped us up with this plan, and we're going to be stuck with it.'

They had learned in the *Theseus*, before setting out, that the French landing on Port Fuad, on the eastern side of the canal, had been based on a colossal mistake.

General Massu was supposed, this morning, to land his tanks on the Port Fuad workshops and make a dash down the eastern bank of the canal to Suez, his flank on that side protected all the way by the Israelis, who occupied all the Sinai. That was supposed to be the *pièce de résistance* of the landing this morning. But already, yesterday, the French parachutists had discovered that the road down the eastern side of the canal was hopelessly cut and blocked by a recent widening of the main canal, only a few miles out of Port Said. Why hadn't their brilliant Intelligence known about that, Peacock had wanted to know. There would be no sudden French dash to Suez down that side.

'And now the French want to move their AMX's and stuff onto our side,' George had complained after a conference with the General on the *Theseus*, 'but the General won't hear of it. He just told them that they'd have to stew in their own juice. They were not going to start sharing ours.'

'That's why they're so anxious to get this place surrendered now,' Peacock pointed out as they moved on again. 'So they can get on to Suez I suppose.'

'Well, we hold this side,' George said, 'and we're not going to move down the Suez road with this porcupine of a city on our backs, no matter what the crazy French want.'

Port Said was just that, Peacock decided—a porcupine. Even as they walked through it there was a front line. There were tanks knocking down houses on one side of them to the north, and on the other side there was heavy Egyptian fire from every window. They had to run for shelter at some corners, then suddenly there would be a block of perfect peace. But the nearer they came to the Coptic church and the native quarter, the blacker the sky and the heavier the sound of fighting ahead. They could hear the rattle of the Russian-built rocket-platforms, the *Katyushas* which sent banks of rockets off the back of a truck, like coal off a chute.

'Somebody's getting a packet of that,' George said as they stopped to make sure it was not directly ahead.

'What happens,' Peacock asked then, 'if they don't surrender the garrison?'

'There won't be much of this town left, because we'll have to smash it up. But they'll give it up after a while. They haven't the stomach to stick it out for too long.'

'I still don't see how there can be any kind of formal surrender,' Peacock pointed out as they were sniped at again. 'Most of this Egyptian fighting is nothing to do with any organized command. It's anybody with a gun in his hands. Who is going to tell them to give up?'

'Silly bastards,' George said as someone fired at them with a noisy little hand-gun. 'They must believe that rumour about the Russians arriving any minute. What would the Russians do here?'

'Not here. They were talking about putting rockets on London.'

They had heard it themselves that morning; and in Peacock's estimation it was not a rumour. It was much more serious than a rumour.

The B.B.C. had said that the Russians, in a note signed by Bulganin, had asked the English how they would like rockets descending on English cities. Would that be any different from the British attack on Egyptian cities?

'The more I think of it,' Peacock said now as they waited for one of the corporals to go ahead and clear out the sniper who was picking at them from a second-floor window, 'the more it sounds like a potential Russian declaration of war, if we continue here. When the Russians say they cannot remain indifferent, they're not likely to stop there. They're talking war . . .'

'Well, we'll soon know,' George said cheerfully. 'Let's wait here until the squad cleans up that corner. Anyway,' he added, 'the Russians would be out cold themselves, because the Americans have their atom bombs in the air, twenty-four hours a day, ready to drop one.'

But Peacock listened to it with one ear of the soldier, and the other ear of the politician. His political ear now recognized danger, so much so that he had already lost his view of what was happening in this burning, smashed-up city, which hardly seemed important any more. What would happen, in a world sense, if the invasion continued and if the Russians acted as violently as they talked?

Would the Russians actually rocket Britain?

'They usually mean what they say,' Peacock concluded sadly, 'in which case this whole bloody mess ought to stop now.'

But George was too casual a companion for this sort of political thinking. He was shouting orders to the squad to be careful of any civilians . . .

Peacock sat patiently in the doorstep now and began to think of the House again. If only he could hear what was going on in there now, he would know how bad it was. The Opposition would have a good grip on Bulganin's letter by now. Opportunists! They were quite happy for the war to start, providing they didn't have to take responsibility for it. The B.B.C. had already reported that the U.N. had demanded a cease-fire, and

654

had also decided to send a force to the area if necessary. Also, there had been a big demonstration in Trafalgar Square on Sunday with Opposition support, which had practically aspired to the heights of bringing down the Government. Even Canada was now against the landing. In fact, only Australia seemed to be in favour of it, and Peacock was not sure that such a brave ally would be adequate, in what amounted to a third world war with the Russians. And the Russian threat was really the only thing that counted now: that was what would decide it.

He thought then: 'Damn it! Damn and oh, Christ! I'm in the wrong place again. This will all be settled in Westminster—today. For sure. And I'm sitting out here in this rubble. What a bloody fool I am, really.'

Amin Fakhry was now feeling so helpless that he was beginning to suspect the adequacy of being a soldier. What hope did the soldier have in this catastrophe? And if the soldier wasn't adequate for it, then who was?

He had lost his band of Sudanese as they ran for shelter to the bare mouth of the Manzalah lake. They were picked off by a British carrier plane which caught them in the open, and only Amin himself and a tall Sudanese rifleman had escaped the bloody mess. How could the simplicity of soldiering count when you were so overwhelmed like that? Defence was helpless against such odds. As he had laid low during the rest of the day to await nightfall, he had wept with childish tears to see two lonely Egyptian jets suddenly, miraculously, appear over Gamil airfield and make one wild running attack on the British.

He did not shout: 'Oh, my brothers!' as he wanted to through his tears, but instead: 'You're marvellous. Unbelievable. But you haven't a hope. Go home. What hope have you got here? They'll overwhelm you. Save yourselves.'

He had escaped that night over the marshy lake in a fisherman's boat and he had gone around the Manzalah canal into the city in time for its bombardment by British destroyers next morning. The poor packing-box hovels of the Manach, which were built over the swampy edges near the old native district of the town, were set alight before his eyes. He watched the people crush into a panic to get away from the fire and from the occasional and almost casually indifferent shelling.

What hope did the soldier have here?

When the landings started that morning he had been looking for the Governor, the authority who could organize the military resistance in the streets. But the Governorate had been destroyed, so under the pressure of the shelling he tried the hospital and was appalled at the sight of a building packed with dying and dead. It was impossible to move in the corridors or even on the staircases, they were so full of wounded men and women and soldiers and children awaiting attention, just lying on the floors. In

655

the courtyard they were stacking corpses under the arches where it was cool. They could not bury them fast enough.

Where was the soldier adequate here?

When the street fighting began against the British commandos, who had landed on the northern beach, he could see that every building was already an outpost of unorganized resistance. There were hundreds of men with rifles and machine-guns who knew nothing about the weapons they were firing. They were hiding in the windows and on the roof-tops, and he thought: 'How can I run about trying to organize their resistance, when it's much better by its unorganized nature, by its own dispersal and its silly recklessness?'

The soldier was not needed there.

And the soldiers, where they were organized, were simply adaptations to the thing they did—the rocket racks they fired from the Russian trucks, or the Bofors they swung around like toys to make hopeless attempts to catch the low-flying jets.

There was no need for him there.

Where, then, were the real soldiers who plotted over maps and moved sections, squads, battalions and regiments into, or out of, organized action?

He could not find them in the city, because he knew they did not exist.

He only found other officers, lost like himself, organizing a dozen or twenty men at a time to do what they were already doing. It was not going to be a military operation which faced the British here, but a clumsy and inadequate mob who served without orders and fought without discipline.

Yet in all the heroism and sacrifice of it, how helpless it was. How inevitable its isolated end, when the British planes came over one by one and cleared out the roof-top resistance.

'But there must be somebody!' he insisted to a subaltern who had stopped him and asked him where the Headquarters had gone to.

The more he had sought, desperately, for the ruling authority behind the city (there must be at least some government, some decision) the more he doubted the reality of it.

A Security policeman told him that Rashid, the chief of the Security police, and the Governor or General Moguy were in the Eastern Hotel. Amin ran down by the canal sea-front, under British fire all the way, and turned off into the hotel, breathless. He found them arguing. But they were not arguing like soldiers, they were on the telephone to the British and to Cairo, playing a cunning game of keeping the British guessing about their intentions, swearing in the stubborn silences (between these fantastic phone conversations with the enemy) to defend the city to the last.

'Defend!' Amin shouted. 'You aren't defending the city. They are!' he said and pointed out of the window.

656

They did not see his point.

'The Army will defend itself on the Delta and behind the irrigation canals, but they won't get trapped in the desert and in the cities to oblige the Jews and the British,' Hakim had insisted.

It was better this way, Amin admitted: house by house, man by man, shot by shot. Even schoolboys were firing from the windows now.

It was therefore not his army he could find here, but at best his own people.

'You are right. You are absolutely right,' he wanted to shout to them in encouragement, as if he had just discovered them. 'I am wrong. Even if they kill you, you are right.'

What else could he do? He left the hotel and picked up a Bren-gun he found under a dead policeman; he took the bag of magazine clips and ammunition and then he found a lift which took him to the top of a shipping company's offices. There he set himself up on the roof to wait for the British.

His neighbours on the surrounding roofs were soldiers, military policemen, civilians, and one or two obvious foreigners of Port Said, which did not astound him. He knew how they would feel also. Anybody must feel it, seeing what was happening here. The town was being wantonly wrecked by the British. But it was painful to watch these amateurs firing these strange weapons they had never seen in their lives before. They fired them wastefully at any plane that went over, and when suddenly they saw a British Commando section doing its efficient house-clearing work on a far-away street, they shouted excitedly and let off their carbines and rifles. At this range they could do no damage at all, but would simply tell the British where they were.

He tried once to shout to them, to tell them to concentrate their fire at a given order, but there were not many soldiers, and though the soldiers among them obeyed him, the rest fought with some other spirit, some other intention.

Was this what Hakim had counted on? Was this what his own argument with Gamal was about—this reckless temper of the ordinary unsoldierly Egyptian, angry at the terrible things being done to him?

'No, no, no!' he told himself, leaning over this frightening parapet to catch the first glimpse of where he knew the next British section would appear. 'Hakim didn't mean this. He doesn't even know about this. He doesn't even feel this.'

Nevertheless he knew where he had been wrong, and Hakim right.

'Look, look!' a youngster in a coca-cola shirt, who had joined him on the roof, shouted.

It was not the British squad he was waiting for, but a British fighter

657

plane which had come through a few puffs of anti-aircraft and was sliding in on their area. Somebody was going to get it.

Amin knew who it would be. He had watched the British technique on the smashed streets below. When the covering section of their squads drew fire from the windows, the accompanying tank obviously radio-telephoned the planes. Their co-ordination was so perfect that the plane could choose a target a few yards wide on this conglomeration, and demolish it at five hundred miles an hour.

The professionals were at work.

But Amin ignored the plane and waited for where he knew the first squad of these baggy-panted British soldiers would appear, backs to the wall in best professional method, Bren-guns well down, and grenade-bags loose enough to get at easily.

He could wait for them.

The rest of his roof-top companions fired at the plane as it came back very low over their heads. They could see the pilot. All around the roof-tops there was fire at it, and Amin knew it was only a matter of time before the plane returned, on its own initiative, and sprayed them with cannon or machine-gun or rocket fire.

But he waited for the British Commando section to appear.

These were the professionals. Yet, even admiring them, he knew it was not their professionalism which would win this. Erratic and foolish as most of the Egyptian fire was, it would make movement difficult for these English soldiers who might otherwise have been very frightening, with their organized movement, their young clean faces, their disciplined method. What gave the English such an advantage here? Was it simply their good order?

Or were outside forces, more powerful than the soldier, at work here —the power of the nation itself? Had Hakim's politics won another round?

'They're on the other block behind us now,' someone shouted.

Amin waited a little longer, and then he lifted the barrel of his Bren-gun on its tripod, up to the parapet. He had to stand up, and he adjusted it to maximum range. There was already some fire from windows opposite, but it was useless. He waited until the young British soldiers below were near enough together to make his fire worthwhile, and he adjusted the sights again.

When the two British soldiers reached a corner together, Amin pulled the trigger. Nothing happened. He had forgotten to push the cocking handle forward. These two English boys had lived another five precious seconds, a few heartbeats, before he snapped the handle forward and fired it, holding it firmly and watching the tracers cut across the two British soldiers, to bring them down so quickly and so surely.

There was a blossoming of erratic fire all around him from the others, who were simply firing at dead men.

Amin the soldier had never killed a man in his life before, but as he waited again he knew that he did not regret it. It was just. There could be no regrets in this situation. He had seen their red English faces. They were young men. They were doing their soldier's duty—what they knew of it or what some other men had decided was their duty.

'Come, *ya Bey*!' one of the militiamen told him as the machine-gun fire from the British raked over their head. 'Shouldn't we go now? It's going to be bad up here. The planes will come now.'

'Go!' Amin told them. 'I'll wait awhile. Go on.'

But two men stayed at the other corner of the parapet, trying to hit some vulnerable slit in a British tank which was now too close to elevate its guns on them. It would undoubtedly call up the planes, which came over regularly in single file. The planes could find them now.

And knowing it, what were these men up here waiting for?

Amin did not know. What did men die for? Why was he behaving in this unsoldierly and disorganized fashion? Why was he doing this stupid and hopeless thing among men a soldier should call rabble—these angry, unshaven, dirty wretches from the street, with their tremendous hands and peasant minds and coca-cola shirts?

'Don't fire!' he shouted at the men in the other corner. 'Wait, wait, wait. You'll see them in a minute—coming from the other side of you.'

'Here are the planes,' one called to him. 'Be careful . . .'

Amin could only think how foolish and crude it was to be here at all, and yet he knew that this time he would not leave. He knew he would never give up this filthy, damp, paper-strewn roof-top. Never.

Roberto and Captain Fernand had reached the Port Fuad side of the canal on a native bum-boat which they had rowed across the canal in the darkness from the Sherif basin. (The Arab vendors had brought their boats right into the canal to avoid the bombing on the sea-front higher up.) They landed on the Port Fuad side opposite the No. 2 workshop, and it was not easy. In their midnight departure they felt exposed to all the sudden shooting which was still going on up and down the mysterious edges of the canal.

'Which way now?' Captain Fernand demanded as they climbed up the tarred wooden steps of an old coaling wharf, once used for the steam tugs. 'We've got to reach the Sporting Club, or somewhere near to it.'

'It's best to stick close to the canal then,' Roberto told his Captain. 'You don't know what will be happening in the streets.'

'Vraiment!' the Captain said sarcastically.

659

They worked along the dockside edges of the Port Fuad frontage, keeping away from the villas; but they were challenged in the darkness in French before they had gone very far. A red beret appeared with a strong torchlight which he shone directly in their faces until the soldier recognized Captain Fernand. This *para* told them that Colonel Maretti had set up his command post on the mole

'How long will it take to reach there?' the Captain asked.

'Ten minutes,' Roberto answered.

'Is it clear all the way?' the Captain asked the *para*, ignoring Roberto.

'It was up till an hour ago.'

It was still clear. They went through the streets without trouble and found Colonel Maretti in an old coastguard hut on the mole, trying to contact the British or the French Headquarters ships at sea, to call off the next morning's (*this* morning's) bombardment of Port Fuad.

'We now have the whole of Port Fuad,' he explained to Captain Fernand, who had come to consult with him about the advance along the Suez road. 'But if the Admiral or the English don't know it,' the Colonel went on, 'and if we can't get any radio contact with anyone, we won't be able to stop them shelling us. They're still preparing the way for the sea landings.'

It was almost morning now, and there seemed to be no doubt that they would be shelled by their own ships. But they sat down on the mole while the radio-operator of the two-way set tried to make his few words intelligible to the *Gustave Zede*, the French command ship anchored many miles off the canal. But the static and interference from a radio storm made it impossible, and by dawn they had decided to give up and move out of the way.

'If we could hold off the bombardment,' Maretti told them, 'there's a fair chance the Governor will still surrender the city by this afternoon!'

Roberto believed it, but as they retreated in first light from the moles, they heard the first shells landing across the canal on Port Said. Before they had passed the narrow passage from the mole to the streets of safe French villas they too were shelled by torpedo boats which had come into the canal mouth and were clearing the way for the French LST's, which were following in half an hour.

Where (he must decide, as he ran with the others) were Françoise and the children now?

Perhaps they had left Port Said days ago and gone to Cairo to Françoise's Jewish cousins. Or perhaps she had sent the children to her friends in Ismailia. She surely wouldn't have kept them in Port Said. Roberto must decide, but he had no means of asking himself such devastating questions. He had never been able to inflict cruelties like that on himself. And having avoided the doubting habit all his life, it was too late to begin doing it now.

When they had established themselves farther back—the officers and the small H.Q. section—he was told-off by his Captain to go back and help their own wounded—victims of their own shelling. He must also report at the double to their new command post in the police caracol when the LST's were seen approaching from the sea.

Excrement was heaped on the English for their stupidity.

'They're going to plod through this muck like oxen,' he heard Captain Fernand complain as he went back to the mole. But complaints hardly mattered when he saw the first wounded *paras* being brought into a villa where the medical officer had set up a clinic for the wounded. They were not badly wounded, but an ear torn off in strips by small shrapnel was as beastly a sight as any he had seen in his life, and he began to feel ill with the unasked questions, the unavailable answers.

Where were they?

He decided that he must go, later on, and look for Beauvoir. He would go the moment he could ask to be let off this waiting-to-be-useful. He would explain to Captain Fernand that his wife and children might be in those streets on the other side, although he did not really believe it. Could he contact someone in order to find out?

Not now, because the LST's were arriving, and General Massu was showing how calm he could be in the face of all this confusion about a cease-fire, although the General had hardly arrived when he decided he would need to cross the canal and find the British H.Q. Since he could not make his dash down this side of the canal, he would try to make it on the British side.

So far, if radio talk across the canal meant anything, the British would not listen. But General Massu would ask them for some Centurions, or even the French AMX's Stockwell had on the other side. He needed to hurry before the whole invasion was called off, which seemed to be possible now. It was not going at all as planned; the UN were beginning to make trouble, and the Russians were threatening.

'You hold yourself ready in case the General needs you to do a little guiding on the other side,' Captain Fernand warned him.

Roberto did not resent orders, any more than he resented himself. He obeyed. He sat down on the steps of the wooden staircase in the caracol, holding himself ready, but he still did not ask himself any questions.

'*Merde* on the whole thing,' he decided calmly.

But he was able to listen to their problems with a certain amount of pleasure. The General had gone off again, so that Colonel Maretti and Captain Fernand were free to discuss their own ideas. They not only cursed the English for holding up their drive to Suez, but they expressed their fears that the politicians in London or Paris would call some sort of truce, and they mixed their doubts with bravado about Russian intervention. They were also worried about one of their own *paras* whose chute had tangled in the rudder of a Nord. He had dropped off into the sea by releasing his parachute harness as the plane flew low and slowly over the water. He had been seen to wave, but a patrol had been sent out yesterday to look for him on the Sinai side. They were waiting for news. A patrol had also been sent out to make contact with the Israelis, and the messenger had come back already in a captured Egyptian jeep borrowed from the Israelis. The Israelis were also waiting to go. So the Colonel and the Captain tried then, over their maps, to find a way to Suez by going out wide into the Sinai and coming down through Israeli-held country.

'The English won't hear of that either,' Colonel Maretti said.

'Why don't we just take a jeep from the waterworks on the other side and go down towards Ismailia as far as we can?' the Captain suggested. 'Whether the British like it or not, we can be at Ismailia in a few hours.'

Could it be done that way?

There was a great deal of discussion, and based on Captain Fernand's knowledge of the situation at the waterworks they made it their plan. They must get as far as they could before the war was called off. They all felt now, every man (including Roberto) who had heard about the Russian Notes to Britain and France—they all felt that either this war stopped today or tomorrow, or there would be a world war, and France and Britain would be rocketed by the Russians. That was the choice now.

Roberto did not wonder if this frightened them or not.

He was simply aware that it didn't frighten them. Here, they were local soldiers with a local situation to consider, and with local minds to apply to it. Even so, who knew what they thought behind their nervous eyes as they piled plan upon plan, courage upon courage, and smoked their Gauloises like men who knew the value of their bravado? The whole world knew.

'Sergeant Rolland!'

Captain Fernand called him in, normally angry. General Massu had returned and was going to cross to the Suez Canal and go down to the waterworks. He was going to make that his advance command post for the dash on Suez in a jeep.

'Come along,' Captain Fernand ordered him, 'and keep your eyes open.'

Roberto said *Yes, my Captain*, and began to follow the five officers who walked quickly towards the canal.

'Go and bring the maps,' the Captain told him, as if he should have known it.

Roberto gave him the maps and began to hate Captain Fernand, not with any particular emotion but simply with the logic of their relationship.

He decided it was going to be a hard day. When they reached the landing-stage, which the old Port Said–Port Fuad ferry had once used and which had so many other memories for him, there were still dead Egyptian officers jammed in a car which the *paras* could not get out of the water. A Staff Colonel told some of the men who had arrived in the LST's to do something about it. Then the launch came. But there was no room for all of them, and Roberto was told to stay behind.

'You can wait here for further orders,' Captain Fernand told him, 'and put yourself at the disposal of Colonel Maretti.'

'Certainly, my Captain,' Roberto said obligingly, knowing now what he would do.

There could always be a long way round to the caracol where the Colonel was. He would go back by Beauvoir's house, where he might find out what had happened to them. There, the unasked questions might be answered.

It was already afternoon, and Roberto realized that he had not eaten at all since they had broached the ration-box on the mole. One thing his heart leapt upon as he walked quickly through the dusty gardened streets. He had always been a clean eater and a clean person. At least, on that point, on that same force in Françoise, they had found a great deal in common. Their clear skins and healthy hair had always admitted their common taste in carrots and milk and lightly-cooked meats. He hated these army rations.

If only he could be left to himself, Peacock felt that he could finally take up this role of genuine observation. He must try to get back to the House as soon as possible now, but first he ought to see for himself exactly what had happened in Port Said, because the war would possibly be over very soon or it would be worse. The General had said confidentially that London was already talking about a cease-fire, which meant that Peacock ought to hurry back to the House as soon as he could, to take part in the running debate (running war, probably) around the Government's policy.

Was Eden right or was he wrong?

That would be the question, and George had already told him, bitterly, that the Cabinet was supposed to be split on whether to continue the war or not, because the Americans were telephoning Downing Street every day telling the Prime Minister it ought to stop.

'The bloody Yanks!' George said unbelievingly. George had been in Korea. '*They* talk about stopping a war. Oh, my good God!'

Some of the Ministers, it was said, also wanted to go on until they had occupied all the canal; Anthony Head the Defence Minister was resigning, and one of the Generals had said that Rab Butler had also threatened to resign if there was not an immediate cease-fire. The politicians were turning white. The Russians had them scared, and Britain had suddenly become isolated in world affairs—except for France, and France did not count. Nobody counted now. Nobody counted, least of all the man doing the job on the spot. And if the Russians *did* move . . .

'They're all so bloody terrified of the Russians,' George complained. 'A Canberra bomber was shot down over Syria a couple of days ago by a Mig 17, and the Navy keeps getting Russian submarine scares. By the time all this gets back to Whitehall it's practically the whole Russian army. There isn't a Russian-manned plane or sub in the whole area. I swear it.'

'But there might be,' Peacock pointed out. 'That's what the Cabinet has to think about. Have a heart, George. You can't just sit out here and imagine that this little war goes on in a world of its own. What about those bloody Russians? Put yourself in Eden's place.'

'No, thanks,' George said. 'I wouldn't be a politician if you paid me half my weight in gold bars . . . Ah, my weight,' George complained.

They had been billeted in a sagging green Headquarters tent which had been set up on the grass verge of a public garden, facing the esplanade, open to the sea, but near enough to a bunker the Egyptians had dug in the gardens to be fairly safe if something unexpected came over.

They had already spent half the night with the General, without the General, with the French, without the French: talking. Somewhere down the straight streets under the damp night in the salty dark breeze from the canal, the house-to-house war for Port Said went on. But they had almost ceased to hear the cough and crack of the carbines and the rifles, the watery sound of grenades. Instead they were trying to speculate their way into the mentality of the men who would decide what happened next: the politicians in Whitehall and the Quai d'Orsay.

'But if I listened to you long enough,' Peacock complained to George, 'I'd begin to hate your idiotic mentality. What's the use of blaming the politicians for the mess, when half the bloody mess is military?'

'How can you say that?' George argued incredulously.

'Don't forget that I'm both. I'm a politician and a soldier. I know the confusion the Army has been trying to cope with. But look at it now. You can't even get on to Suez because you haven't taken this town yet . . .'

'That's because we can't demolish it.'

'You haven't done too badly at that,' Peacock pointed out. 'The native quarter is gone, and practically all the sea-front on this side—right into the town.'

'That's not the point, anyway,' George said, eating a tin of American pineapple, which he had gently looted from a battered food-store. 'You were talking about confusion.'

'All right,' Peacock said. 'Take the idea of using ships as Headquarters. Whose idea was that? Not the Minister's, I'll bet. So look what's happened. Nobody is in touch with anybody. The Navy hears that the

Russians are massing planes in Syria, so they pull your precious Head-quarters ship out to sea, like scared rabbits. Miles away. What contact have we had for five hours with the *Tyne*, or what contact have the French had with the *Gustave Zede*?'

'That's the Navy, not us.'

'Even Cyprus doesn't know what's happening here,' Peacock went on, 'so London doesn't know either. That's not the politicians mucking it up, but the planners, old boy . . .'

'Oh, I know that, Tim. War is nothing but confusion, anyway.'

'So are politics,' Peacock admitted, 'but you can't always blame it on us. That's all I'm saying.'

Peacock already felt that arguing with George was not very rewarding, and he longed to be alone to think. He could laugh at that desire himself. But he had lost track of this. The liaison of the French had broken down, so had the supposed surrender. They had finally discovered the Egyptian General commanding the area and that was all. The Egyptian General had been captured near the Gamil airfield, but nobody had recognized his rank until he had announced himself to the Commando officers who held him. The French had allowed him to telephone Rashid, the chief of the Security police, in the Eastern Hotel, and Rashid had simply shouted at him over the phone:

'Where in God's name have you been, General? We expect the Russians over any minute to bomb the British fleet. Nobody is going to surrender the city now. Nobody . . .'

The General had asked to be excused after that. God protect everybody, if the Russians were coming.

The hoped-for surrender had failed. They had all heard the Egyptian loudspeaker vans going around the city. The Arab experts had translated its announcements as joyful claims that London and Paris had already been bombed, and that the citizens of Port Said, therefore, should not give up. 'To arms . . .' they were shouting.

It was getting worse instead of better, and nobody knew what it would be like once this Anglo-French army moved down the roads into the Delta. No one was sure how far they could get towards Ismailia and beyond. Nobody knew the strength of the defences there, and it was better not to take a chance rushing into it with unconsolidated ground in the rear.

'Stockwell is right,' Peacock said.

But George was still in favour of pressing on, even though he had lost patience with French opportunism. He had just heard from a Marine Commando officer that the French had landed five hundred extra men on this side of the canal, greatly exceeding the agreed division of total forces, so that the French must now be here in equal number to the British instead of the two-thirds to one-third proportion agreed on.

'Oh, damnation!' George cried, fed up with the waiting. 'Something has to happen soon. Anything . . .'

Brigadier Butler was now the land commander because General Stockwell and George's General had gone back to sea to look for their Headquarters ship. They must make contact with Cyprus or with Keightley to see what should be done. Should they press on, regardless?

'Let's go and see the French at the waterworks,' George said. 'We might be able to move the tanks down the Treaty road anyway. There's plenty of natural protection on both flanks down there. Let's go, Timmo. I'm fed with this fanny-sitting.'

Peacock and Astley followed the Centurion tanks in a captured jeep driven by a Marine, and twice they were shot up by machine-gun fire from the buildings near the railway station, but they took no notice and went straight through the golf-course, where there had obviously been a battle between tanks and Egyptian artillery or rocket launchers. Two Centurions were still burning, and the sand fairways were spotted with irrelevantly dead Egyptians.

'How far have you gone?' George asked a French officer who looked very tired, very torn and scarred in his parachute blouse. He had halted them on the roadway.

'Kilometre 24,' the Frenchman said.

Brigadier Butler was already ahead of them on the road, and when they drove into the waterworks villa the plan had already been decided on. The Centurions had left, they were heading south, and the French Foreign Legion *paras* were following in jeeps. But, as George had feared: 'They're bloody well turning *their* reconnaissance into a conquest, and they're going ahead in the jeeps and forgetting the British tanks behind.'

The French had almost reached el Kantara. They were jubilant. But even the French knew that after Kantara they might be entering defended territory, particularly at el Gisr which was a small pass between sandy hills —the highest ground in the canal. The English had warned them that the Egyptians might have well-camouflaged defences on the high ground, which would block the way to Ismailia, which the French wanted so desperately to reach.

'Press on! Press on!' the French Colonel shouted into his radio to the jeeps, ignoring his English allies now.

'Tell them not to lose contact with the tanks,' George told the Colonel in French.

'Ça va! Ça va!' the Frenchman said disinterestedly. 'They know.'

They went back to the waterworks villa to wait for news. A messenger came from the town and told George he must contact the Marine Commandos immediately, so they drove back north into Port Said as night fell. They were strafed near the station again and almost shot up by one of

666

their own tanks which couldn't tell in the early night whose jeep it was. The angry tank commander shouted at them:

'Blink your —— lights when you're challenged, you silly bastards, or you'll get a —— shell up your arses, you silly bastards.'

'That's all right, old chap,' George answered cheerfully 'Bastards often enjoy having shells up their arses.'

Peacock laughed so loudly at this unexpected ribaldry that George was stunned with his success, and they heard the tank crew laughing and repeating additions to the same theme.

'Such bloody good chaps!' one wanted to say. But that was not said any more. It was only felt, and drawn upon when necessary—in battle.

At the Command tent now they saw the gloom on the faces of the signals officer and the Staff Major. The signal which George was handed had been received from the command ship.

'Overlord advises prepare for cease-fire commencing 1730 or 1930 Port Said time,' it said. 'Cease-fire means no firing unless fired upon. Continue to press on while awaiting time limit, keeping losses to a minimum and advancing southwards mostest and consolidating rear. End of message.'

It was the end of the message and the end of the day, it would be the end of the war.

George swore heartily now and turned to Peacock helplessly, saying: 'If the politicians were going to get so scared at the first sign of outside interference, why the hell did they start the thing in the first place? That's what a military planner wouldn't do,' he said angrily. 'He'd calculate the opposition and its likely effect before he started moving in. But look how your politicians have mucked it up this time. We didn't even get started. We didn't have a chance.'

'You're hopeless,' Peacock argued. 'What else could we do but call it off? Try to use your head, Georgie. It isn't only the pressure from America and the Russians. It's what is happening here and you can see it yourself. Nobody can use this city yet as a base. Not safely, anyway. You can't just breeze on down the canal with this unfinished mess behind you. And you haven't even met the Egyptian armour yet . . .'

'Oh, *that*!'

'You can't tell. You haven't had to fight a battle even. How do you know it would be so easy?'

'Look at the Sinai.'

'The Sinai doesn't count. Wouldn't you have pulled out of the Sinai under the same circumstances?'

'Of course. But they didn't pull out. They ran out.'

'Same thing,' Peacock said as they walked up and down the sea-front to resolve this somehow before acting on it any further. 'The only way we ever pulled out of the western desert in a hurry was to run like hell. I don't see how the Prime Minister could help calling it off. Already the Russians are going to drop something if we don't. Everything is piling up against it succeeding. Why continue?'

George shrugged angrily. 'Why start then? That's my complaint. They put us into a fine mess. I *knew* it would happen. That's why Alan Dawnie thought of you. I could feel the politicians building up scares behind our backs. So you ought to bloody well tell them off.'

'It's not that simple . . .'

'At least the French were game enough to have a go the hard way,' George went on recklessly. 'I'll bet they still are. I just can't see those Foreign Legion *paras* taking any notice of a cease-fire.'

Peacock knew he could not argue with that thought. The French would be more reluctant to stop than the British. Yet they would stop. He was sure they would because they couldn't go on with it alone. The whole thing was over. The Russian threat had put finish to it.

But it was not yet over in the streets. A messenger had already been sent to the waterworks to tell the British and the French commanders to hurry up and get as far as they could. Now it was simply a matter of waiting until 2359 hours, two o'clock in the morning Port Said time, for the war to end officially.

'They're serving up something hot in the mess, sir,' a Lieutenant told Peacock as he stood at the open side of the gardens looking at the sea.

The Lieutenant obviously knew him, or knew of him, and Peacock talked to him for a while about the old days on the beach front when the sea used to be much closer in, and the bathing-huts had been a marvellous base for picnics.

'We used to bring ponies onto the sand and have races between de Lesseps and the old light-tower right up the other end. A long way off, believe me, on a pony; lovely little Arabs, some of them.'

It was too dark to enjoy the sea now. He had lost touch with George, who had gone back to the waterworks to see that the British tanks were very close behind the French jeep reconnaissance.

He ate alone; and afterwards, after a mug of thick sweet tea, he thought he would walk into the dark city a little way because he still must see what it was like, clearly, so that he would be able to give some sort of an accurate picture when he got back. He was glad to be alone, and that seemed strange to him under the circumstances because the whole town was a pretty depressing and grim sight now, and he did not particularly like wandering into it. But so much seemed strange and alien to his nature lately. Why was it like that? All that he did, and must do, these days, upset him unnecessarily. But he shrugged off the reluctance and walked on.

Inside the first shattered and tomb-like streets it was fairly quiet.

The password for the night was *Beau Brummel*, and he was safe with it for a little way in the face of the many challengers. He was safe in the rubble of darkness whispering *Beau Brummel* to unseen voices.

'I wouldn't wander too far into those ruins, sir,' a sergeant commando in a little encampment around a Centurion tank told him. 'The Gyppos are beginning to filter back into some of the buildings we cleaned out.'

'Yes, all right, Sergeant. I shan't go far,' he said.

He could see Egyptian dead still lying in the roadways, and the stench was beginning to be unhealthy.

'And you ought to have someone with you, sir. It's against orders to be alone.'

'I know. I know. But I'll just go to the end of the street.'

These lads did not know about the cease-fire yet, although it would not be long before the rumours began to circulate ahead of the official announcement.

'Take a Sten-gun with you, sir,' the Sergeant insisted.

'Oh, I'd forgotten.' Peacock had left his little carbine in the Command tent, but he refused the offer of a loan and decided to walk just far enough to see the canal. There were easier ways and safer ones of reaching the canal, but he wanted to see how much of this side of the city had been knocked down. Someone was sure to make an issue of that.

He took out a notebook from his battlejacket pocket and wrote, conscientiously and as well as he could in the scraps of light:

1. Native quarter, 90 per cent accidental. Wood.
2.
3.

Two and three would have to wait. He had been picked on by a sniper in the damp night and he moved into the archway of a ruined mosque. He didn't like the idea of the mosque, he felt guilty about that, so he moved on.

'The one big problem we faced in Port Said,' he was pointing out as he went along, analysing now what he would have to say in the House when he returned, 'was always the problem of the civilian population. It's no use saying that the city was wantonly destroyed. It was not. If there had to be a military operation to capture the city, then in this case the destruction was only military. That is why we never took the whole city. We did not want to demolish every house in it—which we could have done. The British soldier did not behave like an invader or a vandal. He simply tried to clear a way through the city for the whole reoccupation of the canal. What else could a soldier do?' (He wondered, though, if this was the soldier defending the soldier against the politician.) 'What else could the commanders in the field do? They were told to take over an area with orders not to fight too hard for it. So how can they be blamed for the

669

result—the unhappy result? Something had to be done about the canal, and we did our best on the spot to restore some kind of authority to the area. What would have happened if the Jews and the Egyptians had been allowed to go on fighting it out?'

There were more shots from some dark window almost at street level, and Peacock did not like that, so he abandoned his defence of the operation. It was probably the last speech he would ever make in the House. He knew, quite definitely, that he would ask for the Chiltern Hundreds when he got back. He was sure that he had decided it.

He walked on carefully, afraid of grenades. He did not mind being shot at from high up, but he hated the thought of direct contact with someone on his own level, face to face.

'No, I don't think I'd like that,' he told himself with a slight shiver.

He realized, too, that everyone had forgotten about the Jews. He had clean forgotten about them being on the other side of the canal, only a few miles away. What would they say to this cease-fire? And even if the British did stop, would the Egyptians and the Jews follow suit?

'Halt!' someone shouted in English almost in his ear.

'Beau Brummel,' Peacock said quietly. 'It's all right . . .'

'I thought you were all right, sir, but I had to be sure.'

'You were very clever to wait until I was so close,' Peacock told him.

That was the first requirement of the sentry challenge: wait until the unknown got very close before you challenged him, then he couldn't run away. Such marvellous lads, really. He stood with this one for a while, thinking he ought to question him a little to find out what he felt about all this. But he couldn't be so cold-blooded about it. The feeling was too warm to cheat on it like that. He was offered a cup of tea from a pot the relief had made inside a knocked-about native coffee shop. They had started the primus, and the radio was playing Arab music from a subdued miserable corner. He sat down with them and made jokes about his ride in the helicopter, parachuting, and the French. When they had to leave him he sat for a while drinking their tea in their mug, looking at the pictures of Nasser on the coffee-shop wall and the Arabic inscriptions and the magazine covers and the jokes torn from magazines, and he thought about the House.

'I suppose I'll definitely give it up after this sitting,' he decided again.

He had never been able to escape that feeling since Eileen's last visit. She had infected him with something. He didn't know what. But he knew that it was not the same any more. She had taken something out of it. He was certain it was Eileen and not something else. What else could be causing this depression? Could there be any other reason? No. No. The House had begun to depress him, so he ought to get out. He had no intention of staying if it was beginning to get him down like that. God forbid!

He went outside and he could just see the canal.

'Seems fairly quiet,' he said to the relief, smoking in the darkness.

'They're all over the place,' the relief said unhappily.

'Then I'll just go to the end of the street,' Peacock said, and walked on carefully in the darkness by the intact shops, shoe shops, gift shops, the old shops for the tourist trade which used to have natives outside the brightly lit doors at all hours of the day and night, drumming up trade from the tourist who had come in on the P. & O. boats.

But he had finally reached his destination, because he could see the canal quite clearly.

'Shall I send someone with you?' the sergeant shouted after him.

'No. I'll just go to the canal bank and walk back the other way,' Peacock told him. 'Good night, you chaps.'

They said *good night* and he waited near the shoe shop and thought again of Eileen. It was so extraordinary to be so much in love with his own wife. He had thought, even as he formulated his final speech in Parliament, that there would come a moment in his speech when he could look up into the gallery and see her there—joyfully cynical and unbelieving, and preparing to tease him unmercifully at lunch or dinner: but wonderfully there. He resented it a little. He could never escape her, really. When he looked at another woman, as he liked to do, he could not overcome the power of her existence in him. He remembered that lovely Egyptian Helen Mamoon, who had tempted him enormously, even the way she walked; but at the last moment it was always the view of Eileen, damn and blast it, that got in the way.

'Poor old Sam Hassoon,' he thought then. 'He must be getting the sticky end of the stick now. I really must get him something, somehow. Scotty too. They must be in a frightful mess.'

He had reached the canal banks, and he had two views of it in the night —the wide simple channel which went on into Egypt, and the other end which widened out into the Mediterranean, from whence all this had come—the British and the French.

'It looks so lovely now,' he said simply.

He had forgotten the war for a moment, until he saw the body of a dead sniper hanging grotesquely over a balcony just above eye-level. He was little more than a boy, but his face had swollen in death so that he looked grimly like a child blowing up a balloon.

'I wish they'd clear these bodies away,' he muttered aloud, feeling very lonely, quite suddenly. 'There'll be typhoid if we don't watch out.'

But it wasn't the thought of typhoid so much as this heavy feeling of personal depression which had reached him again—the same feeling he

671

had experienced in the House. He looked at the boy and felt something terribly sad about him, and he almost panicked.

'There must be something wrong with me,' he said. 'Why am I feeling like this these days . . .'

But he did not quite reach the end of the thought.

He heard snipers firing again, and as he turned around to move into a more sheltered place, he was hit several times by Bren-gun fire from the windows of the tattered houses overlooking the canal.

'Oh, no . . .' he cried softly as he felt these terrible blows.

It was such a brief and inconsequential burst of fire in the night, and yet it sounded so personal, so powerful, that he was astounded—that he personally should be the person who received it.

'Oh, no . . .' he said.

He had fallen over on his back, and he groaned in agony.

CHAPTER EIGHTY-THREE

FROM ultimatum to cease-fire the war had lasted five full days. But the actual landings had taken place at dawn on a Monday and the cease-fire had ended the war early Wednesday morning: only $43\frac{1}{2}$ hours, which had already given the war its character in history if one can think of history as that calm abstraction of the anguish we live with.

So much had happened, so quickly, that Scott sat in the November sun on the last step of his brick staircase staring at the newspapers he could no longer read. The war was over. The whole extraordinary thing was done. What did he have to worry about now? Was there anything else of comparative proportions worth even thinking about?

He was worried about Françoise and her children.

The train he had expected them on, the Monday morning train from Port Said, had never arrived, and the news of the attack that same morning on Port Said had left him feeling so helpless, so unable to do anything at all to rescue them (how could he?) that he could not imagine any decision being possible ever again. Yet he must do something. He must surely be able to do something to get them out of there, if they were still alive. Leo Lieberman had telephoned. Why hadn't she come? Perhaps she had reached Ismailia at least, Leo said. Was there any way of getting news?

The phones were dead. All private communication with Port Said had ceased. And, having seen one dead child, he was not thinking so much of Françoise herself but of her two French children whom he hardly knew, who meant so little to him personally, and yet who had suddenly grown to such proportions in his life that he could think of nothing else.

'If only she managed to get them out of the way,' he said to Leo.

If he could believe the Egyptian papers, Port Said had been battered to ruins by air and sea bombardment. Thousands of men, women and children had been killed.

'Good morning, Captain Scott.'

Helen Mamoon, standing near him, was astonished at what she saw in this Englishman's quick glance. Everyone looked miserable sometimes, but this Englishman looked almost sick with it. He hardly seemed to recognize her for a moment; but almost instantly his English face was once more the same normal face he would live his life with—the aspect he wore for others.

'Hello,' he said. 'I was just reading the news.'

'It's all over, *el humdulillah*,' she said to him. 'Thank God the UN stopped it in time.'

'Do you think they stopped it? Do you think it was the UN?'

'I don't know. I suppose they did. But I don't care who stopped it. I'm so thankful it's over.'

He nodded, hardly focusing his eyes on her. 'Have you come to see Sam?' he asked.

'No. I've come to stay at Madame Salz's until all this trouble is over.'

She explained what Sam had already told him: that Quartermain had been interned and that Nona was not allowed to leave their flat. Hanna, their other sister, had gone to live with Nona. Helen herself had come to stay at Madame Salz's, because she did not want to be alone in their own flat. So far the Egyptian Security police had not done anything more than tell her not to leave Cairo; just as they had told Sam to report to the local caracol every two days. Did Hakim consider them unimportant, now that the real enemies and assassins had shown their hand so crudely in Port Said?

But why had she come to Madame Salz's?

'It's convenient,' she had already told Hanna convincingly. 'I shan't have to worry about my meals. Also, if they do take Sam or me away again, someone can ring you up and let you know. And you can bring the children to play in Sam's garden, which will be safer than the public gardens.'

It was very useful, but she could not hide her own cunning or her own feelings from herself. She knew that she had come here partly because of Scott, which surprised her but did not really impress her. Wasn't it logical? She would at least feel partly safe, partly protected, partly attached to some responsible person, if she were even in the same house as this man.

'Everybody else is so helpless,' she explained to herself, wondering at the same time why this strange man should suddenly represent so much to her security. 'I've got to have someone. I can't be alone any more.'

They must all have someone. The end of the war was by no means the end of the worst trouble for people like herself. But she had already been under suspicion, and the aftermath was obviously just beginning, only this time it was the frightening possibility of reprisals on those who were reputed to be on the other side: people like herself for serving the English,

674

or people like Sam for being a Jew. Even Quartermain, Nona, her children. Perhaps no one would be safe if the Egyptian hatred of those who had attacked began to look for an outlet.

'The real terror might now begin,' she said, explaining it to Scott, leaning against the sunny brick wall with her hands behind her back to protect her skirt from the dirt.

'I don't think so,' he said. 'So far the Egyptians are being very tolerant and they're not bothering anyone yet.'

'Oh, I don't blame them,' she went on. 'If I felt as they did I'd want to blame or punish or hurt someone. But this time they'll throw us all out.'

Scott had not given that aspect of it any thought, but she was too obviously right. Would the tragedy never end?

'I only hope, *insha'allah*, that they don't get out of hand again,' he said to her. 'That could be ugly.'

He thought of Sam, who was still incapable of defending himself. If they arrested him now he would certainly admit his guilt, his spying for Bateman. He would accuse himself and they would shoot him. Sam's desire to show his anguish for Zareef had now reached the pitch where he would not hide from anyone. He must tell. Even Madame Salz and little Becky had heard a dozen times his accusations against himself: that *he* had caused poor Zareef's death and that *they* (the world) had forced him to do such a terrible thing. If the Egyptians ever heard him admit that much, after what had happened, they would not doubt him. They would believe him gladly.

'You'll have to watch Sam,' he said to Helen Mamoon. 'He's very upset.'

She told Scott that he had been very good to Sam, and thanked him.

'If only they don't take him away again,' he said, 'he'll be safe.'

'I wish I could get him out of Egypt,' she told him. 'He can't stay safely in Egypt now.'

'Is that why you wanted to get him out of Egypt once before?' he asked. 'You must have known what he did.'

She nodded.

'Did he actually tell you about Bateman?'

'Yes, he did,' she admitted calmly. 'But I told him then that it was absolutely insane. He was so desperate. That was at the time when the Security police were looking for everyone who had no papers. Sam had nothing—no documents of any kind—and he was just waiting every day for them to catch him. It was too much of a strain. He couldn't help doing what he did for Bateman, because he thought he would get British papers out of it.'

'You ought not to know about it,' he warned her then, and stood up. 'No matter what happens, even if Sam admits it to the Security police, you must not know. Nor should Becky and Madame Salz know. They must be absolutely ignorant of anything Sam says.'

She looked gratefully at him for that, even though his advice was naïvely behind her own understanding. But she knew, with overwhelming relief, that she had done the right thing to come here.

'For once,' she felt, realizing how tense, how worried and how frightened she had been—how drawn her whole life had become, 'for once in my life I can let someone else do it. He will know what to do.'

But Scott did not know what to do about Sam at all.

He was wondering what he should do about Françoise and the children. When he glanced down at the Arabic newspaper which called the British and the French and the Jews barbarians for what they had done and insisted that they should all be punished for their brutality, he knew he must somehow get to Port Said, and as quickly as possible.

He had not been near the barracks for two days, knowing that Hakim was finished with him. There was no point in embarrassing everyone by pretending he had a function or a purpose left there.

Yet he must get to Port Said.

He was sorry now that he did not own a car. He could probably have driven most of the way there up the Delta roads, which would not be so blocked by military police.

But he knew that ultimately all the roads leading to the canal would be blocked somewhere; on the one side by the Egyptians and on the other by the British and French. He would have to go through both sides, undetected, if he wanted to reach Port Said itself and to move about in the streets.

He was so used to preparing his own decisions without recourse to anyone else that he was surprised now to find himself discussing them with Helen Mamoon.

'Won't the Egyptians give you a pass?' she said when he told her what he wanted to do.

He looked at her and laughed gently instead of feeling irritated, realizing that this myth of his influence among the officers would remain to the end. 'I don't think so,' he said. 'I have a Frontier Corps pass, but I don't suppose that will be valid for an Englishman any longer.'

'Who will know that?' she said to him.

He almost said that *he* would know it. That was the real invalidity of it.

'It isn't any different from the passes of Egyptians in the Frontier Corps, is it?' she asked.

'Not at all, except that my picture and name are obviously foreign.'

'But everybody must know you, anyway,' she said. 'And they won't care about who you are as long as you have a military pass. Why don't you try?'

He had walked with her outside the garden, outside the gate, and they were standing on the old street, talking quietly.

'I'm wondering what will happen with the British if I get into Port Said,' he said. 'They'll want to know what the devil I'm doing there, if they get their hands on me. I would be very quickly under suspicion, with my reputation!'

'Surely you could cope with that?'

He said he didn't know. 'I don't want to be whisked off to Cyprus by some zealous field-security officer,' he said.

They stood at the gate looking at the house.

'Is that where Hakim Abdul Hakim shot you?' she asked him. 'At this gate?'

He nodded casually. It was not a particularly important thought to him at the moment. In fact, it had always meant much more to other people, including Hakim, than it had ever meant to him.

'What did you say to him when you saw him? I mean after you had recovered?'

'I didn't see Hakim for many years,' he told her.

'Didn't you? But when you did see him, what did you say?'

'About the shooting? Nothing at all. It was a bit late by then, and it didn't really matter.'

Her neck stiffened, and her rather too-proud eyes and face (with its rich bundle of hair framing it) went up sharply. 'But it did matter! I know I would have said something to him. What right did he have to shoot at you? At anyone! All this killing. Why must they always think of winning by killing?'

'He thought I had betrayed Gamal to the British,' he said, amused despite himself at this late indignation, almost understanding it.

'Pht . . .' she said impatiently. 'Anyone even looking at you would have known that idea was impossible. He must have been very stupid.'

'He was very young.'

'Do you love this old house?' she said then, curiously.

'Which? Madame Salz's house?'

'Yes. You have lived here so long.'

He had never thought of it that way, and before he could give it a conscious thought he felt a real flood of affection and affinity come over him when he looked at the old brick walls, waved and buckled; the unpainted window-frames with Madame Salz's front-room curtains behind them, the shutters which Sam had fixed, and the front door with a wooden porch which looked like an unmixable mixture of French and British Colonial styles in argument. That worn wooden porch, which had already had its floor eaten away twice by beetles, was very much the door to his

677

home, even though he normally used the outside staircase direct to his room. But he felt the whole house.

Madame Salz had not changed it much. Sam and Becky lived in Aunt Clothilde's downstairs room, where she had moved when she had eventually been too blind to risk climbing the stairs. The tiled steps were cold, the kitchen was large and fly-blown, filled perpetually with the roar of the primuses. The plastered walls were so dried out in most of the rooms that a small punch would produce a calcified dust-storm. There were always cockroaches creeping in from the garden, and once there had been bedbugs in the ticking of his bed, brought in by a careless servant. He had wanted to burn the mattress, but Aunt Clothilde had poured kerosene over the seams and for weeks he had suffocated with the smell which had soaked the mattress, but he had put up with it to please the old lady; he could still smell it in his memory of it. He realized that he did not think of his own room at all, because it was a comparatively barren unsocial place. He thought of the rest of the house, which had always been filled with boarders, changing with the changing character of Cairo life, mostly Jewish. Madame Salz had taken over the character which Aunt Clothilde had given the house, as well as Felu the tortoise. And finally, Sam and Becky had made it the family house which it was now—a not very economical proposition for Madame Salz any more, but a happy one, and Helen Mamoon was not at all an outsider, being Sam's aunt.

'I suppose I am fond of it,' he said, unable to hide the surprise in the discovery, the identity which her question had forced on him. 'I had never given it much thought before.'

'It looks so well-built, and yet it must be ready to crumble,' she said dispassionately, and told him about the house her family had once owned in Matarieh. It had almost collapsed because the local archaeologists had thought there was a rich Pharaonic tomb somewhere in the vicinity and they had excavated all round the house until her father had put a stop to it because the floors were beginning to tilt and the stairs had slipped out of place.

'We sold it to Azmi Pasha,' she said. 'You remember that old Egyptian ear doctor who used to keep bees and had a tall English wife who dressed like a missionary.'

'I can't ever forget Mrs. Azmi,' he said. 'She used to give a school prize every year for the best essay on an English garden. I won it myself one year . . .'

'Did you ever taste his honey?' she asked.

He never had, but it would be difficult to touch a memory in this city of Cairo which they could not share like that, particularly when it concerned the shadow of the old life. She too still lived half-way back in that English Cairo, which had gone for ever.

He looked at her closely and tried to guess her age. She was very well preserved, so careful of herself and so perfectly held that she might have been no more than thirty. Yet her breasts were deepening and her whole manner was not that of such a young woman. She must be his own age— forty—and yet it astonished him. Was he that old? Was she that old? Where had life gone? It was not a new thought to him any more, but it struck him now in her likeness.

'I went out to our old Matarieh house with my sister Nona a few weeks ago,' she was saying, 'just so that she could see the place. You can't imagine what she did. She started to call her cats. She used to have five or six of them when she was a girl. They all lived in the fields by day and in the lemon tree by night. Imagine thinking you could call up cats after twenty years, even if they were still alive. She was convinced their children would understand her. I suppose that's because we all know about cats, and look a little like cats, don't you think?'

'Who?'

'Why, all Egyptian women.'

He had forgotten that she was Egyptian, yet her face could be nothing else. She had perfectly pointed Egyptian eyes and hard full cheeks and strange smooth skin—the colour of some local and purely Egyptian pigment. Yet she was not quite Egyptian. The European in her manner was too apparent. Only when she spoke Arabic did it disappear completely.

'Look,' she said. 'There's Alicia and old Madame Hassoon.'

The Hassoons were hurrying down the street. They had come to visit Becky and Sam and to sit in Madame Salz's dry old salon drinking milkless tea and talking of friends and enemies, of Sam, and the fear of the morrow when the Jews would be punished for what they had tried to do to Egypt. Those far-away Israelis.

Helen excused herself and went to meet them, and Scott went inside to change his clothes, deciding that he would try to look—near enough—as if he were a soldier, having formed a rough plan of action already.

Was the Frontier Corps jeep still at his disposal? That was the first requirement. If only Amin Fakhry were back it would be simple, but he found the sergeant in the quarantine hut sipping coffee in luxury, surprised to see him, but shamed into a quick salute.

'Where is the jeep?' Scott asked him in Arabic.

'Over in the workshop I think, y'effendim,' the Sergeant replied.

It was obviously somewhere else where it should not be. But Scott told him to get the jeep ready, to fill it with petrol and water and supplies for two men for a week, and to have it ready by six o'clock that night.

'And the two men?' the Sergeant asked cheekily.

'The driver and myself,' Scott told him. 'We will probably bring Colonel Amin Fakhry back with us.'

'Is he alive?' the Sergeant asked, his face suddenly human.

Scott's rare lie had already caught up with him so quickly that he knew instantly that even a small lie would not work for him.

'I don't know,' he said. 'I will try to find out.'

That was true. He had heard from Hakim's office that Amin Fakhry had been alive on Friday in Port Said. Hakim had been decent enough to have someone phone him with the news. But that was before the invasion.

'You will leave here at eighteen hours, *y'effendim*?' the Sergeant asked. He said 'eighteen hours' in clever English.

Scott hated his cheek, but said, 'That's right. Make sure it's ready.'

He had decided to travel at night so that his face, his English oddity, would not be quite so conspicuous at the road blocks.

Then, faced with the sergeant's insolent suspicions, he decided to be bolder about it, and he told the man to type out a movement order for himself and his driver, ordering both to proceed to Port Said in vehicle so-and-so, adding that there they would report to Colonel Amin Fakhry and place themselves at his disposal, returning only if they failed to find him.

'Certainly, *ya bey*.'

That was outright mockery, but Scott felt already that what he had set in motion was a genuine mission, and he did not care if the sergeant ran off to check up with Hakim or not. He would even convince Hakim of its validity if necessary.

It was easier than he had thought.

During the war, bold behaviour in the middle of enemy deserts had often succeeded where caution would have failed; often they had gone hundreds of miles into enemy space by doing it openly, by attaching themselves to the tail of a German convoy, or simply by driving down the main enemy road at night.

He found the road blocks, the usual ones just outside Cairo, but they were very easy to pass because there was so much military traffic on the roads. One more Frontier Corps jeep was not going to inspire a careful check. He had deliberately left Cairo this way for that reason, instead of going up the less important road to Benha.

He did not know his driver well, had forgotten his name ('Farouk, *y'effendim*'), but Scott was pleased to see that he was a neat driver, clean and organized in his person and efficient with that quiet confidence which a good driver can create at check-points, where he addressed all military policemen with the same intimate familiarity.

'Saida, ya sidi,' a quiet joke that.

680

'Where to?'

'Bilbeis, *insha'allah*. What's it like?'

'Not bad now. Yesterday it was bad.'

'How do you keep it going?'

'In God's name, I don't know,' the military policeman said, his voice no louder than the driver's, their mutual understanding obvious. Farouk might have known all these Abdus and Achmeds all his life, and Scott felt much better about his hopes. He explained to Farouk, as they moved slowly behind a convoy of tank transporters, that they would turn off at Bilbeis and go north to Zagazig.

'You can choose your own road,' Scott said, turning around to push down his kit or a spare box of something which had worked loose. 'We are going on to Manzalah on Lake Manzalah. But I think your best way will be through Mansura.'

Farouk agreed and said it would be better the moment they left the canal road, which had already been cut up more than usual by heavy lorries and tanks. It was blocked every few kilometres by queues of convoys without lights pushed over onto the dirt shoulders, which Farouk passed recklessly but effectively with full lights on, so that Scott knew he was in dangerously good hands.

When they had turned off north at Bilbeis into the wet green Delta roads, the cold night air from the fields made them shiver, and they stopped to put on their jumpers. Scott pulled his khaki jumper over his head. They had not yet been questioned closely at all, but even a khaki army jumper might help if they were.

They travelled all night, compacted in silence, over the dirt and gravel roads which cut through the Delta and the villages, going north with only an occasional blockage, usually by a bridge being closed, or a few military lorries blocking the way, but when they came towards the large town of Mansura on the Nile, Scott woke up from a doze and suddenly remembered his father bringing him here to test the back flow of the salinity into Bahr es Sahir—the canal which joined the Phanitic arm of the Nile to the salty Lake Manzalah.

'The Saracens were always better soldiers than the Crusaders,' he could hear his father telling him as he watched the dim street lamps flit by, 'because the Christians always stamped about the country like soldiers, whereas the Arabs took it all in, like good survey engineers. They could smell a shift in barometric pressure a mile off. When the Crusaders tried to cross this canal (this same Bahr es Sahir canal) to take Mansura, the whole lot were knocked to pieces by the Saracens, who soon had them boxed in between the canal and the river: a little detail in the terrain which the Frenchman, Louis, had forgotten to reckon on.'

He could smell the river and smell the cotton warehouses. All these

z*   681

provincial river towns had the same river atmosphere: poorly lit streets, broken footpaths which were deserted after dark, their trees, empty old hotels, silent railway stations. He had stayed in the old Station Hotel with his father, who had always despised the French in Egypt and laughed (unjustifiably) at all soldiers. And here he was riding through the town, and out along the Sahir canal in the footsteps of the Saracens and his father and heaven knew who else.

'If my luck holds,' he told Farouk as they left the town, 'I might be able to get a fishing-boat on the lake to take me into Port Said.'

They shaved and ate breakfast out of town on the dirty green edges of the canal. Scott had brought his own primus and he stewed coffee and reheated some black beans. Their sergeant at Abassia had put in a European loaf of bread for him, but he preferred the native bread, which he stuffed with *ful*, and as he ate it hot he felt, despite himself, the joy of the early green morning bursting over the glistening fields. Nothing could quite equal its beauty, and yet he was feeling too guilty to enjoy anything.

Must he think of Françoise now? All the time?

'What's the use of that?' he told himself unhappily and ate his beans.

He had not made up his mind yet what to do with Farouk. He could not take him into Port Said, because after all he was an Egyptian soldier, and that would be dangerous for him if he were caught.

He had not decided on anything when they reached the fishing village of Gamallih on Lake Manzalah, just before noon. Twice they had been stopped and questioned, which signified some sort of military activity along the dirt road. But Scott knew that the Egyptians must have prepared any advance defences in this area along the lake itself, and it was not until they were right into the large village of Manzalah that they were held up suspiciously by a field-security patrol. They were taken to a young officer who was standing on an old wooden pier looking out over the milky coloured water of Lake Manzalah through field-glasses, and consulting a map held by a soldier.

He had to ask them questions, he said apologetically to Scott.

What were they doing here, and by what authority?

Scott handed him the movement order and his Frontier Corps pass, and told the young Lieutenant who he was. The young man in his eagle-peaked cap looked at him curiously, then with great interest, and then at the driver.

'There's no traffic to Port Said,' he warned Scott in French. 'They're already patrolling the lake to keep us out of the town.'

'Can you give me a boat?' Scott asked him.

'I haven't got one,' he said to Scott.

At his feet, under the pier, were a few fishing-skiffs and a large flat-bottomed launch.

682

'I can't give you that unless I ask permission from Cairo,' he told Scott. 'But if you go on to el Matariya you might find a fishing-boat with an outboard motor.'

Scott took that as permission to move on to Matariya, which was a village at the complex tip of a soggy peninsula jutting into the marshy edge of Lake Manzalah like a hand with wizened little fingers.

The dirt road was hard-baked mud with marsh water on either side, and Farouk was afraid they would run into a bog.

'Don't worry,' Scott told him. 'The road is firm enough. It used to be a good road. There was once an old flat-bottom paddle-wheel boat running a service across the lake to Port Said from this fishing village, so there ought to be some kind of boat there we can have.'

He was not sure yet whether Farouk knew that the journey was a private one, but in any case Farouk was obviously going to help. The most difficult part was yet to come. But in the fishing village of Matariya there were so many military and civilian refugees from Port Said that it wasn't necessary to move cautiously. They could not even attract anyone's attention or help, until they found a coastguard officer who had obviously come from Port Said. He was noisily organizing, with the help of some fishermen up to their waists in water, the erection of sharp stakes in the muddy shore, where the British might still try to land their LST's.

'What do you want to go to Port Said for?' the coastguard asked. He was a high enough officer to ask the question and expect a good answer.

'It's very important that we find out if Colonel Amin Fakhry of the Frontier Department is still alive. That's part of it,' Scott said, as mysteriously as he could.

'But there is still the telephone to Port Said. The Governorate has been talking to Cairo.'

'I don't think this can be discussed on a telephone,' Scott said calmly. 'I have to find him personally.'

'The British have brought armed launches from their ships into the lake,' the coastguard said, 'and they stop everything coming or going. And yesterday a whole boatload of refugees turned over and a hundred people were drowned.'

'I'll travel at night.'

'You ought to be rowed there. But you wouldn't get far enough rowing at night to avoid detection the next day. They'll shoot you up,' the officer warned, 'if they catch you.'

'I'll have to take a chance on a motor-launch, anyway, if you have one. I'm in a hurry.'

There was no launch available, but there were two flat-boats belonging to the steamship company. They had outboard motors which would crack open the day or night for miles around.

'Do you want someone to go with you? A fisherman?'

This was the *fessikh* village of Egypt, and it smelled of rotten fish. Even the people and the roads and the houses smelled of it.

'No, no,' Scott said, reluctant to risk anyone except himself, and afraid of suspicion also. 'I know my way there. I'll be all right.'

He looked over the marshy water, which was part water, part hillocks, part reeds, with a channel cut through the middle and staked on the sides —which was the direct water route to Port Said itself.

'Please yourself,' the coastguard said and told one of his fishermen and a gendarme to punt over to the outboard boat and bring it alongside.

'You ought to go to General Wahabi's headquarters,' the coastguard said. 'He is in the little railway station two kilometres back. You should see him first.'

'I haven't time,' Scott said and went quickly back to the jeep and told Farouk what he was about to do.

'You can wait here for me,' he said quietly and urgently. 'If I am not back in four full days, by Monday night, then take the movement order and go back to Cairo and report to General Hakim.'

He packed a knapsack with a jacket and food, and he endorsed the movement order for the return journey and signed it. He knew, by Farouk's self-protective silence, that this soldier would have gone on to Port Said with him quite willingly if asked, but being a soldier he knew when it was foolish to do more than was expected of you, and Scott realized it and was sorry that he had to leave Farouk behind. He was a good man to have.

He was surprised when he crossed the first part of the lake to see some fishermen in skiffs working old seine nets off the reed channel. They looked up curiously as he passed by, put-putting in his oil-stained skiff. He hoped the little English outboard motor would hold out, and he checked the caps of the battered jerry-cans of petrol to be sure that they were not spilling his spare supply. Then he crouched down on an old carpet seat, keeping his feet out of the rank bilge water, and he tried to think of what he was doing here, on this fishy stretch of white water.

'If the British catch me this time, I suppose they'll consider me an Egyptian spy,' he said carelessly to his feet. 'In which case, they might be right.'

But he could not feel worried about it yet, as he huddled down into this salt-dried, stinking boat. He had almost ceased to care now what happened to him.

Why did he do it, then?

684

He had asked his questions, and he tried to feel that the answers were simple. They must be simple.

But he became very depressed, and the flat saline waste of what had once been (ages ago) the most fertile plain in Egypt did not help his mood. He could not help feeling now that he was going nowhere at all. What was he doing, put-putting across this dismal wet wilderness in the middle of two different worlds, going away from what was his lost but normal life, into something remote and unknowable?

'I'll have to get them back to Cairo somehow,' he decided, 'or I'll never get back myself. Go on,' he admonished himself then. 'Get on with it. Just get on with it.'

He did not give himself any clearer mission than that because he began to think of Ali Zareef and of the fireman's small son, dead in the rubble at Gedida.

'Children at least ought to be safe in the world, whatever else happens,' he decided sadly.

Was that why he was making this journey, simply to satisfy his pained English conscience that two more children (his stepchildren-to-be) had not been murdered by a casual English bomb?

'Perhaps,' he said, and tried to wear the thought off.

But he knew that all this doubt might simply be the appearance of his anguish. Emotion for him was never going to be borne without pain, so he could never be sure of anything he felt. How could he trust it? He had held down his feelings all his life, he knew that; he had imprisoned them against pain. But now that they were trying to force their way out again, he was looking around helplessly for the real means to open the gates.

He drifted for a few moments on this empty waste, eating corned-beef and considering what to do—not wanting the barrenness behind him, yet wanting more ahead of him than was really there, considering the risk.

'If only Françoise would give me a chance,' he thought.

The night wafted it away, but he knew that all he needed was one heart-felt embrace awaiting him in Port Said, and his entire life would be changed. If Françoise could only manage that much, something would emerge . . .

He started the motor, feeling now as if he were simply giving himself one more chance.

He came into the burning edges of the native quarter after eleven cautious hours on the lake. Sometimes he had stopped the motor and pulled into the shallows when he thought he heard activity. The fishermen on the lake had warned him about planes, mines, and a machine-gun on a hillock called Tennis, so that he approached the city carefully, blind in the darkness yet guided by the dull glow of the native quarter which was

685

still burning, and by the gleam of a green arc-light over the canal.

He had stolen a net-pole from a mud landing on one of the marshy banks, and he had poled himself through the shallows for the last hour, getting stuck now and then on the silt banks, wet to the shoulder with the water which ran down the pole, and barked across the shins by his clumsy falls, caused by his frequent running aground.

But he had arrived at the city, and it was almost six o'clock in the cold morning. He moved away from the channel on his left and ran up a bank of the lake near the municipal nursery garden. He realized how lucky he was to have chosen this spot when he saw a half-dozen lake skiffs on the sandy fringe. He unbolted the motor to pull the boat up, leaving its stern in the water so that it did not dry out, because he might still want to come back the same way.

'Who's that, the devil take you? Stop, or I'll be merciless!'

Someone had shouted at him in Arabic, and a noisy shot was fired near enough to be frightening. ('So much for the cease-fire!' he thought.)

'I am the guard here. Beware!' a quavering voice said from a hiding-place.

He replied to the challenge boldly. 'If you're the guardian,' he said in Arabic, 'I want this boat looked after. Come out here where I can see you.'

An old gaffir in a long black overcoat and a scarf around his head, carrying a shotgun, came out of a lean-to on the beach, very frightened. Scott told him firmly that he must look after this boat, and its motor and the petrol cans until he came back. Otherwise (did anyone ever believe his threats?) it would be the worse for him. He gave the old man fifty piastres to quieten his complaints, and resisted a temptation to ask him how he could get into the European part of the city.

'Have you any food in your little sack, *ya basha*?' the gaffir begged as he followed Scott up a narrow-gauge railway-line around the end of a basin which was full of barges. 'There is no food to eat in the town, not even fresh water.'

Scott gave him a tin of bully beef and hurried on until he realized he was in the open space near the main station. A dozen anti-aircaft guns were scattered around the perimeter, helpless and deserted. Piles of small-arms were stacked in the middle of the road, guarded by a soldier who was dressed in a crazy-looking uniform. Scott was near enough to see his face and his stance, which were unmistakably British—a parachutist or a marine, a young man very much in occupation.

It was a shock, suddenly, to see a fellow-countryman standing there on guard, in this deserted place, and he turned off quickly into a side street.

The little cylindrical mezuza—that container of God—was still nailed o the front door of Françoise's apartment, and though he had walked down this street on a carpet of glass and rubble, he could see that the building itself was intact. The main windows were blown in and the staircase was littered with clothing from an abandoned suitcase. It did not look like Françoise's clothing. But he could not get into the flat, and he could not break down the door. Questions of the lethargic servants below the stairs produced no coherent answers, and he went up the back stairs and smashed the wooden panel of the back door with a dustbin from the landing and let himself into the kitchen by unlocking the bolts.

'Good God!' he said aloud.

The mess of the place frightened him. The unmade beds and the packed, abandoned suitcases frightened him. He could see no signs of blood, but he could see that Françoise had been caught in bed by the bombardment, and had fled. If Françoise had left calmly, before the bombardment, the beds would have been made, he knew her fastidiousness for such things. A small blue plastic handbag, obviously Mireille's, was lying on the floor near the front door.

'She must have dropped that in a panic,' he decided.

He picked it up, and as he did so he was swept up by the sentiment of it—the reminder of the affection which this little girl had shown him—or rather had shown anyone who was willing to be a father. How willing Mireille was to be a daughter, his daughter, and to press against him as she always did when he had come unexpectedly and Françoise had said, warningly to him, at the door: 'Ah! It is Captain Scott come to visit us.'

Where were they now?

He did not even know where to look for them.

The hospitals? Could he wander about in the occupied city so freely, hoping to find them? He had seen the British patrols in all the streets. So far they had ignored him, perhaps because he wore a sports jacket which he had brought in the haversack, perhaps because he looked like a local foreigner.

The obvious thing to do was to ring Monsieur Beauvoir, her friend and enemy of the Canal Company, if the phone worked. He picked up the receiver, and though there were many sounds in it the line was useless. He looked up Beauvoir's address in the directory and wondered how he could get across the canal to Port Fuad where Beauvoir lived.

'Must be something going across,' he decided, still forced on by a certainty that he must get there: simply to find her now.

As he walked again through the streets towards the canal, the wreckage was something he hardly had any feelings for. He felt the recklessness of it, the shambles, but he did not think about it. One street would be damaged and another untouched. He asked a black-coated Egyptian policeman, who was inspecting a gharry laden with a large chandelier on the edge of the canal, if there was a ferry plying to Port Fuad.

'Not yet,' the policeman said, and looked at him with such surprise and suspicion that Scott decided to ask no more questions of policemen. He hurried off, looking farther up the canal.

Though he had money he was reluctant to offer too large a bribe to the bum-boatmen who were fiddling with their boats. But he found one who was piling his boat with splintered wood, collected from the bombed streets in a coca-cola cart. He asked the man if he was thinking of going to Port Fuad with it. The boatman began to defend himself aggressively for collecting his pathetic loot, and Scott said it didn't matter about that if he would take him across the canal. He would pay. They bargained over a pound note, a hundred piastres, and the boatman told him to get in.

The two Egyptians loading the boat had quickly left, and Scott was getting into the bow to sit on top of the wood when two British soldiers shouted at them in English.

'Hold on! What d'you think you've got there?'

'Oh, my God,' the boatman cried in Arabic. 'They're coming. They're going to steal my wood. They won't even let us have a miserable piece of wood, not a piece! They'll burn it on the street.'

He began throwing the wood into the canal, until Scott shouted at him to stop it and to keep quiet.

'Come on! Let's see what you're hiding,' the soldier said. 'What's under that stuff you've got there, chum? Have you been stealing flour from the warehouse?'

Scott looked at their English faces and said in English, without thinking or caring about it: 'He's got nothing under there except this old wood he's been picking up off the streets.'

'Where's he going with it?'

'To Port Fuad.'

'What about you?' the second soldier asked. 'Are you French or Greek?'

'Greek,' Scott said.

'I wouldn't hang about too much if I were you,' they said. 'Nobody's very particular at the moment who you are. Everybody is shooting at everybody else. Savvy?'

'Oh, yes,' Scott said and told the boatman quickly in Arabic to move off. 'And don't say a word. Just cast off and go.'

They negotiated the mess of small boats which hemmed them in, the other boatmen shouting complaints and pushing them off while the soldiers still watched them. It was only when they were free and into the open canal that Scott realized how reckless he had been, speaking English like that.

The French were also tolerant. On the Port Fuad side of the canal they

688

questioned him in French—those red berets with strained eyes. Had they been drinking, or were they simply lacking sleep? 'Sleep!' he decided, and told them in French that he was on his way to the villa of M. Beauvoir of the Canal Company to see if his wife and children were safely there.

He still held Mireille's handbag, and unwittingly it became his pass.

'What's all that shooting on the other side?' a *para* asked him.

He listened and realized that he had been hearing the odd shots and the occasional burst of an explosion ever since he had reached Port Said. Only now did it seem important, because this side seemed so tranquil and un-touched and certainly not wrecked.

'Snipers,' he said.

'They say the Egyptians are fighting each other. Is that true?'

'Why should they?' he said and paid the boatman and pushed the boat off, because the boatman, who was becoming frantic, gesticulated silently to Scott to set him free in case these Frenchmen seized his load of plun-dered wreckage.

The French *paras* let him go then, and he walked about carefully until he found the house. He looked at his watch. Was this the time to worry about propriety? It was barely eight o'clock. But Port Fuad was already emerging, quite normal. People were in the streets, shops were just open-ing their shutters, and boabs were sweeping around these thickly gardened French villas. But he felt now like an interloper, and it was only by shrugging slightly in a reckless impatience with himself that he could actually push at the gate of the villa.

It was locked.

He pressed the bell on the stone gate-post and he heard it jangle inside. He realized he was unshaven. There was a native in the garden putting empty flower-pots under a seat. The gardener looked up when he heard the bell, but he went back to his work. Scott watched the front door open, and without any doubt about it he knew he was looking at M. Beauvoir: a small, rather shaggy-eyed Frenchman looking quite startled as he walked quickly down the path. And in M. Beauvoir's eyes it was clear that he too recognized a man he had heard of, scandalously, but whom he had never met.

'Monsieur Beauvoir?' Scott asked.

'Yes.'

'Is Françoise here?'

'Are you Captain Scott? Is that who you are?'

'Yes, it is me. Is she here?'

'Come in,' M. Beauvoir said, unbolting the gate. 'Françoise is here with the children, but she is not well.'

Where was the embrace?

689

He was kept waiting in a cold French salon, the one aspect of genuine French bourgeois culture which had survived longest and which instinctively turns up its nose at any stranger trying to live out a few valuable moments of his life in it.

Françoise was still in bed, but the children were allowed to come in from breakfast, and he felt one burden go, one weight of life he could not have supported. They were safe and he had never been so close to them as he felt now, simply seeing them. Were they all right? What had happened?

Mireille accepted her handbag and leaned on him gently, and André reported clearly all that they had experienced—his small lips forward, his eyes alert and experienced.

'My father came to see us,' Mireille told him at last.

'Tu sais,' André said, 'mon père est un officier para.'

'Your father? Is he here? Is he here now?'

'Of course not,' André told him. But his knowing eyes seemed to realize the damage he was doing, and he lifted his small French heart above it. 'Mireille, and even I, did not really remember him, monsieur. That is to say, not at first. But afterwards . . .'

That was a consolation, wasn't it?

Madame Beauvoir also appeared, and she looked at him briefly from a standing position (what an extraordinary thing it was *not* to be French) and said, 'Bonjour, monsieur,' and disappeared, while Beauvoir returned and took him upstairs, telling him not to stay long.

'Françoise is all right, but she must not move,' he said. 'She has hurt herself very badly.'

The creaking floor-boards under the carpets announced him to Françoise who was lying in a large bed in an honoured-looking French *chambre* —a beautifully barren room without any spare clothes lying about, without any human presence at all except Françoise herself, who was pale and relaxed but very still.

'What's happened?' he said as he reached her, upset by her appearance and realizing how ready, how necessary, how much he could love her if she would only allow him. He had forgotten everything now save Françoise herself.

'I fell,' she said calmly, taking his hand but looking beyond him carefully at Monsieur Beauvoir who was still in the room.

The children had followed, but Monsieur Beauvoir spoke firmly to them and took them out and they were alone. Had she seen a doctor? Was she badly hurt? Was she in pain?

She replied to his anxious, hungry questions with a dull kind of resistance, which denied him the right to be so worried. And yet she was looking accusingly at him as if she owed him a very intimate

690

reprimand. He thought it was his unshaven face, and he apologized for it.

'I had to come a roundabout way,' he explained. 'But tell me what the doctor says.'

'He doesn't know. Perhaps it is my ribs, or perhaps I have hurt my back or . . .' she hesitated . . . *'quelque part plus bas.'*

She would need an X-ray. But at least, she said, she was not in pain any longer, and he realized that she must be relaxed like that with a sedative or a drug. Her arms were limp on the covers, her face was smooth, her cheek-bones clear, her eyes soft. She had never looked so acceptant nor so beautiful nor so French in this French atmosphere.

'Did you come all this way to see me now?' she asked softly.

'I didn't know what to do when you didn't come on the Monday train. I read about the bombardment . . .'

'Pauvre anglais,' she said and her smile relaxed her whole face, so much so that she almost became tender with him and he thought: *Why can't she always be like that? Is that for me? Is it?*

But he could not help doubting because he felt that she was not quite normal in her present state.

'Did the children tell you that Roberto came?' she asked him.

'Yes, they told me. But did he see you? How did he come? With the French?'

She nodded. 'He and Monsieur Beauvoir are arranging for me to be put onto one of the French Navy ships going back to France, with the children.'

He did not know what to say to that astonishing idea, that calm intention.

'Will you go?' he asked, staring at her.

'I will go,' she said to him, 'because I *must* go. I can't stay here . . .'

'But . . .' he shrugged, helpless. 'I don't understand yet what you mean, Françoise.'

'We saw such terrible things,' she went on, her face quite still but her lips gone soft and her eyes burning with tears. 'The people were killed on the streets. The children saw them . . .'

'I was also very worried about the children,' he told her.

'I don't ever want to go back. Never again. It was all so terrible.'

'Don't get upset,' he begged quickly, trying to calm her. 'It's all over . . .'

'No, it isn't!' she answered sharply. 'Now they will start killing all the Jews in revenge.'

'Why do you always think like that, Françoise?' he said in a gentler reprimand. 'Nobody has done anything to the Jews yet.'

'But they will. And if we stay here now we will be caught in it, and it will be just as horrible. You didn't see what I saw . . .'

Françoise had become Françoise again. She was frightened first and tender afterwards, and she looked at him accusingly again.

'Is that why you want to leave?' he asked carefully, realizing how much was at stake now. 'Are you still so frightened? Surely it isn't so bad yet?'

'But you would be frightened too, if you were a Jew.'

He knew she was right to be frightened. Nobody knew yet what would happen if the Egyptians did seek revenge. But he was indignant and jealous because he could guess already what had happened, or he fancied he could.

'What about Roberto?' he asked.

'He came to see Monsieur Beauvoir, to see if we were safe. He is in the Army, but I didn't know he was coming. I swear I didn't know.'

He knew he must have looked upset and accusing, because she looked away.

'You will never understand, *anglais*, what it is like,' she said, her eyes closed for a moment. 'Never! Never!'

He wanted to ask what she meant. Did she mean what it was like to be a Jew, or what it was like to be a woman in her predicament, or any one of many secret dreads she lived with in herself? But he knew he was at a disadvantage already, and he could not press the point when she was like this—part cold and part helpless.

'I am sorry you came all this way. I would have written you a letter explaining . . .'

He waited, but she was in tears again.

'Explaining what, *chérie*?' he said gently.

'Pauvre anglais,' she said through her tears. 'I didn't think this would happen. If it hadn't happened, everything would have been all right. I could have gone to Cairo, and it would have been all right. But what can I do now?' She was trying to stop her tears, but she looked very weak. 'I can't help it. I don't want to hurt you, but I'll never go back now, and I don't want the children to be wrong. They *are* French. They must be French. How can they be anything else? I can't risk them any more. What will happen to them? André is too much for me already. He could never be English, and neither could I. You see?' She looked at him, and yet she avoided his eyes. 'Oh, you don't understand. I can't be anything any more. Those terrible things we saw. Those dead soldiers. If you had only seen them. I can't tell you. I didn't think it was like that. Was that what you were doing in the war? I couldn't bear to be here any more. It's so terrible. Everything was smashed. I don't want to remember it even. You don't know what it's like to be Jewish. Jewish women are all born like me. We have to be. I don't care what happens, I don't want even to live in this terrible part of the world any more. Everybody is going to kill each other. It will go on for ever. It will never end.' She was exhausted, but she was sitting up holding her hair back with tight fists. 'I hate it. But you like it here. You will always be here. You will never leave . . .'

'But I was willing to leave.'

'Oh, that's not it!' she cried, although she had almost regained her composure, so that she did not look so weak now. 'I can't manage André now. I don't care what Roberto did any more, I don't even hate him. And he didn't try to divorce me. So it is no good hiding anything from you, *anglais*, because I could not bear to hurt you. But think of me! I don't know what Roberto is really like now, but I can't forget what it is like here. In any case, I am still his wife. Perhaps he couldn't help being cruel that other time. Perhaps it was my fault. I didn't want him to go away. He said terrible things before he went away, but I can't help being *frigide*. It is me, and I don't blame him, even though he was cruel. You don't understand a woman, either. He said when he saw me that he had done a terrible thing; but I don't really believe he is sorry. It's so difficult to know what he thinks. But I don't really know what I think myself, most of the time, and we are alike. Oh, I am not like you, *anglais* . . .'

'I don't want you to be. That was not what I wanted.'

'Yes, you do. But I couldn't be. I trust you more than I trust anyone, except Leo, but I couldn't be like you, and I can't bear you expecting me to be. I hate you just waiting for me like that. Why did you wait? If you hadn't waited so long it might have been easier for me. But you didn't *do* anything.'

'You would never allow me. I couldn't even touch you!'

'But that's the point,' she said tiredly. 'You don't understand a woman.'

'Did you want me to be cruel also?'

'But it wouldn't have been cruel, no matter what I said. If you had *forced* me to love you it might have been all right by now. But you didn't!'

'Now I don't even understand you,' he said harshly.

'I know you don't. Even Roberto understands more than you. Please don't be angry. I know I am always frightened, but I don't want to be. You would be too kind and too gentle, too patient. Don't you see?'

'Are you going back with Roberto?'

'I will do it for the children,' she said, sitting back a little as if it were all over, decided, done with.

'And yourself. Don't you consider yourself?'

'I don't care about myself,' she said, closing her eyes. 'I will be safe. I simply don't want any more of what I have been through. And I want to be married to *one* man. I don't always want to be someone-else's-wife. I don't care any more what it means. I simply want to go with him now, quickly, and take the children and let them be normal. And myself—oh, I'll think about myself then.'

He could not argue with her because she was staring at him with her

693

troubled semitic eyes, denying him with a force which he could not understand.

If he could have understood—even for a millimetre's division of a second—that she had given him the clue to his own victory, he could have had her back in an instant.

She waited.

She waited for him to sweep Roberto away, to accuse her as angrily and violently as he could of cheating him, to insist that she was already rightly his and that her arguments were dangerous and silly, and that, in a moment, he would take the children away and send someone for her; and like that—no matter what happened—they would make their way somehow, even in Egypt, even now, even as a Jew, even as another man's wife, even as a frightened woman—they would succeed.

Why didn't he do it?

She saw the secret of her own life suddenly disappear from view. It was lost in the hurt, the disappointment, the resentment and the defeat in his face. He had already failed her, because he did not have even that amount of self-interested cruelty, which would have overcome her and won him a great deal more affection than he had ever known in his life.

'What did Roberto say to you?' Scott asked her cynically then. 'That you were French after all, and not Jewish? That you were desirable and not *frigide*?'

She almost sat up. If he would go on for just a little longer, if he could only go on saying the very things that were unworthy of him, he might rescue them both. To insist, to overwhelm, to crush her resistance, even to violate.

'I'm sorry,' he said brusquely. 'I didn't mean that.'

That was his strength and his weakness—that he could not hurt her.

'Roberto wept when he saw the children,' she said calmly, goading him a little, trying to stir him.

But her calmness only convinced him that it was over, and he nodded understandingly and acceptantly.

'After all,' he said, defeated finally by the children—by Mireille and her small blue handbag and warm hands. 'He is their father, not me. He ought to weep over them . . .'

She did not shout, 'It doesn't matter what he ought to do, *anglais*. It's you . . .'

'Yes,' she said coldly. 'They will be happy now.'

He gave up, losing his ability to speak, afraid for the first time in his adult life that he might be overcome by an emotion of something not yet born, but still striving beyond its term to emerge as part of him.

But nothing emerged at all, and he felt, on this very brink, on this edge of discovery of how much he loved her, that he had never loved her at all.

He could retreat, he could say good-bye, he could promise to tell Leo everything, to manage all her affairs in Cairo for her, and he could close the door behind him without changing his mind.

Did Françoise sorrow for more than a second, he wondered.

He would never know what disappointment or what hopeless but strange feminine resiliency he had left behind in that room. She might have run after him if she could have moved; but she wasn't sure, she did not know. More likely she would go back to herself inwardly and solve it that way whereas Scott could not help remarking cruelly to himself at the first sight of a French soldier in the glaring golden morning of Port Fuad:

'She throws herself into the arms of a French parachutist. He's the civilized protector of reluctant woman, is he? But what good will that do her, or her children?'

CHAPTER EIGHTY-FOUR

HE knew he was very vulnerable now, because he did not know what he should do.

Vaguely he still worried about Amin Fakhry, but he realized how impossible it would be to find out anything. Where could he start looking in this occupied city? Or did it matter, anyway, since Amin was probably in some safe place, hiding?

He sat down near the canal, watching a small war going on across the other side. Policemen were firing their ancient shotguns at youths who were running away, and the stench of unburied dead and of smouldering ruins and burning oil was a nauseous mixture.

He avoided the French soldiers who were driving about Port Fuad with a great deal of character in jeeps. Some of them were also looking across the canal and joking about the English. He moved away and by chance found a boatman who was painting the canvas awning of his small hire craft. He was willing to take Scott across the canal for a pound, he said. That was a fortune, considering that the usual price for a private boat was five piastres.

'I must find Amin,' he forced himself to think.

But he had only a dull sense of determination about it, and he was still so confused that, when he crossed the canal, he wandered around the streets of Port Said, wondering who to ask, where to look. Only the shock of the desolation brought any feeling to him. Even Europeans begged him for food. The shops were shuttered up, and there was no food or milk or drinking water. Though the cease-fire was days old, nobody was clearing up the mess or putting out the fires or removing the dead from the more difficult places in the ruins. He felt that he was walking about in a battlefield of primitive recklessness. The streets were littered with weapons, and a few bodies were still hanging out of open rooms, high up where the walls had been blown right away to the innards.

A truck went by with three or four Egyptian soldiers in it. There were some European and native women crowding around a broken water-main with pots and buckets to collect water; and there the soldiers tipped out a crate of canned food and condensed milk, which all the women fell upon with desperate violence, tearing the crate apart with their hands and snatching at the tins from each other while the children were abandoned on the footpath.

A sugar warehouse had been attacked, and though a British tank guarded it now, Scott walked over a gritty teeth-grinding footpath mixed with broken glass, sugar and donkey excrement, which the street urchins were sweeping up, filth and all, to rescue the sugar.

It was already an anarchy of near-starvation, and he began to see its point.

The walls were already painted with Arabic slogans threatening fifth-columnists with death and disembodiment if they co-operated with the British. The British soldiers, who understood nothing, were nervously patrolling the streets looking for the snipers who were shooting at them from time to time, or were hidden in difficult outposts and dropping grenades on their trucks.

Scott had seen Egyptian soldiers, but he knew he dare not approach them, because now, in the presence of the English, he realized how English he would appear himself, and he began to make his way to the native quarter, which seemed to be the most logical place for any non-co-operative Egyptian to disappear in, even Amin.

He was almost there on a quiet and safe-looking street when he was stopped short by a British commando patrol.

'Where do you think you're off to?' one of them said.

Scott did not think quickly enough, and he answered their questions in English instead of in French or Arabic. They asked him for his passport, which he showed them. They didn't believe him. They looked at his filthy clothes stained by the boat and no doubt smelling of the lake, and they searched him and found his Frontier Corps pass. They looked into his knapsack and found his Egyptian map, and they glanced at his khaki trousers and his Egyptian Army shirt.

'Better take him along,' the Corporal said.

He was taken under guard to the Provost Marshal's office, which had been set up near the canal, in one of Port Said's famous patisserie cafés.

'Put him in there,' the Provost Captain said without looking up.

The Captain had his desk at the wrapping and cash counter, and the café itself was now a detention centre filled with a dozen Egyptians and local foreigners and even young street boys, sitting on the floor and on the tables and chairs, waiting.

'Only a check-up,' they said with their firm young English authority. 'Won't be long.'

Scott did not protest, he did not explain. He had seen what he had seen,

697

and he knew already that he would never explain himself to these British soldiers. He did not care what they did to him. He realized how careless he had been, but he was almost glad of some outside interference with his confusion. At least it would give him a valuable pause, some time to think.

He had shared his food, and he waited. They had kept his passport and his Frontier Corps pass, and when a British soldier called out: 'Which one of you goes by the name of Scott?' he got up from a group of four Egyptians and an Armenian lorry driver, all of whom had been relating to each other what the invasion had been like, and he went into the shop part of the patisserie.

'I'm sorry,' the Provost Captain at the wrapping counter said, with the politeness of a man who has been instructed in it, or is following a superior policy of it, 'I didn't know you were a British subject until I picked up your papers. I wouldn't have kept you waiting with that lot. My lads on the street are a bit on edge. Anyway, what are you doing here? Do you live in Port Said?' He was handling Scott's Egyptian Army map of Manzalah and Port Said, the lettering of which was entirely Arabic.

'No.'

'Where, then?'

'Cairo.'

'What happened? Were you caught up in it when it started here?'

Scott shook his head. 'No.'

The Provost, who was a red-headed man of about thirty, had been looking through the passport and inspecting the Arabic Frontier Corps pass, and he asked what it was.

'It's a Frontier Corps pass,' Scott said.

'The Egyptian Frontier Corps?'

'Yes.'

'I didn't know there were any Englishmen left in the Egyptian forces,' he began to say; but then a moment of recognition showed in his face and he looked up in another way. 'Are you that Captain Scott?' he asked. 'The one who was in the western desert?'

'Yes. I'm that Captain Scott.'

'You don't say!' He looked at the Arabic pass again. 'That puts another light on it altogether. Did you come to Port Said for the Egyptians? What are you supposed to be doing here? I didn't realize who you were at first.'

'I'm not going to answer any of your questions,' Scott told him. 'You're the one who is here illegally, not me.'

'That's what *you* say,' the Provost said, stung out of his politeness to an angry defence. 'Anyway, you can go back inside. I'm not turning *you* loose on the streets, not by a long shot.'

698

He waited again, all day. He had forgotten how to wait like this—for punishment, catastrophe, accusation; for doubt; or simply for the long wait of any soldier expecting some decision from authority.

He settled down for the night on the floor, lying on a small carpet and leaning against a piano. A native street-seller, who looked too wild and frightened to be trusted by anyone, slept on top of the piano and wept sometimes and pitied himself in Arabic, so that Scott felt sorry for him, but annoyed.

All the others in the café had been released or taken somewhere else.

Scott was tired by now and he decided to move away from the piano. But the ragged noisy figure on top moved with him and spread out miserably on the cold stone floor near the chairs which Scott had set up for himself, so that Scott was sorry he had brought the poor fellow down from a wooden bed onto a stone-cold floor. He told him firmly to go back, but the youth said he was afraid the English were going to shoot him. They were shooting everybody they had found with a gun, or near a gun, or even those with friends who had guns.

'You hear them shooting our brothers?' he said.

The night was spotted with occasional shots, but Scott guessed it was a little of both sides: snipers versus occupiers, and he lay down on his chairs and tried to sleep, wondering in a masochistic, self-punishing way, what they intended to do with him.

He slept soundly and tiredly and in the morning he did not have to wait long for his future. A soldier brought him a mug of tea; and on a plate of thick white bread two rashers of tinned bacon, a lump of butter and a dob of jam.

'Here it is,' he said. 'Tuck yourself into that.'

Scott sat up stiffly.

'What do you think that bundle of horror will eat?' the soldier asked him, indicating the Egyptian.

'Anything you give him,' Scott answered.

'They say he won't eat bacon. He's a Moslem, isn't he? And I can't give him a mug of tea. He'd contaminate the bleedin' cup.'

But he brought the Egyptian a plate of bread and butter and jam. It was a thicker piece of bread than Scott's, and the youth leapt on it and then stopped. He looked frightened and then he knocked it off one of the little marble-topped tables onto the floor.

'Don't eat it,' he cried to Scott. 'It's poisoned.'

'Shush!' Scott told him. 'Don't worry. They're not going to poison us. Go on and eat, otherwise they'll take it away.'

The youth hesitated and then picked it up from the floor, butter and jam together. He spread it out as best he could with his horny fingers and he ate it noisily while Scott tried to make up his mind which of these two powerful worlds was his.

He need not have wondered, for he would soon find out more tragically what it must be.

They took him after breakfast to a small office in a water-front shipping agency building, where a Major told him to sit down on an old stuffed horsehair sofa. Scott wondered what all that paper-work on the desk could be, in only six days of war. So many signals and movement orders, boxes of files and intra-cross-references, priority lists and security regulations and heaven knows what. A soldier brought in Scott's knapsack which had been confiscated at the café and the Major looked at his passport, map and pass, and put them into a yellow envelope and looked up.

'Smoke?'

Scott shook his head.

'Won't be a minute.'

The minute was a long time, and then a General arrived and walked through into another room. This was the famous bluff and good-natured General Wilson. Scott had recognized him, and after a few moments he was shown into the General's room. The room overlooked the canal: a comfortable shipping manager's office or the bureau of some ancient French authority.

'You look a bit the worse for wear,' the General said to him as if giving Scott a manageable size and shape. 'What've you been up to? Wandering around the Egyptian countryside?'

Two days without shaving or washing and he knew how he looked in his khaki pants which were stained with petrol and oil. His shoes were patterned white with the dried fishy salt of Lake Manzalah. He waited.

'I don't suppose you would tell me what you were doing in Port Said, would you?' the General asked cheerfully. 'It would help, you know.'

'No, it wouldn't,' Scott said. 'And I can't tell you anything.'

'That's a bloody pity. I know you, Scott.' The General looked worried but interested. He played with his nose. 'Why did all you fellows who worked with Pickering end up as cranks?' he asked thoughtfully. 'Although I suppose that's what took you into those long-range groups in the first place. Look at Pickering himself. I knew him well. He was as mad as a March hare, as far as I could see. Wasn't he?'

'Everybody could see he was mad until they wanted something done. Then they asked Pickering to do it,' Scott said savagely, almost feeling like the Scott he had forgotten, the man he had been thirteen years ago when he had resented Pickering's casual death and had grown bitter enough with the blunder of it to seek a retribution which had since cost

700

him so much of his life. He had almost forgotten that feeling until now, except so briefly with Church.

'Well, I'm not going to go over old ground on that score,' the General said, his pudgy cheeks blowing out with an effervescence of good, practical sense. 'I always thought Church was a silly fool to court-martial you, although I can't agree with what you did. You can't get away with that in any army. Refusing an order in the field just won't wear, right or wrong. And, anyway, right or wrong is what you leave to the courts, or to records, or to history for that matter. You ought to have known that. Some expert a hundred years from now would have decided in your favour, anyway.'

'That wasn't what we wanted at the time,' Scott said, flushing. But suddenly he felt cunning. He watched this General's calm eyes, and he realized that the General was using an old device to gain a confidence, and he had used it skilfully.

'What have you been doing for the Egyptians all these years? Survey, wasn't it?' the General asked quickly.

Scott nodded. 'More or less.'

'What a bloody waste of a good man,' the General said. Then he drew a deep breath and walked to the window and looked out at the canal and said, 'However, that doesn't concern me, I don't care what you've been doing for Nasser. That's your business. I don't say, even, that I blame you.' He turned around. 'All I want of you, Scott, is some help in stopping this vile slaughter that's going on in the streets. Cease-fire? Christ all-bloody-mighty—they've got idiots with guns in half the windows of the city, just waiting for my lads to walk into them. I can't have that. It's getting worse. They even dropped a mortar bomb in our signals' tent last night. It can't go on . . .'

'Then why don't you get out?' Scott said, determined to resist that kind of appeal. He wasn't going to fall for it.

'Now that sort of talk is not going to help,' the General said firmly. 'So you might as well listen to me, Scott. I'm going to ask you to help us, simply as an Englishman. Never mind about anything else. You must have some influence on these people, otherwise you wouldn't be here.'

The General waited for a confirmation, but Scott refused to give it.

'You've helped Nasser. That's all right. So now you can help us a little. Do you know what's happened here?'

'Only what I've seen for myself, and that . . .'

'We have agreed to a cease-fire,' the General interrupted. 'But your Egyptian friends are taking a dangerous advantage of it. We have even left the Governor in charge of the city, and even Rashid as the head of the police. We've tried to persuade them to respect the cease-fire. But they talk nicely with one hand and act dirtily against us with the other.'

'I don't know anything about that,' Scott said.

701

'I lost a man yesterday, and two wounded. For nothing, damn them. Absolutely nothing. These schoolboys and gangsters with machine-guns are making it impossible for us to move about in the city, and if we can't move freely we can't clear it up and get it going again. They've also organized a boycott against opening shops and going to work, and the city is going to starve very soon if something isn't done. You follow?'

'I've seen the town,' Scott said. '*You* made the mess of it, General, but now you're complaining.'

'All right, all right!' the General said patiently. 'But why can't you go to Rashid or Riad the Governor and persuade him to stop this nonsense? Telephone Nasser if you like. Do what you want. We don't care what you do, but let us at least have a quiet city so that we can spare its population more horrors.'

'Perhaps the population is angry enough to starve rather than be pleasant with you,' Scott answered. 'They certainly must hate you for what you've done to their town. Doesn't it occur to you?'

'That's irrelevant now,' the General replied, as if he were determined to stick to the point. 'We have agreed to a cease-fire. The UN is talking about sending a force. We shall possibly withdraw within a few months...'

'A few months!'

'It's possible. And until then, I say, it's going to be safe in the streets for my men, otherwise I shall have to take measures to make them safe. Something I don't want to do, because it will mean more bloodshed. You ought to help, Scott. I don't see how you can refuse. This isn't politics, it's humanity, man.'

Scott did not point out that he had no influence. He had forgotten the truth himself. He even felt that he was rejecting something he was able to do if he chose to. But he would not do it.

'You don't understand, General,' he said pointedly. 'What would you do if you were in an English city, and the Germans or the Russians bombarded it and occupied it? Wouldn't you set yourself up in a window and snipe at them?'

'No. I would leave it for the army. That's the trouble. Nasser never had any army here to do the dirty work. He left the fighting to the police and the civilians, which is a criminal way to fight a war, a coward's way. No matter who is right or wrong.'

'Do you think Nasser is telling them to fight now?'

'*Someone* is,' the General said, and in his strange look, Scott realized that he might be that someone himself as far as the General was concerned.

'They probably want to make sure that you don't settle down and stay another fifty years,' Scott said cynically.

'That's not impossible,' the General retaliated. 'The more the trouble, the longer we stay.' The General had lost his practical world in bad temper for a moment, but he was not going to lose it for long. 'In any case,' he said persuasively, 'you can't blame the poor bloody British soldier for what's happened. Yet he's getting the worst of it. That's all I care about, and I appeal to you to spare a dozen young soldiers their lives. You simply can't blame them, no matter who you think is right or wrong. They simply do as they're told.'

'Who cares about that?' Scott said, resenting this argument more than any other. 'If the British soldier can do what he did to this city simply because he was told to do it, or because he doesn't know what he's doing, then he's as much to blame as anyone else.'

'Don't be such a bloody fool,' the General shouted. 'You know it's never a soldier's fault.'

'Who's fault is it, then?'

'Mine, if you like. But I'm not going to debate responsibility with you, Scott. There's a simple humanitarian issue at stake.'

'You're too late to call on that,' Scott said blindly. 'You should have thought of that a few days ago when you bombed the city. Did you care about a hundred lives then—a few thousand men, women and children? Do you think they should spare your soldiers now?'

'I won't hear that kind of talk,' the General said, equally angry. 'Do you refuse to do anything to stop this guerrilla war against us?'

'I certainly refuse,' Scott said, refusing also to follow the General's peregrinations around the room. 'If I were an Egyptian,' he said, addressing the spot which the General had just left, near the window, 'I would not give up shooting at you until the last British soldier had left. The Egyptians know very well that you'll stay in Egypt if you can. You always have. And unless someone goes on making trouble for you, there'll be some other trick, some other device you'll think up to stay on in Egypt. I'm not going to tell anyone to stop firing at the British Army, even if I could. Let them go on doing it. You deserve it. Get out, General, that's the answer to your problem. Simply get out.'

'You're a silly fellow,' the General said. 'And a crank. But crank or no —you're a bit of a menace, and I'll have to treat you as one. You're under suspicion already, and I can't ignore your presence here. You're up to no good . . .'

Scott did not deny it, determined not to argue any further because he was sick with his own resentment and anger. He only wanted it to stop before he got the worst of it again.

But the General turned impatiently to his Major, who had been listening calmly at the wall, which was covered with a yellow glazed map of the world showing all the shipping lines and their routes.

'Alan . . .' he began, and then hesitated.

It was a strange pause. They were all strangers and interlopers in this room, and Scott suddenly felt open and exposed to this feeling of temporariness which made their continued presence here more or less an act of fate. This room was nothing to this General. He had come into it as if he would walk out of it again, cracking his little stick and poking at things with it. It was not even an office for him. The General would never sit at this glass-topped desk with its beautiful ink-stand, and this Major would never be able to give it an air of occupation, permanence or authority. A captured place to walk in and out of, to make a decision in. The General would walk in and out of ruined streets in the same way, looking at his men; and in the same way he would sleep in some local tent or billet with no more than a temporary intention. Scott felt the vulnerability of it, because he and these two men were suddenly rootless men with rootless values which were concentrated in here for just a moment. And he knew then that it was not only a city which was at stake here, but himself, and he must escape it before he was overwhelmed again by the casual moment's destruction, which could easily deal him another blow, harder this time than he could hope to survive. They had him again . . .

'You'd better hand him back to the Provost,' the General said after a second's thought, 'and inform the Adjutant General or somebody.' He looked at Scott. 'Or better still, put him on a ship and send him back to Cyprus or Malta, where he can be dealt with legally, and send someone a signal about it—I don't know: Hetherington or somebody like that.' He had not taken his eyes off Scott. 'Are you sure you won't help us here, Scott? This has now gone beyond a mere casual request.'

'Do what you like,' Scott said, terrified none the less of what was about to happen. 'I'll never help you stay here. I'm sorry . . .'

'You *do* want trouble,' the General said. 'Perhaps all that miserable business all over again. It can happen, you know,' he said cheerfully.

Scott realized again how clever and how psychologically acute this practical war-minded man was. Perhaps a little of the old terror of his court-martial and punishment was clear in his face, so that his fear advertised itself.

'You don't want to help me, I can't help you. So take him off, Alan.'

'Yes, General,' the Major said and led Scott out into the little office which was not so temporary but was vitally permanent-looking because it had boxes of files, a typewriter and a guard. The Major went back to consult the General for a moment and then he emerged with a friendly smile.

'One more stop,' the Major told him, and he took Scott under guard, in the headquarters Land Rover, to a tent on the beach front, where Scott was allowed to sit on the grass and was offered a cigarette by the Devonshire boy guarding him. He was taken into the tent, and he sat down at a long trestle mess-table where he was given a cup of tea by a Colonel who had obviously been briefed already on the conversations with the General.

'Damn!' the Colonel said when he spilled tea in his own saucer. 'Saucers are a luxury, I suppose, but I can't stand a sloppy saucer.' He poured the slop back into his cup and looked at Scott. 'You're certainly an odd-bod,' this one said, also cheerfully, 'but you've actually popped up here at a good time.'

When Scott looked at him seriously, he laughed.

'You don't know me, but I know you. My name is George Astley . . .'

Scott's silence in the face of all these cheerful approaches seemed to be that of a man who did not even speak their language any more.

'I can't believe, you know, that a chap like you could actually agree with all this wild shooting by street louts and schoolboys,' this one said, 'because it's not doing anybody any good. Nobody at all. Even your friends.'

But Scott was only half-listening because he was already looking for a means to escape. And because he felt his intention showing in his eyes, he looked away guiltily.

'I thought so,' the Colonel said, boldly misunderstanding it. 'You don't like it, do you? Incidentally you must have worked with Tim Peacock when he took over Tracks and Survey in 1942. You do remember him, I suppose?'

Scott became cautious again. 'Yes, I know him.'

'Did you know he was here?'

'In Port Said?'

'Yes. He came out with me. Perhaps you'd like to see him?'

Scott tried to think quickly. He was upset and embarrassed at the prospect of seeing Peacock under these circumstances, yet certain that he could explain to Peacock why he had come to Port Said and thus settle this dangerous situation he was in. He doubted now that he could ever get out of it any other way, and Tim would surely help.

'I'd like very much to see him,' Scott told Astley. 'Where is he?'

'Good,' Astley said. 'If you've finished your tea, let's go. I have an idea that Tim may change your mind.'

There seemed to be more of an edge to that than this robust man really meant, and Scott went with him in the Land Rover straight down Shareh el Suez, through the ruins of the bombed streets to the corner where the British had once had their Sporting Club.

Two colonial-style buildings of the old club had been turned into a hospital for wounded, but the jeep stopped under the palms above the garden entrance, and Colonel Astley told him to follow on foot. Instead of going inside the club-house they walked along the shaded gardens until they reached a freshly dug flower-bed under an old banyan tree.

'There,' Astley said, like an angry schoolboy revealing the grim proof of an exploit to an unbelieving friend. 'That's where poor old Tim is. Right under there!'

It seemed to be a special sort of bad luck which dogged a man. Perhaps a man with his need for friendship would never be able to accept fully the normal extremes of the elation and the devastation of life. He didn't understand them. If he had seen Peacock lying there on the ground bodily dead as proof of his death, the tragedy would have been simple. But a man already dead and buried is only a man who has ceased to exist. The tragedy had to come from something else, from the evocation of the living person. And it was only too easy in Peacock's case.

'Oh, no . . .' Scott groaned, just as Peacock himself had protested at the realization that he was about to stop living.

'That was one of your snipers sitting up in a window with a carbine,' George was saying. 'Tim didn't even know what hit him. He hadn't fired a shot or thought of killing anyone, and one of those reckless Egyptian bastards simply got him in the back, the way they're shooting at our youngsters in the streets now. We can't blow them out with tanks, because we've agreed to a cease-fire. So for God's sake have a heart, man, and use your influence on them before there's a worse situation which will probably get out of hand.'

But George Astley was talking to a frightened man who hardly heard. Scott felt as if he were personally responsible for Peacock's death, and for all their deaths; not because of the sniper's bullets but because he had never been able to solve this conflict of responsibility, of Peacock's and his own, and of everybody else's: this old conflict of what was humanly right and what was humanly wrong. Look what it had done . . .

'He shouldn't have been here,' Scott protested. 'He was too old to be here, surely. Why did he come to Port Said?'

'He was doing what he thought was necessary.'

There it was again. Scott winced at the impossible contradiction and tragedy of it. He looked at Astley miserably, trying to fathom for a moment what George Astley must be feeling, so that they could exchange at least one word which could be valid between them. But they were hidden men. They had hidden themselves so effectively that they were complete strangers to each other and could never be anything else.

'I'm sorry, Scott,' the Colonel said sympathetically, seeing how it had affected him, 'I didn't want to make a point of it like this, but I don't want to see any others shot down. You can go free, you know, and without any questions asked, if you give the General your word that you will use your influence with your friends to stop all this dirty guerrilla shooting. That's not much to ask, is it?'

706

'It's not much at all,' Scott agreed, turning away sadly. 'But it's more than I can do. I don't think I have any influence. But even if I did have, I know I wouldn't use it. You ought to go. You ought not to be here,' he said dejectedly. 'There'll be peace here only when you have all gone and never come back.'

Astley listened and felt sorry for Scott, but he did not argue. He could recognize stubbornness.

'Take him back to the Provost,' he told the soldier who attended them with his eyes outside these private, cubicled emotions.

They went away and left Peacock lying under his banyan tree.

It was an old tree, but perhaps, under Peacock's influence, its dusty leaves would flutter a little more gaily from now on. The real pity of it was, from Peacock's point of view, that he would never know now whether Eileen had beaten that red-faced huntsman or not.

She might at least have had the decency to send him a telegram to the House about it.

CHAPTER EIGHTY-FIVE

SCOTT hoped anxiously that they would not move him to a ship before nightfall, because he knew he would have little chance of escape now, during daylight.

But he was alert, and his chance came in the afternoon when four more suspected snipers were brought into the café and there was a violent struggle with several more in an army truck outside. It was so desperate that the Provost Captain and the lone guard at the door rushed out to help, and were occupied for a few moments with it.

Scott saw his chance and walked quickly into the shop and out of a side door, which was locked. The key was on the inside, and he opened it and walked out. Nobody had seen him.

Once outside he did not know for a moment what to do.

'But don't run, not yet,' he warned himself.

He took off his coat and carried it, and when he had hurriedly turned a corner he cut through a narrow gap in a ruined school with a blackboard hanging out of a window, and then he ran as hard as he could, heading towards the native district where he thought he could hide until dark. He avoided a group of Egyptian firemen, who were beginning to clear the broken wires and rubble off the roadway, and he hoped that he was not too conspicuous on an otherwise empty street.

He walked slowly for a while when he saw a British Centurion tank parked at a cross-roads, but the soldiers near it took no notice of him, even though they probably had radio. He was just out of their sight when someone else challenged him.

'What are you in such a hurry about?' a young British marine asked him, a flimsy little Sten-gun held menacingly in his hand.

Scott took it in quickly. *'They're obviously trying to block off the native quarter from the rest of the town to isolate the snipers,'* he decided.

His appearance was against him. It was too much of a contradiction— his large and educated European head, against his filthy clothes and un- shaven face.

'What's up?' the second marine commando asked from a doorway across the street. He had found a little puppy which he had tied up with string, and it was yelping unhappily. They had also strung up a barricade of tables and chairs, making it impossible to pass in a hurry. An Egyptian in striped pyjamas was watching curiously from a window in the block of flats below them.

'I don't know yet,' the questioner said.

Scott knew that his absence must have been discovered by now, and even though these soldiers knew nothing about it, he could not risk wasting time here. The soldier was already a little unnerved by his strange catch, and Scott remembered that most unnerved men fired quickest.

'Well?' the young soldier said. 'Don't you savvy English? Where are you going?'

That wicked little gun was pointing straight at his heart. The young marine was aggressively sure of himself for a moment, and yet Scott's forty-year-old eyes on him were too much for a normally frightened young soldier to ignore.

Something was bound to happen, they sensed it.

'You go back. Back up!' the boy shouted nervously, backing away himself a little. 'Bolley! Look out for him.'

'What's the matter?' the other one asked.

'This one is up to something.'

Scott tried to stop the fury of the world sweeping over him again. Wasn't restraint always better, always safer, always right? But at what point did outrageous fortune become simply the dead hand of a total defeat?

'If you don't back up I'll let you have it,' the boy said.

'Stay where you are,' the other one told him now.

The marines were standing almost together gripping their little Sten-guns and Scott stood unmoved, not taking his eyes off them and yet allowing the fury to sweep up and take over his whole soul. He had killed men, he knew, but he had never hit a man; even as a schoolboy he had been too hard and strong to be bothered with challengers. But now he must knock these soldiers down, even kill them if necessary, otherwise he would be delayed and caught.

Yet it would not come easily. He could not hit a man, even now . . .

'He doesn't look like a bloody Gyppo,' the youngest of them said then.

That silly, unimportant English phrase did too much damage.

What exonerated a man from responsibility? His uniform? Did his young and innocent English face? Must the whole world always forgive the innocent-faced and the uniformed for what they did? Was the soldier never guilty, the ignorant mouth never responsible? Did Englishmen never owe the responsibility for their actions to each other? Was there no guilt at all? Or did it—all this violence—begin with their ignorance and their innocence?

'Bloody Gyppos,' he cried out.

He rushed them in his fury before they could raise their frightened eyes onto a safe target. He was going to kill them, he knew. He knocked them over with his shoulders as he hit them and they fell so heavily that they were tangled up helplessly for a moment. But he had a grip on them, with the Sten-guns squashed between them, and he simply lifted the soldier up and threw him bodily like a doll clean over a low wall and down into the ramp of a basement garage under a block of flats. He heard the horrible moan when the boy hit the cement ramp, and he turned to the other, who lay on his back in terror, weaponless and helpless.

Scott bent down to pick him up and break his back, his whole body shaking with the fury of it: 'Bloody Gyppos!' he was saying. 'Bloody Gyppos. You murder people for a few words like that, you little gangsters . . .'

As he picked him up the soldier offered resistance with his feet and arms.

Scott struck him so hard with the back of his arm across the neck that he thought he had killed him, because he collapsed to the ground like a frightened child.

'You go home to your English mother and tell her that you came out here to murder innocent people. Tell her that. You innocent soldiers. When will you learn that you can't do it any more?'

He saw the boy cringe and hold his arms up to protect his face.

Scott kicked him hard as he lay there, kicked him across the buttocks, and then he picked up the little Sten-guns and held them by the barrel and smashed them on the kerbstone.

'I'm not a bloody Gyppo,' he was bellowing, 'but a bloody Englishman like you. But you disgust me. You all disgust me. It isn't your fault? Isn't it!' he cried as he smashed the guns on the kerb. 'Isn't it! You go and tell that to your general. Tell it to the Egyptians who are shooting at you from the roofs. You shout out to them: *It's my fault* . . .'

Scott was bending over the boy and shaking him angrily.

'Do you understand?'

The boy was white with pain and fright, and his eyes looked helplessly at Scott to understand what was happening, and in those eyes Scott retreated and ran, breathing furiously and pounding the road with his whole body as he wore out the fury which had only half-emerged, half-satiated itself on the rules of the world which said that the soldier was not to blame and the responsibility lay elsewhere.

'Bloody Gyppos . . .'

The innocent English phrase, that stupid normal English sentiment

710

about the world, had become a death sentence in the mouth of any man who held a gun in his hand when he said it.

Let them all die!

'It has to end somewhere,' he cried as he ran through the wreckage of a thousand native huts which had been burned to the ground.

But his fury was gone already, and he was hoping now that he had not hurt the soldier too badly when he had thrown him over the wall.

It was not difficult to get away at night.

He had spent the rest of the day hiding in the old gaffir's hut on the lake shore. The old man had given him a soft tomato and a piece of white cheese, and Scott had given him two Egyptian pound notes, which were a useless fortune at the moment because there was no food to buy with it, but he knew the old man would keep the money until it had recovered its full value.

Now he was back on the lake, returning in the night; and far from having any clear idea of what he was doing, he could only face immediate worries. Did he have enough petrol to get back? Would there be British motor-boats on this side of the lake? Could he hear them in time?

They were desperate necessities now because he was fleeing in terror, and he did not want to be caught. Not again, never again.

Yet what was he returning to?

He told himself it didn't matter. He simply felt that he was going home; and though he realized that he no longer had a passport or even his Frontier Corps pass (and no doubt it would be almost impossible to get either again) he knew he must go back.

There were searchlights sweeping beams of powdery light across the western end of the lake, and he instinctively ducked; but the whitewashed patches of night sky over his head were only a sure proof of his safety. The searchlights were far away. He started the little motor again and put-putted out of the reeds, disturbing water-hen into frightened explosions of flight.

He was going back to the only life that was safe; and yet what was so safe about it now?

CHAPTER EIGHTY-SIX

THE Suez war had been a confusing mirage of different rivalries and different tragedies; and also of universal disgust.

Some men were disgusted at the whole idea of two large nations attacking a small one; but there were those who were disgusted because the Anglo-French-Israel invasion had been stopped too soon, convinced that if it had gone on, even two or three days more, Cairo would have fallen, Nasser would have collapsed, and peace would have been restored to the whole Middle East by a sensible reminder that old interests in the area were not quite dead, and further—that democracy must reign instead of dictatorship and nationalism. And, of course, the canal could be returned to its rightful, mutual owners.

Two French Zionist authors would also suggest, in their disgust, that a ground swell of revolt against Nasser would have won the war, adding: 'This would have been the case if the Canberras that were equipped to carry the atom bomb had turned Cairo into another Hiroshima.'

Men did not mean to be bloodthirsty, but some men felt that in order to be right it was often necessary to be humanely inhuman—if your conscience could stand the terrible strain of that contradiction.

It was already being reported that Sir Anthony Eden had wept when he had left the Cabinet meetings which had ended the war. He had soon afterwards fallen dangerously ill, and had gone on a holiday to Jamaica to recover from this tragic expedition, which had absolutely ruined his health.

The allied withdrawal from Port Said had been slow, the British were obviously reluctant to leave, and because there had been so much guerrilla activity against British troops, a little dawdling was necessary in order to maintain dignity. There was also a sad argument about who should clear the canal.

What shocked most, in this aftermath, was the tragedy of two men. The first was the death of Peacock, a British Member of Parliament shot by the snipers. He had been such a lovable, brave and gay Englishman that half the population of England soon felt, reading their newspapers, that they had known him personally, and had somehow lost a close friend. The value of a man had penetrated everything—even through the House of Commons and the newspapers, even through the antagonisms of the Suez war.

The other shock was the disappearance of Lieutenant Moorhouse, a young British officer who had been captured by the Egyptian guerrillas in Port Said while doing his duty. Bitterly the British had demanded his return, and though the British forces had left Egypt by Christmas without him, they had been assured, through the good offices of the UN with the Egyptians, that he would be found and repatriated. When the Egyptian authorities did find him, where the guerrillas had hidden him, he was tragically dead, and all England mourned for a second man lost, another personal tragedy which would remain, like Peacock's death, as a reminder of the numbness and pain of that curious little war.

The confusing mirage went on.

The Egyptians insisted on behaving like the victors, denying that they had really been defeated in the Sinai, and taunting the allies with a claim that the British and the French had not even been able to subdue one un-defended city with all their might, let alone frighten a small, backward nation which would have fought them to a standstill if the war had continued.

Ben Gurion, the Prime Minister of Israel, had spoken proudly of the Jews' single-handed campaign, their proud return to the Sinai—to the land of their fathers. Not a man of the entire Diaspora could fail to understand the significance of a Jew standing once more on the Mount of Zion, this ancient Jewish sanctuary, this sacred symbol of the Kingdom of the House of David.

Give it up? Give it back to the Egyptians?

Never! Not at first, anyway, although they did give it up; even Gaza which was, they said, a thorn in their side which they would never give up unless the world agreed to demilitarize it. Nobody agreed to anything except evacuation; so the Israelis, feeling the unfair pressure of events upon their very existence, demilitarized what they could themselves, withdrew to their borders with tons of captured Egyptian and Russian material, and thereafter threw themselves once more upon the sympathy and ability of the world to understand their proud struggle for a difficult existence.

The mirage would not disappear. It would go on for a very long time, long after the reality had departed with the last foreign soldier and long after the last angry Egyptian eye, sighting over a rifle, had pulled the trigger on a patient British soldier doing his well-known duty.

CHAPTER EIGHTY-SEVEN

MADAME SALZ'S *pension* had now become a house of strange exiles who lived together like a family which did not want to be disturbed and which did not want to venture out into an unsafe world.

There was no point in any of them doing so.

They behaved as if they were all waiting for something, living out their daily lives in the old house, or in the garden, and impatiently anticipating meal-times when they would all sit together at the big table in the salon. Madame Salz would sit at one end of the table nearest the kitchen so that she could supervise the servant, and Sam would sit at the other end where he belonged. On one side sat Becky and Scott, and on the other Helen Mamoon and old David Kosnoff, who was the only real boarder left, although Helen Mamoon and Scott were paying enough to keep the house going, in this safe but temporary existence.

Every day they would talk together over a lengthy lunch about the situation surrounding them outside, isolating them. What could possibly happen next?

It was not a terror they felt. There had never been a terror against anyone in Egypt, except on that one day when Cairo was burned down and the British had been thrown out of the Turf Club windows.

It was a sad and more frightening fear: simply that the foreigners and the Jews should all go, or that they could not profitably own businesses any longer, or find secure work, or be left in peace in their comfortable flats and houses. They could not collect their pensions from British and foreign firms, nor move money out of the country, nor buy gold without it being discovered. The Jews at least had not been interned, except those suspected of being communists or ardent Zionists, and they had not been molested, although some had suffered indignities from neighbours and officials.

But the air was against them, against all foreigners. The very air. That was the trouble for all of them.

714

Even Madame Salz felt it, and she began to think she would leave Egypt when it became possible to leave. She would join her daughter in Italy. It was not her idea at first, but the idea of so many friends who came to drink coffee or tea at her table and tell, each day for weeks, the latest occurrence to the Limburgs or the Schenazis or the Cicurels, or to that Lieberman girl. Everybody knew (though heaven knew how, since the telephone to Port Said was not working) that she had already left Egypt with her children and her husband in a French ship.

It did not need a deliberate policy to make its point in this atmosphere. Foreigners and Jews were not wanted. They told themselves so every day because they felt it so, and because official eyes were firmly closed against them.

Sam still worked for Leo Lieberman, but at home now. Leo's shop had been sequestrated and sealed, but Sam (a watchmaker's glass in his eye) was still prone to heavy sorrows, to sudden temper and tears at the slightest frustration, which was really the frustration of not knowing what it was all about, or what had really happened, or what the forces were which had made it happen to him, to his friends, to everybody—to this whole nation and every other nation.

In despair he had gone once to the synagogue to see if that might make him feel better, if it could help him understand. Though he had solemnly mounted his hat and his face, and though he took Becky's arm and called a taxi (it would have been disrespectful in Sam's eyes to go to the synagogue modestly and casually) he had found no satisfaction in giving his grief and his puzzle to God. Instead, he had found most relief in his garden, where the first bulbs and flowers of winter were beginning to sprout, and every blossom was a delight to him (he showed each one to Becky as if he had persuaded it out of the ground himself).

And though December was not very cold, he had plastic sheets ready to cover the young buds in case it turned cold and frosty one night. Little Abdulla said frost was impossible. But Sam did not trust God to spare him even that, because he knew now that he was up against a superior but vindictive force, omnipotent and pervading all, even his garden. At Christmas he had extravagantly bought the children a tricycle to ride around the paths of the garden. It was a cast-alloy copy of an English tricycle, made locally. One look at it should have convinced Sam's experienced eye that it would break up in five minutes, but Sam had always had such a faith in the dynamic expression of his own affections that he could not possibly believe it would break, and when it did he suffered a disillusionment with the world as if someone, everyone, were trying to deceive him.

'Even a little bike!' he complained.

It made him look sadly at Becky every day because he knew that they

715

too would soon have to leave what he now called in self-defence, 'this bloody country'.

Scott had returned to Cairo as suddenly as he had left it. Everybody at the *pension* knew where he had been, even though Helen Mamoon had not told them, but they had been very careful and sympathetic with him for a week, or until they forgot their sentimentality about *le pauvre anglais*. He had returned one night in the train from Mansura.

Farouk the driver had waited for him at Manzalah village and they had driven the jeep as far as Mansura so that Scott could catch the ordinary passenger train to Cairo, because this way he could cleverly avoid being asked on the roads for his confiscated pass. No one needed a pass to arrive by train at Cairo station. Sam and Madame Salz had seen him arrive home by taxi that night in a badly-fitting grey suit he had bought in Mansura, but no one had asked him where he had been, or what he had done, although Madame Salz had to ask on his own behalf if he had heard any news of the Lieberman girl. He simply answered that she was safe, and that her French husband had come back.

'Comme j'ai toujours dit,' Madame Salz told Becky afterwards. 'Elle n'a jamais été constante, cette fille. Jamais!'

Scott was now a man with nothing, and he could sit in their company and listen to their Cairo talk and feel no different from any of them. He could look at Sam and tell himself, 'I'm no better off than he is now.' Like Sam he had no papers. The British had seized them, and like Sam he had no predictable future.

He had not gone back to the Frontier Department, because he knew quite well that Hakim had finished and done with him, with his old conscience; and it was more than he could face—to present himself to a man who had so finally disposed of him for ever. He had simply let it lapse. Nobody had telephoned him from Abassia, nobody had asked for him, nobody had sent for him, and he helped Sam in the garden or sat quietly in the windy sun or read whatever he could find on Antarctica, of Shackleton and his namesake Scott, and of all the men who had become so fascinated with that white continent, the men who had invested their whole lives in it, just as he would now, given the chance.

He was quiet, which was normal, but he listened to the gossip at meal-times and joined in sometimes when they reminisced on familiar ground or when old David Kosnoff began to ask him whether he thought the English would give him a resident's visa for Britain if he showed them that he could bring substantial assets (several thousand pounds) into the country and a skilled knowledge of the import and export of carpets, textiles and silks.

'I should think it would help,' Scott said, unable to be ignorant

716

when such a hopeful, helpless question was asked. 'Yes. You must tell them.'

But he became irritated with them sometimes, when they talked incessantly about those who did or did not get their money out. Even Helen Mamoon. He would retreat from them impatiently and swear to mind his own business thereafter. He would be quiet for a day, but then Sam would begin to feel sorry for him, and anything seemed better than that, so he would cheer up and sit on the outside stairs in the winter sun, talking often about pre-war Cairo to Helen Mamoon, or playing unskilled games with Quartermain's children, because Quartermain was still interned and his wife Nona was not yet allowed to leave her flat. The children were brought around by their Aunt Hanna, who told them not to run over Sam's flower-beds.

'Yes, please!' Sam begged her in Arabic. 'Don't let them pull up—in the name of God—anything; or trample the beds down.'

But Scott had been talking to Helen Mamoon one day when her friend Dr. Buelli had arrived from Alexandria, and he had watched them later talking intently together in the salon. He had felt a sudden division again, as if even this amount of friendly talk from Helen Mamoon was really outside her life and everybody else's. That was how it was. He was outside everybody else's life now.

Yet she told him, sitting on the steps one day, what Dr. Buelli had asked of her.

'He's leaving Egypt,' she said. 'He's going to Italy and he wants me to go with him. They've taken away his Egyptian passport after all these years, after all that effort to get it. Poor Buelli. He has to leave. They're going to throw him out.'

'How can he leave without a passport?' (Wasn't that Sam's problem?)

'He's getting an Italian passport.'

'Is he an Italian?' he asked, surprised. He knew of Buelli—a stateless Jew who was a good doctor and a brilliant speculator and a generous man among his own people.

'No, he's not Italian at all, but he's going to get a Livorno passport,' she said, and her defiant look across the cool evening at Scott seemed to record that as a sort of victory for Buelli. 'It just shows you,' she said revengefully, 'how stupid all this passport and nationality business is. You can get anything if you are willing to pay for it. There is now a whole colony of Livorno Jews in the world who have never even been there. They all come from Cairo. Someone found out a little while ago that the town hall of Livorno was burned down and all the records with it. Now all you have to do is to pay a large sum of money to an Italian bank manager or somebody in Cairo to swear that you were born in Livorno, and the priests help too, and you can go to the Italian consulate and get an Italian

717

passport. That's what Buelli is doing. That's what he wants me to do . . .'

'You!'

'Yes. Don't you think the Egyptians will try to take my passport away also? They've asked me for it every week since the Suez war, but I refuse to go in with it. I won't part with it—not unless I have to leave . . .'

'But are you thinking of leaving—with Dr. Buelli?'

'I don't know,' she said very calmly, looking at him provokingly to see what he really thought of such a possibility. He looked away. 'I can't decide until everything else is settled,' she went on, 'until Quarts is free and until they can leave with the children. I might. Oh, I might! I might have to. But I can't decide yet. And, anyway, why should I pretend to be an Italian? Why should I have to do that!'

He felt accused by her outburst, but he kept his head down to avoid it.

It went on like that—as a hiatus, a forced wait. Yet he did not know what he was waiting for. He knew he would have left Egypt long ago himself if he had possessed a passport, if he had somewhere to go. But he was closed in now. He tried to avoid Helen Mamoon after that particular day, and he went to the cinema too often instead of talking to her so much. He would stand in line with a hundred young men who also looked for safe, unqualified evasion as surely as he did. Fantasy was safer than reality at all times.

But he knew he was gradually losing a vital thread of himself, and he longed more and more to talk to someone intimately, to Françoise or to Lucy Pickering. He could not believe that he was now completely alone, or that he could not open his heart even by that fraction he had allowed himself.

'Sam . . .' he had started to say once, but he had given up.

It was no good telling Sam anything these days and the only other person available was Helen Mamoon, but with her he carefully avoided any talk about personal problems, or even about difficult ones, such as Nasser, on which they could never agree.

But he had to come back to her, desperately, and told her, in broad daylight one day, what had happened to him in Port Said, although he left out the real point of it—Françoise—which she could guess anyway. The point he did make was that he no longer had any documents of any kind. The British had kept them all, and now he was no longer able to decide what he could do or where he could go.

'Surely you can get another British passport,' she said.

He doubted it. 'Not after the attitude they took. As far as they were concerned I was an Egyptian spy, sent there to organize Egyptian resistance.'

'But you *know* you did nothing wrong,' she said indignantly.

'They think otherwise,' he said, 'so what's the use of that?'

'But it's your right. Surely the British, of all people, can't take a passport away from you, if you've done nothing criminal or against the state . . .'

'But that is what they do believe,' he repeated. 'I would have, anyway.'

'But you *didn't*,' she persisted, 'and you ought to claim your rights. I spent two years getting my Egyptian passport. I'd never give in. Don't let them convince you that you're guilty when you're not. They have no right. You ought to insist.'

He could laugh sadly at her determination on his behalf, but he did not feel like laughing. He said there was no one he could apply to, anyway. There was no British Embassy or Consulate left, and there wasn't likely to be one for a very long time.

'What will you do?' she asked.

'I haven't decided,' he admitted, trying to be casual about it. 'It's very difficult to decide now.'

'Do you want to stay in Egypt?'

That was a perpetual question for all of them, always requiring an answer, even if the answer changed from day to day.

'I don't think I can do anything here now,' he said. 'They can't really trust any of us ever again. Not one of us.'

'Not even you?'

'Particularly me,' he said. 'I waited too long before I showed them how I felt.'

But she felt sorry for him, because she could see by his manner, by his eyes, by his air of defeat and helplessness that something more terrible than he would admit had happened to him in Port Said. She wanted to stir him out of it—to hit back at whatever it was. She couldn't help it. She could not bear to see a man like this in such confusion. It was wrong.

She tried to encourage him with her own solutions, her own arguments.

'I brought you this to read,' she told him one day, when the light of a January day had followed a discussion which had gone on long into the night over the dining-table. They had been arguing—the two of them—about this cursed, all-powerful force of uncontrollable circumstance which seemed to rule them all. Wars, uncertainty and misery. What hope did any human being have any more? She had lost her temper; not with Scott but with the incredible helplessness of everyone. 'All over the world,' she said. 'But everywhere!'

She told him that she had decided to join a local branch of the Rosicrucians, because there must be some way of living without all this hatred and fear and violence. Somebody must be doing something about it.

He wondered why she had decided of all people on the Rosicrucians,

719

but he did not ask. He had no real interest. Simple courtesy made him take the Rosicrucian book she had offered him.

'They at least say that they want to improve mankind without any of these terrible politics and organized religions,' she said. 'They say that they can do it simply by discovering and propagating a true philosophy. If one could only do that, don't you think it would be marvellous?' she said.

The cabbals, the magical signs and the power of ancient Egyptian symbolism did not seem to be as important to her as the prospect they promised of the marvels man could achieve, if only he could rid himself of his inner failing.

Scott read the book for an hour, through the history of Rosenkreuz, of the rose and the cross, until he came to the explanation of the universe, which, it said, was permeated with the essence of the creator, so that every rock was instinct with life, and every plant and tree was imbued with a sense derived from the Master mind, and each living thing moved and thought in accordance with the supreme design.

'I don't know that it's any good for me,' he told her at lunch-time, handing it back to her and joking with her. 'It's a little hard for me to work on that premise of the universe at this late state. I mean,' he said apologetically, seeing the disappointment in her face, 'it contradicts necessary scientific facts.'

'But that part doesn't matter as much as the idea itself, surely?' she argued.

He nodded and passed Becky the salt. 'That's true. Yes, you are right,' he said gently.

'. . . because there *must* be something that explains all that is happening in the world, and at least tries to right what is wrong. If there isn't, what's the use of anything? There surely must be something . . .'

He watched her temper and impatience and her indignation stimulate her face into tiny lines, which took away the old Egyptian look and made her appear quarrelsome and ready to dispute anybody at all, the world itself if necessary.

'Don't you think it ought to be a *little* more scientific?' he suggested.

She did not seem to hear, and she asked him instead to go with her for her second visit to the lodge of the society, which held an open weekly meeting for initiates in the old sandy building of the Society for Prevention of Cruelty to Animals. He could not say 'No' without facing her contempt or her disappointment, so he went with her in a taxi.

They joined a dozen men and women in a small stale room and listened to a lodge master reading extracts from a translation of a document found in Tibet, which was surely a work originally written by Amenhotep IV, Pharaoh of Egypt, in 1360 B.C., and in which the obligations of man as an

720

individual were listed under the simplest requirements: modesty, application, emulation, prudence, fortitude, contentment and further prudence.

Scott looked at his neighbours and began to wonder what he was doing here. But how could he feel indifferent to these people when he could easily recognize these strange mixtures which Cairo, or any Egyptian city, could produce—not only racial and religious mixtures but men and women who only fitted into Egyptian life with a whole piece missing somewhere: a religion or a status or a quality, or even a hope. Yet they looked serious and dedicated, particularly the women, and they were depressingly convinced.

When he looked at Helen Mamoon in this company he knew it would be short-lived. He did not have long to wait, because she became angry when they would not allow her, in the free discussion, to ask direct questions concerning the attitude of the Rosicrucians towards the inequality and starvation and injustice in the world. The misery, the wars. Was that part of the grand design?

'Misery,' the master read out in reply, 'is the character of thy body, the prerogative of thy flesh. In thy thoughts alone it resideth, without these there is nothing of it. And behold, what is its source but thine own physical passions?'

Helen had said briefly: 'That's not the point I'm making.'

But their point was too gently evasive for her and she had taken his arm and said, 'Oooofff!' and they had left in disgust.

'How did I ever think they would be able to tell me anything?' she said to him as they walked home along the blue-lit Nile, angry again at herself, at the world, at the impossibility of it all, at this wretched elusive *something* which would explain all, if only she could find a clue.

'I suppose they're just another sort of religion,' he said consolingly. 'I read somewhere the other day that there are about a thousand different religions now at work in the world. Most of them go back a long way. Most of them explain the troubles of the world by saying it is divine will, therefore you can't do much about it except forbear and take your punishment . . .'

'Oh, but that's silly,' she said, sounding like Nona. 'Why should we forbear? That's what makes me angry. I simply don't understand it. Why does everybody simply lie down and die when someone in authority tells them to? Why do we accept all this terrible uncertainty, simply because someone else says we should? We ought not to . . .'

'That's true,' he agreed warily, 'but we all do.'

'Then it's wrong. There must be a way not to accept.'

'If one could really understand *why* it all happens,' he said. 'I mean scientifically understand . . .'

Was there a science to uncertainty?

721

'I don't care *how* we understand,' she insisted, 'so long as we can do something about it when we do understand. Oh, if only we had a clue . . .'

She wanted illumination. But he held her arm and guided her carefully over the darkened footpaths where the pot-holes were filled with damp mud. A light evening rain brought them the faint smell of Egypt, the old Nile smells seeping up through the earth.

But the atmosphere tightened on them every day now.

A tax-assessor found Madame Salz. She had never paid a piastre tax in her life, although she had been running her *pension* for ten years.

'But I've never heard of it,' she complained. 'Nobody has asked me for tax before.'

'There are laws which should have warned you, which have been widely published,' the inspector answered in Arabic.

The laws applied to everyone, foreigners and Egyptians alike. All business income must be declared each year for tax purposes. It was very simple. Nevertheless, some people had lived all their lives in Egypt and had never heard the word before. Madame Salz protested and protested.

'I'm sorry, *ya sitt*, but you should have been paying your taxes,' the inspector replied insistently. 'And you haven't paid a piastre. You will have to be assessed and fined accordingly.'

'How much?' she asked him, feeling already like a criminal in her own comfortable salon, where the inspector was drinking coffee reluctantly.

'Mmmm . . . .' The inspector had also discovered that the conveyance of the house and property from Aunt Clothilde to Madame Salz had been irregular, with false values being declared, although at that time everyone had done the same thing. He understood, but nevertheless he could not possibly assess what she owed at less than four thousand pounds, although it would be subject to official confirmation.

'But that's cruel!' she protested. 'It will ruin me. I haven't any money, even four hundred pounds.'

The tax-inspector was a plump, family-looking Egyptian whose salary was probably not enough to keep him, so that he did another job as well somewhere. He shrugged unhappily and said: 'It is not as cruel as it could be, Madame Salz. Technically, you should have been sequestrated.'

'But that's worse,' she cried.

He nodded, and his nod seemed like a terrible warning.

All Jewish businesses had been sequestrated as enemy property—a normal procedure during a war. The Jewish-owned shops had been closed and sealed, and Jewish bank accounts (whether the Jews were Egyptian subjects or foreign subjects) had been blocked. Only enough money to live on could be withdrawn. Jewish directors had been expelled from mixed businesses and from leading positions, the managers of the hotels,

722

and the floor-walkers in shops. The same rule applied to the British and the French as enemy subjects. An enemy was an enemy. But it hurt the British so much less, because so much of their business was big business, like the Shell oil company or the big import houses, whereas the Jewish businesses were large only in a small way, although the biggest land concentration owned by any one man in Egypt (since the end of Farouk) was the holding of the Jewish Smouha family in Alexandria, which ran into eighteen or twenty million pounds' worth of agricultural and urban property.

But *pensions* like Madame Salz's had not so far been classed as business, nor had private houses, and the Jews and the British and the French were safe in their own houses in Egypt, except that British and French subjects had been confined to quarters, whereas the Jews had been allowed to go free, for the most part.

Was a *pension* a business?

'I can't help it,' the inspector said sadly. 'I am only doing my duty.'

That most perforated aspect of the civilized ethic was at it again.

It seemed fair and just, under the circumstances, and yet it was also manifestly unfair and unequal and unjust.

They comforted Madame Salz as best they could, but she could only weep helplessly for hours and cry out that she was ruined. Four thousand pounds! Where would she ever get a few hundred pounds? And even if she had a thousand pounds—what if the sequestration authorities discovered her, anyway, and declared her a business and closed her down, like the Shell company? They would seize her house and then she would lose everything. Were all the laws of state so recklessly lacking in any sort of compassionate selection between human beings and property?

'What shall I do?' Madame Salz begged them over dinner of fessikh and onions and pickles.

'Ah . . . but let us *leave* this bloody country!' Sam bellowed angrily.

'Shhhh!' Becky said, blushing.

Could their friend, Captain Scott, help?

Scott had put a great store in friendship all his life. Hadn't it been the only sure and definable and worthwhile value—that only real value between individuals? But what happened when friendship became impotent, and when individuals were crushed?

He knew he could not run frantically around the country rescuing his friends any longer, because he was as badly off as they were. Thus the importance he had given it (to depending, as well, on one man above others) had now become simply a means of torture. He could not really help Madame Salz, even if he gave her the money himself.

'Yet the Egyptians complain,' Helen Mamoon said with the spirit of her own Christian minority rising in her, 'when the Jews, who suffer this sort of thing, decide to set up their own state where it can't happen any more.'

'It never used to happen here,' Scott argued in the cool night, sitting on the stoop and feeding Felu a night supper of crushed lentils. 'It was Europe that persecuted the Jews, not Egypt and the Arabs. They never did . . .'

'But they do now.'

'Blame Israel this time,' he said.

They had forgotten Madame Salz and they were finally arguing on a forbidden subject, because Scott could not become reconciled to Israel, whatever his sympathies for Madame Salz. And his sympathies were obvious. Not the classical Christian condescension of his best friends—the Jews—but the true value of the people he loved and respected most and could not do without. Sam and Becky were the best link he had with life, and Madame Salz was vital to him now. It was not a friendship, it was his total absorption into their ancient and generous family.

Yet it was not that simple.

He knew that to be a Jew you did not have to be an Israeli or a Zionist. Sam had always refused to consider himself either, even during the war when old Aunt Clothilde and her frail school-teacher friend had called on the Jewish Maccabees to be the world's revolutionaries against great injustices and terrible wrongs, insisting that Jews should not create a narrow political sect out of being Jewish, or seek a new religious homeland where they had no longer any right to it. 'We belong to the world,' these old ladies had said. 'Why should Jews want to go to Israel which has been dead for thousands of years? Palestine is not Israel.'

The problem could not therefore be solved by the mere existence of Israel. He knew—he had settled this much clearly in his mind—that it would only be solved when this hatred of Jews was eradicated from the hearts and minds of men everywhere, especially in Europe where it had reached its cruellest apogee in civilized, humane, cultured Germany.

'But surely Israel has solved *something* for the Jews?' she argued.

'Perhaps,' he said, giving Felu another lentil.

But even in Israel there were still rich Jews and poor Jews. 'I suppose there are ambitious Jews and aggressive Jews and dangerous Jews and peaceful ones and helpless ones and frightened ones. That's all right,' he said. 'That's normal!'

But Israel therefore had the same problems and responsibilities as anyone else, and must therefore be judged in that light. Couldn't you call the Israelis downright aggressors without damning the Jews for being Jews?

'But it *is* a religious problem also,' she insisted, 'even outside Israel.'

He agreed, and he said that the true Jewish religion (the true Judaism)

724

was the only religion he had ever found to be universal and liberal enough to embrace all. It did not demand redemption, it did not thirst for converts and absolute rulings. It accepted the humanity of other ideas and religions willingly, but above all it often concerned itself (unique among religions) with the possibility that man could better his lot on earth materially, even perfect himself. But even this sort of religion had been adulterated with prejudices and with self-inflicted wounds; ridiculous dogmas. Which meant that it no longer answered the problems of this complicated modern world. Look at Sam. Was political and military Zionism the answer for Sam? And look what it was doing in Israel—breeding all those frantic youths who would cruelly cut down all before them in the ferocity of their ignorance, and in the narrowness of their own zealous conviction in themselves.

He argued bitterly and stubbornly, and she listened, but it all foundered for both of them on the morality of the Suez war.

'What else could the Israelis do?' she said. 'You tell me.'

'I don't know,' he had to admit. 'Anything, perhaps, but what they did do.'

'And Madame Salz? Why should it all come down on her?'

'If I could solve that I could probably solve everything,' he said helplessly, unhappily, guiltily.

Madame Salz had brought them out some yaourt, which she had made herself of buffalo milk, and they stopped the argument in deference to her feelings. She sat with them on the porch for a little while, listening to the radio of a neighbour which blazened on the night an old Egyptian popular song which had just been revived. It was a mimicry of man calling up the operator of the central telephone exchange, trying to get a number but receiving only very silly answers. They could not help but laugh, and though Madame Salz did not understand enough Arabic to appreciate it, she laughed with them, and then went inside when her unhappy tears got the better of her.

'There ought to be a universal law leaving old people safe at least!' Helen cried vehemently. 'In every country . . .'

'Also the children,' he said to her.

But who would ever be able to implement *ought* into a social necessity? That was their real problem.

Also, there were shades to it outside their own sun, beyond their own heat and their own light. Ishaak, his desert driver, came to Scott at the *pension* one day and told him how he had escaped from the Sinai and reported the terrible scenes he had witnessed as a *Feldscher*—the bodies burned by the Jewish planes with napalm—burning, jellied petrol. Not the ones *killed* by the napalm, he said, but the ones who had survived.

725

Scott pointed out that they were French planes, dropping French napalm . . .

'That's worse!' Ishaak had shouted ferociously. 'Every religion says that it is even worse to employ a murderer than it is to murder for yourself. Even the Christians and the Jews (God curse them) believe that. But if you could have seen those men, ya Capten,' Ishaak said, one hand to his own delicate face. 'They were burned black all over—all their skin was completely burned and they were still alive. I can't tell you what they looked like. And every time they moved, a little piece of black skin would come off and there was the raw flesh under it. Every time they moved an arm or touched something or cried out, their face, even, would begin to fall to pieces, and it would be raw flesh like a piece of meat in a butcher's shop. Ah, Capten, this isn't human! I don't believe any more in the Jews being human. Nobody human could use things like that, for any reason. Yet that was how they won their battles. Everybody knows it. All our wounded were like that. At first I was sick and I fainted, and then I cried and then I wanted to kill them all—and now I want to go back. I can't be this nurse any more. I have finished. You must speak to General Hakim for me, and I will go with the tanks now. I must go back. I don't care if they kill me now but I will go back and do away with them. I will kill as many as I can. I will never be at peace now until I can do that. So you must please ask them to let me go into the tanks or the rocket-launchers the Russians use. They say they are terrible things. But I want to kill as many of them as I can . . .'

Scott looked at this soft Palestinian face and wondered if it had gained a hard heart, a worldly courage, a real desire for revenge and hate: so that this time it would last and might carry him through the real wars, even in the face of death—which he would normally have fled from, having more intelligence than he had courage.

'I don't see General Hakim any more,' he told Ishaak.

Ishaak screwed up his forage cap. 'But you must!'

Scott shook his head. 'I have left the Frontier Department,' he told Ishaak. 'I can't help you.'

'Then where is Colonel Fakhry?'

'He was killed, they think, in Port Said,' Scott told him.

'Ahhh . . . you see! And look how young and handsome he was. Ya Capten, you can help me with someone. I must go back . . .'

Had Ishaak suddenly become a man, very quickly, in the burned flesh of his fellows? Scott had also seen burned flesh—when his friend Moses Brodie had been burned like that on the minefield Church had sent them on by mistake. He had shot Moses to put him out of his fantastic pain . . .

'I know,' he said to Ishaak, feeling the horror of that day come back as he thought it never would again in his whole life. It had been buried too

726

deep, so deep that he had forgotten it. Yet Ishaak was dragging it out with that violent, revengeful eye.

'You don't believe me!' Ishaak was saying bitterly. 'You don't think I am serious. You think this time I am just like before—being childish, ya Capten! Do you think that?' he said threateningly.

'No, no,' Scott said sadly. 'I know you're serious, Ishaak. I can't blame you. If I could help you, I would. Why don't you simply ask to be transferred?'

'I've asked, but they say they have trained me to be a *Feldscher*, and I can't change. It's difficult to train *Feldschers*.'

'Why don't you go to General Hakim yourself?' Scott said. 'He'll understand.'

'Nobody will understand,' Ishaak said bitterly, tears in his eyes now.

But Scott understood, and yet here was Madame Salz bringing them tea, and Ishaak thanking her in the deepest politesse of his Arab soul. Where was the revenge here, the violence, the justification?

Yet Ishaak went away determined, and Scott knew for sure that he would never be the same Ishaak again, and that this time he would go on without running away, until he had made some final attempt to recover what was, to him, the lost homeland which had been stolen by the Jews.

That was the problem also.

CHAPTER EIGHTY-EIGHT

QUARTERMAIN'S internment in the Semiramis Hotel had not been difficult. They had not questioned him unduly about his sympathies, his politics, his friends.

They had asked him several times if he was a communist, and he had refused to answer; but when they had softened it to 'Aren't you sympathetic to communism in Russia?' he had said as dryly as he could: 'I suppose so. Didn't Russia make Egyptian independence possible?' They had not pursued it any further than that, and they had given him a room overlooking the river, which, they said, he would have to pay for eventually, and they allowed him to telephone his wife once a day to see that all was well.

He ate well. He relapsed—not into bitterness but into 'understanding'. He warned himself every day: 'No bristling and no going off half-cocked,' and he taunted no one but himself. He humoured his nerves instead by playing cards with his fellow British and French correspondents and arguing calmly. But not taunting, never taunting; he had given up taunting anyone, even when he had significance at his elbow urging him on.

Instead, he simply argued them firmly into the ground. That the British should win the war? Impossible, if you understood it. That the Egyptians would, quite logically, be overwhelmed by sheer weight? Not a hope, if you realized what would happen here. That the Egyptian tanks they heard in the streets of Cairo were to suppress a revolution brewing against Nasser? (This was the French view among them.)

'Don't be a bloody fool,' he said, with no disparagement intended.

He rang Nona at six o'clock every evening when the sky was the colour of a dark orange desert, and he talked to the boys and told them not to make trouble for their mother, who reported that they were really behaving very well, particularly Benjamino. They seemed to be better behaved in fact than they had been for years.

Was it because their father was not there to undermine the mother's strict authority by his reasonable approach to them?

Nona did not suggest it, and Quartermain did not bristle at the possibility even in his own mind. They were calm. They were not getting on each other's nerves. They were determined, on the telephone, to be helpful; and Nona told her children every night what a unique and determined father they had, because he would not abandon the clue he had found to the truth of the world—that it was divided universally and unjustly between exploited and exploiters—and she explained that he clung to his belief no matter what happened or what threatened him.

'Where is he?' Benjamin had asked the first night.

'He's gone away for a few days,' she had replied casually. 'And now get your shoes off before you try to take your pants off, otherwise you'll tear them and I won't buy you any more.'

They did not believe their mother, because everything else was so extraordinary. There was no school, and their mother never went outside. Hanna was living with them and she took them out to the gardens. They had heard the gunfire and the bombs, and they had seen their Aunt Hanna's unhappy eyes, as puzzled as their own at the confusion and disruption.

'Be good, children,' she told them every time she brought them back, just before opening the front door to go in, 'and be nice to your mother.'

Benjamin would look at her in amazement. Wasn't he always nice?

'Who do you love?' she would demand of Hilal who was always willing to be asked—to be cradled and cuddled while he sucked his fingers.

He would reply, with two fingers blocking his mouth, by pointing silently to her, to his mother, to his brother, to himself, and then to any door which would represent his absent father.

'Oh, you darling!' Hanna would say and bury her head on him.

Jack de Brazio and Ella had called on Nona with delicacies and presents for the children. There was a policeman outside the flat door, to whom Nona sent coffee twice a day, and who talked Arabic to the children—a great deal of which Benjamin already understood. But little moon was frightened of it because the policeman had a black face, and though no one—as far as Nona knew—had said anything to frighten him in this way, Hilal walked the long way around that beaming dark face and asked his mother inside: 'Why has that man got a white face?'

Nona, who was not going to hand herself over to any Freudian interpretation of inversion, was worried for a moment that he might be colourblind, so she made sure that he could distinguish one colour from another by asking him the colour of the sky.

'Blue!' he said firmly.

Nona was relieved and satisfied.

The de Brazios were impressed with her sanity, with her beauty, with her forthrightness, and with the power she must have to cope with the dry but sharp elisions of her husband.

'Do you need any money?' Jack asked her, having learned already that directness with her was better than delicate hypocrisy.

'Not yet, thank you,' she said.

'You know, I really owe Quarts for his help . . .'

She had cut him short. Americans embarrassed her, particularly generous ones. She did not allow anyone outside her family to be that generous or helpful.

'I don't know about that,' she said. 'You'll have to settle that with Quarts when he comes out.'

The war had ended many weeks ago, but they were still interned, still waiting for the other war, that mirage of it, to go away.

In fact, this aftermath for Nona and Hanna, and Helen too, was already worse than the reality, because now the bitterness would show. It wasn't so much the British who would suffer now but the old enemies—the local foreigners and those Christian Egyptians like Helen who had worked so closely with the British but who were still not free to leave the country if they wished to.

But in the New Year, Quartermain was allowed to go home. It was like coming out of a hospital, and though it was not complete freedom, he was permitted several hours' circulation per day in which to arrange his own evacuation from Egypt.

He was given two weeks in which to leave, and now that 'Swissair' and other neutral airlines were operating on the repaired runways of Cairo airport, there was no excuse he could offer for delay. All that remained for the family consideration was to decide whether Hanna and Helen should leave with them, and how it could be done.

There would be very little choice, because Hanna's renewed *laissez-passer* would run out in a few months' time and the Ministry of Interior would not renew it again if they could possibly avoid it, or they would certainly make so much trouble and delay about it that the very thought of having to go through all that again made Helen's face close up in grim preparation for a battle she already felt she could not win.

'And you, darling?' Nona told Helen when they discussed it over the preparations for the special pigeon dinner which Nona had prepared for her husband's return. 'You can't stay here, and you know it.'

'That's all very well. But what can I do abroad at my age? You said so yourself. We discussed it.'

But she had not told Nona or Hanna about Buelli's offer. She did not know why she had kept it a secret from them even though she had told Scott about it. Also, now that Quartermain was coming out, Buelli had telephoned her from Alexandria because he dared not wait any longer.

'They will find out soon about these Livorno passports,' he warned her, 'and then you won't be able to get one. And I must leave . . .'

He had a week left. He would go to Italy. He had managed to get a great deal of his money out, years ago. He was safe. He was secure. Why didn't she think of that as a solution? She could be very happy with Buelli who was gentle and cultured and intelligent and lively also. To be well-off; not to worry any more about money or passports or countries or nationalities. Buelli would gladly look after her . . .

But though she could speculate and provoke herself with this perfect solution, she could only think, realistically, of how she could survive abroad on her own, and how she could manage here on her own.

It was the same old problem of work, except that this time she had been living on her savings. She had already tried to find other work in American companies and Unesco projects, and in the other foreign organizations—the only kind which could absorb and pay for her capacities. They were already over-employing, and there was no other role yet for women in Egypt, and even if there were she would not be accepted, being a Christian. Her only hope now would be to leave Egypt and ask the Anglo-Egyptian Oil Exploration Company to give her the job they had promised her in England. She had been loyal to the last. She had closed their office and sold up their furniture, she had even sold up the lease and the private possessions of her boss, Jolley, his cash possessions—his tape-recorders and radios and cocktail cabinets and his motor-car. Every piastre of it was in Barclays Bank in his name, over three thousand pounds, although it was now a blocked account—an enemy asset.

But she knew she could count on Jolley's goodwill to give her a decent job in England. There, at least, the family could all be together. Hanna would never leave Nona's children now, and there was no point in Helen herself being left alone in Egypt.

'I suppose I'll have to go this time,' she decided miserably. 'I ought to know when I'm beaten. But there's still Sam. We'll have to do something about him.'

She did not know yet what she could do about Sam, but she went next day to the Swiss consulate to ask for visas for herself and Hanna because there was no direct route to England. Along with the world's loud protests at the terrible revenge being carried out by Nasser on the foreigners and the Jews in Egypt, there was a strange reluctance on the part of the free-dom-loving countries (so Quartermain declared in his new composure) to help them with a little thing like a visa.

But the Swiss at least were being liberal with the Jews, so that they would probably be helpful to an unwanted Christian. Also, the Egyptian

731

Security police had asked her again for her passport, and she said that this time she would leave Egypt rather than hand it over to them.

But Quartermain *had* changed.

'How can a man change himself?' affectionate cynics like Nona would ask.

Quartermain would argue people into oblivion about this.

'It's just a matter of conviction,' he would begin, 'of adaptation . . .'

'Oooof!' Nona would say helplessly and abandon him. 'You and your theories!'

Nona would feed him well, and she had made the children prepare a special welcome in the form of good behaviour, so that father and mother did not have to be unhappy because the children had provoked them with their naughtiness and silliness.

'You can be silly tomorrow in the garden,' she warned Benjamin, 'but not tonight when your father comes come. And if I allow you to stay up late, don't come in at dawn tomorrow morning and jump on him in bed. Do you understand?'

Benjamin understood, and Hilal fell asleep appreciatively, and he was put to bed before his father arrived.

He *had* changed, and Nona herself noticed it.

His eyes, she remembered in a second's glance at him, were not so much angry as worried, and yet they were so friendly. Was that new? Or was it something she had not noticed lately, or until he had been a month out of sight? He was really so gentle, too, in his lank, dry way. Was that new, or had it always been true? His hair was dryer and greyer, and too thick. He did need a haircut. But above all things ('Oh, my God, what a difference!') he had shaved off his moustache, and there was his mouth, courageously exposed.

'What did you do that for?' she asked in amazement.

'Couldn't help it,' he said.

She realized that it was his mouth which had changed him. She had never seen it before, and there it was. It was not so much his eyes that were braced against pain but his mouth which revealed a haunting fear of it, only subtly hidden by his determination to put up with it.

She loved her husband very much just then.

He ate his welcome-home dinner very slowly, and Nona thought it was probably his uncomposed, decomposed stomach giving him trouble again.

'Aren't you well?' she asked him

'Quite well, sweetheart,' he said calmly.

'Aren't you hungry?'

'Starving,' he said. 'You know, I've stopped eating lunch lately.'

'Then why don't you eat your pigeon?'

732

'I am eating it,' he told her. 'I'm eating slowly.'

'Why? What's the matter with it?'

'Nothing!' he said. 'I simply came to the conclusion a couple of weeks ago that the diaphragm is the source of all the trouble, and that people get stomach-aches because their nerves are tight all the time, particularly when they eat. Composure—that's all one needs.'

'When you eat?'

'All the time,' he said. 'But when I eat now I build up a little wall of composure around every mouthful, and that means I relax. I let go. It takes time to finish a meal, that's the only trouble.'

'I'd love to see you relaxed,' she said. She had not changed.

'Ah, but I am relaxed,' he told her, teasing her gently with his eyes—with all their struggle and secrets dammed back by a world of his own, a rather hard world. 'And what's more, my darling,' he said, 'I'm going to stay relaxed. See . . .' he drooped a hand lazily on the table. 'Before I met you I was always like that. But I decided one day, in 1943, it was a miserable way to go through life, being so unresolved; so I became more responsive and much tighter. It was a rotten thing to do to my stomach though; so now I'm going back to the old idea. It's much better at my age. I shan't quarrel with you any more.'

'You want to be an old man before you're forty.'

'I'm going to be a young man at forty,' he argued firmly, getting ready to defend his position. 'No more arguments and stomach-aches.'

Helen Mamoon—that searcher for any kind of illumination to explain the world—agreed with him, but she added: 'If only one could stay composed. But how can you? Only this morning an official tried to call me a foreigner, so I had to lose my temper with him. I get so angry . . .'

'Don't let them upset you,' Quartermain advised. 'Don't let them provoke you, that's all.'

Nona laughed at the miracle, and Benjamino asked impatiently what she was laughing at, thus reminding them of his presence. He was taken off by Hanna who brought him back in his pyjamas to kiss his parents and his Aunt Helen good night.

'Can I keep the light on?' he asked his mother.

'All right, sweetheart,' she replied, 'but go to sleep.'

He delayed departure again as long as he could, but when his mother said to him: 'Go to bed *now*! At once!' with her irritated command, her husband winced and kept his eyes on his coffee, holding tight to his diaphragm, his nerves, and his determination to prove that he had changed. He would not even interfere between Nona and the children.

733

THE first mail direct from England had begun to arrive freely and Scott received a letter from the Antarctic Committee of the Royal Geographical Society telling him that they were disappointed that he had not been able to appear in London for an interview, presumably owing to the recent hostilities, but they would still be quite willing to consider him in the replacements being sent to assist Dr. Vivian Fuchs, if he still wished to offer himself. He had ideal qualifications for many tasks in Antarctica, and they would be only too glad if they could include him in the short list.

'Some people could go to the South Pole and it would do them good,' Helen Mamoon told him when he showed her the letter (was there any pride in him doing a thing like that?), 'but I don't think it would be good for you at all.'

'They've been very decent to me,' he said, 'and this time I must definitely accept the offer or turn it down. I have to go through with it somehow, because I can't sit about here much longer, doing nothing and being nothing. Do you think I could risk going back to England?'

Helen Mamoon would like to have fathomed that immobile but weathered and troubled face and deep eyes; and when he took his steel spectacles off he looked like a man peering into the void of his own life without finding any sign of an objective or a purpose left in it. Why did he peer like that? She longed to help him with a sudden laugh, or a teasing intimacy of some very funny Arabic story. But he would probably blush and look at her in amazement if she did that now.

'He needs somebody,' she wanted to say, but could not say it to him; she could not even say it to Nona who would never understand the compassion this man was evoking in her. Yet she could not suppress it entirely.

'Don't go to the antarctic,' she said so suddenly that she surprised herself.

He looked up. 'Why not? What do you mean?'

'Isn't it dangerous?'

He laughed. 'Not at all. It might be too cold, but it's not very dangerous these days.'

They had both rippled quickly over her sudden insertion, and she asked him what he thought about Sam, particularly if Madame Salz now lost her business by a tax debt and sequestration.

'Leo Lieberman is only being generous to Sam out of the goodness of his heart,' she went on. 'When Leo leaves Egypt what sort of work will Sam get? And they're sure to rearrest him sooner or later. He *must* leave Egypt, don't you think?'

'But where can Sam go?' he wanted to know.

'Why not with Madame Salz?'

Madame Salz (in her sorrow and worry about her own future and still under the influence of her gossiping friends and of the air itself) had taken out her old Austrian passport and had gone to the Austrian consulate and asked if she could return to Austria, which she had left as a very young girl of nineteen at the end of the first world war.

She was genuinely an Austrian citizen by birth, but her husband had been a stateless Jewish printer who had owned a small press in Alexandria until he had died of glandular fever when her two daughters, who had been born in Egypt, were still quite young. She had kept one *pension* after another ever since, mainly in Alexandria, which she had left to set herself up in Cairo because she was sure that the damp sea air had caused her husband's death.

She had kept her Austrian passport until Austria had been forced into Anschluss with Germany under the Nazis. Being Jewish she had no desire then to be German, even if they would have had her. She had then been issued with a *laissez-passer* by the Egyptians. But now her old passport might be valid again; and in fact the Austrians said it was valid enough not only for herself but for Becky as well, and quite possibly for Sam, as Becky's husband; and perhaps they might look favourably on the rest of Sam's family—Alicia and his grandmother.

'But what would Sam do in Austria?' Scott asked Helen Mamoon in the corner of the garden where Sam had recently placed a wooden seat he had mysteriously acquired. 'He can't even talk German. Can you imagine Sam trying to make a go of it in a country like that?'

'Can he make a go of it here?'

Scott shrugged.

'What happens when they arrest him again? They'll never give him papers now, and there won't always be someone like you or Leo Lieberman to help him . . .'

'Or yourself,' he said, admiring her determination but unwilling to hand Sam over to the Austrians. It was simply an impossible thought; yet who else would take him?

'I think if Tim Peacock had lived, he would have got Sam a British passport somehow, once I told him the facts about Bateman. But Sam's hopes in that direction died with Tim in Port Said.'

Scott had not commented on Peacock's death to her before. Quartermain had been shocked into an outburst and so had Sam. They had both been so upset, talking about it, that she wondered why Peacock, whom she had known only briefly, had been so deeply regretted by these men when he quite clearly had nothing much in common with any of them. For that matter, why had she liked Peacock herself, and why had she felt the tears singe her eyes when she had heard the news on the radio that he was dead? She wanted to ask Scott about him, about his wife and what sort of a life he had lived. But even Quartermain was too secretive at this point to be broached by a simple question, and Sam was too dramatically indignant to get any sense out of.

But she had learned something about Sam as a result of it.

Despite his indignation, she realized that Sam was too innocent to believe in death. His sorrow for his friend Zareef, and now for Peacock, was something Sam did not quite understand himself, or even believe in, because he could not find any overwhelming act of respect to bring to it, such as taking a taxi to the synagogue. He wept, but he simply did not understand.

How could a man like that ever survive in some harsh Germanic country?

'If he has Becky he will be all right,' she said to Scott, trying to convince herself, 'and perhaps he can go on from there to another country.'

'To Israel?'

'No. No,' she said quickly. 'Australia, perhaps.'

'I suppose you're right,' he admitted reluctantly.

They did not think it strange that they of all people should be sitting in the corner of Sam's garden deciding his fate for him. It seemed to be perfectly normal.

But it was a sad disturbance for Scott when Buelli found her there.

Scott was introduced to Buelli who was polite, but he was obviously impatient to talk to Helen. Scott left them, and from his staircase on the way up to his room he saw them already talking earnestly, Buelli holding both her hands.

He could guess what Buelli was asking.

But what would she reply?

Helen looked up briefly as he went into his room, and then she gently withdrew her hands from Buelli's and put her arm in his and walked along the hard path with him, listening to him.

'I am leaving the day after tomorrow,' he said with his normal indignant

affection. 'And you must please reconsider it, my dear Helen. But you must! You can't stay here like this. Come with me into Cairo now and I will fix it up with Enrico, who will sign the document at the bank for you. It's not too late. Enrico will talk to the consulate, and you will have an Italian passport . . .'

She stopped and appealed to his reason. 'But everyone *knows* I'm an Egyptian,' she said. 'It would be silly.'

Buelli saw reason. 'Everyone knows that I'm not Italian,' he said excitedly. 'But that doesn't matter. It's simply a device to help . . .'

'I know it is,' she said, 'and I can't blame you for using it, *mon cher Docteur—mon cher ami*. But I can't do it.'

'Why not?'

Why not? What could she ever say to this man who would be so decent and so genuine with her? She looked briefly at his pink, shaven head and saw his golden teeth, his golden eyes, his golden heart. Why not? She had asked herself that question so often in her life. Why not Buelli? Was it some other face that held her? Some other golden heart? Or was it some long history of defiance and struggle which made it impossible for her to go through with a pretence like that? How could she be Italian? Or was she afraid of the shame it suggested—to go away like that with Buelli? Why not? It could never be shameful. Buelli would divorce his wife and marry her, of that she could be sure.

'I should!' she said to him earnestly, appealingly. 'I know I should go. I want to go. But I simply can't do it like that. I don't know why. I can't just give up like that . . .'

'Give up what? Your Egyptian passport? It's useless now, Helen.'

'Oh, it's more than that. I know I'll have to leave Egypt, but if I give in like this on what I am, it's giving in too much. But I would . . .' She gripped his arm. 'I would if I could. Perhaps I will later. I don't know.'

He shook his head. 'Today is the last day, Helen. Enrico will not do it any more after today. He says the Italian consulate will stop issuing any more Livorno passports after tomorrow. And I will leave after tomorrow. Don't you see? It must be now . . .'

'I thought of Sam,' she began to say.

Buelli shook his head. 'I thought of that a long time ago. Enrico won't do it for Sam. It's you, Helen. I can persuade him for you.'

They had been speaking in English, and now she broke into Italian. She could always speak to him affectionately in Italian providing she made it a little exaggerated and gently lighthearted. But they would both know how much she meant it.

'Caro mio,' she said to him with her heart in the language. 'Carissimo!' she said. 'All my life you have helped me. Look at the times we have had together, and how we have been together in the Ministries. Look how

much you have helped me and advised me, and how much you have helped so many friends too, and Sam and Alicia and Mamma Hassoon. Only *I* know how much you do. I know everything, and I know what a wonderful man you are. But it's hopeless. I have thought about it so often. Oh, I spend hours thinking about it. I told myself long ago what a fool I was not to go with you. But I know my mind is made up, and I can't change it, even though I want to.'

He looked at the sky and threw his hands towards it a little in a gesture of accusation. 'I knew!' he said. 'I knew it always. But I never lost hope of persuading you . . .'

To part in this garden with Buelli was not easy and perhaps she could hate the place hereafter. But he did not insist any more. He could see it in her firm, full-bodied determination. He knew her very well, and he admired . . .

But would she at least come to Italy to see him, if she did leave Egypt by some other means?

'Yes, I swear I will,' she said. 'I will come first to you.'

Was that still a hope for him?

Buelli kissed her gently on the cheeks and took his heart away with him from Madame Salz's garden, and Helen Mamoon wondered why the world and the emotions had made a likeness and a difference of them. They had the same spirit, the same determination in the face of the world—the and Buelli. And yet there was a difference, a stroke of bad luck somewhere in their creation which made their total emergence in each other impossible.

She would honour Buelli all her life, but that was hardly enough hope to defy the world with.

She would miss him, though, more than anyone else in her whole life.

When Scott had returned from Port Said, he had not visited Leo Lieberman in his flat. He had simply reported to Leo on the telephone that Roberto Rolland was back, and that Françoise had decided to go back to him, and that the French would evacuate her and the children from Port Said.

Leo had been disappointed; but in the flat misery of Scott's voice at that time he had detected a warning not to ask questions, to leave well alone. Since then, Leo had been out to see Sam once, but he had not moved out of his taxi, and Scott had been in Cairo anyway.

But now he had telephoned to say that he would like to come and say good-bye to them all, because he was going away. When his taxi arrived Scott watched him struggling inch by inch to the gate, and in his present isolated state, in the over-sensitive world he lived in now, he felt sick with the pain of Leo's effort.

738

He could not help himself.

'Hang on, Leo,' he said, warning him.

He picked Leo up, and though he was amazed at the weight of this twisted diseased body, he carried Leo to the garden seat where he now spent all his days, unwilling even to go outside the gate, afraid (he told Helen Mamoon, who had noticed it) that some policeman would ask him for his papers.

Madame Salz saw it from her kitchen.

'Cet anglais,' she said in amazement, and then for Leo: 'Pauvre homme.'

She rushed out on her short legs with a cushion and tripped over Felu who had found a new basking place in the middle of a path. 'Ah, cette bête!' she cried. 'It will kill me one day.'

'Bonjour, Madame Salz,' Leo said to her in his rasping French.

He had not protested to Scott, he had relaxed and let himself be carried, as if sometimes one had to admit a complete confidence in a man.

'Where are you going?' Scott asked him when Madame Salz had left them.

'I heard yesterday,' Leo dropped his voice for Scott's ears only, 'that Françoise had arrived in Lyons, to my cousin's place. I shall go there myself. I know I can get a French visa in Geneva.'

'To stay in France permanently?'

'I think so.'

Not only had they closed up Leo's business, they had forbidden him to buy gold in the *sagha*, which could be more of a death blow to his kind of business than closing his shop. They had not confined him personally in any way, and because of his condition they had allowed him a generous portion of his sequestrated bank account to live on.

'But I don't want to rot away here,' Leo said. 'So I shall take what I can and go to France and see what I can do for Françoise and the children. I think she needs some help.'

Leo obviously decided to be forthright with Scott about Françoise, and Scott himself felt no embarrassment any more, only amazement that this crippled figure could go on. Yet it did go on, clinging and fighting and never giving way at all; and certainly never stopping to contemplate itself. Even a second's self-contemplation would probably have been suicide to Leo, and Scott felt ashamed of the problems he thought he had.

'How will you go?' Scott asked, wondering how Leo would survive any journey.

'By air to Geneva first. I leave tomorrow night. I'm sorry I left it so late to see you, but I only decided yesterday.'

'But your flat? Everything?'

'Oh, that's all under sequestration, anyway. They're going to allow me

739

to take some money and things with me. But I have not been sitting all these years just waiting for this, you know . . .'

He looked puckishly at Scott from his pipe-muffled face, and Scott knew that Leo, in a disinterested sort of way, had been able to get enough of his wealth out of Egypt to be comfortably off abroad. Scott felt relieved. What could this man have done without that facility which money gave him to overcome his great handicap? Yet Scott could look at him and realize that Leo would overcome it anyway; in his calm face there was no fear at all. Fear of anything to Leo was obviously a very stupid thing.

Yet his body was worse; he was surely and slowly dying as always, although he was also slowly living it out to the last, and Scott felt the insulting healthiness and force of his own body which seemed to contribute nothing to his will at all.

'Anyway,' Leo said, 'I've left enough private repairs for Sam to last him a few months. Someone will bring it out and collect it also, only Sam must be careful. No one should know.'

Sam emerged with a table, saying: 'Eh . . . Leo!' and Madame Salz sent Becky to get some English biscuits from the Greek grocers. Then, as they sat down to tea in the sunshine, it was not at all like a farewell party but a moment for Madame Salz to begin some surprising reminiscing on her girlhood in Linz and Vienna, where she had worked in a porcelain factory packing up sets of dinner-ware to be shipped all over the world.

'Even here to Egypt,' she said, and added: 'If only I'd known then that I'd follow the dinner plates . . .'

Leo remembered Linz very well, and said that the Danube was very dirty there because of the factories, but it had an interesting Carolingian square.

'But I worked in Vienna, not Linz,' Madame Salz said, rejecting outright any such taint of provincialism.

With Leo Lieberman gone, Scott felt more aware than ever that the safety of this wounded and isolated life was coming to its end. And yet he was unable to abandon it. He still needed it.

Here he was, still willingly cooping himself up in Madame Salz's house and Sam's garden with no desire at all to go outside. But how long could it go on? It was too painful to anticipate the end of it. He had read through Frank Cowperwood's life again, because he admired the man's determination. But he realized, on this second reading, that it was not Frank Cowperwood who attracted him as much as Theodore Dreiser, the author himself, who seemed to have chiselled his masterpiece out of the hardest granite. (Someone had said so in a preface.) He felt as if he understood Dreiser thoroughly. He recognized a likeness, his own values. But Dreiser must have been a very dedicated and compact man, he thought; a better-equipped man than he could ever be himself.

Meanwhile, Madame Salz was definitely in serious trouble: so much so that Scott felt he must do something about it urgently, because there was no one else to help her, and he could not sit still and let it happen to her. So he telephoned Helen Mamoon, who had gone back to her apartment now that Quartermain was at home, and he asked her if she knew of anyone in the Ministry of Finance to whom he could talk. The inspector of taxes had sent Madame Salz an official assessment for four thousand and four pounds, and they were pressing Madame Salz for payment. They had also warned her, in a letter written in Arabic which he had translated for her, that she must go to the local sequestrator's office with all the deeds and documents of her property before the fifteenth of the month.

'The sequestrator's office!'

Madame Salz had almost fainted, and Becky had put her to bed.

'Is there someone I can talk to in the Ministry first?' he asked Helen. 'She's going to lose everything if this goes through.'

Helen said she would try to arrange it. She knew several officials in the Ministry who might have the courage to help her as an old friend, and she would even go with him if necessary to see them.

'In the meantime, Nona wants you to come to their flat tomorrow night for dinner, to say good-bye. They'll be leaving in five days' time, and I think I'll be going with them.'

'You're going?' he said, unbelieving. 'You've definitely decided?'

'I think so. I *have* to go sooner or later. Now that I know that Sam and his family have somewhere to go to, even Austria, and now that Leo Lieberman has promised them help when they get to Austria, I don't see any point waiting for Nasser to starve me out. I must go,' she said. 'Even if I go my own way, and not like Dr. Buelli . . .' she added as an assurance, a defence perhaps, an appeal for understanding.

But over the phone she sounded brusque and certain, and he could not blame her. Even so, he felt disappointed in her. Something he had come to depend upon had suddenly given way.

741

CHAPTER NINETY

In their last days in Egypt, Quartermain's new composure found a willing response in the arms of his wife, who loved him despite himself, even if she remained calm and inflexibly real about it.

But how could his stomach survive the arguments of the world?

That was going to be the problem even at Nona's farewell dinner for his friends. Jack de Brazio brought up Hungary again, and there was a moment when it looked as if Quartermain would backslide dangerously, because of the hypocrisy (he said) and the credulity of a world (he said) which could weep for Hungary and contribute twenty million dollars in pennies to its unhappy refugees, without ever questioning the nature of the events. And anyway, who had helped the refugees of the Suez war? Nobody. It was almost too much for anyone's composure, and he almost lost his temper. But at the last moment his control was magnificent, although Jack (sure that their friendship was safe again) said, provocatively:

'You know, you get worse instead of better. You're even more rigid-minded now than you were before you were locked up.'

But Quartermain ate slowly and denied inflexibility.

The only thing he had become inflexible about lately, he said, was Zionism, which was now one of the world's most dangerous philosophies. To accusations of anti-semitism he remained inflexible, and he said that if he must hate Israel for what it had done he would hate it for its bourgeoisie, not for its Jews. It wasn't the race that was wrong, but the class. That was the trouble with people abroad. Too many Jews, and too many people with safe but guilty consciences, made the mistake of supporting Israel without questioning its policy. The Jews of Europe had brought their European bourgeois world to make a state, not their Jewish world. The same German and European society (not race) which had produced the Nazi philosophy had produced the Zionist philosophy, and being a Jew was only an unlucky accident to it. The Israelis' policy towards the Arabs was a European and a colonial one. In Israel, Arabs had no rights, could not vote, could not get equal pay, could not join a trade union, could not have opportunities of education, of health, or of anything but degradation. Ben Gurion wanted to expand at the expense of the Arabs. And if he ever talked peace, he kept talking about Israel's superior know-how 'helping' the Arab world. But the Arabs in Egypt had far more 'know-how' than the Israelis, because they had more doctors, more scientists, more heavy industry, a more complex industrial development, and a better-educated bourgeoisie than Israel could boast. So what was this mystical 'know-how' which made the Israelis so superior to the Arabs? Was it the know-how of being European, of being German or Polish or Russian—as against being an ignorant Arab? It was no good arguing. Zionism was the curse, not semitism. Zionism was politics; semitism was race. Until Jews all over the world could recognize the difference, they would be helping the worst elements of their own people. . . .

'All right, all right,' Jack said. 'So you've wrapped up Israel . . .'

'I don't want to wrap up anybody,' Quartermain protested. 'And, anyway, this is a sort of last supper, so let's not argue. There is never any point in arguing anyway.'

But they all ridiculed his pacifism with laughter.

They were all due to leave Egypt soon, even Jack and Ella de Brazio, who had seen the war through. They had just returned from the Canal zone where an American general, with the help of British and German salvage vessels, was unsinking all the wreckage.

'Nasser and the Russians did a marvellous job of blocking the canal,' Jack said, 'but Eden and Mollet did an even better job of making Nasser a popular hero. Before Suez he wasn't all that divine; but now the Egyptians everywhere think he's God almighty.'

'I was just thinking,' Quartermain said innocently, 'that Nasser will now become the best friend Eden and Mollet ever had. That's almost a certainty.'

They laughed, they ridiculed, because the bitter hatred after the Suez war between Nasser and Eden and Mollet was obvious to them all. Everyone knew how impossible it was. How could Nasser ever trust or even tolerate the English or the French again?

'Nevertheless it's true,' Quartermain insisted with a restraint which he could not help admiring in himself. He looked at his wife for approval. Nona, however, was making signs to hurry him up with his eating so that she could tell Ali (who had come back) to bring in the salad. 'Nasser will become their man,' he said.

'I don't see how,' Scott ventured. 'He must still hate them bitterly.'

'Oh, he hates them at the moment,' Quartermain agreed. 'But he hates and fears one thing even more than he hates the British, for instance.'

'Don't tell me,' Jack groaned. 'So he hates the communists.'

'Well, doesn't he? Nasser arrested only a few Englishmen and Frenchmen and Israelis during the Suez business. But he locked up about a hundred communists, even though they were all for him. And, anyway, now that his Anglo-French enemies realize that they can't break him as a patriot and a nationalist, they'll come running to join him as decent-minded anti-communists.'

'If he'll have them,' Scott said.

'You actually sound bitter,' Ella said to Quartermain joyfully.

'But it's normal,' Quartermain answered, unprovoked, finally putting down his chicken bone so that Nona called Ali. 'Don't you see? Sooner or later all anti-communism ends up on the same side, whatever the rivalries. Terrible enemies eventually become marvellous friends. All sorts of things will happen. You'll see. Sooner or later Nasser will end up by doing exactly what the British and French are doing, because once you face communism as the only alternative you either have to come to terms with it, or you have to try and eradicate it by any means. So Nasser is going to do what he can't help doing. He's going to try to tear it out of his mind and then smash it to pieces.'

'With Russian help?' Jack asked cynically.

'Don't try to embarrass me with talk about the Russians,' Quartermain said, his composure erecting another confident barrier. 'That's the contradiction the Russians will have to face themselves . . .'

'You mean—how much help do you give an anti-communist when he is in fact beating his own communists' brains out?'

'That's right,' Quartermain agreed and sighed.

'So,' Jack said, 'you're now against Nasser?'

There was a green salad which had to be eaten slowly, but Nona was so fascinated with her husband's shaven mouth—which now argued the same old argument but which revealed (for the first time) the man who was using the arguments—she became so fascinated for a moment, watching it, that she forgot to pass the salad along. Hanna got up and handed the bowl to Ella, and though they served themselves and began to eat the salad, every one of them and even Nona herself seemed to be waiting on Quartermain's answer—for or against Nasser; while Quartermain was beginning the slow, silent grind of composed salad digestion.

'I'm not against him,' he said. 'I mean—not yet.'

'That's not good enough,' they accused heatedly. 'And what do you mean—not yet?'

'Too complicated,' he said, absorbed in his plate.

'Really, darling,' Nona said firmly. 'Don't be rude.'

'Come on,' Jack insisted. 'You're avoiding it.'

'Honest I'm not,' he said. 'Why must I be for or against something, even Nasser?'

'Because you always are,' Jack said, 'so don't, for God's sake, change that now.'

744

They all laughed so derisively at the possibility that Quartermain looked hurt.

'I haven't changed *that*,' he said, almost showing that he was upset. 'If I have to be for or against him, I suppose I'm against that part of him. . . '

'Why?'

'Nasser is putting my friends in gaol. I'm not willing to go along with that any more.'

It seemed to be a very simple answer for Quartermain, and they would have gone on with it; but the salad had to be eaten and other worlds had to be investigated, so they left him alone.

Why, he asked Nona, wasn't Sam here?

'Becky isn't well,' Helen reported, and revealed a surprise for them. It seemed (in the helpless nature of all things to do with Sam) that Becky was, perhaps, pregnant.

It meant nothing to the de Brazios, who did not know Sam personally, but it meant a great deal to everyone else, who thought it a specially happy piece of news. They could already picture the solemn and responsible father Sam would make (until his children pulled his ear or his nose). But they were also worried.

'If only it hadn't happened just now,' Helen said.

'Why not now?' Hanna asked indignantly. 'Becky's able . . .'

'It will make things so terribly complicated for them when they leave, or rather when they arrive in Austria.'

It was too intimate to discuss it too far, so they left Sam and Becky in privacy. And it was during the polite silence that followed that Scott found himself afraid to talk at all, even to Helen Mamoon who tried to draw him out for his own good. He could still remember his previous experience with de Brazio, and now he hoped—suddenly aware of himself —that no one had mentioned, outside the Quartermain family circle, that he had been in Port Said. The British authorities hadn't mentioned it; nobody had. But de Brazio might know.

He felt Jack watching him closely now. He guessed that it was only out of politeness to Nona Quartermain that Jack refrained from asking him that fascinating and important question: *What had Captain Scott been doing during the Suez war?*

It was already in de Brazio's attitude. To Jack, Scott was still a mysterious and secretive fellow who must have been playing a very important role in events somewhere, surely. If only one could discover the nature of what he did, or open him up somehow to get it all out. It was probably too secretive anyway, which made it all the more remarkable that Scott should be sitting here so casually among them.

The evening passed, and nobody asked him anything.

But on the way home, in the Chevrolet, Jack said to his wife rather sadly:

'Scott is one of those things you have to pass up and leave unfinished. But some day, somebody will scratch that man deep enough to find out what he is all about; and they'll probably find a frightened ant-heap under all that solid lump of . . .'

'Of what?' Ella asked.

Jack restrained himself and said he did not know. It was too late anyway to torture himself with unravelled and unfinished stories like that. Furthermore, once he and Ella left Egypt, in a few weeks' time, he was going to forget the whole bloody episode, which had stretched his objective forbearance far beyond comfort. He would be glad to get out of it.

'If I stayed in Egypt another couple of weeks,' he told Ella, 'I'd probably start talking like Quarts does, because what else can all these poor bastards in Asia see any hope in, except communism? Nasser isn't going to get even half-way to solving their miseries, whichever way you look at him. And all that Europe will ever offer these countries is kind words and parachutists.'

'We *are* leaving just in time,' Ella said sympathetically.

746

CHAPTER NINETY-ONE

THERE were only a few days left and Nona Quartermain still watched her husband in his new mood to see how long it would last; and though she did not quite believe in it yet, she realized that she would never fathom her husband. She knew now, looking at him like this, that he had always disguised (all these years!) everything that had hurt him. She knew now that the things he argued about most, actually did hurt him most, whatever his annoying and derisive way of dispute suggested to the contrary. He was not as cold-blooded as he pretended to be.

He had already told her, and she remembered the visit, of Rushdi the communist. Now he told her about Sophie Mourad, the young woman he had taken coffee with. Sophie Mourad and many other communists were in gaol, and so far (he had now contacted Rushdi again) they had not confessed anything, even under unpleasant and often brutal police questioning.

'So what would you say,' he asked his wife, sitting on the bath near her, while she washed her long black hair in the hand-basin, 'if I decided to take that money out for them?'

Nona's habit of panicking first and recovering afterwards was not an easy habit to overcome, particularly when family life was threatened.

'What will it mean?' she asked, pouring an enamel cup full of water over her hair and squeezing the soap out of it.

'I'll have to smuggle the money out.'

'I suppose you know,' she said sharply, 'what they'll do, if they catch you?'

'Ah, yes,' he said with a sigh. 'You would obviously have to go on without me. They caught a chap the other day trying to get a few hundred pounds out to Greece and they gaoled him for six months in Alexandria. Oh, well . . .'

'You see!' she said.

He shrugged. 'The other problem is, even if I get it out of Egypt, I'm

747

not allowed to take more than five pounds into England, so I would have to smuggle it into England illegally also.'

'That's worse,' she said, pummelling the soap out of her scalp. 'Isn't there any other way?'

'That's what I've often said to myself. But how will things ever get done if you wait for other ways to turn up? I shan't try to do it unless you agree.'

She was irritated with him, and she did not know why. But she tried not to be. 'Even if you do get the money into England—will it be worth all that risk?'

Quartermain's hand went up to his disguise, which was no longer there; so he pushed his long fingers up to his dry eyebrows and began to twist them.

'You ought to be able to tell me that,' he said to her, as if he still needed to be convinced, watching the rivers of soap and water running off her hair. 'Rushdi swears it's the only way. The fellaheen haven't even reached the printing-press level yet. "*Pictures*," he says. Only the simplest form of graphic art, cheaply printed and in colour, is going to be effective. That's what he says.'

'Effective for what?' she demanded, pouring water mixed with oil and vinegar over her hair. 'What can he ever teach the peasants, even with pictures . . .'

'Why do you put that stuff on your hair?' he said, and went on. 'Someone has to begin somewhere. A few people do it, and they go to gaol for it. All right. That's when you know the value of a man. If they don't betray you or themselves then that's when you owe them something yourself, don't you think? Can you see what I mean?'

She had learned a great deal about that mouth now, lifting her wet head to watch him as she flung back her hair. But it still surprised her to see it so revealed. He could say the same mocking words, but he could no longer hide that it actually upset him—that his friends were arrested for doing what he had long announced as the only way for the world to solve its problems. It was driving him, finally, into hitting back.

But why, she wondered, had he left it so long? Had he kept out of it all these years in a natural distaste for conspiracy, or was it because of herself and the children?

'I wish I knew,' she could say to herself now. He had always hidden his motives in his dry mockery of himself and others, even of her.

'Don't you think I have feelings too?' she said impatiently to him then.

He looked a little astonished by her selfishness, misunderstanding it as another display of her terror.

'Don't you think I can be upset too, by what you see? Do you think I can look at this country, which is after all my own, and agree that any-thing is really being done for it . . .'

'Ah . . .' he began.

She wrapped her hair in a towel and pounded her scalp again. 'You don't even know the half of it,' she said sharply. 'You haven't even seen misery. You don't even have a clue to what life does to the fellah and even to the ordinary clerk in this country. It's nothing less than a slow torture —from the day they are born to the day they die. If you could speak even a hundred words of Arabic you might begin to understand . . .'

'But I do know . . .'

'You only *think* you know. You and your famous theories. But you ought to feel it the way we do, and then you would really know. Haven't I lived my life with it, horrified by its cruelty and awfulness? That's what you forget.'

'No, I don't.'

'Yes, you do! Otherwise you would have had more confidence in me. But don't you think *I* know that nobody, not even Nasser, will do very much to lift them out of their filth and their poverty? It would take twenty revolutions more powerful than his even to start it, and I *know* that,' she said.

He simply listened now.

'And, anyway,' she went on, 'what do you think I was feeling all this time, sitting here all day and night with the British and the French drop-ping bombs on us? Do you think I didn't feel ashamed and bitter also? And do you think I didn't say to myself: *I must do something to hit back. Oh, I must!*'

He nodded, but she would not be interrupted.

'I know you don't believe in revenge,' she said as if that were one of his great weaknesses. 'But I do. I certainly do. So I decided then that if *you* didn't do something to hit back, I would. I'm tired of this endless talk; of being right; of knowing what is right but doing absolutely nothing about it. Take the money! Do it, for heaven's sake. Let us be communists, if it is so right. I don't understand half of it anyway, and I'm sure you're quite silly and wrong half the time. You can't be that right always. But at least communists *do* something . . .'

She had been drying her long black hair vigorously with each word, and now she flicked at it angrily with a sweeping movement of the towel, taking her revenge on it, until she finally threw it back over her shoulders.

'And I'm tired of watching all those Europeans, who drop bombs and condescend and vote. That's all their wonderful western world is,' she said, in a temper about it now. 'They're such brutes. Egyptians may be stupid and childish,' she said, 'but we aren't savages the way Europeans are. And if my sons must be Englishmen, then let them be humane

Englishmen, because I'm not going to be frightened any longer of those people . . .'

She wrapped up her hair in the towel again and Quartermain let her go on, which seemed to unnerve her again because she was upset now.

'Oh, I know I'm terrified. I know that. But I'm not going to give in to them. So long as I don't have to live in one of those grimy streets in London where you think the English people are. They're all just as bad and as ignorant as anybody else, and they'll *never* understand the real suffering of a country like this, so it's no use living with them. But you might as well try to tell them, so long as *I* don't have to live among them, that's all. I can't bear those depressing streets . . .'

Nona could not help her tears which slipped down her cheeks without consulting the rest of her face, but Quartermain was finally an understanding man.

'That's all right, sweetheart,' he said gently, patting the damp shoulder he had embraced, avoiding as best he could the wet strands of clean black hair, loose on her neck. 'I couldn't agree with you more.'

CHAPTER NINETY-TWO

FAR down the corridors of the Ministry of Finance, an old servant in a faded khaki uniform greeted Helen Mamoon so effusively that Scott looked at her in surprise and she whispered to him:

'This used to be the Ministry of the Interior also, on the other side, when I worked for the Labour Office, and this old servant used to sit outside my door and wait for me or the Englishman I worked for to ring.'

The old man's effusions were greetings from his whole family, for whom Helen seemed to have done many favours. All were married, thanks be to God, he said; and he had fifteen grandchildren. Four sons had died (it was God's will) and of the rest one was a blacksmith, one was a waiter on a Nile steamer (that achievement was obviously her doing because she said: 'That was so long ago, when I knew my father's friends at the Nile Company's dockyards'), and one was an Army officer.

'Wait here, *ya sitt*! Take your ease! If you would be so kind!'

They waited in a room soaked with Ottoman ink blots and English dust, and they marvelled about Egypt between them: that there were no real class divisions between poverty and wealth, except the wealth of course. But it had always been true. A poor man's son, like this man's son, could become an Army officer and once he achieved that level his background would not count against him, as it probably would in any European country.

Helen Mamoon told him, sentimental in the sad nostalgia of this old Ministry, of her days as a Labour inspectress in the Ministry.

'I always had to have two policemen with me,' she told him, 'because in those days the sight of a woman inspectress simply made them laugh, and quite often I would have to tell one of the policemen to break down a door to some miserable and filthy workshop so that I could get in. They used to threaten to kill me quite often, particularly the Cypriots and the Greeks who used to make those sugared almonds for feasts and weddings. One of them had twenty Egyptian girls working in a dirty black kitchen fourteen hours a day and if one of the big vats of boiling sugar had really caught fire (as they sometimes did on the edges) they would have all been burned alive. The girls were always being burned, and they used to come to me with terrible wounds, until I threatened to close the whole place up with a *procès*, if they didn't improve the conditions . . .'

'Did they?' he asked, fascinated with her active face.

'At first . . .' she began.

But the official they had come to see had emerged from his inner office to greet her, and to hold one of her hands in both of his.

'Ahlan, ahlan!' he began.

Scott stood politely aside until the long greeting was over, and when she finally introduced him to the official, Scott felt that quick look of curiosity and interest which all Egyptians gave him, and which he never got used to.

'And this is Sabry Bey!' she said. She was still respecting and insisting on the old titles because (she implied) he *was* a Bey.

The lavish politeness of the preliminaries was long, because Sabry Bey (who, in the days of Farouk, would have worn a tarboush and perhaps fingered a string of amber beads) had not seen 'Miss Helen' for a long time.

He said he was about to leave the Ministry, to take over control of one of the financial committees Nasser had set up to co-ordinate the financing of the contractual work for the Aswan Dam, which would be paid for now by the Suez Canal. (Who remembered that source of subsequent events? Scott wondered, thinking of Zareef and Peacock and the others.)

'Mabrouk,' Helen said to Sabry in compliment.

'Merci . . .'

And Madame Salz? What of her problem?

They drank coffee while the file was sent for and he looked at it and said he had already spoken to a colleague and there was little he could do.

'As you know, Miss Helen,' he said in Arabic, 'there is no way around our laws these days, even in the Ministry, and Madame Salz *should* have paid her taxes, whether she is Egyptian or not. Even if she had paid one year's tax they probably would never have bothered her. Or at least I could have done something about it. But no taxes!'

'But the sequestration of her house?' Helen said. 'Can't that be stopped?'

Sabry Bey looked at Helen and at Scott. How much could he say when whole phrases and meanings had to be avoided? He could not even say, in the simplicity of facts, that Madame Salz was Jewish and that the recent war had made her, technically, an enemy subject. Nobody could use such honest and therefore such cruel language, and nobody would hurt the old tradition of toleration and politeness by such crude versions of the facts.

752

It was not even half the truth, anyway. There were too many other sides to this problem.

'Dear Miss Helen,' he said in perfect English, as if he did not want any casual office servant to understand what he was saying, 'it's the law, and I'm afraid nothing can stop it, unless she sells her property quickly. Then it might not be so bad, because she can at least get a good price on the open market.'

'But the sequestrator's office has forbidden her to sell,' Helen pointed out.

Sabry Bey thought about it for a moment, looking admiringly at Helen. Scott wondered then what the long friendship really meant, because Sabry was obviously doing this for Helen Mamoon rather than for Madame Salz, whom he did not know. He was not avoiding it politely, but thinking helpfully about it.

'Yes,' he said thoughtfully, as if he had not heard her. 'I think I could persuade the local sequestrator to waive all the taxes, if she sold the house quickly . . .'

'But she's forbidden!' Helen reminded him again.

'I know that, Miss Helen. But I could probably persuade him to allow Madame Salz to sell her property. It's an unusual case, because the sequestrator is very late with it. But if she did sell, to avoid paying taxes, she would have to sell before the fifteenth of the month . . .'

'That's only five or six days away.'

'. . . and she would have to sell it to a fully resident Egyptian subject —you realize that—otherwise it would be definitely forbidden.'

'But even *that* is practically impossible, Sabry Bey. She would never get a fair price if she sells it now on the public market. It might save her paying the taxes, but she'll get nothing out of it, anyway. She'll lose all her money, or her house.'

'Then she must find an Egyptian privately who is willing to pay a fair price for it.'

Sabry Bey said sadly that, under the circumstance, getting Madame Salz's permission to sell was the best he could do. He was begging her to understand how limited his influence was now. She did understand and did not press it. She nodded and thanked him and changed the subject.

They talked on a little, about the complications of it, and then gently complained to each other of the high cost of living. But he had done all he could do for her and she was grateful.

For a moment the power of their farewells became significant, in Scott's eyes, because Helen Mamoon seemed to be saying good-bye not only to Sabry Bey, but suddenly to this old room, to the building, and to her own past which the manner of this man and the character of the meeting must have brought back so forcefully. The Ministry might have changed under

Nasser, but her sensitive fingertips could pick up the flimsiest memories in the corridors as she walked out, gripping Scott's arm while the old servant danced ahead of them.

'Welcome, welcome!' he was saying, as an appreciative sign of farewell.

'All we have to do now,' she said in her usual attitude of being ready for anger yet not quite angry, 'is to find some genuine Egyptian who wants to buy that old tumbledown house in five days and at a fair price: at least three or four thousand pounds.'

They got into a battered taxi and the door banged.

'Even before that,' Scott pointed out, 'we'll probably have to persuade Madame Salz to sell it, because she doesn't really want to give it up, and I doubt if she will.'

'What if she doesn't sell it?'

'She'll lose it anyway—sequestration *and* taxes.'

'But she *does* intend to leave, doesn't she?' she asked.

'So she says; but she can't believe it yet, and she's not going to give up her house until the very last moment, until she realizes she must. But by then she will be too late, and she'll lose everything. That's the trouble.'

'You see!' she said to him indignantly. '*You* solve it. You tell me that Nasser is right. He's not right, I don't care how you look at it. Old and helpless women without husbands ought to be left alone . . .'

'The law never leaves anyone alone,' Scott argued sadly. 'You know that.'

'Oh, *merde* on the law!' she said ferociously.

He could not help laughing as he dodged such an unusual vulgarity.

'Do you know anybody who might think of buying that house?' he asked her. 'Anybody at all?'

'Oh, plenty of people,' she said bitterly. 'But how much would they pay her, when they know they only have to wait until it's under sequestration and then they can buy it for nothing?'

'I wonder, though, what it's really worth?'

'The legal market price can't be more than a few thousand pounds . . .'

'Four thousand at least,' he said. 'After all, it's a good house.'

'I suppose it is—for some foolish and fully resident, pure, one hundred per cent Egyptian who is naïve enough to part with that much money for it. Oh, it's so hopeless anyway.'

So it was, and what had seemed like a concession from Sabry Bey had in fact become the confirmation of a death sentence.

'I don't know what to do about it,' she told him the next day when she came to talk to him about it. 'I can't find anybody. I can't even bear to think about it.'

She also had her own worries. She was definitely going, she said. She had already sold her furniture at a ridiculous price, and she had handed back the lease of her own apartment. In the afternoon she would move all the china and family goods that must not be sold to a cousin's house, with her father's books. Leo Lieberman had already arranged, before his departure, to get most of her money out through a secretive dealer in surgical goods for hospitals, and all that was left for her now was to go to the Ministry of Interior, on the last day but one, and give up her Egyptian passport. She would receive in exchange a bloodless exit visa on a worthless and stateless *laissez-passer*.

That was the price you paid if you were an Egyptian and wanted to leave Egypt now.

'That will make it complete and final,' she told him. 'I won't be able to turn back then. Even to leave here I have to give up my nationality.'

Now it was Scott who wanted to say to her, 'Don't do it. Don't go!' But he had no right to say it, and not enough hope or impulse to overcome his own sense of defeat anyway.

'I'll leave you to Gamal Abd el Nasser and his friends,' she said, not sparing him, and yet trying to show him the helplessness of her predicament, explaining why she could not help giving in. 'If he's going to turn this into a purely Moslem country, and that's what it's going to be, it will only get worse.'

He could not disagree. He sat on the outside staircase with her (it seemed to have become their private areopagus), feeling sorry for her now.

'I simply can't go on fighting just to survive—simply to hang on to a piece of paper called a passport,' she was saying. 'What sort of a life is that? There must be something better than that to do, and if I stayed here I'd only get into more trouble, because I couldn't keep quiet for long. I simply couldn't.'

'I know,' he said sympathetically. 'I know.'

'What will you do?' She looked up at him from the step below him. 'Have you decided? And when will you leave?'

'I'll wait for everybody to go,' he told her, 'then I shall go too. There'll be nothing for me here, either. But I can't do anything about it yet. I don't even know how to go about it. I haven't any kind of a passport, and I can't get one.'

It was also an explanation, and he needed to explain to her.

But he was a very sad man these days, and apparently too stoical and acceptant, which seemed to her to be too easy. Why was he like that?

Scott felt her disapproval, but he knew that he was only waiting for Helen Mamoon to leave Egypt before he too stepped out into the darkness. When they sat together like this on the staircase they could hear the far-away sounds of Cairo, and feel their own city fleeing before their eyes. It was moving away from them with its jangling bells and its hard-pressed people who laughed into their eyes because, after all, *they* would stay. But for those who must leave Egypt there was an air and an atmosphere of dying, because they knew that this life, in its minutest detail, would all go on without them.

That white-armed traffic policeman on the corner would go on waving at his traffic, regardless.

CHAPTER NINETY-THREE

HE thought when he saw Lucy Pickering that he might have another chance.

He had not panicked yet; but when the old Pharaonic kings had supervised the erection of their own tombs, stone by stone, there must have been a moment when they realized that the work was finished. To occupy it was the only thing left for them to do. That was when they must have searched anxiously for a new flutter of life in their hearts—the sort he looked for now.

He tried to tell her about Tim Peacock.

'I don't even understand what he was doing out there,' he said, watching her masked English face which was wrapped in a blue voile scarf against wind and dust and (she said jokingly) the falling flower-pots which the Egyptians felt like dropping on anyone who even looked English.

'It was Tim's own fault,' she said. 'Some idiot in the War Office offered him the trip, so he took it.'

'I meant why would he have wanted to go to Port Said in the first place?' Scott said, as if digging his own grave a little deeper.

'Why not?' she said. 'Tim was always game for anything, wasn't he? That's what he was like. That's what you were all like.'

'I suppose he was like that, but I don't think he meant to be that game.'

'Anyway,' she said, agreeing with him, 'he should have thought of Eileen and his children. But men never do . . .'

'Why didn't he! That's what I really mean.'

'Because a man is always so stupid,' she told him calmly, but she stamped her high-heeled foot a little where they stood outside the Swissair office in Cairo.

They had met here accidentally and yet not surprisingly, and they were already like lovers who had knowingly changed paths although they had not yet finished with each other. 'You are all such silly fools,' she said contemptuously to him.

'I'm certain we are,' he agreed willingly, 'but some men ought to go on for ever, and I always felt Tim was like that. Why did he have to do such a silly thing?'

'Why did Peter Dukes have to commit suicide?—it's the same thing.'

'Peter Dukes?'

'Surely you knew? Didn't you go to see him in that hospital? Weren't you being terribly chummy with him?'

'I went to see him about Sam . . .'

'He won't tell you anything more about Sam, or about me either. He took a handful of pills and put an end to it that way.'

'But why? Was he so ill? He looked all right when I saw him.'

She shrugged. 'Who knows? They say that skin trouble he had was finally too much for him. It was jaundice or something to do with his kidneys. But I think you probably know better. What fools men are. He did it the night of the landings on Port Said . . .'

Scott understood. He could see all of Peter's machiavellian future in ruins. He could guess the extent of Peter's feeling of defeat at the hands of Bateman and the schoolboy Ministers he had hated so much for their ignorance and stupidity. It had obviously been too much to live with—their final act of folly. Was it that, the wreckage of a lifetime? Or had his sunless life finally robbed itself of some essential life force? Perhaps the pigment had failed him just once too often. Even so, another link with this old life had gone—this Cairo English life.

'I suppose there wasn't much future left for him here,' he said. 'But even so . . .'

He watched a sign in the window which flicked on and off and showed an airline stewardess walking happily to an aeroplane holding a prosperous and happy Swiss child by the hand. That far-away world. '*Swissair looks after you!*' came on and off in letters of red, gold and then green.

'Nobody looks after you,' he commented bitterly to himself, 'not even Swissair.' But he was struggling to say something else to Lucy. 'It might have been more logical if it had been me they buried under that flower-bed in Port Said,' he told her. 'It might have been better that way.'

'But you *won!*' she cried indignantly. 'So why should you feel so sorry for yourself?'

'Won what?' he wanted to know. 'Nobody wins,' he said, 'and nobody seems to escape either; not even poor old Tim. I would have thought that he was always safe . . .'

'Oh, you don't understand. And, anyway, I have to go in here to pick up some tickets,' she said, and told him that she had come down from Alexandria to arrange with Swissair to take Church and Professor Maudie to London via Geneva. They had all been under house detention, but now they were free again.

758

'Is she all right?' Scott asked, as the clerk made out the tickets which would take Church and his victim home. 'Can she walk?' he asked.

'No, but we will have an ambulance to take her to the plane.'

'Is Church any better?' he also wanted to know, genuinely concerned.

'You mean has he got over the shock of seeing Professor Maudie so damaged? Not at all. He'll probably never get over it. That's because Professor Maudie is being so decent about it. I thought he would break down and weep with relief when he heard the radio from Cyprus telling the Alexandrines that their city would not be bombed. He was terrified for her.'

'I suppose he expected Alexandria to be bombed. He probably knew...'

The Swissair clerk had everything ready and she began taking a large amount of money out of her handbag.

'Perhaps he did know,' she said, pushing the notes carelessly across the counter. 'And we probably would have been bombed, if the Americans had not kept some of their destroyers in the harbour deliberately. But he hardly knows what has been happening anyway. I don't think he paid the slightest attention to the war, and he doesn't seem to worry about its outcome either. That's what makes him quite pathetic.'

'What's he going to do now?' he asked.

'Nothing. What can he do? He sits with her all day talking archaeology and making plans for her which they both know will never come off now. I didn't realize he knew so much about it, but Maudie says that he has a real feeling, even a rare gift for finding his way through a period, particularly here in Egypt. Did you know that?'

He shook his head. She had her tickets. She folded them and put them into her handbag, and she walked out of Swissair on her lovely shoes with the exodus accomplished.

'Are you going to leave with them?' he asked her. They stood outside again as if they had both decided to go no further together.

'Of course I'm leaving. I only stayed here this long to make sure he was all right.' She looked at him almost sensually then, and yet denied him (in that same look) the touch of her golden flesh—ever again. She was throwing him off. 'In his own way,' she said, 'Jack Church was always the only dedicated man among the lot of you.'

'Dedicated to what?' he almost asked indignantly.

But he thought about it, and he realized it was true. Church, in his own way, had never wavered in his own convictions. '*Conviction in what?*' one might also ask indignantly. Well, Scott answered himself, in serving what he had chosen to serve as a soldier, or simply as a white Englishman doing his well-known duty, even if he sometimes did it incompetently. At least he had never lost his certainty in his behaviour, even though he had

759

changed (as they had all changed) in his understanding of what it was about.

It was simply bad luck that a terrible last-minute error had brought him to this final abnegation. Although it might also be the worthwhile abnegation of a whole, lost lifetime.

'Church is lucky to have Professor Maudie,' Scott told her. He meant that Church had finally found a way to pay back his mistakes.

She knew what he meant. 'That's because he has been decent and consistent to the last,' she said, 'which is more than most men are, even the worthwhile ones.'

He felt for a moment, standing so casually in this Cairo street, that Lucy was now admiring Church in order that he, Scott, would challenge and ridicule her. But he agreed with her. She had always been generous, even if she had not been constant. And if she had decided to adopt Church like that, then Church would never again want for help and understanding.

'So you've finally given in,' he said to her.

'What do you mean?'

He blushed because he had not meant to provoke her, but he could not help showing her what he meant. 'I mean that after a lifetime of striving never to give in, Lucy, you've settled for nothing; nothing at all except the decency and dedication and constancy of Jack Church . . .'

'You needn't be so smug,' she said. 'It's the best thing I've ever done.'

'I'm not being smug,' he said, stung. 'It's not like you, that's all I'm saying.'

'How do you know?' she said sharply. But she was not really angry. She did not really care what he thought, and she tied up her blue scarf and waved to a taxi.

'I'm sorry you're going to leave so soon,' he said mechanically.

'No, you're not,' she told him, 'because it's your fault entirely, and you know it.'

'No . . .'

'Oh, you were always too stupid to understand.'

He shrugged a little in defence, but it shocked him and frightened him to see her so defeated, because he realized how close he was himself to arriving at the same despairing condition. But he recognized some final touch on her. It warned him, like a flame, that he too must now finally enter this tomb he had built for himself—this frightening defeat and isolation, or he must fight his way out of it to stay alive.

He said good-bye and left her hurriedly, suddenly afraid of this last contamination; fleeing before it.

CHAPTER NINETY-FOUR

His plan to ask Helen Mamoon's help seemed simple enough, once he had decided on it. But would it work? 'It depends entirely on her now,' he told himself doubtfully.

The Bank Misr in Sharel Emad el dine told him that his own funds had not yet been blocked, even though they were partly in a foreign transfer account. His monthly salary, also, had not been stopped and there was nothing to prevent him withdrawing several thousand pounds if he wanted them.

'Is that because I have banked all these years with an Egyptian bank and not Barclays?' he joked. He even wrote his cheques in Arabic.

'No,' the manager told him seriously. 'We had special instructions, Captain Scott, that your account was to be left alone. You cannot transfer any money abroad without special permission, nobody can, but you can have as much Egyptian money as you like.'

It amazed him about his salary, and it reminded him guiltily of the fact that he had simply washed himself out of the Frontier Corps quite un-officially. There had been no formal parting, no resignation. He had never gone back to the isolation hut, that was all.

'I'll probably come in tomorrow,' he told the manager.

He could get the money, and now he had one day left to carry out his plan, because Helen Mamoon would leave tomorrow, and after that it would be too late. He knew where she lived, and if she wasn't in her own apartment she was probably at Quartermain's, or she might be at the Ministry today, handing in her Egyptian passport.

He found a taxi rumbling up Emad el dine, and he told the driver:

'Go over to Gezira, and I'll tell you where to go when we get there.'

He needed (he warned himself) to be sure of what he was doing.

'What *am* I doing?' he asked the eyes of the old taxi-driver in the mirror.

The desire to ask the question and find the answer to his life had taken this final turn, and what he was doing now seemed to be so drastic and so

761

sudden that he must first take time to find out if he was deciding it the right way.

'I wonder why she loses her temper so quickly,' he asked himself.

That was quite irrelevant, but no other formula for decision would come to him. He knew that some men could make their life's decisions on the most intangible flutters of the intellect; but he knew that he was not like that. If he could only put his head down—like Beethoven abandoning the servile Goethe and ploughing through the ranks of the royal court with a determined and republican tread—he would do it; and he would do it with all the force of his powerful body, although he may lack the flashing, illuminated eyes.

'She's not an easy woman to approach,' he warned himself, 'so watch out. What possible right have I got to suggest it at all? How do I do it?'

But by now doubt was simply a dark hole in the earth into which he threw every second thought as he went along. It could not stop him. It could not affect him. He had his head in a good position.

'I can decide the rest when I see her,' he told himself and said to the driver: 'Go to forty-one Shareh Mohamed Kamel.'

'Iowa, ya effendim,' the old grey head replied.

She was in, but he had forgotten that her apartment would be devoid of its furniture and filled with tea-boxes and suitcases and undone parcels. Sam let him in, and they stood together for a moment in the stripped salon of the flat—in which there was nothing left except dusty papers strewn over the floor.

'I didn't know you were here,' Scott said, disappointed to find Sam.

'I'm helping them clear the place out,' Sam told him. 'They've sold up everything, even the beds. People having to give up their own homes!' he complained, and kicked a bundle of newspapers across the room. 'Why does it always have to be innocent people, I ask you? Why do they always blame us?'

But Sam had not yet recovered from what Helen had called his latest *impulsion de conscience*.

Sam had felt depressed the day before, looking at some old photographs he had taken of Ali Zareef and himself at Gedida airfield, right under the control-tower in the very mouth of the firemen's hut, where a grinning face was edging into the picture from the fire-engine—Said the driver. Sam had felt so depressed and bitter, looking at this picture, that he had immediately taken a bus into Cairo and then hitch-hiked over the river to Gedida and faced there his old friends.

It had been a rash thing to do.

'*They* had forgotten how horrible it was,' Sam had reported unhappily to Scott when he came back. 'Only I remembered. When I saw Said's

762

friends and I said, *Misqueen, Said!* they told me that Allah was merciful for not taking Said away as well as his small son; for who would have provided for the rest of his children if he had been killed; who was going to provide for Hefney's children? What could I say? Nobody understands it at all. The students began to make fun of me, sitting up in the control-tower, and the officers didn't stop them. They shouted at me through the windows: *"Go to Palestine and fight the fedayeen, Sam."* They thought it funny, until I told them to come down from up there. I wasn't going to keep quiet when they said things like that to me. I shouted at them: *"Why should I go to Palestine?"* I told them I'd fight the whole lot of them instead, if they came down. But they only laughed.'

'What's the use provoking them now, Sam?' Scott had said calmly. 'It's all over.'

'I didn't provoke them. They provoked *me*. The Director and Captain Selim even came over and told me not to make trouble. They told me I must leave. I said I was going, but I said the students had no right to shout at me like that. Captain Selim simply laughed in that sly way he likes. *"They've got nothing else to do, Sam,"* he said. *"We've only got one plane flying. They're angry."* Then he asked me how it was that Captain Scott happened to be on the airfield at the exact moment that the British planes bombed it.'

'Me?' Scott said.

'Yes, you, Capten. And why was *I* there at that moment too. *"Eh?"* he said, like that. What did he think I was there for? Did he think I knew the exact time it was going to be bombed? How could I know? I didn't know. But the students came right down then and they all began to insult me and ask me questions, and every time I said I knew nothing about it they laughed and tried to snatch the fountain-pen out of my jacket pocket, like silly children ...'

'That's what they are sometimes,' Scott pointed out.

'I know. But then Fahid Rahman kicked one of the students in the backside and so they turned on him, and they began knocking him about, kicking him and punching him hard until Captain Selim and I separated them. Then they were kicking at me until I flung one of them into the flower-bed. He was an officer's son, Gamal Anwar's son, and he said he would have the soldiers come and arrest me, so I shouted: *"All right, arrest me, I don't care. You can't insult me like that,"* I told them.'

'Oh, hell, Sam!'

'But they threw a coca-cola bottle at me, even at the Director, because he was telling them to go back inside. One of the bottles hit Captain Selim, so *he* said he would call the soldiers if they didn't go back into the control-tower where they were supposed to be taking a lesson in flight rules, and then he turned on me and told me I was lucky they didn't kill me. He told me to go away and never come here again. But I was so angry I said I wouldn't move. I refused.'

'You should have got out of the way quickly,' Scott said. 'What happened?'

'I was trying to explain to them that I had just gone there to say I was sorry. So Captain Selim insulted me again and said nobody wanted my salty tears; no Egyptian; not even Captain Ali Zareef. You see? So I had to insult him then, because everybody knows he hated Captain Ali. He called the soldier at the gate and told him to throw me out, so I went.'

'You're lucky he didn't have you arrested again. Why did you go there at all? You must have been mad.'

'I would have killed Selim,' Sam groaned, 'if I hadn't thought of Becky.'

'You shouldn't have gone there!' Scott repeated angrily.

'That wasn't all,' Sam reported further. 'I was walking back along that dirt road by the beet refinery, through the village, when that boy Fahid came along on an old motor-bike and offered me a lift. I was fool enough to accept it, because I didn't want to walk all that way. But all the way home he kept shouting silly things at me at the top of his voice, even in the streets of Cairo.'

'What sort of things?' Scott had asked. 'Was Fahid insulting you also?'

'No. He was shouting out, right down Soliman Pasha (and it was a terribly noisy motor-bike—not new at all) he was shouting at me: "*Well, Sam, what do you think of the English now? Don't you think they play dirty tricks on you?*" and he laughed. "*Don't they always run away,*" he said, "*when the trouble starts, so that you get the worst of it, Sam?*" he was saying. This was all in Arabic,' Sam said incredulously, 'at the top of his voice, all the way down Soliman Pasha. And when he dropped me off near the Ezbekieh gardens he said that some day the Egyptians were sure to shoot me, if I didn't get away before they found out everything. He said I was a bit of a haboob myself, but I was also a big fool if I thought *nobody* knew I had done splendid work for the English. Then he drove off laughing at me. He was talking in Arabic like that where everybody could hear it, and I still don't know what he meant. How could *he* know what I did?'

But Scott knew what Fahid meant, and he told Sam not to tell anyone about Fahid, although he knew Sam would report it to Becky, who would console him for the good friends he had against the silly ones. *Why worry about those silly students?*

That had happened yesterday, and now Sam seemed to be suffering the bitter reaction. He walked around the bare salon of Helen Mamoon's flat saying helplessly: 'They can't frighten me. They can't insult me like that. Why should I leave? What right have they got to throw me out of my own country? Why should I be an Austrian? Whoever *heard* of an Austrian? People being torn up from their homes, even my own sister and my grandmother and my wife, and even Helen who is all Egyptian. What have we done, except try to live here because we were born here? I shan't go. I've made up my mind.'

'Oh, Sam, please don't keep saying that,' Helen Mamoon told him now. 'Think of Becky.'

'But she doesn't want to go either.'

'If you're going to upset all our plans,' Helen said angrily to him, 'I shall never forgive you. Go home, go on! I can't stand any more of this . . .'

Sam did not hesitate. He picked up a large tea-box full of kitchen pots and crockery which he had to take to Madame Salz's, and he walked out of the front door, banging it after him by pulling it with his foot.

'If he goes on behaving like that,' she said to Scott, 'I don't know what I shall do. He's silly enough to just sit here, when I leave Egypt, and get into more trouble.'

'Don't worry,' Scott told her, 'I'll see that he doesn't.'

She began to take more notice of Scott himself then, surprised to see him, and already he felt how annoyed she was that he had come into this mess unannounced. 'I was going to come over late and say good-bye at Madame Salz's,' she said.

'I'm sorry,' he apologized, 'but I wasn't sure that this could wait.'

'But you can't even sit down.'

'That doesn't matter.'

But it did, in the formal rules she believed in. She found two broken and bleached and abandoned cane-chairs on the half-hearted balcony, and she brought them into the empty dining-room with his help. When she was seated he sat down carefully on one of them in this heartless empty room, feeling certain that he would eventually go through the seat.

'Have you handed in your passport?' he asked her in this void.

She nodded grimly. 'This morning,' she said.

He was too late. She was no longer an Egyptian and his plan (or this part of it, as far as he could allow himself to think) had already failed.

'Why?' she was asking him, realizing now that he had come here with an air of urgency and decision. 'What's happened?'

'I've just been to my bank,' he told her.

'Did they release your account?' she asked him.

'They didn't even block my account, although they were entitled to . . .' He had a lengthy explanation ready about banking, but it also seemed pointless now.

'Are they going to let you take your money out?' she asked, and for a moment she thought he had come here to ask her to take some of it out of Egypt for him; but that was incredible and impossible.

'No, no!' he said. 'But I can draw out all the Egyptian pounds I want. I thought . . .' He could not remain seated because he knew he was about to crush the chair into a ragged grass heap, so he got up.

She waited—wanting to tell him not to ruin his jacket by putting his massive fists into the pockets so that they bulged out from his hips like sacks filled with small wild animals.

'It's too late now, anyway,' he was saying, trying to get out of it and yet blushing because the force was gathering momentum and he could not stop. 'I was thinking that I would buy Madame Salz's house,' he said. 'I could give her a fair price. But that's not much use now, is it?'

'Why isn't it?' She was always ready to be impatient, but he hoped she would not be too quick with him now.

'The fact is, I'm not an Egyptian subject . . .'

'But you never were, so how could you have bought it?'

'No, I'm not, but . . .' Scott's tongue was almost lost; but the digger must dig and the mason must build even when the king has decided not to die '. . . you are. Or you were Egyptian.'

'Me? What have I got to do with it?'

'I thought I might have been able to buy it in your name. Somebody's got to buy it quickly.'

'Even then,' she said, refusing to get up, insisting that she or someone in the world must remain seated ('If only this man would not stumble now!'), 'I'm about to leave Egypt,' she said, 'and the law says that Madame Salz must sell it to a resident Egyptian. *Please* sit down . . .'

He sat down, frightened of the chair but determinedly polite about it. 'I know that . . .'

What *did* he want, she asked herself. What was he trying to say? She dare not answer herself because it seemed obvious and yet dangerously obscure.

'What would have been the point of using me?' she asked him.

Ages ago, Scott's real heartbeat had disintegrated; and all that he was depending on now was this palpitation of a fantasy, which he could not hold nor feel because he could not believe in himself, even now: that he was doing this.

'I had thought,' he told her, 'that you might stay in Egypt after all. But it's too late now, and I'm sorry that I . . .' he shrugged to finish it.

'How could I stay?' she said. 'You mean stay here alone?'

'It would have been your house,' he explained meticulously. 'I didn't mean to simply use you. No! No! I meant that you could have kept it, if you had wanted it. I thought it might be possible. You could have lived there, if you had wanted to stay. I didn't think you wanted to leave Egypt, really . . .'

'I didn't, and I don't!' she said, hardly believing her own emotions. 'But what about you? You said you were also going to leave.'

'I changed my mind. I intended to stay, if you would.'

She could not avoid it any longer and she longed to stand up herself now, but she sat still and begged for simplicity and clarity and no stumbling and no dark holes in the world. *Illumination!* Oh, just a little . . .

'Why do you say a thing like that? *You would stay if I would.*'

Scott had not yet looked at her, and even when she turned a bundle of old gas bills over and over in her hand he kept his head low, his eyes covered by a careful discipline against dismay, against hope, which no one ever saw, although she might see it now if she looked.

'I don't suppose I should really come here to you, like this, when you are already packed and going.'

'Why not?' she asked him gently, but mistrusting herself now. 'Do you think it's too late to ask me now?'

'I don't want to upset you any more. If it's too late . . .'

She laughed erratically, unbelievingly. 'Perhaps it is,' she said. 'I have to be an Egyptian to be of any use to you, don't I? But I'm not an Egyptian any more. As from this morning . . .'

'Yes, I see. And I'm sorry I said it like that. I didn't mean it like that at all. I didn't want to give you another problem, you see . . .'

'So that ends it?' she said.

She was not teasing him, although she could not resist the temptation to evaluate his offer by stretching all reasons for it to breaking-point. She had to know. She could not risk a confused man fumbling beyond himself. He must also know for himself. Yes, he must.

'I don't know if that ends it or not,' he persisted helplessly. 'It depends on you.'

But he could not move beyond that point, and she knew now that she must help him or it would never be done. Already she could not recognize him any longer as the man she had known this far. He had already turned (on this instant and in his manner) into somebody quite different. She knew how great his need really was, if only she could rise to it herself, and if she only had the courage to try it and to ask one question and to allow her own emotions to go out to him.

'Do you still want me to stay?' she said firmly, too firmly, but not hesitating because the light was before her and she must look at it. 'Is that it?'

One gentler flutter and Scott would have fallen like a leaf before her, without hope of retreat. But she too could not give way so easily. She seemed cold, yet he knew she was not, and she knew he was frightened of making a mistake. ('If only this chair doesn't collapse,' he groaned to himself.)

But he had already gone too far to turn back, having set in motion this hope which he had only partly understood and not knowing how far it would go or what the real end would be. Perhaps she guessed it. Perhaps she realized that he had pushed the idea off, alive, and here it was roaring away with him. In any case, he blushed. He opened his lips. He wished the chair would not sag on one side and perhaps collapse under him; and he knew he was hot and excited.

'Yes, of course I would like you to stay,' he told her. 'Why don't you, Helen? Why should you go? Why should any of us go?'

'Are you sure?' she asked, still firm—too firm—but more helpfully and teasingly firm. ('Oh, good heavens!' she had whispered.)

They had not even put their finger-tips together; they were still crossing voids of unknown worlds; and yet they were by no means sure to arrive.

'I'm quite sure,' he said, 'otherwise I wouldn't be here.'

But Helen Mamoon hesitated then. It was almost a sudden terror of what was happening. She would never know what stopped her—whether it was the curious little river of cold blood which women always have ready to defend their helpless emotions with, or whether it was simply the old tradition she sometimes felt—this fear she had inherited from all those women of the East who had been so crudely taken and then so cruelly locked away by holocausts of men. Or whether it was the need for this man to be sure of himself, and to be sure herself also, so that when she looked at him hopefully there could be absolutely no doubt, no cloud; so that no other alternative was conceivable.

'I don't know whether it's too late or not,' she said and stood up with the gas bills in her nervous hands. 'Everything is so disorganized. I can't think. Oh, I can't think yet. You must go,' she said. 'Please go. You must give me time to think about it calmly. I don't know what to think. I don't know what to say now. You're such a strange man. Please let me think . . .'

She was suddenly standing before him looking puzzled and unhappy.

He got up quickly, rescued from that tilting chair, and he said something apologetic in farewell and emerged into the street blind, but not without a sense of astonished reality. He even felt a moment's weird humour, which turned instantly into fear.

'In about two minutes,' he decided sadly, 'she will have told Nona and her other sister Hanna. Then I suppose they will all be in tears, or they'll be laughing at me.'

He could not blame them. After all, he really was (he decided, he supposed, he granted, he admitted—he gave her everything), he really was a strange man.

Nona was packing the last case of children's clothes and laying out all the washed curtains, determined to leave the place clean tomorrow, cleaner than she had found it, and arguing with herself by shouting at the children.

'Benjamin. Get your shoes on!'

Who could be sure that it was best for Helen to remain, if that was what she decided to do? What if this Englishman Scott turned out to be like the others, and made her unhappy? It was so dangerous, because even Helen herself obviously didn't know what to do. That was a bad sign.

'It's not everything,' she told Hanna. 'Women don't *have* to have a man. It's silly to think like that.'

'Helen doesn't think like that,' Hanna corrected, 'so please don't say it to her. Please . . .'

But Nona had already told Helen her feelings. 'I know, darling,' she had said to Helen, 'that you think you're going to be a burden on the Quartermain household if you come to London, but you won't be. There's plenty of room in the flat in London.'

'In Q's workroom?'

'Only until you find something else.'

'It's not even that,' Helen replied impatiently. 'You don't really understand.'

They were on edge with each other; delicately, but on edge.

'All I'm saying is that you mustn't do something silly, simply because you think that anything is better than being a burden. I still won't leave here if it means leaving you like that. Don't just grab at anything in desperation, that's all I ask.'

She always knew what was in Helen's mind. But this time Helen had become a total stranger, with her own thoughts and her own secrets, and she had gone out without saying where she was going.

'God undo that man!' Nona said helplessly in Arabic when she had gone. 'Why did he leave it until the last minute like that?'

Hanna listened to her and disagreed. She had never questioned Nona's authority (mother of children) before, but now she took Nona quietly aside from the children, into the bedroom, and said:

'Helen may want to stay here on her own. You must remember that.'

'I know that too,' Nona argued, 'but does he mean to marry her?'

'I don't know,' Hanna said firmly, 'but I think Helen has to stay if she wants to, even if she thinks it's her last chance, and even if he doesn't mean that much to her, or breaks his word. She has to *try* to have something for herself, just once, which she has never been able to do, because she brought you up, and kept a house going, and then supported me. And now that she is not young any more don't you think anything is better than giving up and being an old maid?'

'Oh, that's silly, Hanna. Don't talk like that. Why must people always think it is so terrible not to be married? Living with a man isn't so important.'

'Perhaps not,' Hanna agreed in her respectful way, but stubborn. She had also served her family selflessly, and anything said of Helen was true for her too. Yet no man could have been worth half the love she now bore Nona's children, excepting perhaps her own father. 'But this might be important to Helen now,' she insisted. 'Don't try to make it difficult for her to decide. She has struggled all her life, and now she ought to be able to struggle for herself. Let her make up her own mind.'

Hanna was acceptant, but Nona hated to part with a safety factor.

'I don't know,' Nona said. 'I simply don't know . . .'

'That's the children,' Hanna said then.

The children were hammering at the door to get into the bedroom, because their father had come home. That was another problem for them. Nona knew where he had been. He had gone to get the illegal money from Rushdi. When she went out, however, she did not say anything special to him about it and she did not ask, because tomorrow's departure would be difficult enough without knowing in detail what else it might have in store for them.

CHAPTER NINETY-FIVE

SPARROWS were chattering noisily in their early-morning dust-bath, and Abdulla hosed them down and laughed at their swift confusion. 'Who will pay the next water-bill?' Scott asked himself as he listened to Abdulla lavishing the hose on the walls of the house, chasing the sparrows up the roof and across the windows in a flood of impossible rain. He could smell it. If it only would rain.

He had received his wooden boxes from Ghurdakha. Someone down there at Amin's old headquarters had sent up his three cases, and as he looked at them he wondered if he should open these dusty desert store-houses of implements and old records and reports, or whether he should simply walk out on them when he left Egypt.

In any case he had not been down to breakfast yet, and it was late.

'Are you all right, Capten Scott?' Madame Salz called up from the outside stairway. 'Vous n'êtes pas malade? Dites!'

'No. Not at all,' he said. 'But I don't think I want any breakfast, Madame Salz.'

'But that's impossible. You must.'

He knew she would prepare it and bring it up herself, fussing over him. So he began to shave hurriedly in cold water, excruciatingly. When his eyes began to water with the torture of a blunt razor on a hard beard he allowed these easy tears to flow over his cheek into the soap and he noticed that he was turning greyer every day now. It would be difficult to emerge today . . .

'Could I come in? I have your breakfast.'

It was not Madame Salz, it was Helen Mamoon.

He could not make himself perfect in one minute, but he dried his wet face and pulled on his shirt and opened the door and took the tray from her, noticing nothing except the coffee spilled in the saucer.

'I am returning your surprise visit,' she said confidently.

'You shouldn't have bothered. I could have come down.'

She must come in. He hated unmade beds with a soldierly hate, and he

771

put down the tray on one of the boxes which crowded the room and pulled up the Indian cloth cover and pushed open the window and heard Sam shouting angrily at Abdulla for making a river down a pathway which was still waiting for shingle or something to cover the dirt. Pebbles were expensive and difficult to get in Egypt . . .

'Now, please sit down,' he told her.

She was gently amused. 'We are so polite. Why do we always insist that people sit down, no matter what they feel? Can I stay here near the window? I shall just lean here while you eat. It's such a perfect day . . .'

Today she would go away and it was in the air outside. He understood her. She was being very nice to him. She would explain as cheerfully as she could.

'Have you eaten breakfast?' he asked.

'Merci.'

'You must have some coffee then,' he insisted. 'I can't eat alone.'

'Give me a little piece of toast,' she said and took a knife and cut half a slice of toast and leaned on his desk (she could not be untidy enough to sit on it), urging him to eat, which he had to do. He cut the egg in half, slid half onto the other piece of toast, and dropped sugar into his coffee without splashing it over, while she watched with new reasons to watch. Was this how he ate always?

'Whatever is in these boxes?' she asked him.

'My books and instruments. They just arrived from Ghurdakha.'

She picked up a book on the desk beside her. '*Terrestrial theories*,' she read aloud. '*A digest of various views as to the origin and development of the earth and their bearing on the geology of Egypt.*' She looked through it so that he could swallow his egg without embarrassment. 'It seems odd to think that the origin of the universe all comes down to deciding what Egypt is made of. Who thinks of it like that, ever?'

'You must have learned something about the earth's structure,' he said, 'when you worked in Anglo-Egyptian Oil Exploration.'

'Not a thing,' she replied. 'I spent most of my time fighting with the various Ministries over legal exploration and exploitation rights. I only knew what the areas were, and who could be bribed and persuaded in the Ministries.'

'But didn't you work for old Barker-Danderson before?' (He gulped a mouthful of soft egg.)

'That was ages ago, and that was pumps and hydraulic engineering. I became very clever at *that*, at maintenance methods anyway. I never made a mistake in pipe and valve sizes.'

'But your father was an engineer.' (He sipped again and gulped again, and it was almost finished.)

'He built Kitchener's gunboats,' she said. 'That was how we began to

772

be so close to the English, I suppose. So strange, looking back on it now.'

That was your beginning with the British, he wanted to say, *and I suppose this is the end.*

But he had hurriedly swallowed the last of his egg and wiped his mouth, and there was no telling what this casual and thoughtful mood of Helen Mamoon would reveal. She was a dark-eyed woman this morning, as if one night's lack of sleep could play havoc with her health. He could only catch sharp glances of her and then retreat.

'It's such a lovely day,' she said again. 'January can be so nice in Cairo.'

The winter sun had stripped the morning very clean. Abdulla and Sam were still arguing in reckless Arabic below in the garden, and Abdulla's childish laugh rose through the open window and sank into Scott like the talons of some new, republican eagle.

'Are you going today?' he asked her very calmly. 'Did you decide to go?'

She crossed her feet at the ankles. 'You didn't even telephone me,' she accused.

'You told me to let you think it out quietly. That is . . .'

'I know I did,' she interrupted. 'But if you'd really wanted me to stay, wouldn't you have tried to persuade me, no matter what I said?'

His confusion was painful and she wanted to laugh in delight or to rush in to his aid with sudden affection and relieve him instantly and tease him perhaps. She did not know yet how to behave with him, but she could not help playing a little of the coquette.

'I didn't think of it like that,' he began. 'I took you at your word.'

But she rescued him quickly and painlessly then, smiling at him.

'It doesn't matter,' she told him, 'because I've decided to stay anyway.' She was looking carefully at him. 'That is, if you haven't changed your mind.'

'No, no, no!'

'I suppose you guessed it anyway, when I came here.'

'Guessed? I don't think so. No. I was afraid you would tell me you were leaving today. I didn't guess . . .' He did not look at her, or he would not.

She knew what she had felt instinctively already—how difficult this would be, how patient and how helpful she would have to be. He was keeping his head down, and yet he had an air of stubborn determination, as if he would not let her go.

'But you'll have to say it all yourself,' she thought, looking down on him where he sat so still, as if he expected to be condemned by some surprising twist to this. *'You'll have to force him into it.'*

'You haven't said anything to me at all, you know,' she said softly. 'I still don't know what you want, except that you wanted to buy this house; and that you wanted me to stay. But what happens next?'

'What happens next?' he repeated and stood up to look quickly at her and look away again. 'We'll have to talk to Madame Salz . . .'

She laughed, the way any adult would laugh at a child. She was delighted. All very well—but her sense of humour was hardly enough. She was a tidy and handsome woman with an organized mind, but she was still looking for the light, and she must look for it somewhere near him now.

'When did you make up your mind that you wanted me to stay?'

'I don't know,' he said with difficulty, looking around the room as if he had mislaid something important. 'I simply felt you didn't want to go. I thought it was a pity. But that wasn't all . . .'

But she interrupted him by giving him his necktie. Was that what he was looking for? Suddenly she no longer wanted to hear his reasons, or to force any definitions from him.

'*Don't turn him inside out,*' she warned herself. No matter how hungry she was to understand him, it was too soon. She went on looking at him and advising herself. She felt her strong feminine position, her sense of protection for him and her common sense coming to his aid. Let him find his own responses. Let him use his own words for his own desires. But what a wonderful thing it was, just now, this very minute, to be a woman. She thought so, she felt so, and she watched him. It was the only thing to be—a woman—at a moment like this. How glad she was. He had even given it a reason in some way.

'Khaki suits you,' she said to him as he tied his tie.

He looked at her in surprise. 'You're the first person who has ever approved of it,' he told her. 'It's mainly habit . . .'

'But it does suit you,' she said encouragingly.

It was not going to be easy, but she was not going to let him escape one responsibility—the vital one of her own life. He must make at least one outright demand on her, the only one; and at the same time make one clear declaration of himself. She needed that much from him.

'You don't know how glad I am that you asked me to stay,' she said casually. 'I would have gone away, even though I knew it was wrong to leave Egypt. So you see—you have rescued me, although I haven't a home any more. When Hanna goes with Nona, everything of my family is gone.'

'But you will live *here*. That's what I meant.'

'I just can't live here like that. After all, it won't really be my house.'

'But I thought you understood that I meant—if you would marry me, and we could live here in this old house. Didn't you understand that?'

'Oh, no! Oh, no! I didn't know at all.'

It was impossible to prevent one tear deceiving her, but Helen was a fully inspired woman, brought up to think of marriage, brought up to the reality and formality of life as it should be led—not to love by faint-hearted

774

whispers, but to enjoy the official and powerful acts of life which had meaning, so that when she leapt off the window-sill and onto Scott's surprised shoulder, into the nerves of his unfinished tie, she was not behaving like a sentimental girl. She was meeting him half-way to herself.

'You do mean it, absolutely mean it? Please don't say it if you don't . . .'

'Yes, of course,' he said, amazed, relieved, puzzled that he had reached this point at last.

'At my age,' she would report to him later in life, through her own tears of joy, 'you must actually hear the words to believe them. You must actually hear them.'

It was in her mind already how she would say that to him, but she had already forgotten how other men had asked her to marry them, because in her heart she knew that this was the only man worthy of the suggestion, the only one as sincere in his intentions and hopes as herself. And if marriage and love were partly formal, and only partly elation to begin with, loyalty was absolute already, and she knew that she would love this man without question until the day she died.

It was a lovely afternoon, they were saying, for the family to fly away.

Nona, Hanna and Helen and the children were in one of the Packards which Sam had ordered from his Greek chauffeur friends, one of whom flowed all over the driver's seat. He was driving with one hand and playing a game of gruff idiocy with Benjamin who was entering the silly stage. Mitropolous would oblige. He was teaching Benjamin double-Greek back-slang, he said. So that while Hanna and Helen and Nona clung to each other in the upholstered apartment in the back, Benjamin was being given his first lesson in the classics.

'I do wish he would watch the road,' Helen said.

Sam and Quartermain and Scott were following in a normal taxi, which dropped behind in the groaning volume of muscle and bone it carried. The taxi-driver complained of his petrol bill for pulling these monsters, but nobody listened because Scott and Quartermain, who tapped his inside pocket every now and then as if to be sure that something valuable was safe and intact, were arguing about Nasser for the last time.

'You ought to read a little history,' Quartermain told Scott shamelessly. 'Then you would realize that Nasser is a sort of latter-day Cromwell. It was Cromwell who brought about a capitalist revolution in a feudal world. Nasser is doing exactly the same thing, except that by now capitalism is on the way out, and communism is on the way in, so he's too late . . .'

'That's not what the Egyptians think of him,' Scott argued. 'They don't know anything about history. They simply admire him for what he's done.'

'That's because they're too ignorant to understand him yet.'

775

'Then so am I ignorant,' Scott said. 'Because I think he has saved Egypt.'

'So he has!' Quartermain agreed impatiently-patient, because it was clear now that his diaphragm was not so relaxed. Perhaps he was trying to save his composure for later—for the last ordeal at the customs barrier when some officer would ask him if he had any foreign money on him and he would say 'No!' In the meantime, perhaps his nerves were backsliding a little, and he was irritable.

'You'll always be as ignorant as a peasant,' he told Scott, 'until you start staring at words like capitalism, feudalism, socialism, communism, nationalism, Zionism and colonialism in the face. What's the matter with a mind that is frightened off by words or theories, even before it begins to work on them? If I had to know about cartography, what would you think of me if I retreated from idiotic words like geodosy or cadastre or geomagnetism? Why allow your brains to be washed out, even before you've begun to use them, stripped by idiots who haven't the courage themselves to stand up to an idea, any idea, particularly the ones that scare them stiff?'

'But you've spent a lifetime thinking like that,' Scott protested, 'so it's all very easy for you.'

'That's so . . .'

'But you ought not to insist that everybody else thinks about politics as much as you do. There are other things in life . . .'

'*I* don't insist,' Quartermain said. 'But any man who feels lost in this world, or who is puzzled, or who complains, or who is angry, or who hates the mess the world is in—any man who puzzles or even contemplates the world has no right to open his mouth to complain about it unless he looks for his answers first, and the answers are all political, aren't they?'

'That's only what you say.'

'What else decides our entire existence now?'

Scott shook his head because he could not answer that.

'Okay,' Quartermain said. 'Don't think about politics. But don't ever complain about the world either.'

Sam had already been bored by this and he began talking in Arabic to the driver, soothing his complaints and promising him a few extra piastres, swearing that if he couldn't get a return passenger at the airport, they would pay him some portion of the fare back. 'Only I warned you before we left,' Sam told him, 'that we may not be coming back to Cairo with you. I told you.'

'But think what a poor man I am, *ya effendi*. What in God's name can I do right out there where nobody lives, nobody, not even a Bedouin and his camel; and what would he be wanting with a taxi anyway? What a God-forsaken place they choose to say goodbye to the foreigners in. What good is it to us Egyptians, I ask you?'

776

'What's he saying?' Quartermain asked them.

'He's complaining about the distance,' Scott said.

'About coming back,' Sam said.

'You'd better tell him to hurry,' Quartermain suggested. 'We'll be late. Anyway,' he said, turning to Scott to recover his nerves, 'if you're now going to be my brother-in-law, and Sam's uncle as well, you'd better start looking closely at what you've married into.'

Scott had not thought of that aspect of it before and he laughed and felt a mystery disperse, one of thousands which had gone already and left only a few million more.

'It's a strange world,' he said. 'I shall also be uncle to your children.'

'*I* hadn't thought of that,' Quartermain said.

Sam turned around. 'We shall all call you *Amm*!' he told Scott.

But Scott corrected him. 'That's for the brother of your father, Sam. You'll all have to call me *Goz khalti . . .*'

'What's that, for God's sake?'

'That means husband of my aunt.'

Nevertheless, it seemed that he would be their uncle and they thought it very funny.

Nobody was looking for reality.

When they arrived at the airport they stood around in the lounge waiting and trying to fill in the gasp of inconsequence between the dramas. The one final drama to come was what they were waiting for. Sam gave the children folders from an Air France stand outside their closed office, and Scott and Quartermain were watching a plane being loaded on the tarmac.

The loudspeaker system had just announced the moment of departure, and as they turned to obey it they saw a stainless-steel stretcher being wheeled towards them, heading through the main doors out towards the plane. Even before they could see who it was they had pulled open the glass doors so that it could pass through.

Briefly, Scott recognized Professor Maudie lying on it, still alive and fascinated by what was happening to her. She had gone too soon, and only Church was there, following her through the doors, a pale grey man with a small intent head and a military man's face. His short and nervy body seemed to be kept rigid now only by a powerful will. It might hold him up for a few steps more, or it might survive another thousand.

'Oh, Scott,' he said in surprise. 'Yes, again it's you. Are you leaving on this plane?'

The stretcher was pushed ahead by two male nurses in washed jackets.

'No. But Quartermain is, General.'

Quartermain was unseen. He always had been.

777

'Yes. Well, as you see, Professor Maudie is much better,' the General said thoughtfully, already a man of fragments. 'She's not on her feet yet, but I think she'll be all right when we get her home and arrange for some of our specialists to see her. She's doing very well, really.'

'I'm glad of that . . .'

The stretcher was already far away over the black tarmac.

'I must go,' the General said. 'I'm sorry, Scott. It's a pity our meetings are always so brief like this. Good-bye, then . . .'

'Good-bye, General.'

Church had broken into a short vigorous run which enabled him to catch the stretcher before it reached the plane, and he went on ahead to prepare the way for it.

'The same man?' Quartermain asked, astounded as they turned around to the passport section.

'The same man,' Scott assured him as they joined the family.

The Mamoons said their farewells while the Greeks, Armenians, Maltese and Jews and English passengers crowded them onto the passport barrier. The women were not bothering to be western about it; they allowed their older emotion to get the better of them. Nona clung to Helen, and when Quartermain prised her loose and the children were kissed and Hanna and Helen had said the longest and final farewell of their lives, Scott said: 'Good-bye, Nona,' so calmly that Nona suddenly remembered him and put a sister-in-law's kiss on his cheek, although Hanna, even in all her respect and affection for a new brother-in-law, could not do such a thing yet. But she held Scott's hand tearfully and appreciatively so that when the Egyptian soldier pushed them through the barrier there was no time for consoling them, and Sam too was in tears as he was embraced by the children.

It was only when this delicate family tendril had stretched and snapped that Scott saw Lucy Pickering watching him closely from the other side of the passport barrier. He stood now with Sam on one side and Helen Mamoon on the other.

He felt his body crushing and his heart turning over and over.

Lucy said nothing to him, neither moving an inch towards him nor changing the direction of her eyes and her face and her hands.

He nodded his head slightly in embarrassment, and then Lucy quickly looked at Helen Mamoon—the wasted look of so many thoughts already lost and gone. She could know nothing of Helen because she had never seen Helen Mamoon in her life; but in that look she had already guessed and decided and dismissed.

'Is that Mrs. Pickering?' Helen was asking—not Scott but Sam.

'Yes. Yes, so it is,' Sam said excitedly, pleased and betraying himself happily through his family tears.

778

But Lucy had been lost in the queue with her passport and Scott felt a hand gripping his sleeve, as Quartermain bowed a little ironically to Lucy Pickering and greeted her in his new calm, which so far was working very well in the face of the real test to come.

'I wonder what they'll ask him,' Helen said.

They could see the passport officer looking at Quartermain's passport and asking him a question, to which Quartermain replied with a shrug while he slapped Benjamin's hand to stop him fiddling with a label on a stranger's suitcase. The Egyptian passport officer looked at Benjamin and gave him a broken ball-point pen which was on the table near him, and Quartermain received his passport back while Nona and Hanna were passed on.

Helen thanked Allah. 'He's through the first one,' she said, leaning on Scott.

'Why? What's the matter?'

She had not told Scott what Quartermain's world had come to; but when the passengers had all disappeared deeper into the customs hall, where they could not be seen, Helen told him quietly that Quartermain had a thousand illegal English pounds in his jacket pocket, 'simply in his pocket', and when Scott asked in astonishment why he was doing a dangerous and stupid thing like that, Helen whispered her explanation: 'A man wanted it for a printing press—an Egyptian communist friend of his.'

'And he does a silly thing like that?'

'I know,' she agreed.'

'Does Nona know?'

'Yes, but I'm not supposed to know. But I was so afraid he might be caught, I had to tell you.'

He could still be trapped in the customs' inspection.

Sam had gone to the glass doors that led to the tarmac. There was an open-air visitors' enclosure beyond the doors, and they followed him to wait there—to wait. She held Scott's arm and looked over towards the passenger exit, and she looked at Scott with whom she was falling in love by a simple transmutation of old values. Everything about him was suddenly recognizable and desirable: his enormous head, his hands, and his spotless cleanliness which she loved. His extraordinary patience was suddenly apparent. Why? She had never thought of it before. So was his strength, which must have been obvious—but not his containment of it. And when his burnt, troubled face and lost eyes were hardened for a moment into anger or concern at Quartermain's stupid risk, he was quite decidedly the man she had seen all her life, yet had never seen before now.

'Somebody's out,' he said.

It was Lucy Pickering who had been released. She walked alone across the tarmac ahead of two young men who did not hurry. He watched her English walk for a moment, and that was all.

'There's Nona,' Sam said, 'and the children. But where are the others?'

There was some delay. Everybody else seemed to be free. Sam walked up and down, cursing the customs.

'I suppose they're looking at everything Hanna's got,' Helen said. 'Simply because she has a *laissez-passer*.'

But Hanna emerged, and a large trolley of luggage was already at the plane unloading. Then Nona was waiting at the door, but she went back in again, out of sight, while the children ran after an empty trolley.

'Why did he take such a risk?' Scott growled. 'Surely there was another way—*if* he had to do such a foolish thing. Why did he do it?'

Perhaps he had forgotten that all his life he had taken great risks himself. Or perhaps they seemed different to him. But considering the fact that Quartermain would be gaoled if he was caught (the Egyptians were very strict about this) it seemed disproportionate—a few pounds. What made a man risk such a thing?

'I don't know,' Helen said. 'I don't understand him, either. But I don't blame him. You would do the same if you believed in the same things, I suppose. Wouldn't you?'

'I doubt it,' Scott said morosely.

He held her arm impulsively then. Quartermain's sparsely erected figure emerged slowly and confidently, and he called firmly to his children. Nona, looking tense, walked beside him as his diaphragm carried him through to safety.

'Oh, my God,' Helen said. 'It's all right. It's all right . . .'

They waved. Scott felt more upset by Quartermain's risk than he had realized. Sam, who knew nothing, had gone to express himself by buying urgently three or four packets of peanuts. He threw them over the wire fence of the enclosure to the children, which was strictly forbidden but nobody noticed, and Sam had to do something. The children and their father were last into the plane, and they waved until the engines had been started and a white face appeared at a window to wave.

'It's little moon,' Helen said. 'Hillooolu!'

It was little new moon, little change of luck on Hanna's lap, and when the plane swung around to make its stately, turkey-like advance down the runway, Helen wept for the lonely days that were done and the lonely days that were to come, but she also wept in the pleasures of both worlds which were now saying a final farewell to each other.

'Let's go now,' she said. 'I hate to see planes taking off.'

But Sam could never be so casual. He insisted on waiting until the plane had taxied across the airfield, had revved its engines, had plunged like a frightened dinosaur down the hazy black runway and was off.

And while Sam waited for it to disappear utterly, Helen Mamoon opened her handbag to wipe her eyes and organize her face, and she said to Scott with a look from those Egyptian eyes:

'I have a surprise for you.'

'Oh? Yes? What is it?'

She took out her Egyptian passport and held it in front of him until he realized what it meant.

'Is that yours?' he asked. 'Really?'

'Of course.'

'You got it back.'

'Of course.'

'But when?'

She smiled and put it back into her bag. Sam was satisfied. He was ready to go—the plane had disappeared.

'I rang up the very moment you left me that day in my flat,' she told him, 'and my friend in the Ministry rushed over and got it back before they had stamped it and cancelled it. Does it make any difference?'

'Yes. Heavens, yes. Now we can get it all done after all. I was worried . . .'

CHAPTER NINETY-SIX

THERE was a great deal to do.

Madame Salz had the right to feel suspicious of some trickery in all this, but her belief in Scott was so automatic that she did not question what was happening.

'Mon Dieu,' she said resignedly to them, 'je suis contente. Je suis tellement contente.'

They would look after her. The house would no longer be hers, technically, but Helen Mamoon's. 'Ça va!' If she allowed the sequestrator to get it, then it would become worthless. She understood. They would buy it and she would have enough money—four thousand pounds—to live on, or to go away: to do what she liked. 'Yes, yes,' she said. 'That was so cruel of them to tax me and sequestrate me. Why did they do that to me? Must I still go away?'

Scott looked at Helen Mamoon and did not know yet where his responsibilities began and ended. Did Helen want this house to herself? He could not know, and yet he knew what he must reply.

'If you want to stay here,' he said to Madame Salz over the piles of letters in French, and the documents and deeds she had given him to arrange the transfer with, 'you could go on keeping the *pension*, Madame Salz.'

'But you will marry Helen. You'll want your own house,' she said.

Scott looked at Helen Mamoon expectantly then. She would have to answer now.

'If we could have one of the big rooms upstairs, that's all we need,' Helen told Madame Salz. 'We can manage perfectly.'

If he had not begun to love her already, he could love her for that sort of generosity.

'And Sam and Becky? Must they still stay in Egypt? I can't stay without them. What would I do . . .'

That was quite another problem, because it was dangerous for Sam to stay in Egypt now. He had no papers and would never have them now, and he had no work that would last, and he was still a danger to himself, because his hurt conscience always forced a public confession out of him whenever he thought of poor Ali Zareef and Hefney the prop-swinger and Mish-mish, and Bambo the mechanic. It would be better and safer for him to leave. But it was not easy to explain this to Madame Salz. She had heard Sam blaming himself for the disaster at Gedida, and sometimes for the whole war. He blamed himself for his friend's death and wept, but it meant nothing real to her because she did not understand it. Couldn't Sam stay also, even without papers?

'We'll see,' Scott said.

But he knew that he must soon talk to Sam about it, calmly; something he had been avoiding.

'We'll see tomorrow,' he said to Madame.

There was so much to do tomorrow.

Tomorrow was the last day of Madame Salz's time limit and they must arrange the conveyance of the property in Helen's name. At least twenty complicated documents and ten Damgha forms must be filled in, the transfer of the money arranged, and the house itself must be reorganized so that life could go on as before.

Helen and Scott sat outside now in the January night on Sam's bench. It was not cold, and the garden was a deep dark blue, as if the moon had grown weak and old over Egypt and could not quite meet its brightest obligations. 'Never mind,' the old mother goddess could say, 'I'll be re-born again in a month, and then watch me. Pale, pale the stars, when I am risen.'

'Are you cold?' he asked her, feeling her arm through his.

'Not yet,' she said. 'I have two thick jumpers on.'

'Cairo is much warmer than the desert at night,' he informed her.

'Is it?'

'Yes. The one thing I hate about the desert,' he said, 'is the condensation at night—on everything. I never got used to it. You feel it even through a blanket.'

'Why do you like the deserts?' she asked as a bat flew back and forth near them. She took a scarf from around her neck to cover her hair against it. They were supposed to be full of lice. 'I've lived all my life in Egypt and I don't think I've ever spent one night out on the desert.'

'You probably had no reason to,' he said.

'But a desert seems stupid, when you think of it,' she protested. 'If there is a God, why should he waste all that vast area of the earth on nothing? It's such a waste.'

He knew she did not understand. 'Most deserts are quite rich. I mean in natural wealth,' he said. 'Most of them have enough water under them if you can get it up. All a desert really needs to be useful are roads and people.'

'Then I'll wait until they have roads and people,' she said firmly. 'I hate the thought of those vast lonely wastes, and at night especially.'

Scott was not sentimental enough about the vast lonely wastes to defend them, but he felt something go out of his life, because he knew he could never go back into those wastes again. She had so easily closed that empty view behind her, and though he almost longed (this very instant) to be somewhere on the endless limestone plains where they drew off into the old basalt hills, pitch black and slaty, even in the daytime, he could let the view die away in his mind, simply by sitting here. It was over, it was done.

'Tomorrow,' he said, 'I'd better go and talk to that boy Fahid about Sam . . .'

'Is he the one at the airfield? Old Maître Rahman's son?'

'Yes.'

'You can't go tomorrow,' she told him. 'If I know the lawyers it'll take *all* of us all day in their offices, or at the Ministries, to arrange Madame Salz's affairs, and the house.'

'All right, the next day,' he said. 'I'll have to find out if he does know about Sam and Bateman.'

'Do you think he knows?'

Scott nodded. 'You know what his father is like. He's an old intriguer; and I wouldn't be surprised if Bateman was connected with him also. But the boy probably hates his father for it, and Sam too.'

'Would he be mean enough to tell the authorities about Sam? The boy . . .'

'He hasn't done it yet,' Scott pointed out. 'But that night when Gedida was bombed he walked over and hit me.'

'He hit *you*? But what for?'

'If I'd been an Egyptian, and seen those bombs tearing up the place, I'd have taken a shot at anyone near by who happened to be English.'

'But weren't you helping them?'

'What difference does that make?' he said to her. 'I'm wondering how he will ever trust me again. I mean, how any of these Egyptian youths can feel anything but hate for the English. Although this one is quite different. I used to think he was quite mad. Ali Zareef did too. But Ali had a curious way of admiring and helping the boy, and I suppose he must have been worth it. He has a very mean tongue, but I keep realizing now that he was never deceived by anything, and he hated the sillier students. I suppose because they were just ignorant young fools who questioned nothing. He seemed always to be questioning everything, which might be a good thing.'

'Do you think so?'

'I don't know, but I keep remembering many things he used to say in his cynical, mocking way, and I'm amazed that I didn't see what he was getting at then. But now he'll be very hard to approach.'

'Not if he's that intelligent.'

'I'm not sure,' he said thoughtfully. 'But in a way, if he does know about Sam, then Sam's hopes of staying depend on him. Do you think it will be worth Sam's risk?'

'Would you trust the boy now not to say anything?'

'I think so. I don't think he'd hurt Sam. But what happens if there are other crises with Israel? He may lose his temper with Sam next time.'

The bats worried her, but she would not go in yet. She liked to sit like this with him in the quick Cairo twilight which would disappear any minute.

'You know,' she said, 'if they arrested Sam again, and actually put him on trial, even now he'd probably spend the rest of his life in prison. Even if they don't actually discover what he did. But how could he help doing such a thing? *You* tell me who has the right to judge Sam. He didn't want to be a spy for the British. He didn't want to be stateless. He didn't want to be persecuted. Yet look how they could actually try him for being a criminal. How can they do a thing like that? When I even think of it! Sam's whole life has already been a trial. From the day he was born, he has had to justify and defend himself every second of the day, simply for being a Jew. He was guilty even for existing as Sam Hassoon . . .'

'The trouble is,' Scott said practically, 'he did help Bateman.'

'I know. Oh, I know. But he didn't mean to or want to.'

He knew that what she was saying was the truth of Sam's life. Sam was simply an innocent man, but he was a guilty one as well.

'But who has the right to try him?' she said again.

'Perhaps only Sam has the right to try himself,' Scott said carefully. 'Perhaps that is what he is doing anyway, when he protests and loses his temper and weeps and blames other people or blames himself. He's probably struggling to understand.'

'How can he understand?' she wanted to know, still indignant.

'I don't know. But I hope at least that he realizes that he is neither innocent nor guilty, but simply ignorant and alone. That's all it is . . .'

He knew he had learned a great deal himself by watching Sam suffering, and he knew now that (despite all his old Greek friends) Sam was quite alone, because he did not know how *not* to be alone; and he was ignorant because (like everyone else) he would never be able to find the secret of his difficult existence simply by registering the joys and the pain of a life over which he had no control.

'What's the solution, then?' Helen said, with her old search tightening on him as she held his arm. 'Aren't we just going round in circles?'

'I don't know,' he admitted. 'Perhaps it's what we should all begin to find out. Otherwise what will happen to us?'

'Who knows what will happen?' she said impatiently. 'But I do know that I'm not going to just sit and watch it any more. I'm going to find something that will give us some sort of hope. I don't know what it will be, but I'm not going to be helpless any longer. I've made up my mind. I don't care whether they call me a true Egyptian or not, or whether they think I'm a traitor like Sam. I don't care . . .'

If only it was as simple as that, he thought: to decide the truth of the world and then follow it through without being called a traitor by anyone, or at least by those you called your own. If you even knew who were your own. Look at Sam. Were the Jews of Egypt his own, or the Jews of Israel? Were the Moslems or Christian Egyptians his own? Too obviously they were not, because being a Jew or a Christian or even an Egyptian did not solve it at all. Wasn't he, Scott, an Englishman, in exactly the same predicament? So what was loyalty to either of them? To whom did they owe it?

'In a way,' he told Helen, trying to understand it, 'Sam is his own answer.'

'What do you mean? You mean that he must do it by himself?'

'No,' he said.

Sam was Sam: once a sailor, then a mechanic, then a soldier, then a wireless operator, and finally a watch-repairer and the husband of Becky. The race was quite irrelevant, the religion useless. Sam's loyalties were questions far beyond either. He was Sam-the-mechanic first, and anything to do with his race or his religion came a long way afterwards.

'Perhaps it's the same with all of us,' Scott told her. 'Look at me. I've wasted most of my life trying to deny that I was a traitor to my country because I refused to take men into a bad situation during the war. When they punished me for that, I thought I had probably deserved it, and I have felt guilty all these years, even though I knew I had done the right thing. They make you feel guilty. But I've never known, any more than Sam knows now, who owes loyalty to whom, or why; because I'm as ignorant as he is. And do you know why?'

'No,' she said finally, holding his hand to encourage his longing and his difficult attempt to explain himself.

'I was always afraid,' he said simply. 'In that, at least, Quartermain was right. How will I ever know what is right or wrong or loyal or disloyal until I find out what the world is made of—not geologically, but simply in its human beings? What are we? Why do we do these terrible things to each other?'

'But you have always been a kind and a generous man yourself. Surely that counts for something,' she told him. 'Or it should.'

786

'Do you think it does?'

'It must,' she insisted, 'otherwise what's the use of living?'

'I know it counts, but is decency enough? I think I must have lived all these years, Helen, on one value only—friendship; because it was the only one I trusted. But even that isn't enough. What happens when you are impotent to help your friends, or they to help you? Can you hold up the world alone on your back like that? You can't. There must be other trustworthy values, some other sort of understanding, some sort of comprehension which is realistic and responsible and decent. If there isn't, then it means that one just lives a day-to-day existence, being knocked about at will by unknown forces. And that seems to me to be an animal way of living.'

'But,' she said, 'they *do* try to turn us into animals. That's the trouble...'

'Who does?' he asked, squeezing and squashing her fingers.

'Somebody does,' she insisted, 'because that's how we live. Like beasts.'

'That's the trouble, then. Somebody causes it. But who? One by one my friends have been slaughtered in wars. Yet I've never really decided why. People like me see it happening, we even take part in it, and we feel hurt and sick for a little while; but then we forget. Although I don't think I can forget any more. I had never seen a dead child in my life before, but when I found Mish-mish under that rubble I thought then that if a man doesn't understand the reasons for this, then he doesn't deserve to be called a man. The reasons. Even a beginning. Are they right—whoever decides to drop bombs? They think they are, but I know they are not. But then look at what happens to Sam. Are the Egyptians right to have refused him papers? They think they're right, and yet I know it's wrong when I look at Sam. You see...'

'Of course I see, my darling. Why have I been driven quietly mad myself, in my own country?'

'I know. I think of you too.'

'Do you really?'

'Often. All the time now.'

'Why? What suddenly made you think of me like that? Tell me!'

'I don't know,' he said, still holding her hand tightly. 'I think it was because we had both lived here, and I could talk to you about anything and you would know what I meant. We might never agree on some things, on Nasser for instance, but I know that when I talk to you I am talking to someone who knows about this country and the life I know best, and so much more besides. As much as I know myself. Do you see?'

They suddenly heard Sam laughing inside the house, and when Sam laughed these days there was usually a good reason for it. Possibly some latent prank of little Abdulla's had just reached him.

Helen sighed. 'At least he's happy for the moment,' she said.

787

Scott embraced her hand again and she winced. He apologized and blushed and tried to take his hand away, but she held it tight. 'Oh, no,' she said to him.

'Anyway,' he said, 'perhaps that boy Fahid is extraordinary enough to understand about Sam. I hope he is. It might all depend on him.'

He seemed to expect confirmation from her, as if he desperately wanted it to be so. But Helen Mamoon did not confirm anything so calmly.

'Only you know what to expect of him. I've never seen him,' she said.

'I'll talk to him,' Scott said. 'I'll see what he says. I'll try to show him what it means. He doesn't think much of Gamal Abd el Nasser either, like you, but that's something else. He probably has very peculiar ideas too. He's quite an extremist. In fact, he's possibly under the influence of the communists or somebody like that, if he isn't one already. I only hope he isn't . . .'

'Why do you say that?'

Scott thought for a while as he picked up Felu who had been scratching at their feet in the dark. 'I don't know,' he said. 'I suppose communists always frighten me off. They're so sure of themselves.'

'It's only these bats that ought to frighten you,' she cried and dipped her head close to him as an old and shaky mammal (the only relation so far capable of true flight) squeaked over them nervously in a crashing dive from the roof of the old house. She clung to him and covered her head.

'We'd better go in then,' he said, helping her up. 'There'll be dozens of them flitting around here by the time the moon goes down.'

They left the garden seat. Scott still held Felu and he scratched her neck in the way Aunt Clothilde had taught him to, and he thought of that blind old woman and of himself, in this house, in this city, in this country.

'We had better start early tomorrow,' Helen said as they walked. 'At eight o'clock. There's so much we have to do.'

Yes: there was a great deal to do and to decide.

Could Sam stay? Would Becky be able to have her baby in safety? And where would he and Helen Mamoon marry, since there was no British consulate? In a church? No, he couldn't face that. That would be wrong, a repetition of their visit to the Rosicrucians. Perhaps Gamal Abd el Nasser had introduced civil marriages into the Egyptian code, although it seemed unlikely. That was something else to face—the fact that she did not like Gamal at all, and assuredly never would. But they would settle that also, somehow. Perhaps he must settle it himself first. Was Gamal absolutely right? Did Gamal really understand what he was doing?

He felt sorry now that Quartermain had gone. He needed to argue with someone, and no one else ever stimulated these things in the way Quarter-

788

main did. However, he would begin to make a serious study of all their arguments, which might not be so easy to begin with; but like the study of any science, surely it was just a matter of approaching it the right way.

'The big thing,' he told himself again, 'is not to be frightened. She's right. She's not frightened of anything . . .'

'Listen,' she said to him. 'Isn't that strange?'

They had heard the far-away clang of a bell.

'It's a tram bell,' he told her.

'I know. Fancy hearing it all the way out here.'

They were both reluctant to go in, and they walked slowly down the path.

'And you will definitely go to see the Swiss?' she said to him. 'You promise!'

'Yes, I promise.'

The Swiss consulate was the guardian of British affairs now, and she had already made him swear that he would go there and demand his right—his passport.

'And no matter what they say,' she said to him, 'you won't let them make you feel wrong. You *must* demand your rights . . .'

He nodded.

'And Nasser too,' she said determinedly, taking full advantage of this night, this old-starred sky, this warm hand. She had made him promise also to go to see Gamal Abd el Nasser himself and to ask (not beg) for something useful to do. 'If they're going to start building dams,' she said, 'surely they'll need people like you. Go and tell him so . . .'

'I thought you didn't like Gamal,' he teased for a moment.

'I don't. I'll never agree with him. But let him do something right for once.'

He laughed. There was so much to do, if only he could do it all.

'I think I love this old house too,' she said to him at the door. 'Let's go in. I'm a little tired.'

She thought the house looked lovely now, not tumbled-down at all but firmly set on this hard Nile mud. She knew she was being sentimental, but the old brick building seemed to be creaking and groaning and cracking as if it were stretching itself to the limit in order to shelter them all safely. Was that like this man himself?

'I'm an idiot,' he said to Helen as they were entering the back passage, preparing to part company for the night, respectably and surely and regretfully, but in what they expected of each other—necessarily. 'I've brought Felu in with me.'

She waited at the door while he took the old tortoise back to the garden and put her under the mango tree. He stood for a moment to enjoy again the slow emergence of his heart, but Felu was restless and she crawled out of her hole.

'You silly chump,' he said to her. 'The cats will get you.'
But he let her go.

The prowling cats might get her, or tomorrow the kites might swoop down from the trees and nip off her head; but on the other hand she might still outlive them all, if she could survive Sam's aggressive threats and little Abdulla's joyful pranks.